Western Shore

Western Shore

Juliet E McKenna

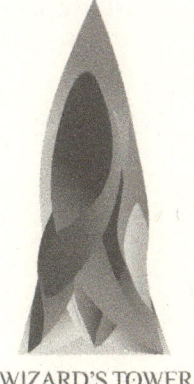

WIZARD'S TOWER

Wizard's Tower Press

Trowbridge, England

Western Shore

Book 3 of the Aldabreshin Compass

Text © 2021 by Juliet E McKenna
Cover art & design by Ben Baldwin
Map by Oisín McGann

All Rights Reserved
First published in Great Britain by Orbit in 2005
Second edition by Wizard's Tower Press, October 2021

Paperback ISBN: 978-1-913892-16-6

http://wizardstowerpress.com/
https://www.julietemckenna.com/

Contents

Acknowledgements	9
Foreword to the Digital Edition	10
Map of the Aldabreshin Archipelago	13
Chapter 1	14
Chapter 2	44
Chapter 3	77
Chapter 4	88
Chapter 5	119
Chapter 6	146
Chapter 7	158
Chapter 8	184
Chapter 9	212
Chapter 10	237
Chapter 11	248
Chapter 12	278
Chapter 13	312
Chapter 14	346
Chapter 15	357
Chapter 16	391
Chapter 17	424
Chapter 18	456
Chapter 19	469
Chapter 20	497
Chapter 21	519
Chapter 22	544
Chapter 23	568
Chapter 24	580

JULIET E MCKENNA

In memoriam

Angela Alvey
1943-2004

For Stephen, and for Lucy
together with Emma, and Mike

Praise for the Aldabreshin Compass

Southern Fire

An original and intriguing setting, impressive world-building and compelling writing set McKenna's work apart from a field thick with far less ambitious fantasy works. Fans of Rosemary Kirstein and Robin Hobb will enjoy this book. — *Publishers Weekly*

McKenna is the thinking fantasy reader's author, the kind who dreams up fantasy elements and then works out the implications of those elements with the precision and thoughtfulness of a scientist, or, well, an SF writer. — *The Dragon Page*

Northern Storm

Northern Storm is an intriguing, even at times exciting, tale that grips the reader from start to finish, and possesses a twist to the tale that has surprised more than one reader. – *Scholar's Blog*

Western Shore

As I've come to expect of Juliet McKenna the world-building is of the highest quality. – Martin Owton, *Infinity Plus*

Eastern Tide

This is a tense, thrilling, moving and thought-provoking finale to a fascinating series. I cannot recommend it highly enough. – Michele, *Scholar's Blog Spoiler Zone*

...an exciting read; McKenna creates fascinating tensions between magic and different societies. – *Publishers Weekly*

JULIET E MCKENNA

Acknowledgements

Any on-going series is shaped by new ideas and unforeseen events. I am grateful to Steve, and to Mike and Sue, for supplying essential feedback, mostly on the vexed question of the final rewrite. For sharing their very personal perspectives on the arrivals of Scotty, and of Jaimee, my thanks to Matt and Trisha, and to Iain and Nici, and also to Liz B for midwifery lore. I'm also indebted to Declan for technical details on eye trauma.

The generous support of many people helps ensure home life keeps ticking over when professional calls on my time come thick and fast. Gill and Mike are pals above and beyond the call of duty. Ernie and Betty continue to provide essential assistance for which I am most grateful. The usual circle of friends helps me keep a sense of humour and a sense of proportion; most notably, Liz, Helen, Corinne and Penny.

On the business side, my gratitude as always to Tim, Gabby, Jess and the Orbit team. I'm indebted to Lisa for both her professional skills and her friendship and my affectionate thanks go to my agent, Maggie, and to Camilla and Jill.

Writers on other genres often tell me that they're envious of the well-established SF&F convention circuit and fan networks. They should be; fan enthusiasm is a constant source of inspiration and motivation and here I'm particularly grateful to Michele, Matt and Toby. I would also like to thank those hard-working convention committees here and abroad who've given me so many enjoyable opportunities to meet other authors, artists and keen readers of all manner of writing. Never doubt that your efforts are appreciated.

Foreword to the Digital Edition

Where do the monsters come from? By the time I embarked on writing the third book in this series, that was the central question. And it's a question of two parts because there's more than one sort of monster here. There are the dragons and then there are the wild men responsible for the atrocities committed in the Archipelago. The nature of evil in epic fantasy fiction was something I wanted to explore, following on from the first two books in the series examining the burdens and limitations of the feudal, hierarchical power that's so often central to such stories.

Answering the dragon question was straight-forward, in the writing at least. It's been established that these elemental creatures are drawn to significant focuses of elemental power. In terms of the natural world that means they would live in places where air, earth, fire and water are doing something dramatic, so volcanoes along the edges of tectonic plates, the confluences of ocean currents and the areas where global weather systems meet would all qualify. I expanded and updated my geographical knowledge and my researches into Indonesia and other tropical islands such as Madagascar gave me further resources to draw on. My maps of the world of Einarinn expanded to include oceanic and climatic data; to establish the situation as it had been, and to explain the abrupt changes which had driven the dragons to cross the western ocean.

Though one major complication arose between me writing the book and it going into print. I delivered the manuscript in mid-December 2004. It wasn't due till the end of January 2005 but it was done, so I was happy to get that item off the To Do List. Then I watched the news on Boxing Day, appalled like the rest of the world to see the cataclysmic tsunami devastating shoreline communities around the Indian Ocean. Once my editor read the Western Shore manuscript we immediately agreed that the final chapters must be rewritten. Because I'd drawn on the history of Krakatoa's eruption in 1883 to devise an earthquake and tidal waves putting Einarinn's dragons to flight. In light of this very real and catastrophic human tragedy, that fiction could no longer stand. At worst, readers might think I was callously exploiting recent events and at best, inevitable recollection of the news coverage would throw them right out of this fantasy world. So I headed back to my geography books to find a different natural upheaval.

On the other hand, news coverage of conflict around the world was an essential resource as I sought to answer the other half of this question. Why were the wild men so murderously brutal? I was determined to find answers that lay between the equally unsatisfactory fantasy clichés of 'they're not so bad when you get to know them, they're just misunderstood' and 'well, they're evil so they do evil things, that's all you need to know'. The history of atrocities, ancient and modern, shows us that humanity can find reasons to justify the most appalling deeds. When resources are in short supply, when they're being crushed by tyranny or besieged by fear, the most ordinary people can be persuaded to find those reasons acceptable — or will consider the costs of challenging them are simply too great. Looking at current and recent strife in the Middle East, post-colonial Africa and Central/South America, to cite only a few sources, it was sadly easy to create a society which explained the wild men's brutality without ever excusing it.

At that point, I realised this book had come full circle, as both Hadrumal's wizards and the Aldabreshin warlord Kheda were forced to confront the reality of what they could, and could not do, and indeed, what they should and should not do, to change this situation. As a writer I found myself considering what I could and should not do in terms of the narrative. A decade ago, diversity issues were far less widely discussed in SF&F but thankfully I was able to draw on both my experiences of reading Victorian and Edwardian British Empire fiction and of visiting modern West Africa. Consequently I was very well aware that wise and knowledgeable white folk turning up to save the poor helpless brown people is a pernicious historical literary device that has no place in contemporary fiction.

In the decade since this book was first published, the news media have continued to report on far too many instances where the savage inhumanity of a tyrannical elite debases and degrades a wider population. It has become more important than ever that the rest of us rigorously examine whatever actions our own leaders insist will put an end to such atrocities. As we see time and again, in fact and in fiction, there are no infallible wave-of-the-magic-wand solutions. Consequently Western Shore still continues to fulfil one of the most important functions of fantasy fiction: holding up a magic mirror so that readers may reflect on the world we live in by means of an action-packed and enthralling story!

— *Juliet E McKenna 2015*

Map of the Aldabreshin Archipelago

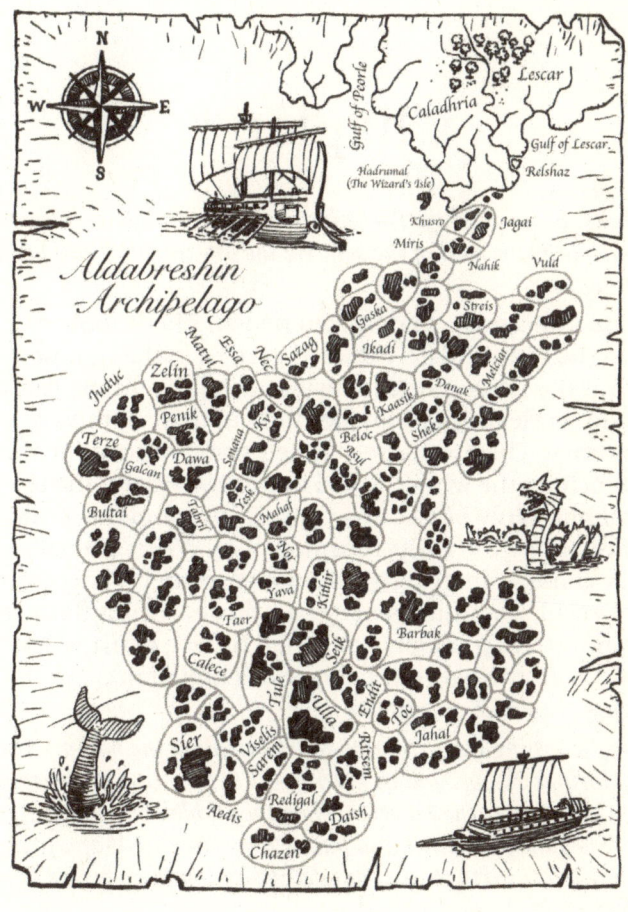

Chapter 1

What a beautiful day. The rains are long past, all malaises driven out by the heat of the sun, yet the dry season is still far from punishing us.

Seated on a wide, low-backed bench, Kheda looked around the immaculately tended garden in the hollow square at the heart of the luxurious dwelling. In the centre, grey and scarlet shadow finches sang merrily in their spacious aviary. The turquoise-painted wood echoed the roof tiles adorning the white-walled buildings. Above, the sky was the soft blue-grey of a courier dove's wing and the garden still husbanded the early-morning cool. When the heat of the day came, spinefruit trees would cast their generous shade. Vizail, jessamine and basket-flower shrubs flourished in the moist, fragrant air, nourished by rich earth, black in contrast with the paths of pale sand. Though none of the bushes were flowering as yet.

They're saving their strength for the trials of the hotter weather. Their glorious blooms will be harbingers of the rains to come when the first clouds blur the horizon. Then they'll blossom and this garden will be full of sunbirds and butterflies. Then seeds and fruit will fall to the moist earth to wait out deluge and mildew before sprouting to drink in the sunlight.

'Are you sure it's not too early?' Beside him, Itrac shifted and tossed a silken cushion petulantly onto the raked sand. 'It should be a year less a hundred days—' She broke off, catching her breath.

Kheda laid a gentle hand on the light cotton gown swathing his wife's swollen abdomen and waited for the contraction to pass. Eyes closed, her face twisted with pain as she groaned and rocked back and forth. Kheda allowed himself a grimace as she gripped his hand.

At least I remembered to take my rings off. And Itrac's hands are barely swollen.

He looked at her slender fingers crushing his fingers atop her gravid belly, hard as rock as the contraction racked her. With blood from northern and western domains in her lineage, her skin was more golden than bronze. Her knuckles showed white. Itrac drew a shuddering breath and opened her eyes, sweat beading her forehead.

'Twins always come early,' Kheda said gently.

'You really think it is twins?' Itrac brushed a stray wisp of hair from her forehead with a shaking hand. The thick plait of her waist-length black tresses was tousled and uneven after the long night of her steadily progressing labour. Stripped of the intricate cosmetics expected of a warlord's wife, she looked very young.

As young as my eldest daughter, very nearly. Born half my life ago. When life had none of the complications that have so beset us both and forced us together like this.

'Your womb grew by more than two fingers for every turn of the stars.' Kheda resisted the temptation to press harder as her belly softened with the passing of the contraction, to try to feel which way the babes were lying. 'I'm sure I could feel more than one head.'

Was I right? Is one of them safely head-down? What do we do if they are both head-up? I can't feel any movement. But there's rarely any kicking this far into a birthing.

He resolutely thrust away half-formed fears and used a scrap of muslin to mop Itrac's forehead. 'You're already as big as any woman bringing a babe through ten full turns of the stars.'

As big as any of my former wives when the birthing came upon them.

'But it's taking so long,' Itrac wailed. A weary tear escaped one hazel eye to glisten on her cheek. 'If I die, you must bury me here.' Her voice trembled. 'In this garden, so your next wife will be able to bless the domain with children—'

'The first birth always takes the longest. Many women labour much longer—' Kheda swiftly changed tack at Itrac's mordant look. 'There is no reason to fear any danger to you or the babies.' He wiped away the tear and cradled her face in his sword-callused hand. 'Look at me.'

Itrac obeyed, her face shadowed with fear.

'Every turn of the stars has seen you in good health,' Kheda continued, reassuring. 'You've eaten well and rested as you needed to. I've done this before, many times—'

'No you haven't!' Itrac's face contorted at the onset of another contraction. 'You may have watched. I watched—' She bit her lip, unable to continue.

True enough; I have only watched, like any man. But I was there to receive my children wet with their birth blood as they slid from Janne, from Rekha. Such is the most intimate expression of a warlord's duty to care for every man, woman and child of his domain. But my former wives and children are lost to me, along with my former domain. Now all I can do is see Itrac safely delivered of these innocent babies that I have begotten on her with undoubted affection but no real love.

16

The dull ache of loss gnawed beneath Kheda's breastbone as the contraction passed and Itrac's ragged moans gave way to weeping. 'I'm so tired,' she sobbed. 'I wish Olkai was here, and Sekni.'

'It won't be much longer,' Kheda soothed as he put an arm around her shoulders. 'Jevin!' He snapped his fingers and the youth who'd been waiting motionless beneath a flame tree hurried forward, bearded face anxious. Like Kheda, he wore an unadorned tunic and trousers of unbleached cotton. This wasn't a day for the finery expected of a noble lady's body slave. Unlike Kheda, he had the straight black hair and compact physique of these southernmost domains.

'Yes, my lord.'

'A drink for your mistress.' Seeing the uncertainty in Jevin's eyes, Kheda frowned at the young man.

Do you remember I told you you're to show no fear? No one must voice doubt as to a wholly favourable outcome.

The youthful slave immediately forced a cheerful smile as he proffered the brass ewer and goblet he had been clutching. 'My lady?'

'It's izam juice.' Kheda helped her take the goblet. 'Your favourite. Do you want another of the rosehip sweetmeats?'

'I don't think I'll ever want to eat rosehips again.' Itrac managed a watery smile before sipping obediently.

'Not too much.' Kheda's hand hovered, ready to ensure she didn't drink too deeply.

Rosehips crushed with quail berries and yellow-fan seeds to ensure you don't labour in vain, just to feel the pains fade and the babies die with them, within you. Those herbs have done their work and better an empty stomach for what is to come. Izam juice with its sweetness to give you strength, with just enough poppy syrup to take the edge off the agonies for you without putting the children at risk. I learned to mix those doses precisely after Rekha and Janne's early labours.

17

'Twins born to the domain will be a powerful omen.' Jevin was clutching the ewer so tightly he was in danger of leaving dents in the metal.

'A portent of fertility and fair weather for all our islands and their people,' Kheda agreed robustly.

As long as I can deliver them both safely and see Itrac through all the perils of childbed. These people could see few worse omens than the death of any one of them.

'What do the stars say?' Her voice faint, Itrac looked up at the cloudless square of sky framed by the roofs of the pavilion.

I never even thought to look at the skies when her pains first began. No matter. I could draw the jewels and constellations in every arc of the heavenly compass blindfold. I might as well be blind, for all the truth they can show me.

Kheda looked up as he drew her close, feeling her trembling within the circle of his arm. 'The Pearl is in the arc of death—' he spoke resolutely over Itrac's inarticulate murmur of distress '—which in its positive aspect is also the arc of inheritance. With the Pearl waxing so close to its full, its talismanic properties make positive aspects dominant. Of all the heavenly gems, the Pearl's the most potent charm against death and for the present it's set among the stars of the Sailfish. That's always a symbol of fertility, all the more so when it swims with either moon.'

'The Lesser Moon as heavenly Pearl must be a talisman for you, my lady.' Jevin looked at Kheda with uneasy hope. 'With our domain's pearl harvest so fruitful last year.'

'In claiming that arc of the compass, the Lesser Moon also forms the point of a triune reading of the whole sky.' Kheda smiled confidently at Itrac. 'Today, of all days in the year, the Opal, the Amethyst and the Diamond are all in the heavenly arc of parenthood.'

'Truly?' Itrac's wonder momentarily relieved her near-exhaustion.

'Opal is a talisman for truth, while Amethyst counsels calm and humility. Believe me — we'll need both as parents.' Kheda handed the goblet back to Jevin. 'Diamond, talisman for all warlords and symbol of long life. The stars with them are those of the Horned Fish, a powerful emblem of life and renewal.'

'They live and give birth in the open seas,' Jevin said encouragingly, 'even though they breathe the same air as us.'

'If that's two points of the triangle, what's the third?' Itrac shifted, her bulk unwieldy, so unlike her usual elegant slenderness.

'The Ruby is in the arc of life.' Kheda brushed a kiss across her clammy forehead. 'Talisman of vigour. In the arc of life where the stars of the Vizail Blossom are particularly bright at this season, and that's one of the most potent tokens of the hope all women carry within them—'

'And the Ruby is a powerful talisman against blood loss,' Jevin interrupted.

'Indeed.' Kheda shot a repressive look at the anxious youth.

Weren't you listening when I told you all she needs from you is constant reassurance? Perhaps it wasn't such a good idea to warn you about all the things that can go wrong in childbirth.

Another contraction seized Itrac. She moaned, low in her throat. Kheda took her hands and braced himself as her nails dug deep into his palms. Her groan rose to a howl that startled a cooing pair of glory-birds out of the nearest shade tree.

That's a new note in her agony. It won't be long now, for good or ill. Jevin can put his trust in rubies and heavenly conjunctions if he likes. I'll rely on all I was taught and all I've seen and all the preparations I've made.

19

Kheda watched Itrac intently as the contraction passed, leaving her panting. A shiver ran through her and clear liquid darkened the cotton skirt of her loose dress. 'Oh, Kheda,' she gasped, suddenly scared.

'My lord?' Jevin was equally alarmed.

'That's the birth waters.' Kheda rose, lifting Itrac to her nerveless feet. 'It's time to go inside. Jevin, take her arm.'

With the young slave supporting her other side, the warlord guided his wife towards the rear of the garden. Double doors stood open revealing a handful of apprehensive maidservants hovering inside.

'Touai.' Kheda nodded to the foremost among them. He noted that two of the girls shared the older woman's lean build, their angular features softened by youth but still marking them as Touai's daughters.

She brought her own living proof of successful childbearing, if Itrac's in any fit state to take comfort from their presence.

Itrac's personal withdrawing room had been stripped of its customary lush carpets, the banks of silken cushions and low tables of polished and inlaid wood. Only the pale-pink walls painted with a riot of colourful birds flitting among nut palms and lilla trees remained the same. A sturdy bed with a firm cotton mattress had been set against one wall of the airy room and the cool lustre floor tiles were covered with swathes of calico. The morning sunlight filtered through thin muslin drapes tightly secured to bar entry to any flies drawn to the scents of blood and birth to come. As Kheda escorted Itrac inside, the maidservants circled around to close the door behind them and refasten the curtain, hiding the garden outside.

'Let's get you to the bed.' As he spoke, another brutal contraction gripped Itrac, forcing them all to a halt. 'Where's Lihei?'

'Here, my lord.' A sturdily built woman with tightly braided greying hair stepped forward and smiled reassurance at Itrac. 'Most honoured to be here, my lady.'

I hope you got some sleep last night.

Kheda set his jaw against his own fatigue. 'Let's get her to the bed.'

Itrac collapsed onto the mattress as the next contraction seized her. She crouched on her hands and knees, keening wordlessly. Lihei hugged her shoulders, crooning soft reassurance. 'It'll pass, my lady, just let it pass.'

Forcing himself to leave Itrac to the grey-haired woman's tender care, Kheda crossed the room to a wide table covered with more calico.

She should have sister-wives to support her, offering that understanding no man can hope to match. All we have is our steward's new wife, a widowed weaving woman until she caught his eye. But Olkai and Sekni are dead and gone and I'm done with marriage for alliance or advantage in trade or territory. I wouldn't have married Itrac if there had been any other way to see her safe from those who would have abused her.

'Touai, you're certain there will be plenty of warm water when we need it?'

'Yes, my lord.' The older maidservant filled a basin from a tall ewer, her hands steady.

Kheda felt a tremor in his own hands as he scooped soft soap from a shallow dish and rubbed it to a lather. As he scrubbed his hands and nails scrupulously, he surveyed cotton cloths neatly folded, ready to swaddle the newborns. A silver tray held smaller squares of muslin as well as a handful of brilliant red ribbons weighted down by a small set of gleaming steel shears. A copper box hid its contents from view.

Needles cleansed with flame. Boiled thread for sewing, inevitably.

'It hurts so much,' Itrac moaned, turning her head into Lihei's accommodating bosom.

'I know, flower.' Lihei hugged the young woman close. 'You rest a moment and let me see how we're doing.'

With Jevin's anxious help, the grey-haired woman persuaded Itrac to sit up against the head of the bed, propped on firm cushions, her feet planted wide. Itrac's head lolled forwards, her chin on her chest, her eyes closed. Kheda rinsed his hands as Lihei sat on the end of the bed and lifted Itrac's skirts up over her knees to see how matters were progressing.

Jevin came to meet him as he approached the bed. 'She's exhausted, my lord,' he said, low and fearful. 'How can she go on?'

'She's past the point where she has any choice,' Kheda said with compassion.

Itrac gasped before Jevin could say anything. 'I have to push.'

'That's as it should be,' Lihei agreed calmly. 'I'll be easing you with warm cloths and oil, my lady, to see if we can't do this without leaving you too sore.' The older woman glanced over her shoulder at Kheda. 'It won't be long now, my lord.'

The warlord nodded. 'Jevin, open that blue bottle and sluice my hands.' He held them over the bowl. As the young slave obeyed, the sharp alcohol stung small scratches on Kheda's hands that he hadn't even realised were there. 'Empty the basin,' he ordered. 'No, not in there!'

About to empty the basin into a shallow ceramic bowl underneath the table, Jevin froze.

'That's for the afterbirth,' Kheda reminded the slave, curbing his own irritation with some difficulty.

Jevin's face was already muddy with weariness after the long, sleepless night. He went positively ashen before scurrying away to empty the basin into a slop bucket standing by a far door.

Kheda glanced at an ebony coffer tucked away beneath the table's calico drape.

Blue casque in case the pains stop altogether; we shan't need that now. Saller rust, perhaps, if there's too much bleeding, but not before the afterbirth is delivered. Hind's herb and black bark, to bring on her milk and ease the pains after the babes are born; that can wait awhile. The root of the yellow earth star will be the most important, to strengthen her blood against childbed fevers. But we have to see these children born first.

Kheda refused to contemplate the other contents of the physic chest: the thin-bladed, razor-sharp knives brought out when all hope for the mother was gone and only the child could be saved; the bright slicing wires used when the babe must be given up for dead and the only thing worse than that loss would be the woman dying with the child un-born within her.

My former wives were safely delivered of ten children between them. I don't intend taking up such butcher's tools now.

He looked at the bed where Jevin was sitting behind Itrac. Her fingers dug into the slave's muscular forearms as she leaned against him, secure within his embrace. Her eyes were closed, her feet set wide, her toes digging into the mattress.

Kheda glanced at Touai, her daughters behind her. 'Stay out of the way but be ready to bring me swaddling cloths and the ribbons to tie the birth cords.' He joined Lihei at the end of the bed and saw that Itrac's labour was indeed proceeding apace. He glanced up at Jevin and managed a bracing smile. 'Just hold her and keep telling her how well she's doing. En-courage her to push until I tell her to stop.'

The slave looked back as Itrac's head rested on his shoul-der, her unseeing eyes rimmed with white. 'She seems so distant, my lord.'

'That's as it should be.' Another contraction seized Itrac and her feral cry drowned out Kheda's words. He rubbed her cramping feet, adding his own meaningless endearments to Jevin's encouragement as she struggled with the merciless demands on her body. The spasm passed and Itrac went limp, sucking down deep breaths.

'You'll be surprised how little she remembers. Janne—' Kheda bit down on the name of his former first wife.

'Women would never do it a second time if they did.' Li-hei chuckled before another contraction put an end to such levity.

And men and women alike lose all sense of time. I was aston-ished, when Janne finally delivered Sirket as my firstborn, to find that it was already evening.

Itrac yelled, pushing with all her strength. Successive contractions came harder and faster, each one arching her back more brutally than before. As Kheda and Jevin encour-aged her, the labouring woman showed little sign of hearing them. With every new spasm, her energy and understanding turned inwards, the dictates of instinct driving her body and brooking no denial.

Lihei continued diligently applying warm, oiled com-presses. Kheda watched intently past the woman's calm brown hands for the first sign of the first child.

This could all still go horribly wrong if the first thing I see is buttocks.

Some indeterminate time later, relief flooded him at the sight of black wispy hair.

'Itrac, try not to push, just for the moment.' He spoke loudly and firmly. 'I can see the head.' As he heard Jevin pleading with Itrac to hold back her straining, Kheda cradled the tiny crown, ready to ease the wrinkled little face gently into the air.

Not too fast, to save Itrac damage. Not too slow, to be sure the baby thrives. Not pulling, not twisting, just guiding as I will do for the rest of this child's life.

There was a moment of total stillness in the room as the baby's head emerged. No one spoke. Kheda found he wasn't even breathing, stunned by the marvel before him.

As astonishing as the first time I saw a child of mine born. You always forget how small they are.

The tiny form slipped sideways as Itrac's womb inexorably expelled it, first one pale golden shoulder emerging, then the second. In a rush of blood and fluid, the baby was in Kheda's hands, the cord still linking it to Itrac thick and blue and pulsing.

'Bring ribbons,' Kheda called hoarsely. 'And swaddling.'

'Is it all right?' Itrac rasped.

'She is.' Kheda held the baby in his cupped hands, keeping her low beneath Itrac's hips. 'You have a daughter, my lady.'

Now we wait, just a moment, until the thread of blood linking you to your mother stills. How strong are you, little one?

The tiny girl drew her first breath with a faint mewling noise and then began crying, a high, reedy sound that was encouragingly robust. Her little arms and legs waved, congested face screwed up against the light and this strange new place.

'Let me, my lord.' Lihei was ready with a soft cotton wrap.

Reluctantly surrendering the child, Kheda turned his attention to the birth cord, watching it shrink and grow pale.

'My lord.' Touai was at his elbow with the silver tray.

Kheda tied a ribbon loosely around his newest daughter's fragile wrist, making sure the knot was secure. 'We need to be careful she doesn't lose this, so we know she was first,' he warned all the women as he tied off the birth cord a finger's length from the baby's round belly. Taking up the shears, he cut through the cord.

Tough as sinew, just like always.

Itrac moaned as a new contraction ran through her, her feet flexing.

'Clean our new daughter while we wait for her brother or sister,' Kheda said softly.

As Lihei withdrew with the newborn, Touai at her side, Kheda looked up to see Itrac smiling through her utter exhaustion. Behind her, Jevin's face was wet with tears, eyes wide with wonder.

Kheda realised his own close-trimmed beard was damp, his eyes full. Another contraction gripped Itrac and he wiped his face awkwardly on one shoulder before turning his attention to waiting for the second baby. It wasn't long in coming. As Kheda received the tiny buttocks, he smiled. 'It's another girl.'

She slid easily from Itrac now that her sister had opened the way. Touai was ready with the ribbons for tying the cord when the moment was right and Kheda cut it deftly. Both babies' cries filled the room; rising above the shaky congratulations the maidservants were offering their lord and their lady.

'Let her suck, my lady.' Lihei returned with the firstborn baby clean and lightly swathed in soft cotton.

Dazed, Itrac obediently opened the front of her gown and brought the baby to her breast. After a moment's nuzzling, the questing mouth found her nipple and one of the quavering cries was stilled. Itrac gazed down at her daughter, oblivious to anything else.

'Do you want to take her, my lord, while I wait for the afterbirth?' Touai offered Kheda cotton cloth to wrap the new baby.

'Yes, thank you.' He carried this second new arrival to the swathed table, close to his body with one hand supporting her tiny head.

You have more hair than your sister, little one. What am I to do now? I was so determined to leave you both to your mother's rearing, to save myself from the pains of loving you lest I lose you. Yet how can I do anything but love you and your sister both?

He laid her gently down in a nest of soft cotton and took up a clean cloth as one of the maids poured fresh water into an unused basin. Dampening one corner, he began carefully wiping the blood and fluid from the baby's flawless golden skin. His own hands were dark and creased in contrast.

Will you share your mother's colouring or will your complexion darken to resemble mine? Will you have her beautiful eyes or will they be green? Will your hair stay black and fine like your mother's or grow brown and curly?

Once he was satisfied the baby was quite clean, he accepted a spotless white cloth from the attentive maid. 'Come and let your mother see you,' he said softly as he wrapped his new daughter securely.

Over on the bed, Itrac was still rapt in adoration of her firstborn. She looked up, disconcerted, first at Kheda and then at the steward's wife. 'Can I give them both suck, at the same time?'

'Of course.' Lihei snapped her fingers at Jevin who was gazing wide-eyed at the baby already suckling at Itrac's breast. 'You can move now, my lad.'

As Lihei saw Itrac settled back against her pillows with a baby at each breast and supported with cushions, Kheda noticed Touai waiting patiently at the foot of the bed with the shallow ceramic bowl.

'Each came with her own afterbirth my lord.' The gaunt maidservant showed him the basin's gory contents.

So there'll be none of that nonsense about them being two halves of one whole and wondering whether the good and the bad in their character has been evenly distributed.

'Good.' Kheda steeled himself to be certain nothing had been left behind to poison Itrac and rob these children of their mother before she was anything more to them than milk and comfort. Finally satisfied, he nodded, and drew a cloth over the basin with relief. He glanced over at the table where the copper box holding needles and sutures waited. 'Does she need...?'

'No, my lord, thankfully.' Fellow-feeling with the new mother was evident in the older maidservant's eyes. 'That's often the first blessing of twins, with them being so small.'

'Not too small?' Kheda asked, watching Itrac's face lit with wonder at the strange new sensations of suckling her babies.

It's early days. Janne's second son didn't live beyond his first half-year, despite all we could do for him...

'No, my lord, not too small.' Touai smiled. 'And they're strong.'

'As is Itrac.' Holding his bloody hands away from his sides, Kheda tried to ease a stiffness in his neck and shoulders that he hadn't felt until now. Tiredness threatened to overwhelm him. Relief that everything had gone so well seemed to have broken down his defences. 'But don't keep her here too long. She needs to be in a clean bed—'

'Leave me and Lihei to our duties, my lord.' Touai flapped her hands at him. 'As you do yours,' she prompted. 'The omens?'

Kheda did his best to hide his reluctance. 'That can wait until I've given Itrac a draught of childbed herbs.'

He returned to the table, where Touai's diligent daughters brought him yet more hot water and he scrubbed his hands until they tingled. Bending to retrieve the ebony physic coffer, he felt all the weariness of the long night in his back and legs as he lifted the heavy box and set it on the table. 'Bring me a small goblet of izam juice, please,' he asked one of the two beaming girls.

'Hind's herb, to begin with,' he commented to Touai as the maid scoured her own hands clean, 'and tincture of earth star.' He took up a silver spoon and measured out crushed, dried petals and then the pungent liquid. 'Is she bleeding too much?'

Touai shook her head, angular face relieved. 'Not with the two of them sucking so readily.'

'Keep a close watch and let me know as soon as you suspect she needs something to stanch the flow.' Kheda stirred the medicines into the izam juice.

Itrac stirred herself to smile at him as he walked back to the bed, though she looked wholly exhausted and more than half-asleep. 'Twins,' she murmured drowsily.

'You were as strong and as brave as I knew you would be.' Kheda kissed her on the forehead, strands of hair still plastered across it.

'I had no idea it could hurt so much.' Itrac bent to nuzzle her second daughter's fluffy black head. 'But it was all worth it.'

Jevin was perched on the edge of the bed beside Itrac, still lost for words. Kheda handed him the goblet as both of Itrac's arms were fully occupied. 'Make sure she drinks it all, and some water.'

'I am thirsty.' She sounded surprised. A yawn interrupted her, drawn from the very depths of her being. The movement dislodged the elder babe from her suckling. Tiny eyes tight shut, she sought the comfort of her mother's breast for a moment, then settled to sleep instead.

'You give that to Touai and strip off your tunic, my lad,' Lihei instructed Jevin.

29

'You heard.' Touai took the goblet from the startled youth and edged him aside as she helped Itrac drink from it.

Jevin obediently tugged his tunic over his head, puzzled.

'For the next ten days or so, if my lady's nursing just one of them, you must keep the other warm.' Lihei wound a length of soft cotton deftly around Jevin's ribs. 'Sit down.' As Jevin obeyed, Lihei handed him the sleeping elder baby. Wide-eyed, he held her with infinite care as Lihei bound her gently and securely against his tautly muscled abdomen.

'We'll need you to take your turn, my lord.' Touai glanced at Kheda. 'When my lady takes her first bath.'

Kheda nodded. 'Naturally.'

'Can I go to sleep now?' With a faint wince, Itrac shifted to lie more to the side where the second baby was still intently feeding.

'Yes.' Kheda leaned forward and kissed her forehead again. 'I'll be back in a little while.'

I wouldn't mind a chance to sleep myself but I had better do what is expected of me.

He headed for the doors opening into the garden, where a little maid had armed herself with a feathery grass whisk to make sure no flies got past her guard. As he stepped outside, trying to stifle a yawn, Kheda was pulled up short. A silent, anxious crowd was clustered in the garden. Almost all the household servants and slaves were there, creased and dishevelled silk tunics identifying those who had kept vigil throughout the long night. Cotton-clad gardeners were clutching hoes and rakes and porters held baskets or brass ewers to their chests.

Beyau, the steward of the extensive residence, stepped forward. His blunt features were uncharacteristically vulnerable, though his stance was still that of the warrior he had been before all the upheavals that had swept over this domain. 'My lord?'

Kheda composed a confident, triumphant smile. 'My lady Itrac has given the Chazen islands two beautiful daughters.'

The garden rustled with exultation dutifully stifled to spare the exhausted mother within.

Beyau beamed at him. 'The beacons are ready, my lord.'

'Then light them.' The crowd parted to clear a path for Kheda across the garden and some eager hand opened the door to the hall on the far side of the pavilion. 'While I see what the omens say.'

Kheda kept smiling and nodding to acknowledge the murmured congratulations as he passed through the garden. Eager hands patted his arms and shoulders in tangible approbation. As he passed into the long, high-ceilinged audience hall, he noted five times the usual number of maids busy brushing the thick, soft carpet and polishing the tall, elegant vases that lined the walls. They all turned hopefully towards him.

Kheda tried to make his smile a little less stiff. 'My lady Itrac is safely delivered of twin girls.'

The women curtseyed, their individual congratulations merging with the gathering swell of relief and celebration that followed Kheda out into the bright sunshine in front of the pavilion. He blinked and shaded his eyes with one hand as he saw the sparkling sea before him crowded with boats. Some might be dutifully ferrying necessities to the warlord's household from the outlying islands with their comfortable huts of tight-fitted wood and closely woven thatch. Most had no such excuse.

I don't think I've ever seen this harbour so full.

This most southerly residence of the Chazen warlords was built on a chain of small islands at the heart of a broad expanse of reef. Those who had ruled here before Kheda had put their trust first in the open waters and then in the tortuous channels among the corals that barred the way to any ship whose master wasn't privy to the anchorage's secrets.

He watched the news sweep through the assembled boats, like the breeze that bellied the triangular sails of the fishing skiffs and the mighty square-rigged masts of the fat merchant galleys. Delight surged through the ships like the waves toying with the rowing boats. Signal flags were raised and Kheda heard the distant note of brazen horns sending word to the ever vigilant triremes patrolling the deeper blue seas beyond the turquoise waters of the lagoon.

Word will soon be carried from one end of the domain to the other. And to every neighbouring domain beyond.

The crowds outside the pavilion were more voluble in their exultation, their words an unintelligible jumble of congratulation. Those further away contented themselves with raising a cheer that soon spread out across the harbour. Feet and oars drummed on decks and thwarts, swelling the tide of jubilation.

Itrac is truly bound to this domain now, not just as wife to their former lord. The threads of her daughters' birth blood are a better and stronger bond than her role as only survivor of the disaster that overthrew her dead husband's authority. Now she has given Chazen an heir and a second daughter sharing the same birth stars, should any calamity befall the elder.

Acknowledging continued congratulations, Kheda walked down the neatly raked path leading away from the pavilion and crossed a small bridge of ropes and wood swaying on piles driven deep into the reef. Any attacker would find themselves wrong-footed and exposed to arrows from all sides as they fought across these narrow walkways that the defenders could cut at will.

I'd forgotten how tightly one of those tiny hands can get a grip upon your heart. A grip that cannot be broken. And I am bound by my duty to make sure no battle or other woe blights those new lives.

I have no one to blame for that but myself. I chose to take on this role as defender of Chazen and Itrac's protector. The domain I was born to was lost to me. Can these births help me finally put Daish behind me and look to the future? That might be easier if I had any confidence in what the future might bring.

A nub of coral supported a square platform where more bridges ran away across the crystal-clear waters. They linked islands where more low pavilions of white stone were roofed with tiles like a reflection of the brilliant sea. Flashes of red and orange sunset fishes in the water beneath his feet caught Kheda's eye as he crossed to the next island.

Everyone is so pleased at present. Will there be any dissenting voices, once the village soothsayers have taken time to consider the implications of a girl as heir to the domain? Will there be whispers of regret behind discreetly raised hands that I could not give the domain a son, to be a true-born lord of Chazen when he grew to manhood?

A few slaves and servants clustered on the wide steps of the building here, shaded by the broad eaves. Kheda glanced at the humble dwellings where the servants were quartered and the shuttered, more opulent and spacious buildings beyond.

Beyau will soon have every maid and manservant cleaning and polishing, fitting out those halls with every luxury to welcome the dignified lords and gracious ladies of the domains that border Chazen. They will soon be discussing the news that these islands are now fated to pass into the hands of a ruling lady. So if my first duty is to hold this domain secure for her to inherit, my second must be to teach her all the intricacies, contradictions and deceptions necessary to rule once she has reached an age of discretion.

As Kheda crossed the next bridge, he accepted further profuse congratulations with smiles and nods. He felt his smile becoming irretrievably fixed and crossed the final swaying walkway across the reef with carefully concealed relief. The slaves and servants of his personal household were gathered on the steps of the warlord's pavilion. There was one warrior in chain mail among the silk and cotton tunics and dresses.

'Ridu.' Kheda nodded as the armoured youth came clown the steps.

'Congratulations, my lord.' Ridu bowed low.

'Thank you.' Kheda couldn't restrain a jaw-cracking yawn.

'You're tired,' Ridu observed unnecessarily.

'I'm also crumpled and stale,' Kheda said frankly. 'Have them fill me a bath while I visit the observatory.' He nodded towards the very last building on the chain of little islands. 'Then I'll sleep.'

Ridu bowed again. 'Do you want anything to eat, my lord?'

Kheda was already walking towards the observatory. 'Nothing special, just some steamed saller grain and meat, perhaps some fruit.'

'Very good, my lord.' Ridu turned and clapped his hands at the attentive servants as Kheda continued on his way to the observatory.

For my guard captain, Ridu makes a competent personal attendant. Not that I'll convince Beyau it's acceptable to use him as such. Nor that the last thing I want is a body slave shackled to me and my fortunes ever again. He'll start pressing me on that again soon; especially now we can expect visits from all our neighbouring lords.

The long shadow of the observatory reached across the dusty ground. The tower rose three times the height of the single-storeyed building surrounding it whose half-circle halls held the accumulated wisdom garnered by generations of Chazen's warlords. The topmost level of the tower was open to the sky.

How long do I have to stand up there to convince everyone I've studied the patterns of the clouds and the flight of birds, the ripples

34

and shades of the sea, to determine what lies ahead for my new daughters? The whole household would wait patiently for days if I said I needed to read all the books within, searching out interpretations of every conjunction of the stars and the bright jewels that circle through the heavens, checking through the records left by each warlord interpreting the validity of each construction placed on the concatenations of signs and stars. Can I bring myself to dissemble like this for much longer?

He opened the solid wooden door. Ignoring the spiral stairs curling upwards through the core of the tower, he passed through the archway leading to the eastern-facing hall. Star circles in bronze and silver hung on the walls, glinting as shafts of sunlight piercing the oiled wooden shutters fingered them. The paths of every constellation were incised on each plate, heavenly jewels inlaid on the net of pierced metal overlaying the circles, a measuring bar precisely aligned across each one.

Kheda halted, taken quite by surprise. 'Risala?'

A young woman was sitting on a stool at one of the long tables set in the middle of the room. She had a small ivory circle before her, one of those marked out for reading the heavens as well as registering the path of the sun and taking directions for setting sail.

'I picked this up on a trading beach in the Tule domain.' She rotated the disc this way and that. 'I thought it would make a nice addition to the Chazen collection.'

Kheda surveyed the extensive array of stargazing apparatus. 'Chazen Saril's collection.'

Risala waved a thin hand at the euphoria still ringing round the anchorage outside. 'You're the only person in this entire domain who still has qualms about your claiming dominion here. I've made it my business to be certain.'

She stood up, brushing back a lock of unbound black hair that fell to her shoulders, and looked at Kheda with fond irritation. 'Do I have to remind you what Itrac's fate would have been if you hadn't offered her marriage? She would have fallen prey to some monster like Ulla Safar, ready to rape her and call that a wedding. What would have happened last year, even if Chazen Saril had still been alive? No one I've spoken to is under any illusion that he could have saved them from one dragon, let alone two.' She narrowed her sapphire-blue eyes at Kheda. 'So was it twins? Boys or girls or one of each?'

'Two girls.' Kheda scrubbed his face with his hands, trying to stave off his weariness. 'Each will be her own woman — they're not mirrored twins. They're small but strong and healthy. Itrac's exhausted but she suffered no damage in the birthing. There's every reason to believe she'll recover fully and fast.'

'So now you've come to read the signs in the skies and the earthly compass to be sure of that, and to see what lies ahead for the children.' There was an unmistakable note of command in Risala's voice as she came over to Kheda.

'You're here to make sure I do my duty?' The bitter mockery in his reply wasn't directed at her.

'We can see that as an omen; that I just happened to arrive on the day Itrac gives birth.' She slid her arms around his waist. 'You know what you have to do.'

'While you alone of this whole domain know that I think it's a wholly futile exercise.' Kheda clasped her narrow shoulders with his broad hands and looked at her.

You're much the same age as Itrac, and as my lost eldest daughter. And I love you with more passion than I ever thought possible.

'Do you plan on telling anyone else?' She stiffened in his embrace and stared up at him, her blue eyes clouding. 'No, I didn't think so.'

'Why do you still wear this?' Kheda stroked a finger along the chain of small silver-mounted shark's teeth around

Risala's neck. 'Can you honestly tell me you still believe the portents we imagined were woven around it?'

She looked stubborn. 'I know it's a token of your faith in me. It tells me I can trust you with my life.'

'As I trust you with mine.' Kheda bent to kiss her.

Risala's lips were soft and eager, the flicker of her tongue prompting a spark of desire in him. A spark that faded and died as another yawn would not be denied. Kheda drew her close nonetheless. 'Everyone's eyes will be turned to Itrac for a good long while. We'll be able to find some time for ourselves.'

'As long as we're discreet,' Risala warned. 'The lords and ladies of Redigal and Ritsem will be visiting soon enough. I'll be no more use as your confidential agent if their spies hear gossip that I'm your concubine.'

'I won't have anyone visiting too soon.' Kheda stifled another yawn. 'Itrac needs time to regain her strength and the babies must build up theirs. I suppose I must consult the star circles for an auspicious conjunction of the heavenly compass for visits.' He scowled with distaste.

'Especially from the Daish domain,' Risala said neutrally.

Daish, where I was warlord until a malign succession of disasters convinced my formerly faithful wives that I was no longer fated to rule over them. There was no brooking their determination to see me driven out, short of taking up arms against my own son. Some thanks that was for risking my life to bring them some means of salvation from invaders who had already laid waste to Chazen and slaughtered Itrac's sister-wives and their children.

When Kheda didn't answer her, Risala twisted in his arms to look back at the ivory star circle on the table. 'It's forty days until the new-year stars align. That would insure Itrac a generous recuperation.'

Kheda nodded reluctantly. 'I imagine I can read some lies into the sky to argue for such a delay.'

'Go and read the omens for your new daughters, for their sakes.' Risala rose up on her toes to kiss him. 'It's not their fault your faith in such signs is wavering.'

Kheda looked unblinkingly at her. 'The only signs I look for are hints on the wind or in the sea's currents that we're to be invaded by those wild men and their magic once again, or worse still, see another dragon land on Chazen soil.'

Risala shuddered involuntarily. 'Then look for those signs as well, as long as you read the sky for your daughters' births. Or do you want to scandalise the gossips around the island cookfires, and have them looking askance at the babies from their birth?' A new thought struck her. 'What are you going to call them?'

Kheda shrugged. 'Itrac said, if it proved to be twins and they were girls, she wanted to call them Olkai and Sekni.'

Olkai and Sekni who were so well loved and respected. That didn't save them from death at the hands of the invaders who ravaged this domain for their own foul purposes. None of us saw any portent that presaged such disaster. With all she's seen since then, how can Risala wonder why I no longer have faith in the signs of the heavenly compass?

'That'll be popular among the islanders.' Risala was biting her lower lip absently. 'And it's news I can trade—'

Kheda frowned as he belatedly saw something else in Risala's expression. 'What is it? You didn't just come here to make sure I didn't scandalise the domain and blight my daughters' lives by declaring my abandonment of portent.'

'I picked up something else in Tule waters besides that ivory compass.' She wouldn't meet his eye, looking down. 'I got a message from Velindre.'

Kheda's blood ran suddenly cold. 'What did she say?'

Has that strange barbarian woman seen some sign that fire and magic and death are about to overturn all our lives once again?

'Nothing to send us running for the boats and fleeing the domain.' Risala laid her cheek against Kheda's chest, her hands linked in the small of his back. 'She wants to meet me on the most northerly of the Endit domain's trading beaches, on either of the days bracketing the Ruby's passing into the arc of wealth.'

'She's been brushing up on her stargazing,' Kheda commented cynically. 'What do you suppose she wants?'

'There's only one way to find out,' Risala said ruefully. 'I'll take the *Reteul* and visit the other main trading beaches on my way to see what news is being bought and sold along with word of Itrac's new daughters. I can get there and back before the new year if the winds stay in my favour. Which would be an omen,' she added lightly.

'For those fool enough to put their trust in such things.' Kheda allowed himself a moment's comfort as her body pressed against his. 'Still, the trip will certainly be a chance to read moods in the domains you pass through.'

'Such as Ulla waters. You can't avoid inviting Ulla Safar to celebrate Chazen's good fortune,' Risala warned.

Kheda sighed. 'Not when the venomous slug can snap his fingers to summon more armed men than any two other domains could muster from all their islands.'

'Not when his ill will would close so many sea lanes to stifle Chazen's trade,' Risala pointed out more prosaically.

'Let's hope he'll content himself with finding spiteful portents in his reading of the heavens over Chazen's new daughters' births.' Kheda reluctantly released Risala. 'I supposed I had better go and see what's to be seen, if only to confound his malice.'

To match Ulla Safar's undoubted lies with lies of my own. What does that make me?

Risala reached up to take his face in her hands. 'I need no signs to tell me those girls couldn't wish for a better father.' She drew him down to kiss him soundly.

'That remains to be seen,' he said tersely. 'All right, I'll go and see what I can make out. Wait for me here.'

Heaving a weary sigh, he left the room with its myriad star circles and climbed the spiral stair to the open observatory with leaden feet.

Do my other children still think I have been a good father to them? How do they judge me, forced to abandon them thanks to my own choices and those of their mothers? I won't be able to avoid inviting Sirket, any more than I can shun Ulla Safar. Daish Sirket, my son, my firstborn, forced to assume rule of the Daish domain when he's barely older than Itrac. But if I hadn't allowed everyone to believe me dead, so I could forswear all I held true and bring a wizard to fight the invaders' magic, Sirket and everyone else in Daish would have suffered the same slaughter as Chazen. Does he know that? Has Janne told him? What exactly has she told him?

Kheda squinted as he emerged onto the open observatory level. The sun was growing hotter and the black and ochre tiles dividing the floor with the cardinal lines of the compass were warm beneath his bare feet. He turned and looked to the north, where the Daish domain lay hidden far beyond the horizon.

Will Janne or Rekha come with Sirket? Will they deign to tell me if Dau is married yet, without my knowledge or consent? How much will Mesil or Efi and Vida have grown? Would I even recognise Mie or Noi, barely more than babies the last time I saw them? I've never even seen Yasi, Sain's firstborn, and he'll be walking by now.

He walked slowly around the waist-high wall, one finger tracing the carvings on the wooden rail that delineated aspects of the particular omens to be read in each third of the quadrant. He paused at the curling script marking out the arc of marriage.

What would Sain Daish say of me as a husband? Does she still trust in omens? Fearful as she was, she came to marry me trusting in the portents that I and her brother saw promising her a long and successful marriage. Look how that turned out. But everyone will be expecting me to tell them how the portents promise a long and happy life for each of my newest daughters. Risala is right about that.

He sighed and returned to the centre of the open floor, fixing his attention on the south and east where the successive arcs denoting the fates of children, parents and siblings ran round the compass towards the west. A steady breeze blew in from the open ocean.

Below the horizon at this season, the stars of the Winged Snake writhe in the arc for children. Its restless nature is said to bring hidden things into the light, as well as being token of courage. Shall I tell everyone I saw a rainbow there, to be certain that all possible positive interpretations can draw the sting from whatever signs village soothsayers claim for this day?

Kheda gazed out over the ocean. Where the green and gold of the waters around the reefs faded to mysterious blue, a puff of spray caught his eye. He saw another, then another, at odds with the ruffles of white rising and falling.

Whales. A sign of vitality and of determination, also of mystery and an unknown fate. Though the whale is always read as a positive sign by the sages of Chazen. This is the only domain where men are brave enough, or sufficiently foolhardy, to take to their boats to pursue the great beasts. Will they try to catch up with those I see and drive some laggard into the shallows where meat for a birthing festival can be harvested along with fat and bone? The whale's a sign of plenty in this domain, isn't it? I can tell Itrac that our elder daughter is born to the expectation of her resolute rule bringing fruitful times for Chazen. She'll be happy to hear that and I won't be telling her an outright lie.

That didn't particularly relieve the heaviness weighing down his spirits.

There's no earthly omen in the arc of parenthood. That's no great concern. The heavenly conjunction of Amethyst, Diamond and Opal will keep the soothsayers hunched over their books of lore until the rains come. And the Horned Fish's stars swim there. Those beasts have been known to succour drowning mariners if the books in the libraries here are to be believed. I can tell Itrac that augurs well for our care of these babies.

He looked past the point of due south marked on the observatory's tiled floor to the next arc.

The Net's myriad stars shine in the arc of siblings. If I stress the aspects of unity and cooperation, Itrac can hope our daughters' life together will be harmonious. Though nets can entangle and subdue. How difficult will it be for this second daughter when she realises she isn't the heir, when the two of them are so nearly of an age? Will she fret over whatever twist of fate held her back to be born second? Girls born when both moons are waxing are said to be precocious.

An unexpected flash of white caught the warlord's eye. This time it wasn't on the sea but rising into the far blue sky. A zaise spread long white wings with a span as wide as a tall man as it soared above the boundless ocean, spurning the land.

All white birds are a sign of beauty and fertility. I can claim that as well as the zaise's stamina and constancy for the younger girl. And mariners say the bird is an omen of returning safe to harbour, even if it's rarely seen to rest on the waters and never known to land on solid ground. Some even say it builds a nest that floats on the waters beyond the outermost islands.

I suppose there will be those who would say that was a valid omen for a girl who must fly away to some other domain to fulfil her destiny. Still, with a bird portent for the younger one, and the whale omen for her elder sister, I can argue that each girl should be treated as an individual from the outset, not as two halves of some whole. And both omens carry an element of mystery, so perhaps I can pro-

tect them from the burden of false expectations wrenched from the heavens.

Abruptly weighed down with weariness, Kheda turned away from the vast sweep of the southern horizon to go back down the stairs.

That's sufficient nonsense for the soothsayers and everyone to debate over their cookfires. I just want some sleep.

Chapter 2

I won't be able to escape inviting these noble warlords to share my observatory. How will they read these new-year stars? I'd better not give any of them reason to suspect I no longer share their trust in portents plucked from the heavens. Though there should be plenty of distractions. I haven't seen the anchorage so crowded since the day little Olkai and Sekni were born.

Kheda stood on the steps of his personal pavilion where the wide eaves cast welcome shade from the hot afternoon sun. He looked out across waters thronged with the un-decked shallow galleys that came and went between the islands of the domain. After dutifully obeying his decree securing an extended respite for Itrac, it looked as if half the loyal populace had seized this opportunity at the turn of the year to bring gifts to their warlord, his lady, the domain's new heir and her sister.

And everyone, rulers and ruled, slave and free, expects to see me in all the elegance of my position.

Immaculately groomed, Kheda smoothed the front of his azure-shot emerald tunic, resisting the temptation to fold his arms across his chest. It wouldn't do to crease the silk. His mouth watered as the breeze brought tempting scents of broiling fish and spiced saller grain. Roasting pits and cook-

44

fires on the shallow islands across the lagoon were readying a lavish feast to impress the rowers bringing their warlords and noble ladies to Chazen. A slew of bright awnings were also rigged and ready to offer shade for other guests on one of the outlying islets.

Traders trusting in the new-year stars will be warmly welcomed by Chazen. The merchants who sail the domains have shunned these beaches for too long. Though we can hardly blame them, when these last few years have seen Chazen battered by invasion and terrified by monsters. I hope Risala gets back soon enough to gauge the value of the transactions. If the scales tilt even a little in Chazen's favour, that'll be an augury I can trust beyond anything imagined in the heavens.

Absently, he twisted one of the many rings he wore: a heavy silver band carved with intricate sigils and set with a massive uncut, highly polished emerald. More emeralds glinted in his earrings and in the gold bracelets binding the full sleeves of his tunic. Looking beyond the trading galleys with their single tiers of oars, he gazed at the high-sided triremes patrolling deeper waters beyond the reef, lean and menacing. Kheda identified the distant warships as the *Brittle Crab* and the *Stilt Bird*.

That's something else I can trust in — the dedication and skill of the mariners, warriors and archers manning Chazen's defences. They won't let opportunists make free with our sea lanes. I even believe they'd face down foes backed by magic again, spitting in the wind to defy the evil. Chazen men have killed a dragon. No other domain can make that boast. But let's hope we don't have to fight any kind of invasion again in our lifetimes.

Steps sounded on the walkway leading to this easternmost island at the heart of the Chazen warlord's residence. Kheda saw Beyau approaching with a purposeful stride and nodded to acknowledge the steward. Scarlet glory bird feathers were embroidered across the shoulders of his cerulean silk tunic

45

and down the sides of his trousers, and he wore a heavy gold chain around his thick neck.

'My lord.' The burly man bowed his head briefly. 'A gift for your daughters has come from a village spokesman called Isei. He speaks for the people on Gisaire.'

'Isei?' Kheda reached out an open hand. 'Is he here?'

'No, my lord.' Beyau handed him a small box of pale-green silkstone. 'He sent his apologies that his duties called him to the outlying reefs.'

Where the first fruits of the pearl harvest are being gathered. Everyone is wondering how rich the harvest will be this year. That's an omen that will be pondered in Chazen and beyond. All I want to know is whether the seas will give up the wealth we need to restore Chazen.

Kheda studied the box, carved from a single block of soft, translucent stone. Canthira leaves made from slips of the nacre that lined pearl oyster shells were expertly inlaid into the closely fitting lid. He looked over the lagoon to the hopeful awnings on the trading beach. 'Is this the quality of the craftsmanship that visitors will find over yonder?'

'Along with choice trinkets in turtleshell and hakali wood, as well as pearls strung in all different fashions.' The steward smiled broadly. 'The rains were long and gentle, the saller harvest the best we've seen in ten years. Storms spared the vegetable plots and fruit trees and the forests are full of game.' He glanced along the chain of islands linked by bridges and walkways, his stern face softening with affection. 'My lady Itrac traded last year's largesse from the pearl reefs to good effect, for iron and cloth and more besides. Even after rebuilding their homes and filling their families' bellies, Chazen folk have had leisure to turn to profitable use.'

'Indeed.' Kheda nodded approvingly, keeping darker thoughts to himself.

Of course, there are far fewer bellies to fill, after the disasters of the past few years. But this is a new year. Let's look to the future — especially the next few days.

'I take it everything is quite ready for our guests?' he said lightly.

'Naturally, my lord.' Beyau grinned. 'We'll be putting my lord of Redigal and his retinue in the marble pavilion. Those of Ritsem and their entourage will be sharing the ebony hall while we'll be giving Daish the golden pavilion. The Ulla contingent can make what they will of the turtleshell hall. Would you care to see?'

'I'm sure everything is just as it should be.' Kheda weighed the pretty box in his hand and realised something was shifting within. Prising the lid free, he found two fine discs of whalebone threaded on silk ribbon iridescent as pearl. One was expertly carved with a horned fish, the other with a sailfish.

'The same but different, my lord,' Beyau said approvingly. 'Just right for twins.'

Isei obviously made note of the stars when the girls were born. That's to be expected: a village spokesman watches for conjunctions of the heavens. And he didn't shirk his duty in setting his people's difficulties and needs before me last year. What does he expect of me under these new stars?

Kheda nodded thoughtfully. 'I had better make plans for a tour of the domain as soon as we're done with these celebrations.'

I can undertake my duties as law-giver, arbiter and healer in all good faith. But will I still be convincing playing the part of augur, reading the portents and omens for every isle and village? I shall have to be. No warlord can hold onto power without his people behind him, not without ruling through fear and brutality like Ulla Safar.

'Your people will be glad to see you,' Beyau agreed. 'Though you'll have to find a new body slave before you can make such a voyage,' he added firmly.

'Not for travelling within my own domain.' Kheda shot the steward a quelling look. 'I'm mindful of the ill-fortune that beset my last two body slaves. Telouet was nearly killed saving me from Ulla Safar's murderous plot.'

'He made a full recovery from his injuries,' countered Beyau.

And now serves his new lord Daish Sirket. At least one good thing came out of that disastrous night; there's no one I would rather trust to care for my son.

'What of my last slave?' Kheda challenged. 'Dev followed me into the fight against that first dragon's foul magic and died in the fires the beast summoned.'

At least, that's the story everyone believes, apart from the three of us who survived.

'Dev was a barbarian from the unbroken lands. Who knows what choices in his past might have led him to such a fate?' There was a hint of uncertainty in Beyau's voice. 'Sorcerers do as they please in the north, tainting everything there with evil.'

Do you suspect that Dev was in truth a wizard? Do you suspect that I brought a mage here against law and custom that condemn magic from one end of the Archipelago to the other? Would you have helped me shelter and protect him, for the sake of his spells that were the only effective weapon against the invaders' magic, and then against the dragon that followed them here? Would you have denounced me for those crimes, demanded my dishonoured death and seen Dev skinned alive?

Kheda looked impassively at Beyau, his face betraying nothing of the turmoil in his mind.

No, you still trust me, Beyau. You'd never have followed me into battle against that second dragon, if you hadn't trusted me with your life.

'It's just not fitting, my lord,' the steward pleaded. 'You must have a personal body slave.'

'When I read omens assuring me I do not risk condemning an innocent man to an undeserved fate, slave though he might be, I'll find one.' Kheda realised he was knotting his fingers so tightly his rings were digging in painfully and forced his hands apart. 'Until then, Ridu can serve as my bodyguard as well as captain of my personal warriors.' He gestured towards a figure crossing the next island but one.

'Yes, my lord.' It cost Beyau visible effort to smooth the dissatisfaction from his face.

Kheda looked up to check the position of the sun above the wheeling coral gulls. 'Do you suppose something's delayed Ulla Safar? His shipmasters aren't usually this far adrift of their tide.'

'We're expecting Redigal Coron's galleys for the sunset high water.' Beyau let his exasperation show. 'If Ulla Safar's galleys can't cross the reef when they arrive, they'll just have to stand off in the main channel while we see the Redigal flotilla anchored.'

Kheda shrugged. 'Ulla convenience is the least of my concerns.'

By tomorrow Ritsem Caid and the contingent from Daish will be here as well. Irrespective of omens, I must start this new year by renewing my ties with those domains I hope will remain my allies. And by getting the measure of those who at best wish me no good fortune, and at worst would happily see me dead. Is Itrac up to the challenge of besting their women in their silken combats?

He carefully fitted the lid back onto the box. 'We'll see if Ridu has news and then I'll take this gift to my lady.' He walked down the steps of the pavilion and headed for the bridge to the next islet, Beyau falling into step beside him. 'What are we serving our guests tonight?'

'Spotted deer from the forests of Boal. Bristle-mouthed fish from the knot-tree swamps. Silver fowl from Esabir. Green turtle from the shallows of Dalao.' Beyau ticked off delicacies on his fingers as they crossed the swaying planks. 'Purple conch flesh from the Snake Bird Islands—'

'My lord.' A young warrior halted on the sandy path and bowed low. Straightening, he took off his steel helmet and tucked it under one arm, the veil of fine chain mail fixed to the shining brass brow band rasping against his brass-inlaid vambraces.

'The residence warriors are looking forward to testing themselves against the honour guards escorting our quests?' hazarded Kheda.

The grin widened on Ridu's cheerful brown face. 'We must uphold Chazen's reputation, my lord.' He rested one hand lightly on the hilt of the scabbarded sword thrust through his wide belt. Bronze inlay on the steel plates inset into his gleaming mail hauberk to protect his vitals caught the sun with a flash of fire.

'As dragon slayers?' Beyau smiled reluctantly as he reached out to straighten the ridged grey scale hanging from a sturdy copper chain around the young swordsman's neck.

'We of Chazen owe those of Ritsem and Redigal a debt of gratitude for their help in driving out the wild men's invasion the year before last,' Ridu said with dignity. 'But we killed that second dragon ourselves last year. None can say doing so did not reclaim our standing as warriors in full measure.'

What would you say if you knew that cloud dragon we killed was a northern wizard's simulacrum, summoned to kill the true evil? The only real dragon was the one that came before it, linked in some mystery to the wild men who invaded in its vanguard, all of them

50

wielding foul magical fires that no Aldabreshin could withstand. We could never have defeated a dragon without me forswearing myself and making that pact with Dev and then with Velindre. I wonder if Risala's found her yet.

Kheda set such concerns resolutely aside. 'Test yourselves against the Ritsem guards, by all means. Ganil, Ritsem Caid's body slave, will be in command.'

'He's a good man,' Beyau allowed grudgingly.

'The Redigal warriors will test your mettle as well.' Kheda frowned slightly. 'I don't know who Redigal Coron's body slave might be. I imagine he still changes his personal attendant with each season.'

'Are you sure you don't want to come back to serve in the residence contingent?' Ridu regarded Beyau with spurious innocence.

'Spend the heat of the day in full armour taking orders from a whelp like you? No, thank you.' Beyau sounded almost convincing. 'Though I might dig out that talon I won from the dragon,' he mused.

'The Daish contingent will be led by Telouet, Daish Sirket's body slave.' Kheda succeeded in keeping his voice calm. 'Look for his help, and Ganil's, to make sure no one responds to provocation offered by Ulla Safar's entourage.'

'My lord.' Ridu hid his surprise at Kheda's candour with a bow.

Beyau showed no such discretion. 'You think they'll cause trouble?'

'They'll make the most of the least opportunity to do so,' Kheda said frankly, 'but I don't think even Ulla Safar would have his men start a fight wholly without justification. Not if you make it clear that Chazen, Ritsem and Daish stand shoulder to shoulder.'

Our neighbours may not see the same portents in the upheavals of these past two years but they agree that Ulla Safar overstepped the mark in trying to have me killed.

Ridu drew himself up to his full height. 'Yes, my lord.'

Kheda nodded to Beyau. 'Send word to my lady Itrac's pavilion as soon as any galleys are sighted.'

'Very good, my lord.' Beyau bowed low before turning a stern eye on Ridu. 'I'll show you just where visiting warriors will be accommodated, in case of trouble.'

Ridu followed Beyau away across the island and Kheda took the walkway that led towards Itrac's pavilion. Household slaves and servants were in evidence but there wasn't the bustle that had reverberated around the lagoon for the past few days. Today, suppressed anticipation hung around maids dusting already immaculate steps and the water carriers de-livering shining brass pots.

The sand before Itrac's pavilion was raked with elegant lines and an old man stood ready to smooth away Kheda's footprints. He bowed low and pushed open the tall door. The warlord acknowledged him with a brief smile and won a wrinkled grin from the old man.

Jevin was standing just inside. 'My lord.' Like Ridu, he wore a burnished hauberk of fine chain mail. Unlike the guard captain, he could boast no dragon scale around his neck, though rock crystal gleamed in the silver brow band of his helmet, on his broad silver-studded belt and on the pommels of his twin swords and crescent dagger.

If my deceits are ever discovered, no one will be able to condemn you as tainted with magic. You were guarding Itrac when Ridu, Beyau and I were killing an already dying dragon. You will guard her against any accusations that she shares my guilt.

Itrac's audience hall was ready for their anticipated quests. The floor tiles were the soft green of water over sandy shal-lows, while hangings of translucent silk echoed the countless shades of blue uniting sea and sky. Brightly coloured fish decorated a thick carpet of mottled blue silk. They swam in shoals and pairs and spirals through a deceptively simple pattern of drifting sea grass, bordered by clusters of sea stars, pearl oysters and parti-coloured clams. Kheda smiled as he placed the little box on one of the low ebony tables set at each corner of the carpet. All were painted with intricate scenes of busy pearl divers.

No one is to be left in any doubt that the seas are rapidly replenishing this domain's wealth.

'Are you thirsty? Shall I send for juice?' Itrac was sitting cross-legged on a bank of cushions at one end of the carpet. She wore a full-skirted, long-sleeved gown of white silk shot with all the colours of the rainbow.

'Not on my account.' Kheda took a moment to flatter Itrac with his full attention.

Where her dresses had usually been designed to flatter her modest bosom, this one proudly celebrated the splendid cleavage granted by her new motherhood. She wore a collar of pearls touched with pink and blue and gold, lustrous against her copper skin, and bracelets of those same prized coloured pearls. More glistened in the midnight of her hair, drawn back to fall in a cascade of ringlets around her shoulders.

'Do you approve, my lord?' She smiled, her lips carefully outlined and glossed with coral softness. Subtle silver cosmetics brightened her eyes and highlighted her fine cheekbones.

'I do,' Kheda assured her. He sat down beside the twin babies who lay kicking their legs contentedly on a thick rug of stout white cotton prudently spread to protect the rich carpet from mishap. Each little girl wore a simple shift made from the same silk as Itrac's gown, along with a sturdy clout about her little bottom.

'Is it time to pretend we're happy to see Ulla Safar and whichever vicious shrews he's seen fit to bring?' Itrac twirled a twist of polished coral on a cord as baby Olkai watched with bright curiosity. The baby reached out, her wrist now adorned with a solid silver bangle. Little Sekni's wrists were bare as she chewed on one plump fist, fascinated by the silken hangings flickering in the breeze that filtered through the high louvred windows.

'Not yet.' Kheda waved back the elder of Touai's daughters who'd promptly stepped forward from her post by the far door.

'I had a courier dove from the western reefs this morning,' Itrac announced with ill-concealed glee. 'This year's pearl harvest promises to be as rich as last year's.'

'That's good news.' Kheda searched Itrac's face for undue weariness concealed by Jevin's skilful cosmetics brush. 'But this isn't a visit for trade. I don't want you tiring yourself out.'

Not that any two warlords' wives can ever get together without at least making some exchange of promises. But you don't look too weary. Touai's daughters are certainly proving their worth as mistresses of the nursery.

Itrac smiled serenely. 'I shall plead fatigue if anyone hopes lack of sleep has blunted my wits and tries to inveigle me into a disadvantageous deal.'

'By which time they will have given away their bargaining position?' Kheda grinned.

Was I wrong to think Chazen Saril only married you for your youth and beauty? Had he seen the seed of this acumen that's come to full flower?

Itrac's smile hardened. 'My main concern is determining the state of the Daish pearl harvest before I make covenants with any other domain.'

'You think their reefs will be barren for a second year?' Kheda's stomach felt hollow.

Which would be a truly disastrous omen for Sirket's rule.

'If they are, I see no reason to help them conceal it this time. Last year, we needed so many things to rebuild the domain—' Itrac shrugged, an unconsciously voluptuous movement. 'I won't let Janne Daish force my acquiescence as she passes off Chazen pearls as Daish's again.'

How will you manage that, when my former wife has twenty years and more experience in the tortuous negotiations between domains?

Kheda traced a thoughtful finger along sea grass swirling around a steel and sapphire blade fish. 'You'll need passage for Chazen ships through Redigal sea lanes secured before you risk having Daish waters closed to us.'

'I will be inviting Moni Redigal to extend her visit here.' Itrac twirled the coral and smiled at Olkai as the baby cooed.

'I don't want you asking too much of yourself—' Kheda began.

'We won't allow her to tire herself out, my lord.' Jevin spoke up from his place by the door.

Kheda looked at the nursemaids and saw all three were united in determined agreement.

'Satisfied?' Itrac queried dryly. She nodded at the green silkstone box Kheda had put on the table. 'What's that?'

'Gifts for our daughters from the island of Gisaire.' He showed Itrac the pendants.

'They're lovely.' Itrac smiled with delight before snapping her fingers on sudden recollection. 'Jevin, where's that offering from Sechel?'

'Here, my lady.' The slave retrieved an unassuming roll of cloth tucked away behind an alabaster vase holding dried afital grasses.

Kheda was startled to see a wholly different material wrapped within the cotton. 'Is that cloth of pearl?'

'A length for each of your daughters, my lord.' The slave proudly displayed the shimmering fabric wrought of countless small pearls, each one pierced and invisibly woven together with fine links of silver wire.

'So the Chazen folk that Janne Daish's people sheltered as they fled north from the invaders brought valuable craft secrets back with them.' Kheda smiled down at Sekni so that Itrac wouldn't see a qualm on his face.

What will it mean for your future, little one, if Janne Daish becomes Chazen's outright enemy? Because I find I am bound more surely to your future with every passing day, and to your sister's. While your mother seems to need me less and less now she has you two to fill her days and her heart.

The baby stared back, dark eyes solemn. Then her gaze fixed on the carved pendant dangling from Kheda's lingers and she charmed him with her pink, toothless smile.

'I suppose I will owe her some recompense—' The warning cadence of a signal horn beyond the lagoon interrupted Itrac.

Kheda got to his feet with relief mixed with apprehension. 'That must be the Ulla ships.'

'Put that somewhere out of sight.' Itrac gestured to Jevin to roll up the priceless gift in its concealing cotton and beckoned to the nursemaids. 'Take Olkai and Sekni back to their own apartment. It's too hot to take them into the sun.'

'You're coming with me?' Kheda was a little surprised.

'I am.' There was no sign of any weariness in Itrac as she handed her babies to their doting nurses. 'We'll begin as we mean to go on and that means not giving Ulla Safar or his wives any reason to think we're not wholly prepared to meet them.' She kissed each tiny girl and stood patiently while Jevin repaired some invisible smudge to her lips with a deft finger. 'I wonder what gift they will be offering our daughters.'

56

Kheda offered Itrac his arm. 'That will certainly be a significant sign.'

Never mind the empty symbolism of the gift; I'll want to read the intent behind it. I still don't know why Ulla Safar tried to have me killed. Custom forbids such open questions, especially when he took such pains to be sure he could deny all knowledge of the assault. I can't complain. That same custom is what keeps the other warlords in these reaches from asking me outright why I fled that chaotic night and left everyone thinking I was dead. But they want to know. Risala's web of informers hears their questions whispered on all the trading beaches.

The warlord and lady walked out onto the raked path. The confusion of boats in the lagoon had cleared to leave a broad-beamed galley picking a careful path between the outcrops of coral. The square-rigged ochre sails on the three masts were furled in heavy swags and the vessel was in the hands of the oarsmen toiling unseen on her middle deck. The lithe Chazen triremes that had escorted the galley wheeled around in a flurry of foam and headed back out to deeper water.

'The *Yellow Serpent* should return from the eastern sea lanes tomorrow.' Itrac glanced over her shoulder to Jevin, following a pace behind. 'Bring me the shipmaster's messages as soon as they're anchored.'

'Yes, my lady.' The slave bowed obediently.

My lady Itrac Chazen follows the tides of opinion these days as skilfully as her sister-wife Olkai ever did.

A chill struck Kheda as he saw that a single-masted boat with a triangular sail had slipped between the two triremes. As the lesser vessel dutifully dipped the pennant signifying its right to travel these waters, he saw a golden-haired figure at the distant tiller. A cold grip tightened around his heart.

What is Velindre doing sailing the Reteul? *Where's Risala?*

57

'Which galley is that?' Itrac was concentrating on the Ulla domain's ship making its way towards an anchorage cut into the reef.

'The *Velvet Fowl*.' Kheda dragged his wits back to more immediate concerns and frowned. 'I'd have expected them to bring more than one ship.'

Is this some insult? What do we do if Ulla Safar is openly setting his face against us? Can I strengthen ties with Redigal and Ritsem sufficiently to blunt his hatred? I need to know whatever Risala's learned of the moods in Ulla waters. I certainly don't want Velindre within a day's sail of my new daughters.

The *Velvet Fowl* wallowed, ungainly, as her helmsman turned her stern to the anchorage. Deep within the ship, the pipe that governed the oarsmen could be heard. As the Ulla rowers eased the high-sided vessel close to the piles driven solidly into the coral, Chazen men threw ropes up to the crew on deck. The *Velvet Fowl* came to rest against the floating walkway with barely a crunch of the bulbous fenders of woven saller straw. Ridu immediately led a double column of Chazen swordsmen to line the landing stage with glittering steel as the fat-bellied vessel was securely tied to the dock.

'My lord.' Itrac looked expectantly at him.

Kheda was trying to see past the vast bulk but the *Reteul* had vanished as the comings and goings across the lagoon resumed. He forced a smile. 'My lady.'

Arm in arm, they walked down the raked path and onto the immaculately swept planks of the dock. A knot of richly dressed women were descending the stair-like ladders fixed on either side of the great galley's stern. Their nervous expressions were at odds with their finery as they turned to curtsey to a grotesquely fat man making his ponderous way down to the landing stage. A sizeable contingent of armoured men waited up on deck, blank-faced as they surveyed the Chazen warriors.

'Ulla Safar.' Kheda bowed, not acknowledging the unusual number of visiting swordsmen with so much as a glance.

'Chazen Kheda, thank you for inviting us to your domain.' Ulla Safar's courtesy was perfunctory. Sweating profusely, he mopped his brow and long black beard with a white silken kerchief before tucking it into the heavy silver belt girdling his golden tunic. The fabric was richly embroidered with the dusky velvet fowl for which his galley was named. His sleeveless overmantle was finest transparent gossamer embroidered with the fire creeper such birds wove into their bowers deep in the forests cloaking the massive central island of the Ulla domain.

'You and yours are most welcome, my lord,' Kheda assured him with pleasure.

Safar looked suspiciously at him. His pale yellow-brown eyes were veined with red and half-hidden in the folds of fat disfiguring a once-handsome face. 'My wives are delighted to congratulate you on your safe delivery from the trials of childbed, my lady.' He spared the gaggle of women fawning around him a cursory gesture as he turned to Itrac. His smile turned to an open leer as he took in her décolletage. 'You're looking well, my dear.'

Look all you like, you fat lecher, but lay a finger on my wife and Jevin will cut off your hand.

'Indeed.' Mirrel Ulla advanced hastily, hands outstretched, silver and onyx bracelets bright against her ebony skin. Her brittle smile didn't reach eyes as blank and secretive as the dark gems studding the silver collar she wore. 'We are so glad to see you so obviously recovered.'

Kheda bowed and made sure his eyes didn't stray to Mirrel's generous bosom, seductively displayed by a dress of fine silvery gauze.

That gown's more suited to a boudoir than a boat. What game are you playing now? Shall I let slip that I wouldn't let my least-valued slave soil himself satisfying your lusts?

'I have my household to thank for that,' Itrac replied with nicely calculated ruefulness. She turned to indicate a long roof. 'You will have the turtleshell pavilion—'

Chay Ulla stepped forward. 'We trust your new daughters are consolation for all the bereavements you've borne so bravely these past few years.'

Kheda cut her off smoothly. 'The new year reminds us above all else that life must go on, my lady.'

Spiteful as always, Chay, but clumsier than you're wont to be and you're looking daggers at Mirrel, not Itrac.

Itrac's composure was unshaken. 'Those gone from us are never wholly lost, not while we honour their memories.'

'Indeed.' Dark-brown eyes clouded, Chay's smile took on the same fixity as Mirrel's. She twisted an unconscious finger among the ropes of striped golden agates hanging to her waist. The Ulla domain's second lady was taller than her sister-wife, her skin a warm brown against the gold silk of tunic and trousers that flattered her long bones and solid build.

What's going on? Chay's lost weight since we last had the dubious pleasure of Ulla company, and her slave's best efforts with the cosmetic brushes haven't hidden whatever strain is carving those new lines around her eyes.

Kheda let his gaze slide to the nameless huddle of lesser wives and concubines behind Ulla Safar and caught glimpses of open apprehension. The women's body slaves were uniformly blank-faced, though Ulla Safar's massively muscled attendant glowered beneath the rim of his ruby-encrusted helm.

'It is certainly a time to look to the future.' Ulla Safar smiled sweetly at Itrac before turning a look of honeyed malice on his own women.

If Safar's malevolence is focused on his own household, does that mean the rest of us will escape it? Will Jevin catch hints dropped by the Ulla wives' body slaves? But he's bound to Itrac and besides, he won't be looking for things I need to know as warlord.

'You must be tired after your voyage and the heat of the day is upon us,' Kheda said artlessly. 'My steward will show your retinue to your accommodations, if you would care to take some refreshment with my lady and myself.' He waved a hand to summon Beyau from the Chazen servants waiting beyond Ridu's honour guard.

'My thanks.' Ulla Safar thrust his broad hands into his belt, spurning Chay and Mirrel who had both reached out fruit-lessly to claim his arm.

A signal horn sounded out beyond the reef and Beyau looked askance at Kheda. 'That's the Redigal ships, my lord.'

'Then we must wait to greet our friend Coron.' Suddenly jovial, Ulla Safar turned around with an alacrity belying his bulk. 'I can suffer the sun for a little longer.' He turned an un-expected sneer on his wives. 'You all make yourselves scarce, and make yourselves presentable before you shame me any further.'

'Show our guests to their accommodations.' Kheda nod-ded at Beyau. The steward was frozen with astonishment at the Ulla warlord's overt discourtesy to his women.

'At once, my lord.' Beyau bowed low and departed with ill-concealed relief. The Ulla wives hurried after him like whipped children.

Ridu caught Kheda's eye with a discreetly questioning look. The warlord answered with a minute jerk of his head and a contingent of the honour guard on the quay peeled off to follow the Ulla retinue. The rest waited for the Ulla warri-ors to disembark and an equal number detached themselves to escort the visitors to their temporary barracks.

'I wonder which of Redigal Coron's wives will be accompanying him.' Kheda offered his arm to Itrac before smiling at Ulla Safar and leading the way towards the next anchorage along the reef where Chazen men were waiting, ready for the rapidly approaching Redigal galley. The two warlords strolled along the planks with every appearance of amity, Itrac gliding between them. Ridu and the remaining Chazen swordsmen followed behind. Kheda noted Ulla Safar mopping his brow again.

I know it's hot but you're sweating more than I'd expect and if Chay has lost weight, you've gained it, my lord slug. Your body slave was watching your wives' slaves with more mistrust than Ridu was. How many discarded concubines has that faithful brute beaten to death for you?

The remaining Chazen honour guard drew up with a rattle of armour to receive the new arrivals, the thud of their feet making the landing stage tremble. Everyone stood in silence as the galley drew closer.

The Redigal warlord was standing by the stern rails, broad-shouldered and long-legged, a head taller than any other man on deck. While Coron was Kheda's elder by nearly ten years, hair and beard now more grey than black, his dark skin gleamed with health. He moved with the vigour of a man in his prime as he came down the stern ladder as soon as the ropes were secure.

'Chazen Kheda, we're delighted to join you in reading this new year's auspices.' He held out both hands, topaz and amethysts shining around his wrists and in his rings.

Kheda matched Coron's firm grip. 'You honour us with your presence.'

'My dear!' Moni Redigal slipped past her lord and embraced Itrac with due consideration for the finery they both wore. The silk of her gown was precisely the shade of her husband's topaz, the colour flattering a complexion paler

62

than any Kheda had ever seen other than on a barbarian slave. Sparkling filigree adorned her wrists and the tight curls of her distinctive russet hair. Her necklace was a web of gold dotted with garnets and diamonds.

'Elio, Hinai, it's so good to see you.' Itrac's smile took in Redigal Coron's other wives, resplendent respectively in emerald and sapphire silk and jewellery. Both were pretty rather than beautiful, with the long black hair, warm brown complexion and light-boned build common among the seafaring islanders of the Archipelago's southern reaches.

'And you, my dear.' Elio held out her hands to take Itrac's with evident affection.

You all look a great deal happier than Ulla Safar and his wretched women.

'Chazen Kheda, you'll remember my son and heir, Redigal Litai.' Redigal Coron beckoned to a youth who was making a creditable effort at matching the poise of his elders.

'Now of an age of discretion.' Kheda smiled warmly at the boy.

He was born half a year before Mesil, so he's into his fifteenth year. Does Mesil have a beard shadowing his jaw now too?

'Ready to begin learning how to rule wisely and well.' Coron laid an encouraging hand on his son's shoulder.

Ulla Safar cleared his throat with a hint of displeasure at being overlooked thus far. 'It's good to see you, Coron.'

'Ulla Safar.' The curtness of Coron's tone and the briefness of his bow were equally insulting. 'You haven't brought Ulla Orhan to share this joyous occasion?'

'My son is indisposed.' Safar bit off the words, sensuous lips thinning.

'I am sorry to hear it.' Itrac stepped into the awkward moment with a tranquil smile. 'Coron, our steward is attending to the Safar retinue. As soon as he's free, he'll make your people comfortable. In the meantime, shall we retire to my pavilion for refreshment?'

'That would be most welcome.' For Itrac, Redigal Coron was all courtesy.

Kheda took the opportunity to look beyond the warlord, his wives and their faithful slaves. Chazen servants were busily unloading all the chests and coffers that held everything necessary to keep the Redigal nobles richly dressed and perfectly groomed throughout their stay.

But where are the zamorin *who've attended Coron so assiduously since before his father died?*

Kheda realised that Ulla Safar was also looking for those plump, smooth-skinned counsellors. Unguarded anger twisted Safar's heavy features as he glanced at the tall, well-muscled slave at Coron's shoulder. Redigal Coron's man was watching the thick-bodied brute shadowing Safar warily.

Coron has a new body slave and he's clean-shaven. Does that make him a lover of men or a castrate? Either way, he's certainly not another blunt-witted swordsman like those the faithful zamorin *counsellors always foisted on Coron and replaced so frequently. This day is full of puzzles.*

'I see you've only bought the one galley,' Ulla Safar commented brusquely.

Kheda smiled deprecatingly at Coron. 'Chazen is a small domain, but we could have accommodated more than one of your ships.'

'We set out with a second vessel.' The Redigal warlord shook his head with transparently spurious sorrow. 'It foundered as we crossed the deep channel north of Ocal.'

'That's a tragedy, my lord.' Kheda allowed some of the shock he felt to show on his face.

'Your family are all safe?' Wide-eyed, Itrac looked at the Redigal wives for confirmation.

Moni Redigal nodded, unconcerned. 'We left the other children at home with our sister-wife Uva.'

'We look forward to the day when our daughters can become friends with yours.' Hinai Redigal seemed equally untroubled by the calamity.

'All your counsellors were lost?' Kheda took pains not to notice that Chazen's curious slaves and servants had given up any pretence of being busy about their duties.

With these eager ears on every side, this news will travel the domains faster than froth on the tide. How will you want this omen read, Coron?

'What of that galley's oarsmen?' Ulla Safar held Redigal Coron's eyes with a challenge just short of accusation.

Coron looked levelly back. 'As soon as we saw the ship was in trouble, we sounded our signal horns. Boats from the closest islands took almost all of the mariners from the water.'

'Yet none of your counsellors lived?' Itrac asked artlessly.

'The stars and choices that had brought them to that day decreed otherwise.' Coron gave a perfunctory shake of his head.

'A sad loss,' Kheda managed to say.

If the mariners were all rescued, the Redigal islanders must have left the zamorin *to drown. They wouldn't have done that unless they were forewarned. What can have driven Coron to rid himself of his lifelong counsellors so ruthlessly?*

'It's too hot out here.' Ulla Safar was mopping his brow again, the white silk kerchief obscuring his face. He lowered his kerchief and addressed Itrac with scant politeness. 'My lady, you offered us refreshment—'

'The heavenly compass had been indicating some threat to our household.' Redigal Coron continued as if Safar hadn't spoken. 'I turned all my attention to ensuring that my wives and children were safe.' Coron shook his head with apparent

65

regret. 'I never imagined catastrophe would befall my counsellors.'

*Did you have travelling seers visit the islands around Ocal with
such ominous prognostication that no one dared pluck the drowning
zamorin to safety?*

'There is seldom opportunity to avert disaster, if the
heavens decree it,' Kheda lied evenly, 'as we know only too
well in Chazen. Just as we know those who suffer misfortune
and survive it are in no sense to blame for what has befallen
them.'

*Which is simple truth, and if you want my support in whatever
you're plotting, my lord of Redigal, you'll do all in your power to
give the lie to rumours of bad luck still hanging around Chazen
waters like foul air.*

Coron promptly swept a hand around to encompass the
islands of the residence, the lagoon and the whole domain
beyond. 'The good fortune that has blessed Chazen since
you drove out the curse of magic makes that plain.'

'Let's see what the new year brings.' There was a hard edge
to Ulla Safar's words as he tucked his kerchief back in his
belt.

*The rest of us will be more than satisfied to see a permanent
breach in the long alliance between the two of you.*

Kheda smiled cheerfully at both warlords. 'Let's see what
refreshments await us.'

Redigal Coron turned to indicate three armoured swordsmen drawn up a few paces apart from the Redigal honour
guard. 'I know this visit is to read the new-year omens and
to welcome your daughters, but we've brought you a gift,
Kheda.'

'We know you've been looking for a new body slave.' Moni
Redigal dimpled a smile at the warriors anonymous behind
the face plates and chain-mail veils of their helms. 'Your lady

Itrac bade us bring the best of our warrior slaves for your consideration.'

'I'm honoured,' Kheda managed to reply with barely any hesitation.

'Prai has tested them all in single combat.' Coron glanced at his own new body slave with guarded affection. 'He vouches for their skills, though you'll have your own guard captain verify that, of course.'

Kheda inclined his head to the young warrior, who was grinning with open satisfaction. 'See they are suitably accommodated, Ridu.'

Ulla Safar subjected the three warriors to scornful examination. 'I could have brought you an excellent selection of slaves, had you only asked.'

'I'm sure I mentioned it to Mirrel.' Itrac held out a hand to Redigal Litai, who was watching the three warlords with some trepidation. 'Let's retire to my audience hall.'

Stiff with courtesy, the warlord's son offered her his arm and the two of them led the other Redigal nobles away from the landing stage, Coron with one wife on either arm. Ulla Safar stumped up the path alone after them, scowling blackly. Kheda offered Moni his own arm and followed. As the slaves formed an armoured phalanx behind them, Kheda saw Moni Redigal's slave shoot a conspiratorial grin at Jevin. The younger man answered with a knowing half-smile. Redigal Litai's slave looked as nervous as his young master as he fell into step beside Jevin.

If the boy has his own attendant, he can travel to other domains without his parents. Coron is serious about training him in his duties as heir. He looks a promising lad; he won't equal his father's height but there's an encouraging breadth to his shoulders. I wonder how much Sirket will have changed when I see him—

'My lord Chazen.' As they reached the shade of the nut palms beyond the landing stages, Beyau reappeared to interrupt Kheda's painful thoughts. He promptly subjected the three unknown armoured slaves to a penetrating scrutiny.

'I take it the Ulla contingent are all settled in?' Kheda prompted after a moment.

'Indeed, my lord.' Beyau recollected himself and handed Kheda a fine slip of paper. 'A courier dove brought word from Daish Sirket. They expect to arrive early tomorrow morning.'

'We shall be very glad to see our friends of Daish,' Moni said warmly.

'Indeed.' Kheda glanced down at the message slip and schooled his face to immobility as he realised it said something else entirely.

Who does Velindre think she is, summoning me to her presence? Why is this wizard woman here? Where is Risala? I need to know what she's heard about this breach between Redigal and Ulla, about Coron's drastic removal of all his zamorin, *and if she's heard any rumour of Ulla Orhan being unwell. What I don't need is any more dealing with wizards and certainly not with so many inquisitive eyes around here.*

He screwed up the ciphered slip of paper and smiled at Moni Redigal as they continued on their way towards Itrac's pavilion. The sun's glare struck up from the white sand of the paths as the shimmering sea's inadequate breezes played with the fronds of the nut palms. As the path split into branches leading to Itrac's pavilion and away to the other islets of the residence, Kheda forced himself to halt, feigning sudden recollection.

'Moni, that mishap on your voyage here might just make sense of an omen that's been puzzling me for days. Will you make my excuses while I just go and reread the record? I'll rejoin you all as soon as I can.'

Just as soon as I've sent Velindre on her way.

'Of course.' Moni Redigal looked at him with lively curiosity before going on alone readily enough.

'My lord?' Ridu paused with the hopeful newcomers at his heels.

'Get yourselves to the barracks and out of all that armour before you faint in the heat.' Kheda waved the swordsmen away with a careless smile. He waited, looking expectant, until Ridu had no choice but to obey. Then Kheda took a deep breath and made his way towards the distant observatory isle as fast as he could without attracting too much attention. He waved an absent hand to acknowledge the bows of the servants on the steps of his own pavilion before disappearing into the cool hall at the base of the tower.

It's all very well Beyau and Ridu and Itrac all expecting me to find myself a new slave, but how can I encumber myself with some unsuspecting shadow? How would I explain this meeting, never mind my more lethally incriminating secrets?

He went through the open archway into the west-facing room where closely packed bookcases stood back to back in a line broken by tall sloped reading desks of carved russet wood. 'Velindre, I didn't expect to see you here.'

'No, I don't suppose you did.' The wizard woman was examining a cabinet of black lacquered wood packed with rows of tiny drawers. As self-assured as ever, she was as tall as Kheda, and much of an age with the warlord. Her blonde barbarian hair had been bleached to palest silk by the Aldabreshin sun, in striking contrast to her deeply tanned skin. Only her brown eyes could suggest she had any Archipelagan blood in her, along with her fluent mastery of the language. 'Congratulations on the birth of your new daughters, my lord.'

'Where's Risala?' Kheda asked, peremptory.

'I know where they came from, Kheda.' Velindre stuck her hands inelegantly in the pockets of her creamy cotton trousers. Cut from the same cloth, her baggy tunic hung loosely on her spare frame, effectively concealing any hint of femininity about her.

Kheda glanced involuntarily over his shoulder to be quite certain there was no one to overhear them. He looked back at the magewoman. 'The savages? The dragon?'

'Both. At least, there's no reason to think they came from different places,' Velindre amended.

Kheda folded his arms obstinately. 'Make this quick. I have to rejoin my guests.'

'As soon as the last rains ended, I sailed for the western-most reaches of the central domains.' Velindre gazed out of the window, one hand idly resting on the Chazen dagger she wore on her plaited sharkskin belt. 'I've been making the most of this disguise you foisted upon me. You'd be amazed what people will tell a travelling *zamorin* scholar.'

I'm still amazed that no one's seen through your disguise. Then again, everyone knows to give zamorin *due privacy lest their condition is the result of particularly savage mutilation.*

'What did the people of the western reaches tell you?' demanded Kheda.

'Sailors' legends of men from ships thought long lost washing up on their shores on rafts of broken timbers,' Velindre mused. 'Some telling stories of escaping a distant perilous land that no one could ever find. Those who sailed in search of it were generally never seen again.'

'What makes you think that's anything more than a poet's fiction?' Kheda asked sceptically.

'Strange trees have fetched up on outlying reefs after deadly storms have lashed the deep,' countered the magewoman. 'Unknown birds are occasionally blown ashore by those same storms. Those aren't stories — they're taken as omens and recorded as such. I've seen talismans made from such wood and feathers plucked from the birds and they're like nothing else found in the Archipelago.'

70

'You've visited each and every domain to be certain of that?' interjected Kheda.

'I have ways of being sure of such things. Would you like me to explain in detail?' Velindre's hazel eyes challenged him.

Kheda answered with a curt shake of his head.

What must it be like, to be able to read the very essence of nature and have the ability to warp it to your will?

'Such occurrences are all precisely recorded as omens of the earthly compass.' Velindre gestured towards the accumulated records of every event Chazen warlords had deemed significant throughout the turning aeons. 'Along with unknowable lumps of scaled and spiny creatures washing up in stinking pieces when the currents shift north for no readily apparent reason. Not readily apparent, that is, to anyone unable to read the elemental currents of air and sea,' she added with satisfaction.

What trouble will it bring down on our heads if you're discovered to be a wizard while you're here?

'Just tell me what you think you know.' Kheda found his throat was dry and not just from the heat of the day.

'There's a sizeable piece of land far out to the south and west of here,' Velindre stated with absolute certainty. 'In the ordinary course of things, ocean currents and the prevailing winds make it nigh on impossible to reach the Archipelago from there.'

'Those savages managed it,' Kheda reminded her bitterly, 'on rafts and boats made from hollowed-out logs.'

'Because they had their crude but undeniably powerful magic to help them.' Velindre was unperturbed. 'And latterly, the winds and currents have swung to the north. Otherwise those wild men would have been eaten by the ocean sharks and no one would have been any the wiser.'

71

Kheda shrugged. 'Then let me know as soon as the currents shift back so we can all sleep easier in our beds.'

'That's all you want to know?' A brief smile deepened the crow's-feet around Velindre's eyes. 'When you have how many questions about those wild men and their wizards and just why they came to plague you? The only way we'll find the real answers is to go there; you know that.'

Kheda shook his head stubbornly. 'I cannot leave Itrac. I owe her—'

'Don't you think you owe it to Dev to see this through?' Velindre's words were icy cold. 'After he died in your service, saving your domain from the destruction that dragon was wreaking?'

'I didn't ask him to sacrifice himself,' Kheda retorted.

'What has that to do with anything, my lord of Chazen?' Velindre countered with infuriating confidence. 'I've learned every custom governing obligations great and small while I've been sailing the Archipelago. That debt lies on the ledger, Kheda, until you've repaid it by securing the future Dev laid down his life to protect.'

'So I'll honour him by guarding Chazen's islands and people and not leaving them unprotected,' said Kheda with some heat.

'How do you propose to protect Itrac or get your newborn daughters to safety if another wave of wild men washes up on your islands?' Velindre asked bluntly. 'I'll tell you for nothing that those wind and ocean currents are still curling north out of their usual paths and I see no sign that they'll revert to the south any time soon. What will you do against another dragon landing on your beaches?'

'What will happen to my wife and daughters and to Chazen, if I'm away on some half-witted hunt for an unknown land with you?' Kheda shot back.

'If you're here and taken unawares like last time, you'll have just as little chance of defeating savages or dragons as you did before,' Velindre overrode him. 'Certainly without me or some other wizard to fight their fire with magic of our own. If you come with me now, we'll know if there's any such danger heading this way long before it even darkens the horizon. I can use my magic to send you back here in the blink of an eye, faster than a dragon can fly. You know that. Forewarned, you can be forearmed. And while you're getting your people out of immediate danger, I'll go straight to my own people in the north. I told you — we barbarian wizards take grave exception to the abuses of magic that these savages obviously delight in. All things being equal, all you'll see of the savages is a few corpses washing up in the westernmost isles of the Archipelago.'

'Then carry the fight to them on your own account,' Kheda protested. 'Don't involve me.'

'You involved yourself when you bound Dev's fate to Chazen's.' Velindre looked at him, unblinking. 'If you don't come, I won't go either. You can deal with whatever comes your way on your own. I'll go home to the north and not look back.'

'Do all barbarians do business with threats and coercion?' Contempt curled Kheda's lip. 'Or is it just wizards? I don't believe you.'

'I don't know about other wizards.' Velindre's sudden smile almost disarmed him. 'But I know I can't do this on my own and I won't risk it. I'll need more than magic on such a voyage. I need you,' she continued ruefully. 'You're used to reading the slightest signs of something amiss in the flight of birds or the run of the sea's fishes, even if you assign them entirely spurious meaning. You may well see things that I'll overlook just because they have no elemental significance. You're also used to foraging and hunting, which I'm certainly not, and you're an expert swordsman while I'd be dead inside a few strokes of a knife fight if I couldn't use my magic.'

She looked at him, wholly serious. 'I don't want to use my magic unless I absolutely have to on an island where our experiences suggest wizardry would draw every wild mage and any dragons straight to me.' She shrugged. 'Besides, I trust you more than anyone else I can think of taking on such a voyage.'

'I don't find your flattery any more convincing than your threats,' Kheda said coldly.

'Don't you want to know what prompted that dragon to fly and drove those savages to come here?' the mage-woman challenged him. 'Whatever that was, it happened around this time of year. Don't you Aldabreshin believe that fateful things come in threes?'

Kheda looked down at the russet tiles cool beneath his bare feet and then back up at the tall barbarian in her androgynous garb. 'Where's Risala?'

'Waiting for you and me to join her and sail for the west,' Velindre assured him. 'All I'm proposing is that we find this island and go ashore discreetly to learn a little more about these savages. If we can determine just what their relationship might be with any dragon still there, we can come back and decide what to do with such knowledge at our leisure.'

'Why can't you just use your magic to learn what you need to? Or to take you to this island?' Kheda asked stubbornly.

'Because, as I know I have told you, I cannot use magic to go to a place I've never actually visited. No wizard can.' Her composure wavered just a little. 'And as for scrying, you do recall that fire dragon insinuating itself into my spell when I came looking for Dev? I don't want to risk that happening again.'

'You don't suppose there might just have been the one dragon?' Kheda wondered with faint hope. 'And we killed it?'

'Possibly.' Velindre ran a hand over her cropped golden hair with a grin that lifted the years from her angular face. 'But I wouldn't wager my hide on it.'

She risks her hide sailing these waters. If she is ever discovered to be a wizard, she will be flayed alive. Her skin will be nailed to some warlord's gates to turn aside the evil of her magic lest it distort the omens of the earthly compass.

'I have to entertain Chazen's guests. I certainly can't leave without arousing suspicions. I'd come back to find I've no domain to rule.' Kheda scowled. 'I don't want to risk that happening again.'

'Do you want to risk wild men or dragons assailing Chazen with no time to do anything about it?' demanded Velindre. 'I'm not leaving here until you agree to come with me, Kheda.'

Curse her, and curse all wizards. But she's right, and curse her thrice for that. If there's any chance murder, fire and magic could threaten Chazen again, I have to know about it in time to defend the domain. There's no one I can send in my stead, not with a mage. But how can I find an excuse to leave here for some voyage into the unknown ocean?

'We'll see about that,' said Kheda curtly. 'Very well, I'll consider what you've said. In the meantime, you stay here in the observatory or on the *Reteul*. I'll tell my steward you're a visiting scholar who's to be fed and watered and left alone in the library. With everything else he's got to keep an eye on at present, he won't look beyond your disguise. Others might. Go nowhere else. And don't count on me coming with you.'

He turned and walked back out into the warm sun and the clean salt scented breeze playing over the island. The freshness wasn't enough to rid him of the sour realisation that the magewoman had powerful arguments on her side.

Where is Risala? Would she think it was her duty to go on this voyage alone, if I refuse and Velindre is determined to go regardless?

I truly believe all wizards are mad. Some just hide it better than others. Mad and perilous to know.

Chapter 3

They would come for her. The old woman knew it. Not tomorrow, with the old man's death still a raw wound for the whole village. Perhaps not while the younger men recalled his stories of hunts long ago and still used the knives that he had shaped. But knives didn't last for ever.

The women would spare her what scraps they could. Until the weather turned hotter and drier and they must save what little they could forage for their hungry children. They would forget that she had helped them through the travail of bringing those children into the light.

She had no children left to offer her a grudging corner of their hut. Her daughters were all gone; some bright-eyed and willingly, others reluctantly bartered, one simply vanished, seized in some raid. She had never given the old man a son to stay in the village and hear his forefathers remembered in the lists of names recited by the painted men.

He had never reproached her for bearing only daughters. She turned away from the doorway of the hut to look back at the old man lying dead on the earthen floor, wrapped in hides. He had not beaten her. He had not given her up to be fodder for the beast, as some would have done. After all, he had not chosen her for his woman, not wooed her away from the maidens' dances beneath the eyes of the sky. She had just been his share when his raiding party had ransacked the village she could barely recall, somewhere through the dark forest and beyond the green grassland.

She returned to the doorway, looking out into the rapidly darkening twilight. They would come for her. When they decided she offered the village nothing in return for whatever food and water she consumed. When the beast came, and the painted man demanded fodder for the creature, in return for his favour for the village. No one would risk his disfavour.

Should she just wait patiently? More than one old woman or old man had done so, in the long years she'd lived here. They had lived out their last days with full bellies and soft hides to sleep on. When he had come, the painted man, whichever one it had been, he had praised their courage and their devotion to their children in offering up this last good deed.

Others had chosen a quicker end to life's trials. Could she throw herself into the flames when they came to burn the hut around the old man? He had earned that much respect from the hunters — his body would not become fodder for the beast or be cast out into the forest to sate some lesser scavenger. Besides, the dwelling was dead now that he was dead and could never be lived in again.

What else could she do? She looked back once more at the old man lying still and lifeless in the gloom. He had been kind and he had been brave. He had hunted the great birds of the grasslands and the wily lizards of the muddy rivers. He had never returned empty-handed from the chase. He had never given in. Nor had she. He had taught her that much. She had fought to save him from the fever that had laid him low, cooling him with poultices and bringing gourd after gourd of water from the river, her burdened back aching from the long walk.

She fought back tears and despair. Was she just going to wait here until they ushered her out of the hut, their eyes averted? They wouldn't want to see her weeping as they brought an ember from the communal hearth to fire the walls of woven lath and the parched grass thatch.

No. She would not. Her stiff knees and hips protested as she rose from the hides she had been sitting upon. Bending painfully, she picked up the topmost hide, a length she had scraped and soaked and oiled to a thin softness none of the other women in the village could match. She wrapped it around her desiccated nakedness, knotting the corners over one withered breast. Moving slowly around the hut, she amassed a small pile of prizes in the middle of the second hide, a thicker piece with scurrier's mottled fur still clinging to it in matted patches.

Her face fell as she considered a knife that the old man had made, the black stone rippling along the cutting edge. Some young hunter would have had his eye on that. He might even now be offering to help burn the hut, in hopes of finding that knife and keeping it for himself. If she took it with her, someone would know and they would pursue her. Such a treasure wasn't to be lost along with some useless old woman.

She could take the lump of black stone, though, half-used but still worth having. Together with the bent length of thick bone, battered with use. Her finely tapered digging stick, worn smooth and well fitted to her swollen-knuckled hand, was certainly of no interest to anyone else. Nor were the few scraps of hide, the skein of cord twisted from pounded bark and the best of the gourds she had diligently gathered throughout the long hot season. She and the old man had feasted on the soft flesh that was so much easier on their gums and remaining teeth. Then she had dried the carefully emptied husks and offered them to women tied to the village by their crawling and suckling children. The mothers had traded eggs that their older children had dug from the sandy banks of the river or sometimes even a portion of the meat that their men had brought them.

Her stomach rumbled at the recollection of sweet, slippery liver, so much easier to chew. She was hungry. How could she leave with an empty belly? Would someone take pity on her if she joined the circle around the hearth? Perhaps. Perhaps they would come and burn the hut while she wasn't here. Perhaps the hunters had already decided who would keep her tied like a dog to a post of his hut until the painted man and the great beast came again.

Careful to stay in the shadows, she looked out of the doorway once again. Men and women alike were unidentifiable shadows crossing the firelight of the communal hearth. The noise of the naked children running around rose like bird chatter above the crackle of the flames. She heard the occasional chink of one stone pot against another as the women set their families' meals in the outer ring of embers. The adults' conversations were too quiet to hear, men and women standing with their heads close together, some being shaken with regret. Others wiped tears from their eyes.

The defiance that had set her shouting at the old man in the days of their youth rose within her. Could she steal an ember from the hearth unnoticed and fire the hut herself? That would deny those who relished the prospect, and would spare those who would weep a few discreet tears for her fate, and out of fear of their own old age.

It would also draw unwelcome and immediate attention. Besides, she had nothing to carry an ember in. The stoppered hollow bones that the old man was wont to carve were all gone. Everything had been traded for food to sustain him through his slow decline and that final cruel fever.

She glanced behind her towards her own stone cooking pot lost in the darkness beyond the old man's body. There was no way she could carry that away with her. All the same, the water it held would deceive her hungry belly for a little while. She slipped back into the darkness to kneel stiffly down by the heavy stone bowl. Cupping her hands, she drank as much as she could of the water she had so laboriously brought up from the river.

When she felt uncomfortably full, she returned to the mottled scurrier hide and gathered up the corners. Trussing the whole bundle with a fraying rope of plaited bark, she clutched it in her fleshless arms and edged close to the doorway. Peering out, she satisfied herself that everyone else was busy around the hearth or their own dwellings. The old man's hut was on the edge of the village. It had been in the middle when he had first brought her here. When the changing seasons saw them all return to this place, the old huts were repaired and new huts built but never on the same spot where a previous dwelling had died with its builders. So, as the years passed, a gap had opened up as the huts that had surrounded theirs were burned and the rest of the village edged away. The old man had outlived everyone else in the hunting party that had brought her here as a captive.

She stood by the corpse for a moment. There was only the faintest hint of decay in the still darkness. He had been kind to her, even when she had tried to run away. He had taken care that her bonds weren't too tight and had refused to listen to the older men insisting that he beat her into submission. One of the girls taken with her had died from such a beating and two others regularly bore bruises until they had proved their worth by bearing children. He hadn't even forced himself on her, waiting until she finally turned to him in loneliness and despair and surprising her with tenderness that offered at least fleeting gratification to lighten her misery. Eventually she had been happy enough in her way, with her daughters, and when they were gone, with the old man.

He had made no secret of sharing her sorrow at the loss of their children.

She looked back out to the distant fire in the centre of the village. She had never given up in her youth. Even in the darkest nights she had never been tempted to do the same as that girl who had refused all food and secretly eaten dirt from the floor of her hut until she had died. She wasn't about to give up, even in this wretched old age.

Clutching her bundle, she stole out of the doorway, pressing so close to the fragile walls that splinters from the laths caught at her skin wrap. Heart pounding, she slipped into the shadows by the side of the hut and waited. No shout of surprise or greeting came and she slipped further round to put the whole hut between her and the rest of the village. Still no one seemed to have noticed her.

Scrubby trees and bushes had reclaimed the deserted plots where those long dead had once built their huts. Beyond the rustling undergrowth, the taller trees of the dark forest rose up black against the star-filled sky. The twin eyes of the sky looked down on her. Half-closed, they still shed enough light to show her the faint scar of the path worn by women and children fetching kindling from the forest margins and water from the distant river in the cool of each morning. She hurried away down the track, moving as quietly as she could lest she startle some ground-roosting bird into raising a shrieking alarm.

Ignoring the fork where the path branched off towards the river, she took the hunters' trail into the depths of the dark forest. She had never done so before, but what did she have to lose? If they looked for her, they would look by the river first, so this way she might avoid notice just long enough to escape.

The blackness beneath the sprawling canopy of the trees was absolute, giving her no choice but to stick to the main path. Mysterious feet pattered alongside her from time to time or scampered in the branches overhead. Menacing snarls and pitiful cries spoke of battles for life and food won and lost. She hugged her pathetic bundle tight to her breast and hurried on as fast as she could, her old bones aching with the exertion.

She lost all sense of the night passing. There was only the endless darkness. Once she heard something larger than a man moving slowly through the trees. Saplings creaked and snapped as it forced its way through a thicket. She could hear its rasping breath and smelled a rankness she had never encountered before. Frozen with terror, she stood trembling on the path, face buried in her bundle to muffle the impulse to cry out in sheer terror.

Whatever it was moved away unseen, uninterested. She stumbled onwards on numb feet, shaking with relief. Gradually her calm returned. She wouldn't have made much of a meal for whatever the creature had been. Old age had dried her to skin and bones. But she wasn't ready to die just yet. Not that she knew what she was going to do, or where she was going to go. That didn't matter, not yet. A curious peace filled her as she walked on through the night. She just had to keep on moving. Every day she kept moving was another day gained. Life was hard but she wasn't done with it yet.

Little by little, the sky paled up above the treetops and she could see further into the grey colourlessness beneath the trees. She began searching for some animal trail leading off the main path. Hunters from other villages would be up with the dawn and she was a prize to be captured without mercy or malice. A prize to save them from giving up one of their own when a painted man came and demanded tribute for his beast.

The path curved around a mighty fallen tree that was fast subsiding into decay. Green tufts growing along the length of the mouldering trunk spread their leaves to the open sky above. The old woman moved more cautiously in case birds were browsing on the tender shoots in the transitory glade. In case men lay in wait for the birds with their spears and slings.

She looked along the void ripped into the forest by the falling of the great tree. Beyond, the green shadows led away towards the higher ground. Fewer people lived on the higher slopes, that much was certain. Life was harder up there, with less water and food for hunting or foraging. What was that to her? She was leaving one death behind her. If she ran into another, she was no worse off. And if there were fewer people on the higher slopes, surely there was less chance of her being seized? And if there was less prey for the hunters, there must surely be fewer creatures that might hunt her.

Her stomach gnawed within her and she felt lightheaded with hunger. If she didn't find something to eat, and soon, she might as well just lie down to die here. Hands shaking, she untied the rope around her bundle. Setting down the scurrier hide, she took out her digging stick and gave the rotten wood of the fallen tree an experimental prod. It crumbled to damp splinters. She dug harder beneath the edge of a sheet of bark, ignoring the hot ache in her gnarled knuckles.

She snatched at the fat white grubs squirming in the unwelcome light, biting down hard on the pulpy blandness twisting on her tongue and swallowing hastily. She managed to eat a couple of handfuls before the rest writhed in blind terror away from the daylight. Drawing a deep breath, she spat out a few fragments of sour wood and wished fruitlessly for a drink of water. At least the meagre meal had dulled the worst of her hunger pains.

Where should she go now? The sunlight was strengthening and this was a well-trodden path. Better to trust in the concealing gloom of the forest. She peered cautiously around the tangled mossy roots before leaving the shelter of the fallen log and picking her way through the tangled vines and bushes enjoying their brief tenure of the open glade. She would make for the higher ground, she decided. Though the underbrush was scant beneath the mighty trees blocking out the sunlight, the leaf litter lay thick under her feet. She walked carefully, alert for many-legged stingers and poison snakes. The few patches of open ground were smudged with marks that she could not identify, ripped up by vicious claws.

She noted fallen wood here and there out of old habit. Would a fire protect her when darkness fell again and the forest's night dwellers came hunting? She dismissed the notion with caustic self-censure. Where would she get an ember from? Besides, a fire would surely snag the all-seeing eye of a painted man or a great beast.

The forest grew quiet as the day progressed. Only the birds were busy, flitting from tree top to tree top high above, serenading each other. She stopped when she heard a harsher note of disagreement. Picking her way towards the sounds of yellow birds squabbling, she found a tree ripe with brown furry fruit.

A scurrier was already feasting on the fallen bounty, cramming food into its mouth. It looked up, its dark muzzle clotted with fruit pulp. Lashing its fringed tail, it raised one clawed hand towards her and snarled, its sharp teeth white and pointed.

The old woman retreated, but only far enough to find a rotten bough lurking beneath a sprawl of leaves. She edged back towards the brown-fruit tree and saw that the scurrier had forgotten her, more interested in filling its already bulging white-furred belly. Gritting her teeth, she hurled the length of crumbling wood at the scurrier. It screeched, surprised, and scampered away up the tree trunk, claws digging deep into the ridged bark.

It settled on a high bough and looked down. The old woman watched it for a while. It showed no signs of moving.

Cautious, she approached the fruit tree, careful of the striped
stinging flies. The scurrier chattered angrily in the tree top
and threw twigs and leaves at her. The old woman ignored
it as she poked through the glutinous mess with her digging
stick. She was more concerned about the noise the scurrier
was making. Hunters could be coming to see what was caus-
ing such a commotion. And the creature had had the best of
the fallen fruit. Still, she found a few fruits fallen or knocked
down before they were too ripe. Better yet, they showed no
worm holes or signs of gnawing.

She jumped as a stinking lump of scurrier filth thudded
onto the leaves beside her. Leaving the scolding scurrier to
its tree before the creature showered her with its piss, she ate
the brown fruit as she walked away, savouring the sweetness.
She spared a moment to hope that some hunter might hear
the spiteful beast and come to claim its hide for his bed, its
meat for his children.

She was still thirsty, though. Thirst killed long before
hunger, every child knew that, and everyone knew there was
less water the higher up the slopes you went. She began looking more closely at the smaller trees clustered in the spaces
opened up by the death of some long-dead forest giant.
Finally she spotted the thick ridged fronds of a drought tree
and pushed her way through the undergrowth towards it,
doing her best to avoid thorn scratches that would fester and
kill her.

Setting down her scurrier skin by the tree, she picked
up the least rotten length of fallen wood she could find and
thumped the nest of feathery fronds sprouting from the
stubby trunk as hard as she could. She didn't want to disturb
any snakes or stingers lurking in the depths. Untying the
bark rope around her bundle, she spread out the hide and
sat down. She picked up the broken lump of black stone and
looked at it this way and that. Gripping the angled piece of
bone tight, she set the black stone down on the hide and,

catching her tongue between her dry, cracked lips, she hit it hard. A flake split away, one good enough to do the job. The old man had taught her well. Protecting her palm with one of the scraps of hide, she looked for the best cutting edge and smiled triumphantly.

Getting to her feet, she circled the drought palm looking for a frond thin enough to yield to her failing strength. Seeing a likely prospect, she pressed close to the tree, the prickly trunk jabbing painfully at her old skin through the gap in her scant leather wrap. She pulled the frond down as far as she could, using all her meagre weight to bring the tip lower than the base. She worked slowly, cautiously, sawing at the stubborn green skin with the cutting stone. Dark sap from the outer layers stained the pale fibrous inside. It tore loose with an abruptness that surprised her. Doing her best not to spill the precious water on the uncaring forest floor, she sucked frantically at the hollow stem of the frond. The water was pure and faintly sweet and soothing.

Thirst quenched, she sat for a little while on the scurrier hide, absently swatting away the flies instantly drawn by the breath of moisture. Some while later, she got up with a sigh and, cutting a second frond, she managed to pour more than half its hoarded water into the bigger of her two gourds. She plugged it with a twist of greenery torn from the discarded frond and knotted a sling for it from her skein of bark cord. The gourd sloshed at her side as she went on her way, bundle balanced on her other hip.

The ground was definitely rising. She walked doggedly onwards. There were fewer villages in the uplands. All she had to do was stay out of sight.

Chapter 4

That rich scent is purple poppy and that drier astringency is red-lance. I'm surprised it penetrates the dense spiciness rising from the clumps of aspi leaves.

Refreshed by the night's dew, the physic garden surrounding the observatory tower breathed a heady mix of perfumes into cool air barely stirred by the new day's breezes. It was still early enough for the stone steps of his pavilion to feel cold beneath Kheda's feet. He was already dressed in fine indigo silk embroidered with silver, his silver and sapphire jewellery dull in the muted light.

'I don't know that Daish Sirket will expect you to greet him when they're arriving so early,' Itrac said neutrally as she padded over the smooth tile on soundless feet. Her night plait was unbrushed and she wore a crumpled pink robe over ungainly padded breast bands and supportive binding wrapped tight around her belly.

'I couldn't sleep. But you should rest all you can.' Kheda put his arm around Itrac's shoulders and gave her a gentle hug to make it plain he wasn't rebuking her. 'And don't exhaust yourself entertaining all our guests today.'

'I was awake to feed Olkai and Sekni.' She tugged absently at the front of her gown. 'Has Ritsem Caid said what omen he sees in Redigal Coron's loss of his counsellors?'

Nothing to give me a clue as to what mendacious interpretation I should be concocting for best advantage.

Kheda answered her with a question of his own. 'Did Sekni and Olkai sleep well?'

'Well enough for me to be sufficiently rested for today. Jevin says you're permitting some travelling scholar to consult the Chazen archive,' Itrac persisted with some concern. 'Does he bring some contrary portent for Olkai and Sekni's fortunes from some other domain?'

'No, no,' Kheda assured her. 'He's only interested in mariners' histories.'

She laid her head on his shoulder. 'You'll rest more easily when you read the new-year stars. It'll be interesting to see something of what lies ahead for the Ulla and Redigal domains,' she added thoughtfully.

'Indeed.' Kheda glanced towards the shuttered observatory, satisfying himself there was no sign that the magewoman within was stirring.

Will there be the slightest chance I can read some false omen into the heavens or the earthly compass that would justify my departure on this cursed voyage into the unknown with Velindre? To think I would once have sooner cut off my sword hand than tell such lies.

'The Ritsem slaves are already awake,' Itrac observed. Servants were emerging from the shadowed portico of the distant ebony-doored hall and heading towards the kitchens flanking a lofty storehouse on the next islet. 'Despite their late arrival.'

'Ritsem Caid said he'd welcome Daish Sirket with me.' Kheda turned his attention to the drifts of mist beyond the outermost edge of the reef, trying to discern any hint of a ship. 'Which will demonstrate Ritsem's closeness to Chazen.

Not that he needs to, even if Ulla Safar made so much of his surprise that he had only come with one of his wives.' He didn't hide his irritation.

'They brought Zorat with them.' Itrac was unperturbed. 'Ritsem Caid would hardly take his heir to a domain he didn't trust, and Taisia's his first wife.' She spoke more softly, for his ears alone. 'Taisia Ritsem is with child. She told me and the Redigal wives, and Chay and Mirrel, when we were in the nursery last night. Isn't that proof that Ritsem are our faithful allies? Taisia would hardly risk any lingering shadow of Chazen's misfortunes falling on her unborn child. I'm not surprised Mirrel Ulla and Chay ate so little at dinner. The news must have curdled their stomachs.'

'Why?' Itrac's evident pleasure in this diverted Kheda from the empty seas beyond the lagoon.

'Because they are both desperate to find themselves with child. It seems Ulla Safar is hoping to breed himself a new son.' Itrac's nose wrinkled with distaste. 'He has kept them both shut up in Derasulla along with his lesser wives and concubines since the end of the rains, and the first woman to give him one will be raised to first wife over Mirrel.'

'Ulla Orhan must really be ill.' Kheda stared out across the lagoon.

I'm going nowhere until I know what Ulla Safar is up to. Velindre can protest all she wants. And I want Risala back here, not least to learn what rumours she's picked up in Ulla waters.

'Safar obviously misread whatever signs led him to poison every other boy child his women were inconsiderate enough to bear him.' Itrac shuddered.

What omens convinced my father to raise all his sons to the brink of manhood instead of allowing our mothers to send us away as infants? How difficult was it for him to set his seal to that final decree declaring me his heir on his death? How could our mothers enforce his wishes, offering the rest the choice between castration and life as zamorin slaves or a quick and simple death? How could they do otherwise without throwing Daish into chaos? Were they glad that custom demanded they quit the domain after they had condemned their own sons to such a poisoned choice? How could I ever have believed the circling stars could sanction such a thing?

Kheda grimaced. 'So how many of his women are brooding swollen bellies inside that fortress?'

'None,' said Itrac with vicious amusement. 'And from what Elio Redigal was telling me, indulgence in his barbarian liquors and intoxicant smokes generally leaves Safar too limp to make good on his intentions, no matter how firm his resolve to get himself another male heir.'

'Let's hope that omen unmans him still further, or he dies of an apoplexy between some concubine's thighs.' Kheda's gaze drifted to the hall whose doors were patterned with turtleshell plaques. 'But what about Tewi Ulla? If Orhan dies, she's next born and becomes the heir, and there's that whole gaggle of girls to come after her.'

'All those girls have had any courage or wit in them crushed by Mirrel and Chay's inventive cruelties.' Itrac shivered and folded her arms beneath her milk-heavy breasts. 'Besides, Safar's trying to marry them off, even the ones barely of an age of discretion. Hinai Redigal says he doesn't care who he gives them to, as long as wedding into another domain gets them out of the line of succession.'

'Who has he palmed them off on?' Kheda realised the breeze was rising and moved to shield Itrac.

'He's had precious few takers.' Itrac was torn between satisfaction and pity for the hapless Ulla daughters. 'Didn't you see how Ritsem Caid and Redigal Coron both changed the subject when he mentioned that their heirs were now of an age to marry?'

'Is that what's caused this breach between Ulla and Redigal?' Kheda wondered doubtfully.

'I don't think so.' Uncertainty drew out Itrac's reply. 'That new slave of Coron's is involved somehow, and Moni made a point of letting us all know he's sharing Coron's bed, not just sleeping at the foot of it.'

Kheda frowned. 'It's been a long time since Coron last took a male lover and he's never done so openly.'

'Moni was saying she shouldn't be surprised if Coron went clean-shaven before long,' remarked Itrac. 'Let me know what Ritsem Caid makes of that notion.'

'Daish Sirket might know something, or Janne Daish,' Kheda said reluctantly. 'And here they are.' He pointed to the unmistakable shape of a fast trireme coalescing out of the distant mist. A signal horn from the wider, taller galley following the warship startled a flurry of coral gulls from their roost.

Itrac hunched her shoulders inside her pale-pink gown. 'I had better go and prepare myself.'

'They've yet to dock and their servants must settle everything in their accommodations,' Kheda said firmly. 'You don't need to receive them until mid-morning if you don't want to.'

'I don't need to antagonise Janne Daish.' Itrac surprised Kheda with a pert smile. 'Not until I choose to. Not until we've found out what they know about Ulla Safar's preoccupations and Redigal Coron's new boldness.' She walked away towards the bridge leading to the next island and Jevin detached himself from the shadows of the portico to follow.

Kheda watched the fast triremes curl away to leave the mighty Daish galley picking its way through the reefs of the lagoon.

'They're only bringing one ship.' Beyau appeared at Kheda's side. 'Do you suppose that was the young warlord's decision or has that bitch of a mother of his still got his sash knotted around her hand?'

'Watch your tongue,' Kheda advised tersely. 'I don't want to be forced to have you flogged if Daish Sirket takes offence at that kind of talk.'

To think I used to worry about the people of Chazen being too reticent to speak their minds. They certainly trust me now. What will they think of me if some menace reappears from this island Velindre has found beyond the western horizon? What will my lords of Redigal, Ritsem and Ulla make of it, and read into such an omen for my new daughters' futures? What will Janne Daish think or say? Will she finally choose to betray my secrets and reveal just how I drove such foes away before? What will that mean for little Olkai and Sekni?

Kheda watched a contingent of Chazen warriors march swiftly down towards the empty anchorage as the Daish galley drew closer. Ritsem Caid followed after them, his faithful slave Ganil one pace behind. Kheda began walking along the paths and walkways towards them. Ritsem Caid saw him and waited where three bridges met on a lump of rock ringed with slow ripples.

Kheda inclined his head in greeting. 'My lord, I appreciate you making this early start with me.'

'I was already awake, brewing a ginger and wax-flower-leaf infusion to settle Taisia's stomach.' Caid ran a hand over long curly hair tamed in rows of tight braids. The rising breeze flattened the dove-grey silk of his tunic, showing muscles built on his lithe frame by years of practice with sword and bow.

'Congratulations, my lord.' Kheda grinned as they walked on together.

'It was unexpected news,' Caid confessed, hands clasped loosely behind his back. 'But it's every woman's right to decide when and if to bear her children.'

'Not according to Ulla Safar, it seems,' Kheda said caustically. 'Have you heard anything about Ulla Orhan being ill?'

'No.' Ritsem Caid was plainly puzzled. 'Talking of Safar, I know you won't heed his nonsense but Trya and Ri will visit as soon as they've balanced their ledgers.' As he gestured, the strengthening sunlight caught the carnelians studding his gold rings. 'We've just entertained Toc Faile, and before that, Jahal Luso's household. All too soon we expect Endit Fel and his ladies to join us for the transit of the Emerald across true east.'

So Trya and Ri are doing all they can to undermine the Ulla domain's grip on trade to the north and east of here, seeing Mirrel and Chay so distracted.

'They will be most welcome.' Kheda waved away Caid's explanations. 'We're sufficiently honoured that Taisia was prepared to make the journey now she is with child.'

'Taisia is determined to bid for the oyster shells from your pearl harvest,' Ritsem Caid admitted ruefully.

So Ritsem can burn the shells for the lime they need for smelting the iron ore they have so recently discovered in their domain. Ulla Safar's influence over my lords of Endit and Jahal must be slipping now that his stranglehold on the trade in metals has been broken.

Kheda smiled. 'Itrac will be happy to make such a trade.'

In return for a fair share of Ritsem iron.

'We see it as a potent omen that Itrac named your daughter and heir for Olkai Chazen who was born my sister.' Ritsem Caid's voice tightened. 'And that your domain is blessed with twin daughters.' He rubbed a hand over his neatly plaited beard. 'If Taisia's baby is a boy, Kheda, would you consider him as a husband for your daughter Olkai? As long as he shows the necessary talents for a warrior consort? Taisia has already given up two sons to live other lives under distant stars to save Zorat from any challenge by a credible rival. I'd like her to keep this new child close, boy or girl.'

'Itrac and I would give such a match every consideration,' Kheda said cautiously.

Ritsem Caid sighed as he watched the Daish galley draw near. 'We are both blessed that our first-born sons were so well fitted to be our heirs.'

'Sirket is warlord of Daish and acknowledges no kinship with me now that I am of Chazen,' Kheda said distantly.

The two men walked on in silence broken only by the stirring of rowing boats setting out with stealthy oars to fetch the day's necessities from outer islands around the lagoon.

Ritsem Caid looked sideways at Kheda as they crossed another bridge. 'There must have been whispers from some who'd rather have seen a son born to be the next warlord of Chazen in his own right.'

'Chazen Saril's final year as warlord was a disaster,' Kheda said bluntly. 'And my accession hardly took place under ideal circumstances. Most see such omens arguing that it's a good thing little Olkai will be able to choose a husband sanctioned by favourable portents for the domain.'

As long as there's still a domain for her to inherit and we haven't all been eaten by a dragon.

'You've done well enough by Chazen,' Caid said robustly.

'There are still those with doubts.' Kheda abruptly changed the subject. 'What do you read into Redigal Coron's loss of his *zamorin* counsellors?'

'I never trusted any one of that nest of lizards.' Ritsem Caid shook his head and his slave Ganil let slip a wordless grunt of agreement. 'Though I'm surprised at Redigal Coron's equanimity over their deaths.'

'He seems confident the domain will not suffer for lack of their counsel.' Kheda chose his next words carefully. 'I wonder if Daish Sirket foresaw any hint of the disaster.'

Will you tell me if he tells you anything, Caid? Because I don't imagine he'll want to speak to me any more than he absolutely has to.

95

The Daish galley approached with the creak and rush of oars rolling over the calm waters. Voices floated from the stern platform as the helmsman in his high seat called out to the rowing master as he deftly used his twin steering oars to guide the broad-bellied vessel.

'The *Rainbow Moth*.' Ritsem Caid studied the pennant at the top of the central mast as the ship wheeled around to present its wide stern to the anchorage. 'Rainbow for new light cast on old certainty,' the warlord mused idly. 'Moth for change and new beginnings.'

All I see is Janne's favourite ship commanded by her most loyal shipmaster. What does Janne know about Ulla Safar's new obsession or Redigal Coron's unexpected ruthlessness? How can I expect her to tell me?

Ritsem Caid halted as they reached the landing stage. 'Redigal Coron can look to that new body slave for wise counsel instead of those *zamorin*.'

'Let us hope so,' Kheda agreed.

Janne is the only other person who knows that one of those drowned zamorin *was born my brother. Will she find a way to use that against me?*

Ganil spoke up behind the two warlords. 'Prai joined us on the practice ground yesterday evening, my lords. He knows how to handle a blade.'

'I'm glad of that.' Kheda watched the Chazen islanders securing the vast galley. Brown-skinned and black-haired, the Daish crew with longer, straighter daggers at their belts were otherwise indistinguishable from those of Chazen with their crescent blades.

'Is Daish offering any slaves for your consideration as you look for a new personal guard?' Ritsem Caid was studying the armoured men lining the ship's rails.

'I don't know if Itrac has requested their help.' Kheda forced an amiable half-smile as a young man and an older woman descended the stern steps with their personal slaves a few paces behind.

I don't imagine Itrac would offer Janne the chance to plant a spy in our household. Will that snub have put Janne Daish on her guard or on the attack?

Clearing his throat, Kheda walked forward to greet his former wife and erstwhile heir. 'My lord of Daish, my lady. You are both most welcome.'

'My felicitations on your new daughters' birth.' Daish Sirket's response was stilted and emotion shadowed his eyes, as green as Kheda's. He was plainly his father's son, with the same high forehead and oval face, cheekbones and nose more sharply defined than was usual in the southern reaches. Janne's blood showed in Sirket's fuller lips and darker skin, in his jet-black hair and close-trimmed beard. He wore a red silk tunic a shade darker than his mother's gown, embroidered with soaring brindled eagles. Rubies glittered in the woven gold of his intricate collar and diamonds caught fire at his wrists and fingers in the sunlight.

Rubies for courage and strength and diamonds to clear a warlord's mind of emotions that would cloud his purpose. I swear you're taller, my son, and you're certainly broader across the shoulders.

Kheda smiled over the tightness in his throat. 'Thank you.'

'It's good to see you, Sirket.' Ritsem Caid stepped forward to offer his hands to the young warlord. 'Taisia and I have brought Zorat with us and he's eager to see you again.'

Daish Sirket addressed himself to Ritsem Caid with ill-concealed relief. 'I'll be glad to offer whatever advice I can to Zorat. I trust it will be many years before he has to take up care of the Ritsem domain,' he added hastily.

'Let's hope so,' Caid agreed with amusement. 'Redigal Litai is here as well.'

Kheda inclined his head to Janne Daish. 'I take it the other ladies of Daish chose to stay close to home for the new year?'

What do you know about the recent changes in Redigal's fortunes, my lady? I see you're wearing ropes of the finest pink and grey pearls that the Daish reefs can boast. Is that to remind us of your shrewdness as guardian of Daish's trade? Or are you hoping that they will soothe your emotions? I'm not about to place any such reliance on talismans.

'To support Mesil as he reads the stars in his lord and brother's absence.' Janne calmly smoothed her ruby silk dress over her hips. It was simply cut and loosely flowing as befitted her status as the warlord's mother, and a long over-mantle of dull crimson embroidered with white basket flowers further concealed her shapely figure.

We taught Mesil to be loyal to Sirket since his birth. I thought the omens spared me my father's choices. I thought I would be there to see them grow to manhood and guide them through any quarrels that would threaten the peace of the domain. So much for predictions.

'Ri and Trya send their regards.' Ritsem Caid tried to lighten the awkward silence. 'And you must take their best wishes to Rekha and Sain.'

'Gladly.' Janne spared Caid a brief smile. 'Excuse me, my lords, but it's very early and I'm not as young as I was. I would like to rest a little before paying my respects to Itrac Chazen. Lend me your arm, Sirket.' Her expression impenetrable, Janne walked away, not so much leaning on Sirket's arm as leading him.

Beyau and Ridu took that as their signal to come forward, falling instinctively into step. A few words sufficed to impose their separate authority on the armoured men and cotton-clad servants now spilling onto the landing stage from the galley.

Janne and Sirket's respective slaves bowed low to the two warlords before following their mistress and master. Like Ganil, they wore simple silks and twin-scabbarded swords thrust through double-looped sashes, as well as two and three daggers apiece on their brass-studded belts. Birut, Janne's attendant, looked impassively at Kheda, a fear-some-looking warrior with the more curly hair and stockier build of a hill man, though with more height than most. The other slave was equally well muscled, his broad face made distinctive by a flattened broken nose. He bowed and turned away, not giving Kheda any hope of catching his eye.

Will I ever be able to make things right with you, Telouet?

'The swordsmen will be out on the practice ground by now,' Ritsem Caid said briskly. 'Let's go and see how those slaves Taisia brought are faring against Moni Redigal's offer-ings.' He didn't give Kheda the chance to demur, leading the way off the landing stage. 'What particular qualities are you looking for in your body slave?' Caid asked as they took the convoluted path towards an island where long wooden huts roofed with palm thatch surrounded an expanse of hard-packed sandy ground. 'You'll be wanting someone good with children, obviously. I'm sure Taisia took that into account. Ask her any questions you might have as to the provenance of each slave.'

The dew on the planks of the swaying walkways had dried apart from a few patches where the shadows from the nut palms fell.

Caid continued talking. 'If you find you're not happy with your choice, you can always trade him on. We won't take offence and I'm sure Redigal Coron won't either. There were some likely prospects in Jahal Luso's household according to Ganil.'

'I'd be honoured to advise you, my lord Chazen,' offered the slave following behind them.

Kheda glanced over his shoulder. 'How long have you been with your master, Ganil?'

'Sixteen years, my lord,' the burly slave replied.

'Telouet served me for more than twenty years,' Kheda said quietly. 'More than half my life. I find it difficult to im-agine anyone else at my back.'

'You have to look to each day and its omens, Kheda.' Ritsem Caid stopped and gave him a hard look. 'And to the future above all else.' The warlord started walking again, picking up the pace.

As they arrived at the practice ground, the Chazen swordsmen were emerging from their wooden huts, bare-chested and wearing mismatched cotton trousers.

Kheda did his best to gather his thoughts. 'Ganil, tell me about the two you brought here.'

'Kiba was traded out of the Seik domain by my lady Trya.' The slave followed Kheda and his master into the dappled shade of a flame tree. 'He had been body slave to Soi Seik until she married into the Mahaf domain and decided to choose herself a new attendant. He was with her for three years.' He pointed to a mature man with a wiry beard. Heavily built, his dark eyes were alert as he scanned the other swordsmen making practice swings with empty hands.

'My lady Taisia acquired Aitu from Masoal last year,' Caid chipped in, pointing to a solidly muscled young man with fine black hair slicked back with oil and a beard precisely shaved along the line of his determined jaw. 'We've been training him up. It won't be long before our daughters are looking for slaves of their own,' he added ruefully.

'I wonder sometimes where the years have gone.' Kheda searched the sandy expanse for unfamiliar faces. 'Where are the slaves Redigal Coron is offering?'

'Over there, my lord.' Ganil nodded to three men standing a little apart from the Chazen men.

Kheda eyed the trio. 'What do you know of them?'

Ganil frowned. 'I think Haro—'

'They are called Luri, Haro and Capai.' Ridu appeared at Kheda's side. The young guard captain had shed his armour for faded blue cotton trousers and a sleeveless oarsman's tunic. 'Luri's originally from the western reaches.' Ridu pointed to the closest, whose ancestry was obvious in his dark complexion and the sparse hair dotting his skull with tight black curls. 'His father's crimes saw the whole family enslaved and he became attendant to a Galcan daughter who married into Tabril. He was traded on to Yava a few years later, then on to Calece and Viselis.'

'If I were you, I'd want to know why so many warlords and ladies were happy to see the back of him,' Ritsem Caid observed.

'Haro was slave-born in the northern domains,' Ridu continued. 'He came to Redigal through my lady Moni's sister who married into Kithir.'

Kheda studied the man whose raw-boned frame and paler skin spoke of barbarian blood somewhere in his line. 'I don't recall him ever serving Redigal Coron.'

'Those unlamented *zamorin* counsellors can't have considered him suitable,' the Ritsem warlord said dryly. 'Which could be a recommendation.'

'Capai is from the Aedis domain.' Ridu pointed to the youngest of the trio, who had the coppery complexion and lithe build of a fisherman. 'He gave himself up to Aedis Harl after his village was overwhelmed by a tempest and nearly everyone drowned.'

'That's hardly the best of portents.' Ritsem Caid frowned.

'He survived,' Kheda pointed out.

'And had the courage to give up mastery of his own life in hopes of escaping further misfortune.' Ridu studied the youth critically.

Or just gave up, when no portents or soothsayer could make any sense of the troubles that beset him. I could sympathise with that.

'Their skills are more important than their pasts,' Kheda said tersely. 'Let's see what they could offer me.'

'Yes, my lord.' Ridu strode out onto the practice ground, adjusting swords thrust through his doubled belt of plaited cords.

'He's certainly grown into the role, your young captain of warriors,' mused Caid.

'He proved himself against the wild men and then against the dragon.' Kheda watched Ridu directing the swords-men into pairs. 'As for his youth, well, we lost nearly all the domain's experienced warriors to those savages and their wizards.'

'Chazen Saril lost them,' Ritsem Caid corrected Kheda firmly. 'You saved this domain.'

'My lord.' There was a warning note in Ganil's soft words.

Kheda turned to see the unwelcome sight of Ulla Safar approaching the practice ground, massive in mossy green robes, with his brutish attendant and two unknown slaves following behind him.

'I didn't expect to see him here.' The Ritsem warlord scowled,

'Nor I.' Kheda made sure his own expression was suitably opaque as Ulla Safar arrived.

'My lords.' This morning, Ulla Safar was smiling broadly, his pale eyes keen. 'I've brought two of my own swordsmen for your consideration, as you look for a new body slave.'

'I didn't know you had slaves in your guard.' Ritsem Caid frowned again.

Ulla Safar's smile hardened. 'Every day we discover things that we don't know.'

Whereas we all know you show scant consideration for the nice-ties distinguishing free islanders from slaves. These men know better than to protest or they'll see their whole families clapped in irons. Do

they hope they can win a place in Chazen and bring all their loved ones beyond Ulla's malign reach? If they buy them back by spying on me.

'Let's see their paces,' Kheda said neutrally as he gestured towards the practice ground.

Each visiting slave faced a Chazen warrior. At Ridu's command, every sword flashed from its scabbard, the lethal tips of the leading blades just touching, secondary swords held low by each man's off side. At Ridu's second shout, every warrior slid into practised routines of thrust and sliding parry, counter-thrust and hard block. Kheda found himself counting the steps while Ritsem Caid shifted beside him, following the drill once, twice and then a third time.

'Cease!' Ridu's voice cut through the slither and smack of steel and all the men stood motionless.

'They've barely broken sweat.' Caid studied the Ritsem slaves with satisfaction.

'Indeed.' Kheda noted that the Redigal and Ulla slaves were equally unwearied by this brief exercise.

'Turn about,' barked Ridu.

This time the Chazen warriors who had played the attacker waited for the visiting slaves to launch the first thrust before side-stepping out of the line of danger. Some came closer than others to rolling their own leading sword up and over their foe's killing blade to threaten his throat. The swordsmen on the defensive withdrew a pace to retaliate with murderous side-swipes of their secondary blades. Each man repeated his moves and the drill ended in a rattle of clashing steel.

'Now they're sweating,' Ganil noted with satisfaction.

'What did you say that one's name was?' Kheda pointed to the copper-skinned youth, who was showing a deft turn of speed.

'Capai, my lord, and I don't think much of his footwork,' Ganil said disparagingly.

'No one doubts the excellence of your warriors, Chazen Kheda,' Ulla Safar observed thoughtfully, 'but you are looking for a new body slave, not more guards. Surely you should be testing them against each other.'

He pulled a pale-jade kerchief from one full sleeve and dabbed at his dry forehead. The supposed slaves he had brought with him immediately turned from Chazen swordsmen to face the Redigal and Ritsem candidates.

Ridu looked to his warlord for instruction, jaw clamped tight on his irritation.

'Let them make one pass against each other,' Kheda called out.

Then perhaps we'll see what you want out of this, my lord of Ulla.

This time Capai was forced onto the defensive by one of the brawny Ulla slaves, but he held his own against successive thrusts to his face. When it was his turn to attack, however, the youth barely made his first move before falling back. He was bleeding from a deep slice to one shoulder where the Ulla man's blade had nicked him.

'You need a body slave who can move faster than that.' Ulla Safar tucked his kerchief back in his sleeve.

'Cutting a man on the practice ground suggests your man can't control his blade,' countered Ritsem Caid.

Ridu said something to the Ulla swordsman, who bowed low. Plainly determined to stay on the sand, Capai shook his head as the young captain gestured back towards one of the huts. Ridu shrugged and walked away, raising his own sword to the rest of the Chazen swordsmen.

Kheda watched Capai complete the sequence of moves without mishap this time. As a result he missed seeing exactly what the other Ulla slave did to send the ebony-skinned Luri sprawling in the dust. The Redigal man was back on his feet in an instant, spitting abuse at the Ulla slave.

'He tripped him, my lord,' rumbled Ganil with disapproval.

Ridu separated the belligerent slaves with an upward sweep of his sword, his expression scathing. As Luri stepped back, raising his hands to protest his innocence, he stumbled and stooped to clutch at one knee, face twisted with pain. Ridu shook his head, dismissal from the practice ground unmistakable. Capai had his hand clamped to his wounded shoulder. Ridu ordered him off the practice ground as well, denying the youth's futile protests with a shake of his head.

Two Redigal slaves wounded and humiliated. No one could consider them a well-omened choice for my body slave. Is this about punishing Redigal Coron for whatever has come between you, my lord of Ulla? Or do you plan on having your men wound every slave on offer so that I'm forced to choose one of your spies? What are you plotting if I refuse to oblige?

Kheda's frown deepened as two newcomers in ragged cottons appeared between the palm-thatched huts.

'Word reached Telouet quick enough.' Ganil grinned. 'And Prai's curious as well.'

Kheda wasn't amused. 'I hope they have their masters' permission to be here.'

'You can ask them yourself.' Ritsem Caid turned to bow politely to Daish Sirket and Redigal Coron, who were coming to join the gathering of warlords beneath the flame tree.

The young Daish warlord bowed politely to Kheda. 'My lord of Chazen, we were thinking it would be a good idea to test your potential body slaves against men who know just what is asked of them.'

Redigal Coron said nothing, simply staring stony-faced at Ulla Safar.

What is going on here?

'I see no harm in that.' Kheda watched Ridu exchanging a few words with the two experienced slaves. The rest of the Chazen warriors were standing with their swords hanging loose by their sides, faces alight with interest.

Ridu snapped his fingers to indicate that Telouet should take on the man who'd injured Capai. Telouet planted himself in front of his foe, both hands on his sword hilts, face impassive as he waited for Ridu's shout. Prai drew himself up in front of the slave who'd tripped Luri. Bare-chested, the Redigal slave bowed without ever taking his eyes off his opponent, oiled muscles glossy in the morning light.

The next pattern of sword strokes was woven around disabling thrusts and cuts to thighs and knees. The Ulla slave moved fast, both blades scything down and round. Telouet moved faster, blocking and twisting to turn all four blades back against the Ulla man time and again. Kheda held his breath as the Ulla slave managed to lock the hilts of his own swords with Telouet's, digging his feet into the ground. Telouet pushed hard and broke free with a feint that threatened to hamstring his opponent.

The startled slave sprang backwards, all his attention slipping downwards. Telouet took an unexpected pace forward, deftly reversing his second sword. He struck the man hard between the eyes with the polished pommel stone. Blinded by painful tears, the slave slashed one sword round at Telouet's midriff. The Daish slave met the threat with a rapid parry and followed up with a shove to the Ulla man's chest, knocking him down onto his rump.

'You should discipline your slave, Daish Sirket,' Ulla Safar said angrily, 'with a good flogging.'

'An assassin intent on the Chazen warlord's life will hardly be obeying the rules of the practice ground.' Sirket kept his eyes fixed on Telouet as the slave stood waiting for Ridu to examine the Ulla man's forehead.

Has Telouet told you about that night in Ulla Safar's fortress, my son? When the fat snake tried to kill me and Janne and all our retinue with a supposedly accidental fire, and sent some club-wielding murderer to dash out our brains in the smoke for good measure. When none of these noble lords could set aside their immediate rivalries to join forces against the savages already devastating Chazen. Nothing's changed there. But at least Ulla Safar seems on the back foot now. Could I persuade Ritsem, Redigal and Daish to join forces now, if I come back with proof that the savages are still lurking over the horizon?

'Your man is forced to retire, Safar,' Ritsem Caid said with satisfaction as Ridu waved the slave off the sand, still rubbing his eyes and blinking.

'He's the lesser of the two.' Safar looked at Redigal Coron with an unpleasant sneer.

'Prai has the measure of him.' Coron looked confidently at his slave, who smiled back with open affection.

All the men on the practice ground withdrew to fighting distance again. At Ridu's nod, they circled and sidestepped in a new pattern of thrust and parry. Now that Telouet was safely paired with one of the Ritsem slaves, Kheda watched Prai's adroit evasions of the second Ulla man's merciless attack.

So Coron and Sirket are taking this chance to humiliate Ulla Safar for some reason best known to themselves. If I had a body slave, I might have some chance of finding out why. But I can't have a body slave, certainly not while Velindre's lurking in the observatory library. I have to find some excuse for putting off making a choice, no matter how set everyone else is on helping me.

Prai's bout with the Ulla slave ended without mishap and Coron's handsome body slave stepped back, weight lightly balanced on the balls of his feet, his beardless face alert.

'You've a fine slave there, Coron.' Ulla Safar scowled and tugged his kerchief from his green sleeve to dab at beads of sweat catching the light on his forehead.

Redigal Coron showed no sign of hearing him. 'All the omens have been telling me I must look to a new direction, Chazen Kheda, for myself and for Redigal.' He watched the fighting men intently as they embarked on another series of sword drills. 'That dragon was first and foremost a dire menace to you and yours. But it was a powerful omen for the rest of us as well.'

'Many sages say a dragon's outline in the clouds presages disaster driven by discontent and false reasoning,' Ulla Safar interjected darkly.

'Poets weave dragons into their epics as a symbol of untrammelled power choosing a capricious path that leads to destruction.' Coron was still following Prai's every move. 'Whatever prompted those beasts to come to Chazen last year led directly to their deaths. Since then, Chazen has prospered. I felt it right to address various discontents within Redigal, both in the wider domain and in my own household.' He smiled as Prai wheeled stylishly around the Ulla slave's rapid sword strokes and left the man baffled, unable to keep up. 'Now we all seek a fresh direction under the new year's stars in hopes that we might prosper.'

'Who knows what the new year will bring.' There was no mistaking the menace in Ulla Safar's words.

Sirket spoke up unexpectedly. 'I hope it will bring a visit from Ulla Orhan to Daish.'

'What?' Safar's head whipped round to stare at the young warlord. He swiftly recollected himself. 'I think not. My son is unwell with a most debilitating fever.'

'I am sorry to hear that.' Redigal Coron dragged his eyes away from Prai to show every appearance of concern. 'What are his symptoms?'

'We will all be happy to share our healing lore, my lord,' Ritsem Caid chimed in with spurious sympathy.

'There are no symptoms of particular significance,' Ulla Safar said curtly. 'Which is what makes it so difficult to treat,' he added with spiteful satisfaction.

'Is there much fever on Hakere?' Sirket asked. 'Perhaps some village healer there has had success treating the sickness.'

'What has that to do with anything?' Ulla Safar's eyes fixed on the young warlord.

'That's where his last letter came from.' Sirket looked uncertain. 'If there's no other disease in Derasulla, he must have caught the contagion there.'

'He sent you a letter?' Ulla Safar took a step towards Sirket, his face ugly.

Kheda moved to block his path. 'I trust there is no widespread fever in Derasulla, my lord Safar,' he said sternly. 'If that were the case, you and your wives visiting this domain when our daughters are still so young and vulnerable would be a most unfriendly act.'

Give me that justification for throwing your fat carcass back onto your galley, with orders to quit my waters by sunset, taking your vile wives with you.

'What?' Safar was momentarily distracted. 'No, it's only Orhan who's ill.' He looked back at Sirket, pale eyes narrowing. 'And he's been kept apart from everyone else for a full cycle of the Lesser Moon.'

'But his letter arrived just before we set sail.' The young warlord looked quite bemused.

'Was it dated?' Ulla Safar asked quickly.

'I don't think so.' Sirket sounded unconvincing.

'Ridu has concluded this practice session,' Ritsem Caid said loudly, gesturing towards the youths appearing at the far end of the practice ground carrying brightly polished brass water jars.

'If you'll excuse me, my lords, I should return to my lady mother.' Sirket raised a hand to Telouet, who made a brief bow to Ridu and disappeared between two huts.

Kheda noted a swift look of complicity pass between Redigal Coron and Sirket.

What is this all about? I can't ask you directly because we never discuss such things openly, do we? And one never questions another warlord's management of his own affairs.

'How do you rate them, my lord of Chazen?' Ritsem Caid nodded towards the sweating swordsmen now quenching their thirsts.

'You'll excuse me as well.' Ulla Safar watched Sirket's rapid departure with a glower. 'I should join my beloved wives for breakfast.' He snapped his fingers at his thickset slave and hurried after the youthful Daish warlord.

'You don't think his presence in that black mood will give them all indigestion?' quipped Ritsem Caid. 'Kheda, do you see a slave to your liking?'

Kheda fell back on the excuse he'd been using to fend off Beyau, 'Given what has befallen my previous personal slaves, I don't want to make this choice lightly.'

'You don't think you'll be seeing a dragon here again, surely?' scoffed Caid.' When every scale of the beasts who died here is a talisman to ward them off.'

You can believe that if you like, Caid. I don't and I don't suppose Velindre does either, curse her. If she did, she wouldn't be here plaguing me.

'You should look for a portent to help guide your choice,' Redigal Coron said seriously.

'The simplest augury would be just spinning a blade between them and seeing where it falls,' Ritsem Caid suggested.

Coron looked askance at him. 'You don't think a blade-bone divination would be more fitting? This is a weighty decision.'

You don't seriously think any truth can be read in the patterns of cracks appearing on some animal's shoulder blade laid across a fire? I might as well be landed with a slave on the haphazard fall of a sword.

Kheda tried to hide his growing irritation. 'It is indeed, so I will take my time to consider it.'

Redigal Coron frowned. 'It would be best if we hunted a deer specifically for such a divination. Then you could read its entrails as well.'

'There are no deer on any island closer than a day's hard rowing for a fast trireme and I don't see how we can take ourselves off on a hunt without annoying all our lady wives,' Kheda said apologetically. 'Not to mention disrupting my lady Itrac's plans for the new-year festivities.'

'Let's go to the observatory,' Caid suggested with a shrug. 'If there's a relevant omen, it should be plain to see.'

Velindre will be plain to see if we go over to the observatory now. You've spent your life surrounded by zamorin, *Coron. I don't imagine her disguise will fool you.*

Kheda cleared his throat. 'The new-year stars aren't yet fully aligned. That must surely be the best time to consider my choice of a new body slave and look for omens to guide me. Let's breakfast, my lords, and see what entertainments my lady Itrac has planned for our day. Our work tonight will come soon enough.'

When every interpretation will be as open to debate as the maze of cracks appearing on a blade bone set over afire and I'll have had some time to consider what lies I can get away with to justify my refusal to burden myself with a slave.

'It'll be the omens around the earthly compass that will be crucial for all our domains.' Redigal Coron abandoned the subject of the slaves. 'There are no patterns being drawn in the heavens, in triune, square or any other figure.'

'I'm inclined towards hope nevertheless.' Ritsem Caid's expression lightened. 'The Topaz is moving into the arc of life and self to join the stars of the Bowl. With both moons all but full, we can look to the positive aspects of faithfulness that Bowl and Topaz both share.'

'The Diamond is in the arc of children.' Redigal Coron smiled at Kheda. 'With the twin moons meeting at their full three times this year, such aspects are propitious for you and your daughters.'

Will you still be so optimistic if some new invasion washes up on Chazen's shores or another dragon blights our skies?

'Go and breakfast with your lady wives, my lords.' Kheda smiled. 'I'll see if my guard captain has anything to say that has a bearing on my choice of a slave.' As he looked towards Ridu, deep in conversation with Prai, the Redigal slave noticed his movement and promptly headed towards them.

'I hope Taisia's stomach is a little more settled or I'll be breakfasting on dry saller and cold water. I'll see you when my lady Itrac summons us all.' Ritsem Caid nodded to Ganil and departed without further ceremony.

'You fought well, Prai.' Redigal Coron greeted his approaching slave with a faint smile.

'Thank you, my lord.' Prai's gaze lingered on his master's face, his eyes fond.

As the two of them departed, Prai barely the requisite pace behind his master, Ridu walked across the sand to join Kheda. His bow wasn't deep enough to hide his chagrin. 'I don't know that we learned a lot from that, my lord. I'm sorry—'

'You've nothing to apologise for,' said Kheda firmly, 'not if Redigal and Daish choose to take the opportunity to settle some score with Ulla Safar. That alone makes me disinclined to accept any of these slaves.'

Ridu was taken aback. 'My lord, you must have a new slave—'

'Bloodshed on the practice sand is hardly a good omen.' Kheda shook his head, feigning concern. 'I'm going over to the observatory. I may see matters more clearly for some solitude. Tell Itrac to send Jevin to fetch me when she wants me.'

'Yes, my lord,' said Ridu unhappily.

'This practice may have been ill-omened but that's not your fault,' Kheda said firmly. 'Put it behind you and ready the guard for the rest of the day.'

'Yes, my lord.' Ridu bowed again, still looking unconvinced.

Kheda left the practice ground and made his way over the bridges linking the scatter of islands. Overhead, coral gulls wheeled and mewed across the lagoon.

Courier doves will soon be flying north as Ulla Safar tries to find out just how Orhan could have sent Sirket a letter. Is Orhan ill or imprisoned? What are Redigal Coron and Sirket up to? There's plainly some agreement between them. Could Janne Daish shed any light on this if I could secure her goodwill? What would her price be? How can I possibly leave on some voyage with Velindre with so many questions unanswered? And I still have to find some justification to avoid being lumbered with a new body slave without offering insult to Redigal or Ritsem.

Frustration quickened his pace sufficiently that he was grateful for the cool within the half-circle halls when he finally reached the observatory.

'My lord Chazen Kheda.' Velindre appeared in the arch leading to the east-facing library and bowed low with all dutiful courtesy.

113

'We'll be reading the new-year stars from the tower this evening,' Kheda said bluntly. 'You'd better make yourself scarce. I doubt Caid will give you a second glance but Ulla Safar is a notorious lecher and Redigal Coron might well see through your pretence given his long familiarity with *zamorin*.'

'Surely he only has eyes for that new slave of his.' Velindre was amused. 'I had no idea he sharpened his sword on both edges.'

'I had no idea you listened to gossiping maidservants,' said Kheda curtly. 'Regardless, we don't want to be taking any chances.'

'I'll hide myself away on the *Reteul*,' Velindre dismissed the matter with a flick of a long-fingered hand. 'How long before we can set sail for the west? You do realise you have no real choice in this?'

'Everyone else is trying to force me to choose a new body slave.' Kheda scowled. 'At least Dev could pretend to be a swordsman and play that part.'

'I apologise for my lack of forethought in being a woman,' Velindre said sardonically. She paused for a moment, 'You know all manner of herb lore. Dose these slaves with an emetic to lay them low or something to raise a rash. That would be an ill omen and you'd be free to refuse them.'

'Which would lender those slaves valueless at best and suspect at worst,' Kheda retorted. 'What have they done to deserve that? Besides, Janne would smell something fishy and so would Itrac. They were both there when Ulla Safar poisoned Telouet to leave my back unprotected.'

Velindre gnawed at an already bitten thumbnail. 'Very well, then. Choose a slave and we'll get rid of him on our way.'

Wizards. Though you're not quite as callous as Dev. He would have suggested that from the start.

114

'You'll cut an innocent man's throat?' retorted Kheda. 'That's the only way to be certain he won't make his way back here or to Redigal or Ritsem and tell everyone exactly what I'm doing and who I'm with. Besides, I haven't even agreed to come with you. As matters stand—'

'There must be some barren rock where we can strand him where he won't be found.' Velindre spat out a fragment of nail.

'Without water or food?' Kheda challenged. 'Why not just cut his throat and be done with it?'

'You have the power of life and death over your slaves, don't you?' Velindre said with reluctant distaste. 'Besides, wouldn't his fate lie in his stars?'

'You don't believe that any more than I do,' Kheda snapped. 'And a warlord's power of life and death over his slaves is a responsibility he accepts because their fortunes and choices have brought them so low that they cannot be masters of their own future. Hasn't travelling the Archipelago this last year taught you that much?'

'I've learned more than you know, and I've seen more than a few domains where such niceties are barely observed.' Velindre coloured beneath her tan. 'Then find some way to put off making a choice, as well as an excuse for leaving as soon as possible. We don't want to delay and find that whatever prompted last year's dragon to fly has come again while we've been dithering. That would make all Redigal and Ritsem's manoeuvrings look pretty trivial, along with whatever quarrel Daish is looking to foment with Ulla Safar.'

'You have been gossiping with the maidservants.' Kheda shook his head obstinately. 'I am not about to consider leaving until I'm sure Itrac and the domain will be secure without me. Which would be a lot easier to ascertain if Risala were here,' he growled.

'Risala considers the wild men and their dragons a more pressing priority than your neighbouring warlords' bickering.' Velindre shook her head. 'Besides, she's more use keeping my ... associate company.'

'You've brought another barbarian into the Archipelago?' Kheda stared at this unexpected revelation. His blood ran cold. 'Another wizard?'

'Who might possibly betray that fact, left unchaperoned.' Velindre raised her chin defiantly.

'Who might betray you, at the threat of the flensing knife?' spat Kheda. 'Is that why you're in such a hurry to leave?'

'There's nothing to be gained by delay.' The mage-woman looked back at him, unblinking. 'And if he's taken for a wizard, what do you suppose will happen to Risala?'

Curse you, wizard, you know exactly where to stick your knife. Well, perhaps I will come with you, just far enough to get Risala out of your clutches.

'Supposing I can come up with some excuse to leave, we will have to move fast.' Kheda tried to sound as if he were genuinely capitulating as he reached for the chain of keys threaded on his belt. 'You had better stow a few things aboard the *Reteul*, if you can manage that without being caught for a thief.' He walked round the curve of the inner wall to a wide, deep chest and unlocked it. He threw open the lid and lifted out a small silver-bound ebony coffer. 'This is my travelling physic chest, and no one will miss these swords. They're not my best blades.'

Velindre took the scabbarded weapons and looked closely at one. 'Wasn't this Dev's?'

'Yes.' Kheda wondered if he was imagining the gleam of a tear in her eye. He dismissed the notion and reached into the chest to pick up a small circular brass box. Opening the physic chest, he tucked it between the tight-packed, tightly sealed vials and little lacquer containers.

'You can spend the rest of the day in the library before hiding on the boat tonight,' he ordered her brusquely. 'You've been brushing up on your stargazing, haven't you? Look for any justification in the current state of the heavenly compass for using more methods of divination — candles, mirrors, molten metal in water, the more obscure the better. The more predictions we seek, the more contradictory answers we can concoct.'

'How will that help us?' Velindre was curious.

'The more uncertainty I can stir up—' Kheda hesitated. 'I might just be able to argue that I need to travel somewhere else in the domain to look for greater clarity.'

For a few days at least. For long enough to find Risala.

The magewoman looked unconvinced. 'Then you'll be expected elsewhere in the domain. What happens when people realise you're nowhere to be found?'

'Probably at least as much trouble as I got myself into the last time I disappeared,' Kheda snapped, exasperated. 'But you're the one who wants me to do this. Why don't you put some of the learning you're always boasting about to good use and find me some kind of excuse for abandoning all my responsibilities here?'

Velindre smiled sweetly at him. 'As you command, my lord.' She took a book bound in dull grey leather tooled with gold from a shelf and opened it to the first page. It was a volume of exquisitely drawn and coloured pictures of flowers.

Kheda didn't bother to identify them. 'Where is Risala?' he demanded. 'And this associate of yours, exactly?'

Velindre looked levelly at him for a long moment before unexpectedly capitulating. 'There's a burned isle three or four days' sail from here. Risala said it was the first place you encountered the wild men's magic. She said no Chazen islander would be sailing there.'

Kheda stared at the magewoman. 'No,' he said eventually. 'They wouldn't.' Turning abruptly, he walked rapidly out of the tower.

Chapter 5

'Your mariners' displays this afternoon were most impressive, Chazen Kheda.' Redigal Coron saluted him with his golden goblet of velvet-berry juice. The drinking vessel's silver inlay shone in the soft light cast by lamps set on tall stands around the edge of the thick mossy carpet softening the grey marble floor of the vast dining hall.

'Indeed.' Ritsem Caid echoed the gesture before drinking deep. 'And now another splendid feast. Taisia will be tested to be certain our hospitality equals yours when you next visit.'

As the warlord lowered his goblet, Ganil promptly stepped forward to refill it from a ewer of beaten gold.

'The bounty of your domain is an excellent omen.' Coron held out his hand and Prai replenished his lord's drink. The slaves were standing the requisite few paces away on the interlaced pattern of striol leaves that framed the flower-studded carpet. Chazen household slaves and servants hovered further back in the shadows. As the dusk deepened, the palm fronds carved into the beams of the painted ceiling high above were already becoming indistinct.

'Indeed.' Kheda sipped at his own richly scented sard-berry juice.

119

I wonder when this dining hall was last this full? Probably not since Itrac came here to wed Chazen Saril.

Kheda glanced at his wife, but her face betrayed no such memories as Moni Redigal shared some amusing tale. Elegant in aquamarine silk brocaded with pale flowers and wearing ropes of pearls of pristine purity, Itrac's laughter floated above the lively chatter filling the hall. The two women shared a bank of cushions with Elio Redigal beside a low table bearing remnants of the sumptuous dinner. Elio's remark prompted new hilarity, lamplight flashing from the garnets on her bracelets as she illustrated her point with indecorous gestures around her silk-swathed bosom. Moni Redigal fanned herself, laughing. Her dress of red-shot violet silk was elegantly draped to flatter her figure, while her intricate coiffure, studded with jewels, declared her power and status.

Across the table, Mirrel Ulla and Chay sat in forced unity, their laughter striking a false note. Mirrel wore another revealing dress of white gossamer and a profusion of diamonds set in flowers of gold while Chay's black gown was relieved by a girdle, collar and bracelets of vivid enamelled silver. Both women's faces were impenetrable masks of paint and powder.

'Such a shame Ulla Safar finds himself indisposed this evening,' Redigal Coron remarked inconsequentially as he reached for a dish of rustlenuts. 'I suppose he got too much sun.'

'Which can be no one's fault but his own.' Ritsem Caid dismissed the absent warlord with a flick of his hand. 'Zorat and Litai were paying close attention to the triremes and I was pleased to see Sirket sharing his knowledge with them.'

At a table on the opposite corner of the carpet, under the gentle supervision of Hinai Redigal, Litai was striving to join in the lively exchanges between Daish Sirket and Ritsem Zorat.

'They look as if they're ready to take a turn at a galley's oars.' Kheda managed a smile as he brushed crumbs of nut cake from his emerald tunic, brocaded with the same jade avahi flowers as Itrac's gown. His belt was crafted from the finest turtleshell.

All three youths were wearing tightly fitted sleeveless tunics, albeit of richly embroidered silk. In silks to match their masters, their slaves stood alert for any sign that their service was required.

You haven't looked in this direction once, Telouet.

'I wonder what Taisia and Janne Daish are discussing.' Kheda looked towards the far table where his erstwhile wife and the Ritsem warlord's lady were absorbed in conversation.

'Babies, doubtless,' said Caid fondly.

Taisia was absently smoothing her rich saffron gown over her barely rounded belly, her rings studded with yellow jasper and her bracelets with polished pebbles of golden chrysolite. Janne Daish wore a dull gentian dress belted with a single gold chain and an unjewelled necklace of twisted gold wire. Plain ivory combs held her greying hair off her face, and with her lips and eyelids no more than glossed with gold, all could see that her years easily equalled Redigal Coron's.

Because you're no longer first wife of Daish, Janne, just the unwed warlord's mother.

'They'll be talking trade.' Ritsem Caid reached for a bowl of sliced lilla fruit dusted with crushed sweet-pepper.

Redigal Coron went to pick the few remaining palm kernels from a dish glutinous with honey then changed his mind, laying down his spoon. 'So, Kheda, are you any closer to deciding which slave you'll take for your new attendant?'

'I would choose sooner rather than later if I were you.' Ritsem Caid rinsed sticky fingers in a shallow bowl of water proffered by Ganil and dried his hands on linen draped over the slave's arm. He leaned back on his cushions to loosen the azure sash around the waist of his full-sleeved sapphire tunic.

'It would be best to have decided before we read the new-year stars,' agreed Redigal Coron, tugging at the vivid ochre mantle overlaying his scarlet tunic.

'All in good time, my lords.' Kheda saw Itrac trying to catch his eye down the length of the hall. He nodded briefly and she signalled to Beyau. Kheda rose to his feet as the household servants came forward to clear away the emptied bowls and platters. 'Excuse me, my lords — I'll take a little air before we're delighted by Itrac's musicians.'

Just to be sure we won't be tripping over Velindre in the observatory. I wonder if her gossiping with the maidservants has turned up any clues as to why Ulla Safar has shut himself away this evening. Does Beyau know anything?

Taking care not to hinder the sturdy slaves bodily picking up and removing the low tables from the carpet, Kheda caught the steward's eye. They moved to one of the pairs of tall doors set along the side of the hall to admit cooling breezes when Chazen's warlord sat there in judgement. For now, the slatted doors were draped with pale-yellow muslin curtains, denying the night's insects.

'I take it Ulla Safar's retinue have been suitably fed in their pavilion?' Kheda raised a brow.

'Fed and watered, my lord.' Beyau lowered his voice. 'Safar's locked himself away in an inner room with that thick-necked slave of his and a whole cage of courier doves.'

'Send a hawk handler out on a fast trireme.' Mirrel Ulla was watching him suspiciously so Kheda smiled amiably

122

back. 'If we can bring down one of Safar's birds, we might learn what messages he's sending to Derasulla.'

Because I cannot leave here, even for a few days to extricate Risala from these wizards, unless I know Itrac will be safe.

Beyau looked at the busy slaves, indecisive. 'Give me a few moments, my lord—'

Kheda shook his head. 'I'll go to the observatory and write a note for the *Brittle Crab*'s shipmaster. You can take it later.'

'Make your choice of body slave, my lord, and he can take it.' Beyau walked away to rebuke a maidservant for spilling water from a brass ewer onto a marble step.

I need a body slave for a warlord's duties but I cannot risk one betraying my association with wizards. Because that is a betrayal of every law and custom that a warlord is supposed to uphold. But there would be no domain for me to rule if I hadn't betrayed that trust. Am I ever going to be free of this paradox?

Kheda descended the broad, shallow steps that surrounded the hall on all sides. His stride lengthening, he crossed the short bridge leading to the island where his personal pavilion stood dark against the clear moonlit sky. Honeycanes planted around clusters of palm saplings rustled in the night breeze and he relished the cool air on his face.

'Searching for omens on the horizon?' Janne's dress rustled as she stepped onto the planks of the bridge. 'Birut, return to the hall. Chazen Kheda and I wish to talk alone.'

A shadow behind her, Janne's faithful slave muttered something under his breath as his heavy tread retreated down the sandy path.

The night breeze teased Kheda with Janne's familiar perfume and the soft radiance of the twin moons high above stripped away her years. He could see the beauty he had married half a lifetime before, He spoke before she could. 'How are my children?'

'Settled for the night, as far as I know.' Janne sounded faintly surprised that he should ask her. 'A nursemaid
brought word to Itrac just before she had the tables cleared.'

'How are my elder daughters?' Kheda found his grip tightening on the plaited rope of palm bark strung either side of
the bridge. 'How are my sons?'

'The younger children of Daish are very well,' Janne replied smoothly. 'Our sister-wife Sain has proved a loving and
devoted mother to them all.'

'Leaving you and Rekha free to concentrate on trades and
intrigues.' Kheda's tone was accusing despite his best efforts.
'Where is she? Doesn't Itrac warrant the courtesy of a visit
from both of you, after she let the two of you pass off the
bounty of Chazen's reefs as Daish pearls last year?'

'Rekha is on an extended tour of the Aedis, Sier and Tule
domains,' Janne said more curtly. 'She will pay her compli-
ments to your new daughters in good time.'

'She will if she doesn't want her discourtesy to jeopardise
Daish trade with Ritsem or Redigal,' Kheda shot back.

'They plainly have no qualms about renewing their ties
with this domain.' There was just a hint of anger in Janne's
words.

'It would make your life easier if Chazen was shunned,
giving you an excuse to avoid me.' Kheda tried to curb his
resentment. 'But you and I and Rekha and Sain are tied
through our children, Janne. Don't think I have forgotten
them just because Itrac has given me new daughters.'

'According to custom—' Janne snapped.

'Custom?' Kheda spoke over her. 'What custom? If we had
divorced, you would have been the one to leave the Daish
domain. Those of our children of an age of reason would
have stayed with me. Those below it would have gone with
you but they'd have been given the choice of returning when
they reached it. How many times do the histories record a

warlord separated from his children in circumstances like these? If you've found precedent, do share it. I've found none.' Kheda waved a hand at the dark observatory and swallowed hard. He managed to moderate his tone as he continued. 'How are Mesil's studies progressing? Is Sirket teaching him his stargazing and herb lore and all the history of the domain?'

Is he going to prove an ally for Sirket as he grows into his full strength, as you and I always hoped and planned? Or need we worry that he might turn out to be a rival? How could I turn such a circumstance to Chazen's advantage without hating myself?

Janne answered his unspoken question after a moment. 'Mesil is still happy to leave questions of warfare and lawmaking to Sirket while he studies healing and divinations.'

'I'm glad to hear it,' Kheda said with frank relief. He found he couldn't hold back more questions. 'What about Dau? Does she have any plans for marriage yet? What about the little ones? I take it Efi and Vida are learning their letters and their numbers? What about Noi and Mie and Sain's son, Yasi?'

He's my son, too, even if I wasn't there for his birth.

Kheda fell silent, choked by the bitterness of his losses. Waves sluiced over the corals with a low murmur of surf. Songs and laughter echoed across the lagoon as Chazen islanders made merry with the visitors come to trade and the crews of the warlords' great galleys.

'Turn your hopes to your new daughters, Kheda.' Janne cleared her throat, her voice unexpectedly gentle. 'You can leave the Daish children to my care, and Rekha's, and Sain's. The choices you made took you from them. There's no going back.'

'It was the choices you made that denied me any hope of going back to Daish.' Kheda couldn't help himself. 'Your choices have denied a father to our children.'

'Your children had already mourned you as dead.' Janne's tone hardened, her arms folded tight below her bosom. 'Daish had a new warlord in Sirket. All Chazen had was Saril who was utterly broken by fear and doubt.'

'Who never had a chance to go back and redeem himself,' Kheda retorted. 'Not after you fed him white mussels gathered in a red tide that killed him stone dead.'

'All three of us ate from the same shellfish,' Janne said steadily. 'If Saril had been fated to return to Chazen, he would have lived. If I had erred in reading the dreams that guided me to that place and that deed, I would have paid for it with my life.'

She glanced involuntarily over her shoulder. The white sand paths were empty in the moonlight and no motionless shadows lurked among the gently shifting stands of nut palms beyond. She looked back at Kheda and he was surprised to see vulnerability in her face.

'Just as if you had been the one in mortal error, when you sought out that foul barbarian to help you fight the invaders' magic with northern sorcery, you would have been the one to die on those sands. How can you doubt the omens of that day, Kheda?' she went on, strain tightening her voice. 'And what of last year? Chazen Saril could never have stood up to a dragon arriving in these waters, even if he had managed to reclaim his domain after he had disgraced himself by fleeing from the invaders who came before it. As for two such creatures—' she shuddered. 'And that sorcerer masquerading as your slave proved your salvation a second time. Chazen was even cleansed as his evil poisoned the beast when it consumed him. That is what really happened to him, isn't it?'

Kheda made no move to answer her.

So you didn't believe the tale that Dev was burned to ashes by the dragon's fiery breath. Not that you would ever believe the truth, even if I could share it with you. Once we shared everything.

126

'So yes, Kheda, I'll allow that your choices cannot have been as corrupt as I thought them.' Janne spoke through gritted teeth. 'Not if you were able to lead the men of this domain to kill that second dragon with sword and spear. The poets will be composing epics around that feat for generations to come. They're already singing your praises from one end of the Archipelago to the other now that you have been so plainly vindicated by Chazen's prosperity and your new wife's fertility.'

Kheda heard the faintest of tremors running below Janne's words.

Your faith in the heavens and the portents of the earthly compass hasn't been shaken in the least. You seize on the random turns of chance as justification for what you have done. Whereas I can no longer believe in any such guidance or excuse. If nothing else had come between us, this would have driven us irrevocably apart.

'I'm glad to see Itrac so happy again,' Janne Daish said with clipped neutrality, 'because Chazen Saril couldn't bear to have her near him at the end. Did she tell you that? Her devotion to this domain was a constant reproach to his cowardice in fleeing Chazen. He rejected her utterly. He could barely live with himself, never mind anyone else. But of course you know that. Why else would you forbid him a resting place among the honoured dead of the domain? What did you do with his body, Kheda?'

'That's none of your concern.' Kheda drew a breath. 'As for his death, all right, I'll allow you thought you acted in the best interests of the Daish domain, Janne, as you have always done.'

'I'd prefer the unequivocal reassurance of the heavens or the earthly compass.' Janne moved to the little bridge's rope rail and stared out over the open sea.

You're not just playing the part of the dowager to throw the other wives off balance. You are truly dispirited, and more weary than

127

*I can ever recall seeing you. It would be so easy to take you in my
arms, to offer you comfort. But I must be satisfied that your weakness
will strengthen Itrac's position. I must not let slip how wearisome I
find all this manoeuvring.*

'Let's hope Sirket sees hope for Daish in the new year's
stars.' Kheda looked away over the silken waters. 'Ritsem
Caid believes the earthly compass will counsel faithfulness
between allies. Daish and Chazen will always have interests
in common.' He drew a bracing breath of the salt-scented
air. 'And common enemies. Why do you suppose Ulla Safar
snubbed us all with his refusal to dine in our company?'

*What inside knowledge can you offer me? You always had the
most well-informed network of eyes and ears of any warlord's lady.*

Janne Daish rallied, squaring her shoulders beneath her
gossamer wrap. 'I imagine our hurt feelings are the least of
Ulla Safar's concerns.'

'How so?' Kheda prompted.

Janne considered her reply. 'You may as well know,' she
said at length, twisting the fringe of her wrap around her
fingers. 'Ulla Orhan has been actively seeking support among
the spokesmen of the domain's villages and islands. It's whispered he is looking to overthrow his father. So Ulla Safar had
him locked in Derasulla's deepest dungeon.'

The back of Kheda's neck prickled as if a chill breath of
wind had blown from the north. 'And Orhan will be sliced to
quivering shreds for the fat snake's entertainment as soon as
he's got a new son who looks healthy enough to live to an age
of reason.'

'More likely it'll be a death leaving a presentable corpse,'
Janne said dryly. 'Safar's predicament is complicated by the
affection of the Ulla people for Orhan, despite their fear of
Safar. Safar has had plenty of practice using venoms to make
it seem as though someone has died of a fever. Remember
Orhan's mother.'

'Hence the tale of him being unwell.' Kheda shook his head. 'But Sirket said he'd had a letter—'

'I take it he let that slip with appropriate clumsiness?' Janne's smile gleamed in the moonlight.

Kheda was puzzled. 'It wasn't true?'

'It was true.' Janne tossed a shred from the fringe of her wrap into the silent water beneath the bridge. 'But the letter didn't come from anywhere on Hakere, so Safar can waste all the time and men he chooses beating the bushes on that isle.'

'Orhan has escaped his father's clutches?' Kheda frowned as he tried to make sense of this unexpected news. 'Is that what you were telling Taisia Ritsem?'

'That and warning her not to take any food or drink from Chay or Mirrel,' Janne said with distaste. 'They're frantically trying to dose each other and any other wife or concubine they suspect of receiving Safar's attentions, to be certain any babe he begets slips away. I wouldn't put it past either one of them to ruin Taisia's happiness out of sheer spite.'

'They are truly vile.' Kheda didn't hide his disgust. 'I've always thought they deserved each other, those two and Safar.'

'They're reaping a full harvest from the misery they've sown in the past.' Janne settled her wrap anew around her shoulders. 'With any luck they'll poison each other and Safar for good measure, while Orhan thrives on saller pottage and spring water out in the forests.'

'Wouldn't we all be safer if Orhan were recaptured?' Kheda picked at the rope rail. 'If he dies, Tewi Ulla becomes the heir and there's no way she could hold that domain together.'

'Orhan has been paying court to Dau for over a year now.' Janne folded her hands deliberately across her golden belt. 'Sirket, Rekha and I all agree that it would be a good marriage.'

'You want Dau to marry Ulla Safar's son?' Appalled, Kheda pushed himself away from the rope and set the whole bridge swaying.

'Not unless she chooses to,' Janne said with asperity, putting a hand on one of the posts to steady herself. 'I know you always thought Orhan a fool, but we've come to realise that was a feint to divert his father's suspicions.'

'It was a convincing deceit.' Kheda picked at the frayed palm rope again, biting back more heated words.

He's still not fit to wash the dust from my daughter's feet. But I have no say in such matters now that Sirket is warlord of Daish. Does he know anything more of the plots inside Derasulla's labyrinthine walls? Another of my lost brothers chose to serve the Daish domain as a zamorin *slave in that termite hill. Who does he send word to now?*

'Ulla Orhan played a significant part in saving you from Ulla Safar's assassins,' Janne said pointedly into the silence.

'Is all this what's caused the breach between Redigal Coron and Safar?' asked Kheda abruptly.

'No, that was Ulla Safar overreaching himself once again,' Janne said with satisfaction. 'Coron discovered that those *zamorin* counsellors of his were plotting to overthrow him—'

Kheda searched his memory for some half-recollection. 'There was rumour—'

'This was no rumour,' Janne said tartly.

Kheda looked towards the silent darkness of the observatory, '*Zamorin* are supposed to be less interested in worldly ambition than whole men, cut off as they are from fathering their own posterity.'

'Which is why Redigal Adun sought such scholars as tutors for his sons,' agreed Janne. 'I don't suppose he foresaw that those *zamorin* would become such a powerful clique, renewing their number through adopted sons and co-opted nephews.'

Kheda shook his head slowly. 'What kind of man would willingly undergo castration? When so many die—'

'Which is partly what prompted this plot, as I understand it,' Janne said delicately. 'Those counsellors looking to retire to enjoy the luxuries they've amassed have been finding it difficult to secure replacements.'

'If their numbers dwindle, so does their power.' Kheda nodded. 'Whereas if the domain was thrown into confusion by the loss of their beloved warlord, at sea perhaps, with his senior wives and his heir—'

'It wouldn't be so remarkable for one of their own to take power, to save the domain from anarchy.' Janne finished his sentence. 'A warlord need not necessarily beget his own children, as long as they are born to his wives and acknowledged as such. Several of the Redigal daughters are of age to wed—'

'With those trusted and uninterested *zamorin* servants ready to advise them in their choices of lovers to bring new blood into the noble line,' concluded Kheda.

'Or whoever the *zamorin* put forward as warlord might still have been in possession of his personal jewels.' Janne shrugged. 'Rumour also has it that several they have recruited in recent years haven't been fully qualified. Or overly astute, apparently,' she added with asperity.

'How do you mean?' Kheda was intrigued despite himself.

It's so easy to slip back into our old complicity. It was so easy to love you, Janne. I'll never love Itrac in the same way. But it's so much simpler to love Risala. She knows all my secrets and still loves me, even if I've yet to convince her I cannot believe in omens any more.

'You've seen this new body slave of Coron's, Prai.' Janne drew closer, lowering her voice. 'Moni acquired him to be a new guard for her daughters. One of the newer *zamorin*

131

counsellors saw Prai going clean-shaven, assumed he was another eunuch and let slip something that puzzled the boy. He went to Moni and she warned him not to reveal himself as a lover of men, but to play along with the foolish *zamorin* to learn what he could of their plots.'

Kheda nodded his understanding as Janne continued.

'She soon learned enough to blackmail the relevant counsellor into promoting Prai to be Coron's body slave. Obviously Moni knew Coron was more inclined to men than to women when she married him. Prai had come to admire Redigal Coron, so it was a short step to loving him once he had Moni's blessing.' Janne adjusted one of the ivory combs in her hair. 'Prai could pass messages to Coron in the privacy of their bedchamber without the *zamorin* counsellors interrupting or becoming suspicious. When Moni had proof of the plot and Ulla Safar's complicity, Prai told Coron and helped stiffen his resolve to rid himself of the *zamorin* in one stroke.'

'I would never have thought Coron had it in him,' Kheda said frankly. 'He's always been so in thrall to those counsellors.'

'They played no small part in guiding Redigal Adun to choose him as heir.' Pity coloured Janne's words.

'Out of six or seven brothers—' Kheda grimaced at unwelcome recollection.

When the old Redigal warlord knew he was on his deathbed, he had the rest strangled in their sleep. Our mothers told my brothers that tale to prove our father was offering them more mercy than some warlords.

He cleared his throat. 'And Ulla Safar knew of this plot?'

'And decided to enter into discussions with the leaders of the *zamorin* rather than tell Redigal Coron,' Janne confirmed. 'When Coron found out, Moni says that was the stone that set the landslide in motion. Coron's been increasingly troubled by the upheavals in these reaches, suspecting some disaster lurking unseen ahead of him.' She shivered though the breeze wasn't cold. 'He's been especially concerned by the appearance of those dragons. Such a potent symbol of the twisted evils of magic and his *zamorin* could offer no answers as to why they had come.'

'No dragon overflew Redigal waters.' A qualm hollowed Kheda's belly.

What will Coron and the other warlords make of it if another dragon comes? Or more savage invaders?

'Coron saw their arrival as a dire omen.' Janne pulled her wrap tight around her shoulders. 'Then he discovered this murderous plot that was putting his whole domain at risk. So he offered equal weight in topaz for vials of creeth-tree resin.'

'Why?' As soon as Kheda asked the question, he realised the answer. 'Because it's called dragon's blood when it's burned for divinations.'

What would he have traded for the real thing?

'Exactly.' Janne shrugged. 'Whatever he saw reassured him that all the good he had done as warlord hadn't been in vain, since Prai had been there to forewarn him of this plot.'

Kheda frowned. 'Moni Redigal told you all this?'

'She wanted to be sure I knew why the Redigal domain is loosening its ties with Ulla.' Janne pursed her lips. 'She'll be making it quite clear to Itrac and Taisia Ritsem as well. Besides, now that Safar has lost his monopoly on the supply of iron in these reaches—' Whatever Janne was going to say was lost as a sweep of music rang out through the night.

Kheda saw lamplight spilling through an open pair of doors in the side of the great hall. 'We had better get back to enjoy my lady Itrac's musicians.'

'I'll go first.' Janne's face was unreadable in the moonlight. 'So no one suspects we've been indulging in some tryst.' As she walked away, the moonlight turned her gown to dark silver, outlining the seductive fullness of her hips and hinting at her long, shapely legs.

Kheda started a slow count to a hundred as she disappeared into the darkness beneath the nut palms. A shadow detached itself from one of the upswept trees and Kheda saw the sharp line of a scabbarded sword cast on the ground by the all-seeing moons. His hand went to the crescent Chazen dagger at his own belt.

'You shouldn't be out here alone, my lord.' Telouet stepped onto the moonlit path. Not quite as tall as Kheda, he was appreciably wider across the shoulders. 'Not when you still haven't chosen yourself another body slave.' His tone was accusing.

'I've yet to find anyone who could hope to be your equal,' Kheda said lightly, hooking his thumbs in his turtleshell belt.

Not only with a sword. Who could take your place after I had shared more of my life with you than with anyone else but Janne? But I couldn't burden you with the secrets I'm hiding now.

'You don't need my equal, my lord,' Telouet said brusquely. 'You just need someone big and strong enough to guard your back. Ulla Safar might be rutting like a hog in his wallow but he could well send out spies and assassins again when he sees his influence cracking like mud in the sunshine.'

'Then I'm glad Sirket has you to guard him.' Kheda hoped the half-light hid the pang those words cost him. 'Shouldn't you be in the hall serving your master?'

'He wants to see you.' Telouet nodded past Kheda, his beard jutting belligerently. 'He's gone to the observatory.'

The observatory? What if he's found Velindre? She should be able to talk her way out of it but what if he tells Janne? What does she know or suspect?

Kheda hesitated as another swirl of music floated out through the open doors of the great hall. He made a swift de-

134

cision. 'Walk with me. You can escort him back to the dining hall when we're done.'

'Yes, my lord.' As Kheda turned, the slave slipped instinctively into step a few paces behind the warlord, into the position that had been his for so many years.

'You've made a full recovery from the wounds you took at Derasulla?' Kheda forced himself to keep his words amiable.

'Thanks to Sirket, when the wound festered.' Telouet's voice was tight. 'Your son was certainly paying attention when you taught him his healing herbs.'

'I am sorry, Telouet, for your wounds and for everything else you suffered.' Kheda was glad the slave couldn't see his face as they walked on. 'For leaving you to believe I was dead.'

'I would have followed you, my lord.' Telouet's voice cracked with emotion.

And a journey to procure a wizard would have been the death of your trust in me, even if mischance hadn't killed you outright.

'Did Sirket heed his other lessons?' Kheda distanced himself with dispassionate questions. 'How is he managing Daish's alliances?'

Telouet acceded grudgingly to the change of subject. 'When he gets the chance, he reminds my lords of Aedis, Sier and Tule how far Safar overreached himself in trying to have you killed. My lady Rekha lays the groundwork in her travels and then Sirket exploits any weakness he sees in Ulla Safar's pacts. His reading of the heavenly compass makes a powerful argument that it's time other warlords addressed Safar's malice,' Telouet said suddenly. 'He sees a potent omen in the way Chazen has successfully defied even greater evils.'

Whereas if Safar hadn't tried to have me killed, I'd never have been able to let everyone think he had succeeded and disappear to go in search of the magic Dev brought to defeat the invading wild men. I even believed that was some sign that I was doing the right thing.

Kheda couldn't find the words to continue the conversation and they reached the observatory in silence. He halted, turning to look Telouet in the face. 'I'm glad to know Daish is in safe hands. There's something else I want to ask of you. Will you swear to me that you'll keep it to yourself, for the sake of all the years you served me so faithfully?'

'No.' Telouet folded his arms across his barrel of a chest. 'I am Daish Sirket's slave now.'

'Then I'll ask anyway and it'll be for you to decide whether you tell Sirket.' Kheda smiled wryly. 'If some dark day comes when Itrac needs a true friend, if she needs more than just an ally and I cannot be at her side, make sure Sirket knows I want him to take my place, as he has done in Daish.'

Because there's always the possibility that I won't break free from this entanglement with wizards before I'm discovered or betrayed. If there's no one I'd rather have ruling Daish in my stead, there's certainly no one else I'd trust to cherish Itrac and our innocent newborns.

Confusion creased Telouet's broad brow. 'My lord—'

'I had better talk to him before someone comes looking for us' Kheda strode away towards the dark observatory. 'Watch the bridge for us.'

The darkness inside the entrance hall was nearly complete. Just enough moonlight filtered though the door for Kheda to see Sirket sitting on the lower steps of the spiral stair.

The youth stood up. 'My—' He choked on his words.

'My son.' Kheda put his hand into a niche in the darkness and took up a spill of wood tipped with fluff from a tandra tree seed pod. Finding the waiting spark-maker, he squeezed it to snap the toothed steel wheel over the translucent grey firestone. A spark ignited the tandra silk and Kheda touched the burning spill to a wick floating in an open oil lamp. 'You can't begin to imagine how I've missed you.'

'Father.' Sirket stepped forward. 'I don't know—'

'I'm sorry.' Finding himself unable to look his son in the face, Kheda concentrated on nursing the fragile flame. 'Sirket, I am so sorry for everything I've put you through, you and your brothers and sisters. I had to save Daish, for all of you. Can you believe me when I tell you I couldn't see any other way of doing that?'

Could I have seen some other path if I hadn't been blinded by staring at portents and omens?

'You were talking to my mother just now.' Sirket's voice was raw. 'Were you as cruel to her as the last time you met?'

'We've made —' satisfied the lamp was well alight, Kheda blew out the burning spill '—a truce, if not our peace.'

'She's tired and she's worried.' Sirket's own voice shook with anxiety. 'You may as well know sooner rather than later. The Daish pearl harvest has failed again.'

'No!' Kheda stared at his son, aghast.

'Do you know what the travelling seers are saying?' the youth said roughly. 'I'm sure you can guess. It seems my rule is proving inauspicious. They're not giving up on me just yet, though. Evidently this new family of yours is giving some of them ideas. Plenty of soothsayers are seeing unmistakable signs that I should be looking for a wife, to bring a new beginning to the Daish domain.' He drew a long, shaking breath before going on, his words tumbling over each other in an unstoppable torrent. 'They don't care that would deprive me of my mothers as well as my father, never mind the grief that would bring Mesil and Dau, never mind we'd see the littlest ones taken from us, to wherever Janne and Rekha and Sain chose to go. How will the middling ones ever forgive me if my marriage means that Sain must leave them all alone, handing them over to some stranger who's probably only married me for power and status and will soon find she's made a startlingly bad bargain?'

He broke off and looked abruptly away, composing himself with visible effort. Then he glared at Kheda, accusing. 'How is the domain supposed to flourish if Janne and Rekha aren't managing the trade? It wasn't supposed to be this way, father. I should be able to wed at my leisure, and learn to rule by watching your example, just as my wife should learn what will be asked of her by travelling with your ladies. What am I supposed to do?'

'Have more faith in the people of Daish, for a start.' Seeing the gleam of tears in Sirket's eyes, green as his own, Kheda felt his throat tighten. 'They will trust you to make the right choices, over when and how you marry, whatever the soothsayers are muttering into their beards. Ruling is difficult. I always told you that. When you next make your progress around the domain, have Telouet take the spokesmen of a few key villages aside, to point out how Daish trade would suffer if you were to marry. You're hardly likely to find a wife the equal of Janne or Rekha.'

'You always told me to look for the signs and portents that would guide me.' Sirket scrubbed angrily at his eyes with the back of one hand. 'You never foresaw this.'

'No.' Kheda looked steadily back at the young man. 'Just as no one foresaw my father's death in the collapse of his own observatory tower, least of all himself. I wasn't that much older than you when I had to learn to rule alone without his guidance. Plenty of seers were claiming that his fate was a deadly omen for Daish, within our own waters and in neighbouring domains. I was lucky no one saw some portent encouraging them to invade us.'

There are probably some even now who are harking back to that catastrophe as the start of all these misfortunes. At least now I'm no longer tempted to agree with them.

'That was different,' snapped Sirket. 'You were already married to my mother for one thing.'

138

'The right wife is a great comfort in such difficult times,' Kheda agreed. 'The wrong one would be worse than no wife at all. Don't rush into anything because that's what you think the people want. Take your time and make your choice when the time is right for you. See what me and your mothers got right in our marriages, and see where we went wrong. Try not to make the same mistakes,' he added ruefully.

Try not to find yourself married to a widow half your age because you feel guilty for the death of her husband and it's the only way you can protect her.

'If I marry, Janne and Rekha and Sain must leave—' Sirket protested.

'Why?' interrupted Kheda.

'Why?' Sirket stared at him. 'Custom—'

'Custom says that you're the warlord, Sirket, and that means the power of life and death and everything up to that in Daish is yours to use as you see fit.' Kheda cut the youth's words off with a sideways sweep of his hand. 'Custom is for customary times. There's nothing usual about the days we're living through. You said yourself that no one predicted any of these catastrophes. If you choose to marry, for the sake of the domain or for love or for something in between, ask Janne, Rekha and Sain to stay. If you refuse to deprive your sisters and brothers of their mothers' love and support, who's to gainsay you?'

'What—' Sirket's mouth hung open for a moment.

The lamplight in the hallway enclosed them, the stairwell and the open arches to the halls on either side black voids framed by vines painted on the plastered stone work.

Kheda made an abrupt decision. 'I need you to hold Daish securely, my son. I need you to be Chazen's ally. I need you to be the warlord I raised you to be, the man I have always known you would become.' Kheda rubbed a hand over his beard. 'I have to go on another journey, alone. I'm glad of this chance to tell you ahead of anyone else, even Itrac. I'm leaving here, tomorrow or someday soon. I don't know quite when I'll return but hopefully I won't be away for too long.'

'You're leaving again?' cried Sirket. 'Why?'

'The first time I left you, I was looking for some means to fight the wild men who brought such destruction out of the southern ocean. I can't tell you the whole truth of what I found and what I did but I won't tell you any lies.' Kheda looked steadily at his son. 'I came back with the means to kill their wizards and it wasn't just that blend of narcotics to stifle their magic that I showed you and Redigal and Ritsem. It was what gave me the means to fight the dragons when they came last year. It's what has helped me learn why the wild men came here. They came to wait for the dragon. That's why their wizards were fighting among themselves, to see who would be left, who would be strong enough to harness the evil of the dragon's magic for his own fell purposes.'

'You killed the dragons.' Sirket's emerald eyes were rimmed with white. 'Both of them.'

'I cannot be certain another one won't come flying out of the open ocean.' Kheda's face was as grim as his words. 'There are hints that we could see another wave of wild men come ahead of another such beast, driven by the same lust for the unbounded power of magic. I don't think Chazen's fragile prosperity will persuade the domain's people to stay and face such disaster again. If Daish confidence is balanced on the knife edge you tell me it is, such a calamity will throw all its islands into chaos. I won't stand idly by and let that happen, Sirket. There's a chance I can learn whether this danger truly threatens to return to plague Chazen and Daish and all the other domains of these southern reaches. Or if we can look to a future free from such fear.'

'And you can only do this by going away on your own again?' Sirket's incredulous words echoed back from the

140

white walls washed with golden lamplight and floated away into the darkness beyond the empty doorways.

'I won't be wholly alone.' His hands behind his back, Kheda clenched his fists. 'But don't ask me who I'm going with.'

'My mother Janne shared certain suspicions about that dead slave of yours,' said Sirket slowly. 'Was she right?'

'Do you really want to know?' Kheda challenged the youth. 'I won't lie to you if you ask me those questions. Do you want the burden of such knowledge?'

'No. I don't think I do.' Sirket looked away before snapping back, face accusing, 'What about Itrac? You're going to abandon her with two infant daughters, just like you abandoned us?'

What is that note in your voice? Was there some truth in those rumours I heard when I was travelling without a name that you were looking on her with growing affection, when she and Chazen Saril were given sanctuary in Daish waters?

'Itrac married me, above all else, to safeguard the Chazen domain.' Kheda drew a steadying breath. 'I'll tell her I am going away to be certain we are all safe from any new threat. She won't ask any more of me than that. I'm asking you to be a friend to Chazen in any dealings you have with other domains. Rally your triremes and warriors in her defence if it comes to it. I hope it won't. Ulla Safar looks to have plenty of concerns to keep him close to home. Redigal Coron seems absorbed in his own affairs, while Ritsem Caid is busy extending his domain's influence to north and east. But you said it yourself — a lot has happened that no one's foreseen.'

'When will you be coming back?' Sirket asked with growing apprehension.

'As soon as I can, but there's always the chance I won't return. I chose that risk when I sought the means to save Chazen and Daish the last time and I must choose it now.' Kheda studied his son's face intently. 'I wish these days had

141

never come upon us and that I had been able to see you married and grown, inheriting Daish from me in the fullness of time. If it was my choices that have made that impossible, forgive me.'

'I don't blame you, not any more.' Sirket struggled for words. 'I did, I mean, at first. I mourned you and everyone was so upset. When I learned you weren't dead, I was so angry, and my mother Janne wouldn't tell me—' His voice broke and a glistening tear ran down his face. 'Then she did tell me, but not all of it, I could tell, and that made me more angry still.'

'My lord.' Telouet appeared in the entrance, a dark shadow falling between them.

'Yes.' Sirket and Kheda spoke in the same breath.

'I can see your steward going into your pavilion, Kheda,' the slave said quietly. 'He's looking for you.'

The warlord pressed the heels of his hands into his eyes and found his own face was wet. He drew a deep breath. 'Then it's time to smile, Sirket, and make believe we haven't a care in the world. We'll go and enjoy whatever intricate follies Itrac's musicians have rehearsed for us and then we'll come and read the new-year stars with my lords of Redigal and Ritsem, and Ulla Safar if he deigns to join us.'

And I will be lying through my teeth as I pluck spurious justification from the stars for what I intend to do regardless. And tomorrow will be the last day I'll feign and mislead anyone like that.

'Yes, my father.' Sirket's voice was unwavering as he wiped tears from his own cheeks.

'I am so proud of you.' Kheda laid a hand on the youth's shoulder as they stood in the open doorway. 'I want you to know that.'

'I won't fail you,' Sirket promised fervently. The moonlight gilded his determined face, unexpectedly strengthening his resemblance to Janne.

'I won't be long.' Kheda encouraged him with a gentle push. 'I have to write a note for one of my shipmasters.'

Sirket strode away, Telouet at his heels. Kheda slipped back into the vestibule and took the lamp from its niche. He carried it carefully into the black shadows of the western hall. Chazen Saril's collection of star circles gleamed dully on the walls. 'Velindre?'

'He didn't see me.' Her voice came out of the darkness. 'I was ready to disappear but he stayed by the stairs.' She emerged into the dim light, indistinct in her loose grey clothes. 'I heard you tell him you'll be leaving with me. I'm glad you've come to your senses.'

'We'll see about that. I need to write a note for the *Brittle Crab*'s shipmaster.' Kheda set the lamp on a table and opened a drawer, searching for reed paper, pen and ink.

'What's so urgent?' Velindre came forward another pace.

'I want a hawk-handler to bring down one of Ulla Safar's courier doves. I'm not going with you until I have some idea of what he's intending.' Kheda began writing. 'You can carry this for me and stay out in the lagoon on the *Reteul* when you're done. Then stay away. I don't want you here when we come to read the stars at midnight.'

'Ulla Safar is planning to leave here at first light, him and his whole retinue.' Velindre surprised the warlord with her ready knowledge. 'One of your mariners came here looking for you earlier, from the *Green Turtle*. He'd overhead Safar's men whispering on the beach. He recognised me from last year, so knew I could be trusted with the news.'

'Did he?' Kheda stared at her, not overly pleased.

'So I bespoke my associate to ask Risala if she had any idea why Ulla Safar is sailing north,' the magewoman continued. 'She says there's rumour that the people want Ulla Orhan to overthrow his father.'

143

'Yes, I know,' Kheda said tersely. 'You worked magic, here, with so many visitors in the residence? Did anyone see you doing anything suspicious?'

'No.' Velindre shrugged. 'Trust me, Kheda — I've no wish to give up my skin to decorate your doorposts. The important thing is that Ulla Safar is going to be far too busy with his own affairs to threaten Chazen or anywhere else. Now you just need to find some justification for your departure and we can go. I've found endless obscure divinations for you to play with.' She gestured into the darkness and Kheda saw the faint reflection of gold tooling from a stack of books.

'We'll see.' Kheda finished writing and folded the reed paper. He found a stick of sealing wax and held it carefully in the flame of the lamp. 'Take this to the shipmaster of the *Brittle Crab* and then make yourself scarce. Meet me back here at dawn.'

If Safar is rushing back to scour all the Ulla islands for Orhan, I could call that a sign, to reassure Sirket. After all the conversations today, I know I can trust Daish and Redigal and Ritsem to be more concerned with their own affairs than with Chazen's, if I can only find some unexceptional reason for a brief absence.

'I am yours to command, my lord.' Velindre's reply was sharp with sarcasm.

'For the moment you had better be, for both our sakes.' Kheda let a blob of wax fall on the paper and used a sapphire seal ring he wore next to the uncut emerald to press it flat. 'And don't you dare work any more magic until we're well away from here. I'll come with you just as far as I must to find out if savages or dragons are threatening me and mine again from this wild isle beyond the horizon. As soon as we know what we're dealing with, you can use your magic to bring me straight back here. Me and Risala.'

And I might just believe in signs again if we find there's no threat and I can end my association with you and your magic once and for all.

Chapter 6

It was a hunting party. They weren't hunting her but that didn't matter. If they caught her, she was fodder for whatever beast soared over these thorn-covered hills, to be taken bound hand and foot to whatever painted man held sway here. She needed to get back to the thorn scrub that cloaked the dry, broken slopes. It didn't offer the easy concealment of the dense green forests she had left behind but she could find somewhere to hide herself.

At least she had heard the men shouting to each other, their words punctuated with laughter. If they had been silently slipping through the grasses in pursuit of some quarry, they would have come across her digging in the dry river bed, forced down from the undulating ridge by her burning thirst. If they were intent on tracking some prey, they would have wondered who had disturbed the sand and followed any footprints she might have left. Scrambling to hide beneath the crumbling overhang of the river bank, the old woman drew in her scrawny arms and legs and crouched behind her mottled bundle of scurrier hide.

Earth pattered down in front of her face, falling from the underside of the overhang. A voice sounded loud above her head. It was a boy, his shadow long across the pale stretch of sand between her and the darkness where she had been digging, drawn by the treacherous promise of water hidden from the devouring sun beneath the flood-carved channel. The boy shouted again. His words sounded strangely made to her ears. She had never met anyone from this dry face of the crumpled hills where she had discovered that the giant forest trees couldn't sustain a foothold. She had never known anyone who had ventured this far.

The boy was still calling back over his shoulder. He had seen the darker upheaval out in the middle of the river bed and thought lizards had been digging there. He had hopes of newly buried eggs. The old woman heard scorn in the reply ringing back to the boy and allowed herself to breathe more easily. It seemed this hunting party had no need to dig for lizard eggs. The boy petulantly kicked a clod of earth threaded with grass roots off the overhang and rejoined the men of his village. Gradually their voices faded away into the distance.

The old woman's shrunken stomach griped with hunger at the thought of rich, meaty lizard eggs. Her mouth was as dry as the sand that clung to the crusted wrinkles around her sore, reddened eyes. She dared not return to the hole she had been digging. Faintly on the breeze she could hear the hunting party raising a hoarse, triumphant song. They were leaving the perilous grasslands for the comparative safety of the thorn-covered hills.

She waited for a long while, ignoring the pain in her cramped arms and legs. Finally, she crawled out from beneath the overhang, brushing the sandy earth off herself and looking warily around. The boy was no fool. There could well be lizards coming to dig in the sandy river bed. A hunting party could afford to shout out to each other and sing heedless songs. They had slings to deter attackers and clubs and spears to deal with anything that chose not to be deterred. Her digging stick wouldn't stop a big lizard making a meal out of her. All the same, she clutched it in her gnarled fist as she began walking cautiously upstream. She bent low to keep below the level of the crumbling bank. There might be more hunters around, not singing their songs.

The river bed narrowed and sloped more steeply as the land rose up ahead of her. Tall grasses waved on either side and she halted more frequently, straining her ears to try to determine if the wind was chasing her or whether something more dangerous was stalking her unseen through the rustling clumps. She decided it was the wind but moved more quickly all the same. On the high banks to either side, the dark-green thorn scrub was growing more thickly now. She picked her way through a tumble of broken and dusty rocks scattered across the river bed by the last torrent of rainwater to scour this cleft. Some were as tall as she was and she could not have reached round any of them with both her arms. She kept a wary eye out for anything lurking in the shadows.

Lesser lizards watched her from the tops of the rocks as they basked splay-footed in the westering sun. She scowled back at them, their dark eyes glittering in the black stripes that ran down their blue hides from their noses to the tapered ends of their tails. One wasn't watching her, though, its eyes half-closed as its head bobbed up and down in mindless enjoyment. It was on a low rock that she could reach. Lizard meat was as good as lizard eggs. The old woman bent slowly down and found a heavy rock that fitted her fist. As she straightened up, her protesting knees gave a loud snap and the sun-drowsed lizard darted away with all the rest.

She closed her eyes tight, furiously begrudging the tears forcing themselves out between her sparse, gritty lashes Opening her eyes, she hurled the useless rock viciously at an uncaring boulder. It bounced back to strike another rock and rolled over a bed of broken rubble. The rattling crack of stone in the sunken river bed startled her back to her senses.

That had been a foolish thing to do. She couldn't risk drawing unfriendly eyes or ears this way, of man or animal.

Hampered by her unwieldy bundle, she hurried upstream, the empty gourd in its sling bouncing on her hip. Her breath was rasping in her throat and her heart was pounding. Unreasoning panic threatened to overwhelm her. She had to force one trembling, dusty foot with its cracked and flaking toenails in front of the other. Finally she reached the steep wall of the dry cataract she had come across earlier, which had tempted her down into the flatter land, tormented as she was by thirst.

The thorny forest grew thick on either side of the crumbling banks. Knife plants flourished in bushy clumps of green and brown blades. Fat, fleshy spine plants sprawled among the rocks of the cataract, pale yellow-green and studded with thick black barbs, smug and impenetrable. Thorn spikes rose up from their nests of tangled roots and immature stems. Dark green and glossy, twice as high as a man was tall, they were scaled like the leg of a monstrous bird, each flat leaf tipped with a vicious prickle. Here and there, one was topped with long, narrow flowers that clawed at the sky like talons, crimson as blood.

The sun was sinking. She had to get out of the river bed before night fell and more dangerous creatures than the blue and black lizards emerged from their lairs with the darkness. She had to get up into the thorn forest to find herself a thicket to hide in while she still had enough daylight left to weave its branches around herself. She had to do that without pricking herself with spines that would catch in her flesh to fester and poison her. She must avoid the slicing leaves that would scent the night air with her blood and draw predators that could rip apart a thorn thicket.

The old woman realised she was whimpering.

Something rustled up above and she smelled a damp, musky odour. The old woman ducked behind a trailing mass of roots hanging over the edge of the cataract where a thorn spike had been half washed away by a wet-season downpour. The noises up above faded as whatever creature it had been took some unseen path away through the ferocious landscape.

As she clung to the roots, the old woman realised that the thorn spike was in no immediate danger of falling into the dry cataract as it waited out the endless days of the heat. The half-exposed roots clung grimly to the earth supporting them, offering hand- and footholds. She choked on a sob of relief and began climbing painfully upwards, her bundle awkwardly crushed between her chest and the dry, dusty earth. She scrambled, panting, onto a small barren expanse of the river bank between two sprawls of yellow spiny plants and forced herself to consider what she must do next.

If she stopped, she would die — and more quickly in this harsh landscape than she might have done in the green forest. So she was determined not to stop, not to die, not until lack of food or water left her too far gone to care.

She saw a way through the low malice of the fat spiny leaves and edged along, sliding her feet through the dust to avoid treading on some crippling barb. Beyond the spread of yellow spiny plants she found a well-worn track and saw that patches of thorny brush had been stripped for firewood here and there. There was a village somewhere close by. Perhaps that was where that hunting party had come from. She followed the path unwillingly, looking for some lesser track that might lead her away from discovery and capture and death.

The track curved along the hillside, the tall tips of the thorn spikes level with her head on one side where the ground fell away so steeply. Parched rock broke through the dusty soil and curved up like a wave on her other hand, its crest bristling with knife plants. The old woman strained her ears for any sound of people, her eyes darting in all directions.

The path divided at the end of the stretch of rock. One fork led downhill, threading through clusters of truly enormous thorn spikes. Little yellow birds fluttered around the crimson flowers, perching lightly on the blooms as they feasted on the nectar. Deft russet birds with forked tails pursued the clouds of insects drawn by the heady scent.

The other path led uphill through clumps of knife plants and spiny sprawls of fat yellow leaves and disappeared around another blunt shoulder of rock jutting out from the starveling ground. The shadows were lengthening and darkening. It would soon be night.

The old woman looked nervously from one route to the other. Going downhill would offer more immediate concealment among the thorn spikes, but that path looked dangerously well trodden. Safety lay in solitude. Gritting her teeth against the hot agony in her shoulders, she wrapped her arms around her bundle and scrambled along the upper path. She rounded the rocky outcrop and stumbled to a halt, her bare feet slipping in the slick dust. The rock had concealed a deep gash in the land and she had been lucky not to fall from the ledge she was standing on. Below, a mass of thorny forest lurked in tangled green shadows. She had no hope of reaching it.

Voices floated up from the gloom beneath and firelight flared. The old woman's heart pounded in her bony chest as she shrank back against the rock. She stumbled, falling backwards into a dark void she hadn't thought to look for. Biting her lip against the pains shooting through her back, she lay still on the stony cave floor and watched sparks drifting up from the fire below. She heard wood and dead thorn spikes being tossed into the makeshift hearth and the firelight strengthened.

The rocky ledge's shadow cut a black line across the cave wall. Above it, figures danced in the flickering light. The old woman pressed her hands to her mouth to stifle a moan of despair as she gazed at the fierce faces and dread beasts drawn out of the curves of the rock with charcoal and ochre and stains of coloured clay. She had fallen into a painted cave.

Down below, some amicable dispute arose over who precisely had played the greater part in the day's successes. The succulence of roasting meat floated up on the night air. The smell set the juices in the old woman's mouth running where it had been dry with dread. It was a hunting party, she realised. Was it the hunting party who had nearly run across her earlier? Did it matter? She sat upright and waited, silent, biting her dry and cracked lips as the good-humoured conversations were replaced by the muffled intensity of eating, broken only by brief exchanges.

She closed her eyes to the stark, accusing gaze of the cave paintings and concentrated on the muted sounds of the men at their meal. They were alive and relishing their food. She was still alive. She would be dead if anyone found her in this painted cave, but her life was forfeit anyway if she was captured. While she was alive, she could hope for another day, and another after that.

Her silent defiance faltered at a new thought. How had the men lit the fire that was cooking their prey? Had one of them been carrying an ember in a hollow bone tightly sealed with mud? Or did they have a painted man with them, to summon up a flame with a snap of his fingers?

She listened and dared to hope. Would they sound so carefree if a painted man was with them? No one laughed like that with a painted man at hand, jealous of his dignity and demanding that all obey him. She lay down, pillowing her matted grey head on her bundle. If the hunting party didn't have a painted man with them, they wouldn't be climbing up to this painted cave. She would just have to stay here till they left. Exhaustion overcame her fear of the unseen men below in the gully and dulled the pain of her aching bones, and she dozed.

When some unknown noise woke her, she was startled to realise she had slept for some considerable while. Even in the cave she could feel the settled chill of deep night. Slowly, stiffly, she shuffled to the edge of the cave, trusting in the concealing darkness. The eyes of the sky were high above, both still half-closed but shedding enough light to show her that the unseen hunters had gone. Their fire had been doused with sand, the detritus of their feast strewn around.

The old woman grabbed her bundle and hurried back along the treacherous path as quickly and quietly as she could. Something skittered away from her to be lost in the blackness as she made her way along the lower path. As she had hoped, it curled around to the hunting party's temporary hearth. This was a regular stopping point judging by the old, dry bones piled up in the hollow beneath the rocky outcrop. Perhaps their village wasn't so close, if they had to travel through the night to get home. The journey had obviously been worth it, though. A sizeable scurrier carcass sprawled half-dismembered across the remains of the fire, covered with sandy earth. It was already drawing ants and tiny black lizards to scour its bones clean.

The old woman grabbed a well chewed shoulder-blade bone and scraped the earth off the carcass. There was still meat to be had and marrow in the bones. Those men must have hunted well indeed to be so wasteful with this kill.

The makeshift hearth was still hot beneath her hands. Sparks floated up and sullen cinders glowed sluggishly. The old woman prodded the heap of old broken bones cautiously lest snakes or stingers were lurking there. Snatching at wind-blown dead leaves and twisted scraps of dry hide, she piled them onto the brightest of the embers, crouching to blow softly on the tinder. A fledgling flame shed enough light to show half-burned scraps of wood and she soon had a modest fire burning.

What would she do if someone saw the firelight in the night and came to see what it was? Well, she would die, most likely, but she would die with a full belly if she possibly could. Untying her bundle, the old woman took out the lump of black stone and used the bone hammer to make herself a new cutting shard. She crouched over the scurrier carcass and, slicing and pulling, got a rib loose. The hunters had feasted on the creature's meatier limbs and flanks. Passing the rib swiftly through the fire seared away the importunate ants and she gnawed the remaining flesh as best she could. Then she smashed the bone open with the lump of black stone and sucked out the meagre marrow, relishing its richness.

Her spirits rose. She took a burning stick and went over to a yellow spiny plant. Satisfied no snakes were lurking beneath the plump leaves, she used the shoulder-blade bone to hold down a succulent barbed leaf and carefully cut it away from the main stem with her shard of stone. Careful not to catch herself on the curved black spines, she carried the fat leaf to her little fire. Sap hissed and the spines crackled and flared in the flames. While she waited for the leathery skin to blacken and soften, the old woman set about scavenging the rest of the meat from the scurrier's ribs.

Movement in the darkness at the edge of the firelight caught her eye, Movement and black shining eyes. Something had been drawn to the scent of blood and meat. The old woman flung the broken rib bone she was sucking on at the eyes. They disappeared with a scuffling sound and something else ran, too. Something had been foraging in a newly dug pit over there. Getting reluctantly to her feet, the old woman went to investigate.

She discovered that one of the hunting party had been digging up the swollen roots of a black-fingered plant. No wonder this was a favoured halting place on their journey home. Working more by feel than sight, she quickly cut a string of the bulbous tubers loose and carried them back to her little fire. Head back and mouth open, she held up the roots and sliced into them, gulping down the woody-tasting water they were hoarding. Thirst finally quenched, she tossed the fibrous hollow tubers onto the fire where they hissed and burned as she returned to the scurrier carcass.

By the time she was contemplating how best she might break open the scurrier's hips to get at the marrow in there, the spiny yellow leaf was soft and charred. Using the shoulder-blade bone to save her fingers, she hauled it onto the cooler earth and sliced it open with her new stone shard. Peeling back the slimy skin, she blew on the bland, pale pulp to cool it a little and pulled out as many of the harsh fibres as she could. Then she began eating, sucking at her fingers when the heat threatened to scald them.

When had she last eaten her fill like this? Not since the old man had been able to leave his hut. And there would be more meat to salvage when the daylight came. She could cut more yellow spiny leaves and lay them on the fire. She could pack the pulp into one of her gourds and fill the other with water from the black finger plants' roots. Finally scraping the last of the pulp from the inner corners of the fat spiny leaf, she sat back and gazed sleepily at the flickering fire.

Something moved behind her in the darkness and hissed. A surge of fear restored her to full wakefulness and she scrambled to her feet, the shoulder-blade bone held out defiantly before her. Whatever it was lurked just beyond the meagre light cast by the fire. Something else hissed and the first creature replied. Whatever it was, it wasn't alone.

The old woman gathered up her belongings with one hand, still clutching the bone. Not that she had much hope of fighting off anything that attacked. And if she fell asleep down here, she'd wake up to find a lizard chewing off her foot or her hand. If she woke up at all.

But where could she go in the middle of the night, with no light to guide her, in this unknown land? The chittering of some night flyer drew her eyes upwards. She looked reluctantly at the dark edge of the cave mouth just visible above the out-thrust ledge in the rock.

She could sleep in the painted cave. She'd set foot in there, albeit by accident, and had not died of it — not yet, anyway. She'd even fallen asleep in there. Was she going to die of it? If so, what more did she have to fear? If not, well, that would be something to think about. And if she didn't die in her sleep, she'd be hungry when she woke up.

Defiance lending her strength as well as courage, she ignored the menacing noises lurking in the shadows and swiftly cut two more of the yellow spiny leaves. She wedged the fat slabs into the dying fire. Perhaps the lizards and ants would leave her some of the softened pulp to salvage in the morning.

The hisses in the darkness were growing louder, with something growling deep in its throat. She had to be alive to see the morning. The old woman drew a deep breath and snatched up her bundle, trying not to run. The old man had always said that if you ran, you'd be chased. Not that she could have run in the darkness that engulfed her as soon as she left the firelight.

She picked her way painstakingly back along the path to the fork and retraced her steps to the painted cave. Steeling herself, she went inside, deliberately this time. No beast appeared to immolate her. No painted man peeled himself off the walls to strike her down. She lay down, using her bundle for a pillow once again, and cradled her full belly. Trying not to listen to the snarling quarrels between whatever creatures had come to scavenge the rest of the scurrier, she went back to sleep. If a painted man did appear to wreak his revenge on her, she'd be dead before she woke.

Chapter 7

'You'll be fit for nothing if you don't get some sleep tonight.' Itrac tilted her head quizzically as she joined Kheda beneath a cluster of nut palms between his pavilion and the observatory. 'Beyau said you've been out here since before dawn.' A silver-ornamented band of turtleshell pushed her unbound black locks off her face. Close-cut trousers of soft pink flattered her long legs beneath a loose scarlet tunic and a gauzy mantle embroidered with trumpet flowers.

Kheda smiled briefly at her. 'I wanted to see Ulla Safar's galley safely out of the lagoon.'

'Was there any portent?' A faint crease appeared between Itrac's precisely plucked brows.

'No,' Kheda said slowly. 'And we could come to no firm conclusions as to the meaning of the new-year stars.'

So I have no lies ready to persuade you that I must leave here, just for a little while. Will I have to stay? What will Velindre say to that? What will happen to Risala if I don't go with her? Would she go off with these wizards alone, without me? I wouldn't put it past Velindre to come up with barefaced lies to convince her that's what I want her to do.

'Did Olkai and Sekni sleep well?' he asked briskly.

'Yes, thankfully.' Itrac gestured towards an open-sided silken tent erected on an islet across the sparkling lagoon. Blush coloured hangings fluttered in the breeze that carried laughter across the water. 'Are you going to join us for breakfast?'

'Naturally, my lady.' Kheda smoothed his white silk tunic, bright with coppery embroidery mimicking red-lance fronds.

'It would be more fitting if you had a body slave at your heels.' Itrac began walking. 'Jevin says you've sent those hopefuls to join the swordsmen in their morning drills again. How do you propose to choose between them if you don't let them attend you?'

'Their practice yesterday was marred by possible ill omen.' Kheda looked sternly over his shoulder at the hapless slave. 'I want Ridu to get their measure without distraction, now that Ulla Safar has gone. As soon as we see some clearer portent, I'll make my choice.'

A truth that hides a lie and a still deeper truth. I won't see an omen telling me which new slave to take because I no longer fall for such foolish self-deception.

'Very well, my lord.' Jevin's self-possession faltered a little.

Itrac looked out across the lagoon. 'Then let's join our remaining guests for breakfast.'

'As you wish, my lady.' Kheda cordially offered her his arm. As they walked on together, Kheda noted the discreetly approving glances of residence slaves and servants.

These islanders of Chazen adore Itrac, and not just for standing by them after disaster overtook Chazen Saril's rule. She could have refuted her marriage after such ill omens and lost herself in some obscurity where no one could have found her, even if her birth domain refused her sanctuary out of ignorant fear of the taint of magic.

The people of Chazen even approve of me, though I wasn't born to their domain and took power under such dubious circumstances.

What else could they do, after I rescued them from such evils? And now I have supposedly secured their peace and prosperity with my astute rule guided by earthly portents and readings of the heavens.

What would I tell them if I knew the savages were about to invade again, with or without a dragon? What could they do? Wouldn't they be better left in ignorance?

As they crossed the walkways towards the tent, Redigal Litai and Ritsem Zorat appeared, running across a beach of white coral sand and stripping off their tunics. They dived into the sea barely a breath apart. As their dark arms cut the water to white foam, the Redigal wives abandoned their cushions within the shade of the breakfast tent and came to shout their encouragement.

'Who won?' Itrac shaded her eyes with one hand as she tried to follow the swimmers disappearing under a bridge.

'Litai.' As the boys clambered up onto the planks, Kheda saw the taller boy bow low to the younger.

'That's a pleasant portent for him,' Itrac said cautiously as they walked on. 'Could you and the other lords truly make nothing of the new-year stars?'

'A lack of omens isn't necessarily bad news. It may just mean one has to look further afield for guidance.' Kheda did his best to make this sound like an idea that had just occurred to him.

'You see nothing to guide you close at hand?' Itrac sounded more surprised than alarmed.

'Until I do, I must let my duty guide me—' Kheda broke off as he saw Sirket leaving the Daish contingent's luxurious accommodations.

And my duty has always been to safeguard my people, my family. All of my family.

Itrac looked at Sirket with keen pity. 'The omens for Daish are clear enough and surely undeserved.'

'Has anyone deserved the sufferings visited on us all these past two years?' Kheda said unguardedly.

We delude ourselves looking for signs in the sky that promise certainty for the days ahead when the only certainty we might have, for good or ill, can only come through me associating yet again with wizards. What am I to do, beyond getting Risala out of their clutches?

'My lord?' Itrac was looking at him, taken aback.

Kheda tried for a reassuring smile. 'Perhaps we will see something in the earthly compass today to clarify the puzzles of the heavens.'

'Let's hope so, my lord.' Itrac quickened her pace on the white path they had reached. 'We have had many wider portents of good fortune to sustain the whole domain,' she said bracingly, 'and there will be omens in the gifts our friends have brought for our daughters.'

'Indeed.' The warlord watched Redigal Litai and Ritsem Zorat dive into the water again, swimming across the narrow strait to beckon to Sirket as he walked across a bridge. Sirket turned to say something to Telouet, his hand going to the gold chain belting his violet tunic. The slave shook his head firmly and Sirket waved Litai and Zorat away with a rueful shrug.

You're playing very different games, my son, while they're still free to enjoy their boyhood.

'I hope Mirrel Ulla remembered to do her duty by little Olkai and Sekni before Safar dragged her away,' Kheda asked suddenly.

'Grudgingly.' Itrac frowned.

'What was Ulla's gift?' asked Kheda.

'A pair of swords and daggers for each of them to bestow upon their body slaves when that day comes,' Itrac said thoughtfully.

161

'The blades are watered steel, my lord,' volunteered Jevin, 'as fine as any Ulla swordsmiths have ever made.'

'I will have to see what can be read in the patterns in the metal,' Kheda said neutrally.

A double-edged gift in every sense, given the vast and contrary breadth of lore concerning blades.

'Let's hope our daughters both grow to such beautiful girlhood that they warrant body slaves to match such handsome swords,' Itrac said resolutely.

'To remind their many suitors to pay them all due courtesies.' Kheda managed a wry smile.

'I shall drive a dagger into the nursery doorpost for each of them,' Jevin assured him, 'for the protection that bestows.'

They reached the bridge leading to the isle with the blush-coloured tent. Itrac stopped and looked Kheda straight in the eye. 'Ulla Safar is gone, taking all his vileness with him. Our other guests wish our daughters nothing but good, so let's enjoy this breakfast and the rest of the day.'

'As you command, my lady.' Kheda looked away to search the inner islands. 'It seems we're still waiting for Redigal Coron and Ritsem Caid.'

'There's Coron.' Itrac pointed and Redigal Coron waved back blithely, faithful Prai one pace behind.

'And Ganil's got Caid out of bed.' Kheda saw Telouet draw Sirket's attention to the approaching Ritsem warlord and Sirket slowed to allow him to catch up. The two men walked on more slowly, dark heads close in conversation. Litai and Zorat followed with discreet interest.

How easy it proved to leave our debate last night so inconclusive. Coron has never yet taken the initiative in any such discussion, while Sirket was too preoccupied as well as too conscious of his recent elevation to warlord to insist on his interpretations. I only hope

162

Caid wasn't too irritated with me casting doubts on all his efforts to read some meaning into the sky.

He was relieved to hear that the Ritsem warlord was talking about something entirely different as he approached with Sirket.

' ...And now we have Barbak Moro's wives making overtures. They're eager to work their alchemy on our iron and give us a handsome share in the steel they win from it,' Caid concluded triumphantly.

Sirket looked more cautious. 'Looking to the south is a new twist for Barbak.'

'Because Toc Faile has married another of his sisters into Barbak's household.' Ritsem Caid grew still more animated. 'I know Sain Daish has largely withdrawn from trade to attend to Daish's younger children but she's another of Toc Faile's sisters and ties of blood are never broken. Use her good offices to renew your links to Toc and come to an understanding with Barbak through Faile. Then we can persuade Endit Fel to turn his back on Ulla—'

'We can discuss this later.' Sirket cut Caid off apologetically. 'My lady Itrac.' He bowed low.

'Good morning.' The Ritsem warlord bowed in turn and then grinned at Kheda. 'If we can bring the Mivai domain into line, we'd have a solid bulwark all along Ulla Safar's eastern sea lanes. What do you say to that?'

Redigal Coron arrived in time to hear this suggestion. 'Have Taisia talk to Hinai Redigal.' He waved a hand towards the women laughing together in the roseate shade of the pavilion.

Kheda nodded his understanding. 'One of her sisters married out of the Seik domain into Mivai.'

Threaten Ulla Safar's eastern borders all you want, Ritsem Caid, and do it with my blessing. I want as many things as possible distracting him before he thinks to look south and sees me gone, even for a little while.

'You can discuss such things after breakfast.' Smiling, Itrac nevertheless ordered an end to the men's discussion.

As they entered the open-sided tent ideally placed to catch the morning's cooling breeze, Kheda noted Janne's absence from the gathering of wives. 'I hope your lady mother isn't indisposed this morning, Daish Sirket.'

'No.' Sirket's face was as unemotional as his father's. 'Here she comes.'

Everyone turned to watch Janne and her slave crossing the lagoon. Birut was carrying something large and square wrapped in white cloth. Janne swept ahead of him, elegant in a plain grey silk dress. As she moved, the side-slit skirt revealed her elegant legs and Kheda noted how the gathered bodice subtly enhanced her voluptuous bosom.

After playing the dowdy dowager, you've decided to remind everyone just how stunning you could look at the height of your influence. Why is that?

'What do you suppose she's got there?' Ritsem Zorat speculated incautiously as he and Redigal Litai helped themselves to skewers of spiced turtle meat.

'Daish's gifts to Chazen's new daughters.' Taisia Ritsem surprised her son with a minatory glare. Her misty mantle embroidered with butterflies fluttered over a sleeveless tunic and wide trousers of pale-yellow silk. The Redigal wives wore flowing gowns in differing shades of blue brocaded with emerald vines, their jewels discreet gold-mounted sapphires.

Beyau appeared at Kheda's side. 'Honeyed curds and pitral?'

'Thank you.' Kheda accepted the unwanted bowl and took a spoonful. The aromatic honey cut through the tartness of the curds and complemented the fainter sweetness of the sliced pitral fruit. 'I hope Ulla Safar didn't manage to leave any slave behind, not even one begging for sanctuary from his brutality?' he asked the steward in a low voice.

'None of them even tried,' Beyau confirmed. 'The *Yellow Serpent* is following them.'

'I want to know exactly where the Ulla galley makes land-fall before leaving our waters.' Kheda dug into his breakfast. 'Have all the village spokesmen send word of any unexpected merchants or poets turning up, or seers. Especially seers. I hope Daish Sirket's people will be as alert as the Ulla ship passes through their waters.' He shot Beyau a significant look.

The steward glanced swiftly at Telouet to show he had taken Kheda's meaning. 'I'm sure they will be, my lord.'

'We would benefit from knowing more about Ulla Orhan's current situation,' Kheda continued in a low tone, 'but Orhan will hardly be trusting anyone he doesn't know to be a true friend just at present.' He gave the steward another significant look.

'Indeed, my lord.' Beyau looked a little puzzled.

Will you believe I'm seeking news of Orhan if I disappear for a little while and return with Risala, whom you know to be my link with all Chazen's eyes and ears? But that's not an excuse I can offer up for wider consumption.

After a swift glance to be sure the Chazen servants were keeping her guests well served with food and drink, Itrac stretched out her hands to welcome the first lady of Daish. 'Come and have some breakfast, my lady.'

'Thank you.' Janne graciously accepted a plate of sliced pitral and sard berries from a maidservant.

'Now we're all here.' Moving to the centre of the rich red carpet covering the palm matting laid on the sandy ground, Itrac claimed everyone's attention with a winning smile. 'Moni, would you like to show us what tokens you've brought for little Olkai and Sekni?'

Swaddled in white silk, Sekni was sleeping peacefully as her nurse cuddled her close on a cushion in a corner of the tent. Olkai was quietly wakeful in the arms of Touai's elder daughter, sucking at the silver bangle around her chubby wrist.

Moni Redigal smiled at the twins as she summoned her personal slave with a snap of her fingers. The swordsman knelt to present her with a finely carved casket of white halda wood. 'We bring your daughters opals, talisman gem of the Greater Moon, for intuition and understanding, most especially of dreams.' Moni opened the coffer, turning it so everyone could see the unset gems nestling in pale-blue velvet within. 'For Olkai, who is heir, we offer the white, for balance and truthfulness. For Sekni, who is to be her sister's support, here and wherever marriage might take her, we offer the black, for inner strength and self-knowledge.'

Even in the muted light filtering through the soft silk, iridescent flecks glowed within the stones. There were ten of each, pale and dark, all the size of Kheda's thumbnail.

Moni closed the box with a muted click and handed it to Itrac. 'Of course, opals need careful tending if they are not to spoil, just like children. Let that be a token of your duty, as parents and for Chazen as a whole. All children are in part the responsibility of the whole domain.'

'This is a handsome gift, my lady.' Itrac passed the casket to Jevin and embraced Moni.

'Redigal is glad to make it.' Moni kissed her cheek fondly.

'Ulla Safar will be spitting venom when he hears about this,' Kheda murmured to Beyau.

'I fear our gift hardly matches such munificence.' Taisia Ritsem held out a hand and her slave helped her to her feet. A second slave who had been patiently waiting outside the tent came and set a tall box covered in reddish leather on the floor before her. Taisia opened the lid and lifted out two

166

lanterns of brilliantly polished silver. One was small, no larger than Kheda's clenched fist, while the other was twice the length of his hand. The smaller one had ovals clear as glass set into its sides, while the larger was faceted with translucent misty-white shell.

'We have found crystal oysters in our rivers once again.' Taisia showed both pieces off.

'A rare find, and a splendid omen,' Redigal Coron congratulated Ritsem Caid.

'It's no myth that the young oysters live in shells so clear their beating hearts can be clearly seen. It's only as they grow older that the shell becomes even barely opaque,' Taisia continued, smiling at the murmurs of surprise and approval from the gathering. 'As it's said the light from such lanterns reveals truth, we offer a pair, large and small, for each new daughter of Chazen. We hope they will always see clearly by their light, especially in matters of affection since every oyster can be read as a sign of the female heart.' She grinned. 'And naturally, we trust that they will both always see their dealings with Ritsem in the most favourable light.' She set the lanterns back in their box as everyone laughed.

'My lady of Daish?' Itrac turned to Janne, who composedly passed her empty fruit plate to an unobtrusive maidservant.

Everyone fell silent at the realisation that Janne hadn't laughed. 'My lady of Chazen,' she began slowly, 'I trust you'll forgive me for not bringing my gift within this tent. It's not the happiest of offerings but I couldn't think of anything more appropriate.'

Kheda noted that Sirket was looking resolutely at his dusty feet.

What by all the stars in the skies are you up to now?

There wasn't a sound in the tent beyond the idle flapping of silk and the shuffle of some slave's nervous feet on the palm matting.

Itrac's smile turned a little brittle. 'Please do explain.'

Janne looked out over the lagoon to the westernmost reef. 'A domain is guided by its lord, who is guided in turn by the omens he reads in the heavenly and earthly compasses, supported by all the wisdom his forefathers have recorded. Only one divination is a woman's prerogative and that is the reading of dreams, bound as we are by the plaited threads of marriage, blood and birth. The dreams of a daughter born to rule must be more potent than any other.'

She paused as everyone looked to the far island where a tall wall with a single gate ringed the solid pillar of stone where open stairs spiralled up to the platform where the most honoured dead were laid.

Turning back to Itrac, Janne's voice strengthened. 'You named your elder daughter for Olkai, who was first wife and beloved friend to so many of us in the days of Chazen's peace and prosperity before the upheavals of these last few years. Those upheavals cost Olkai her life and cost Chazen even more dearly, in that she died as she came seeking refuge in Daish, despite all we could do for her—' Emotion apparently overcame Janne and she closed her eyes for an instant.

Kheda did his best to hold his own feelings in check.

Despite all I could do for her, my knowledge of healing little more than a curse when I saw how little chance Olkai had of surviving such horrendous burns. Are you looking to remind everyone of my failure, Janne?

'Olkai was so cruelly cut down in the full bloom of her wisdom and beauty.' Janne opened her clear, dark eyes. 'Sekni, too. Yet their virtues remain, as the perfume of the fallen flower lingers. Sekni's bones were lost among the carnage but Olkai's remains at least have lain atop a Daish tower of silence. Their presence has honoured our domain, but the time has come to return such vital talismans to Chazen. As you raise your daughters, you will be guided by your dreams, Itrac, and in time, they too will sleep beneath the towers to see what truths may come through the mists of sleep and dawn. So your sister-wife Olkai's bones are Daish's gift to Chazen's newest daughters.'

Janne gestured towards Birut, waiting patiently just outside the tent, and he withdrew the white cloth from a brass-bound coffer. Kheda saw it draw thoughtful glances from the other warlords and ladies. The Ritsem warlord was looking tranquil enough, though grief for his dead sister darkened his eyes and his knuckles showed pale as he clasped Taisia's comforting hand.

'A most considerate gift, if wholly unexpected.' Itrac's voice was tight. 'Chazen is most grateful to the Daish domain.'

So this is why you were wondering what I had done with Chazen Saril's corpse, Janne. And now everyone else will be thinking along those lines. Not that anyone will ask me, because warlords don't ask one another such questions. Even Itrac hasn't asked me.

Kheda shot a swift glance at Sirket and saw utter bemusement on the young warlord's face. A knot beneath his breastbone eased.

If Janne means mischief, you've no part in it, my son. Are you looking to make mischief here, Janne, or are you truly sincere? Either way, you've given me a most unexpected opportunity, my lady, to twist this to my own purposes. There was a time when I would have taken this for a most powerful omen. Now I just have to manage not to choke on my own hypocrisy.

'I am more grateful to Daish for this gift than you can imagine, my lady.' Feeling curiously calm, Kheda stepped forward. His words broke the tense silence beneath the silken canopy. He smiled warmly at Janne and was rewarded with a flicker of uncertainty across her flawless face. 'Olkai was ever a woman generous with her wisdom and her affection.' Kheda gestured towards the distant tower of silence. 'We of Chazen gratefully recall her virtues, as we cherish too our memories of Sekni who died at the hands of those foul invaders. Both women never faltered in their duty to the people of Chazen.' He took Itrac's hand and squeezed it tight. 'Just like Itrac Chazen, whose faithfulness to the peace of the past has been wholly vindicated by Chazen's present prosperity and the future promise of her twin daughters.'

Muted agreement ran around the gathering and Itrac held her head high, a threat of tears retreating as the colour rose on her cheekbones.

'I am not so confident on my own account.' Kheda's sombre words instantly silenced the sympathetic murmurs. 'I have faced difficult decisions over these last few years. I allowed you all to believe Ulla Safar had indeed killed me, believing it necessary at the time. My choices were vindicated as I led Chazen to victory over magic-wielding savages coming out of the empty ocean to plague these islands, but that doesn't alter the fact that my deceit laid undeserved suffering on the innocent children of Daish. I have paid for my deception — those children are now lost to me, as I found that my choices had bound me to Chazen.'

Not daring to risk catching Sirket's eye or Janne's, Kheda pressed on. 'I have been blessed with Itrac Chazen as my wife. We were able to evade the first dragon that came in the wild men's wake, and then to kill the second monster after it was wounded in its battle to slay the first. But in doing so, I led many brave men to their deaths.' He broke off to take a deep breath, looking out across the lagoon.

'Ulla Safar has chosen to leave us, so I can be frank with you all, as friends of Chazen. I am burdened by so many deaths laid to my account. I tell myself that the ledger is balanced with the lives my choices have saved, but I still wonder if there might have been a better path for me to take that would have cost fewer lives and spared even a few some measure of pain. I have come to suspect this is why I am failing to see the omens that should guide me towards the best future for this domain, and in the choices I must make as husband, and as father to these new daughters of Chazen. My life has taken a new direction with their birth and I do not wish to go astray.'

Let's hope the ring of truth in that drowns out the lies I've been so carefully preparing. I won't find a better time to deceive you all, thanks to this unexpected assistance Janne Daish has handed me.

'I have been tempted to go into seclusion to meditate on these things, but I hoped the new-year stars would give me some guidance without that proving necessary. Yet we could not agree on our interpretations last night, my lords. Now I see the sign I have been looking for in the return of Olkai Chazen's bones.' He gestured towards the casket that Birut was guarding. 'This is a sign that it is Itrac who will find answers to her questions in this residence, in her dreams beneath the tower of silence. Now I see clearly that the heavens are telling me to look elsewhere. The Lesser Moon rides with the stars of the Sailfish, emblem of good fortune in voyaging, in the arc of the sky where travel leads to new knowledge. I must never forget that the twin moons will be symbols of these twin girls for Chazen throughout their lives. And the Greater Moon rides in the arc of honour where the stars of the Hoe remind us of every man's honest labour in service of family and domain that binds him to the land.'

He saw that Redigal Coron was about to say something, so turned away to gesture towards the south. 'All the other heavenly jewels are in arcs of the sky where the stars are beneath the horizon, which speaks of things hidden from view. We couldn't see any potent conjunctions, yet the symmetry in the heavenly compass must signify something. The Amethyst that counsels humility rides in the arc of duty with the Winged Snake, symbol of deeds bringing things into the light.'

Is this what I have spent all my life doing, reading whatever was most welcome or useful into the meaningless patterns of the sky? Deluding myself and others? Whatever, I cannot stop now, not and get away with this.

'Beside it, the Diamond bringing clarity of purpose looks over the Horned Fish, symbol of nurturing in the arc promising omens for our children. Across that hidden half-circle, the Ruby promises strength and longevity in the arc of wealth, blessed with the Vizail Blossom that symbolises all our wives and daughters. Next to that, the Topaz that balances head and heart guides us towards new ideas, moving with the turn of the year into the arc of life where the stars of the Bowl promise not only sustenance for the body but food for thought as well.'

Kheda paused, blood pulsing in his throat. 'My lords, my friends, I must go in search of peace and solitude to come to terms with these past few years, to regain my perspective on the future. Now I understand why there has been no omen to guide me in the choice of a new body slave. I must do this alone. The omen of the return of these bones cannot be gainsaid.'

With everyone else stunned and silent, he turned to Itrac and caught her face in his cupped hands, kissing her. Embracing her, he drew her close, apparently burying his face in her neck. He spoke softly, for her ears alone.

'You have never asked me where Chazen Saril's bones lie, Itrac, and I honour you for that. But I fear I have dishonoured the domain with that secret. If I travel alone, I can bring his remains back to join Olkai's on the tower of silence and no one else need know.'

I would never have thought of this without Janne's gift. And the irony is it need not be a lie. I can bring Chazen Saril's bones back here. It's surprising how easy it is to weave truth and circumstance into a tissue of lies embroidered with a little wishful thinking.

172

Itrac stiffened in the circle of his arms. 'I have seen how troubled you have been, my husband, even though you have tried to hide it.' She spoke loudly enough for the assembled warlords and ladies to hear clearly. Her voice was calm and level, though Kheda could feel her trembling. 'I believe you are right. This is something you must do for all our sakes.'

Kheda saw a single tear running down Janne's cheek. He covered his confusion by kissing Itrac's hair in apparent affection. 'I am honoured by your confidence in me, my lady.' He surprised her by unclasping her necklace of silver-mounted lozenges of turtleshell and deftly securing it around his own neck. 'Honour me with this talisman.'

Redigal Coron managed to find his tongue. 'We appreciate your confidence in us, my lord of Chazen.'

Kheda looked directly at him. 'We ask more than that of you all, my lord of Redigal. While I am gone, Chazen could be seen as vulnerable by any who wish the domain ill.' He managed a thin smile. 'Perhaps we can see an omen in Ulla Safar's unexpected departure, which allows me to be frank. We all know his malice of old, my lords. While I'm encouraged to learn that malevolence is being repaid with a host of troubles keeping him close to home, I ask all of you to stand as Chazen's allies if his vicious eye turns this way. Who knows, I may learn something or see some portent that will be of benefit to us all in our dealings with him. More than that, I ask you not to wait for some move against my wife and daughters but to pre-empt any attack, if you learn of one.' He looked briefly at Beyau.

Make sure you let them know you suspect I'm going to try to make some contact with Orhan.

Ritsem Caid spoke up suddenly. 'Chazen can count on Ritsem's friendship and protection until your return.'

'There have been portents in Redigal advocating new honesty to accompany this new year,' Redigal Coron said slowly. 'I welcome your frankness, Chazen Kheda, and you may trust in Redigal's defence of your waters and your people while you seek new clarity for yourself.'

'You may treat our sea lanes as your own for purposes of trade,' Moni assured Itrac.

As Hinai added her agreement, Kheda saw Elio Redigal looking expectantly at Janne Daish. Janne looked blandly back at the Redigal wives before turning to her son, her face unreadable.

Sirket squared his shoulders. 'Given all that Daish owes the Chazen warlord and his lady, our promise of alliance is scant repayment. I offer it nevertheless and we'll make good our debt with ships and men if need be.'

'Your goodwill eases my mind more than you can know, much as I hope there'll be no need for anyone to raise arms in Chazen's defence.' Kheda was glad to be speaking the truth again. 'I'll take my leave of you, with my heartfelt thanks.'

'You're leaving now?' Ritsem Caid was quite taken aback.

'There's nothing to be gained by delay.' Kheda walked towards the nursemaids cradling Olkai and Sekni, Itrac at his shoulder.

Redigal Coron sounded uncertain. 'As long as one has taken appropriate time for reflection.'

Kheda took Olkai from her nurse and held her close, breathing in her soft, seductive scent. 'If I am to regain my faith in the future, I must put myself in its hands.'

I am doing this for you, my new daughter, for you and your sister, and for all my children and everyone else in this domain and Daish. Even if no one can know just what it is I'm doing.

He kissed Olkai's feathery dark hair and handed her back to her nurse, feeling a raw pain barely assuaged by the solid weight of Sekni replacing her in his arms.

'Where will you go?' Sirket asked with barely masked distress. 'You'll need a ship—'

'I know where I need to go. Do you see that small boat anchored over by the observatory?' Kheda looked up at Itrac as he kissed Sekni, still sleeping soundly, and handed her back to Touai's second daughter. 'It belongs to a *zamorin* scholar who brought me lore about dragons last year, lore that helped us find where they were laired after they had wounded each other in their battles. Now I understand the omen in the *zamorin*'s unforeseen return. The boat is called the *Reteul*. Zorat, Litai, do you understand?'

Ritsem Zorat looked wide-eyed at him. 'The reteul is a bird of good omen,' he stammered, 'a reminder to trust in the past and hope in the future because each bird sings the same song as those that laid them in the egg and teaches it in turn to those as yet unhatched...' He fumbled to a halt and looked desperately at Redigal Litai.

'The birds of any one island share a particular song that no others know.' The youth twisted his hands around one another. 'We can see a good omen for your safe return in that.' His voice rose to a question as he looked desperately at his father.

Kheda smiled broadly at the other warlords. 'My lords of Redigal and Ritsem, you can be proud of your heirs. And even though I find I must leave, my lords, my ladies, please stay awhile to enjoy my lady Itrac's hospitality.' Kheda indicated the islands of the residence with an expansive hand. 'You're welcome to use my library to help you divine whatever meaning the heavens hold for your own domains.' He looked from Coron to Caid and then around at the whole gathering. 'I hope to see you soon with a clearer understanding of what the future holds for Chazen.'

And I'll be going now, at once, while you're all too stunned to really take this in. Before one of you comes up with all too many good reasons why I shouldn't.

Seeing Itrac was too occupied with presenting a serene countenance to the gathering to speak, he kissed her swiftly and walked rapidly out of the pale-pink tent. He had crossed the first walkway towards the observatory isle before rapid footsteps came up behind him.

'My lord,' protested Beyau, 'let me see that this *Reteul* is properly supplied with food and fresh water. You can't be leaving without so much as a change of clothes—'

'Go back to my lady Itrac, Beyau.' Kheda kept his eyes on the path. 'She'll have ever more need of you while I am away and you've never failed in your duty to Chazen. Don't start now.'

Beyau halted, stricken. 'Yes, my lord.'

I'm sorry, Beyau, I know you don't deserve that, but I have to shake you off. I'll just have to share Velindre's wardrobe.

Stifling a wholly inappropriate smile at that notion, Kheda lengthened his stride and left the burly steward standing in the middle of the short bridge. Slaves and servants slowed in their tasks as he passed them, looking at each other with shrugs of incomprehension. Kheda ignored them all, heading straight for the *Reteul* rolling gently in the modest berth beyond the observatory.

Where is Velindre? She had better be aboard. We're only going to get away with this if we leave at once.

He jumped over the rail and landed on the *Reteul*'s deck with a solid thump. A tanned and bony hand instantly threw open the hatch to the single hold below. 'Who's there?' the magewoman barked.

'Stay down there.' Kheda saw that the sail was rigged and the little boat ready to depart. He moved quickly to unlash the ropes securing the *Reteul* to the mooring posts.

'What did you do?' the unseen magewoman asked. 'What are they all doing? I thought we were going to spend the day bamboozling everyone with divinations.'

'Circumstance played into my hands and I took the chance it offered,' Kheda said curtly. 'I've convinced everyone that I will be better off seeking insight on my own for a little while. For the moment, I hope everyone's busy agreeing with everyone else that this is plainly the only course open to me. That and reassuring Itrac that I haven't run mad,' he added caustically.

'So we're leaving before it occurs to anyone that you might be suffering from too much sun?' Velindre sounded amused.

Kheda moved to the long stern sweep and used it to push the little boat deftly out of the coral's embrace. 'Coron will spend the rest of the day in my library looking for omens that might explain my actions. Ritsem Caid won't do anything until he's thought through all the implications this might have for his current campaign to isolate and undermine Ulla Safar. With luck, Beyau will be sure to have Jevin let Ganil and Prai know that I am hoping to make some contact with Ulla Orhan while no one is looking to see what I'm doing.'

'We haven't time for any distractions like Orhan.' Velindre began climbing the ladder up from the hold. 'As soon as we sail west—'

'I'm sailing just as far as this burned isle where your associate is holding Risala,' Kheda said baldly. 'Then we'll discuss what we're doing next.'

Velindre stared at him. 'You said—'

'No,' Kheda cut her off. 'You presumed. This is as much as you're getting from me, Velindre, for the moment at least. Or do I anchor over there and go back to tell everyone I've changed my mind? I don't imagine anything will surprise them today.'

'Very well, my lord.' The magewoman's sarcasm was withering. 'Once we join up with Risala, we shall see, shan't we? Are we sailing straight to join her or do you want to circle a few islands to see if anyone's spies are tracing our wake?'

'If anyone sees us setting our course to the burned island, we'll hope they assume I'm revisiting events of these past two years in hopes of seeing my path to the future.' Kheda grunted as he strove to scull the boat into clear water. 'And I don't imagine Redigal Coron or Ritsem Caid will want to offer the insult of having me followed. More to the point, if they think I might find Orhan, or discover where he is, they'll want to be able to deny any such knowledge in good conscience if Ulla Safar does catch up with him and cut him into pieces.' He leaned into the oar again. 'The Daish domain is in such disarray that neither Sirket nor Janne will think to send curious eyes after me and Itrac certainly won't.' Kheda felt a qualm at his callous deceit. 'She thinks I'm going to retrieve Chazen Saril's bones and we agreed when we married that the wider domain shouldn't ever know where I laid him to rest, in case malcontents gathered there.'

Velindre sat on the edge of the hatch. 'How long will it take for word to reach Ulla Safar that you've gone off on your own again?'

'He doubtless has spies in Redigal and Ritsem.' Kheda slowed in his sculling to catch his breath. 'But they won't know anything until Taisia and Moni have enciphered the news for their courier doves and sent word to their sister-wives. Then some covert bird has to fly north to Derasulla.' He looked at the nut palms to judge the prevailing breeze before fixing Velindre with a stern eye. 'Then you can use your magic to make sure there's no threat setting sail from Ulla waters before we discuss just what we do about this western isle of yours.'

'Naturally,' Velindre agreed with suspicious meekness.

Kheda looked warily at her for a moment. 'You had better see to that sail. I want to be well beyond the outer reef before it occurs to Redigal or Ritsem to look for a merchant galley flying their domain's pennant out on the trading beach.'

'Why would they do that?' Velindre went to adjust the ropes at the little boat's mast.

'To make note of every line and plank of this ship,' Kheda said succinctly. 'So they'll know you the next time they pass you on the sea lanes. And they'll be looking for you, make no mistake.'

'With the intention that I'd enjoy their hospitality until I'd given up everything I knew or suspected about where you might have gone?' Velindre suggested flippantly. 'Along with anything that might possibly explain this aberration of yours?'

'Just be grateful Ulla Safar isn't still here.' Kheda scowled. 'You wouldn't expect to escape him without being tortured to give up your secrets.'

'I heard enough tales about Safar on my travels.' Velindre shivered as she looked around the lagoon. 'Just let that oar trail in the water.'

Kheda felt the deck shudder beneath his feet. 'Magic?'

'None that anyone will notice,' Velindre assured him. 'I know better than that.'

'Just what have you learned about Aldabreshin attitudes to magic, after sailing the Archipelago for half a year?' The oar thrummed in his hands and Kheda realised that a discreetly cooperative current was sweeping them towards the closest break in the outer reef.

'That largely theoretical prejudices have flowered into active hatred of all wizardry, thanks to the arrival of those wild men and the cruelty of their onslaught.' Velindre looked at the triangular sail and it bellied obediently with just enough wind to carry the *Reteul* forward. 'Which gives me reasons of my own to want to put an end to their predations.'

'And what would those be?' Kheda slid a sideways glance at her.

You sound as if you were born in these waters and even if you don't look like the rest of us, you're convincing enough as a zamor-in *slave of barbarian blood. But you're more different from me and mine than even the most barbarous pale-skinned northerner from those unbroken lands. I mustn't forget that.*

She surprised him with her candid answer. 'I like the Archipelago, Kheda. Each domain has a fascinating history and poems and legends as elegant and sophisticated as the most accomplished mainland literature. I've met all manner of wise and friendly people, from highest rank to none. I'd like to be able to sail these waters without hiding who and what I am. I wish I could counter fable with some truths about us wizards from the north,' she added wryly. 'We mages of Hadrumal are nowhere near as numerous and as all-powerful as Aldabreshin tales make us out to be. We keep to ourselves much of the time, mostly debating how to win the respect due to our powers without striking such fear into the mundane populace that they turn on anyone suspected of magebirth. There's no hope of persuading you Archipelagans of the reality of wizardry if those wild mages reappear with all their vile abuses of magic. Come to that, if tales of the invasions here and of dragons overflying these islands reach the mainland, I can see life for some of my associates there becoming far more uncertain.'

'How many wizards are there in the north?' Kheda wondered, not for the first time.

'Magebirth isn't that common.' Oblivious to his curious gaze, Velindre watched the foam framing their path through the outer reef. 'Think about those savages that invaded.

Every wizard was backed by several hundred men without any magic within them. Those men must have had wives and mothers and sisters, and then you can count in the men too old to fight as well as children at their mother's knee.' She grinned with an irritating superiority. 'I don't think we need worry about finding wild wizards standing shoulder to shoulder on this unknown island.'

'I wouldn't bother counting the old and infirm.' Kheda raised his voice as they passed through waters noisy with surf. 'They get fed to the dragon.'

'Which is an obscenity every northern wizard would abhor,' Velindre said with sudden loathing. 'I've read enough Aldabreshin philosophy on my travels to know that your sages condemn the abuse of power, from warlords down to some swaggering bully of a village spokesman. We wizards of Hadrumal condemn the abuse of magical power just as thoroughly.'

'Condemning it is one thing.' Kheda hauled up the stern oar and stowed it by the side rail. 'Doing something about it is quite another. The philosophers are eloquent on that subject.'

'Which is why we should both want to see just what we're dealing with out in that savage land.' Velindre narrowed her eyes as the ship surged forward on the open sea, a strong wind filling the sail with scant need for magic. 'You have to come with us, Kheda. You've done the most difficult bit — getting away from Chazen. You can't waste this opportunity.'

'We'll discuss it when I see that Risala is safe and well.' Kheda watched the *Brittle Crab* turn on her station around the arc of the reef. The fast trireme looked expectant, oars poised and projecting either side of the brass-sheathed beak of her ram. He held his breath but no signal horn sounded from the inner islands to set the vessel pursuing them.

Velindre turned to him with a question of her own. 'What's so ill-omened about this burned island where she insisted we hide up?'

'It's where Chazen Saril's younger brothers were kept after being blinded and made *zamorin* on his accession.' Kheda didn't like the distaste he saw on the magewoman's face. 'It's also where I first encountered those wild men and their wizards, when I brought Daish triremes and swordsmen down to see why Chazen ships were fleeing into our waters with tales of fire and mayhem in the night. I went there with Chazen Saril.' He tensed at the recollection and his voice turned accusing despite himself. 'We were attacked by monsters. Magic twisted lizards and birds and the crabs on the shore into abominations that ripped my men to pieces.'

It's also where we laid Chazen Saril's putrid corpse when we brought it back in shame and secrecy from Daish, on the darkest night in the five-year cycle of the heavenly compass. None of this is omen or portent. You just realised it was the safest place to hide this wizard Velindre wished on you, didn't you, Risala? Because no Chazen islander would dare set foot there or even sail close enough inshore to see who might be anchored there.

'I recall Dev saying you destroyed the monsters by setting the whole island alight?' Velindre queried.

'Fire is the ultimate purification,' Kheda confirmed shortly.

'I don't know how your philosophers are squaring that with that dragon blasting Chazen with flaming breath last year,' the magewoman mused with sly provocation. 'A crude measure, but still, I gather it was effective. I imagine you weren't facing the most powerful wizards in that invasion, if they couldn't quench the flames.'

'I have no idea.' Kheda looked ahead to the white-rimmed lumps of indistinct green dotting the horizon.

Will I find you convinced you've seen some omens on that wretched isle, Risala? Will you be hoping I will see something to restore my belief in such guidance? You're the only one who knows I laid Chazen Saril in the blackened ruins of the pavilion where his brothers had been imprisoned. Did I still half-believe such an act might have a power to influence the days to come? I know you did. But my disillusion with portent and prophecy runs deeper than ever nowadays.

The only other person who knew where we laid Chazen Saril was Dev, and Dev's dead. He was powerful enough to fight the strongest of the wild wizards who came to plague us and he nearly died of it. He tried to turn his magic against the fire dragon and that was truly the death of him. How powerful are these wizards of this unknown isle? How many of them might there be? Just how strong is Velindre, or this new wizard that she's brought with her? Are they equal to whatever perils might lurk on this mysterious island? Can I risk finding out that they are not and dying for their arrogance? What will become of Itrac and the babies?

They'll be defended by Ritsem and Redigal and Daish besides, that's what will happen if I don't return. Can I risk not knowing what lies beyond the western horizon? Could I return to Itrac and try to live in any kind of peace of mind now that I know this unseen land could be nurturing who knows what manner of magical threat?

The vista ahead of him was empty of answers. The *Reteul* flew on over the turquoise waters as if driven on as much by his urgent questions as by the magewoman's magic.

Chapter 8

How long will this place smell of burning? How far does the breeze carry the decaying breath of this place, to remind passing ships of what happened here? Does it keep them away?

Kheda watched the blackened isle rising above a slew of jagged reefs just high enough above the water to give a foothold to tenacious tangles of grey-stemmed midar. The tormented screams of dying Daish warriors echoed loud in his memory.

My swordsmen, my faithful captain Atoun, ripped apart by whip lizards transmuted to something half-way between animal and man by the wild mages. My first encounter with magic that was as foul as I had always believed it. Yet I come here now in a barbarian wizard's company, finding myself increasingly persuaded that she alone can show me what threat to the domain lies beyond the horizon.

'We could have been here last night.' Velindre sat on the Reteul's stern thwart, one hand on the tiller.

'This isn't a shore I wanted to come on in the twilight or with a contrary wind.' Kheda adjusted the angle of the sail.

We did kill all the monsters, didn't we? Surely nothing could have survived.

The *Reteul* continued on her way, the morning breeze negating any need for magic. Both magewoman and war-lord wore the loose unbleached cotton tunic and trousers of *zamorin*.

Not that anyone will take me for zamorin *with my beard. Not that there's anyone to see me hereabouts.*

The little boat skirted the vicious corals. Kheda studied the shore. There were no trees, just stark black stumps still taller than a man where the insatiable flames had devoured the mighty ironwoods. The dense stands of tandra trees and dappled figs hadn't been able to withstand the all-consuming flames, reduced to heaps of charred wood. The clusters of nut palms that had edged the beach were just a memory, their ashes a stain spread across the white sand by the storms of two successive rainy seasons.

Velindre shook her golden head at the devastation. 'If I didn't know better, I'd have said elemental fire did this.'

'It was sticky fire,' Kheda said shortly. 'We don't set such blazes lightly, but there are times when only the purification of burning will suffice, especially in times of disease.' A shift of the wind brought a richer scent to mingle with the memory of burning and he noticed swathes of fresh green among the dark ruination.

Renewal. I could have called that a favourable omen, if I still believed in such things.

Coral gulls walked splay-footed and unbothered along the sandy shore. Unseen among the newly grown low brush, crookbeaks squabbled raucously. Looking over the side rail, Kheda saw a school of sunset fish flash from yellow to orange and disappear into trailing sea grasses.

'There's our anchorage.' The magewoman waved a hand towards a blunt headland defying a sizeable reef not far out to sea and the *Reteul* veered obediently inshore.

'That's your ship?' Kheda looked at the blue-hulled vessel lying at anchor in the shallow cove. 'You've certainly applied yourself as a scholar to have sufficient learning to trade for something like that.'

'I'm flattered that you think I could do so,' Velindre said, a trifle sarcastically. 'No, I took a leaf out of Dev's book. I've been trading, which incidentally gave me an excellent excuse for idling around the beaches to listen to sailors' tales of mysteries out on the deep.'

'You didn't think such stories were just prompted by your barbarian liquors and dream smokes?' Kheda tried to keep the distaste out of his voice.

'Hardly, given that's not what I trade,' Velindre retorted acidly. 'Dev was a fool to risk being caught with such contraband.'

'What is your cargo?' Kheda was curious.

Velindre didn't answer, studying the vessel ahead instead. 'That's how they build ships in the western domains, so it's robust enough to take out onto the open ocean. We wouldn't survive this voyage in a cockleshell like this one.'

The blue-hulled vessel was nothing like the *Reteul*. Kheda certainly hadn't seen many similar ships in these southerly waters. The twin masts were much of a height and each carried a creamy triangular sail hanging half-furled from a raking yardarm. Bright with yellow paint and carving, a six-sided platform rose solidly above the steering oars at the stern, its angularity incongruous. Kheda would have been hard pressed to tell which was the prow or the stern without the steering oars and the cant of the sails. Both ends of the ship were equally rounded, blunted with a layer of double planking. Solid clinker-built panels were fixed to shield the steering oars from violent seas.

'You can sail that yourself without arousing suspicion?' he asked dubiously. 'Without magic?'

'It's a two-man ship.' Velindre wasn't offended. 'The sideways sweep of each sail can be governed from the stern platform as long as there's a second pair of hands to adjust the pitch of the yardarms. You see those ropes running to the pulleys on the side rails?'

Kheda lost all interest in the complexities of the unfamiliar rigging when he saw two figures on the raised stern platform.

Risala.

'We'll beach the *Reteul* up above the high-water line. If anyone does sail by, they can assume you're ashore communing with the past.' Velindre took a firm grip on the tiller and lifted one long hand towards the sail. 'Hold on to something.'

Kheda grabbed at the side rail as the *Reteul* accelerated towards the shore. Velindre's magic drove the little ship swiftly up the sloping sand, shells grating beneath her hull.

'Don't spring any planks,' he warned the magewoman sternly. 'I shall want to sail home in this boat.'

The *Reteul* slowed to a halt. As Kheda waited a moment to be certain the deck wasn't about to shift beneath his feet, he saw one of the figures on the blue boat dive off the stern. Fetching anchors from the lockers in the *Reteul*'s prow and stern, he swung himself over the side and down onto the sand. He had the little boat firmly secured by the time Risala reached the shallows.

She stood waist deep, wiping wet hair out of her eyes and smiling. 'Good morning, my lord.'

Taking a moment to appreciate her slenderness outlined by her clinging wet tunic, Kheda grinned back before a faint noise inland sent a shiver down his spine. He turned to look at the burned trees and clumps of new brush. 'We did kill all the monsters, didn't we?'

'The biggest thing on this island is a chequered fowl,' Risala assured him. 'Naldeth — the other wizard — he's been ashore several times and scried across the island besides.'

'Has he had any more success scrying out to the west?' Velindre called down from the *Reteul*'s deck.

Risala looked up, shading her eyes with one hand. 'Not really.'

'Why has he been ashore?' Kheda demanded, frowning.

Never mind any thought of portent, I won't have any barbarian mage disturbing Chazen Saril's bones to satisfy some macabre curiosity.

'Because his elemental affinity is with fire.' Velindre leaned over the *Reteul*'s rail, unconcerned. 'He was curious to see how the burning spread once you'd set your fires, and how the land is recovering.'

Kheda looked at Risala. 'He's a fire mage like Dev?'

'He's nothing like Dev.' She chuckled, running her hands through her damp hair to leave it a mass of unruly black spikes.

Kheda looked back up at Velindre. 'Is he your lover?'

'Oh no.' The magewoman laughed. 'He's not to my taste and I don't imagine I'm to his.'

Risala giggled. 'He's far too much in awe of Velindre to lay a finger on her.'

Kheda shrugged. 'I shall want to get his measure before I agree to sail anywhere with him.'

'Then come and meet him.' Velindre stood up and swung her meagre bundle of clothes tied with a leather strap over one shoulder. Kheda saw she was also carrying his little physic chest and had his twin swords thrust through her belt. 'If you don't want to be away for too long, the sooner we start this voyage, the better.' Velindre vanished in a spiral of twisted air to reappear on the stern platform of the blue-hulled ship.

Kheda stepped close and slid his hands around Risala's narrow waist. 'I've missed you.'

'No more than I've missed you.' She drew his face down to kiss him long and deep.

After some indeterminate time, Kheda reluctantly broke free. 'What do we do now?'

Risala raised one black brow and pressed her hips against his. 'I can tell what you want to do.'

'I can wait.' Kheda kissed her again. 'I meant, what do we do about this voyage Velindre's determined on? I haven't agreed to go with her. I only came here to be sure you were in no danger.'

'We'll all be in danger if those wild men come again, or another dragon.' Risala laid her hands flat against Kheda's muscular chest and tucked her tousled head under his bearded chin. 'I don't particularly want to go with them but surely forewarned is forearmed.'

'That's what she keeps saying.' Kheda tightened his embrace. 'But how can I leave Chazen and Itrac at a time like this?'

'The domain's quite at peace,' Risala said slowly. 'People have plenty of food, and new trade and newborn children of their own to occupy them. But they're still afraid of fire in the night coming to overthrow it all again. They need to know they are safe. Or if they're not, this time they need to be told to flee before they're slaughtered.' She shivered involuntarily.

Kheda heaved a sigh. 'A warning is not much to offer.'

'It's better than nothing,' Risala muttered. 'Naldeth says we can reach this strange isle by the dark of the next Lesser Moon.'

Kheda looked up to the morning sky where a pearl sliver indicated that the Lesser Moon would still be with them for a handful of days or more. He frowned. 'That's impossible, if this island is so far—'

'Not with their magic,' Risala reminded him. 'And that magic can bring us home with no need for ships.'

'Both wizards will know this place at least,' Kheda conceded grudgingly. 'But how can I disappear for a whole turn of the Pearl?'

'What did you tell Itrac, to explain coming away with Velindre?' Risala toyed with the laces at the neck of his tunic.

'That I needed time and solitude to consider the omens for the domain,' Kheda said sourly, 'since I find I can't read any clear meaning in the earthly or heavenly compasses at present. At least that's no lie.'

Risala took a moment to answer. 'No one would think a turn of either moon was unduly long to spend on such an important thing. Besides, all Itrac's attention will be focused on her babies. She'll barely know that you're gone.'

Kheda grunted. 'Perhaps. But Ulla Safar will know as soon as word gets back to Redigal and Ritsem.'

'Ulla Safar won't spare you a second thought,' Risala said with conviction. 'He'll be lucky to still have a head on his shoulders by the time we get back, if Orhan's supporters have anything to say about it.'

'Truly?' Kheda leaned back so that he could look at her.

'That was the word on every second beach where I made a stop on my way to meet Velindre,' she assured him, no doubt in her blue eyes. 'And anyway, what would Safar do? It's not as if you're leaving the domain, as far as anyone knows or even suspects. I take it you said you were coming here?'

'I told Itrac,' Kheda said slowly, 'but no one else.'

'Jevin will make sure Ritsem Caid and Redigal Coron know.' Risala bit her lip. 'What of Daish?'

'I told Sirket I was likely to be away for some time,' Kheda admitted. 'That I needed to know if the wild men or any dragon were coming to threaten us again.'

'Then why make that a lie?' Risala slipped out of Kheda's arms and walked back towards the sea. 'Come on. Come and meet Naldeth.'

Kheda followed, wading and then cutting through the waves with powerful swimming strokes. Risala at his side, he trod the chill water by the swelling side of the western-built ship. 'Velindre? A rope?' he called out.

A woven ladder slapped down the blue planking. Kheda steadied it with his weight as Risala climbed nimbly up. He followed, wiping water from his hair and beard as he swung his legs over the rail.

'My lord Chazen Kheda.' The unknown man standing just in front of the aft mast bowed courteously.

You're certainly nothing like Dev.

'Naldeth.' Kheda bowed briefly in reply. 'So you're playing the slave to Velindre's *zamorin* scholar?'

'Slave or servant,' the mage replied easily. 'We say whatever suits the beach we land on.'

Perhaps a year or so older than Risala, Naldeth was only a little shorter than Kheda. He had the rounded features of a true barbarian and had evidently not been sailing the Archipelago as long as Velindre, for his pale northern skin was still more ruddy than tanned. He wore his unremarkable dun hair drawn tidily back in a short braid, sun-bleached to a shade just lighter than his mild brown eyes. His somewhat sparse beard was neatly trimmed along his jaw line. He wore the same unbleached cottons as Kheda.

He wears a Chazen dagger, like Velindre, but here in the south he must turn heads, he's so plainly barbarian. In the central and western domains, northern slaves are more common, so I don't suppose he warrants more than a passing glance. Apart from his lack of a leg.

Having made his bow, the wizard was leaning on a well used crutch. One cotton trouser leg was drawn up and tucked through the belt on his tunic, making it plain that limb ended abruptly at mid-thigh.

At least he has his knife hand free.

Kheda turned to Velindre, who was descending the steps from the stern platform. 'What's your vessel called, shipmistress?'

'The *Zaise*.' The magewoman smiled. 'It seemed appropriate, from what I've read of bird and ship lore.'

'Would you call that a good omen, Chazen Kheda?' Naldeth's attention was fixed on the warlord.

'Kheda will suffice.' He glanced briefly at the youthful wizard. 'I don't look for omens for this voyage.'

He felt Risala stir at his side and resisted the urge to look at her.

'Did you know that western mariners venture out into the deep to catch currents running along the outer edge of the Archipelago?' the wizard persisted. 'One comes down from the north and another runs up from the south.'

'If those western mariners are lucky as well as bold, they avoid the point where the currents meet and will sweep them out west to die of thirst and madness on the open ocean,' Velindre said sardonically.

'Is that the route we're to take to this strange isle of yours?' Kheda raised his brows. 'If I agree to come with you—'

Naldeth scowled. 'You must—'

Velindre shook her head to silence him before answering Kheda. 'There's another current in the southern ocean beyond Chazen's waters that'll carry us west and then curl north to bring us to the savages' isle.'

Kheda noticed that the space beneath the stern platform had been made into a low cabin, its door tied shut. The wooden grates that would normally shed light into the ship's holds were cloaked with sailcloth held down with tightly nailed battens. 'Just what cargo have you been trading through the domains?'

'We're carrying naphtha and rock tar.' Velindre's smile widened. 'And the sulphur and resins that go with them to make sticky fire and suchlike.'

'That's a volatile mix.' Kheda looked down involuntarily as if he could see the barrels of potential blazing death beneath his feet.

'Not with a fire mage on board.' Naldeth shifted his crutch noisily on the planking. 'Kheda, when Dev—'

'It gave us an excellent excuse to anchor well clear of every other ship on the trading beaches.' Velindre spoke over the young wizard again. 'And with incendiaries always a warlord's secret, I was trading with their most trusted stewards and guard captains, which made it all the easier for me to ask about curious omens washed up from the deep or blown in on storms.'

'I gather you set that inferno with sticky fire?' Naldeth continued, gesturing with his free hand towards the blackened isle.

That's not what you were going to say, young wizard. What do you know of Dev?

'It's the only thing that will burn long and hot enough to set fire to a whole island.' Kheda turned back to Velindre. 'This is a risky cargo to take out into the open ocean. What if some barrel springs a leak in a storm?'

'My elemental affinity is with the air, Kheda,' she said with faint rebuke. 'I don't propose to fall foul of any storms.'

'Why do we have to sail all the way to this island?' Kheda looked around the ship. 'If you can't use your magic to carry yourselves there, why can't you look for it with your bespelled waters? You could find Dev all the way from the northern wastes.'

'We've tried, believe me,' said Naldeth with feeling.

'There's magic there, Kheda, even if it's not being worked by men or dragons,' Velindre said slowly. 'It's in the earth and the air, in the seas and the rivers. There's some confluence of power—' She broke off, shaking her head. 'Whatever it is, it foils all our attempts to scry for wild wizards or dragons. We'll just have to go and see with our own eyes.'

Kheda looked at her for a long moment, searching for any hint of dissembling or falsehood. 'You say you can get us there in the next cycle of the Lesser Moon?'

Velindre looked at Naldeth, her lips thinning. 'Perhaps. Certainly it shouldn't take much longer than that.'

Kheda rubbed a hand over his beard. 'And you could use your magic to send me home at any time? Me and Risala?'

'Oh yes.' Velindre had no hesitation about that.

'Dev said you can scry for someone you don't know if you have something of theirs.' Kheda reached into the neck of his tunic and unclasped Itrac's silver and turtleshell necklace. 'Show me that my wife and children are happy and secure.'

Velindre narrowed her eyes at him. 'If you insist.'

She took the necklace and coiled it in her palm. Moving to the barrel of water lashed to the stern mast, she dipped a handful to cover the gleaming links. The liquid lay obediently in her palm, not a drop escaping. The mage-woman passed her other hand over the necklace and the water cloaking it glowed turquoise. 'See for yourself,' she said simply.

A scene like a painted miniature was caught in the circle of silver and mottled turtleshell. Itrac was lying on a wide

194

day bed set beneath the shade of a bower in the garden at the heart of her pavilion. She was holding little Olkai on one side and Sekni on the other as they drowsed together. Jevin stood watchful while both nurses sat placidly sewing tiny garments of shining white silk.

Kheda watched for a moment. 'I'll come with you if you show me at least once a day that all's well at the residence,' he said with resignation. 'You'll scry for the trading beaches too, to look for any upheaval that might signify trouble between the domains. If we see any such thing, I want your oath on whatever you hold sacred that you'll send me home. Me and Risala.'

'At once.' Velindre nodded. 'On my honour and my element. Is that enough for you?'

Would I have believed Dev if he'd sworn such an oath? Doubtful, and I wouldn't necessarily have believed whatever he had shown me in a spell. But Velindre is different, isn't she?

Kheda nodded curtly. 'Then if you can be sure this cargo won't be the death of us, let's get under way. As you've been saying, there's nothing to be gained by delay.'

Naldeth looked as if he wanted to respond to that but Velindre waved him forward. 'See to the foresail. Risala, show Kheda how we set the aft sail.' The mage-woman turned to climb the ladder-like stair up to the stern platform.

Naldeth stumped away, his crutch loud on the decking. Tossing the prop aside, he leaned against the side rail, needing both hands to adjust the ropes that angled the yardarm.

Risala tugged on a rope and cursed under her breath. 'Something's stuck.' She swung herself up onto the ladder-like ratlines stretching up from the side rail to the top of the mast. Kheda watched her run up the tarred rope rungs and reach carefully out across the spar to free the rope hampering the billowing sailcloth. The scrape of Naldeth's crutch brought his attention back down to deck.

The young wizard was waiting. 'So are you going to ask me about this?' He gestured towards the stump of his thigh. 'You're not worried that I won't be able to play my part in this voyage?'

'I'll take Velindre's word that you'll be more help than hindrance,' the warlord answered calmly.

'You don't want to know what wrongdoing or folly brought me to such a mischance?' Naldeth persisted. 'Such accidents are seen as omens in the Archipelago, aren't they?'

'I told you, I don't look for portents concerning this voyage.' Kheda's voice hardened a little.

And these past few years have disabused me of any belief that any man's future is inexorably determined by his past choices.

'It was pirates.' Naldeth wasn't to be deterred. 'I was doing no one any harm, sailing to help settlers making a new life in a wilderness. We were captured and thrown into the ship's hold. When they were pursued, the pirates trailed me in the water on the end of a rope, cutting me to bleed till the sharks came. They said they'd carry on till I had no arms or legs unless our rescuers withdrew. Do you think that's a just fate for someone as evil as a wizard?' There was a distinct edge to his question.

'You were evidently rescued before you lost all your limbs.' Kheda met the youth's hot stare with cool equanimity. 'I assume these pirates met a death appropriate to their crimes?'

Don't you know that one of the first things a warlord learns is not to respond to contentious challenges?

'I was rescued by my fellow mages, as it happens.' Naldeth scowled. 'And yes, the pirates were hanged.'

'It's not for me to make sense of such things for you.' Kheda gave a single shake of his head. 'I don't know you. You're the only wizard I've met besides Dev and Velindre and I've no idea which of you might be typical of your breed or even of northern barbarians. I've met none of them either.' He surprised the taut-faced youth with a grin. 'I suspect you're all noteworthy in your own way. I know you've at least enough courage to sail waters where your magic would condemn you to be skinned alive. For this voyage, I'll judge you on the evidence of my own eyes.'

Naldeth stared back at him for a long moment, unblinking. 'And I'll do the same.'

'I thought we wanted to get under way,' Velindre called down irritably from the stern platform.

Kheda turned his back on the youthful wizard and scaled the stern ladder to join the magewoman by the steering oars. 'We want to pass well to the south of that isle.' He pointed to a distant lump of land. 'Otherwise we'll spend the next three days wallowing in knot-tree swamps.'

'I know.' Velindre was leafing through a newly sewn book of reed paper filled with annotated sketches of coastlines and sea lanes.

'You've made up your own route record,' he said with some surprise.

'Naturally. What Aldabreshin shipmistress would be without one?' Velindre traced a course across the page she had sought with a nail-bitten finger. 'Then we leave that reef to the north.'

She tucked the precious book into an ample pocket inside the waist of her trousers and pulled on the ropes canting the aft-sail mast. As she adjusted the steering oars, the *Zaise* turned obediently away from the shore.

'Just make sure our course takes us well away from the pearl reefs,' Kheda insisted. 'Chazen's safety depends at least in part on people thinking I'm still in the domain. I can't be seen to be leaving.'

'Don't worry about that,' Velindre said confidently.

197

Would it be any use if I did?

Kheda dropped down to the deck where Risala was sitting in the shade cast by the stern platform.

She looked up at him, her face unreadable. 'Did you bring a star circle with you?'

'Only to count the days.' He sat down beside her.

'Both moons are sharing the arc of friendship with the stars of the Canthira Tree,' Risala observed stiffly, 'an emblem of new life born of fire. Let's hope that means you can be friends with Naldeth.'

Kheda studied the young wizard. He was still by the foremast, making what looked like an unnecessary adjustment of the pulley blocks. 'What have you made of him while you've been waiting for us?' He moved closer to Risala and put an arm round her shoulders.

'There's no harm in him.' Risala shifted position to turn into his embrace and kissed his cheek. 'Other than being a wizard, of course. As far as his leg's concerned, he just needs to be convinced you won't assume he's lacking wits as well as a foot.'

'Then let him convince me,' Kheda said quietly.

It wasn't long before he was at least convinced that Naldeth was practised in sailing the *Zaise*. With Velindre at the tiller, there was little for Kheda and Risala to do. Whether favourable winds or wizardry propelled them, the ship made good speed. By noon they were leaving the most densely settled islands behind, seeing no ships larger than fishing skiffs and none close enough to hail. The sun was gilding the western sky as they escaped the last contrary currents winding around the treachery of coral and sandbanks. The pearl reefs that were proving so valuable for Chazen were barely smudges on the eastern horizon.

They sailed into deeper, darker seas where Chazen ships didn't venture. The waves grew larger, lifting the *Zaise* on ever taller swells. No longer veering at the dictates of islands, the winds blew steadily from the east. As far as Kheda could judge, the barrel-sided ship was cutting through the seas as fast as any trireme.

I wouldn't want to be caught in these winds without a shipload of strong oarsmen to fight our way back. I hope our shipmistress knows what she's doing.

'I'm hungry.' Risala heaved herself up from the deck and disappeared into the low stern cabin. She reappeared holding four lidded bowls close to her chest.

'Saller pottage.' Kheda grimaced.

'It keeps without spoiling for days at a time, and rowers stay healthy on it,' chided Risala handing him a bowl and a spoon.

'And I ate a lifetime's worth when I was a nameless oarsman on a galley.' Kheda dug the horn spoon into the sticky steamed grain mixed with shreds of smoked meat, half-dried pepper pods and oily crushed tandra seeds.

Velindre slid down the ladder from the stern platform and accepted a bowl. 'We can trawl for fresh fish at dusk. Naldeth!' She waved to the young wizard, who had managed to stay busy about the ship all day.

He joined them and thanked Risala courteously as he took his meal from her. He looked thoughtful as he chewed. 'Chazen Kheda, I'm curious about those creatures Risala said were altered by these wild mages. What can you tell me about them?' He filled his mouth with another spoonful.

Kheda found the dense, cold pottage sticking in his throat. 'They were cinnamon cranes and robber crabs grown twice and three time their usual size.'

'That's a curious trick.' Naldeth's brows knitted. 'What about these tales of lizards turned into men? Is that some poet's embellishment?'

'No poet would invent such a lie,' Risala objected.

'There were whip lizards on the island and those are dangerous enough in themselves.' Kheda's stomach tensed at the bloody memory. 'Some spell stood them upright like men, reshaping their bones and flesh. They attacked us like animals, though, with teeth and claws.'

Naldeth looked at Velindre, animated. 'Hearth Master Kalion's discovered a certain amount about altering minerals with fire.' He gazed avidly out to the west. 'I'd dearly love to know how one would go about changing the very substance of a living creature.'

Kheda found he had lost what little appetite he had for the saller pottage.

Is this insatiable curiosity common to all mages? Will it prove as lethal for you as it did for Dev? Was it the pursuit of new lore that took you on that voyage where you lost your leg? An Archipelagan would have taken that for a sign to spend the rest of his life close to home and been grateful to still be alive to realise that.

'Whales,' Risala said with surprise.

'Where?' Velindre scaled the ladder to the stern platform.

'Yonder.' Risala pointed as they joined her. Naldeth followed, dropping his crutch to pull himself up the steep ladder.

Away to the south, white puffs of moist breath shot up from the cobalt waters and dark shapes rose and fell just beneath the surface. A huge barnacled head broached, underside pale and striped with deep grooves, tiny eyes black in the dappled margin between dark hide and light. The mighty beast plunged down in a flurry of foam and its massive black tail swept up. It struck the water with a resounding splash before the whale vanished. Almost at once, a second surged up from the depths and crashed back down.

'Coron will be pleased to see them in Redigal waters if they head north.' Risala looked at Kheda with a smile.

'What's that?' Supporting himself with one hand on the rail, Naldeth pointed to a swell laced with spume just beyond the whales.

Something long and sinuous slid through the ocean, a shadow quite unlike the oval backs of the whales.

'A sea serpent.' Kheda felt cold despite the sun and the sturdily built *Zaise* suddenly felt all too fragile beneath his feet. 'Velindre, get us away from here.'

'I don't think it's after us.' She spoke quietly as if the creature might hear her. 'If we run, there's always the chance it'll chase us instead of the whales.'

'It's hunting the whales?' Naldeth stared out at the ocean, mouth half-open.

'Better them than us,' Velindre said with regret.

'It's after one of the young ones.' Kheda pointed to a black whale blotched with barnacles riding high in the water. A shorter shape was just visible in the white foam beside it.

'There's another serpent.' Risala took an involuntary step back as a rough-skinned loop the greenish-brown of seaweed broached the surface between their boat and the group of whales.

This second serpent twisted in the waters and vanished. The whales were swimming faster.

Naldeth gasped as the greenish sea serpent suddenly shot up out of the sea, straight as an arrow and reaching taller than the *Zaise*'s masthead. A long fin ran the length of its drab body, translucent in the sunlight, and drops of water gleamed on its coarse hide. Eyes like jet shone in a head no thicker than its body with no hint of a neck. Beneath a blunt snout, its mouth was agape, lined with ugly yellow teeth. Bending itself bonelessly in half, the creature dived back into the water, pointed tail finally flicking up a trailing edge of that single fin.

'Is it going to attack?' Naldeth wondered breathlessly.

'No.' Kheda pointed to the distant sea serpent as the whales veered sharply away from the more obvious threat. 'That's the one going in for the kill.'

'It's hunting the slowest.' Velindre nodded as the lithe menace slid behind a solitary black shape now falling behind the rest of the whales.

'She can't leave her young one,' said Risala, distressed. Kheda reached for her hand and laced his fingers through hers with a comforting squeeze.

'Can't she fight back?' protested Naldeth as he saw the smaller beast pressing close to its mother's dark flank.

As he spoke, the mother whale rolled in the water with surprising agility and smashed her mighty tail down towards the pursuing sea serpent. As the creature lurched away, they saw it was darker than the other, with a thick black edge to the long fin running down its back.

'She can't fight both of them,' Velindre said with measured pity.

The second serpent was now cutting a curving course through the water between the chosen victims and the rest of the fleeing whales. As the mother rolled again to put herself between her young and the black-finned serpent still harrying her, the greenish serpent dived. It reappeared snapping at the frantic youngster. Blood blossomed briefly on the turmoil of foam, shocking scarlet amid the muted colours of beasts and ocean.

'We have to do something!' Naldeth looked from Kheda to Velindre.

'Why?' The magewoman looked back, impassive.

'Why let an innocent creature suffer?' the younger wizard demanded with some heat.

'Sea serpents must eat,' Kheda said with mild regret.

'Serpent for danger and chaos,' said Risala involuntarily. 'But twin serpents of any kind can be an omen, of renewal in death or hope after peril's evaded.'

'So we mustn't act for the sake of not altering some omen?' Naldeth demanded belligerently.

He looked back out to sea where the mother whale was now striving to force the persistent greenish serpent away from her youngster. The smaller whale circled on the surface, blowing out a plume of spray snatched away by the wind. The black-finned serpent briefly broached the surface to snap at the ugly raw gash in the youngster's flank before disappearing into the depths.

'I don't see any sense in drawing those serpents this way,' Kheda said curtly. 'Haven't you heard tales of them wrecking ships?'

'Have you ever seen that happen?' snapped Naldeth.

'No, and I'd never seen a dragon before last year,' Kheda retorted. 'As it turned out, the poets' tales didn't tell the half of it.' He looked out to sea. The mother whale was drawing a circle of foam around her youngster, nimble despite her great bulk. The serpents were swimming the other way, looping through the water, drawing gradually closer and closer.

'Velindre, if you won't do something, I will,' Naldeth warned.

The magewoman looked at him, exasperated. 'The antipathy between fire and water—'

Scarlet steam exploded in front of the black-finned serpent as it broke off its circling to dart towards the mother whale. Kheda glimpsed a brilliant streak of white light cutting through the air as Naldeth made a throwing motion. The sea around the greenish serpent boiled furiously as well. The mother whale shrank back from this incomprehensible happening and blundered into her youngster. Both vanished below the seething waves along with the greenish serpent.

The black-finned serpent twisted this way and that, lethal mouth agape. Naldeth flung out both hands. He would have overbalanced if Kheda hadn't caught him with a strong arm under his elbow. The black-finned serpent rose out of the water in looping confusion, snapping at its own coils. The mother whale reappeared to vent a noisy plume of spray and then dived deep, her wide tail smacking down hard on the surface of the sea. There was no sign of her young or of the greenish serpent.

'What have you done?' Risala watched, appalled, as the black-finned serpent's teeth ripped into its own hide. Dark blood stained the frothing water around it and uncanny crimson reflections ran along the creature's coils.

'The other one's making its escape.' Velindre's eyes grew distant for a moment, unfocused. 'The two whales are following the rest. The young one is badly bitten. Are sea serpents poisonous, Kheda?'

'Opinions vary,' he said shortly, withdrawing his arm from Naldeth's elbow. 'What did you do?'

'Burned the oils in its own skin.' The young wizard leaned on the rail, still intent on his magic. The sea serpent's struggles grew more laboured. Its blood was now a black slick on the surface of the water, glinting with scarlet malevolence. He shot a defiant glance at Velindre. 'At least those whales have a chance now.'

Can you do something like that to a dragon?

Kheda decided not to ask.

Coral gulls appeared to hover over the dying serpent with raucous cries of anticipation. Unseen scavengers from the deep pocked the sea with ripples as they tasted the spreading blood. The serpent floated motionless on the swell, then began slowly sinking. As the last hint of magic faded, the gulls dived, beaks tearing. Vicious angular fins cut through the soiled waves and the serpent's hide reappeared here and there, coils thrust up from below. Blunt grey heads broached the surface as the sharks ripped into the moribund sea serpent.

'Satisfied, Naldeth?' Velindre placidly resumed her meal of saller pottage.

Kheda saw that the young wizard had gone pale beneath his tan, eyes wide with the shock of memory as he stared at the sharks. He shook the youth's shoulder briskly. 'The wind's shifted and strengthened. Some slack in those forward lines wouldn't come amiss.'

'What?' The wizard looked at him, bemused, before recollecting himself. 'Yes, of course.' Ungainly as he supported himself with the rail, he slid down the ladder to the deck and retrieved his crutch to stump away.

'How can we read the omens if he does things like that?' Risala looked abruptly down at the planks where Naldeth's discarded bowl was rolling to and fro, trailing saller pottage. 'And we don't want to be wasting food,' she added crossly.

Kheda realised with some surprise that he still held his own bowl. He looked at the remains of his meal. 'I think I've lost my appetite,' he said apologetically.

'Me too.' Risala took Kheda's bowl from him and jumped down to disappear into the stern cabin.

The silence on the stern platform was broken only by the scrape of Velindre's spoon.

'Do you want me to take a turn at the tiller?' Kheda offered after a few moments.

'Not until I'm sure we've picked up that current I mentioned. After that, you two can share watches with me and Naldeth. He has no great feeling for water but his fire affinity gives him sufficient sympathy with air to be sure we're following the course I set him.'

Kheda glanced towards the young wizard, who was now standing in the prow, looking out across the ceaseless barren swells. 'When did that happen to him?'

'Three years ago.' Velindre said unemotionally.

Kheda yielded to his curiosity. 'How did you persuade him to risk himself in Archipelagan waters? What does this voyage to the west offer him?'

'The chance to learn something new about the magics of elemental fire.' Velindre smiled thinly. 'Something sufficiently extraordinary that our fellow mages will want to talk about his splendid new discovery whenever they encounter him, rather than trying to find a way to ask how he lost his leg and was he really a hero who saved those settlers. Either that or they tie their tongues in knots trying to avoid mentioning anything about it.'

The disdain in her answer left Kheda disinclined to enquire further. 'I'll go and see where Risala's got to.'

He climbed down the ladder and ducked his head to enter the low stern cabin. In the dim light filtering through small windows set beneath the aft beams, Risala was scraping the unwanted food into a bucket. 'We can throw this into the water at dusk if you're going to try fishing,' she said curtly.

Let's not discuss whether or not there might have been omens in the struggle between whales and serpents that Naldeth has polluted.

Kheda gestured to the barrels lining the wooden walls. 'What food are we carrying, besides saller pottage?'

'Smoked fish. Duck sealed in its own fat.' Risala counted off the casks with a finger. 'Dried zira shoots and pickled reckal roots. Herbs and spices.' She nodded towards a net of plump sacks hanging from a beam. 'And there's plenty of dry saller grain.'

Kheda contemplated the wooden trap door in the planking. 'What's down there?'

206

'The stern hold where we'll be sleeping.' She managed a brief smile. 'The rock tar and naphtha and the like are in the central holds. Naldeth has the fore hold and Velindre sleeps in here.' She pointed to a tidy pile of blankets in a box bed built against the bulwark.

'I think I'll see just what we're carrying.' Kheda reached down for the brass ring sunk into the trap door. 'And that it's all securely stowed.'

'I'll call if Velindre wants you.' Risala looked upwards, her expression pensive.

Kheda pulled up the trap door and slid down the ladder beneath. This stern hold was shorter than the deck cabin with a reassuringly thick bulkhead built around the cross-beams bracing the hull. It was almost completely dark and he could taste the oily metallic bite of naphtha in the stale air.

'Leave the door to the deck open,' he called up to Risala. 'I'm not sleeping down here unless we get rid of these fumes.'

He tried the door in the solid bulkhead and found it unlocked. He went through to find more light was filtering through the canvas-shrouded deck gratings. Barrels were held back against the curved hull with plank partitions and further secured with nets wound between stout hooks. The scents of tar and oil were muted, which augured well for the seals on the casks. Kheda made a slow circuit all the same, looking for dark stains of seepage. As satisfied as he could be in the dim light, he tried the door to the next hold and found that unlocked as well.

A yellow smear on the chests of rough wood secured along one wall of the hull was bright in the gloom. It tainted the air with sulphur. Lidded baskets opposite held thick glass bottles tightly wrapped in woven straw. They were sealed with corks and twine and wax to be sure none of their viscous golden contents could leak. Kheda recognised them.

207

Barbarian pine resins. Janne Daish would offer equal weight in mother-of-pearl in trade for such bottles. What do these barbarians know of Aldabreshin recipes for sticky fire? Is there any quicklime here, or just sulphur?

As Kheda studied the other unhelpfully anonymous chests, he realised that something else was tucked behind the one wedged closest to the stern bulwark. About the size of a small barrel, it was thickly wrapped in clean sacking tied with new hemp rope. Kheda reached over the inconvenient chest and tested the ropes. They had been knotted tight and not by an Archipelagan seafarer.

He eased the tip of his dagger into the heart of the top-most knot and worked it back and forth, careful not to cut the rope. Winning just enough slack to be able to shift the sacking beneath, he tugged at the coarse weave. The dim light from the covered grating fell on a dull maroon surface, gently rounded, smooth as glass, and beneath it a fresher red, the colour of blood. The web of fine cracks crazing the surface glinted softly.

Kheda drew back, blood pounding in his temples.

How could we have guessed what that dragon flying in from the western ocean wanted with our rubies? We were just relieved that chests of gems would placate it, would buy us time and lives and land. Who could have imagined the dragon could concentrate its magic so fiercely that it could meld the jewels it chose into this unnatural gem and generate a spark of new life in its very heart?

Why was it that this egg burned Dev alive when he turned his own magic to killing that nascent dragon? What enchantment seduced him to that unhallowed rapture even as the flesh melted from his bones and he was reduced to ashes?

Motionless in the breathless hold, he tried to force away the obscene recollection of the mage's death.

Why did Velindre demand the dead dragon's dead egg as her price for betraying the second dragon to me, the simulacrum she wove from air and magic to light the true fire dragon? Why did I give it to her? That false dragon would have died anyway. She'd already told me there was no sapphire at its heart to give it true life. Could I have convinced the people of Chazen that I was a warlord they could trust if my leadership hadn't been sanctioned by that deceitful victory? How many men died believing the lie that they were fighting to save the domain from a second predator?

As he stared at the mystery half-hidden in the shadows, the door to the foremost hold opened, startling him.

'Are you looking for something?' Naldeth stood in the doorway.

'I was just wondering exactly what you were carrying.' Kheda turned his back on the bundle, hoping to hide the disturbed sacking with his body. 'Are all these chests full of sulphur?'

'No.' Naldeth hopped into the hold, steadying himself with one hand on the door. 'We're carrying a fair amount of alum. Warlords who want to buy the stuffs to make sticky fire generally want the means of stifling it as well.' He lowered himself carefully to the floor of the hold. 'Did Risala tell you not to discard the vinegar from the pickles? It'll be more useful than water if I'm not on hand to kill a fire for you.'

'Indeed.' Kheda gazed at the remarkable contraption the one-legged wizard was laying out before him on the planks. 'What is that?'

'I thought such personal questions were considered impolite among you Aldabreshi.' Naldeth looked up from untangling a confusion of leather straps and buckles. He was grinning. 'How many folk do you think have actually asked me outright how I lost my leg since we sailed south?'

Kheda smiled back but didn't rise to the bait. 'Who made it for you?'

Dull steel was shaped into a blunt-toed foot beneath a curved metal calf riveted to a shin plate. Concentric curved plates overlapped at the front of knee and ankle to suggest that the remarkable creation would bend at both joints. The hollow thigh was topped with more straps and buckles.

'An armourer first came up with the idea.' Naldeth rapped the facsimile limb with his knuckles, the noise loud in the confines of the hold. 'We barbarians don't fight the endless battles that Archipelagan poets insist must constantly ravage the north, but there are enough pointless wars to leave all too many men missing a leg.'

'So these armourers profit when they send men to fight and again when they come back maimed.' Kheda propped himself casually on a chest.

'Don't tell me any Aldabreshi smith wouldn't do the same.' Naldeth shifted on his buttocks and eased his stump into the open top of the metal leg. 'If you're not the bloodthirsty savages our barbarian minstrels sing of, you're certainly as avid a flock of merchants as ever traded.'

'Does it bear your full weight?' As the wizard buckled a stout leather belt around his waist and began securing dangling straps to matching buckles on the metal thigh, Kheda reached stealthily behind his back and tucked the loose sacking under the ropes to hide the exposed surface of the dragon's egg.

'The steel skin's mostly for show.' Naldeth pulled a final strap tight. 'A solid wooden post runs all through the middle, down to the foot plate. There's a metal spring in the angle between the foot and the post, and this —' he tugged on a cord that disappeared into the angle behind the knee '— and some hinges inside mean I can bend it when I want to.'

Kheda nodded with admiration. 'Steelsmiths on the trading beaches must have made handsome offers for a chance to study it.'

'Velindre hasn't let me wear it in Aldabreshin waters.' Naldeth got to his feet with surprising ease, pulling and slackening the cord that bent the metal knee. 'She said you people don't wear plate armour, so it would mark me out as too newly come from the north.'

'That's true enough.' Kheda watched the wizard walk slowly up and down the hold, swinging the stiff leg out slightly with each step. 'It's a remarkable contrivance.'

'I still need my crutch if I'm not using a touch of magic to keep me upright.' Naldeth grinned. 'Which is another reason for not wearing it on trading beaches, that and the soft sand.' The wizard twisted to adjust a strap at the side of his waist. 'No Aldabreshi's ever asked me what happened to my leg, not once. Velindre said they wouldn't. No one asked how I was coping with such a loss or what I would do with the rest of my life.' He swallowed his unguarded anger and managed a thin smile. 'There's something very restful about the way you people simply accept a person for what they are. It must make life much simpler.'

'My life's hardly been simple.' Kheda strove to keep his words light. 'And every turn of the heavens seems to bring some new twist, such as Velindre turning up to propose this voyage.'

'We'll just have to see how it all turns out.' Naldeth studied the warlord for a moment. 'Are you sure you won't be looking for omens?'

Something in the wizard's gaze made Kheda a little uneasy. He looked up at the canvas-shrouded grating. 'Do you suppose it's worth trying some fishing yet?'

Chapter 9

How fast is this current carrying us along? How much faster is this ship moving thanks to Velindre's magic? Why is there no wind? Is this more of her magic? Perhaps not. There are glassy seas in the central domains. Risala has crossed the windless reach between the northernmost Archipelagan isles and the seas that lap the unbroken lands. The fickleness of wind is why we Aldabreshi have always trusted in triremes and mocked becalmed barbarians.

He surveyed the sea, flat and calm all around. Without wind to swell the canvas, the *Zaise*'s sails were furled, yet the ship sped on through the water. Kheda threw out his line and leaned over the rail to watch the hooks disappear in the curls of white water trailing alongside the *Zaise*. 'Risala, if I ever complain about saller pottage again, remind me how much I dislike eating nothing but fish.'

'It's going to be plain fish if we don't make landfall soon.' Risala knelt next to him, gutting a silvery handful. 'We've nearly used up all the herbs.'

'There's some saller grain left.' His flesh-and-bone foot tucked under the knee of his half-crooked steel leg, Naldeth sat baiting a line of viciously barbed hooks with rancid duck meat wriggling with indefatigable maggots. His northern features and plait of lank barbarian hair still looked incongruous above the cottons of an Aldabreshin slave.

'And we have all the fresh water we need.' Velindre spread her hands over the barrel lashed to the stern mast and the seawater briefly shimmered bluer than the sky above. She frowned and a battered leather bucket emptied itself to wash the slime and fish blood from the deck planking.

'Have you managed to scry out this isle yet?' Kheda scowled. 'The Lesser Moon has gone right round the heavens, darkened and brightened again—'

'What have you tried by way of additions to your scrying water?' Naldeth looked up from his noisome task. 'Inks or oils?'

'When I need a fire mage's advice about a water spell, I'll be sure to ask you.' Velindre looked out past the prow. 'I can feel the currents of the ocean meeting some land not too far ahead. And it resonates with elemental vigour.'

'Do you suppose the confluence of elements is what attracted the dragon?' A maggot wriggled unheeded between Naldeth's finger and thumb. 'Or that the dragon somehow drew the elements together?'

How much longer before we learn something to justify my making this voyage? All I have done so far is enjoy the peace and calm of days without anyone making demands on me. Was it the prospect of such freedom that seduced me into agreeing to come, at least in part, even if I didn't realise it at the time?

Kheda wished briefly for a thin mantle to wear over his faded grey tunic and trousers. These seas were palpably cooler than Archipelagan waters. 'How much further?'

'I'm not entirely sure.' A frown deepened the fine creases around Velindre's hazel eyes. 'There's considerable turmoil ahead.'

'A storm?' Risala asked with some alarm.

'No.' Velindre shook her head confidently before frowning again. 'I'm not sure what it is.'

Kheda looked up from his taut fishing line. 'Before we get any closer, I want you to scry for Itrac. I want to be sure that she and the children are thriving before we risk any un-known peril.'

'As you command, my lord.' There was no malice in Ve-lindre's quip. She spread her hands over the barrel again and vivid green radiance dripped from her lingers into the water.

'You can do this without that necklace now?' Kheda moved to look into the vision the magewoman was sum-moning.

Velindre shrugged. 'Magic's like most skills — the more practised you are, the more effective you become.'

'A fact the Council and Archmages of Hadrumal are remarkably disinclined to make widely known, even among the mageborn.' Unblinking, Naldeth studied Velindre with a hint of envy hardening his undistinguished features. 'Your touch with water magic these days is truly remarkable for a mage with an air affinity. You learned more than I realized from Azazir.'

'If I'd ever imagined the toll his obsession had taken on his sanity and humanity, I'd never have gone near him.' There was a brief flash of anger in Velindre's eyes.

Anger and fear. Fear of the power you saw or of what you might become, if you let yourself go down that path? But if you hadn't gone to find this wizard, be he mad or sane, we'd never have had his knowledge of dragons to help us free Chazen.

Kheda concentrated on the image in the scrying spell. He was surprised to see Itrac seated in the west-facing hall of the observatory tower. Books were strewn across the table and she was deep in conversation with Jevin. The slave stood just behind her, one hand on her purple-draped shoulder. Itrac smiled at something and looked further down the room to a

214

rug surrounded with cushions where Touai's daughters were laughing and playing with the baby girls.

Who's reading the heavens for you, Itrac? Are you comforted to see the Diamond, talisman for warlords, riding in the arc of marriage with the Horned Fish and the Opal? Are you wearing amethyst silks and jewels as the Greater Moon rises to its full to promote truth in your dreams of me, as the Amethyst rides with the Spear that's token of a man's valour in defence of his family and home?

While in truth I'm just idling away my days and spending my nights in Risala's arms, as if I have no more onerous responsibilities than pleasuring us both. I can't even fool myself that some shift of the heavens tells me I deserve such an interlude after all the trials I've undergone.

'She looks as well as ever and little Olkai and Sekni are plainly thriving.' Velindre snapped her fingers and the vision shifted. 'There are an admirable number of trading ships in the lagoon and no sign of any unrest.' The spell sped around the islets so fast it left Kheda dizzy. 'Does that suffice or do you want me to search the sea lanes as well?'

'If you please,' Kheda said shortly. The reflections in the water dissolved into a meaningless blur as he let his thoughts wander.

Itrac looks well, but is she commanding respect through the domain and among our neighbours? Should I have Velindre send me back to Chazen? But we've come this far.

'Has no Archipelagan ever thought of building a real sailing boat?' Not for the first time on this interminable voyage, Naldeth's thoughts had drifted away on a new tangent. 'A tall ship like those that sail the eastern ocean, out beyond Tormalin and the Cape of Winds?'

'I don't know.' Kheda shook his head. 'I don't know anything about barbarian boats.'

'Triremes and galleys are far better suited to Archipelagan waters.' Risala looked up from scraping another fish's innards into the scrap bucket.

'An ocean ship would find anything but the wider sea lanes of the outermost domains a real trial,' agreed Velindre, 'given the way the winds sheer around the islands.'

'So why not still build ocean ships for those outer reaches?' Naldeth demanded.

'Because no one sees the need.' Kheda leaned against the ship's rail.

Naldeth sighed with exasperation. 'Has it never occurred to any Archipelagan that the barbarians might know something useful?'

'Archipelagans rarely consider barbarians at all,' Risala pointed out, 'unless we're looking to trade for metals we lack or things like pine resins.'

'Most of our seers say our peoples are like oil and water.' Kheda yielded to a mischievous impulse. 'That we're fated never to mix.'

'You can mix oil and water — or vinegar, come to that,' argued Naldeth. 'If you add spice ground to a really fine powder. You people make sharp sauces that way.'

'Which goes to prove philosophers rarely tell the whole story,' Kheda replied without rancour.

Naldeth waved a slimy hand towards Velindre. 'Everyone thinks she's part-barbarian and no one cares.'

'They think I'm an Archipelagan who happens to have barbarian blood in her — or rather, his — recent ancestry.' Velindre's gaze out beyond the prow didn't waver. 'That's quite a different matter. There are some who will assume that's why I was made *zamorin*, to cut out that barbarian bloodline. If they bother to think about it all,' she mused.

216

'Anyone dealing with me is only concerned with who I am in the here and now. My past is my own affair, like my future.'

'I thought the Aldabreshi see time like that star circle of Kheda's,' retorted Naldeth. 'Always chasing its own tail.'

'It's true that the more self-referential aspects of Archipelagan thinking are influenced by Aldabreshin concepts of time,' Velindre said thoughtfully as she fitted the lid back onto the water cask. 'The cyclical nature of the heavenly compass can mean an omen seen a hundred or more years ago can be significant today or a hundred years hence. But in essence Archipelagan time is a constant entirety, a perpetual present.'

'Do barbarians even have records going back a hundred years?' Kheda challenged.

'We do.' Naldeth took up this new discussion with relish. 'But we see those days as left in the dust of the trail behind us. We look to our next step on the path, on the way to something new and better. You've been building triremes in the same way for generations. Every mainland shipwright is searching for some way to improve his craft. Your seers and sages tread the same circles as those who've gone before them, reinterpreting the same stars and omens. Every mainland philosopher is looking for new ways of thinking, towards a more rational understanding of the world.'

'A man who looks inward might come to a better understanding of himself, and his place within the world.' Kheda looked over at Velindre. 'Are you mages all climbing this endless ladder towards some greater understanding?'

'Climbing it and treading on each other's fingers in our haste to be first to reach some new nuance of elemental knowledge,' she said caustically.

'I thought you enjoyed sailing the Archipelago because of the lack of questions, Naldeth,' Risala remarked slyly. 'You've said how restful it must be knowing your place in life and having everyone else know it just as clearly.'

'It's certainly a welcome relief from the exacting expectations of some of our more competitive colleagues,' Velindre agreed.

'You've not stayed in the place you were born to.' The young wizard turned to Risala. 'Shek Kul was your warlord, wasn't he, in a northerly domain?'

'He's a just and powerful warlord who keeps his people in peace and prosperity, as his father did before him.' Risala scraped blood from a gutted fish's backbone. 'They don't have to ask where their next meal is coming from or if some rival warlord's triremes are about to seize their island. They're happy for their lives to follow the same course year after year.'

'But you weren't?' Naldeth persisted.

'The stars marked out a different path for me,' Risala said sunnily. 'We're not all going round in circles.'

'So you became a poet?' Naldeth looked for Risala's nod of confirmation. 'And a spy.'

'Confidential envoy,' Risala corrected him with a grin.

'A new role where you nevertheless trade on the fact that people in the domains you visit will just see the poet and satisfy themselves with all the assumptions that go with such an occupation,' Velindre mused.

'Whose side are you on in this argument?' Kheda wondered.

'I wasn't aware we were taking sides,' the magewoman replied serenely.

Risala looked at Kheda with a smile that melted his heart.

You're the one person who sees me for who I truly am in all this confusion that has overwhelmed my life. You're the one person who doesn't burden me with expectation or assumption. But will you ever accept that I cannot believe in omens any more?

'I'll wager Aldabreshin seers and barbarian philosophers share the ability to tire the sun with their talking.' Kheda walked across the deck to pick up the bucket of fish guts beside Risala, bending to kiss the top of her head before dumping the rank contents over the rail. 'Do you really have no idea how far it is to our destination, Velindre?' Keeping tight hold of the rope tied to the bucket, he let it fall into the sea to rinse itself before he hauled it up again full of clean water.

Risala came to stand beside him and began scrubbing fish blood and slime off her hands. She stopped, mouth open. 'Kheda, look—'

'A bird.' Kheda narrowed his eyes to make out this newcomer more clearly. 'And not another zaise.'

It was considerably smaller than the great white wanderers and more solidly built, akin to the coral gulls of the long-distant Archipelago. Not so closely akin, though. It had dark-brown undersides to its wings and a mottled belly as well as rusty-red legs. As it came closer, squawking on a rising note, Kheda saw a vicious downward hook to the point of its beak. It dived into the residue of fish guts floating on the water.

Velindre came to join them. 'It seems to think it's at least half-fish.'

In the clear seas, they could all see the strange gull folding its wings close to its body to undulate through the waters more like a fish than a bird.

'I don't want to hook that.' Kheda hastily dumped the bucket on the deck and began pulling in his fishing line hand over hand.

'A bad omen?' Naldeth bent to rinse his own hands in the bucket of seawater.

'Did you see that beak?' Kheda retorted. 'Would you like to try getting close enough to beat out its brains and pull the hook out of its gullet?'

He dumped the tangle of line on the deck and looked up from his task to see Velindre hurrying up the ladder to the stern platform. 'That's no ocean bird,' she called over her shoulder. 'We must be closer to land than I thought.'

Risala grinned at Kheda. 'You can take the foremast.'

'Thank you,' he said with a grimace. 'Stow those fish, Naldeth. We don't want to lose our supper if that bird's a scavenger.'

The boat's calm passage made climbing the ladder-like ratlines to the top of the mast easy enough, though Kheda still did his best not to glance down. The deck seemed all too narrow and all too far below him, surrounded by far too much sea for him to fall into.

Though presumably Velindre would catch me.

He braced himself in the rigging and looked out to the west and to the north. On the far horizon he could see a billowing drift of white cloud.

'What can you see?' Naldeth was pacing the deck in frustration, his rocking, stiff-legged gait setting the bucket of fish swinging alarmingly.

'Clouds caught by high ground,' Risala called out from the aft mast. 'There's land ahead.'

The curious gull or one very like it swooped past Kheda, startling him with its rising cry. Choking back a curse, he pressed himself against the knotted ropes.

'Loose the sails.' Some breath of magic brought Velindre's calm words clearly to his ear amid a rush of newly summoned wind.

Kheda did so as quickly as possible and made his way back down the ladder of ropes with a treacherous tremor in his arms and legs.

We Aldabreshin have the sense to stick to oars and square-rigged sails that you can manage from deck. Only mad barbarians would risk climbing up and down masts in ocean seas.

Risala met him on deck. 'Shall we keep watch from the prow?' The rising breeze tousled her black hair and tugged at the hem of her loose blue tunic.

'Let's.' Kheda nodded amid the flap and creak of the newly liberated canvas.

The ship rose and fell beneath their feet as it had not done for days on end. Velindre's magic scorned the natural indolence of the air and lashed it into motion. Glimmers of sapphire blue threaded through the lively gusts filling the *Zaise*'s sails, as the ship left the windless seas and the strange current that had carried them this far. The ocean swells grew taller again, blunt billows rising and falling and edged with the barest lacing of spume.

Kheda held on to the ship's rail with both hands, Risala safe between his arms. The white bank of cloud on the horizon waited motionless as the *Zaise* soared over the dull blue waters towards it. Kheda felt the chill wind teasing his wiry brown hair.

Naldeth came up beside them, peering straight up into the sky.

'Have you seen some more birds?' Kheda squinted upwards too.

'I thought I'd keep an eye out for dragons,' the mage said slowly.

'Look.' Risala pointed down into the water.

'A tree branch.' Kheda's heart pounded with absurd relief. 'We're definitely approaching land. Though that's not from any kind of tree that I recognise,' he added doubtfully.

'Do you want a closer look?' Naldeth raised a ready hand glowing with ruddy magelight as the branch floated away.

'No.' Kheda concentrated on the clouds ahead, piling high into solid white banks reminiscent of those above the fire mountains and scarps of higher ground on the larger islands within the Archipelago.

Almost imperceptibly, the sea took on a greener hue, and here and there they spotted drifts of weed. More gulls appeared like the first, and other smaller creamy birds with pale-blue heads and darker wingtips, diving after unseen prey. A squabbling trio floated past perched on another sodden tree branch, heedless of the rise and fall of the ocean.

Kheda studied the fluffy fragments torn from the misty bulk growing closer on the horizon. It was strange to see clouds scudding towards them while the wind pressed his tunic to his back. He bent to speak into Risala's ear over the noisy rush of water beneath the prow. 'I want to talk to Velindre.' She nodded and he made his way back along the unsteady deck.

Velindre's eyes were bright as she directed the steering oars with one hand and twisted the easterly wind to her bidding with the other. 'What can you see?'

'There's all manner of detritus in the water.' Kheda paused half-way up the ladder. 'Are you sure there hasn't been some storm in these reaches?'

'No.' The magewoman was adamant. 'Whatever this elemental coil is, it's not a storm.'

'As soon as you know what it is, let me know.' Kheda slipped back down the steps and returned to the prow.

Dark smudges appeared on the horizon below the swelling white clouds. It still took an age to reach the islands, even with Velindre summoning all the elemental air within reach. She abandoned concealment and the *Zaise*'s sails crackled with azure radiance. The wind blew scraps of magelight away to fall into the foaming wake, glittering briefly before the water snuffed them. The waters were turbid now, choked with sand swirling away in patterns drawn by submerged currents. Weed and broken trees thudded against the *Zaise*'s hull and Kheda was glad of the double planking at stem and stern.

'This reminds me of the days after a whirlwind struck Shek waters, when I was still apprenticed to Gedut,' Risala commented speculatively. 'He composed a poem about it.'

'Velindre says she sensed no storm.' Kheda drew Risala back with him. 'Let's see what we can see from the stern platform.'

The land ahead was breaking into a chain of dark islets riven by narrow channels.

If there are wizards or even dragons, I want to be beside a mage I've seen calling lightning out of a clear sky and bringing down a dragon with a rival beast of her own creation.

Risala hesitated. 'You'll keep watch, Naldeth, so we don't run aground on anything?'

'Yes, of course.' The young wizard's eyes were unfocused. 'There's a peculiar tangle of elements here,' he breathed.

Disquiet prickled down Kheda's backbone as he hurried the length of the ship, Risala's hand in his. 'Velindre—' he began as he climbed the steps after Risala.

'Naldeth's enjoying a rush of blood to his affinity, I take it?' Velindre sounded amused. More to the point, as far as Kheda was concerned, she was clear-eyed and wholly composed. 'There's been wild fire magic at work here.'

'How recently?' demanded Kheda.

'It's difficult to tell,' Velindre said thoughtfully. 'Long enough ago for storms to have doused it pretty thoroughly.'

'There's nothing that could set your cargo alight?' he persisted. 'If Naldeth hasn't got his wits about him, we could burn to the waterline.'

'I'd say not,' Velindre replied, offhand.

Kheda wasn't overly reassured.

Could whatever accursed enchantment is rousing Naldeth's wizardry stir that dragon's egg down in the hold? Why did Velindre bring it here?

Kheda chewed his lip as they sailed on and dark rocks rose up on either side of the *Zaise* in the fading light towards the day's end. A few of the blue-headed gulls hopped insouciantly along invisibly narrow ledges, chattering among themselves.

'Can you see anything?' Kheda scanned the broken facets of dull brown stone that seemed to absorb the sinking sun's glow rather than reflect it.

'Nothing bigger than a bird.' Risala was keeping alert watch on the far side of the stern platform.

Velindre gestured at the masts and the sails drew themselves back to the spars to be lashed tight by snaking ropes. 'Let's have as clear a view as possible.'

Kheda's disquiet grew as the channel narrowed and they sailed into shadows the setting sun did not penetrate. The waters grew dark and forbidding, a rank odour floating over the surface.

'What's the draught of this hull?' he asked dubiously.

'I'll know to within a finger's width of water if we can sail on or not,' Velindre assured him.

Kheda looked down over the stern platform's side, the magewoman's confidence notwithstanding. The water was stained dark with rotting vegetation hanging in clumps stirred by their passage. Stirred but not washed away. He realised what he was seeing. 'There are trees under this water.'

224

Risala looked around, puzzled. 'Is this a river in flood?'

'No.' The magewoman looked thoughtful. 'This is salt water, not fresh.'

Naldeth came hurrying back from the prow, his false foot loud on the planks. 'This isn't a channel between two islands.' He climbed deftly up the ladder, scarlet magelight bright in the joints of his steel leg. 'This used to be a valley. This whole expanse of land just sank.'

'How?' Kheda looked from the young wizard to Velindre.

She chewed her chapped lower lip. 'I've really no idea.'

'Let's find out,' Naldeth urged impatiently.

The *Zaise* slid silently over the drowned trees. The channel or valley, whichever it was, turned an abrupt corner around a shattered cliff where a steep scree tumbled into dark shadows. The sky opened up above them as the heights retreated on either side. A long expanse of sluggish water stretched ahead to a sloping shore rising out of the lapping sea. Dead trees bristled with split and broken branches. Those closest to the water were stripped of all branches and bark to leave bare spikes jutting up from muddy ground that reeked of decay. The *Zaise* slowly advanced, faint blue magic shimmering like marsh light around her. Something grated along the underside of the hull.

'Velindre?' Alarmed, Kheda couldn't help himself.

'I told you, I can gauge the depth of the water beneath us,' she reminded him. 'And whatever happened here happened long since.'

Kheda surveyed the desolation. 'Did magic do this?'

Naldeth shook his head. 'I've no idea.'

Something dropped into the water with a plop that echoed around the valley.

'There.' Risala pointed at ripples in the murky water.

A blunt scaly snout caught the light. A lizard as long as Kheda's arm was swimming across the drowned valley. It reached a dead tree and climbed rapidly up it. Pot-bellied and short-tailed with sprawling legs, its stubby toes were tipped with needle claws that dug deep into the lifeless wood. A ridged red crest ran down its back.

'That's no beast I know,' said Kheda.

'There's no magic to it.' Naldeth sounded disappointed.

Odd angularities among the stubs of a handful of storm blasted trees caught Kheda's eye. 'What's over there?'

The air shone oddly around Velindre's eyes. 'Something was built in the trees,' she said slowly.

'So there were people here.' Kheda searched the shore with new intensity, his hand going to his belt knife. He remembered his weapons stowed unheeded down below. 'Risala, fetch my swords for me, please.'

'Are these people still here?' She didn't wait for an answer, dropping down the ladder and disappearing into the stern cabin.

'You won't need those.' Naldeth turned in a slow circle, one hand raised with a scarlet flame dancing on his palm.

'These wild mages can sense some new wizard working his magic in their territory,' Kheda rebuked him.

'Then they can learn who they're dealing with,' retorted Naldeth, his flame flaring.

'If there was anyone here to be drawn by magic, we'd have seen them by now.' Velindre waved at the sapphire magelight glistening on the *Zaise*'s rails. 'All I'm sensing is the echo of old enchantments among the elemental chaos.'

'Do you remember how fast a dragon can appear?' Kheda challenged.

The boat's blunt prow nosed through the clouded water. As they drew nearer to the muddy shore, they saw that a

226

platform of lashed logs had been fixed into notches gouged deep into the trunks of the stricken trees. Walls of woven twigs were broken and splintered, any roofing long since torn away.

Kheda looked beyond the makeshift building to piles of debris cast up by successive storms. 'Those are the hollowed logs the savages use for boats.'

'The wild men who came to plague the Archipelago lived here?' Risala climbed up the stern ladder and handed Kheda his swords. 'They fled this disaster and came to steal our lands and we killed them.'

'Did we kill them all?' Irresistible hope rose in Kheda's chest. All the same, he doubled his sword belt around his hips and thrust the scabbarded blades securely between the overlapping loops.

The *Zaise* slid sideways through the water to brush up against a mottled grey trunk with a few remaining scabs of black bark. They could all see the ragged marks where the heartwood had been gouged out of the log with crude tools and rough points had been shaped at each end.

'What were they fleeing?' Naldeth sounded disappointed. 'The dragon? Do you think it pursued them?'

'As best we can tell, they were expecting it to follow them,' Velindre reminded him.

'It was only the wizards and their warriors who came to attack us.' Risala gazed around the eerie valley. 'We never saw any women or children or elders. Perhaps they stayed behind.'

Kheda joined her in scanning the barren slopes. 'To die here, without their men or magic to sustain them.'

Have we come all this way for nothing?

Somewhere a bird screeched and drilled into a tree with a resonant burr that shattered the silence.

'But what happened?' Naldeth persisted. 'What about the dragon? Did it live here before it followed the wild men to Chazen?'

'I think we should investigate a little further,' Velindre concurred and the *Zaise* obediently eased away from the dead trees. The ship retreated slowly back along the bright reflection of the cloud-strewn sky between the dark waters mirroring the sombre heights on either side.

Kheda looked up. 'Dusk comes later and more slowly in these reaches but we don't have much daylight left.'

'I can give you all the light you want,' Naldeth said scornfully.

'Setting a beacon to draw anyone or anything that might be curious about us?' challenged Kheda.

'Let's just see what we can before dark.' Velindre guided the *Zaise* deftly down a different channel, the barest suggestion of a summoned breeze stirring her hair.

Naldeth watched the muted ripples of the ship's wake spreading behind them. 'Your studies with Azazir certainly paid off.'

'I wouldn't call it studying with him.' Velindre gave the young wizard a mordant look. 'And he's an object lesson to us all as to what can happen when you become entranced by your own affinity.'

Kheda saw Naldeth acknowledge that caution with a meek nod.

Velindre isn't going to discuss this Azazir with you, boy, accept it. Dev said he had been banished by the other wizards as a danger to any who came near him. Yet she went to find him because he was the only one who knew the secret of weaving a false dragon out of summoned magic. How many wizards die in their quests for learning?

'This place isn't quite as dead as it looks.' Risala came to stand beside Kheda and pointed to the edge of the cliff looming above them.

As Kheda looked up to see a tracery of twisted stems tufted with leaves outlined against the sky, a cloud of pink and grey birds erupted from niches in the rocks. Their whistling cries filled the air as an eagle, or something akin, soared overhead, claws splayed. Circling, it stooped and dived to snatch something from the water in a flurry of spray. It climbed into the sky with powerful strokes of black-and-white-banded wings, pointed tail feathers sharp as shears. A long fish, brown as the decaying leaves, writhed in its grip, trailing silver drops of water.

'That would be an omen,' Risala said with a shiver. 'If we were looking for such things,' she added quietly with a hint of foreboding.

'We're looking for any sign of savages who were left behind.' Kheda peered keenly around as the *Zaise* emerged into a wider channel. 'Or some clue as to what became of them.'

'Velindre, over there.' Naldeth suddenly pointed to a larger lump of land some way off rising steeply out of the water to a peak high enough to snare a skein of mist. 'There's something...' His words trailed away into uncertainty.

'Was this land or sea?' Kheda studied the black waters on either side of the boat.

'Does it matter?' Velindre was peering at the peak ahead, eyes narrowed. 'Naldeth, what do you sense in that cloud?'

'Ash and steam,' the youthful wizard said slowly as they drifted closer. 'That's a fire mountain.'

'We're safe enough as long as it's breathing white smoke.' Kheda searched the plume for any hint of the grey that presaged catastrophe. He caught Naldeth's slight surprise. 'There are plenty of records of the omens seen around fire mountains erupting in the Archipelago.'

'I shall have to look them up when we get back.' The wizard grinned.

'Is it safe to go any closer?' Risala was looking at the strange seas ahead. Ridges of greenish water were surging up from the depths, breaking in ragged trails of white foam.

'For the present.' Velindre was unconcerned as the *Zaise* rocked erratically in the confused seas. 'This is just the currents fighting their way through new paths in the deep.'

'There's fire in the deep as well,' Naldeth said suddenly, 'in the rocks underneath the sea.'

They crossed the uneasy channel and the waters abruptly stilled. Now they were close enough to see the full strangeness of the island ahead. The peak was riven from top to bottom, with a wide central cleft belching out the pale cloud that streamed away over the mastheads. Below the sheer drop of the uppermost rocks, molten stone had congealed in ungainly twists and lumps, sparkling with incongruous beauty here and there as the sinking sun struck some glassy facet. A paler flow overlaid a lifeless black slurry disappearing into the water. The grey column of cooled stone was contorted like a tree crippled by a strangling vine, dividing to thrust rootlike tendrils into the sea, sharp and spiky where they had been brutally snapped off.

'This is close enough.' Velindre waved a hand and a cloud of green magelight gathered around the ship's hull, drawing them away from the waters sucking ominously around the ugly margin of the shattered rocks. They drifted slowly past the cliff, the cloven rock sharp as a knife edge.

'How long ago did this happen?' Kheda asked. 'How many storm seasons does it take to blunt something like that?'

'This wasn't just one cataclysm.' Naldeth gazed at the mottled rocks. 'I would say the trouble began a couple of years ago. There would have been earth tremors and lesser eruptions to begin with.'

'Then the land began sinking and the seas encroached further with each passing season.' Velindre looked back to the drowned valleys. 'So men and beasts alike moved into the heights.'

'Then the final eruption shattered these islands,' muttered Naldeth, keen eyes searching intently among the fissures and bulges.

'So the wild men came to Chazen.' Risala nodded her understanding. 'Looking for somewhere safer to live.'

'But the dragon stayed here for nearly a full year more.' Kheda studied the shore now coming into view. 'Did it do this?'

The long, smooth slope of this side of the island was a striking contrast to the destruction of its other face. It looked no more inviting, though. A thick forest of mighty trees had been laid low, like saller stems slashed with a scythe. Barely a handful were still standing, down by the shallow curve of the beach, white and skeletal amid a choking layer of ash and boulders. The only hint of colour ran along the high-water mark where the brown decay of storm-tossed branches was valiantly nourishing a fringe of feeble grasses, a few tufts of sturdy cane and even an unknown infant tree.

'I can't think why a dragon would destroy its home,' Naldeth said dubiously. 'And it would have liked it here. The elemental fires of the mountain would have buoyed up its magic.'

'Until they broke loose.' Velindre turned the *Zaise* broadside to the beach.

'The people fled first and finally things got too hot even for a fire dragon.' Kheda looked back across the trackless ocean towards the Archipelago. 'So it followed them.'

'But what happened to the women and children?' Risala wondered. 'They didn't come with the wild wizards and their warriors.'

No one could answer her as they sailed slowly past the pallid landscape. Velindre guided the *Zaise* towards a bulging crag thrusting out to sea. The ripples running outwards from the ship's blunt prow washed against the pale rock, staining it black. The stone was pocked with broken edged holes, some overlapping, some deep enough to swallow a man whole. Further up, long furrows had been gouged into the once-molten ridges.

'This wasn't caused by the fire that came up out of the earth to destroy the mountain.' Naldeth sounded pleased. 'Magic's been at work here — though long since, I'm afraid. But this wasn't caused by a fire dragon, either. An earth drag-on must have been drawn to the eruption.'

'You're sure?' Kheda regretted the words as soon as he'd said them.

'Believe me,' said Naldeth sardonically. 'My fire affinity has given me a sympathy with earth magic. Once I got back to Hadrumal after my ... mishap, I spent a year and a half studying with one of the finest stone masters that element has ever imbued. He said—' and Kheda got the distinct im-pression the young mage was quoting this unknown wizard precisely '—"You may as well do something more construc-tive with your time than stare at that empty metal foot of yours and imagine you can feel your toes."'

'The fire dragon would have fought to defend its territo-ry,' mused Velindre. 'I wonder if their feral magic stirred up the fire mountain.'

'I'd say it was more likely the other way round,' Naldeth demurred.

'You're sure it's gone, this earth dragon?' Kheda glanced up to reassure himself that the cloud rising from the narrow peak was still blandly white.

'Yes,' the young mage said slowly. 'Though this is still a very strange place as far as the elements are concerned.'

'Where did it go?' Risala shared Kheda's concern. 'We'd have heard if any other dragon had come to the Archipelago.'

'The news would have run the length and breadth of the domains,' Kheda agreed.

'There are plenty of places in the northern mainland where dragons could find a focus of elemental power.' Velindre shrugged. 'And hide themselves from anyone wishing them ill.'

As if anyone other than a mage could threaten a dragon with the slightest harm.

Kheda held his tongue as the ship rounded the bulbous headland to find a narrow cove clogged with the floating stone that erupting fire mountains threw up into the air and Aldabreshin seers prized for its contrary nature. But these were not the fist-sized pieces that traders offered in the Archipelago. Slabs of the frothy rock as thick as a man's arm was long bobbed in the slack water.

Tree roots and stumps were caught up with the jostling stones, dark and waterlogged yet kept afloat by the strange rock. Paler shards lay atop some of the uncanny rafts, yellow as old bone. Kheda looked more closely. It was bone. He saw sallow lengths knobbed at each end and the shattered fan of a ribcage. The stained bones were dry and free from flesh and there was no smell of putrefaction.

Countless animals must have been killed when the mountain exploded. No wonder there are still plenty of birds here. The scavengers must have feasted till they couldn't fly.

Then he saw the smooth dome of a skull, empty eye sockets vacant, lower jaw gone. Now he knew what he was looking at, his eyes were irresistibly drawn to a ghastly grin just beyond, a smashed brow above the stained teeth.

He found his voice. 'This is what happened to the women and elders.'

'And the children.' Risala pressed her hands to her face, eyes rimmed with white as she stared at a fragile broken skull amid a mess of tiny bones.

'With all the animals dead, and all the people too, there was nothing for the dragon to eat.' Velindre strove to keep her words dispassionate but her voice shook nevertheless.

Kheda looked at the uncanny, macabre scene.

Can this really be the end to it all, after this long voyage and all its apprehension?

'Their mountains were burning and their land was drowning. They had some way of living with one dragon but a second came to fight it.' There was an odd strained note in Risala's voice as she turned her back on the charnel cove. 'The men and their mages sailed off on their logs and rafts, heading east into unknown waters full of sea serpents and whales and all manner of sharks. Did they know how far they would have to go to find somewhere safe? Did they even know the Archipelago lay out there? And the women and children and the old men and women waited and waited, but no one came back because they all died in the fight for Chazen. So everyone here died as well when the mountain exploded.'

We didn't know. We didn't know who they were or why they had come. They attacked us with fire and spears and magic and showed us no mercy. We didn't start the fight. All we did was defend ourselves and our own.

Kheda turned around, but any attempt at words to comfort her died on his lips. There was no more land on this side of the fire island. The eerie waters lapping this drowned domain yielded to more natural seas that stretched out dark and mysterious in the deepening twilight. The indigo sea melted into a lavender sky streaked with all the reds and oranges of sunset. Black and featureless as the sun sank behind it, a vast island lay long and low on the horizon, larger than any Kheda had ever seen or heard tell of, capped with a bank of gilded white cloud.

Risala gazed at it. 'What's over there that's so horribly frightening to people with wizards and even a dragon to call on somehow, that they'd risk the open ocean rather than make less than a day's sail to a certain shore?'

Kheda could only shake his head for an answer.

'Let's find out,' Naldeth said incautiously.

Kheda found his voice. 'Why?'

'Because that earth dragon went somewhere,' Velindre reminded him. 'And we don't know what other dangers might lurk there. Forewarned is forearmed. That's why we came here.'

'Can't you scry from this distance?' Kheda objected. 'Why put ourselves at risk, if the wild men and their mages chose to avoid the place?'

'Hadrumal's magic is considerably more sophisticated than these savages' spells.' Naldeth sounded faintly offended. 'You must have learned that from Dev.'

'Scrying's not the most robust of enchantments.' Velindre silenced the young mage with a wave of her hand. 'There's fire beneath the water hereabouts and both are woven into the depths of the earth where the mountain's eruption has split the sea bed. The steam and the ash are weaving all the other three elements into the air. The best course is to sail over there and see what there is to see with our own eyes.'

'The confluence of elements stretches all the way over there.' Naldeth was looking increasingly eager as he stared at the distant shore. 'We've come all this way. There has to be more to learn here.'

'I suppose so,' Kheda said with deep reluctance.

I had better return with some solid news to set in the balance against the contented indolence and self-indulgence of this voyage so far.

Chapter 10

The old woman liked being by the boundless water. Not just because she could forage among the rocks when the waters receded in their daily dance and fill her belly with the sweet salty shellfish she prised from the damp crevices. Not just because she felt so safe sitting high in the cranny she had discovered half-way up the shallow rocky cliff, which was only accessible from below. She would see anyone walking along the shore long before they saw her and she had pains-takingly stockpiled stones on her ledge to break the heads and hopefully the resolve of anyone who wanted to capture her. Not that she had seen anyone else on this exposed shore in all the days she had been here.

She simply loved to look at the water. It fascinated her. She had never imagined it could be so vast. The painted men had often said that the whole land was ringed with endless waves, so fleeing their supremacy was pointless. She had heard such tales since her childhood in that village she could scarcely remember. She had imagined these boundless wa-ters were like the floods that swept through the green forests when the great storms came and the empty rivers overfilled and overflowed.

Some years the floods came quicker than others. The rivers roared down from the high ground in ravening spate, surging through the trees, felling the forest giants whose day was done and crushing lesser trees with the tumbling trunks. Once such fury was done, the flooded forests were quiet and still. The swamped shrubs were briefly home to swimming lizards and snakes, and to the birds that preyed upon them. Gradually the waters seeped away into the soil to hide once more from the all-seeing sun and the rivers shrunk back into their narrowest courses.

The spectacle before her was so far beyond such floods that there was no comparison. This water was alive, defying the sun with a brilliance quite unlike the muddy clumsiness of the rivers. She couldn't imagine it ever drying up. It scoured the shore with crashing waves, white as a great beast's teeth. It came and went back and forth over the rocks as it saw fit. She had watched its powerful billows shaping the long expanse of dunes where the cliffs fell away. This flood wasn't about to sink into the sand and vanish.

There were mysteries in the depths of this water that she could never have envisioned. Beyond the lowest point where the waters yielded temporarily to the land each day, the shallows shone with all the colours of a butterfly's wing. Out past the strange-coloured rocks that broke the surface with a froth of white, the water turned darker, patterned with lines where swirling greens fought shadowy blues. Every so often, a breaking crest of foam surged across the dappled surface before vanishing as quickly as it had appeared.

She gazed out into the misty blue. She had never lived anywhere where there weren't trees or mountains to be seen on the horizon. If there was a horizon here, it lay too far distant for her clouded eyes to see it. Perhaps the waters simply curved upwards to become the dazzling sky somewhere beyond her understanding. This water was blue as the sky — and water fell from the sky as rain, after all.

238

Other things came from the sky. A shadow undulated across the yellow and brown rocks. She looked up warily and huddled in the niche that protected her from more than the sun's unblinking eye. A few pink-and-black-striped birds swooped and chattered above the vacillating ripples on the beach. She was happy to see them. They would disappear the instant any larger shadow darkened the shallows, proclaiming their alarm. She moved out of the shade, relishing the warmth of the sun-soaked rocks that she found so soothing to her stiff back.

She looked down to her favourite scatter of rocks jutting up from the shallows. It wouldn't be too much longer before she could climb carefully down and walk over the rapidly drying sands to reach them. There would be the tiny black spiral shells she could empty with a twist of a stone splinter and the larger brown ones that clasped such sweet yellow flesh tight in their twin halves. She decided she would gather some of the frilled green weeds today and bring them back up here to dry, held secure with a rock. She had small stones to spare for shying at the pink and black birds who would steal her food given half a chance.

The painted men had never mentioned the strange burning taste of this vast blue water. Why was that? She picked up her gourd and shook it. It was less than half-full. She would have to make her way to the grudging seep of sweet water that darkened the rocks where an outcrop banded with brown and black like a lizard's back rose above the shore. She had burrowed into the flaking stone a little way with her digging stick and that useful shoulder-blade bone she had carried with her but it still took an interminable time for the precious trickle to fill the gourd. Though she didn't have anything else to do, for the first time that she could recall in all her long life. Better fetch water first, she decided, so she didn't have to leave whatever food she might gather exposed to the scavenging birds.

She reminded herself to watch for any birds gathering around one of the pools left in the hollows of the rocks. That meant trapped fish, left behind by the retreating waters. She looked thoughtfully at her bundle of mottled scurrier skin faded to an indeterminate colour somewhere between grey and brown. She needed a sharp edge to slice into a fish and she had precious little of her black stone left. Was there none to be found anywhere on this exposed shore? She had looked, time and again. She certainly didn't want to retrace her steps back inland in search of cutting stones.

The band of thorny scrub between the lower lands and the barren heights had proved remarkably persistent. It had sheltered her long after the green forests of mighty trees below had given way to lush grasslands that had reached out almost as far as this water before her. She had walked on with no expectations, with no wish beyond surviving each day uncaptured, sustained by the faint, unquenchable hope of finding sufficient food and water to stem the worst pangs of hunger and thirst. And as the days had passed, she had managed to keep herself alive and to slip unnoticed along the well-trodden trails that alerted her to the presence of some nearby village. She had stayed on the slopes as the dry scrub grew thinner and sparser and any signs of hunters or women foraging had grown fewer and further between. After all, where there was no other prey, she should surely be safer, she had reasoned.

Soon she had had no choice but to keep to the pathetic remnants of the thorny scrub. The lower land had turned to rolling expanses of sandy dunes bare of food or water. For the first time she had seen the endless waves and realised that the painted men had been speaking the truth. Finally she had looked down on a vast plain where there was nothing but sand and rocks. Great boulders were scattered across it, catching dead drifts of crumbling wood and the strange stone plants that occasionally washed up in the waves here.

The old woman had kept on walking. She had had no reason to stop. Not until she had reached this thrusting point where the land doubled back on itself and the great waters stretched out to the horizon. There was nowhere further she could go. Then she had found this place and had learned that she could both feed herself from the creatures living in the rocks and not die of thirst as she had half-expected. As she laid herself down to sleep each evening, she found herself hoping for the first time in a long while that she might wake to see the new dawn.

She wondered, not for the first time, if anyone else had ever walked all this way to see such a marvel as the great water. Did anyone besides her know of this empty shore? None of the caves along this shore were painted with anything more than bird droppings. Quaking with fear, she had been into each and every hollow beneath the overhang of the shallow sandy cliffs when she had first reached this unforeseen end of the land. If she wasn't alone here, there was nowhere else to go. But there were no painted caves and she had seen no sign of anyone else, not even a footprint in the sand.

Her fears had gradually eased and she had come to hug the knowledge of her solitude to herself. Of course, one day she would lay herself down to sleep in the small cave in the back of this crease in the cliff and not wake up to see the sun again. Still, that was a better death than being fodder for some beast. She had escaped that fate. The painted men had said the land was ringed with endless waves so there was no point in trying to escape their domination. But she had found one remote corner where their feet did not tread, where their followers did not swing their heavy clubs and beat lesser men and women into submission.

The painted men did not come here, even though that great green beast lived down in the waters below. She looked out beyond the line of foaming rocks running parallel with the shore. She hadn't seen the green beast in some days. She had stopped fearing it would come ashore and sniff her out, reaching into her meagre cave with its lurid talons to skewer her and drag her out to crunch her aged bones. She only ever saw it in the water, ducking its ferocious head to dive, its dark-green back vanishing in the depths, or floating idly on the rolling waves, sunning its pale and shining belly.

The closest it had come to the land was climbing out onto the line of jagged rocks to devour the monstrous, gasping serpent that had unexpectedly washed up there in a surge of frighteningly green-tainted foam. The painted men had never made any mention of creatures like that. The beast had broken the scarlet-finned serpent's spine with a single crushing bite of its glaucous fangs and ripped gory chunks from its writhing flesh. It had come back to feast for several days before leaving the carcass to the exultant birds. Now all that was left was a black smear of dried blood and a few white bones wedged among rocks out of the water's reach.

She looked to see if the black stain had been washed away yet and quickly shuffled backwards into the darkness of her rocky niche. There was something out on the water beyond the rocks. Not a beast, nor yet one of the giant serpents. This thing was riding on the water, not swimming in it. The old woman frowned and shaded her faded eyes with one wrinkled hand, squinting to try to see more clearly.

The apparition came closer into the shore. The old woman struggled to make sense of what she was seeing. This strange thing was floating on top of the waves. What could ride on these waters? Painted men could bring down tall trees with fire or lightning, so that their followers could hollow them out. They used them to float through the flooded forests and out onto the broad expanses of the swollen rivers, spearing the biggest lizards and fat snakes as thick as a man's thigh that thought themselves safe beyond the sodden shallows. Sometimes the hunters lashed their logs together and floored them with sheets of bark to make rafts to carry a raiding party across the floods. The painted men summoned shadows and mist to hide their warriors until they fell on some hapless village, to plunder and enslave whoever could not lose themselves in the forest's gloom fast enough. She had not been fast enough, when she was a girl, when her village had fallen to such raiders.

The old woman thrust away all recollection of those horrors and concentrated on the curious thing coming closer still. This was no hollow log nor yet a raft, but all the same, the old woman could see something of the same idea in the thing. It was made of split lengths of wood, though she had never seen a blue tree. There looked to be some kind of hut built on one end of it, though that was also made from pieces of solid timber, not the woven laths and grass thatch that usually made a dwelling.

In front of the hut, tree trunks stood upright, branches stripped of leaves but draped with massive lengths of hide hung out to cure in the sun. What creature had given up so vast a hide? A great beast might be big enough, but who could kill a beast for its skin? And anyway, a beast's hide was coarse with scales and spines. Was this the skin of some monstrous serpent like the one the green beast had killed? How could men hope to kill such a creature?

Because there were men on this wondrous raft. They were standing on the roof of the hut. The old woman gazed at them, astounded. They had made this thing to ride across the great water. Who could do such a thing?

Who were these men? She strained to see them more clearly as the raft turned with unexpected purpose to come closer to the shore.

They looked strangely pale and misshapen. One was wearing a headdress of bright feathers, golden in the sunlight. Another had a more muted cap of paler brown, with a long plume dangling down his white back. Yet another looked pied, like a black-bellied lizard with its white legs. She realised with a start that she had edged out of her niche onto the ledge to get a better view of this curiosity. She crouched lower. She didn't want to be seen. Painted men adorned themselves with feathers and smeared themselves with coloured clays.

Perhaps they had come from the sunset side of the island, beyond the central mountains. The painted men of the green forest had said there was nothing beyond the heights but an arid desert of lethal heat by day and murderous cold by night. But she had already decided that the painted men didn't know everything. She frowned and looked at her wrinkled hands. This point of land thrust into the water almost exactly half-way between sunset and sunrise and this strange raft was coming from the sunrise side of the island.

Had these strange people come from the lands beyond the green forest that she had turned her back on when she had fled the old man's village? What manner of strange creatures lived in whatever unknown lands opened out beyond the vast tracts of tall trees and mighty rivers there?

The pounding of her heart slowing, she concluded she was safe enough. The line of rocks barred the strange blue raft's way to the shore for as far as she could see up the coast. She watched it nosing along, coming closer to the rocks below her cliff. Were the pale men looking for a gap?

An unexpected swell rose up beneath the floating raft and threatened to dash it violently against the rocks. The old woman gasped as green light flared deep in the dark waters. The beast that swam here had come to destroy this intruder. It rolled over and the old woman saw its pale belly, as blue-green as the shallows. Where the shadow of the hides hung on the raft dulled the water's sparkling surface, she glimpsed the beast's head clearly for a moment. The beast's massive mouth gaped, its burning eye bright beneath the crystal waters. Green fire glowed in the depths and a great burst of foam boiled upwards. The beast was trying to drive the strange raft onto the rocks. In a rush of understanding, she realised that was how it had killed the giant serpent.

The raft danced lightly away from the lethal embrace of the rocks. The beast rose up from the depths once more, a green shadow with its mighty wings folded tight against its long body. The waters surged again and the raft rocked violently. It managed to ride the swell, though now it was coming perilously close to the rocks. The beast reared up out of the water before diving back down and its spiked tail struck the raft with a hollow boom that echoed back from the cliffs.

A mighty wind arose from nowhere, whipping up sand and grit all around the old woman. Clouds suddenly coalesced far away out over the water and spun around up in the sky, darkening from white to ominous grey. A murky talon reached down towards the waters and a spine of white foam rose up to meet it. They joined to form a twisting column dancing this way and that.

The beast erupted from the waters, green as weed. Spreading pale-bluish wings, it launched itself upwards with a noise like thunder. As it hovered above the boiling foam, the raft was no longer of any interest. All its attention was fixed on the distant waterspout, clawed feet reaching forward as if it would rend the thing to pieces.

It flapped its wings a second time, striking spray from the waves as it flew towards this intolerable impudence, faster than the swiftest hawk. Then it folded its wings close to its shining green sides and dived, long spiked tail ripping a white gash into the water as it disappeared. The beast's dive roused a great surge that drove the scorned raft hard onto the rocks. The old woman gaped as the waters swelled with green fire to lift the strange blue creation impossibly high and wash it clean over the murderous barrier.

The raft bobbed contentedly in the narrow strip of water between the rocks and the sandy beach. The stranger in the golden headdress was standing stock still on the roof of the hut, like a scurrier frozen by a shadow in the sky passing over it. The rest of the outlandish men ran up and down, dragging at ropes tied to the white hangings draped on the two barren trees.

The old woman watched the beast now pursuing the waterspout mercilessly. The spiral danced tantalisingly out of reach every time the great green creature burst up from the depths, jaws snapping and claws lashing. With each twist and turn, it was luring the beast further and further away.

She looked at the whirling grey clouds drawing a perfect circle in an otherwise empty blue sky. She might not know much about this vast water or what weather might be expected on this shore from season to season, but she was certain that was no natural cloud come up so handily to tempt the beast away. No ordinary wave had carried the blue raft unharmed across the rocks, not even one thrown up by the green beast's dive. These strangers were indeed painted men who could turn the world to their wishes.

She looked down at the pale figure with the gaudy golden head still standing motionless, turned to watch the fast-disappearing green beast. Was the one with the brown headdress his servant? Powerful painted men allowed lesser ones to attend them, all the while on the alert for their treachery, or so it was whispered around the hearths of the villages.

Did this mean that the painted men were going to land on her deserted shore? Would their followers soon be arriving, driving on captives laden with laths and grass to build their huts? Would the painted men be summoning uprooted trees to be split with wedges of stone and hammers of bone? Would the timbers be thrust into the sands to make the merciless wall of a stockade for whatever hapless captives would be offered up to sate the beast's hunger? Did that mean the green beast would be coming ashore? Presumably a painted man would know such things. And the lack of food or water wouldn't worry these painted men. They could always summon such things out of the empty air. How soon would their followers be coming? Had the painted men on the blue raft lured the beast away so they could set up their encampment without it biting their heads off before they had got started?

The old woman sighed with deep, aching regret. She had been content here. Now she would have to pick up her gourd and her bundle and start walking again. Which way should she go? Backwards, retracing her painful steps? She quailed at the thought and turned to look along the sunset side of the point of land. Surely whatever lay in that direction couldn't be any worse than the hostile barrens she had crossed?

But that was where the painted men were going. She watched the blue raft slowly picking its way along the narrow channel between the line of foaming rocks and the sandy coast. But did that mean their spearmen would soon be coming to this point of land? If they did, they would surely find her and capture her, tying her up to be fed to the green beast. Or were they heading up the sunset side of the land to meet their followers? Would they be walking along the sands or along the shallow, crumbling cliffs? If she went that way, would she blunder into their lethal embrace?

Not if she was careful, she concluded. Whereas if she stayed here, there was every chance she would be discovered. She had left footprints in the sand and tossed broken shells plucked from the rocks carelessly from the ledge of her little cave. Not for the first time, her only hope of safety lay in keeping moving.

Chapter 11

'Are you sure it's not following us?' Kheda stared out over the *Zaise*'s stern, trying to see into the sand-clouded water. His gut was still tight with tension.

'Quite sure.' Velindre adjusted their course with a delicate push on one steering oar. 'It'll chase that waterspout till the magic unravels and then—'

'It'll come back to find us,' Kheda concluded heatedly.

'It will go back to enjoying the elemental forces stirred up by the collision of these incredible currents.' Velindre was unconcerned. 'I'm sure of it. It's an animal, Kheda, albeit a magical one. It's not evil or even malicious, certainly not in the way a man would be. It was more curious than intent on killing us and there must be plenty of other prey for it in such rich waters. Think how many sea serpents we've seen.'

'And it'll be finding gems on the sea bed,' Naldeth added thoughtfully. 'There must be rich seams of gemstones given how closely earth and fire are allied under these waters. The nature of rubies—' He broke off, suddenly self-conscious, and stared up at the banded rocks of the cliff.

You thought of rubies because of that dragon's egg stowed in the hold. How can magic fuse such a mass of jewels together and twist itself into whatever unnatural life gives birth to a dragon?

'But why did it chase that sea spout rather than attacking you?' Risala asked Velindre as she ran lithely up the ladder from the *Zaise*'s deck. 'The dragon that came to the Archipelago was set on killing Dev. You said they see any other magic user as a rival. That's why we had to dull your magic, and Dev's, with that potion Shek Kul found for Kheda.'

'That's a very good question.' Naldeth climbed rather less nimbly after her, with a grating squeak from the joints in his metal leg.

'Just in case you're about to suggest it, I have no intention of ever taking those cursed herbs again and being cut off from my affinity.' Despite her caustic tone, a half-smile widened irresistibly on the mage woman's thin lips. 'Which is why I've been practising working my magic at as much of a remove as I can, the better to go unnoticed by dragons or anyone else. Behold my success.'

Naldeth stared at her, affronted beneath his ruddy tan. 'You didn't think to share that with me?'

'I wasn't sure it would work,' Velindre admitted a little ruefully. 'Now we've seen that it does, I can explain the principle and then we'll see if you can grasp it.'

'Oh, I will,' promised Naldeth tersely.

'This is hardly the place for experiments,' Kheda broke in. 'The savages' wizards can sense magic being worked as well as dragons. They came after Dev and Risala that first time, when Dev came across them—'

'Let them come.' Velindre's composure was unshaken. 'Then perhaps we'll finally learn if anyone lives on this desiccated rock. That's what we came to find out, isn't it?'

249

The *Zaise* slid on through the treacherously narrow channel between the vivid corals of the reef and the muted rocks of the shore.

'I'm sure there must be more dragons here.' Naldeth looked up eagerly at the shallow sandy cliffs.

'Won't they be sensing whatever magic it is that you're using to stop us being wrecked?' Risala looked around far more uncertainly.

'I doubt it,' Velindre said easily, 'any more than you'd hear someone whispering on the far side of an island in the middle of a rainy-season tempest. I'm using very little wizardry and there's so much wild magic in the very nature of this place thanks to the elements meeting here. We're sure to go unnoticed.'

Do the times I've found a wizard's confidence misplaced balance the scales against the times when they've been able to fulfil their impossible promises?

Kheda took Risala's hand and squeezed her fingers reassuringly. 'Thus far we've seen one dragon and no sign of wild men.' He turned to Velindre, challenge in his expression. 'How far are we going to sail around this island before we decide it's safe to go home?'

Where I must take up my proper responsibilities once again.

'We're at the southernmost point of the main mass of land.' Velindre's expression grew distant, almost dreamy. 'Water that has circled the whole compass of the ocean collides as one current brings heat down from the central seas and another brings a cold surge up from the far south. The winds meet here, too. Some have travelled with the currents; others are rising from the land here and mingling with them, fighting against them.'

'Each current carries earth run off from rivers in distant lands, as well as all manner of sea creatures—' Naldeth broke off and narrowed his eyes. 'There are definitely fire mountains inland, and hot springs.'

'You're still certain this is just one island?' Kheda interrupted.

Naldeth nodded unhesitatingly. 'One island, several hundred leagues long and a hundred wide at its broadest, near enough. Where the raw elements of earth and fire are remarkably closely interwoven,' he continued thoughtfully.

'There are powerful currents and seasonal wind patterns back in the Archipelago.' Risala looked from the tall, slender magewoman to the stockier younger wizard. 'As well as fire mountains that have blown half an island into clouds of burning dust before now. We're not plagued with dragons. Why should we expect more of them here?'

'Because dragons are creatures born of pure elemental magic. Those Aldabreshin places you talk of are still vibrant with elemental power,' Velindre added neutrally, 'as you would know if Archipelagan custom didn't condemn all mageborn to an undeserved death. The correct question is why don't they draw dragons to them as a matter of course. Well, now we have the answer.'

'Would you care to share it with us?' Kheda asked with some rancour.

'If the magic Velindre's using now is a whisper, those natural focuses of magic in the Archipelago would be a raucous shout.' Naldeth was looking up at the barren cliff tops. 'But the intensity of elemental entanglement here is still a cacophony that would drown them both out. I'm surprised we've only seen one dragon drawn here.'

'So far,' Kheda said dubiously.

'Don't tempt the future.' Risala looked up at the empty skies before continuing to survey the inhospitable shore.

'These wild men lure dragons with prisoners as ready meat, don't they?' Naldeth queried, a trifle callously. 'It can't be any too easy to get a water dragon's attention, if it spends all its time out at sea.'

Kheda glowered at the unrelieved intransigence of the fractured cliffs. 'Does this commotion in the elements you're talking about mean you won't know if any savage mages are working their spells?'

'That's an interesting question.' Velindre nodded. 'We shall have to wait and see.'

'You said their magic is remarkably unsubtle.' Naldeth looked at her. 'And almost solely woven from the element of their affinity. Surely we'll be able to feel that?' He looked at Risala and grinned. 'Like a spider feeling something blundering into its web.'

'Let's hope so,' Velindre said dryly.

'There may be nothing for you to feel.' Kheda looked at the frothing white water beyond the blunt end of the headland. 'Perhaps all the savage mages died in Chazen or on that drowned isle.'

'I wouldn't count on it,' the younger mage scoffed.

'As I said, that's the southernmost tip of the island.' Velindre raised her hand and the *Zaise* idled in the sparkling waters, scorning the insistent winds. 'So, are we turning around to sail back up the eastern face or do we see what lies on the western shore?'

'All we've seen on the eastern side has been destruction wrought by the waves thrown up by that outlying island erupting.' Kheda slipped his arm around Risala's shoulders and held her close. 'If there are people living anywhere here, I imagine they'll be on the far side.'

'Are we going to sail around this whole island?' Risala looked up at the barren crag looming above the mastheads. 'How big did you say it was, Naldeth?'

'Big enough for you to make an epic poem out of such a voyage.' He grinned at her.

'It's not a voyage we could hope to make this side of the rains arriving back home,' Kheda said firmly. 'We'll go on just far enough to see if there are any wild men still living here and then you can use your magic to send me and Risala back to Chazen, back to the burned isle so we can recover the *Reteul*. You two can stay here to try to pursue dragons without getting eaten if you choose.'

'As you command, my lord.' Velindre smiled so serenely that Kheda was instantly suspicious.

They sailed around the broken rocks beneath the headland with emerald magelight frothing around the *Zaise*'s hull. It didn't draw the water dragon back, to Kheda's relief. The western shore was as rocky as the eastern face and Kheda began to wonder if the seas lapped at continuous inaccessible cliffs all around this massive isle. The two wizards stood silent, absorbed in some uncanny communion with seas, skies and coastline. Noon came and went and Kheda and Risala shared a scant meal of wind-dried fish and plain water. Both mages simply waved away any offer of food.

Kheda periodically shifted his gaze from the cliffs to the seas ahead in an attempt to stave off insidious if inappropriate boredom. He blinked and rubbed his eyes, to be sure what he was seeing was real. It was still there: a red stain drifting through the clouded channel like a trace of blood. It thickened, drawing dark lines in the greenish waters that surged around the brown smudges of the corals just beneath the surface. Ashore, the ramparts of banded sandy rock finally gave way to crumbling cliffs of dark mud and russet clay, topped with a parched suggestion of yellowed vegetation. Out to sea, the reefs curled away to vanish beneath the waves and the seas turned to a colour somewhere between ochre and crimson.

Velindre shivered involuntarily and startled them all by inadvertently pulling so hard on one steering oar that the *Zaise* lurched sideways. 'There's a river mouth,' she explained. 'An eddy where the salt water meets the sweet surprised me.'

Scant moments later, the coastline took a sharp turn away from them, subsiding into mud flats and sandbanks. A silt-laden river oozed sluggishly into the sea through countless channels. Sere grasses clung insecurely to patches of dry ground on the larger hummocks, sown by seeds blown from the parched scrub lining the true river banks far away in the distance. Further inland, a line of darker green promised more substantial vegetation. Beyond that, the land rose in a sweep of dun rock streaked with countless mossy, leafy hues, finally dissolving into a blur ultimately topped with the clouds that clung to awesome mountainous heights deep inland.

'Is this navigable?' Kheda asked.

'Just about.' Velindre's hazel eyes were bright with anticipation.

'If we can get even a little way inland, I can try to understand the rocks and the fires underlying this place.' Naldeth's equally unnerving eagerness made him look more boyish than ever.

'Any people living here will be near the river.' Risala didn't share the wizards' enthusiasm.

'Where there's water and food and fuel,' agreed Kheda, unwelcome tension crawling up his spine.

'Velindre, what can you do to hide us?' Risala asked. 'Without alerting any wild wizard hereabouts,' she added tersely.

Kheda didn't speak, straining his eyes as he searched for any sign of movement ashore beyond the wind stirring the vegetation.

If we do run into something we dare not tackle, the wizards' magic can carry us all the way back to the Archipelago. That's what they've promised time and again. Which would mean this whole voyage and all my lies and contrivances to make it will have been utterly in vain. Would that be best, just to go home and put all this behind me?

Velindre glanced at Naldeth. 'Can you draw the haze rising off the land out across the water?'

'I'll make us no more than a reflection of mudflats distorted by the light,' the youthful mage promised.

Velindre gestured at the masts and the white canvas flapped and cracked and furled itself to leave only the aftmast rigged with half its sail. The steady wind coming off the ocean pushed the *Zaise* steadily up the river, scorning the feeble current.

Leaving the braided rivulets and sand bars to the white-crested waves rushing in from the open water, the river gradually collected itself into a broad, curling channel. Mudflats sprawled on either side between the red-stained water and the grass-topped sandy banks some way in the distance. Low islands broke through the flow in the bends on either side, crowned with tangled greenery and crowded with ungainly brown birds chattering peaceably among themselves and preening their ragged feathers with heavy black bills.

If there's nothing to disturb them, does that mean there's nothing to threaten us? But if we scare the birds up, who or what will see them take flight?

'Kheda, over there!' Risala was keeping a lookout on the other side of the stern platform.

Naldeth leaned over the rail, intent on whatever it was. 'I see it.'

'What is it?' Kheda staggered as the *Zaise* scraped on a hidden sand bar and the deck rocked violently.

The wash from the *Zaise*'s hull slopped over the slick mud. The brown birds closest at hand erupted into the air in a raucous cacophony of hoarse squawking and rattling wings.

Does that serve me right, for tempting the future?

Kheda dismissed such foolishness. 'Risala, what is it?'

She pointed. 'Over there, by that dead tree.'

A mighty bole was half-buried in the mud where some flood had wedged it into the inadequate gap between two sandbanks. Velindre eased the *Zaise* closer with a deft hand on the intricate ropes governing the half-sail. The enormous trunk was damp and split, a twisted tangle of dry, grey roots reaching back upstream.

Naldeth studied the indistinct grey-green cloaking the distant heights inland. 'There must be sizeable forests somewhere.'

'Where the savages fell trees for their boats,' Kheda said grimly.

They could all see two hollowed-out, pointed logs wedged in among the splintered roots, half-hidden in a wash of mud. Some of the brown birds settled on the sandbank again, rattling their black bills as they jostled each other.

'They used fire to char out the middle.' Naldeth was leaning over the rail to look more closely at the log boats.

'Magical or natural?' Velindre asked instantly.

'Natural.' Naldeth sounded a trifle disappointed.

Kheda could see black burn marks that had obstinately resisted the river's scouring. 'Was there any trace of fire on that log boat we found on the drowned isle?'

'None.' Naldeth was certain.

Kheda looked inland as the *Zaise* drifted past a broad curve of bank and a new vista opened up. 'If they were made differently, were they made by different people?'

'Naldeth, is that smoke?' Risala asked abruptly.

Kheda located the faint grey smear crossing the darkness of the distant trees as the young wizard straightened up and looked inland.

'You've got good eyes.' Naldeth frowned. 'Yes, it's fire, natural fire. The grass is burning.'

'What starts a grass fire under a blue sky without a cloud to be seen?' Risala wondered aloud. 'It has to be wild men.'

Kheda took a resolute breath. 'I had better go ashore and see what I can find out.'

'Let me scry—' Velindre hesitated.

'If there's anyone mageborn out there, they'll be on us in a trice,' Naldeth objected. He turned to Kheda. 'I'll come with you.'

'No.' Kheda pulled his tunic over his head before stripping off his trousers. He wound them deftly into a loincloth, leaving his long legs bare, his skin dark against the pale cotton. 'I can look like them, from a distance at least. You can't.'

Not with your pale barbarian skin, even if you had both of your legs intact.

'I can.' Risala pulled her red tunic off over her head, blue gaze defiant as she emerged, her black hair tousled.

'Four eyes are better than two,' Velindre agreed. 'We'll sit tight and feel for any tremors in the elements that might betray some mage ashore to us, won't we, Naldeth?'

'Yes, of course.' The young wizard swallowed and looked away from Risala's bared breasts.

Velindre was scanning the unhelpfully low-lying mudflats and sandbanks. 'We'll go just a little further upstream.' She pointed towards a sizeable sandbank huddled in the crook of a sharp meander. 'If you can't see us, you can see that.'

Dragging his gaze from Risala again as she wound her own trousers round her hips, the young mage addressed

Kheda. 'What do you intend doing if you trip over some wild wizard and he throws a handful of fire at you?'

'I don't intend getting close enough to trip over anyone.' Kheda slid down the ladder to the main deck and laid his hand on the door to the stern cabin. 'And their mages have always worn paint or feathers or some such. As soon as we catch sight of anything like that, we'll be on our way back.'

'Do you have your star circle?' Velindre pulled a small brass sun column from her pocket, flicked up the ivory vane and turned it to the brilliant sun. The shadow fell just short of one of the incised curves swooping down around the stem of the instrument. 'If you're not back by the next arc, I'll scry for you and if necessary I'll fetch you back here with magic.' She grinned at Kheda. 'If that brings some wild wizard or dragon down on us, then we'll just have to scurry back to Chazen or Hadrumal.'

'Are you taking a sword?' Risala was tucking her sheathed dagger securely into her improvised loincloth. 'And I'll want a hacking blade for anything we might trip over in that grass.'

'Naturally.' Kheda opened the door to the stern cabin. By the time he had gone down to the stern hold and retrieved a scabbarded sword as well as a wide-ended hacking blade and a brass water flask with a braided strap, Velindre had guided the *Zaise* into the narrow channel pinched between the main river and a long, low island strewn with flood-tumbled boulders.

Risala was on the main deck, leaning over the rail to look at the mud below the sharply undercut bank. 'How solid do you suppose that is?'

Kheda allowed himself a moment to admire the smooth brown curve of her naked back before looking up at Naldeth on the stern platform. 'I take it you'll pull us out if we sink?'

'I should be able to do that without magic.' The young mage waved a coil of rope.

'I'll go first.' Kheda swung his legs over the *Zaise*'s rail and pushed himself off the ship's side as hard as he could. He landed where silty water lapped the mud bank and his feet sank a little. The river water was cool around his feet, though it had an unsavoury stagnant smell.

'I think it'll hold us.' Risala jumped and Kheda caught her shoulders to steady her as she landed.

'You don't have to come with me,' he said quietly. 'You could stay safe on the ship.'

'Where's safe, out here?' She gripped the long handle of the hacking blade in its sewn-leather sleeve. 'I'll be safer with you if some wild wizard or dragon comes looking for them.' She jerked her head back at the *Zaise*.

'True enough.' Kheda found he could barely see the ship through the shimmering distortions Naldeth's magic was wrapping around it. Trying made him feel nauseous, so he turned his back on the disquieting sight. 'Let's get to solid ground.'

He picked his way carefully to the grassy bank, testing each step on the mud. Risala walked carefully in his footprints. He felt thirsty but realised that was only apprehension drying his mouth. Chest-high, the lip of the bank was sharply undercut and the edge crumbled as Kheda tried to pull himself up onto solid ground.

'Here.' Risala braced herself on one knee and offered her cupped hands as a step. With that slight advantage, Kheda managed to haul himself properly ashore. Kneeling, he turned to reach a hand down to pull Risala up. The two of them crouched in the colourless dry grass as something not too far away fled with a rushing rustle.

'Where's that fire?' Kheda stood cautiously upright and looked for the smudge of smoke in the distance. It was thicker now, rising from several points to mingle in a pale-grey line tattered by the breeze coming in off the sea.

'It's heading away from us,' Risala observed.

'Then let's catch up a little,' Kheda said resolutely.

He used his scabbarded sword to push aside the chest-high grasses. Growing in thick clumps, their stems were green at the base but soon bleached to creamy yellow by the merciless sun. The dry blades were coarse and sharp-edged, not quite drawing blood but leaving his bare legs sore all the same. There was seldom room enough between the clumps to take a step without wiry tendrils poking painfully into his feet. Risala tucked herself close in behind him, intermittently biting back a mutter of discomfort. Trying to keep the line of rising smoke in sight, Kheda tripped as he found a narrow path worn through the dense grasses. Risala stumbled into him and he caught her arm with his free hand.

'What do you suppose made this?' She looked towards the smoke and then back towards the river where the *Zaise* should be.

'Men or animals.' Kheda gauged the line that the path took inland across the floodplain. 'If we follow this and then cut across the grass when we get closer to those fires, we can lose ourselves in the shadows of the trees.' He couldn't help glancing back towards the river but could see nothing beyond a punishing glare on the water.

They could move more quickly on this clearer path, narrow though it was. It crisscrossed other equally thin paths worn through the thick grasses. Sweating freely now, Kheda took a drink from the water flask and passed it to Risala. She gratefully took a mouthful and handed it back. Soon he could smell the burning as well as see the smoke and slowed, half-crouching so that the frayed tips of the grasses swayed above his head.

'What can you see?' Risala was looking to either side and back down the path lest anything was watching them.

'Savages,' Kheda said, resigned.

Two lines of dark-skinned men were working together, either naked or clad in scant leather loincloths. They were walking behind the slowly advancing fires, flailing bundles of twigs to make sure the fire didn't run riot instead of following the paths they desired for it. Men with clubs and spears were further away, spread out in the sallow unburned grasses. Their raised weapons were black outlines against the grey-white smoke as they searched the ground for prey fleeing the flames.

'Can you see anyone who might be a mage?' whispered Risala.

'No,' Kheda replied softly, 'but I can't see much at this distance.'

The wild men moved across the lengthening black scars burned into the grassy plain, billows of smoke swirling around them.

What are they hunting?

As he wondered, a great cry went up. The wild men ran after some creature racing towards some illusory sanctuary of unburned grass. Clubs swept back and smashed down. Arms raising long spears thrust hard into the melee.

Whatever it is, it's fighting back.

Kheda saw men reeling away from the fray. As the wind twisted to carry the sounds of battle over the grasses, wordless cries of passion and determination mingled with a tearing sound somewhere between a hiss and a screech.

The group of wild men suddenly broke apart with cries of anguish. Something came racing through the dense grasses, charging through the barrier of the flames. One of the savages who'd been tending the fires tried to intercept whatever it was, a spear raised high above his head. Whatever it was bowled him over, flinging him up so high that his bare legs spun higher than his head before he crashed back down to the ground. Then whatever it was attacked the hapless hunter where he lay. The grasses thrashed violently as his gurgling despair was lost beneath that eerie tearing screech.

Kheda drew his sword and took firm hold of Risala's wrist with his other hand. 'If it comes this way, we just get out of its path.' He could feel her trembling, her skin slick with sweat.

As the hunters raced to their fallen comrade, shouting and waving their spears, the unseen creature fled. It came running towards Kheda and Risala, the thud of its feet breaking through the frenzied rustle of the grass. As it burst out onto the narrow track a perilously short distance away, it froze, staring at them. It was a lizard, as long as a tall man from its blunt nose to the end of its heavy tail. Its head and back were armoured with solid yellow-brown scales, with still thicker scales running down the length of its body to make black horny ridges. Its lashing tail was flattened from top to bottom and saw-edged with vicious plates stained with blood and dirt. Digging its clawed feet into the parched earth, it hissed, a bubbling sound with its jaw gaping. Kheda saw speckled yellow skin inside its maw and stained white teeth, stubby and broad. Strands of dirty green drool hung from the corners of its wide mouth.

Not a whip lizard. I've never seen anything like it.

Kheda kept Risala behind him and held his sword low and ready, the braided silk binding the hilt drawing the sweat from his palm.

The creature hissed again and lurched away from them, crashing through the brittle grasses on wide-splayed legs as it headed towards the river.

'Kheda.' Risala resheathed the blade she had half-drawn and shook his shoulder urgently as he was still trying to see where the lizard had gone.

He looked back to see the savages gathering together, beating out their fires. Some bent over prey or casualties; others were gesturing and shouting self-importantly. A few were standing idle, leaning on spears or resting their clubs over their shoulders. Torn by the breeze, their quarrelsome words were unintelligible.

Kheda crouched as low as he could while still keeping a clear view of the hunters. 'We don't move until they do.' He smiled at Risala and passed her the water flask. As she took it, he saw more fear in her eyes than he would have expected.

Eventually the wild men moved off, some carrying dead animals slung over their shoulders, others with larger prey lashed to spears borne between two or four men.

Kheda noticed that several wounded were being left to make their way along as best they could, limping, using their spears as props.

No one's gone to see what's become of that man who fell foul of that lizard. Which is a relief because they'd come too close to us for comfort if they did. I just hope he's quite dead before any scavengers get the scent of blood.

All the same, the thought of abandoning even an unknown wild man to bleed out his life in the desolate grasses left a sour taste in Kheda's mouth. He couldn't help thinking of his modest physic chest back on the *Zaise*.

But there's probably nothing I could do for him. Even if I could, we'd either have to take him prisoner or risk him betraying our presence here. Besides, he's a savage. These people showed no mercy in Chazen.

The words nevertheless rang hollow inside his head.

'Where are they going?' Risala stood a little straighter.

'Over towards the trees.' Kheda watched the ragged column head for the greenery rising up the sides of this broad, shallow valley.

'What do we do now?' She glanced back towards the river.

'We'll follow them, just for a little while.' Kheda looked after the wild men. 'Let's cut across to the tree line before they do. We'll be harder to see against the shadows there.'

That was easier said than done, as the tussocks grew thicker and more densely packed away from the river bank. Kheda used his sword to cut at the stubborn grass and the blades retaliated by slicing fine cuts into his hands and forearms that instantly swelled and stung. Finally the clumps began to thin as the land rose up. A band of barren earth where the grasses ended soon yielded to tangles of sprawling spiny plants with fleshy yellowing leaves. Beyond, contorted grey trees ran away up the steepening slope, their pale blotchy branches fringed with coarse little leaves.

Kheda crouched in the edge of the grasses and poured a little of their precious water over the shallow oozing cuts that were now tormenting him.

Risala waved away tiny black flies hovering greedily. 'Are you all right?' she asked with some alarm.

'I think so.' Kheda paused to contemplate the possibility that the grasses might have poisoned him.

No fever or chills or tremors. It just cursed stings.

He fought the urge to scratch at the red scores on his thighs and calves and looked at Risala's bare legs. She showed fewer marks but the inflammation was more marked on her lighter skin. 'How about you?'

'As long as the itching stops soon, I'll be fine,' she said through gritted teeth. 'Where are the savages?'

Kheda moved cautiously out into the barren expanse just short of the tangled plants and twisted trees and looked inland. 'They're still fighting their way through the grasses.'

Burdened with game and wounded, the wild men were making slow progress through the dense growth.

'They must have hides like water oxen,' Risala muttered, blowing to cool a swollen scrape on the tender inside of her forearm.

'Let's keep a good way back.' Kheda watched the slowly moving hunters for a moment, then searched the curious undergrowth between the unknown spindly trees for any plants he recognised.

If this was the Archipelago, I'd guess that spiky cluster was some variant of leatherspear. Sap from that would soothe these cursed cuts. But I've never seen leatherspear tainted with purple like that. I could kill us both with ignorance and the best of intentions.

'Kheda,' Risala said warningly.

Refocusing his attention further afield, he saw that the hunters were emerging from the grassland to disappear down the barren strip along the edge of the outlandish trees. They were moving fast now. He saw some carrying a single unknown bird or a lesser lizard breaking into a run. Even those burdened with greater animals were hurrying as best they could. The wounded were left to make their own way, their able-bodied companions deserting them.

'Savages,' Risala muttered contemptuously at Kheda's side. The two of them slowed, wary of getting too close to the struggling men.

'They're scared of something in the woods.' Kheda saw the wild men glancing fearfully into the shadows with every second or third step.

'So why not stay out on the plain?' Risala's hand went to her dagger.

'Where those great lizards are lurking?' Kheda glanced at the impenetrable wall of grass waving idly in the breeze.

Cautiously, Kheda and Risala followed the wounded savages making their best speed along the open ground. He held his sword ready, alert. She had her hacking blade bared, moving along close by his open side.

I'd rather be doing this in a decent suit of armour, regardless of the heat. How far away from the ship are we now? How far are we going to go before we turn back? How long have we been creeping along like this? Will Velindre scry for us and snatch us back with some wizardry before we've learned anything of real use?

They went on still further as the edge of the twisted woodland curved away from what Kheda could recall of the river's winding course. They rounded a thicker clump of the contorted trees and Risala froze. Kheda stopped dead with her and, crouching low, close together, they retreated into the shielding grasses.

A finger of low ground thrust between low hills just ahead, choked with dense tussocks of yellow grass. Beyond, the land swept steeply upwards and an irregular outcrop of pale stone reared up through the strange woodland. Caves pierced the whole face of the rock, black against the variegated stone. Ropes and notched tree trunks offered access to the upper levels where women and children looked out anxiously. Figures armed with spears stood by the lowest entrances where a single broad fire burned low in a hollow scraped across the mouth of the largest cave. A little way down the slope, a substantial screen of branches snapped from the twisted grey trees shielded the half-circle of earth that had been cleared around the rock's base. The barbed leaves of the fleshy yellow-green plants were piled high around the branches.

The wild hunters hurried towards this sanctuary. A strange clattering rang through the woods. Some of the wild men froze, raising their clubs and spears. Kheda caught a flash of movement deep among the contorted trees. Spurred on by the sight, the savages ran as fast as they could, a few dropping their burdens in the dust. Dead fowls' wings fluttered for a moment then lay still. Now left far behind, the wounded huddled together, steps laboured as they pressed desperately on.

Kheda saw movement again, closer to the margins of the trees, and unexpectedly vivid blues and greens. Sinister chattering echoed back and forth, louder and more menacing. Wild men emerged from the lower caves and lit brands of wood tipped with grass clotted with some kind of resin from the fire pit. They advanced outwards in a slow line, spears lofted at shoulder height, torches held out before them, looking in all directions.

'Can you see a wild wizard?' Risala crouched lower in the grass.

'I don't believe so.' Kheda was torn between fear of being spotted and his increasing desire to see what was going on more clearly.

The first of the hunters now had to cross the narrow expanse of grass that separated the stretch of woodland edging the valley from the shelter of the rocky outcrop. For the first time, Kheda saw that the wild men were labouring under the weight of several dead horn-plated lizards slung on spears carried between them. Those who hadn't abandoned their lesser burdens of smaller lizards or ungainly fowls clustered close, clubs and spears raised. Some were staring intently into the denser trees on either side of the rocky outcrop, others looking behind.

The men who had come out of the caves with their own spears and burning brands advanced to the crude barrier defending the outcrop. Kheda saw some using sticks to drag away the thick clumps of fat, spiny leaves and clear paths through the piles of branches. The rest held their spears ready.

Hollow chattering rang through the trees, pierced by screeches from the grasses separating the hunters from the sanctuary of their caves. The blood-curdling shrieks were so loud as to be painful, freezing the breath in Kheda's throat.

Then, his hands clapped to his ears, he stared, discomfort forgotten in his astonishment.

Birds had been crouching hidden in the stands of dry grass. They stood up, as tall as a man or taller, with dark-blue plumage that shaded to vibrant green on the tips of their wings and tails. They bent long necks low, opening menacing black beaks, viciously curved. The red of their thick tongues was shockingly vivid as they screeched both at the hesitating hunters and at the men waving firebrands by the cave's makeshift defences.

More birds appeared between the twisted trees, stalking forward on long, pale, scaly legs, vicious talons clawing at the ground. They answered the rest of their flock, which had been lurking silently in the long grass, ear-splitting cries echoing back from the rock face.

The men with the firebrands shouted defiance at the birds and urged the hunting party on. Pressing still closer together, the hunters advanced into the narrow band of grasses. One of the monstrous fowl ran forward, bating wings that Kheda couldn't imagine ever lifting such a massive bird into flight. One of the savages flung a spear that the bird dodged nimbly. It raised a crest of blue-black feathers, vicious beak gaping, head questing forward. More emerged from the sere grasses. Some were as large as the first one, others smaller, without crests or the emerald flashes that the biggest birds were now displaying on their flailing wingtips.

The hunters were outnumbered. The monstrous birds blocked their way and menaced the men resolutely holding open the paths through the barrier of tree branches and spiny plants. The savages with the firebrands moved slowly outwards from the rock face to the outer edge of their defences, extending their line as far as they dared without opening up too wide a gap between any two men. The birds closest chattered angrily, ferocious heads rearing back from the flames.

Those birds that had lurked in the trees stalked forward to press ever closer to the men burdened with the precious proceeds of the hunt. Without fire to deter them, they snapped boldly at the spears and clubs that were thrust out against them. One fastened its lethal beak on a wooden shaft, splintering it as it ripped it out of the wild man's hand. It gripped the hardwood stave in one clawed foot, flapping its wings to balance itself as it bit clean through the spear and flung the shards away with a toss of its crest.

Another one darted forward and the wild man it menaced threw the mottled red lizard he was carrying full at its face. The great bird plucked the dead lizard out of the air and wheeled away. It had to lift its booty as high as it could to escape the mob of lesser birds that instantly surrounded it. Screeching their desire for the meat, they jumped up and down with their futile wings flapping.

Closer at hand, a man screamed in terrible anguish. Kheda realised that some of the smaller birds had stayed creeping along the edge of the trees. Heads low and noisy cries stilled, their blank black eyes were intent on the wounded men straggling along behind the hunters. One had sprung forward and seized a limping man by the shoulder, its hooked beak digging deep into his brown skin. The savage hammered at the massive bird with his fists, writhing in agony. He made no impression on the thick glossy feathers as the bird lifted one brutal foot and disembowelled him with a single stroke of its claws.

Risala hid her face in Kheda's shoulder as more of the smaller birds slaughtered the wounded. He held her close, swallowing bile as he forced himself to watch. The birds bent to feed, jostling, their eerily soft cries of satisfaction muted as they crammed their beaks full. One tossed its head back to swallow some unidentifiable lump. Another daintily used beak and feet to sever an all too identifiable hand from a bleeding arm. Their pale, scaly legs were soon covered with splashes of crimson darkening to black.

Nauseated, Kheda looked past the feasting birds to the hunters still trying to force their way to safety with their precious meat. The vanguard with blazing branches were holding the birds at bay while more men advanced to defend the path through the barrier. Savages high in the upper caves threw rocks and branches, their harsh shouts defying the murderous birds' belligerent screeching. The hunters carrying the heavy lizards hurried towards the safety of the caves, dodging through the gauntlet of flame. The rest flung the last of the smaller lizards and fowl away into the tall grass. The heads of the deadly birds whipped around and they sprang after the bait.

The remaining wounded, unheeded by birds intent on easier kills, crawled and stumbled as fast as they could after the wild hunters who were now shouting encouragement from the shadows of the lowest cave mouth. Some reached the shelter of the spears and firebrands. The last stragglers died beneath the tearing beaks and piercing claws of murderous birds rushing out of the trees. A handful of the able-bodied hunters charged at the birds, brandishing their burning branches, and the monstrous fowl scattered. At a shout from the rest now dragging the spiny clumps of fleshy leaves together again to reinforce the barricade of blotched tree trunks, the hunters hurried back through the single remaining opening. As they retreated into the gloom of the cave mouth, they threw their burning brands down to leave a ring of fire smouldering on the bare earth inside the defences.

The birds scorned the tangle of branches and spiny leaves with rattling beaks but didn't try to jump the barrier. There was enough food outside to sate them without risking the flames. They bickered less menacingly, tearing chunks of meat apart between themselves as they retreated into the woods. As their noise lessened, Kheda could hear wailing coming from deep in the caves.

There are women and children in there. Do these wild men always risk such losses, for the sake of feeding their families? Why don't they burn that grassy dip to ashes, to deprive those birds of cover? Because they dare not set a fire that could rage utterly out of control? They cannot have a savage mage among them, not and suffer so many deaths.

'Kheda!' Risala screamed as a middling-sized blue-green bird darted out from behind a bulbous cluster of spiny plants. Feet splayed, it stood before them, head thrust low and beak gaping. Kheda pushed Risala backwards into the grasses as the bird pecked at him. He sidestepped to cut its head off with a single sweep of his sword. Its long neck lashed, spraying blood in all directions as it collapsed into the dust. Kheda backed away before he was wounded or tripped by the creature's scaly legs thrashing in its death throes. He looked up at a clattering sound and saw more dark eyes gleaming beneath the twisted trees.

'Come on.' He grabbed Risala's hand, hauling her upright. They backed away as fast as they could down the barren margin between the trees and the grasses, away from the caves and the slaughter. Kheda watched the birds behind them while Risala turned to make sure they didn't run into some new danger. The birds didn't follow, pausing instead to tear into the corpse of the one he had beheaded with delighted squawks.

Risala began running, dragging Kheda mercilessly with her. 'We have to get back to the river.'

He ran, his chest heaving, and saw she was bleeding from fresh cuts inflicted by the cruel grasses he had thrown her into.

'Here,' she gasped, finally stopping. 'We should be able to cut straight through to the bank where we left the *Zaise*.'

271

Kheda caught her in his arms and held her close, feeling her heart beating hard and fast against his bare chest. He realised he was spattered with the dead bird's blood. 'We'll just have to hope the smell of that slaughter over there is drawing any other predators.'

Risala sounded determined. 'There are two of us. We should be able to scare off one of those lizards at least.'

Kheda risked raising himself to his full height to see over the grasses, relieved beyond measure to see a lazy curve of gleaming water turning towards them. 'Velindre or Naldeth should be able to see us once we reach the bank. I assume they'll make themselves visible to us.'

'Let's hope so,' Risala said fervently.

They began forcing their way through the lacerating grasses once again. Kheda barely noticed the stinging of fresh cuts as he tried to make sense of what they had seen.

What is this place, where men eat lizards and are prey to birds themselves? What manner of birds were those? Yora hawks, like those in myth and legend? Are we going to meet mirror birds and winged snakes next? Why not? Horned fish and sea serpents are real enough, if rare enough to be called portents whenever they show themselves.

I've been in border skirmishes and full-blown battles, never mind leading my men against these savages and that dragon of Velindre's. I've seen men die for the causes they believed in, good and ill. I've killed men with my own blade, when I had no other choice. Why is it so much worse to see men torn apart by animals simply intent on filling their bellies?

He realised Risala was talking to him. 'What were those things?' she asked a second time. 'Are we going to find other creatures drawn from constellations walking this land?'

'They were just birds.' He couldn't restrain a shudder despite his resolute tone.

'Just giant birds, along with hideous lizards, in a land where dragons swim in the seas.' There was the faintest of tremors in Risala's voice. 'You still don't believe there are any omens to be read here? What do you suppose any other Aldabreshin seer would make of all this?'

'That's no concern of mine.' Kheda saw the sun shining off the river through the haze of grass. 'I just want to get back to the *Zaise.*'

They emerged onto the crumbling bank and looked upstream and down, trying to get their bearings. Kheda was inexpressibly relieved to recognise the choke point where the low muddy islet split the meandering waters of the main channel. He was surprised to see they had come some distance past it. He was more perturbed to see no trace of the *Zaise*, not even the distorted shimmer of Naldeth's magic wrapped around the ship.

'Where are they?' Risala looked around.

A faint shout from the far bank startled them both. The words weren't in the Tormalin tongue or any Aldabreshin dialect. It came again.

'Can you see anyone over there?' Kheda hid his sword behind his back, trying not to be too obvious about it.

Will we be recognised as strangers at such a distance?

The distant bank was a sea of swaying grass, scored here and there with the narrow paths worn by lizards or whatever else lived in this strange place. The plain extended a good deal further on that side of the river before the swell of the land rose up to meet the fat spiny plants and twisted trees.

'Have they gone to hide somewhere else?' Risala bit off the words, frustrated. 'Do you suppose she's scrying for us?'

'I don't know.' Movement on the far side of the river caught Kheda's eye. Away in the distance, a wide bluff jutted out from the valley side into the grassy plain. Another gang of savages were picking their way cautiously down a bare earthen slope facing the river that was somehow resisting the encroaching woodland. All the spearmen carried burning torches and, despite the bright sun, Kheda saw the unmistakable unnatural scarlet of magefire.

'There.' Risala choked on her relief.

'Where?' Kheda looked upstream but couldn't see a thing.

'Just wait a moment.' Risala stared intently at nothingness.

Kheda saw a shallow furrow carved in the silty water fade and disappear. In the next instant, the *Zaise* blinked into view, Naldeth beckoning frantically from the stern platform. Wild shouts rang out across the grasses from the distant bluff, startled outrage plainly audible. The ship drifted closer and vanished again.

'So much for their magic not attracting any notice,' Kheda commented bitterly as he began pushing through the rustling grasses, heading as quickly as possible for the invisible ship.

'Are we going to be safer ashore or aboard?' Risala wondered with equal terseness.

'I really don't know.' Kheda stumbled as a chunk of the undercut bank fell away beneath his feet to land in the water with a resounding splash.

Risala caught his hand and pulled him back. 'I suppose we'll find out.'

As they approached the last point where they had seen the ship, Kheda tried to make out where these newly arrived wild men and their mage might be. It proved impossible to see where the savages had gone once they'd reached the bottom of the barren slope and disappeared into the grasses.

Does that wild wizard have a dragon to call on? The mages who came to the Archipelago came to woo that fire dragon. What do we do if some dragon appears here? I've seen one sink a trireme, never mind a ship the size of the Zaise. Dev saved me from drowning. We should have made a pact — that Velindre would save Risala, and I'll take my chances with Naldeth.

The *Zaise* flickered into sight once again, looking strangely flat like a reflection in polished metal.

'Come on!' Naldeth's agonised whisper sounded loud in Kheda's ears, as if the mage were standing next to him.

The wild men on the far side of the river were shouting, definitely getting closer. Kheda saw scarlet flames advancing through the distant grasses, along with the fire-hardened points of brutal wooden spears.

The ship disappeared just as Kheda dropped down from the dry bank onto the treacherous mud. Risala landed beside him with a squelch and slid a few paces. He grabbed her hand.

'Run.' Velindre's calm voice floated between them.

'Where to?' demanded Kheda.

'Just do it,' the magewoman insisted, unseen.

With Risala's fingers interlaced with his own, Kheda tried to run across the slippery mud. Inside a few paces, his feet had left the moist slickness, sinking instead into a spongy nothingness that sloped rapidly uphill. It was worse than running in soft sand; his aching calves and thighs protested. He ignored the discomfort and hurried on, trying not to look down. He didn't even want to contemplate the apparent emptiness ahead reaching all the way to the far river bank.

Something caught him across the shins with an agonising crack and he tumbled headlong onto the deck of the now wholly visible *Zaise*. Risala landed on top of him and rolled away, cursing under her breath.

'We have to get out of here.' Naldeth stood on the main deck, a flicker of scarlet light tangled around his outstretched hands.

'I'd say so,' Kheda hissed. Biting his lip, he rubbed his bruised legs.

'Can they see us?' Risala was still crouching on her hands and knees.

'I hope not.' Velindre was standing up on the stern platform, shaking the remnants of a cerulean flame from one hand. She raised the other to the stern mast where the half-sail obediently bellied with a sapphire-laced wind.

'Can you see them?' Kheda got slowly to his feet and headed for the ladder at the stern.

'Stand still,' Naldeth warned. 'Don't disturb the spells.'

All the youthful wizard's attention was focused on the magelight between his hands. He stretched his hands a little wider apart and Kheda saw fine threads of magic catching the light, floating outwards in all directions. The warlord stood motionless where he was.

Slowly easing herself to a sitting position, Risala looked dubiously around. 'Can they hear us?' she whispered. 'If they can't see us?'

Naldeth spared her a brief glance. 'Not if we keep our voices down.'

Velindre's hazel eyes were fixed on the half-furled sail, her other hand guiding the steering oars several paces behind her.

Fighting a pointless urge to sink below the *Zaise*'s deck rails to hide, Kheda watched the wild men reach the thinner grasses fringing the far bank. Savages naked but for loincloths carried the mage-lit torches and their long vicious spears. The wild wizards followed, striding unhindered through the inhospitable grasses which parted before them, sending ripples running away like water.

'Two wild wizards,' Kheda said softly. 'And they are wild women.'

Both wore wraps of soft leather tied just above their breasts and reaching to mid-thigh. Their long, coarse curls were knotted around dense clusters of vivid red and purple feathers and both carried themselves with an ominous assurance.

'Do you suppose they answer to him?' breathed Risala.

A third savage mage strode forward to stand on the undercut lip of the bank, between the feather-crowned women. Where the wild spearmen wore the usual brief clouts of stained hide, this man wore a belt of plaited cords with a panel of wooden beadwork hanging at his groin. All around the rest of the belt scraps of lizard hide were tied, interspersed with what looked horribly like hanks of black, tangled hair. He wore a band of pale-grey feathers tied just below one knee and another around one wrist. Shrugging back a heavy cloak of long blue-green feathers that could only have come from the monstrous birds that had attacked the cave dwellers, he turned to the two women, gesturing upstream and down.

'So that's a wild wizard.' Naldeth stole a quick glance before returning all his attention to his spell-casting.

'Can he see us?' Kheda couldn't see any clue on the savage mage's face. He couldn't actually see his face, he realised with a shudder. The man wore a bleached white skull as a mask, stark against his profusion of dark, matted locks. The empty eye sockets of the skull stared after the invisible ship, framed by the downward curve of the ridged horns once flourished by whatever beast had given up its life for the wild mage's adornment.

'Probably not.' Naldeth didn't sound as certain as Velindre had done, as the *Zaise* slipped silently away downstream.

Chapter 12

Wild wizards, like the ones who burned the fleeing people of Chazen alive. Like the ones who twisted harmless animals into monsters to slaughter my swordsmen.

'Where are we going?' Kheda forced the words out.

'Back out to sea,' Velindre said tersely, 'before that mage thinks of whipping up a sandstorm.'

Because coating anything invisible with dust would leave it plain for all to see.

'The rawest apprentice in Hadrumal would have done that by now.' Naldeth drew his hands together, lacing his fingers tight. The whiteness of his knuckles belied his contempt for the savages standing confused on the rapidly receding river bank.

'Won't he sense your magic?' Faintest blue magelight still shimmered around the half-sail, countering the sea breeze coming inshore. Kheda moved closer to Risala.

'Not unless he's quicker witted than he has been so far.' Nevertheless, Velindre raised a hand and the sapphire radiance faded to a bare memory staining Kheda's vision.

'He wasn't so slow-witted.' Kheda couldn't help himself. 'He found us, didn't he?'

'That wizard couldn't see us,' Naldeth said stubbornly. 'I'll take my oath on it.'

' All he knew was that something was awry,' Velindre agreed. 'He didn't know what.'

'Then how did they just happen to arrive so soon after we sailed inland?' snapped Kheda.

'The smoke could have drawn them,' Risala said reluctantly. 'From the hunters' fires.'

'I suppose it's possible,' Kheda allowed grudgingly.

'Once they were close enough, their wizard could have felt some disturbance in the elements.' Velindre considered the puzzle, ignoring Kheda's irritation. 'Though I'm certain he didn't know what it was.'

Naldeth nodded his agreement. 'If he had any notion, he would have brought down some magic on us.'

'Or some dragon,' interjected Risala.

'At least we know there are still mages here.' Kheda dismissed the cooling remnants of his anger. 'As well as potentially dangerous numbers of wild men. That's what we came to find out—'

'You're proposing we go back to the Archipelago immediately?' Velindre was still gazing back up the river. 'To sit and wait for their attack?'

'We don't know that they will attack again,' protested Naldeth.

'We don't know that they won't,' Kheda said grimly.

And I still don't know what we'd do if they did.

The younger wizard shook his head stubbornly. 'Surely this isle is big enough for their needs. It's not as if a land this size could blow itself apart and sink like that outlying chain.'

'We still don't know for certain why those savages from that drowned island sailed east to Chazen instead of coming here.' Risala grimaced, absently rubbing at a sore welt on one forearm.

'If we took a day or so to get a little closer to those mage-born, we might glean some better understanding of their magic.' Velindre caught her bitten thumbnail between her white teeth, brow clouded with thought. 'Finding some weakness in their wizardry could prove vital if they do come to the Archipelago one day. That masquerader in the feather cloak has an affinity with elemental air but he wasn't drawing on the breezes around him. I'm sure he has some tie to a dragon. I could feel it.'

Instantly Risala looked up. 'Is it anywhere close?'

'Let me read the breezes.' Velindre stared into the sky with disquieting eagerness.

'Just don't bring it down on us.' Kheda turned to Naldeth. 'Were those women with feathers in their hair mages as well?'

'I'd call them mageborn rather than mages,' the young wizard said slowly. 'One of them was keeping the torches alight with a fire affinity but I don't think she could do much more than that.'

'Not without a fire dragon's aura to draw on.' Velindre was still intent on the cloudless sky.

'The wild wizards who came to the Archipelago had lesser mages hanging around them, to begin with at least,' Risala said thoughtfully.

'And we never really understood why.' Kheda looked around dubiously.

'We don't know anything about them.' Velindre was unperturbed. 'Which is hardly surprising after barely a day sailing this coast. We came here to reconnoitre, Kheda. Will you at least spend another day seeing what we might learn?'

'One more day,' he conceded.

Because there are indeed too many questions still unanswered, and I have come too far for all this to be for nothing. And Risala and I are not alone, defenceless against evil wizardry. But is the confidence of these northern mages wholly justified or am I just seeing more of Dev's arrogance?

The *Zaise* slipped back down the muddy channel towards the maze of rivulets cutting through the sand bars defying the surging sea. Kheda's countless scrapes and scratches began to throb unbearably. He realised he was still gripping his bloodied sword and clenched his fist around the hilt all the tighter to fight the urge to scratch at his itches. Finally he lost sight of the savage mage in the receding grasslands.

'We had better find somewhere to hide the ship without magic if we're going ashore,' Naldeth said irritably, 'in case some elemental concealment catches a wild wizard's eye.'

'Or a dragon's.' Velindre leaned against the tiller to turn the prow of the *Zaise* towards the north, beyond the river mouth. 'Let's see how the land lies this way.'

Kheda couldn't decide whether to be reassured or irritated by the magewoman's calmness.

All these scratches are doing nothing for my temper. And I had better clean this sword before we go ashore again.

'If we're going ashore again, what are we going to do?' Risala frowned, rubbing harder at her forearm.

'I suppose we could find out where that masked mage lives,' Kheda said reluctantly. 'Or see how he deals with those wretches in those caves, assuming he crosses the river.'

'Do you suppose he has any dealings with them?' wondered Risala. 'They can't have had any magic, or they'd have used it to drive off those vile birds.'

'Those caves are probably as good a place as any to make for once we've hidden the ship.' Taking Risala's hand away from the score she was absently inflaming, Kheda looked at Naldeth. 'Have you any experience of stalking game?'

'I wouldn't know how to begin without using my magic.' The young mage was looking ahead to the jagged cliffs where the high ground on either side of the grassy plain broke on the seashore. 'Velindre, there are caves inside these rocks.'

This dark-grey stone was unlike any they'd encountered so far, fractured by the ceaseless battering of the ocean and smeared with the white droppings of unfamiliar seabirds that bickered on ledges fringed with meagre vegetation.

Kheda couldn't see any opening big enough for a man to slip through, never mind a boat.

'Getting into some sea cave might be easy enough,' he warned, 'but remember that we have to get out again, whatever the tide.'

'And we may not be wanting to use magic to do it.' Risala moved closer and he welcomed the reassurance of her presence beside him. She pulled away with a hiss as his sweat seared one of her grazes.

Kheda bit his lip against the sudden pain clawing at his own arm. He took Risala's hand. 'Come on, let's find my physic chest.'

They left Velindre scanning the skies and Naldeth absorbed studying the inhospitable cliffs.

Risala followed Kheda through the door to the stern cabin. He set his blood-clotted sword carefully down and bent to pull open the trap door to the aft hold.

'Did we do the right thing, coming here?' Risala asked abruptly.

Kheda let the heavy trap door fall backwards with a thud. 'I don't know. But Velindre's right — we've been in these waters for less than a day. We should see what the next few dawns might bring.'

'Couldn't you look for some portent—' Risala bit her

'I'm more concerned with getting their measure, so we know just what danger they might be to Chazen and the rest of the Archipelago.' Kheda looked down at his muddied loincloth. 'Wait here. I'll pass the physic chest up.'

He could put his hand unerringly on the ebony and silver casket in the gloomy hold. Taking a few steps back up the ladder one-handed, he passed it up to Risala as she knelt and reached down through the trap door. Climbing back up into the stern cabin, he set the chest in the sunlight falling through the open door and knelt to unsnap the catches.

As he reached for a green glazed pot, Risala pointed to a wax-sealed lacquered box. 'Is that the powder that dulls a wizard's magic?'

'It is.' He picked up the green pot of salve. 'Though I don't plan on trying to get close enough to that wild mage to poison his sorcery with it.'

'I don't suppose there's enough there to stop a dragon blasting us with lightning or searing us into ashes?' Risala's attempt at light-heartedness fell flat.

'I doubt it.' Kheda twisted the cork of the salve pot and snapped the wax seal. 'Let's settle for stopping this accursed itching.'

He began applying the ointment, fragrant with herbs, to her numerous lacerations. The feel of her firm flesh beneath his fingertips soothed him.

Risala scooped a fingerful of salve from the pot and gently stroked it along a crusted score on Kheda's chest, 'Did you ever fathom the herbs that make up that magic-stifling powder?'

He rubbed the pale ointment into the scrapes on her narrow shoulders. 'Not wholly, and there are rare earths in the mix besides. I don't know where I might find them here, or the plants I would need to make more of the stuff. I didn't recognise anything growing ashore and the season when such things need to be harvested can make or break any concoction's usefulness. Anyway, do you think we could find a way to feed it to a dragon or a wild mage?'

'We managed to avoid being blasted or burned alive before.' Pulling away from him, Risala's voice was muffled as she dragged her faded red tunic on over her head. 'Let's hope our luck holds, omens or no omens.'

'I'm more inclined to rely on Velindre's magic whisking us away from any danger and sending us home.' Kheda rubbed ointment into the worst of the scrapes on his legs.

Am I ever going to be able to live in any kind of peace in Chazen now, knowing this land is out here, with these wild men and their wizards and dragons, even beyond such an expanse of ocean? Am I any further forward than I was? Was I too eager to let Velindre persuade me to leave the burdens of obligation and family behind, for the temptation of solitude with Risala?

'Just as long as her magic doesn't just bring a dragon down on us.' Risala took the earthenware pot and bent to tend the scratches on her legs, shedding her makeshift loincloth. Straightening up, she handed the pot back to Kheda.

Kheda carefully replaced the empty salve jar in his physic chest. 'Any dragon will go after the two of them before it bothers with you or me,' he said quietly.

Though what would we do then, alone on a hostile shore without hope of magical aid? Was I too easily seduced by Velindre's promises that her powers would make everything simple?

Standing up with new resolution, he stripped off the loincloth he'd made of his trousers. 'We'll track these savages to their lair and the wizards can watch them for a few days.' Pulling fresh clothing from the bundle of worn cottons he had been sharing with Velindre, he dressed rapidly. 'Then Velindre can use her magic to take us to some northern backwater and we'll make our way to Shek Kul's domain.'

'Word of the two dragons seen in Chazen will have reached him.' Risala nodded her understanding. 'He'll have been searching all the northern lore he can get his hands on for anything that the warlords of ages past used to keep barbarian mages out of their waters.'

'Velindre found lore we could use against the dragons before. I'll humble myself before Shek Kul if that's what it takes for him to share such knowledge.' Kheda took rags and a metal vial from one of the nets nailed against the wooden walls to hold oddments and necessities. 'Chazen's safety is more important than my pride, and at least I'll be able to tell him what we'll be facing, if they come again, by way of trade.'

Risala picked up the soiled sword. 'Shek Kul's no fool—'

The *Zaise* lurched violently. Risala dropped the blade and Kheda wrapped her in his arms, both of them fighting to keep their balance. The scrape of rock reverberated through the hull. Kheda kissed Risala's hair as the ship settled to an even keel. She tightened her arms around his chest as much as she dared given all their various contusions.

'Sorry about that.' Naldeth appeared in the doorway, the daylight dimming around him. 'Oh, forgive me.' Seeing Risala half-dressed in Kheda's arms, he retreated bashfully.

Kheda grinned and gave Risala's naked rump a fond squeeze before releasing her and handing over a pair of sturdy trousers. 'I think good stout cottons are called for hereabouts.'

'As well as footwear.' Risala reached for a sack slung on a peg. 'It would be foolish to come all this way and die from a festering thorn.'

'And we'll all carry blades, wizards or not.' Kheda picked up his sword and the cleaning materials and went out onto the deck.

The *Zaise* was edging into a contorted cave reaching deep into the cliff. Seawater slopped over angular ledges as the walls loomed high on either side, and the harsh sound echoed back and forth. Gooseflesh rose on Kheda's arms as they moved out of the sun into the gloomy chill. A faint nimbus of green magelight ran along the *Zaise*'s rails.

Like the cold fire that is a mariner's most potent omen out of sight of land. And I am in a land where creatures of portent stalk the earth as well as the heavens. Yet I have nothing to guide me to the wisest course of action, because I have lost all faith in such signs.

'Can we get back out of here?' Beside him, Risala hugged herself, looking at the fragment of open sky painfully bright against the darkness surrounding them.

'Whatever the tide.' From her vantage point on the stern platform, Velindre anticipated the question on the tip of Kheda's tongue. 'And without any magic strong enough to be felt above the natural turmoil of these waters.'

'See that cleft?' Naldeth pointed into the cold darkness beyond the *Zaise*'s prow.

'No.' Kheda stifled a shiver as Velindre's green wizardry dripped from the ship's rails and faded into the deck planking, leaving an iridescence like the sheen inside a mussel shell.

'It runs nearly all the way up to the top of this cliff.' The youthful wizard raised a hand and white flames flickered on his fingertips to cast hard-edged shadows onto the deck. 'I can make us a way through.'

'Let's make sure we have a ship to come back to.' Kheda set down his sword and helped Risala fetch out the closely woven fenders stowed beneath the *Zaise*'s rails.

Velindre brought the *Zaise* alongside a rocky ledge where wetness caught the light filtering in from the entrance. The fenders rustled and rasped as they were crushed between stone and hull. Stuffed with the silky fibres found inside tandra tree seed pods, their oily scent filled Kheda with an unexpected rush of desire for recognizable trees populated by readily identifiable birds.

'We must all carry blades.' He left the fenders and collected his sword, opening the vial to tip the scouring mixture of fine sand and vinegar onto a rag. Risala slipped back into the stern cabin.

'Don't worry about mooring ropes.' Velindre slid down the ladder as the *Zaise* froze in the midst of the jolting waters. 'Our bird's not going anywhere.'

'So, Kheda, what's it like ashore?' Naldeth asked with keen interest.

'Every leaf is edged like a razor or studded with thorns.' Risala reappeared and tossed a pair of sturdy leather sandals with nailed soles over to the magewoman, dumping an armful of other gear on the deck. 'And there are birds big enough to bite a man's arm clean through.'

Naldeth turned from looking ahead into the featureless darkness, his mouth half-open. 'Shall I take a sword?'

Kheda began wiping the grime from his blade with an oiled rag. 'Do you know how to use one?'

'Not as such—' the young mage began defensively.

'Then no.' Perversely amused by the disappointment on Naldeth's face, Kheda relented a little. 'You'll find a hacking blade will serve if you have to fight with it and it'll be more use against the scrub's teeth around here.'

'We should all carry water flasks, and something to eat.' Risala handed Naldeth a brass water flask on a braided strap almost identical to her own as well as a leather pouch to sling over his other shoulder. 'We don't want to have to go foraging.'

'No,' Kheda agreed, scrubbing hard to be sure he was ridding his blade of every smear.

I haven't come all this way just to have my skull crushed by some savage's club because my sword sticks in its scabbard.

'Make sure you don't lose this.' Risala offered the young wizard a square-ended blade as broad as his palm and as long as his forearm, protected by a wood and leather scabbard. The varnished handle was almost as long as the blade.

'Here, let me show you.' Kheda took a long leather belt from the pile of gear in front of Risala and looped it twice around Naldeth's hips. Kheda's foot brushed against the cold metal of the youth's toeless foot and he looked down. 'How much magic do you use to keep yourself walking?'

Velindre answered for the young mage. 'Not enough to stir the elements beyond arm's length.' She sat down to pull on stout sandals and used the laces to bind her loose trousers tight around her ankles.

I suppose I shall just have to take your word for that.

Kheda looked at Risala. She shrugged at him, her expression unreadable in the dim light. The straps of a water flask and a light leather sack crisscrossed her chest, and she held her hacking blade in both hands, dagger ready at her belt.

'Show us the way out of here, Naldeth,' Kheda said.

The young wizard stood upright and squared his shoulders. He climbed over the *Zaise*'s rail and walked cautiously along a ledge deeper into the gloom. A muted red glow leaked from the joints and rivets of his metal leg.

'I'll bring up the rear.' Velindre's face was more angular and androgynous than ever in the meagre light filtering through the cave. 'Just in case.'

'We'll spend a day seeing what hope there might be of learning something useful.' Kheda's tone brooked no argument from the magewoman. 'If there's any sign of danger, you take us away with your magic at once.'

Faint green radiance reflected in her eyes as she nodded calmly. 'I've no desire to find myself in some contest with a wild mage or being eaten by a dragon.'

'Come on.' Naldeth called impatiently out of the darkness.

Kheda swung himself over the rail. The slick stone felt treacherous under the soles of his sturdy sandals and cast up a damp cold. Feeling his way cautiously towards the pale blur that was Naldeth's tunic, Kheda's outstretched hacking blade found a low ledge the instant before he cracked his already bruised shins on it.

'See up there?' Naldeth raised a hand once more tipped with pale flames that revealed riven rocks making a perilous stair. 'This cleft reaches nearly to the top of the cliffs. I'll only have to open the last stretch with wizardry.'

Kheda began climbing cautiously upwards. He paused when the young mage reached a tumble of broken stone caught between two cracked walls. 'Is that safe?'

'Quite safe.' Kheda could hear rather than see Naldeth's grin.

'I see your time in the Gidestan mines with Planir wasn't wasted.' In the shadows behind them all, Velindre sounded approving.

'You know our Archmage.' Naldeth turned with a scrape of his metal foot on the stones and began climbing again. 'He doesn't tolerate slackness.'

The cleft grew narrower and steeper and the air turned stale and dusty. Kheda looked up vainly for any chink of natural light beyond Naldeth's eerie magelight. As the roof lowered and the deceptive shadows danced around, the warlord found himself cringing, expecting to hit his head on unyielding stone with each step.

Naldeth finally halted and the flames in his hand turned to ochre. 'I will have to use a little earth magic here.'

The light showed they had reached a dead end. One side of the cleft reared up solidly to bar any further passage while the other rolled away to disappear into some empty void echoing with the sound of the clawing sea far below.

'Be as quick as you can, and discreet,' Velindre called from the rear. 'I can sense open air not far above us.'

'Can you sense any people up there?' Kheda asked swiftly. 'Before he makes the ground fall out from beneath their feet.'

Naldeth wasn't listening, already concentrating on the unyielding rock face. Ochre light suddenly filled the air and then soaked into the dark-grey stone, running along the interstices like liquid fire. The young mage pressed himself against the rock, the glowing lines throwing strange shadows on his face. He closed his eyes and breathed deep.

Kheda reached around for Risala's hand, keeping his body between her and the magic. He braced himself and felt Risala hold her breath. The air tasted oddly metallic and warmed rapidly.

A muffled crack sounded deep within the wall of the cleft, and then another. The ochre light flickered with each snapping sound and tremors ran through the stone beneath their feet. The orange light blinked out and Risala's fingers tightened around Kheda's in the darkness.

The rock face disintegrated with a gentle sigh. Velindre summoned a pale-blue flame that showed them countless thin fragments sliding down the long slope they had just climbed, shards drifting more like leaves than stones. By contrast, the dust fell out of the air as fast as metal fragments drawn to a lodestone, leaving barely a mote to sparkle in the shaft of sunlight piercing the darkness. Kheda gazed at the patch of empty blue overhead.

'Careful,' Naldeth warned as he climbed up newly revealed artfully ragged steps.

'Don't go outside.' Kheda released Risala's hand and hurried after the wizard. 'There might still be someone or something waiting up there.'

The velvety slick of powdered stone was disconcerting to walk on and it sifted into his sandals, gritty between his toes. Kheda ignored the discomfort, watching intently for any shadow crossing the opening ahead.

Naldeth halted in a pool of light on a broad stone shelf beneath a last brief flight of magically wrought steps that reached up to the surface. 'I think we're alone.'

'Wait there.' Kheda moved in front of him and discovered that the wizard had opened a deep crevice in the side of a rocky bluff on top of the cliff. The bright sunlight stabbed at his eyes and the heat of the open air was brutal even before he stepped out of the cool of the cave. Gripping his scabbarded sword and mindful of the hacking blade thrust through his double-looped belt, the warlord edged out onto the dusty slope.

Beneath the outcrop of grey stone, the barren earth was patched with grass dried to straw by the sun and crushed by the wind. The slope ran away to meet a sparse expanse of those blotched and twisted trees fringed with paltry leaves. Kheda could see no movement in the dappled shade beneath them. Further down the slope, larger trees lifted thicker canopies of denser green. The forest rose up again to a shallow crest and then sank once more out of sight. A series of low rolling hills marched away into the east. A few birds flapped lazily above the treetops, their fluting calls unperturbed. A little way to the south, the hills yielded to the sere yellow of the grassy plain where the meandering river glinted like steel. There was no longer any sign of the hunters' fires. He frowned as he tried to calculate where their caves might be.

'Is it safe?' Risala asked from the dark opening behind him.

Kheda slid a little way along the side of the bluff, his back pressed to the rock. There was nothing on the cliff top between the bluff and the sheer drop to the unseen surf. 'As far as I can see.'

Risala emerged cautiously, shading her eyes with one hand. 'Where are we?'

'There's the river.' Kheda pointed. 'The caves must be somewhere over beyond that second hill.'

Velindre joined them, followed by Naldeth. 'What caves?' the young wizard asked instantly.

'The fires we saw were set by a hunting party.' Kheda kept looking but the landscape seemed wholly devoid of life. 'They were going back to caves where they live with their spoils.'

'They were being hunted in turn by truly hideous birds.' Risala shivered at the memory.

'You were serious about the birds?' Naldeth was disbelieving.

'Taller than you or me.' Kheda thrust his sword into his belt and drew his hacking blade. 'Able to kill a wild man with beak or talons.'

'Just like yora hawks,' Risala muttered darkly. 'If we were looking for an omen.'

'Let's hope we don't run into any winged serpents,' Velindre said lightly.

'Let's get out of this sun before our brains boil.' Kheda studied the vista before them. 'We'll move slowly and carefully in the trees, to be sure we see or hear any savages before they see us. Naldeth, seal off this stairway as quick as you can. We don't want to leave an open invitation to the *Zaise*.'

He waited, tense, the dust around their feet shivering as Naldeth's magic worked deep in the rocks.

'Done,' the youthful wizard said briefly.

'Follow me.' Breathing more easily now he was moving, Kheda headed for the widest opening between the twisted trees. The others followed close behind, stopping with him when they reached the illusory shade of the foliage.

At least the lad moves freely enough on that metal leg of his.

Naldeth took a pull at his water flask. 'What now?' Sweat already darkened the armpits of his tunic.

'Let's start with those savages in the caves.' Kheda looked at the two wizards. 'We can cut through these trees and find a vantage point on one of the hills. That should keep us away from the skull-masked mage if he's still out on the plain.'

'Those birds were lurking in the trees.' Risala gripped her hacking blade.

'Those armoured lizards were hiding in the long grass, which also cut us to ribbons,' Kheda pointed out. 'The birds are easier to kill.'

'Did you see any sign of a wizard with these cave dwellers?' Naldeth asked.

'No.' Kheda looked at Velindre. 'But you had better be ready to use your magic to get us out of any danger I can't kill with a sword.'

'I've no plans to die here,' she assured him.

'I'm glad to hear it.' Kheda moved slowly through the trees, pushing aside stray branches where he could, only cutting where he had to, careful to avoid any strike echoing through the trees.

Have these forests ever felt the bite of metal? Who are these people, who arm themselves with sticks and stones and go in fear of birds and lizards? I would have thought there was nothing they could not do with the magic they draw from these dragons.

The ground between the trees was pale as sand. Leathery spiky plants claimed any open spaces, thrusting knife-like leaves upwards. Old growth had fallen back to surround each

293

dull green and purple crown with desiccated brown leaves and Kheda froze as he saw movement in one clump.

A small lizard patterned with yellow and red pounced on a crawling beetle. The lizard turned back to its sanctuary, beetle legs fringing its mouth. A mulberry snake with a pale head struck from its lair beneath another crown of spikes. The lizard thrashed wildly in its mouth then went limp, bright eyes dulling. The snake dragged it into the shade and set about the leisurely business of swallowing.

Kheda glanced over his shoulder. 'Watch where you're putting your feet.'

He kept to open ground as best he could. Looking back as they drew closer to the taller, darker trees, he noticed that the others were following his trail so closely that their footprints overlaid his own. He retraced his steps, angry with himself. 'Risala, cut a branch and sweep away our tracks.'

'You think we're being followed?' Naldeth looked around apprehensively.

'We will be if any hunter worth the name comes across a trail like that.' Kheda sliced a leafy frond from a tree, careful of the vicious spines lurking amid the greenery, and swept away the pattern of nails that Velindre's soles had printed clearly in the dust.

Risala shared his chagrin. 'We've never seen any of those savages wearing sandals.'

The magewoman watched Kheda obliterate her tracks. 'I told you we needed your particular skills.'

Kheda looked up to see Naldeth drinking from his water flask again. 'You don't know when you'll get a chance to refill that,' he warned. 'And Velindre won't be summoning up water with her magic unless we're all dizzy with thirst.'

The young mage looked surprised. 'Velindre?'

She looked at him, impassive. 'We're following Kheda's lead.'

Kheda began moving again. Risala dropped back to continue brushing away their trail. Kheda slowed as they reached the thicker band of taller trees that were sheltered from the sea's storms by the slope they had just descended. The trees' trunks were black and brown and deeply buttressed, spreading canopies of broader leaves high above their heads. Vines strung fibrous loops between the lofty branches while saplings and opportune bushes clustered where the shade was less dense. The rest of the ground was covered with a thick layer of fallen leaves. The top layer was dry and crackled as they passed over it, though every step stirred up a scent of rot in the humid stillness.

We won't leave tracks here but it'll be tricky to move quietly through this.

'Watch out for snakes.' Kheda moved cautiously onwards, stabbing at the leaf litter with his hacking blade.

'What was that?' Naldeth halted, mouth open, as he stared at one of the tall trees.

'It looked like a matia,' Velindre mused. 'It was brown and furry with a long nose and a twitching tail,' she amplified for Risala's benefit.

'Whatever it was, it was running away.' Risala dismissed the unseen creature. 'That's all we need to know.'

Kheda turned to silence them all with a sweep of his hand. 'Voices carry further than we can see. Only speak if you must.'

To his relief, the forest grew no thicker. He skirted the patches of denser growth, at the same time using them as cover until he was certain the trees ahead sheltered no unwelcome surprises. Risala followed close behind, constantly scanning the underbrush, with Velindre coming after her, equally vigilant. Naldeth lagged behind, stumbling whenever his lifeless metal foot sank into unexpected softness in the dark leaf mould.

Kheda saw brightness ahead where the tall trees stopped. He pushed carefully through the thorny tangle of scrub on the shady margin of the woodland, grateful for his long sleeves and trousers. The slope they had been carefully descending fell abruptly away and the dry expanse of a desiccated stream bed opened out before them, the crumbling edge treacherous.

He took a moment to orient himself. This watercourse ran away to the south, to join the flow of the wide river they had sailed up earlier and swell it with whatever rain fell on the higher land to the north. It was plainly a seasonal tributary; at present it was a barren stretch of pale sand dotted with tufts of the razor-bladed grass and uneven slews of tumbled rocks and dead and broken tree limbs. On the far side, the next low hill rose up to be claimed by the forest once again.

And those caves and the wild men who fought those vile birds are somewhere beyond that.

'Someone's been digging.' Risala sank down behind the concealing leaves of a sapling and pointed to a dark hole excavated in the pale sandy stream bed. 'Or something. I suppose it could have been some animal.'

'Someone, I'd say.' Velindre narrowed her eyes as she looked at the diggings. 'For water.'

'Using pointed sticks and pieces of gourd.' Naldeth pointed to the detritus scattered around the hole.

'Which they dropped as they ran.' Kheda looked at the darker earth cast aside around the hole. 'And they're not long gone, or that would have dried out.'

Risala looked at him. 'Could they have heard us coming?'

'I think we would have seen or heard them running, don't you?' Kheda looked up and down the dried-up stream. There was no sign of any living creature in the silent and empty valley.

'So what do we do now?' Naldeth asked expectantly.

Kheda stared across the dry valley. There was no obvious trail cutting through the trees on the far side of the stream bed. 'We have to get across this open ground as quickly as we can.'

'Do you want me to wrap a little concealment around us?' Velindre offered.

Kheda hesitated. 'Can you be certain no wild mage will sense it?'

'Not unless he's actively looking for us and scrying this valley in particular,' she assured him.

'Very well, then.' Kheda nodded reluctantly, taking one last look to be certain there was no one in sight.

The air shivered with the disquieting shimmer of magic as he strode into the open. Apprehension prickled down his spine along with a trickle of sweat, though at least there was a breath of cool breeze once they emerged from beneath the trees.

As they reached the patch of dug-up ground, Kheda scanned the soft stream bed for any sign to show which way the unknown savages had fled. All he could see were animal tracks: splayed footprints with the telltale depressions made by taloned toes and the dragging line left by a tail cutting between them.

Is that what they were running from? What was it? A lizard? Where did the lizard go?

'Do we see if we can find whoever was digging or carry on to those caves you were talking about?' Naldeth was struggling to get a purchase on the loose sandy earth with his false foot.

297

Risala walked a few paces away in the direction of the unseen grasslands, scanning the ground. 'They didn't go this way.'

'They went north.' Velindre looked up the dry stream.

'Away from that wild mage with the skull mask.' Risala turned her attention towards the black and brown trees clustered thickly on the opposite bank. 'I'm not anxious to go into that forest, Kheda, not if those birds are there.'

'Then we'll go and see if we can find the people who went upstream from here.' Kheda grinned as both wizards' faces betrayed their surprise at this change of plan. 'A wise leader always listens to those following him.' He pointed to the far bank. 'But we'll use those trees for cover. We're not going to walk up the middle of this watercourse.'

Risala looked at him with a smile in her eyes. 'As you command, my lord.'

They moved on and Kheda tried to curb his exasperation with Naldeth's stumbling progress. Once they were safely within the trees on the far side of the stream bed, he allowed a halt.

The young wizard evidently read something in Kheda's expression. 'If you want me moving any faster, I'll need to use more magic,' he said tightly.

'I'll try to find a path that won't be too taxing.' Kheda tried not to sound curt.

That proved easier said than done and it was an awkward task keeping close enough to the edge of the trees to see the dry stream clearly without drawing too near to the fractured lip of the bank. High above, unseen birds bickered. Now and again one squawked a peremptory warning and Kheda froze. When the idle chatter in the treetops resumed, he moved on, each time with his heart beating a little faster. The dry valley curved around a shallow bend and as soon as he got a good view of what lay beyond, Kheda stopped.

'Not all these savages live in caves.'

Back on the western bank that they had just left behind them, below another of the irregular outcrops where the rocks of this harsh land broke through the meagre soil, the thickly buttressed trees had been claimed by the wild men. Underbrush and lesser saplings had been cleared and platforms built around the sturdiest trunks, supported by branches forced into compliance with thick plaited ropes. Crude sheaves of dry leaves showed up brown among the green, tied to cast shade, while hanging hides foiled draughts, though the dwellings could hardly be called huts. Wild men and women were moving peaceably around the wide bases of the trees with no thought that they might be observed.

'Do you suppose these people have a wizard to call on?' Risala studied them.

'We'll have to wait and see,' said Velindre, her eyes keen.

Are these allies of those cave-dwellers to the east of here? Or does this dry valley mark some boundary? Whose territory are we in? Does it make any difference?

Kheda looked up and down the bank of the stream where they stood, searching for a safe place to hide and keep watch on those new wild men without risk of being seen. A wide-boled tree whose drooping branches were thick with coppery leaves caught his eye. Cautiously, he pushed aside the dangling foliage to find a bare circle of richly scented earth within the curtain of branches. There were no snakes immediately apparent or burrows where some venomous creature might be lurking.

'In here.' He beckoned the others into this opportune hiding place.

'What now?' Naldeth sat down in the aromatic shadows with palpable relief.

'Concentrate on your element.' Velindre moved to get a better view across the dry stream. 'We should be able to sense if there are any mageborn over there.'

The wizards sat still in remote contemplation. Risala edged across the ground to join Kheda. Sitting cross-legged, she delved inside the leather sack she was carrying and offered him stale saller flatbread and a piece of dried turtle meat.

'What do you suppose those wild men are eating?' Kheda whispered as he chewed the leathery flesh.

'Something substantial given the size of that hearth.' Risala dripped a little water from her flask onto the saller bread to make it more palatable.

Time passed tediously slowly as they watched the savages piling dry branches into a hollow dug just above the edge of the stream bed. The substantial stones ringing the pit were blackened with use. With some agreement presumably reached that the pile was big enough, a handful of dark-skinned men in leather loincloths huddled to one side. A sharp rapping noise echoed across the emptiness and after another interlude, pale-grey smoke showed that a fire had been kindled.

'Just a natural flame.' Naldeth stirred to answer before anyone could ask. 'Struck from flint and fool's gold,' he commented with some interest.

The huddle broke up as the wild men carried smoking bundles of tinder and poked them into different places around the edge of the pit. The smoke thickened and darkened and drew together into a single column. Dry wood crackled and split and the first true flames flickered to life. Children appeared to fling bundles of sticks onto the fire. As the blaze rose to a brilliant scar against the darkness of the trees behind, the men shooed the children away. They chased each other around the tree trunks with shouts and laughter that echoed along the dry valley.

The men sat around the fire, watching as the dry wood burned down to a bed of glowing embers. From time to time, women in scanty leather wraps emerged from the shadows beneath the platforms rigged in the trees. They consulted with the seated men before disappearing once more. Finally, the men rose to fetch sticks and raked aside the ashes and stones that had been soaking up the heat of the fire.

The women reappeared in twos and threes. Some held dripping lumps of meat or ungainly burdens wrapped in thick green leaves. Others carried gourds and lengths of stout vine plugged at each end with twisted tufts of foliage. The meat hissed as it was tossed into the middle of the hot stones, while everything else was set carefully in the ring of embers. The fickle breeze carried the taste of roasting meat to taunt the unseen watchers beneath the all-enveloping tree.

If they have no metal for weapons, they certainly wouldn't have it for fire irons or cook pots.

Hunger stirred by the appetising odours, Kheda was trying to estimate how long the food might take to cook when Risala clutched at his arm.

'Look,' she breathed.

Kheda followed her pointing finger to see a familiar figure leading a sizeable contingent of savages up the dry stream bed. It was the wild mage with the cloak of feathers and the mask fashioned from a skull.

'Don't so much as stir your element,' Velindre warned Naldeth tensely.

Kheda noted that the women with feathers in their hair were walking a few paces behind the wild mage. The three mageborn were surrounded by warriors carrying spears of fire-hardened wood and clubs studded with chips of black stone that caught the light.

'Do you suppose he goes to find the source of any fire?' Risala wondered almost inaudibly.

'These people show no sign of fearing attack.' Kheda tried to make sense of this mystery. 'Perhaps this skull-faced wizard is a newcomer to the area.'

'I can feel something stirring the earth.' Naldeth tugged at the cord that bent the knee of his metal leg so he could kneel upright, looking down at the ground.

'I think that old man might object if this skull-faced mage has come to claim his little valley.' Velindre stiffened like a matia catching a threatening scent.

A grey-haired wild man emerged from the shadows beneath the mighty trees. He wore a loincloth like all the rest and a hide cloak slung around his bony shoulders. The skin was pale on the inside and when the old savage turned to face the approaching wild wizard, Kheda saw that the outer side was brilliant with intricate patterns of sewn beads. As other men and women gathered a few paces behind the grey-haired wizard, he noted that many of them wore necklaces of coloured beads while some of the children had strings of polished stones knotted around their waists.

Risala had seen the same thing. 'Talismans?' she wondered, with a sideways glance at Kheda.

The skull-faced mage halted. One of the tree dwellers might just have been able to reach him with a particularly fine spear cast. The skull-wearer turned and beckoned to someone in his retinue. The women with the feathers in their mud-caked hair led burly savages dragging bound and bloodied captives out from the midst of the spearmen. They threw their prisoners onto the sand in front of the skull-faced mage, who called out something unintelligible to his tree-dwelling counterpart.

The mage in the bead cloak shrugged with evident un-concern as he made some reply. It was impossible to see the skull-faced wizard's reaction but the captives writhed in their bonds in frantic, futile efforts to free themselves.

'Here it comes,' Velindre breathed.

A sound like canvas torn in a storm filled the air. The sound of a dragon's wings.

'The source of Skull-Face's power.' Naldeth shivered with anticipation.

I should have brought that remnant of Shek Kul's powder with me. Cramming it down Dev's throat was the only thing that stopped him setting all of us alight when the fire dragon's aura overwhelmed him.

'Make sure you control your magic with the beast so close,' Kheda whispered fiercely, looking from Velindre to Naldeth. 'Or will I have to knock you senseless?'

'I'm all right.' Naldeth's brown eyes were uncannily bright nonetheless, irises tainted with a hint of redness.

The dried-up stream bed and the banks on either side shook as the skull-faced mage's vivid blue dragon landed just behind him.

'I should have been expecting this.' Velindre gritted her teeth, hugging her knees to her chest. She glared at a coil of dust spiralling up beside her and it promptly died.

The dragon was as long as any trireme that sailed Aldab-reshin waters. It stalked forward on long, elegant legs, mus-cular tail twitching and stirring up dust with the murderous spike at its tip. The thick scales on its back and flanks were midnight blue edged with vibrant azure. Smaller scales on its belly paled to the hazy lavender of a rainy-season sky threat-ening thunder, a shade echoed in the membranes of the vast wings it was carefully folding tight against its sides. Arching its serpentine neck, the dragon snapped a fearsome crest of sapphire spines erect. As it opened its mouth, it hissed with an unexpected softness that was somehow all the more menacing. Its head was long and pointed, its teeth glittering crystal blades. Its predator's eyes were the blue of a late-evening sky with pinpoints of white fire shining like stars at their centre.

More lightly built than the fire dragon that was the death of Dev. Vastly more alert than the simulacrum Velindre concocted. How dangerous is it? How dangerous is a wizard with that creature's power to call on?

Kheda glanced involuntarily at Velindre. The mage-woman was still sitting huddled, her eyes fixed on the cobalt dragon. Her ragged breath clouded in the stillness as if the air still held the chill of the dawn but Kheda was as hot as ever.

The skull-faced mage shouted something to his opponent in the beaded cloak. The grey-haired mage shrugged once again, his gesture dismissive. The blue dragon shifted its feet slightly, lethal sapphire talons digging into the sandy soil.

'Oh my,' murmured Naldeth.

A grating noise like the first warning of a landslip echoed around the valley. Kheda looked at the crag above the tree-dwellers' encampment expecting to see rocks tumbling from the heights. There was nothing to be seen. Then there was something there. He blinked, not trusting his own eyes, before looking at Risala. She didn't notice, transfixed as she stared up at the crag, her mouth half-open.

The shape of the outcrop had not altered. It was Kheda's perception that had changed, as if the harsh sound of stone against stone had somehow affected his eyes instead of his ears. Where he had seen dark stains trickling in meaningless patterns down the grey rock, now he saw the outlines of legs and a long, thick tail. Where the edge of the crag had been a random array of ragged stones silhouetted against the cerulean sky, now it was the curve of a dragon's spine, edged with regularly spaced razor-sharp scales. Shadows shifted to become a head rising up from a ledge. Kheda blinked again and the creature was transformed from a painted shape on the cliff to a living beast, not as long as the sky dragon but heavier, deeper in the chest and broader in the haunches.

It sprang down from its perch to land just behind the wild wizard with the gaudy cloak of beads. Its shining armoured hide was black as jet save for its underside where dark steely-grey scales offered no hint of vulnerability. Claws the colour of ancient unrusted iron dug into the stream bed as it crouched low. It snarled silently, showing metallic teeth like newly forged swords as its long black tongue tasted the air. Even the inside of its mouth was black. Against such darkness, the vibrant amber of its eyes was all the more striking. It glowered, spines bristling around its blunter, broader head, its unblinking gaze burning with golden fire.

No wonder these tree dwellers weren't worried about being attacked.

Risala reached for Kheda's hand, her grip crushing his fingers. Kheda looked hastily at Naldeth. The young mage was motionless, hands pressed to his face, mouth open in wonder. He glanced wide-eyed at Kheda. The warlord breathed a little more easily, seeing none of the dangerous thrall in the young mage's eyes that he had feared.

He looked back at Velindre. Her eyes were closed as she sat still hugging her knees, her jaw clenched. Strain deepened every line and wrinkle in her face, aging her cruelly. Moisture condensed out of the dry air to bead her short-cropped hair like cold crystals, trickling down her temples like sweat.

The wild wizard in the beaded cloak clapped his hands together. The black dragon reared upright on its hind legs and extended its wings. Sunlight flashed from silver membranes stretched between the black bones.

The sky dragon reared up to match it, the draught from its outspread wings sending clouds of dust boiling into the air. The skull-faced mage was unbothered. None of the dust came within arm's length of his own people. The bound captives thrown into the space between the two wizards weren't so fortunate. They writhed and coughed as sand blew all around them, filling their eyes and ears.

The beaded mage shouted angrily as the wind raised by the sky dragon's wings spread to set his people's tree-top dwellings swaying wildly. He raised his hand and the air around the platforms fell abruptly still. The black dragon sprang into the air with a brutal clap of its wings, swooping low over its opponent. It breathed an oily black mist at the blue dragon, which recoiled before leaping into flight itself. It spat white fog into the smoky stain on the air and the darkness dissipated, falling down to the earth. The skull-faced mage wheeled around, gesturing. He wasn't quite quick enough and black tendrils landed on two of his retinue. They fell choking to the sand, legs thrashing and hands clutching at their throats for an instant before being stilled in death.

The dragons didn't care. The blue flapped its mighty wings and soared higher. The black pursued it a little way and then fell sideways through the air, cutting a wide circle above the watching savages. Sand rose from the stream bed as the dragon passed overhead, trailing behind it. The dust coalesced into a glittering line cutting through the sky wherever the black dragon's tail flicked. The creature flexed its wings and rose to join the blue dragon, which had been carving lazy circles in the sky, spinning wisps of cloud out of nothingness.

The black dragon rolled backwards and lashed at the blue dragon with its tail. The shining trail of burning sand snapped like a whip and flung fiery droplets at the cloud dragon. It dodged deftly, though its skeins of cloud were thrown into disarray. Hissing, it spat white vapour at the burning drops, which promptly fell from the sky in a rain of hard black crystals.

The beaded mage's people stood their ground and jeered as the skull-faced wizard's retinue flinched and ducked, even though he threw handfuls of vivid blue fire to shatter the black stones. A wind sprang up from nowhere to send the fragments tumbling away through the air.

'It's using the sand to make glass,' said Naldeth excitedly.

'But they're not fighting like the other dragons did.' Risala watched intently, as much fascinated as afraid.

The black dragon swooped low over the stream bed again, looking up at the blue beast. The sky dragon began circling once more, drawing the tattered fragments of its clouds back together. Head outstretched on its long blue neck and tail thrust out behind it, its supple legs extended fore and aft. Suddenly it rolled sideways and curled up so that its pointed muzzle was almost touching the vicious spike tipping its tail. The clouds it had summoned followed obediently, spinning a wreath in the air that thickened and grew. The blue dragon twisted sharply away from the coiling vapours to leave a whirlwind gathering pace and substance as it sank to threaten the black beast.

The jet dragon waited, hovering like a hawk, all its attention on the menacing spiral of cloud. The trees lining the dry stream bed thrashed in the downdraught and this time the mage in the beaded cloak did nothing to still them. In the last instant before the whirlwind touched it, the black dragon shot straight up into the sky. Taloned feet drawn close to its body, its silvered wings ripped through the air so close to the whirlwind that it seemed impossible the cloud would not touch them. But it didn't and, darting up the dry valley, the black dragon rapidly outstripped the relentlessly pursuing whirlwind. The blue dragon went chasing after both its foe and its magic, shrieking furiously.

The black dragon stopped dead in midair before abruptly doubling back on itself to soar up over the whirlwind. Looking down, it breathed a shimmering grey smoke that fell into the heart of the spiral of cloud and melted it away like ice under the sun. The black dragon didn't pause to admire its success, wings pumping as it flew straight back down the valley. For a moment it looked as if it would collide head on with the blue dragon. At the last instant, it soared over its foe's back, head turning to breathe another noxious cloud down the length of its spine.

Slick greyness folded around the blue dragon. It yelped, head and tail whipping this way and that as it fought to escape the miasma coating it. The greyness dulled the blue dragon's vibrant colours, dragging it inexorably down towards the ground. It hissed, breathing white smoke down its own flanks to burn through the cloying murk. Just as it seemed as if the blue dragon must crash into the stream bed, it fought its way free of the clinging remnants. Turning its back on the skull-faced mage, it departed, the strong beats of its powerful wings ripping through the air.

The tree dwellers cheered loudly, with mockery in their laughter. The skull-faced wizard whirled around, his cloak of blue feathers swinging out wide behind him. The mage in the beaded cloak watched him depart with his retinue trailing behind him. The feather-crowned women hurried to catch him up, their shoulders hunched and heads hanging dispirited. The challengers made no attempt to take the hapless captives with them, still lying bound and half-choked with sand in the middle of the stream bed.

The black dragon landed in the dry channel with a resounding thud and looked steadily at the mage in the beaded cloak. The other tree dwellers fell prostrate on the ground, some hiding their heads in their cradling arms. The beaded mage sank slowly to his knees, not taking his eyes off the dragon.

The black beast crept towards the bound captives, steely belly low to the ground, mouth agape and black tongue tasting the air. The wild wizard shuffled backwards, his whole posture one of submission, though he still didn't take his eyes off the dragon for an instant.

The dragon snapped at the nearest captive, cutting the unfortunate in two with a single bite. The wild wizard continued retreating and now all the tree dwellers did the same, wriggling backwards through the dust on their knees and elbows. The dragon ate a second prisoner, turning its full attention to the task. The wild mage got warily to his feet and walked backwards to the shelter of the trees. Another captive died with a whimpering gurgle as the dragon hooked it closer with its lethal talons.

The tree dwellers scurried back to their settlement. Women emerged from the shadows, paying no heed to the slaughter continuing in the stream bed, going instead to check on their fire pit and resuming whatever tasks they had been about. A low murmur of voices drifted across the dry valley, and the occasional burst of relieved laughter, broken only by the gruesome crunching as the dragon continued feeding.

'The dragons didn't want to fight.' Naldeth was sweating profusely but his voice was steady.

'They wanted to see who was most powerful.' Velindre looked up, shivering uncontrollably. 'But they weren't about to risk serious injury to do it.'

'Are you all right?' Kheda reached for the mage-woman's shoulder. She was so cold to the touch that his fingers burned and he snatched them back. 'And what about the savage mages?'

'What about them?' Velindre's laugh had a hysterical edge. 'They have no power over those dragons. The beasts just know that where there are mages, there'll be easy meat. You have jungle cats in the Archipelago, don't you? They're quite happy to trail a hunting party and steal its kill if they can. It's less effort than hunting for themselves.'

'And as long as the wild mages can keep the dragons content with easy meat—' Naldeth's face twisted with distaste '—they have all the power of the dragons' auras to draw on for their own magic, for whatever their own purposes might be.'

'How can you be sure of this?' Risala looked from one wizard to the other.

'You felt it?' Velindre looked at Naldeth, half-shamefaced.

'Oh yes,' he assured her, a catch in his voice.

'You both held your own magic in check.' Kheda didn't know what else to say. 'That counts for something.'

'Where's the dragon?' asked Risala suddenly.

Kheda looked back to find the stream bed empty. 'Where did it go?'

All that was left of the erstwhile captives were gruesome tatters of crimson flesh and white bone amid dark, bloody stains on the sand.

'Naldeth—' Velindre began cautiously.

'It's not back up there.' He peered up at the crag beyond the platforms in the trees. 'But it's somewhere close. I can feel it.' He looked at Velindre, biting his lip. 'And it'll feel us if we move, I'm certain of that. It's on the alert in case that skull-faced mage comes back.'

Kheda looked out at the stream bed. Ridges and rocks teased him, mimicking the lines of the vanished beast before looking as innocent as they had done before. 'We can't hide here until some savage gathering wood trips over us.'

'Then brace yourself,' Velindre said with sudden decision.

White light blinded Kheda as the air crackled with the tinny odour of lightning. He gasped as dizzying enchantment swept all sensation away. He gritted his teeth until the light fled and he fell to his knees, still dazzled. He spread his

310

hands on the ground and felt hot, dry earth. Opening his eyes, he squinted at the unwelcome barrenness of the savages' island. There was no sign of the dry valley or the grassy plain they had visited, nor of the rocky bluff above the cave where the *Zaise* was safely hidden.

'Where are we?' he rasped, his mouth dry.

'I have no idea.' Fear equalled the chagrin in Velindre's answer.

Chapter 13

Kheda wheeled around in a slow, measured circle. He realised he was gripping his sword hilt so hard his knuckles ached and forced himself to slacken his fingers.

Losing my temper is not going to improve matters.

As his first furious impulse to berate Velindre subsided, he registered the sound of surf crashing on rocks and noticed the land falling precipitously away on their western side. The dusty rock beneath his feet was redder than the darker cliffs beyond the river mouth. 'We're still on the coast at least.'

'We passed by here earlier.' Naldeth's eyes were strangely vacant. 'Velindre, what went wrong with your spell?' He sounded simply curious rather than condemnatory.

'I drew the skeins of element around me easily enough,' she said thoughtfully, 'only the air twisted back out of my control and flung me away. Flung us all away to the south.' Her voice strengthened. 'I hadn't realised just how all-encompassing that blue dragon's influence would be. That's a useful lesson learned, if nothing else.'

Kheda bit back a sharp retort and scanned the unhelpful rocks for any familiar landmark. 'Are you saying the dragon wanted rid of us?'

'What about the black one?' Risala searched the sky. 'Is either of those dragons about to come sniffing after you?'

Naldeth stooped awkwardly to press a hand to the ground. 'I don't sense the earth dragon anywhere close.' He stood up, brushing his hands together. 'Velindre, were you more susceptible to the dragon's influence because the air is your element, or was it the spell that was vulnerable in itself, as a working with elemental air?'

'You can discuss your theories later,' Kheda said sharply. 'Velindre, is the blue dragon anywhere near?'

'No. It's headed inland.' Velindre gazed into the sere interior of the island where the wind scoured dull green land riven with dry gullies and backed by the crumpled flanks of copper-coloured mountains.

'You're certain?' Kheda demanded.

'Oh yes,' Velindre assured him, with the sensuous shiver of a woman surprised by a lover's caress. 'I can feel it.'

Disquieted, Kheda pulled the little ivory star circle out of his pocket. 'I'd say we're quite some way south of that river.'

'How long a walk is it back to the *Zaise*?' Risala looked to the north.

Kheda scowled at Velindre. 'Will that wild mage wearing the skull have been caught up in whatever this dragon did? Will he know you're here?'

'The dragon's humiliated and spoiling for a fight.' Velindre spoke slowly, still distracted. 'It failed in its challenge to the black dragon so it's circling its territory, to make sure no other rival is tempted to think it is weakened.'

'How many dragons are there here?' Risala couldn't hide her alarm.

Velindre looked puzzled. 'I can't be sure.'

Kheda was most concerned with the immediate threat. "Can you tell what this sky dragon is thinking?'

The magewoman struggled for the right words. 'I can feel the impulses driving it, through the resonance of the elements. It's a very odd sensation,' she added frankly.

'Why aren't they fighting each other?' Risala wanted to know. 'That's what you said dragons do. That's how we saved Chazen, by setting two dragons on each other.'

'It was enough for that black dragon to display his superior magic.' Naldeth plainly approved. 'He didn't have to risk bodily injury to prove himself stronger than the blue.'

'Like a matia?' Velindre was incredulous.

'A what?' Naldeth looked bemused.

'A small furry beast that hunts snakes,' Kheda explained. 'They never fight to wound each other, because a wounded matia will soon be dead and none of them want to risk that. The males chase each other up and down the biggest trees to prove who's the most agile.'

'And the most cunning,' continued Risala slowly. 'They aim to trap their rivals on some branch too high and exposed to offer escape. When the winner relents, the defeated one slinks off.'

'And sometimes the winner doesn't relent until an eagle has spotted the treed matia and plucked it off the branch to feed its chicks,' Kheda added.

'Which is considered a notable omen.' Risala looked at him, her expression bleak.

'But dragons aren't matia.' Velindre reached for her own flask and gulped down half her water. 'Let's not forget that.'

'True enough, but that black dragon was certainly out to defeat a rival.' Naldeth spoke with complete conviction.

'Will it see you two as a threat if we use magic to try to get back to the *Zaise*?' Kheda looked from Naldeth to Velindre. 'Will it find you out?'

'When the fire dragon came to Chazen, it hunted Dev like a hound on a ripe scent.' Risala plainly shared his concern. 'And it was looking to kill him, not just to prove it could work more impressive magic or chase him off.'

'Maybe fire dragons are different. Fire mages have a reputation for volatility, even if Naldeth here proves the rule by exception. Maybe it just didn't like Dev. He could be pretty objectionable when he put his mind to it.' Velindre's smile was a wry blend of pain and affection. 'All I can tell you is that blue dragon isn't the least bit interested in pursuing me.'

'I don't suppose you look much of a threat when it can snatch a simple translocation spell away from you so easily,' Naldeth commented incautiously.

'My instincts didn't wholly fail me,' retorted Velindre waspishly. 'We didn't land out on those reefs, did we?' She flicked a hand towards the lethal seas foaming beyond the cliff edge.

'Are we going back to the ship?' Risala took a drink and screwed the cap back on her water flask. 'Or somewhere else?'

'Can you use your magic to get us back to Chazen?' Kheda shoved the star circle in his pocket. 'You two could stay to try to fathom the mysteries of these dragons and these wild mages and then come to warn us if there's any sign of them taking to the ocean again.'

And what preparations would we make? What lies would I have to tell my allies to persuade them I'd seen portents foretelling such an attack?

'Let's see what I can see.' Velindre sounded oddly tense as she poured a little water into her empty palm and summoned up a mossy glow within it.

Kheda moved to her side. All he could see was a tangled mass of unfamiliar forest. 'Where's Itrac?'

'Never mind Itrac, that's not even Chazen.' Velindre's brows knotted as she passed her other hand over the uncommunicative puddle of water. The dark-green glow brightened to emerald radiance, obliterating the useless image. The magelight grew brighter in the shadow of Velindre's hand and then dissolved into sickly jade threads that wavered like weed in the water. Velindre cursed as the magical tension holding the water together snapped and the liquid dripped through her fingers to vanish into the thirsty ground.

Naldeth stared at the damp dust with disbelief. 'If she can't hold a scrying together, you don't want her risking your lives with a translocation.'

Kheda reluctantly set aside any thoughts of an immediate return to Chazen. 'What about just getting us back to the *Zaise*, so we don't have to skirt round that skull-faced mage or the tree dwellers and their dragon?'

'I was trying to scry out the *Zaise* that second time,' the magewoman said bitterly.

'What's happening?' Naldeth couldn't restrain his curiosity.

Kheda rounded on him before Velindre could answer. 'Can you try the necessary magics?'

'Me?' The young wizard stared at the warlord. 'My affinity's with fire and scrying's a water spell, so there's the antipathy—'

'Don't even try,' Velindre advised tartly. 'With the turmoil in the elements hereabouts, Hearth Master Kalion couldn't see further than those trees.'

'You don't know—' Naldeth began hotly.

'Then it seems we're walking back to the *Zaise*,' Risala interrupted with deliberate composure.

'Indeed.' Kheda took a moment to gather his thoughts.

This is no time for a quarrel. We can argue when we're back on the ship — where I'll tell Velindre she's to sail us at least as far east as she needs to be sure of sending me and Risala back home with her magic. We're not staying here if these mages can't keep us safe with their wizardry.

The others stood looking expectantly at him.

'We need shade and cover from unfriendly eyes.' Kheda pointed to the sparse greenery a little way inland. 'We're far too exposed on this cliff. But we had better stay alert for any sign of those murderous birds or worse.'

'You and I can do that.' Risala shot a stern glance at the wizards. 'You two keep watch for any dragon or wild mage.'

'I don't know how much daylight we have left.' Kheda started walking, the sun still uncomfortably hot on his back. 'I'm not sure we'll get back to the *Zaise* before dark.'

Risala followed close by his shoulder, her hacking blade held ready. The wizards followed a few paces back, Velindre curbing her long stride to match Naldeth's irregular gait.

At least this ground is hard enough for him to walk fairly easily.

Once they had crossed the open expanse of hard-packed ruddy soil, the dusty green proved not to be trees after all but a bizarre blend of thistly bushes and plants that thrust long fingers as thick as a man's arm into the air. They had no branches or side shoots; they were just stems densely covered with spine-tipped leaves that looked more like the scales of some lizard than the skin of any plant.

'There's cover, if not a lot of shade,' Kheda said bracingly to Risala.

She looked behind her to be sure the two wizards weren't lagging. 'We can hope no one's fool enough to come in among all these thorns just wearing a few scraps of hide.'

It was relatively easy to pick a path between the upthrust spikes and the desiccated thistle plants. The only obstacles were intermittent sprawls of pale yellowy-green plants with thick, succulent leaves studded with curling black thorns.

Kheda kept an eye on the broken line of the cliff edge away to his off hand. The sun sank steadily in the sky, and by the time the western sea took on the golden glow that promised sunset, they had reached a stretch of this strange spiny forest where brilliant scarlet blossoms dotted the scaly green stems. Tiny grey birds fluttered around the flowers, together with the largest butterflies Kheda had ever seen, yellow as sulphur.

'What was that?' Naldeth halted and whirled around, searching the lattice of green pillars casting long shadows across the dry ground. 'I heard footsteps,' he said with complete conviction.

Kheda strained his ears. In the distance he could hear the sea's ceaseless murmuring. Close at hand, at first the silence seemed utterly complete, as the onset of dusk vanquished the day's breezes. Gradually, he picked out the chirruping of some insect and the idle trills of the tiny grey birds flitting overhead from lofty bloom to lofty bloom, burying their long beaks in the flowers. Red scissor-tailed finches snapped incautious flies out of the air.

'Perhaps it was some animal,' he said at length.

'Hunting us?' Risala was still keeping a keen eye to the fore.

'Perhaps,' Kheda acknowledged readily, 'but we're hardly as defenceless as those savages.' He nodded to Naldeth. 'Draw your blade and keep watch behind us. But don't go rushing into the attack, and don't use magic unless something's about to bite your head off.'

'Or someone else's.' Naldeth unsheathed his hacking blade and gripped it resolutely.

Velindre looked up at the vivid evening sky. 'The dragon's still a good way away.'

'Both of them?' Risala's vigilance ahead wavered for a moment.

318

'I'd feel the black dragon coming anywhere close,' Naldeth reassured her. 'Fire and earth are sympathetic elements and given that creature's power—'

'We can discuss all this when we're safely back at the *Zaise*.' Kheda narrowed his eyes as he thought he saw some movement among the motionless forest of upthrust stems.

Was that some brush stirred by a breeze or some animal or just my eyes deceiving me?

He swapped his own hacking blade to his off hand and drew his sword. 'We move as quietly as we can. Sound will carry further than we can see once it gets dark.' He picked up the pace, Risala at his side.

'How are we going to cross that river in the dark?' she asked in a low tone.

'Without using magic?' He glanced at her and shrugged. 'I don't know. I don't even know if we'll get that far. It might be better to find some shelter on this side and cross at first light.'

'That skull-faced mage lives on this side of the river,' she reminded him.

He grimaced. 'And the black dragon lives on the far side, between us and the *Zaise*.'

'I take it we're not stopping for food?' Velindre was rummaging in the leather sack she was carrying. She handed Kheda a scrap of salted duck meat wrapped in stale saller bread.

He chewed it, finding his mouth too dry for comfort. 'We'll certainly have to look for water before long.'

'Will you look for omens at first light?' Risala asked with unexpected insistence. 'Please—'

'Kheda,' Naldeth warned from the rear, 'there's definitely something following us.'

'Quiet.' Velindre hushed him. 'Listen.'

319

A night breeze was rolling down from the hills inland. Faint yet unmistakable, Kheda heard heart-rending sobbing. 'Where is that coming from?' he breathed.

Velindre raised a hand, magelight no brighter than starshine flickering between her outspread fingers. 'Over there.' She pointed inland, not far off the line Kheda was estimating would take them back to the river.

'Do we head back towards the coast?' Risala looked towards the cliffs that were now a black rampart across the golden horizon.

As Kheda pondered their options, a scream tore through the silence, raw with anguish. Gooseflesh prickled down the back of the warlord's neck. 'Wait here while I scout ahead,' he ordered.

'With something creeping along behind us?' Naldeth shook his head. 'Not when you're the one with the sword and the skills to use it.'

The scream came again. Louder sobbing followed, ripe with panic.

'You might need more than a sword to deal with whatever or whoever's inflicting those agonies.' As Velindre closed her hand on her magic, a pale glow within her fingers showed she had not wholly quenched it.

Risala looked at Kheda, her eyes dark as the fading light muted everything to colourless shades of grey. 'I don't think we should split up.'

'Then stay close and stay quiet.' He began picking a careful path in the direction of the screaming.

Better to know what the danger might be and avoid it than leave such uncertainty at our backs.

He halted when he reached an unexpectedly wide sandy track. There was no doubting that this path had been trodden by countless men over many years. Kheda crouched low in the meagre shadow of a cluster of spiky plants and Risala and the two wizards followed suit. Beyond the open swathe of ground that had been cleared of even the smallest thistly plant, a crude barrier had been woven from thorny stems pulled down and lashed together with cords of twisted grass. The yellow-green fleshy plants grew thickly inside the fence.

Another shriek ripped the silence apart. A hubbub of pleading sounded shockingly close before it was cut short by a commanding shout.

No animal is inflicting these agonies, then, or at least, not a four-legged one. Isn't that all we need to know?

Kheda glanced at Velindre. 'Is that sky dragon anywhere close?'

She shook her head, mute.

Naldeth was peering back into the gloom behind them. 'Whatever's following us has no magic, I'm sure of that much.'

'We know what brutalities these savages are capable of.' Kheda looked at Risala. 'We don't need to see it again and we might still get to the river before we lose all the light if we keep moving.'

'But there's someone with magic out there.' Velindre pointed in the direction of the frantic weeping that was still tearing at their ears.

'That skull-faced mage or his women?' Kheda looked along the cleared path and tried to judge if it curved away from the sounds of torment.

That sky dragon wasn't the only one humiliated. Many a man would look to share such mortification around to take the sting out of it.

'Let's get well away before he feels a wizard's presence out here and comes looking for a fight.' Risala stood up in the same movement as Kheda.

Naldeth rose more slowly, gripping his hacking blade with both hands. The last rays of the sinking sun burnished his steel leg. 'So we let whoever is screaming just go on screaming until they die of it?'

'Give me one good reason why we should risk the same fate,' Kheda said curtly.

'A wizard is doing that.' Naldeth looked at Velindre. 'We came here to stop their abuses of magic.'

'A wizard with all the aura of a dragon to draw on,' she pointed out, not unsympathetic. 'How do we fight that?'

'It's not our concern,' Risala said roughly. 'They're savages. And your magic wasn't working as you wished earlier. Do you want to confront some wild mage and find yourself powerless?'

Naldeth stared at her, outraged yet unable to find the words to answer her.

'We came here to learn what this place means for Aldabreshi and mages alike.' Kheda forestalled him, voice low and forceful. 'Which means we must pick any fights carefully, when we've worked out as much of this puzzle as possible.'

Somewhere across the tangled barrier of spiny stems, ragged cheers were now drowning out the fading lamentation. Naldeth looked at Kheda, his mild face hard. 'I'm not sailing away until I know exactly what uses magic is being put to here.'

'We'll discuss it when we're back on the *Zaise*.' Kheda stepped out onto the open path and set a rapid pace towards the river. Disconcertingly, the land sloped upwards and the curious forest of upthrust stems and thistly plants fell back to leave a dry plateau dotted with the strangest trees Kheda had ever seen. Their squat brown trunks were three or four times the height of a man yet ten men would be hard pressed to link hands around the largest of them. Each was crowned with an incongruously small tangle of knotted branches twisted into fantastical shapes and topped with tousled twigs.

'Watch your step.' Kheda noticed hummocks dotting the bare sand that were too regular to be the work of wind or rain. 'Something's been digging here.'

He slowed to move cautiously from the cover of one massive trunk to the next, doing his best to look in all directions as tension pricked between his shoulder blades.

We're far too exposed.

'There's the river plain.' Risala pointed to a pallor beyond the edge of the open plateau and they heard the soft, welcome rustle of grasses.

Kheda realised they were on the bluff of high ground that reached out into the valley. The barren slope that the skull-faced mage had descended must be somewhere ahead.

A scream ripped through the dusk behind them, closer than the sounds of torment they had been trying to leave behind. Running footsteps slapped the hard-baked earth.

Kheda pressed his back against the swollen tree and cursed the thing for having no branches low enough that they might at least try to climb and hide out of sight. The Greater Moon was rising, now at its full and casting cold, unwelcome light on the events unfolding below. He slid down to crouch in the barrel-like tree's shadow.

Risala and I might escape notice but the wizards' pale skins and Velindre's yellow hair will show up like candles in the night.

He looked around to urge the mages to hide behind the tree. They weren't there.

Risala looked at him, white rimming her eyes. 'They just disappeared.'

The running feet reached the open expanse of the trees. Kheda crouched still lower, Risala on hands and knees beside him.

The fugitive was a girl on the brink of womanhood, long-legged and slender, wearing a scanty hide wrap. She dodged between the barrel trees, jumping over the treacherous hummocks. Threatening shouts pursued her. Men appeared and one flung a wooden spear. Narrowly missing the girl, it went skidding across the unyielding earth, coming perilously close to Kheda and Risala.

The girl fell headlong as if she had been poleaxed, not even putting out a hand to save herself. But she wasn't insensible. Kheda could see her struggling against invisible bonds.

Struck down by magic.

Whatever bound her was tightening. Her struggles grew more frantic and at the same time weaker. He could see her mouth opening, the cords of her throat taut as she screamed. No sound escaped whatever foul wizardry entangled her.

Her pursuers came closer and no such spell muted their jeering. Some carried stone-studded clubs and Kheda braced himself to see the unfortunate girl's brains dashed out. He felt Risala pressing close to his side.

To Kheda's surprise, the pursuers didn't touch the girl. After venting their scorn with unintelligible insults, they withdrew. The wizard with the cloak of blue feathers walked slowly through the mob of them, his women in faithful attendance two paces behind. The skull that formed the mage's mask shone red in the light of the handfuls of flame that his feather-crowned women held aloft, making black pits of the empty eye sockets. Turning, the wild mage said something, and Kheda saw that more people were being brought to witness whatever was planned for the girl.

Bold and arrogant, the wild warriors of the wizard's retinue forced the reluctant onlookers forward with clubs and their spears of fire-hardened wood. They sneered as their shoves provoked whimpers of distress from the hapless savages clad in scraps of animal hide. Women cowered, bare shoulders hunched, some seeking to protect their children in a vain embrace. One man pressed his hands to his face, trying to stifle his weeping. Tears spilled through his fingers, shining like blood in the unnatural red light of the magefire.

The girl had given up her helpless struggles. Dust swirled around her as she was lifted up by invisible strings, the skull-faced mage extending his hand to guide his spell. She hung in the air, her arms and legs limp and dangling, her head twisting this way and that in anguish. The wild mage flicked his hand and a waft of blue radiance tore her hide wrap away, revealing her undernourished nakedness. Two of the burly spearmen closest to the wizard let their weapons fall to the ground, eager anticipation on their faces. Now the skull-faced mage let the girl's hysterical sobbing be heard, stirring answering anguish among the onlookers. One of the warriors who was already unknotting his loincloth gave the nearest savage a back-handed slap to the face, chuckling as he did so.

The brute's laughter broke off as he looked down. A tree root had twisted up out of the bare earth and knotted itself around his ankle. As he looked up, mouth open in a surprised shout, a second wiry root snaked around his other leg, reaching up to his muscular thigh. With a snapping sound, more roots sprang up to tie all the girl's would-be assailants solidly to the ground. Blood dripped dark onto the pale sandy soil as merciless tendrils gouged into bare skin.

The skull-faced mage shouted angrily, the dead creature's horns lowered as his head whipped from side to side. A quivering hedge of roots surrounded him, barely held at bay by the sapphire fire flowing from his outstretched hand. The women with their crowns of feathers huddled behind him, holding their balls of scarlet magelight close to their chests.

The unarmed savages melted rapidly away with wails of distress and confusion. The skull-faced mage bellowed with outrage and flung one hand above his head. A spiteful wind flung sharp grit in the eyes of those trying to flee. Here and there, a discarded spear sprang up of its own volition to belabour their unprotected backs.

The cordon of wriggling roots immediately drew tighter around the wild mage. Grit and weapons alike fell to the ground. This time he had to thrust out both hands to hold the squirming tendrils just beyond arm's reach.

The girl fell to the ground, landing hard, a last moan jolted out of her. Two men ran to snatch her up. Flinging her arms over their shoulders, they hauled her away. Cringing as the skull-masked mage screamed his fury, nevertheless they didn't stop and vanished into the night.

The wild wizard snatched a ball of fire from one of the leather-crowned women. As he threw it at the roots hemming them in, the magelight turned from scarlet to cold blue-white. Magic crackled between the roots like lightning, instantly crisping the tendrils to black ash. Shooting outwards, claws of sapphire magelight flashed across the ground to rip away the roots holding his spearmen immobilised. Vicious burns in their tender flesh glistened in the moonlight but few dared cry out.

The unpleasant smell of singed skin and hair caught in Kheda's throat. He fought a desperate urge to cough, gripping his sword in one hand and his hacking blade in the other.

I've never needed a third hand so badly, so I could take tight hold of Risala. We'll have to make a run for it and let the wizards make shift for themselves. Let's just hope we can hide in the grasses without being eaten by a lizard.

Risala's fingers tightened on his shoulder. Her face was determined in the pitiless moonlight and he felt the tension quivering in every fibre of her. He braced himself, ready to spring up as he saw the wild mage turning this way and that, all his attention on the ground.

The wild mage's blue-black magic was burning newly emerging roots to carve dark lines in the pale ground. Kheda watched intently as the ominous blackness converged on one of the giant barrel trees, which burst into purplish flames, the leathery bark spitting and splitting. The wild mage yelled at his warriors, gesturing, and they converged on the burning tree.

One yelped as he skirted a sandy hummock and stumbled. He tried to stand up but the ground betrayed him. The sandy earth flowed away beneath his feet and new fissures opened up elsewhere in the dry expanse. Shouting their alarm, the spearmen dodged and sidestepped. Relentless, the crevices pursued them, gaping ever wider. The wild men were soon struggling in a slough of smothering sand, the solid ground retreating, always a step ahead of their plunging feet, out of reach of their flailing arms. The wild wizard screamed furiously, penned with his cowering women on a shrinking pedestal as the earth around them crumbled.

'Head for the river.' Velindre's dry voice whispered in Kheda's ear.

Slowly, carefully, Kheda retreated, Risala close by his side, their steps matching. Once the bulbous barrel tree was directly between them and the skull-faced mage, Kheda sheathed his sword and grabbed Risala's hand. They ran for the edge of the magic-racked plateau and slid down the scoured slope towards the dubious shelter of the rustling grasses. The tall blades were as vicious as they had been before. Kheda ignored the sting of new slices on his hands and face as he slashed a path through the vegetation, Risala pressed close behind him. He didn't stop until they reached the river.

'What now?' Risala gasped breathlessly.

'Shall we swim for it?' Kheda looked over the lip of the bank down to the mudflats below. A menacing shape

327

broached the water and for an instant the moonlight glistened on rugged scales.

Who knows what could be lurking in the rivers here to pull us down to drown and eat us.

'Follow me.' Naldeth walked stiff-legged out of a haze of crimson that vanished almost as soon as it appeared. He strode towards the central channel where the drought-stricken river still flowed deep. Mud surged up to meet his steps, banishing the water in a flurry of ripples.

Kheda followed, still holding Risala's hand and watching the river with lively suspicion. 'Where's Velindre?'

'Keeping our skull-faced friend busy with a sandstorm.' Naldeth hurried onwards.

Risala looked up into the star-studded night sky. 'What about the blue dragon?'

'There's been no sign of it.' Naldeth swallowed a tremor in his words.

Kheda glanced back over his shoulder to see the river washing away their footprints as the transitory bridge of enchanted sand melted away behind them. Movement caught his eye and he saw a shadowy shape moving in the grasses fringing the river bank. 'Who's that?'

'Not a mage,' Risala said with relief as no spell attacked them.

'Hurry up.' Velindre appeared on the far bank and offered Naldeth her hand. Thrusting his blades through his belt, Kheda hoisted Risala up and then scrambled up the crumbling bank himself.

Naldeth was staring back over the river. 'It's an old woman. She must have run the wrong way in the panic.'

'Let's get clear of here before that wizard sends his minions after us.' Kheda turned his attention to Velindre. 'Now that we know where we are, can you carry us back to the *Zaise*?'

'No wizard with any sense translocates himself or anyone else into a cave,' Velindre said reluctantly. 'Not with the risk of being entombed in solid rock.'

Kheda looked out at the black bulk of the rising land, the trees cutting a mysterious silhouette against the starry sky. 'Then we had better start walking and hope those tree dwellers are fast asleep.'

'And that black dragon.' Risala shot a questioning look at Naldeth.

He was still gazing at the figure on the far bank. 'She's all alone. If those spearmen don't kill her, she's prey for anything else hunting tonight.'

'Those spearmen won't cross the river without their mage, and his dragon for good measure,' Velindre stated with absolute certainty. 'That's the boundary of the blue dragon's territory, which makes it their border as well.'

'Come on.' Kheda gave Naldeth's shoulder a shove.

'In a moment.' The wizard shrugged him off. 'If the wild men won't cross the river, she'll be safer over here.'

He thrust a hand out towards the water and a narrow bridge of glistening mud rose out of the depths.

'You don't think the tree dwellers will just kill her out of hand?' Kheda objected.

'Or those vile birds,' said Risala with feeling.

The young wizard ignored them both, moving to stand clearly visible, beckoning to the hesitating figure on the far bank.

Slowly, the old woman lowered herself down onto the mud and hobbled towards them. She moved awkwardly, hunched over some precious burden, the moonlight silvering her grey hair.

'She can take her chances.' Kheda turned away before she had reached the middle of the river and thought back to the terrain he had seen earlier in this interminable day. 'Let's make for the edge of those twisted trees and hope those birds are roosting deeper in the forest. If we stick to the very edge of the higher ground, we should be able to cut across the bottom end of the tree-dwellers' valley. We'll go right to the sea and work our way up along the cliffs till we reach the *Zaise.*'

He hefted his hacking blade at an unnerving rustle deep in the dense grasses. A furred creature appeared, held startled in the moonlight as it crouched on all four limbs. Its snout was reminiscent of a hound's, yet it had long-fingered paws as if it lived in the trees and it was more catlike than dog in its lineaments. Before Kheda could decide what it was, it vanished into the darkness.

Like a loal, yet quite unlike. How many strange creatures live in this place?

Restraining the impulse to slice and force a path through the grass as quickly as possible, Kheda moved slowly and quietly, alert for any huge lizard lurking somnolent in the cool of the night. He could hear the harsh breathing of the others close behind him, and back beyond that some faint splashing from the river. Closing his ears to such distractions, he concentrated on the grassy plain ahead. He didn't let himself relax when they reached the sparse, spindly trees. Straining his eyes for any sign of the lethal birds, he went just far enough up the slope and into the woodland to gain a vantage over the plain and the river and the bank beyond.

'That old woman's following us.' Naldeth was trailing behind, looking over his shoulder.

'Forget her. There's someone over there.' Risala sank down as she pointed into the deceptive patterns of shade and moonlight beneath the blotched trunks of the trees.

Kheda realised they were closer than he had realised to the dry grass-choked gully where the birds had lain in wait for the hunters. 'I'd guess they're cave dwellers.'

'Come to watch the show,' Velindre murmured.

Kheda breathed a little easier as he realised she was right. The distant figures were all watching the commotion on the far side of the river. Several of the barrel trees up on the barren plateau were still burning with vivid purple flames while shouts and screams suggested that the wild mage was taking out his wrath on some unfortunates. In the meantime, his spearmen were beating noisy paths through the grassy plain to the river bank.

'Let's leave them to it.' Stooping uncomfortably, Kheda led the way stealthily in the direction of the unseen cliffs. The twisted woodland meandered along the margin of the grassy plain. He tried to see if any of the bigger trees were rising up in the darkness, to warn him they were approaching the tree-dwelling wizard's dry valley.

'Wait.' Naldeth startled him with a warning hand on his back. 'We woke the neighbours as well.'

'The dragon?' Kheda was torn between the urge to stand upright to see what lay ahead and a fervent desire to cower in the dirt.

'No,' Naldeth said slowly, 'but his favourite mage has come to see what's going on.'

'This way.' Velindre slid deeper into the spindly woodland. She found a shallow scrape in the ground and crouched down behind an inadequate barrier of the thick-leaved spiny plants. The others joined her.

'Where is he?' Kheda looked westwards along the edge of the trees. He soon made out a knot of people standing beneath a broad-canopied giant that marked the edge of the dry tributary valley. The mage in the beaded cloak stood a few paces in front of the rest, intent on the barrel trees burning in the distance.

'He'll know us for wizards if we move any closer,' Naldeth whispered. 'He probably felt my magic coming across the river,' he added apologetically.

'We couldn't have stayed on the far bank.' Kheda looked around the depression. 'We'll just have to stay here till he gets bored and goes back to bed.'

Does he have anything to do with the cave dwellers? If he sends any messenger to them, or they send word to him, whoever it is will be bound to see us. Unless Velindre uses her magic. But that will just alert the mage in the beaded cloak. So much for a simple day spent reconnoitring this land and then getting back to our boat unscathed.

'I'm more concerned with what might have made this place for its bed.' Risala shifted a clump of dried grass that lay flattened in the hollow and Kheda saw that something with frighteningly large claws had scraped deep furrows into the hard earth.

'We'll just have to deal with whatever it is if it turns up.' Kheda looked from side to side. 'They can't stand there watching all night, can they?'

'We'll just have to see.' Velindre tapped Risala on the shoulder. 'If we all sit facing outwards, we can lean on each other as we keep watch.'

The magewoman sat herself down to look inland along the tree line towards the unseen caves. Kheda settled himself to watch the softly swaying grasses while Risala stared into the gloom of the twisted woodland. Naldeth lowered himself awkwardly to the ground, vigilant in the direction of the tall tree and the mage with the beaded cloak.

The flames of the burning barrel trees eventually began to gutter. The shouts of the searching spearmen faded as they toiled back up the slope and disappeared beyond the bare plateau.

No one spoke. Kheda felt his own breathing slow and heard the inconsequential sounds of the night landscape for the first time. He looked up to gauge the progress of the moon past the fronds of the spindly trees and surprised himself with a yawn. After the long day's walk and the constant tension, he realised he was exhausted. Then he noted just how still Naldeth was sitting beside him, all his weight resting on Kheda's shoulder.

Has he fallen asleep? He had better not start snoring.

The young mage was still awake. 'We're being watched,' he said softly.

'What?' Velindre turned her head towards the plain.

'There.' Kheda focused on a dark shape lurking motionless behind the fringe of grasses. It hadn't been there before.

Risala twisted awkwardly to see. 'What is it?'

'It's more a question of who.' Kheda got slowly to his feet, letting his hacking blade hang loosely by his side. He spared a quick glance to either side and saw that both the tree dwellers and the men from the caves still had sentries keeping watch across the river.

Are we about to be betrayed to them?

The shape shifted and stepped onto the open ground at the edge of the grass. The moonlight showed them the old woman in her hide wrap. Close to, Kheda could see that her bare legs were no more than skin and bone and her grey hair was matted in filthy clumps. She would have been shorter than Risala if she had been standing upright. She was shorter still as she stooped over the bundle cradled in her skinny arms. She stood motionless, head cocked slightly to one side, her expression lost in shadow.

'I don't think she's about to attack us,' Risala said with reluctant compassion.

'She certainly has no magic.' Velindre's level tone never-theless betrayed her relief.

Kheda tensed as the old woman moved. All she did was lay her bundle down on the ground and knuckle her back in an eloquent gesture of weariness. She looked from side to side and then cocked her head at him again. Kheda didn't move. The old woman folded her arms across her meagre chest and thrust her head forward at him. Both wizards and Risala froze as she took a step forward. Surprising them all, she skirted nimbly around the sprawl of fleshy plants and vanished into the dark woodland.

'Where did she go?' snapped Velindre.

'Do you want to risk magic to find her?' Naldeth asked.

Risala was looking at the bundle on the bare earth. 'She left all her things.'

Or made us some offering, to try to buy her life?

'Let's just keep our ears open for a moment,' suggested Kheda.

All he could hear was the same idle night sounds as earlier. Kheda found he was too tense to sit down again. In between glances to check on the patiently watching savages hemming them in, he looked over his shoulder in the direction the old woman had gone.

For no reason he could have explained, he was more than half-expecting her to return. She did so, and sooner than he had anticipated. Hurrying on silent feet, she gathered up her belongings and looked expectantly at the four of them gathered close together in the shallow scrape. She jerked her head and walked back past the sprawl of fleshy plants. When they did not follow, she beckoned insistently, shifting her burden to one bony hip.

'She wants us to follow her,' Naldeth said cautiously.

'It could be a trap.' Risala was dubious.

'If she wanted to betray us, all she had to do was shout to those sentries.' Kheda stood slowly upright.

'Can we assume she wants to avoid them as well?' Velindre rose beside him. 'Where do you suppose she wants us to go?'

'There's only one way to find out, and we're none too safe here.' Kheda took a deep breath and walked up out of the hollow.

The old woman nodded vigorously and moved deeper into the trees, pausing to look back to make sure they were following. Kheda went first, Risala close behind him, Velindre and Naldeth spread out a little further back.

Kheda squinted as he saw the old woman heading un-erringly towards a solid darkness within the gloom. As they drew closer, he saw a low outcrop of grey stone sheltering a black hollow leading down into the earth.

That's surely too small to be some dragon's den.

He couldn't decide if he was reassured or not to see the old woman scramble down what was evidently a steeply sloping entrance.

'Are we going in there?' Risala sounded torn. 'Why do you suppose she's helping us?'

'I don't know,' Kheda admitted, 'but it doesn't sound as if there's anything in there eating her.' He looked around the inhospitable wood. 'That's a better hiding place than any we've found, and as long as we know where she is, she can't be betraying us.'

'I helped her. She's returning the favour. Come on.' Naldeth pushed past them both to clamber down awkwardly into the cavern.

Velindre shrugged and did the same.

'Go ahead.' Kheda nodded to Risala, making a last survey of the encroaching darkness before following her.

The entrance was even steeper than he had anticipated, a slick expanse of rock with some uncomfortably sharp ridges. Inside the darkness was absolute.

'Is this just a cave?' Kheda instantly regretted asking as both wizards kindled flames.

A blue-white feather danced on Velindre's upturned palm. 'It's remarkable,' she murmured.

'What does it mean?' Naldeth's magelight made a candle of his forefinger as he gazed around.

Risala was watching the old woman closely. 'She doesn't seem overly bothered by magic.'

'Just as long as it doesn't bring some wild wizard down on us,' Kheda said tersely. 'Is it safe for you to do that?'

'Don't worry.' Velindre chewed absently on her ragged thumbnail as she walked deeper into the darkness.

'It's only a tiny flame.' Naldeth followed her, the radiance nevertheless filling the cavern.

There wasn't much space between the walls of faceted grey rock and windblown leaves were scattered all along the floor. Kheda didn't have a chance to consider what vermin might be lurking among them: he was too astonished by the riot of colours splashed all around him.

'It's those birds.' Risala traced a wondering finger over a startlingly effective representation of the murderous fowl. It was drawn with just a few deft strokes of charcoal around natural bulges in the rock that shaped the body of the bird. Fingers dipped in some green pigment had been pressed against the stone to make surprisingly realistic feathers.

'And those armoured lizards.' Kheda picked out an ochre shape lurking in pale grass made by rapid scratches scored into the rock and through the picture.

'And a dragon.' Velindre slowly raised her hand and her magelight burned brighter to show a spur of stone thrusting down from the rocky roof. It had been skilfully shaped and painted to bring out the full likeness of the dragon's profile that some unknown artist had seen in the rock. It loomed over them, perhaps a quarter as long as the real thing, every scale painstakingly picked out with red pigment rubbed into the shallow grooves carved into the stone. The jaw was closed, the muzzle a bulbous protrusion, the spiny crest a fan of crevices.

The eye glinted and Kheda saw that a shard of crystal had been wedged into the rock there. Velindre stepped aside and as her magelight moved with her, the answering spark in the crystal eye shifted as if the beast were watching her. The shadows stirred and all the creatures on the walls shared an instant of illusory life with the dragon. Naldeth shivered and Kheda couldn't blame him. The effect was uncanny.

'Why did she bring us here?' the young mage wondered.

Kheda turned and saw that the old woman had gone. 'To trap us after all,' he spat.

He saw instantly that there was no other exit from the cave and leaped up the slope, sword ready as he scanned the darkness. He cursed again as he found himself all but night blind thanks to the magelight in the cave. A step whispered on the dry earth and he turned, blinking as his eyes struggled to adapt to the moonlight.

It was the old woman, clutching an armful of dry sticks to her bony chest. She looked at Kheda with wretched terror. Belatedly he recalled he had had to step over the old woman's pitiful bundle to reach the steep slope of the cave's entrance. He lowered his sword. She stepped closer, still tearfully apprehensive. Dumping the sticks on the ground, she took a hasty pace backwards, wrinkled chin quivering.

'What's she doing?' Risala was close behind him.

'Bringing firewood.' Kheda hesitated for a moment, then sheathed his sword and bent to gather up the scattered sticks.

He stepped aside and nodded towards the open cave mouth. 'Offer her your hand. Let's get her inside.'

'You're sure about this?' Risala still had her doubts.

'We came all this way to find out more about these people,' Kheda reminded her.

The old woman watched them warily as they spoke. When they fell silent, she stooped awkwardly to pick up a stick that Kheda had missed and offered it to him, her hand shaking.

'Come on.' Kheda added the stick to his armful and smiled pointedly at Risala.

She pursed her mouth but held out her hand to the old woman, who walked hesitantly towards her. Kheda took a last look around at the shadowy night before following them back into the cave. Once inside, the old woman took the firewood off him and squatted down to build a neat lattice on a ledge at the foot of the slope.

'Can we risk a fire?' He noted black stains that suggested the stone had been used as a hearth before. Close to, he also noticed that the old woman had a distinct odour, mostly thanks to the hide wrap she wore, and to whatever was matted into her hair.

At least she doesn't smell of any fever or incontinence that would threaten us with some illness.

'How is she going to light that?' Risala was watching the old woman askance.

'Are you sure she has no magic?' As Kheda turned to ask Naldeth, the old woman stood up stiffly and walked towards the young mage. He and Velindre both stiffened. Velindre had set her magelight clinging to the rock wall just in front of the painted dragon and the pale flame flared azure.

The old woman gently took Naldeth's hand, tugging at him. He followed her obediently to the hearth, mystified yet

338

willing to cooperate. The old woman pulled his hand forward and thrust his fingers into the sticks.

Kheda saw unmistakable exasperation in her eyes. 'She wants you to light it.'

Naldeth smiled at her and looked at the others. 'I can keep the elemental aspects confined within the cave without anyone being the wiser.'

'What about the light?' Kheda asked. 'A savage need not be a mage to have eyes in his head.'

'It won't leave the cave,' Naldeth assured him.

Kheda wavered for a moment, then nodded. 'Very well, then.'

Naldeth smiled briefly as he gently removed the old woman's insistent hand from his wrist. Snapping his fingers, he dropped a scarlet flame into the dry twigs. They crackled and the fire rapidly shifted from the scarlet of sorcery to a reassuringly natural gold.

'Do you think we dare sleep now?' Velindre yawned and Naldeth couldn't help but do the same.

'You two can try. We'll keep watch, or I will, if you're exhausted.' Kheda glanced belatedly at Risala.

She managed a thin smile. 'We can sleep when we're on the *Zaise*.'

'Are we taking her back to the ship with us?' Naldeth studied the old woman, who was sitting quietly by the fire, one hand on her bundle, studying the painted walls of the cave. Her expression veered from awe to fear and back again.

'We'll discuss that in the morning.' Now there was firelight to see by, Kheda realised the outer layer of the woman's bundle was a furred and spotted hide faded to a dun between grey and brown.

Not from any beast we've seen so far. Which isn't all that surprising, given that we've not exactly been on a hunting trip. I wonder if the furry beast is predator or prey?

His stomach rumbled with protest at the thought of food. Risala came to sit beside him and tugged her leather sack open. 'Has anyone got any food left?'

'I have a few pieces of saller bread.' Naldeth looked surprised as he investigated the bag Risala had given him before they left the *Zaise*. 'And some meat.'

'Share it out.' Kheda saw the old woman watching with open curiosity. 'Give her some as well.'

'What do you suppose she wants with us?' Velindre accepted her meagre share and sat leaning against the cave wall.

'How are we going to ask her?' wondered Naldeth. He tore a piece of saller bread in half and chewed on his own portion as he offered the rest to the old woman.

'I don't know.' Kheda watched her turn it this way and that, furrowed brow creasing further with bemusement.

She sniffed at it and tried to take a bite. As she opened her mouth, they all saw she was lacking a significant number of teeth on one side of her upper jaw.

'She can't chew that.' Exasperated, Risala shook her flask to attract the old woman's attention and unscrewed the cap to drip a little water onto her own saller bread. 'It's softer this way,' she explained as she bit into it with an exaggerated smile.

The old woman cocked her head on one side and held out her piece of bread. Risala wetted it for her and she tried again. A faint smile deepened the wrinkles on her fleshless face as she evidently found the bread more palatable.

Kheda swallowed the last of his own bread with difficulty. 'Is there any magic you can use to make her understand our tongue?'

'Us?' Unexpected pain twisted Naldeth's face. 'No, we—'

'Elemental magic can't do things like that.' Velindre spoke over him sufficiently hastily to pique Kheda's curiosity.

Is there something you're not telling me? Or do you just want to avoid discussing another instance where all your vaunted powers can't actually solve a problem at hand?

Kheda turned his attention to the old woman, who was steadily chewing the stubborn saller bread. He saw her dark beady eyes slide from Velindre to study him with new frankness. The warlord found himself intrigued.

'What do you want with us?' He tried to put his question into his tone, raising his eyebrows and spreading out his hands in supplication.

The old woman narrowed her eyes, considering him thoughtfully. After a couple of abortive gestures that conveyed nothing to Kheda, she reached for a stick of firewood waiting beside the little blaze. Gnarled knuckles tightening, she snapped it clean in two and set the pieces down on the floor.

'What does that mean?' Naldeth wondered, perplexed.

The old woman silenced him with a peremptory wave of her hand and carefully counted out five more sticks. Looking at Kheda, to be sure he was paying attention, she picked them all up and, with an exaggerated lift of her elbows, tried to snap the entire handful at once. Laying the sticks down carefully next to the one she had already snapped, she folded her thin arms and looked expectantly at Kheda.

He rubbed his beard. 'Do you suppose she knows she's vulnerable alone and that there's strength in numbers?'

341

'It's difficult to think what else she could mean.' Risala handed the old woman a strip of the dried duck meat Naldeth had found in the depths of his bag. 'And she doesn't look stupid.'

'I don't think any of these savages are necessarily slow-witted.' The young wizard surveyed the intricate artwork decorating the cavern thoughtfully.

'But why has she thrown in her lot with us?' Risala looked troubled. 'Where did she come from?'

'Would you throw yourself on the mercy of that villain wearing the skull mask?' retorted Velindre.

'Especially when you're old enough to qualify as dragon fodder,' Kheda agreed with distaste.

'She knows we're wizards.' Naldeth picked a dark shred from between his teeth. 'She must have seen us take on the skull-faced mage. She saw us beat him. She must think we're a fair bet.'

I'd nearly forgotten about that little display of yours. Thank you for reminding me, Naldeth.

'Just what did you two think you were doing back there?' Kheda demanded abruptly.

'Besides saving some innocent girl from being raped or worse?' Naldeth was wholly unrepentant.

'And making sure that villain and his brutes were sufficiently distracted not to stop us escaping,' added Velindre tartly.

'Will he come after us when it gets light?' Risala shivered even though the fire now had the cave cosy and warm.

'Let him,' scoffed Naldeth. 'There's no subtlety to his magic, no sophistication, no true understanding. In Hadrumal he'd be no more threat than some buffoon at a masquerade.'

Kheda was stung. 'We're not in Hadrumal, wherever that may be, and he has a sky dragon's power to call on. These people wrought havoc in Chazen with their crude magics.'

'Only until you had magic to counter them.' Naldeth sounded incautiously patronising.

Fatigue tripped Kheda into an ill-tempered response. 'That masked wizard couldn't brutalise these people without magic. Everything I see here tells me Archipelagan suspicions of mages are more than justified.'

'It's not a question of magic,' Velindre broke in before Naldeth could snap back. 'It's a question of power, Kheda. I'll grant you magic gives that rogue his power, and sustains it, just as long as everyone else is too cowed to club him over the head some night when he's sleeping. But the magic is just the tool he misuses. There are warlords in the Archipelago who rule through fear and violence and they don't need wizardry to accomplish that, just the strong arms and sharp blades of their swordsmen.'

'What about Ulla Safar?' challenged Naldeth. 'And I saw as bad as him and worse sailing the Archipelago with Velindre.'

Kheda stared at him. 'There's no comparison and you know it.'

Naldeth was unrepentant. 'At least we wizards curb our own if they abuse our common birthright. The Archmage and the Council of Hadrumal keep a very close eye on any wizard who shows signs of straying down perilous paths.'

'They know you're here, do they?' Kheda retorted. 'Looking for some arcane knowledge to elevate your standing among your peers? Don't pretend you have no interest in power.' He shot an accusing look at Velindre. 'Dev told me you had ambitions to higher rank among your peers. Any benefit to the Archipelago last year was an incidental dividend as long as your curiosity about dragons was satisfied.'

'Dev didn't know all he claimed.' The magewoman's tight expression suggested the contrary. 'And holding rank among the wizards of Hadrumal is a far cry from imposing this kind of magical tyranny.'

'What are we going to do about that wild wizard?' Naldeth turned to her. 'I don't relish the thought of standing before the Council and telling them we hid in a cave until we could run away from him.'

'Kill that sky dragon,' Risala said bluntly. 'You summoned up a false dragon to fight the fire dragon that attacked the Archipelago. If you think that savage mage is no more than a fool in a mask without its power behind his magic'

'No.' Velindre refused absolutely. 'These dragons aren't evil, whatever your Aldabreshin superstitions might say. They're animals, even if elemental affinities make them magical. All they want to do is to thrive and survive and leave their young to come after them. It's not their fault if these savages have allowed these mages to subjugate them—'

'You think they had a choice?' Kheda waved towards the old woman and was startled to see she had laid her head on her bundle and quietly gone to sleep. Refusing to be distracted, he returned to the argument. 'Facing fire and lightning with bare hands and stone knives? What about that girl who was caught in his spell's clutches?' Kheda turned to Naldeth. 'How should she have fought back?'

'This is getting us nowhere and it's late,' Risala interrupted with sudden weariness. 'There's nothing we can do until the morning. Savage or not, she's got the right idea.' She nodded towards the old woman, who was now sleeping peacefully, curled up like a child.

Naldeth wasn't about to let the argument go. 'What you have to understand about wizardry is—'

344

'Just hush.' Velindre had lost her taste for debate the same as Risala. 'Go to sleep, Naldeth, or you'll be in no fit state to do anything useful tomorrow.'

The younger mage's chin jutted belligerently, though he didn't say anything further. He settled himself against the wall as best he could and shut his eyes with a huff of irritation.

Velindre sighed and her eyelids closed, her angular face softened just a little by the sinking firelight.

Kheda was still too exasperated to think of sleep. 'I'm going to find more firewood.'

Risala nodded resignedly. 'Don't go too far.'

'I won't.' Kheda scrambled up the steep slope towards the entrance. Out in the dark night, the breeze was chill after the warmth of the cave.

This whole day has just lurched from confusion to chaos time and again. Why did I ever come on this voyage? What are we going to do? What are we going to do with that old woman? What if we have to make a run for it, to escape that wizard in the beaded cloak or anyone else on this side of the river? Do we abandon her to her fate? If we don't, is she going to be the death of us, deliberately or all unwitting? And Risala expects me to find the answers in the heavens.

He looked up angrily at the blithely twinkling stars.

345

Chapter 14

When she woke, the old woman had no notion where she was. The walls of the painted cave were a meaningless blur in the half-light, while the smell of old wood smoke stirred confused memories of the village she had left behind. Then someone close at hand stirred and murmured, the sound like a brooding bird.

Stealthily, she rubbed her eyes to wipe away the stickiness of morning. As her vision cleared, she looked covertly around, bony fingers clutching her bundle of precious possessions. Satisfied that the strangers were all still asleep, she sat slowly upright, biting her lip against pain and stiffness. Moaning would bring no relief and might wake the strangers.

So they hadn't been some fever dream as she lay senseless somewhere, her only hope that she would be wholly dead before scavengers found her. Who were they? Where had they come from?

She studied the two closest at hand. The girl was lying on her side, her knees drawn up like a child. The man was slumped against a ridge of stone running down from the roof to the floor of the cave, one hand protectively resting on the sleeping girl's shoulder.

The old woman reached out, careful not to touch the sleeping girl, though. She saw that the skin on her own arm was only a little darker. The girl's flesh had all the silkiness of youth and good feeding while the old woman had long been half-starved, but they were not so different. Apart from the girl's hair. Short as it was, the old woman could see it was as straight as falling water. She ran an unconscious hand over her own tight-curled, matted locks.

Quite the strangest thing about the girl was her garb. The old woman risked a feather-light touch on a fold of the loose stuff that covered the girl's arms and body. It wasn't hide, of that much the old woman was certain. Looking more closely, she concluded it was somehow akin to the ropes everyone twisted out of grass and tree bark, but try as she might, she couldn't imagine how the two things were related.

She gazed at the garb. The most wonderful thing about it was the colour. It was the pink of a sunrise sky or a cliff-bird's breast feathers, and patterned with silver leaves. It was the most beautiful thing she had ever seen. Not even the most favoured women of the most successful hunters had ever had anything so glorious to wear.

The man stirred in his sleep and the old woman hastily withdrew to crouch beside her bundle, feigning sleep. She didn't hear him wake, so she opened her eyes again and studied him. His skin was a familiar hue but he had hair as brown as a tree scurrier's, even if it curled as tightly as her own. She recalled the reddish-brown tint that sometimes appeared in children's hair when the end of a long dry season left them with swollen bellies and shrunken limbs, their cheeks hollowed by hunger. But like the girl, this man was straight-limbed and well fed and showed no sign of having ever gone hungry.

The old woman looked at the man's long knives, hidden in their hide casings. Whatever were they made of, that could be crafted into so long and narrow a blade? A momentary pang surprised her. The old man would have been fascinated by these people and their strange knives.

As the strangers slept on, the old woman shifted to sit cross-legged and considered the other two newcomers. She had never seen anyone like either of them.

The older one, with the golden hair and light-brown skin, was fast asleep in a niche, knees drawn up and head uncomfortably canted to rest on one shoulder. The face was softened in sleep and lacked any hint of a beard, so the old woman concluded this one was most probably a woman, despite her lack of curves at breast or thigh.

She clenched her hand tight against the desire to creep over and touch the golden stranger's hair. It was as straight as the dark-skinned girl's but cut shorter still. Would it feel like the pelt of some animal or like the sun-dried grass it so closely resembled? What lay beneath the stranger's dusty garb? The old woman could see the brown skin end and creamy pallor begin where the fibrous stuff the stranger wore had slipped awry around her neck. Was she parti-coloured like some lizard? Did she have stripes or patterns beneath her strange garments?

The other man — and he plainly was a man, judging by the stubble shadowing his jaw — was as much of a puzzle as the golden stranger. His hair was the brown of leaves at the end of the dry season, his skin a sandy colour with an underlying reddish cast on his nose and forehead. Had he come from the same place as the golden stranger? Where could that be?

They were evidently both painted people with all the power that implied. The old woman watched them sleep on. There was no point in being afraid of them now. They could have killed her last night if they had chosen to. They could just have left her on the other side of the river to take her chances between the lizards and the followers of that painted man with the horned skull. Instead, they had helped her cross over the river. They had even invited her to share the cave's shelter instead of killing her there and then for profaning it.

Why had they done that? Were they keeping her to make an offering of her? Much good it would do them. There wasn't enough flesh on her bones to impress a beast, not if she was offered up alone.

She debated whether or not she should creep away while they were all still asleep. But if she ran away, she still risked being captured by the followers of the painted man with the horned skull. Or by those other people she had seen last night. The skull wearer evidently didn't rule everyone in this valley. No, she concluded, leaving was just too dangerous a prospect.

On the other hand, if she stayed, just possibly, these painted strangers might protect her, for a little while at least. She had made herself useful to them, even if it was only by bringing them firewood. Everyone knew that painted men showed most consideration to those who made themselves useful or held precious knowledge. Besides, now they knew her, they would find her if she ran away. Everyone knew there was no escaping a painted man's power.

She frowned as she considered a new puzzle. She had found this cave easily enough, even in the dark. The moonlight had shone on the scores cut into the trees and on the arrangements of stones that warned of its presence. Since her life was forfeit to whoever caught her anyway, and she had hidden in other painted caves on her wanderings without her skin catching fire to melt the flesh from her bones, she had been ready to risk it again, to escape a night so full of dread.

Yet all the while the strangers had been huddling like addled children in some terrible lizard's scrape, even after

349

they had attacked the skull wearer, after they had humiliated him in front of his followers and the local people. They hadn't shown themselves to claim their victory, nor asserted their authority over this place and any who dwelt there. They hadn't killed the skull wearer nor yet challenged him to yield to their greater power and serve them instead. They had just run away and hadn't even been able to find this sanctuary for their kind.

But then, wherever they had come from must be further away than she could imagine. They didn't understand her words and she certainly could make no sense of their tongue. Their talk sounded like the evening birds chattering back and forth in the depths of the green forest.

The old woman rubbed a thoughtful hand around the back of her neck. Why had she returned and shown them the way to the cave? Perhaps they wouldn't have bothered pursuing her if she had just disappeared into the night. But there had been so many terrors out there in the darkness. Well, the old man had always told her there was no point in regrets. They had helped her cross the river and that meant she should help them, if she could. Because the gratitude of a painted man had a value beyond reckoning in an ordinary life, never mind when you were caught in an ominous valley where a river separated two painted men's territories.

Had they come to drive out both painted men and seize the valley for themselves? There was no doubt that these strangers were painted people. She had seen them kindle coloured light and set tree roots and the ground itself against the skull wearer. The reddish-skinned man had summoned flame out of the empty air to light the firewood. They had the power even if they wore none of the usual adornments to declare it. Unless that was what the reddish stranger's peculiar shining leg was. The old woman looked at that for a while, utterly mystified.

350

Some while later, she looked back at the other man, the dark-skinned one with the brilliant knives. She'd seen no sign of him using a painted man's power. Or the girl in the soft pink garb. Yet the golden stranger and the reddish one both followed this man's lead.

Well, he did hold the most lethal weapons she had ever seen. How many men had he killed or beaten into bloody submission in their unknown homeland? How many would a warrior have to kill to establish such authority over two painted ones?

Reluctant to pursue that notion, the old woman looked at the black-haired girl. She had kept close to the tall man as he had led them all the long way through the spine thickets and down to the grassy plain. Even in sleep they were close together. The girl must be his woman, she concluded. Not the golden stranger, though. There was no hint of such close-ness in the way the two of them had dealt with each other. Or in the way the golden stranger and the reddish one had behaved. They weren't mated, she was sure of that.

Where was their blue raft? This new question struck her with the force of a blow. She hadn't expected to see them again after they had floated away ahead of her up the coast. She had only been concerned with escaping the followers she expected would come after them. But there had been no sign of followers, and now there was no sign of the blue raft. They had been walking through the spine thickets when she had seen them in the distance.

She sighed. Why had she given in to the curiosity that had drawn her to follow them? Why hadn't she gone back to the headland and the emptiness where she had lived unbothered by anyone? It had been an unpleasant surprise to discover that the skull-wearer's territory had been so close, but she hadn't seen his people before. Now he and all his followers and that wide river besides lay between her and that barren coast. And his quarrel with these strangers would only be ended when someone was dead.

Could she possibly get back to her headland without being caught if she abandoned these strangers before they woke? She sighed again. No, she really didn't think so. How would she cross the river?

The old woman rose slowly to her feet and hobbled up the awkward slope, her back aching. Her bladder was uncomfortably full and she was hungry and thirsty. Outside in the dawn cool she relished the fresh scent of the dewy air. Birds twittered in the trees, no cries of alarm ripping through the skeins of mist to warn her of some lurking predator. All the same, she went a prudent distance from the painted cave before she made a scrape in a drift of leaf litter with one foot and relieved herself. She kicked leaves back over the dampness, still looking warily around.

Noticing a clump of familiar leaves, she cursed herself for a fool as she realised she'd left her digging stick and her stone blade back in the cave. She knelt, and tried and failed to dig with her hands, then looked around for some scrap of wood to help her break the hard, dry earth. Movement caught her eye and she froze. But it wasn't some terrible lizard tasting the scent of her urine on the air. The tall man and his woman had woken and were standing by the cave entrance. They went a short distance to relieve themselves as she had done, each keeping watch for the other. Then they walked a little way from the cave, looking around. Looking for her.

The old woman sat back on her heels, motionless. There was another puzzle. These people must eat. They had carried food with them, strange as it was. Now the man was looking around hungrily while the girl was peering into her empty bag with a foolish expression. Didn't they realise they were standing under green-nut trees?

Or were they expecting her to forage for them? Perhaps that was it. Perhaps that was why they had let her live. Without whatever followers they must surely have back in their distant homeland, who else was there to bring them food and water?

But she couldn't dig with her empty hands. The old woman made a sudden decision and beckoned to them, her smile beseeching. As they approached, the tall man smiled back, though the girl still looked less friendly, quietly saying something in her fluting voice.

The old woman pointed down at the dark spotted leaves and made a digging motion with both hands. She gazed at the tall man, willing him to understand her. He nodded slowly and drew one of his great knives out of its covering. It was as long as his forearm and as wide as his hand and the old woman marvelled at the way it shone like water. More importantly, it bit into the dry earth as readily as any blackstone blade.

He soon uncovered a cluster of the plant's swollen purple roots and, producing a smaller knife of the same shiny stuff, deftly cut one free. Holding it to his open mouth without biting into it, he looked up at the old woman, his face questioning. She shook her head firmly and reached out to tap the curious shiny gourd the girl carried slung from one shoulder.

The girl stiffened for a moment, then slowly unslung the gourd and unsealed it, setting it down on the ground. The old woman was momentarily distracted by the marvellous strangeness of the way she took off a piece that had seemed to be part of the whole. Then she realised the tall man was still kneeling there, looking quite addled as he held up the purple root. Carefully she took the root from him and, emboldened, reached for his pale knife. Concern creasing his brow, he pretended to touch the edge before snatching away his finger with an exaggerated show of pain. Then, his expression still warning her, he let her take it.

Amused, the old woman carefully took the strange pale knife and sliced into the purple root. The water the plant had so carefully hoarded trickled into the mouth of the gourd. The tall man said something, smiling like a child delighted by some elder's fireside trick.

The old woman couldn't help herself and laughed. He grinned at her, then his face turned serious as he took the gourd and sniffed carefully at it. He sipped cautiously, holding the water in his mouth to make sure it was good before swallowing.

So he did possess foraging skills, even if he had the status not to have to use them. The old woman dug up more of the swollen roots with the pale knife and emptied their water into the gourd. The tall man and the girl stood watching her. When she was done, the tall man took his pale knife back and knelt to carefully cut a few more of the roots free. He deftly sliced the end off one and handed it to her so she could drink before doing the same for his woman and quenching his own thirst with another.

The girl was still looking askance at her, which momentarily irritated the old woman. She handed her the half-full gourd and went to look for any nuts that the birds or lizards or whoever else lived in this valley might have left among the dusty green leaves of the trees. The tall man and the girl followed her, though this late in the dry season she had to search three different trees before she spied reddish husks hiding behind a thick clump of leaves. She twisted the cluster of nuts free with a grunt of effort.

The tall man and the girl were still watching her with the uncomplicated curiosity of children. The old woman took one of the girl's hands and filled it with the nuts. Taking one of the ripest, she carefully widened the split in the shell with her fingernails to reveal the green kernel within. Snapping the nut open, she plucked out the meat and ate it, looking the girl steadily in the eye all the while.

354

The girl gingerly cracked open one of the nuts and nibbled cautiously at the green kernel. Looking oddly thoughtful, she said something to the tall man. He came and ate a nut, frowning. The old woman waited, apprehensive, until the tall man's face cleared. She smiled hopefully and tugged at the hide sack the girl carried. The girl didn't surrender it and the old woman braced herself for some blow or rebuke. But instead the girl simply opened the sack herself and turned her attention to the trees, rapidly twisting free whatever nut clusters she could find and dropping them inside. The tall man startled the old woman by reaching up to branches too high for her and the girl and pulling down some nut clusters himself. He didn't even eat them, handing them to the girl instead so she could put them in her leather sack.

The old woman began filling a fold of her hide wrap with red shells. Vigilant for any hint of danger as she did so, she saw the tall man was keeping a similar watch as he set about cutting a stout twig from a nut tree with his pale knife. He took a length of cord from some fold in his strange garb and as he twisted a deft noose, the old woman realised he was making a snare.

She watched him trace the faint score of some trail along the hard ground and kneel to tie his snare to a frail nut-tree sapling barely clinging to life in hopes of rain coming soon. He split the stick to hold the noose loosely above the run and, looking up, caught the old woman watching him. He grinned, his shrug eloquent. He didn't know if he was going to catch anything but he thought it was worth a try.

He stood up, still watchful for anything stirring in the early-morning cool. The old woman wasn't worried; the birds were still chattering peaceably among themselves. The girl said something and headed back to the painted cave, sack of nuts in one hand, shiny gourd in the other. The tall man followed her, ushering the old woman ahead of him, still diligently keeping watch.

She had no choice but to obey. She slid a sideways glance at the tall man and wondered if he was kind to the girl. He was certainly a man of puzzles and contradictions. He was a hunter — he'd proved as much setting that snare — and those remarkable long knives he carried must surely signify some notable status. He was no painted man, yet the paler-skinned painted man and woman yielded to his authority. But he hadn't claimed whatever first share he felt entitled to from the root water or the nuts and had shown no fear of undermining his standing by gathering such humble food.

They returned to the cave and the old woman watched the girl pour the nuts they had gathered out onto the rocky floor and begin dividing them. She realised with growing astonishment that the girl was making five equal shares.

Chapter 15

'Do you think you'll catch anything in that snare?' Risala sounded sceptical.

Velindre stirred at the sound of her voice, though Naldeth was still fast asleep.

'Our friend here didn't pull it up and scowl at me for a fool. I rather think she would have if she reckoned I was wasting my time.' Despite their perilous situation, Kheda found that the notion amused him.

Risala didn't smile. 'What are we going to do with her?'

'I don't know.' Kheda considered the old woman, who smiled hesitantly back at him. 'But as long as she's with us, she can't be telling some wild mage where we are.'

'You don't think you should go out and look for some signs to guide us now it's light?' Risala flung a worm-eaten nut away with some venom. 'That skull-wearer will send his spearmen out to hunt down whoever spoiled their sport last night soon enough.'

Do you mean signs of local wild men or signs and portents in the skies and the earthly compass?

Velindre saved Kheda from having to answer as she opened her eyes and yawned. She sat up abruptly as she reg-

357

istered the daylight slipping down the cave entrance, digging her fingers into her stiff neck. 'I thought we were going to try to get back to the *Zaise* before dawn.'

'You needed to sleep yourselves out.' Kheda was unrepentant. 'I learned from Dev not to risk encountering any magic-wielding enemy with a half-exhausted wizard at my side.'

Their voices roused the younger mage. He moved sleepily before coming fully awake and instinctively clutching at his stump. 'Ah, cowshit and cockleshells.'

Kheda saw pain carving a deep cleft between the mage's brows. 'Let me have a look at your leg.'

'It'll be alright.' Naldeth spoke through clenched teeth.

'He's a healer,' Velindre said acerbically. 'Let him see it.'

'You can help me shell breakfast.' Risala tossed another rejected nut into the depths of the cave.

'My pleasure,' replied the magewoman dryly. 'Once I've attended to my own more immediate needs.'

'Can you help me up,' Naldeth asked roughly, 'before I piss myself like some cripple?'

As Velindre stepped past Kheda in the narrow confines of the cave, the warlord offered the mage his arm. Naldeth gripped his forearm and Kheda hauled him upright. Jaw clenched and sweat beading his forehead, the younger man clambered awkwardly out of the cave behind Velindre.

Risala concentrated on shelling more nuts, the only sound in the cave the sharp splitting. 'Have you any thoughts on what we'll do once we've got back to the ship?' she asked at length, not meeting Kheda's eye. 'Will we sail for home?'

Kheda hesitated. 'If we agree that's for the best.'

He saw the old woman looking inquisitively at him and then back at Risala and fell silent.

What would you say, if you could say anything we could understand?

Some moments later, he heard Velindre returning, her voice terse and practical. 'There are enough uncertainties about wielding magic in this place. You don't need the additional distraction of physical pain, not if it can be relieved, even a little.'

'All right, very well,' Naldeth snapped as he slid down the cave's awkward entrance slope and resigned himself to unbuckling the straps around his waist and thigh. 'I'm not used to walking for so long, not over such rough ground.'

'No, I don't suppose you are.' Kheda gently pulled the metal leg aside and looked keenly at the dust- and sweat-stained trousering wadded around Naldeth's stump.

No blood; that's a mercy. A sore might not ulcerate in this dry heat but if it took an infection, I don't know what we'd do. I couldn't cut the thigh bone any shorter without physic or proper instruments and I doubt we could nurse him through such an ordeal, even if we got back to the Zaise.

Velindre considerately turned her back and sat down next to the old woman. She watched her deftly cracking the nuts for a moment and then took a handful of the pile closest to her. Similarly averting her eyes, Risala pulled the mouth of her leather sack wide to receive the green kernels as she began splitting her share of the ruddy shells apart.

Kheda carefully unwrapped the cotton. It stuck and Naldeth flinched. Kheda got out his dagger and looked up to see that Naldeth had blanched beneath his tan. 'I'm just going to slit the seams,' he assured him. 'And a little water will make this go easier.'

'Not out of some muddy hole,' Naldeth said roughly.

'No.' Kheda reached round for Risala's flask slung on his back. 'Our aged friend over there showed me roots that hoard rainwater from whatever wet season this place might have. Trust me, it'll be as clean as if it had been boiled. There

359

are similar plants in the drier isles of the Archipelago's eastern reaches.'

'If you say so.' Naldeth didn't sound overly convinced.

Kheda deftly cut the trouser leg's seams and rapidly moistened the stuck cloth with a trickle of the precious water. 'Whoever doctored this for you did a good job,' he said with well-disguised relief as he laid bare the mage's stump.

Nevertheless, the white scarring where some unknown physician had sewn up the flap of skin to seal the amputation had split in a couple of places. Pale-pink flesh beneath had oozed a little clear fluid into the cotton. Above the scarring, the shrunken muscles of Naldeth's pallid thigh looked swollen and bruised where his weight had borne down into the leather cup concealed within the metal leg.

'What does she want?' Naldeth twitched a fold of cotton over his exposed mutilation and scowled past Kheda.

The warlord turned to see that the old woman had shifted so she could see what they were doing. 'There's no harm in her—' he began.

'Where are you going?' Risala's question went unanswered as the old woman stood up, brushing nut shells from the lap of her wrap, and scrambled out of the cave.

'Not far.' Her bitten fingernails proving inadequate for the task, Velindre was using the tip of her dagger to split the nuts. 'She's left her belongings.'

'And the food's in here.' Briskly, Kheda sliced a scrap of cleanish cotton from Naldeth's ruined trouser leg and moistened it to wipe away dust crusted along one scar. 'Do you have any nuts like those in the north? They're surprisingly sweet.'

'No.' Naldeth cleared his throat and strove for an even tone. 'I don't recall seeing anything like them.'

'Assuming we can eat this splendid breakfast without some wild men turning up to dig us out of this burrow like rats, what do we do then?' Velindre asked.

'Do you feel any wild wizard nearby?' Kheda looked around at her. 'Or a dragon?'

Velindre paused in shelling her nuts. 'No,' she said at length. 'Not anywhere close.'

'Do you?' Kheda glanced up at Naldeth as he continued cleaning the mage's scars.

'You don't want me working any magic while I'm in such discomfort.' Naldeth grimaced. 'We might as well light a beacon to let that skull-faced wizard know where we are.'

'What's she got there?' Risala frowned as the old woman reappeared at the cave mouth.

She made her way gingerly down the rocky slope, waving a handful of twigs each bearing a few withered leaves. Stripping off a few, she tucked them into her mouth and chewed for a moment. Then she bent down to take Kheda's hand and spat into his palm. The pulpy mess gave off a powerful odour.

'What is she doing?' Naldeth was revolted.

'I think she's trying to help.' Trying not to recoil from the stickiness in his hand, Kheda took a cautious sniff. 'It can't be poisonous if she's chewing it.' Familiar notes in the scent teased him but more were wholly unknown.

An astringent? It smells vaguely like one of the pastes that galley rowers use to dress their blisters.

The old woman made an impatient clucking sound with her tongue and bent stiffly to push Kheda's hand towards Naldeth's thigh.

'You're not putting that on me.' The mage shuffled backwards, alarmed.

361

Kheda took pity on him. 'No.' He twisted his hand out of the old woman's grasp, shaking his head. Her face fell pathetically as she stood upright, shoulders drooping with disappointment. Kheda tried to reassure her with a friendly smile as he took the twigs with their scant leaves from her and handed them to Naldeth. 'But you can chew on a few of these and we'll use the pulp on your scars and bruises. It can't hurt and at very least it'll keep dirt out of the broken skin.'

Naldeth regarded the twigs with misgiving. 'Can't we just mash them up with some water?'

'We've scarcely enough water for drinking,' Kheda reminded him. 'Besides, it may be that spittle brings out some virtue in the leaves. That's the case with some Archipelagan ointments.'

'Do as he says,' Velindre ordered from her seat by the spotted hide. 'The lowliest Aldabreshin healers can rival the costliest mainland apothecaries.'

'I don't know who they might be,' Risala interjected, 'but Kheda has an enviable reputation even among other warlords.'

Kheda addressed himself to Naldeth. 'I've got trusted skin salves and decoctions to take the ache out of the bruising on the *Zaise*.'

'How are we planning to get back to the *Zaise*?' Velindre asked immediately.

'I take it you still aren't prepared to shift us all into a cave with your magic?' Kheda discreetly scraped the mess of chewed-up leaves off his hand onto a gritty patch of rock. The old woman was sitting shelling nuts again and didn't appear to notice.

'I might get us safely inside given how close we are.' Velindre contemplated the nut in her hand. 'But any wizard with his wits about him could probably follow us straight there.'

362

'I don't want to trust to magic with that much uncertainty,' Risala said bluntly.

'And we had better assume these wild mages do have a full measure of wits.' Kheda considered the old woman. 'These people may be savages but they're not stupid.'

'They wouldn't survive in a land as cruel as this if they were.' Naldeth reluctantly stripped a few withered leaves from a twig and began chewing. 'I think we could learn a lot from her,' he added round his awkward mouthful.

'Not very easily, since we've no way of talking to her.' Risala scooped up a handful of nuts from one of the heaps and passed them over to Kheda.

'Not yet, but we can try.' Velindre snapped her fingers to attract the old woman's attention and held out her hand. The old woman looked a little bemused. Velindre beckoned with her fingers and the old woman promptly dropped a green kernel into her open palm.

Velindre nodded and held the nutmeat up between forefinger and thumb. 'Nut.' She looked enquiringly at the old woman, who looked even more confused.

'Why do you feel she should learn your barbarian tongue, rather than Aldabreshin?' Kheda felt unreasonably irritated. He prised apart a few nuts and shoved green kernels into his mouth.

'Then let's learn her language.' Naldeth spat a pungent glob of crushed leaves onto his hand and smeared it on his stump, his expression one of distaste.

'What do you suppose she's going to say?' Risala picked up a kernel and mimicked Velindre. '"Nut"? Or "good"? Or "food"?' She dropped it back into the leather sack and spread her empty hand. 'What would this mean? "Hand"? "Hello"? "Five"?'

Despite her earlier terseness, Kheda knew that Risala wasn't simply being contrary, just realistic. 'We could probbly learn something of each other's languages.' He tried to sound neutral as he continued eating his own share of the nuts. 'In time, and doubtless with plenty of misunderstandings along the way. But we don't have time. We need to consider how best to get back to the *Zaise* undetected.'

'And once we're there, we consider how to put an end to the tyranny of that skull-wearing mage and his kind.' Velindre looked straight at Kheda. 'Don't you think this woman and these people deserve better than a mage's foot on their necks? You were outraged on their behalf last night.'

'And dawn brings cooler counsel.' The warlord sat down and helped himself to more nuts. 'All things being equal, I'd agree, but I don't see how losing our lives will benefit these wretches.'

'What are these people to us?' Risala looked up from contemplating her fingers, stained red by the nut husks. 'I'm sorry for them, that they live in such wretchedness, but what can we do? And we have a greater obligation to our own, don't we?'

They all looked at the old woman, who sat placidly chewing on nutmeats and cracking shells.

'She's shown us food and water and shelter. I thought debt and obligation were woven into the endless circles and cycles of Aldabreshin philosophies.' Distaste curled Naldeth's lip. 'Kheda, this stuff is making my tongue numb.'

'Then it should ease the ache in your leg. As for obligation, Risala's right. My overriding duty is to my domain and then to the wider Archipelago.' Kheda shot the younger man a stern glance. 'Certainly before I risk myself helping even innocent kin of people who brought death and torment to Chazen.' He met Velindre's penetrating gaze with a level stare of his own. 'How would you go about putting an end to this skull-faced mage's rule? You were adamant you wouldn't summon up a false dragon to kill the one that gives him his power.'

The magewoman's answer surprised him. 'I said I wouldn't kill it and I won't. But I could conjure up a simulacrum to confront it.'

'What would that achieve?' Risala challenged.

'If it fled, the sky dragon would chase it, I'm sure of that,' said Velindre slowly. 'If it flew far enough away, it would leave the skull-faced mage relying on the natural elements hereabouts.'

'And then?' Kheda prompted.

'Then Naldeth kills him.' Velindre's uncompromising declaration hung in the silence of the cave. 'My magic will be tied up in creating a false dragon, so it will have to be him.'

'Me?' The youthful mage gaped, his mouth unattractively filled with half-chewed leaves.

'Could he do that?' Kheda looked hard at Velindre.

'I think so.' The magewoman nodded. 'If the skull-mage hasn't got a dragon's aura to draw on.'

'You think so?' cried Risala. 'Why risk—'

'Because that mage's rule is the foulest abuse of magic I have yet encountered,' Velindre spat with more anger than Kheda had ever seen her show. 'I may not hold any office in Hadrumal, but all wizards share some responsibilities. The Council has safeguarded the rest of us by culling the rogues since Trydek was first raised to Archmage.' She narrowed her eyes at Naldeth. 'But the Council isn't here and you and I are. You said you didn't relish the thought of going back to Hadrumal to tell Planir and the rest of them what we found here and then admitting we did nothing about it.'

'We fought that brute last night to save that girl, and you didn't set out to kill him. You told me just to tie him up with tree roots.' Naldeth sounded defensive. 'What will the Council say if I admit openly attacking him? They spend half their time disciplining apprentices fool enough to try magical duels—'

'The Council will accept that you had to do this,' Velindre assured him sternly. 'There are times for rules to be followed and times for them to be broken. There's no subtlety in his magic—'

'I thought we were looking to get safely back to the *Zaise*,' protested Risala.

'What is killing this one wizard going to achieve?' Kheda agreed with her. 'Even if Naldeth can kill him—'

Velindre cut them both off with a sweep of one hand. 'Even if we get back to the *Zaise*, I wouldn't take a wager on our chances of getting out of these waters. At very least that skull-faced mage knows we're here and if he's looking for us, we'll need magic to ward him off.'

Kheda frowned and shook his head. 'His rival on this side of the river, that mage in the thrall of that black dragon, he'll soon notice something's happening if you go up against the skull wearer—'

'Then we'll have to make sure Skull-Face is dead and we're gone before any other dragon or mage decides to intervene.' Velindre shot Naldeth a significant look.

Risala scrambled to her feet. 'I need some fresh air.'

'Wait for me.' Kheda rose to follow her.

'Let's think how best to do this. And eat something.' Velindre scooped up the nuts that were left for Naldeth. 'In some ways it is a shame that you never met Dev, or Azazir.'

Kheda left the mages talking as he climbed out of the cave to find Risala sitting not far away, hugging her knees.

'They think punishing that skull wearer for staining their precious magecraft is more important than saving their own skins.' She scowled up at him. 'Please, Kheda, can't you search the skies for some guidance? I can't bear this uncertainty.'

'Just at the moment, I think we're better off trusting to our own common sense.' He tried not to sound too brusque. 'Let's see if anything edible's fallen foul of that snare yet.'

'Will you read any omen in it if it has?' Risala threw the challenge up at him.

'No, I won't,' he said shortly. 'I'd rather try to think through what Velindre's just said.'

'Isn't it folly to go looking for a fight?' Risala demanded. 'We're on our own here, Kheda. You've no warriors to call on, no triremes or archers.'

'It still may be that taking the initiative is our best chance of escaping from here. You said yourself that that wild mage they attacked last night will come looking for us.' Kheda sat down and put his arm around her stiff shoulders. 'I don't think Velindre would attempt to draw off this sky dragon unless she was convinced she could do it. Wizards do not like to fail. You know what Dev was like. He was always going to succeed or die in the attempt.' Kheda swallowed the recollection of that death once again.

'Until finally he did both.' Risala reluctantly laid her head against Kheda's shoulder. 'What do we do if Velindre kills herself?'

'Let's hope it doesn't come to that,' Kheda said grimly. 'If it does, we will still have Naldeth, I hope. And I think we can trust Velindre not to put Naldeth up against someone he couldn't equal. I think I understand a little of what she means about this wild magic being unsubtle—'

'It doesn't have to be subtle,' Risala pointed out acidly. 'A handful of fire exploding inside your head is just as effective as an assassin's knife. We saw that when these savages invaded Chazen.'

'And what do we say, if we can get home to Chazen?' Kheda hugged her tight. 'Do we warn the domains that there's an island out here in the western ocean that's full of wizards and dragons? Do we admit that we have no defence against them, unless we betray all we believe in and make common cause with the barbarian mages of the north?' His voice was harsh with the unpalatable truths.

'I don't know.' Risala pulled away. 'I just want to see some sign, some hint, even, that we might actually survive all this. Whatever the dangers we faced before, at least I could believe that the omens had told us that was the best course of action. That we were risking ourselves for a future, for ourselves and for Chazen.'

Do you want me to lie to you? No, I won't do that, not even for you.

Kheda chose his words carefully. 'Having Velindre and Naldeth kill this skull-faced mage and drive off his dragon may yet serve the Archipelago's future, far more than they realise.'

'Why—' As Risala twisted, her face accusing, she froze, looking past Kheda's shoulder. 'What's that?'

He turned to see a shiver in the scant foliage that had nothing to do with the idle breezes. 'I think that's a sign that time for discussion is past.' He sprang to his feet, grabbed Risala's hand and ran for the cave mouth. Sling stones rattled against the rock face and he heard the thud of an optimistic spear landing somewhere behind them.

We won't outrun a lightning strike.

To his surprise, they made it back into the cave unscathed by crude missiles or deadly magic.

Risala slid down the steep slope, heedless of bruises to her rump. 'They're out there.'

'Coming for us?' Velindre stood up, running a hand through her short-cropped hair. 'Or waiting for us to come out?'

'They're just keeping watch for the moment.' Kheda pressed himself against the rocky mouth of the cave. A shadow not cast by the sun moved beneath a stand of twisted trees and resolved itself into a loincloth-clad spearman. 'They must have tracked us here.'

'Unless she betrayed us.' Risala scowled at the old woman, but her heart wasn't in the accusation.

The old woman looked at her and then at Kheda, her face crumpled with fear and confusion.

He shook his head. 'She doesn't even know what's going on.'

'I imagine they'll wait until their mage arrives.' Naldeth dragged his metal leg towards his stump. It rasped on the cave floor. 'Didn't you say only mages killed mages when they were fighting each other in Chazen?'

'I'd say we're committed, wouldn't you?' Velindre challenged Kheda with a glint in her eye. She turned to Naldeth. 'You keep tight hold on your fire until I've dealt with his dragon.'

'Then I suggest you make ready.' Seeing more movement among the trees, Kheda glanced briefly back into the cave.

The magewoman looked grimly composed, her eyes hard as onyx and her thin lips pressed tight together. Naldeth looked altogether less impressive, with fragments of leaf stuck to his chin and his nerveless fingers fumbling with the straps and buckles.

'Let me help.' Risala moved towards him.

'I can manage.' He warned her off sharply.

'Don't be a fool,' Velindre barked. 'We don't have time.'

Kheda turned back to keep watch on the lurking savages. The old woman startled him as she scrambled up the sloping entrance to peer around him, her claw-like hand grabbing his arm to steady herself. She hissed between her sparse teeth, shaking her head, and Kheda couldn't doubt the intelligence in her dark eyes.

How do I communicate with you? Is there anything useful you could tell us? I assume you don't want to die any more than the rest of us.

He drew his dagger and mimed a discreet thrust at the watchers now standing more boldly beneath the trees.

The old woman shook her head vehemently and, fastening her hand around his wrist, pushed the weapon back down. Kheda hastily resheathed it before she inadvertently stabbed him in the thigh. She tugged at his tunic, insistent on drawing him back into the cave.

Kheda shook his head with a forbidding frown, unpicking her fingers from his clothing before pointing first at his own eyes and then at the wild men now gathering in significant numbers in the dappled shade of the nut trees. The straight lines of their spears stood out clearly among the gnarled branches.

The old woman shook her head, exasperated. She edged her way down into the cavern and slapped a soaring painted falcon on the wall. Sweeping her arm around to encompass all the images, she jabbed one withered finger first at Naldeth and then at Velindre. Looking at Kheda, her face twisted with frustration that almost matched his own. She indicated the outside with a flick of her hand before drawing one hand across her wrinkled throat, eyes closing in a gesture that needed no translation.

'What do you think she means?' Risala asked helplessly. 'Other than they'll kill us as soon as we set foot outside.'

'They can try,' Velindre corrected her.

Kheda watched out of the corner of his eye as the old woman hurried deeper into the cave to point up at the dragon's head fashioned out of the rocky spur. She swept her arms around again to take in the whole cave and then pointed again at Naldeth and Velindre.

'This cave must be somehow sacrosanct to wizards.' Naldeth was balancing on his flesh-and-blood foot as he made final adjustments to the fit of his false leg. 'But I don't feel any undue elemental strength hereabouts.'

'I think she wants us to summon a dragon.' Velindre's smile was chilling. 'We can do that much for her.'

'It's coming.' The cave wall glowed briefly beneath Naldeth's fingertips as he braced himself with one hand while negotiating the uneven floor. 'The blue dragon.'

'I need to touch the breezes if I'm to raise a simulacrum to challenge it.' Velindre sounded almost eager as she stepped past Kheda into the daylight.

Kheda looked down towards the younger mage. 'What about the black dragon?'

'It's nowhere close.' He grinned up at Kheda, disquieting eagerness replacing his earlier reluctance. 'Give me a hand up, if you don't mind.'

'What do we do?' Risala looked at Kheda as he hauled the young mage up to stand in the cave entrance.

'What we always do,' the warlord said wryly. 'Stay out of the way.'

And be ready to run if the battle goes badly for Velindre or Naldeth and I see the faintest possibility that we might escape unnoticed in the confusion. If we could get to the Zaise, would we have any chance of sailing for home without a mage to steer us through contrary winds and waves?

The old woman was trying to pull Risala into the depths of the cave now. Kheda jumped down the slope and shooed her away. He took Risala's hand and pulled her up towards the daylight. 'Whatever happens, I want you by my side.'

'What—' As Risala's voice rose on a note of panic, the reverberation of dragon wings outside drowned out every other sound.

Sapphire light crackled all around Velindre. She was standing a few paces away, looking up into the sky. Raising one hand, she drew down a pillar of light as blue as the cloudless sky above. The base of it hovered just above her upturned palm, bathing her in a painfully bright radiance that bleached all colour from her. Unblinking, Velindre stood still as a statue carved of marble. Only the pillar showed any sign of life. Brighter azure light pulsed down its length from some unimaginable height above, as regular as if it echoed the beat of her heart.

The wild mage's sky dragon bellowed. It was circling high above. With a spiral twist through the air, it flew at the sapphire column, jaws gaping with menace. Veering away at the very last moment, it wasn't quite deft enough and one edge of its wing brushed against the lurid light. The magic shivered in Velindre's hand and she gasped. Above, the sky dragon roared with rage or agony. Kheda couldn't tell which.

What use is foretelling? Every portent that might guide my life has been pored over since the day I was born, yet no omen ever saw my death in an unknown land encompassed by wizards battling with dragons.

The magewoman stretched her hand up higher, her face a daunting mask of determination. Blood trickled down her chin as she bit her lip, looking black against her unnatural pallor.

The sky dragon swooped with another deafening crash of its lavender wings, mouth agape, and this time it bit into the blue light with its crystal teeth. The flash of magic seared Kheda's vision and left him frantically wiping away stinging tears. Trying to blink away the throbbing smudges staining his sight, he grabbed for his sword hilt.

The sky dragon roared with renewed fury and dived low to pass so close to the ground that its wings stirred up a cloud of dust and dry leaves. A second bellow rang out, high above. Kheda's vision cleared and he realised that what he had vaguely thought was some unexpected cloud was in fact a soaring white dragon. He looked quickly towards the savages still lurking beneath the trees.

They were staring up at the skies, hands and weapons limp at their sides, mouths open in astonishment.

The false dragon that Velindre had summoned was as white as the ice coating the most inaccessible peaks of the Archipelago's tallest mountains. Its underside and the membranes of its wings were touched with the blue of a moonlit sky seen from such cold heights. Its claws and ferociously bared teeth were the indigo of those rarest of nights when the stars alone ruled the heavens. Cold white fire burned in its sapphire eyes as it looked down and it hissed with contempt. The cobalt dragon beat its lavender wings and screamed its outrage as it climbed the sky to fight this unexpected rival.

Dragons fight dragons. Wizards fight wizards. Where is the skull-faced wild mage?

Kheda looked back to the wild men but couldn't make out either the skull wearer or the feather-crowned women. He found his gaze drawn inexorably skywards again.

No one's going to be making any move until this is over, one way or another.

The false dragon darted this way and that. The sky dragon was long and lithe; the false dragon was more slender still and smaller, able to twist through impossibly tight circles. The sky dragon drew level with it and bated its wings, hanging in the air like a hawk. It breathed a dense white mist at the false dragon. The simulacrum fell down the sky just ahead of the tumbling cloud. The savages beneath the trees howled their approval. Just when it looked certain that the vapour would envelop it, the false dragon blinked into invisibility. The cheers of the wild men fell apart in confusion.

The sky dragon roared and dived steeply downwards. Scattering the mist with furious strokes of its mighty wings, it searched for its enemy, questing head whipping from side to side. The false dragon appeared directly behind its lashing tail and spat shards of crystalline ice that skittered noisily across the vivid blue scales armouring the sky dragon's flanks. Outrage rang through the sky dragon's roaring, now so loud that Kheda's ears were aching.

The blue beast doubled back on itself in midair, lethal mouth agape. The false dragon flapped its wings to climb higher but looked just too slow to evade it. Then, in the instant the sky dragon was about to sink crystal fangs into its icy white neck, the false dragon vanished once more. The sky dragon hissed and began rolling over and over, wings folded close to its body with head and tail outstretched. Strands of pale vapour began forming around it.

'There he is.' Naldeth hadn't been watching the antics of Velindre's simulacrum. He had been waiting for the skull-faced mage.

Kheda saw the wild wizard standing in the midst of his retinue, his head tilted incongruously backwards like the rest. It was impossible to see the wild wizard's reaction through his skull mask but his people were plainly astounded as they watched the battle going on above their heads. 'Are you ready?' he asked Naldeth.

Can you do this? Truly? And what happens if you can, never mind if you cannot?

'I'll be ready just as soon as Velindre plays her part,' Naldeth murmured, now looking upwards.

The blue dragon had rapidly gathered a dense spiral of cloud around itself and flew unerringly at the false dragon as soon as it reappeared. This time the simulacrum waited, flapping in a lazy circle, indigo tongue lolling and jaw gaping wide in what looked uncommonly like a mocking smile.

Because you've seen it try this trick before, haven't you, Velindre?

But this time as the blue dragon flew closer, it didn't release the cloud as a murderous vortex. Instead, white tendrils reached out from the spiral and sought to entangle the false dragon. In the instant before the clutching white fingers laced themselves tight, the simulacrum vanished yet again. More significantly, the tendrils of cloud flashed into vivid claws of lightning that shot backwards towards the blue dragon. The beast shrieked and writhed as white light crackled along its hide, leaving deep burns scoring its vibrant blue scales.

The crowd around the skull-faced mage gasped, a few shouting out loud in their astonishment. Kheda watched the wild wizard in the skull mask shove his feather-crowned attendants aside. He hurried forward out of the shade of the nut trees to see what was going on up above more clearly. The false dragon appeared and then disappeared again before the sky dragon could attack. It reappeared once more, this time a little further away in the direction of the sea. Bellowing with fury that made the air shake, the blue dragon flew after it more swiftly than the fastest trireme. The simulacrum lured it still further away. Soon both dragons were lost beyond the swell of the land as it rose towards the broken cliffs of the seashore.

Stumbling slightly, Velindre walked backwards towards the shelter of the cave mouth. Her face was drawn and blood from her bitten lips stained her teeth. 'Naldeth, let's see ... if you were ... paying attention ... to Hearth Master ... Kalion's lessons.' Chest heaving as she gasped for breath, she sat down heavily, her head hanging. 'Some water would be nice,' she rasped.

Wordlessly, Kheda handed her the brass flask and watched the skull-faced mage take another few paces away from his warriors. The wild wizard wasn't looking up into the sky any longer. He pointed an unerring hand towards the cave mouth and shouted, shrill with rage. The dry ground exploded with a shower of dust and stones as a spear of lightning landed no more than an oar's length away.

Naldeth walked stiffly forward out of the shadow of the rocks, rubbing his palms against the sides of his tunic. Without any preamble, he threw a handful of burning scarlet towards the wild wizard, and then another and another. The skull wearer waved his hands, each gesture summoning up a gust of blue-white vapour to snuff out the bright fire. Naldeth kindled a crimson blaze on the empty ground between them. Gouts of sorcerous flame broke off to twist through the air towards the wild wizard. The savage dismissed them with a disdainful sweep of one hand and clenched his other fist high above his head. Smashing it down, he summoned a lightning bolt to blow the crimson source of the flames into oblivion.

Kheda flinched as a new wall of fire sprang up and swept towards the trees, hiding the mage and all his retinue. Then a cold realisation pierced the warlord.

The only wizard ever to battle the wild mages was Dev, and Dev's dead. Does Naldeth know all the rules of this warfare? Only wizards kill wizards and wizards only kill wizards. If he kills any of those spearmen, surely the rest of those wild men will attack, and Velindre's still helpless.

The wall of fire swept through the trees to dissolve in the barren space beyond. Not a leaf was scorched as far as Kheda could tell but the wild men were patently disconcerted. Milling around, they slapped at their heads and loincloths until they realised they weren't ablaze.

'Wizards only kill wizards,' Naldeth murmured, 'but Dev didn't say anything about giving the rest a good fright.'

The wild mage strode forward, waving his arms, his long matted locks bristling monstrously around the animal skull. Every feather in his dark-blue cloak stood out straight, rimed with a white light that hovered on the very edge of seeing. Every breeze fled and the still air tasted of thunder. The skull wearer shouted and blue flashes of magic began shattering the rocky outcrop that sheltered the painted cave.

Kheda ducked away from the razor-sharp splinters of stone ripping through the air, shielding Risala with his body. The old woman dropped to lie huddled in the cave entrance, wrapping her skinny arms around her grey head and drawing up her legs like a frightened child.

Velindre dragged her head up to regard the wild mage with weary disfavour. 'Is that the best he can do?'

'Let's see.' Naldeth wiped an open hand across the still air and a defiant breeze sprang up. It scooped dust from the ground which glowed even in the bright daylight. A flick of Naldeth's hand dismissed the smouldering golden cloud and it drifted away towards the trees.

The wild mage threw darts of sapphire fire at this new threat, tearing holes in the shimmering fabric. It made no difference. The tattered magic flowed together again. It parted briefly to flow around him where he stood alone and drifted irresistibly towards the savage spearmen now huddling in the questionable shelter of the twisted trees.

The glowing haze surrounded them and the wild warriors began wailing, rubbing frantically at their faces, heedless of weapons fallen to the ground.

Kheda saw white-hot flashes in the shadows. 'What are you doing?'

'Blinding them,' Naldeth replied calmly. 'Just for a little while. Undermining their faith in their wizard.'

'Just kill him.' Velindre still looked quite dreadfully pale, with smudges like bruises under her eyes. Then she doubled over, racked with coughing.

Kheda opened his mouth to ask what was wrong just as a similar paroxysm seized him. Risala gasped and began coughing too, as did the old woman still lying curled up in the cave. Cough after cough tore at Kheda's lungs until his throat felt raw and his chest burned. Through tear-filled eyes he saw Naldeth send a burning shaft of red gold straight at the wild mage who dodged it with contemptuous ease.

A crack of thunder sounded in the empty sky and Kheda gasped as the coughing fit fled. A fresh salt-scented breeze offered the illusion of relief but in the next instant, the air was as still and heavy as if the worst storms of the rainy season were about to break over them.

Kheda tried to draw a breath but found he couldn't. It was as if bonds had been wrapped tight around his chest. He strained until his ribs ached with the effort and the blood roared in his ears. Velindre slumped over, hugging herself. Risala sank to her knees, panting like a trapped animal. Her eyes widened with terror as she clutched at her throat and Kheda reached for her. Even that slight effort made his arm ache as if he were lifting an iron bar. The old woman lay still as death. Dimly, as his vision blurred, Kheda heard Naldeth talking to himself again, his tone still quite conversational.

'He has some impressive mastery of the air. Still, as Dev told Velindre, these people have no idea of blending elements.'

The fragments of rock that the wild wizard's magic had broken from the outcrop sprang into the air. They instantly glowed as red as if they'd fallen from a furnace. Naldeth sent the incandescent shards shooting towards the skull-faced mage with a flourish of his hand. The constriction crushing Kheda's chest vanished as the wild wizard summoned up a white whirlwind that swept up the stone fragments and quenched their fire.

Naldeth chuckled and the stones began to glow again within the spiral cloud. He raised a hand, palm out towards the wild wizard. The whirlwind writhed this way and that. Naldeth leaned forward and the cloud sank lower. It touched the ground and began sucking up dust and stones. The vapour darkened from pristine whiteness to a dirty, menacing grey. Clinging to the earth, it grew squatter and darker, the incandescent stones pinpricks of scarlet within it.

The wild wizard screamed with rage and thrust both hands up at the sky, calling down a blistering bolt of lightning to shatter the treacherous whirlwind. The spiral cloud exploded into dust and debris that was tossed this way and that by the tortured breeze. But the burning stones didn't fall to the ground. Released from the whirlwind, they flew straight at the skull-faced mage, sure as slingshot.

He flinched and ducked, half turning away. Where the stones struck his cloak, the feathers flared into lurid crimson flames. Where they landed on naked skin, they instantly burned deep holes, black as the sockets of his skull mask. One smouldering stone hit the skull between its empty eyes and the bone split to leave the two halves of the mask hanging askew. Burning gashes were spreading across his muscular thighs and down his corded arms, rimmed with scarlet sorcery. Another strike wholly obliterated one of the horns and then the whole skull fell away in ruins.

Thus revealed, the wild mage looked little different from any other savage. The man screamed and fell to his knees, hands pressed vainly to his belly. His fingers began burning as they sank into the scorched void opening ever wider to reveal his entrails. He looked at Naldeth, screaming, pleading, his face contorted with agony. His whole midriff was ablaze now, the flames licking up his forearms to blacken the skin and melt the flesh beneath.

A death like Dev's. But without the ecstasy.

Kheda turned away, nauseated. Then he saw Velindre sprawled on the ground and all thoughts of Dev's fate fled. Convulsions gripped the magewoman, her eyes rolling back in her head, blind and white, as her mouth frothed with spittle. Blood stained the back of her dirty cotton tunic.

'What's wrong with her?' Risala was on her knees frantically sweeping away the vicious shards of shattered rock lying all around to save Velindre from any further lacerations.

'I've no idea.' Kheda skirted the magewoman's thrashing limbs.

There's more danger of injury if I try to restrain her than if I let the convulsion run its course. If she bites her tongue, with luck that will heal. Only a fool would put something in her mouth. She won't thank me for breaking her teeth. Though I'd risk my fingers if I had a draught that might stop this. But everything that might help is in my chest aboard the Zaise.

'I left enough of them unblinded to witness their mage's fate.' Naldeth sounded unexpectedly sad as he gazed at the savages beneath the trees. 'They can guide the rest back to wherever they live. They'll be able to see again tomorrow.'

'Never mind them.' Kheda was incensed. 'Velindre's ...' he found himself lost for words '... stricken.'

'What?' The young mage wheeled around, horrified by what he saw.

'Can you shift us to the *Zaise* with your magic?' Kheda was watching intently for any signs of Velindre soiling herself. 'Perhaps I can—'

The magewoman's convulsions ceased as suddenly as they had begun. She lay limp on the dusty ground, sweat beading her forehead and soaking through her cotton tunic.

Risala used the edge of her sleeve to clean the dirty foam from around Velindre's mouth. 'Kheda, water.'

Kheda uncapped the brass flask and knelt to trickle a little of the precious fluid between Velindre's lips. The magewoman's perspiration smelled rank, as if she had spent days in a fever. 'Naldeth, what's wrong with her?' he demanded.

'I don't know.' The young wizard's voice quavered.

Velindre startled them all with a groan.

'Help me.' Kheda nodded to Risala and between them they rolled the magewoman onto her back, lifting up her head to rest against Risala's thigh.

'Drink, just a sip.' Kheda held the neck of the brass flask to the magewoman's blood-caked lips.

Velindre squinted up at him, her breathing fast and ragged. 'Did we win?' she whispered faintly.

'I did.' Concern twisted Naldeth's face as he looked down at her. 'You were right. He could use his air against my fire affinity but when I bound the fire to stone, the antipathy of earth to his own element defeated him.'

'You can thank Dev for that tip.' Velindre's grin was ghastly.

Kheda tried to see if she'd suffered any injury beyond scrapes and bruises. 'What happened to you?'

'The dragon.' She tried to sit more upright, clinging to Risala. 'It won.'

'It's coming back?' Dread gripping his gut, Kheda scanned the skies for the bright-blue beast.

'Not his dragon.' Velindre reached for the water flask with trembling hands and took another sip. She peered past Naldeth towards the blackened corpse of the skull wearer, still smouldering and staining the clear air with vile-smelling greasy smoke.

'I don't understand.' Naldeth was confused.

'Neither do I,' Velindre admitted sardonically, 'but the simulacrum defeated the true dragon.'

'Your false dragon defeated the fire dragon that was laying waste to Chazen.' Kheda looked at her uncertainly. 'Then it began dying as the magic unravelled. You said that's what would happen. You weren't affected like this when we slew it.'

When I was leading the men of Chazen to slaughter a dragon that was nothing more than a lie that would have dissolved into mist within a few days regardless. So they could reassure themselves as to their bravery. So their trust in the rightness of my rule might be made absolute by such a powerful omen.

Velindre drew a deep breath and pressed her palms to her face for a long moment. 'The simulacrum defeated the sky dragon,' she said finally. 'Then it ripped it open and ate its sapphire heart. You recall why a wizard-summoned dragon is condemned to die before it's barely tasted life?' She looked from Kheda to Naldeth.

'Because there's a void at its centre,' Kheda said slowly.

'A true dragon's heart is elemental gemstone.' Naldeth nodded. 'Which is why they seek out jewels to form into their eggs.'

'The dragon I made won't die now.' Defiant delight kindled in Velindre's hazel eyes. 'It will live out its days like any other of its kind.'

'Here?' Risala demanded, looking upwards. 'Will it be looking to you to feed it with prisoners and slaves?'

Velindre shook her head cautiously. 'Not as far as I can tell. It's tasted the winds coming up from the southern ocean and flown to find their source.' She blinked away joyful tears. 'It had no expectation—'

Kheda gasped, startled, as wiry fingers clutched at his elbow. As he turned, his hand already on his sword hilt, he realised it was the old woman. She was looking past the remains of the dead wizard towards the belt of twisted nut trees. She pointed urgently and Kheda saw shapes moving in the shadows once again.

'Only wizards kill wizards,' he said grimly, 'but I'll wager the rest of them will do their best to kill us, if they can catch us.' He stooped, lifting one of Velindre's slack arms up over his shoulder. 'Can you walk?'

The old woman clucked, shaking her head and smiling broadly. Turning to Naldeth, she bowed low. Straightening up, she pointed to the lurking figures and bowed once again, withered arm held out straight. As if this were some signal, a few bold savages moved out from beneath the nut trees into the open. They flung themselves prostrate on the ground, hands outstretched in supplication.

Understanding dawning, Kheda saw that none of the wild men now carried weapons. 'When we saw their wizards killing each other in Chazen, a defeated mage's warriors — and his prisoners and his loot — they were all claimed by the victor. They're surrendering.'

'To Naldeth,' Risala agreed, relief warring with apprehension in her voice.

'To me?' The young wizard's words cracked on his astonishment. 'I thought we wanted to do away with magical tyranny.' He looked to Velindre for her agreement.

'I don't think it's going to be that simple.' She glanced up at Kheda as he helped her to her feet. 'As I believe our warlord was about to point out earlier.'

'What do we do now?' Kheda scowled at the old woman, who was tugging at his arm again.

She glared back at him, unrepentant. She pointed first to Naldeth and then to the waiting wild men before looking expectantly at Kheda.

'Can you walk?' Kheda looked closely at Velindre. 'Can you do any magic?'

'I can probably walk.' But as the magewoman tried to step away from his supporting arm her knees buckled and she would have fallen if Risala hadn't caught her. 'But no, I don't think I can work any wizardry just at present.' She heaved a shuddering sigh.

'Naldeth?' Kheda turned to the younger mage and saw an unhealthy pallor beneath his ruddy tan.

'I just need to catch my breath,' he said unconvincingly.

'How far away are we from the *Zaise*?' Kheda looked around to get his bearings.

'It's that way.' Risala pointed unerringly to the dark canopies of taller trees away to the west. 'That's the line of the dry stream where those tree dwellers live. We need to bear to the south, down to the grasslands, so we can cut across the mouth of their valley.'

'Where their mage and his dragon can't have missed either of these duels and we've no magic of our own to call on if they come looking to see what's happened.' Kheda took stock of the two mages; Velindre was still almost faint with exhaustion, Naldeth visibly weighed down with fatigue. 'I don't think we can risk making for the ship, not just yet. They'll never manage that climb up to the cliff top.'

'We certainly won't slip past that dry valley unnoticed, not with all these savages following us.' Risala surveyed the wild men still lying prone beneath the nut trees. A few were lifting cautious heads to see what was happening by the cave. 'So what are we going to do?'

'That skull-faced mage must have had some kind of lair.' Kheda looked for the feather-crowned women and frowned when he realised they were nowhere to be seen. 'Which presumably now belongs to you, Naldeth. That would be some sanctuary, just till you two recover your strength. Once we've had some food and some time for reflection, we can consider how best to get back to the *Zaise*?

'What about the wild men?' Risala looked warily at the prostrate savages. 'Will they let us go?'

'I can't see them stopping us.' Kheda sighed reluctantly. 'And in the meantime, they'll be bodies to stand between us and anyone else's spears until we're rested.'

'Kheda—' Naldeth roused himself to protest incoherently.

'Do you have some better idea?' the warlord challenged. 'And what would you wager on your chances of persuading these people to let the four of us go off alone into hostile territory? Do you feel fit enough to take on that mage in the beaded cloak and his black dragon besides?'

'No.' Velindre was adamant.

'We may end up doing that anyway if we don't move soon.' Risala indicated the closest wild men, who were now getting to their feet.

Then everyone froze as a faint tremor ran through the earth underneath them and a low sound on the very edge of hearing seemed to surround them.

'What was that?' Kheda looked at Naldeth.

'I don't know.' The young mage moved to Velindre's other side, draping her arm around his neck. 'But let's get out of here.'

Unnerved by the earth tremor and the strange noise, the wild men who had been following the skull-faced mage hurried forward to throng around the four of them. With their stained loincloths and mud-matted hair, they smelled sour with fear and filth.

Naldeth backed away, trying to avoid the worst of the odour. 'How do we tell them what we want to do?'

'Just head for the river,' Kheda suggested, but the crowd was pressing around them so thickly that they had no hope of forcing a way through.

The old woman appeared at Kheda's side and seized his elbow yet again, shoving him forward. She said something and the wild men instantly sank to their knees and prostrated themselves once more, chests to the ground, their hands outstretched towards Naldeth.

'I have no intention of setting myself up to be some magical tyrant like that villain,' Naldeth said angrily.

'Then start considering how you might show them that,' snapped Velindre.

As the savages began slowly getting up again, their faces wretched with apprehension, a resonant cry echoed through the twisted trees. Another answered it, followed by a hollow clattering sound. All the savages turned towards Naldeth, fearfully hopeful and expectant.

'It's those birds.' Kheda drew both sword and hacking blade as a new realisation made his stomach churn. 'Those savages you blinded will be easy prey for them, Naldeth.' The horror of that prospect drove him a few paces towards the nut trees where the bespelled unfortunates still cowered.

'It was only supposed to be temporary,' the wizard protested, nevertheless following Kheda towards the belt of twisted trees.

'I don't imagine those birds will care.' Kheda glanced over his shoulder to see Risala drawing her own hacking blade, grim resolve on her face. 'Can you summon up enough fire to roast them, Naldeth?'

Risala drew level with Kheda's shoulder. 'Can't you just undo the spell?'

'I can try,' the wizard offered uncertainly.

As they moved, Naldeth still supporting Velindre as best he could, the wild men scrambled to their feet and pressed close around the four of them. As they reached the twisted trees, the savages snatched up the spears they had discarded in the dirt. Those at the forefront spread out to flank Kheda and Risala, their weapons levelled, expressions hard.

Somewhat to Kheda's surprise, the trees proved to be empty of the vicious birds. As a few of the unblinded wild men began calling to those savages Naldeth had bespelled earlier and gathering them together, the warlord looked across the grassy plain towards the dubious safety of the river. He saw a flash of an emerald crest as one of the vicious birds lifted its head above the swaying grasses.

'I see it.' Naldeth raised a hand and crimson fire flickered around his fingers.

'Can you scare those birds off with your magic and still have enough strength to raise a walkway across the river?' Risala asked suddenly. 'There were lizards as long as the *Zaise* in the water last night.'

'I don't know,' Naldeth admitted, uncertain.

'Then don't risk it.' Kheda gripped his sword hilt. 'Steel will kill these things as surely as sorcery.' He strode forward into the vicious grasses, giving everyone else no choice but to follow.

A great squawking bird burst through the tussocks, murderous black beak gaping. More of the flock flapped their ineffective wings ferociously behind it. Those savages escorting the blinded men raised a despairing wail. Kheda side-stepped the creature's vicious lunge and swept his sword up and around. The bird's lifeless head fell to the ground as its body collapsed with a thud and a flurry of feathers. Kheda heard a second screech behind him cut short, the sound of the bird's fall drowned out by the shouts of the wild men on either side, astounded, encouraging and reassuring the urgent questions of those who still could not see.

Another bird took a lanky stride forward, whether to attack or to try eating its dead fellow Kheda couldn't tell. He dismissed the irrelevance and parried its hooked beak with his hacking blade before slicing through its neck with his sword.

The rest of the birds screeched uncertainly, milling around rather than attacking, disconcerted by the scent of their own kind's blood. Emboldened, several of the spearmen lunged forward, yelling. The birds turned tail and vanished into the grasses, rattling their beaks with alarm.

Kheda looked over his shoulder to see Risala smile thinly back at him. Her hacking blade was smeared with blood and three of the blue-feathered birds lay dead at her feet. She took a pace back and he did the same as wild men clustered around the dead birds, eager to claim this unexpected bounty.

Kheda watched for a moment as the wild men produced crude knives of black stone from the folds of their loincloths. The fluted blades proved surprisingly efficient as the hunters deftly gutted the dead birds.

'Come on.' He beckoned to Naldeth and Velindre as the savages rapidly dismembered the fowl, skewering the legs and carcasses on spears for easier carrying.

Naldeth tried for an optimistic tone. 'I suppose this is one way to learn more about these people.'

'Just be sure to keep your wits about you,' Kheda said shortly.

'And keep thinking about how we're going to get back to the *Zaise*.' Risala looked at the soiled savages as she tried to scour the blood from her blade with a twist of dead grass. 'We're caught between a wall and a sword here, aren't we?'

'I hope not.' Kheda tried to sound convincing. 'Wherever these savages live, we know there won't be a wizard, or a dragon. If they're all in awe of Naldeth, we should be safe enough from them. So we can take some time to eat and rest and then find a way to slip back to the *Zaise* unnoticed.'

388

Risala drew closer to him, surveying the waving grasses with mistrust. 'You don't think those women with the feathers might dispute Naldeth's claim?'

'Let's hope they've had the sense to flee before he can kill them too.' Kheda spoke quietly enough that neither wizard heard him.

Risala fell silent as they hurried on through the grasses. As they reached the crumbling bank, Naldeth pushed past the warlord, leaving Velindre swaying but at least standing unsupported on her own two feet. The young mage drew a shining ridge of mud up out of the water to give them all a safe path to the far side. The wild men's murmurs grew loud with approval.

'I'd say they've got a better deal in a wizard after this morning's work,' Velindre commented. 'And I think they realise it.'

Cries of relief and astonishment drowned out her words. Those who had been blinded by Naldeth's earlier spell were crying out and weeping. Some stood staring at their hands, others blinking wildly or knuckling their eyes as they found they could see once more.

'You undid your spell,' Risala murmured.

Naldeth's smile was brief and crooked. 'It just unravelled when I drew up the walkway. The elements here are so unpredictable.'

The spearmen closest to him threw themselves down in obeisance again.

'It should secure us more goodwill, regardless.' Kheda watched those savages unencumbered by spears laden with fowl meat or busy with reassuring their comrades scramble down onto the mud. More deftly than he had expected, the wild men scooped up fish left flapping on the surface of the walkway and dug nameless wriggling things out of the silt before they could burrow to safety. They turned, smiles broad on their dirty faces, bowing and nodding their gratitude to Naldeth.

'You've sealed their fealty by feeding them,' Risala said with sudden realisation.

Kheda nodded slowly. 'Any slave in the Archipelago knows he's safe as long as his master gives him saller and salt.'

Is this going to make it harder or more easy to leave when we judge the time is right? Are these people going to want to lose this new wizard who saves them and feeds them so readily?

Chapter 16

As soon as Kheda stepped up onto the far bank, he had his sword and hacking blade ready.

What horrors are lurking on this side of the river?

'Where are we going?' Risala scrambled up to stand close beside him.

Kheda saw that all the savages were looking at Naldeth, who was negotiating the awkward climb up the crumbling bank. 'It looks as if we're all waiting on your convenience, Master Mage.'

'All right,' the wizard said uncertainly.

'Just start walking,' Kheda said curtly. 'Let's hope they show you where to go.'

To his relief, he was proved right. As Naldeth took a few hesitant steps, three eager savages who weren't burdened with fish or fowl flesh hurried ahead, half-turning to draw the wizard onward with beckoning hands and anxiously ingratiating smiles.

Kheda saw they were following the path he had cut through the vicious grasses the night before.

Was it only last night? It seems like an age ago.

He glanced at Risala and saw her face tight with tension. 'I think it'll be all right,' he said softly.

'Do you?' She stared at him. 'I'd feel better if we'd seen some sign that suggested as much.'

'I think we can trust the way these people are behaving towards us,' Kheda retorted.

I'll trust that and my own instincts before I rely on some omen of the sky or earthly compass. Can't you accept that?

Risala didn't answer. As Kheda walked on, he concentrated on scouring the clumps of grass for any sign of danger. Clouds of tiny black flies were drawn to the fish and bird meat but nothing bigger had shown itself by the time they reached the steep barren slope leading up to the plateau where the bulbous barrel-like trees stood.

The fissures Naldeth and Velindre had opened up in the ground still gaped, the sandy earth deep within still dark where the dew's dampness lurked beyond the increasing strength of the sun. Several of the trees leaned drunkenly askew, their roots flailing impotently in the empty air. One had toppled over completely, an ugly gash in the sustaining earth cutting its feet from under it. Those mighty trees that had burned had been reduced to ragged black shells, the soil all around them grey and lifeless.

Naldeth clicked his tongue in exasperation and waved a hand at the ruined expanse. Sand began flowing like water to fill up the crevices. The wild men picking their way cautiously across the broken ground halted, their murmurs half-appreciative, half-apprehensive. Naldeth turned his attention to the fallen tree. Its exposed roots writhed and the stunted branches thrashed as it strove to stand upright again. Those savages closest to it sprang away with cries of alarm. The rest halted, some kneeling and others cringing as they all turned to the mage.

'Leave it.' Velindre gave Naldeth a discreet shove in the small of his back. 'Save your strength.'

Naldeth sighed and let the tree crash back to the ground. The savages hurried onwards with visible relief. Once they had left the barren expanse of the mighty barrel trees, they found themselves toiling up an apparently endless shallow slope dotted with thistly plants and the strange scaly fingers of thorny green spikes. The sun was beating down strongly now and Kheda was sweating.

Where are we going to find water in this desert, so far from the river?

As he slowed to mop his brow, savages hurried past him. The foremost began shouting and Kheda saw movement ahead. A gap opened up in the indistinct green as men and women appeared, using sticks and spears to drag aside a woven barrier of thorns and spines.

Kheda took a moment to look around. Behind the tangle of vegetation, the land rose bare and brown, the earth washed away to leave scars of broken rock. Looking inland, he saw that this whole expanse of higher land fell away sharply into deep gullies choked with twisted nut trees and tangled thistly plants. On the seaward side, as best he could judge, the spiny forest sprawled all the way to the cliffs.

So these people at least have the wits to claim land with natural defences on two sides and reasonably open scrub on the other two.

'What do I do now?' Naldeth hovered at Kheda's elbow.

'You look calm and in control.' He pushed the younger man forward. 'And we'll be following you, looking equally confident. Just remember how hounds can rip the throat out of a foe who cowers too low.'

Risala was stony-faced. Velindre still looked drained, though her eyes were brightening with anticipation and a hint of discreet menace. Kheda looked to the old woman, who was still dogging his footsteps, in case her expression might give him some clue as to what to expect. Unfortunately her expression was as impenetrable as Risala's.

Naldeth walked slowly through the rough opening in the spiky barricade. Yellow-green sprawls of the fleshy spiny plants grew along the inside. The wild men separated to pick their way through this low maze. Those who had appeared to greet them waited, spears ready.

As Risala and Velindre fell into step behind him, Kheda used his hacking blade to knock away the more threatening of the fat spiny leaves. A murmur of awe made him look up. Those who had not seen his steel before were gaping at it. Kheda paused and swung at one of the taller paddle-shaped leaves. It fell to the ground with a soggy thud, cleanly sliced in two. He looked around, his face impassive as he held the gaze of any who caught his eye.

Do you understand this? That if you attack me, you'll be cut down?

As the wild men and women within the barrier stood still, suitably cowed, a small child naked but for a string of crude beads knotted around his hips ran forward. Squatting down, he thrust a stick deep into the pulpy interior of the severed leaf and lifted it up, wary of the spines. Licking at the juice trickling down to paint dark shining lines on his dusty forearms, he hurried away with his prize.

Naldeth chuckled. 'I don't think he's in awe of you, my lord of Chazen.'

'I don't suppose that matters.' Kheda was satisfied that all the adults' attention was still fixed on his blade as they walked on, leaving the thorny barrier and the sprawling plants behind.

'Do you suppose this is what they call home?' Velindre wondered wryly.

There was something approximating a village in the midst of the area encircled by the tangled barricade. Low huts spread in an irregular fashion around a trampled expanse of bare earth with a fire pit dug in the centre. The walls of the crude dwellings seemed to have been made from lattices of the nut trees' gnarled branches. As best Kheda could tell, a layer of the razor-edged grass had then been threaded in among the twigs before a haphazard coating of muddy clods was slapped on top. Some had roofs made in the same fashion; others were merely enclosures with an awning of animal hide stretched over one corner.

'Do you suppose that's where the mage lived?' Naldeth looked askance at the largest building in the makeshift village. Where the other huts were irregular in height and shape, this was a precise circle. The wall was made from stakes cut from the twisted trees and planted with care to minimise the inevitable gaps between each one. The roof was considerably more substantial, thickly thatched with grasses and resting on sturdy timbers that must have been hewn from taller, straighter trees akin to the ones in the dry valley back on the other side of the river.

'They didn't run away.' Risala pointed at the two women lurking in the substantial hut's open doorway. 'What do you suppose they are going to do?'

Kheda could see no clue in their expressions beneath their coronets of plumes, gold and scarlet and orange. Closer to, he saw that their hair was caked solid with some shining red substance, vivid among the ebony heads of the rest of the savages.

'What am I supposed to do with them?' Naldeth asked uncertainly.

'For a start, make quite sure they know your magic outstrips theirs,' Kheda said firmly.

Can we keep them in check until both our wizards are fully restored? Or will I just have to kill them out of hand to be sure we're all safe?

As distaste at the prospect of carrying out such dubious executions knotted the warlord's stomach, the men and women of the ramshackle village clustered around those who had returned laden with the unexpected bounty of fresh fish and meat. They were loud with their exclamations of astonishment and pleasure.

No one seems overly concerned about the loss of their skull-faced mage.

Keeping half an eye on the waiting women, Kheda watched as children, as brown and naked as the first, ran to cut more of the thick yellowy-green leaves from the fleshy plants. They had crude knives of black stone hanging on thongs knotted around their necks. Women in sagging wraps of thin hide knelt to strip the fish from the sticks they had been carried on, gutting them efficiently with more slivers of stone. As the children brought the spiny leaves, the women slit them open and packed them with fish and whatever worms or eels or crustaceans had been dug from the river bed. Older boys hurried to bring twisted branches from stockpiles between the huts while two grey-haired warriors set about rousing the slumbering fire to a new blaze. The slabs of fowl flesh and the long scaly legs were simply propped over the flames still skewered on the spears while the women laid the stuffed spiny leaves in the embers around the edge.

'Do I just stand here?' Naldeth hissed.

'They're coming over.' Risala hadn't taken her eyes off the feather-crowned women, who were indeed reluctantly leaving the shelter of their hut.

'Go and meet them.' Kheda coughed as a shifting breeze hit him with the stench of something revolting singeing in the fire. 'Show them you're in charge.'

'I'll be right behind you,' promised Velindre quietly.

'Can you work any magic without falling over?' Naldeth coughed and strode past the communal fire. All anxious smiles, the savages bowed low as he passed them. The feather-crowned women halted to wait a few paces from their door.

Kheda realised that it was beeswax mixed with red ochre caking their hair to hold their gaudy feathers in place. As dark-skinned as the rest of the islanders, the women both wore wraps of thin hide tied just above their breasts and reaching to the tops of their thighs. Unlike the other women, their garb was decorated with swirling patterns of beads sewn to the leather, made from polished fragments of red shell and pale-yellow bone.

A wariness in their eyes suggested they had lived hard and dangerous lives and expected nothing else. Kheda watched them closely for any more immediate clue as to what they might do but their faces were unreadable. Unable to distinguish between them, he noted that one woman boasted a necklace of strange three-lobed teeth while the other had wristlets of dark scales threaded on plaited grass. Both were young enough that their limbs were still firm and smooth and they had an air of good health.

So you've long been used to better feeding than the majority of these impoverished wretches. I can't see how you could be carrying any weapons under those scanty wraps. Why would you need to, if you can kill with your magic?

'Can you tell if they're about to use some spell?' He slid a sideways glance at Velindre and was reassured to see the magewoman regarding the two wild women with open suspicion.

'It all depends how they've been taught to use their affinity,' mused Velindre.

Kheda drew himself up to his full height. The feather-crowned women spared him brief glances which he met with the most intimidating stare he had cultivated through all his long years as a warlord. He angled his hacking blade and his sword with slow deliberation, the polished steel still visible amid streaks of the great birds' blood and catching the sun. Every other savage stared awestruck at this mystery, though the women remained impassive. Kheda stood poised, blades just at rest as if he were waiting to meet a challenge on the Chazen warriors' practice ground.

Like Telouet testing slaves brought for my consideration. I'm even walking two paces behind and one pace to their new master's open side.

The feather-crowned women slowly turned all their attention to Naldeth. The one with the necklace of teeth was just a little quicker than the one with the scaled wristbands in sinking to her knees, head bowed submissively. As she followed her companion's lead, the one with the scaled wristlets glanced upwards through her eyelashes while keeping her face turned dutifully to the ground.

'Get them up. No, don't offer your hand.' Kheda rebuked Naldeth swiftly as the mage reached out. 'Make it an order.'

After a breath of hesitation, Naldeth snapped his fingers, red fire blinking between his finger and thumb. Both women froze, looking up at him. Their expressions were still masks of indifference but Kheda saw a spark of anger come and go in the eyes of the one with the necklace. The one with the wristlets betrayed nothing.

Naldeth coughed and bade them rise with a sweeping gesture. They rose with fluid grace and turned to walk back into the high-roofed circular hut. Neither looked back to see if they were being followed. Naldeth hesitated again.

'On you go, Master Mage,' Kheda prompted. He stepped up behind the wizard and with Risala and Velindre following close behind, Naldeth had no choice but to go forward.

There was more light inside the gloomy hut than the warlord had expected and the gaps between the stakes making up the walls freely admitted the passing breezes, avoiding any stuffiness. The shade was welcome after the heat of the sun outside.

'How do they cut rafters like that without steel?' Risala looked up, wondering.

'Magic?' Kheda hazarded.

'Not as far as I can tell.' Velindre was looking around the hut with growing interest.

The four thick pillars that held up the roof's framework marked out a wide square. Crude panels of woven stick and grass set between pairs of pillars defined three sleeping areas where hides were piled on heaps of dried grass. A few meagre possessions were tucked into the corners between the rough screens: little gourds, leafy twigs presumably selected for some virtue or other, and unidentifiable lumps wrapped in scraps of animal skin. In the space between these crude concessions to privacy, the earthen floor of the hut was scored with interlaced patterns. Some were mere scrapes of colour, faded and scuffed. Others were intense with fresh charcoal lines cutting through older symbols.

'Kheda,' Naldeth said in strangled tones, 'what—'

The warlord looked up from the patterns on the floor to see that the woman with the wristbands had untied her wrap. Tossing the thin hide aside, she stood naked before the young mage, still wearing that same impassive expression. When he made no move towards her, she went over to one of the sleeping spaces. Sitting on the hides, she found a small gourd in a corner and, pulling out a plug of leaves, poured a little oil into one hand. Still expressionless, she looked up at Naldeth, rubbing oil over her bared breasts and belly until her skin gleamed.

'I'd say she's accepted she's yours to ... command.' Velindre didn't sound overly amused.

'I'm not about to—' Naldeth bit off his heated words as movement outside the hut caught his eye.

'That's probably wise.' Kheda saw there were plenty of curious savages pressing as close as they dared to see what was going on within the inadequately opaque walls of the hut. 'Not until we know what she — and they — might make of that.'

'Not now and not at all!' Naldeth took a step forward, stretching out his hand to the naked woman. She misunderstood him and lay back on the hides, drawing up her feet. 'No, get up, get dressed,' he said hurriedly. She didn't obey, simply spreading her thighs wider. Scowling, Naldeth caught up her hide wrap from the ground and threw it at her. 'No!'

Even in the dimness of the hut, Kheda could see the young mage's furious blush rising beneath his tan. A murmur spread through the crowd outside, with undertones Kheda couldn't quite identify beneath the wide-ranging surprise. The woman scrambled to her feet clutching her beaded wrap. She hurried out of the hut, retying the hide with jerky movements that spoke of shame and anger, her pace quickening.

The second woman with the strange toothed necklace gave a slight shrug, her face as expressionless as ever, and reached for the knot securing her own rudimentary garment.

'No!' Naldeth swept his hands across in a cutting gesture. 'I won't have this. Kheda, make them understand!'

'How?' Kheda tried to keep his voice calm and reasonable.

'I don't know!' Naldeth wheeled around and strode angrily out of the hut. The crowd outside hastily withdrew as the mage emerged into the sunlight.

As he did so, some scuffle broke out over by the central hearth. Kheda shaded his eyes with his off hand and realised that the first feather-crowned woman whom Naldeth had rejected was on her hands and knees. A wild warrior struck her hard a second time, smashing a thick stone-studded club down onto her spine. She fell flat with a cry of pain and fear. No one else moved. The man with the club swung the heavy weapon at her head, using both hands and putting all his strength behind the blow. The club connected with the woman's skull with a sound like a melon dropped onto a marble floor. She lay with her face in the dirt, her arms and legs jerking. After a few moments, she was still.

'I thought you said only mages killed mages!' Horrified, Naldeth flung the reproof back at the other three as he hurried towards the dead woman.

The wild man waited, a gap-toothed smile broad on his dark face, the club in his hand smeared with blood.

'That's what I thought.' Kheda saw tufts of the woman's red wax-coated hair caught on the vicious stone shards studding the club.

'Can you do anything for her?' the mage asked desperately.

'I doubt it.' As they drew closer to the corpse, Kheda saw blood sluggishly oozing from her nose and ears. Her eyes were open but unseeing and her skull was grotesquely misshapen. As they stood over her, he could see pale-grey matter exposed among the crushed ruins of her crown of feathers. 'No. She's dead.'

'Why did he do that?' Naldeth raged, turning on the wild man with the club.

The savage's smile faltered and he took an uncertain pace backwards as Kheda raised his sword. 'Do you want me to kill him? Think carefully about that. A death can't be undone.'

'Kill him for doing what?' Risala interjected. 'Murdering her? Or quite properly executing her? We know nothing of their customs, Kheda. Kill him and we could all end up dead.'

'Not while I have breath in my body,' Velindre promised dourly. 'But we can't kill him without knowing why he did this,' she agreed reluctantly. 'He might have been taking some wholly justified revenge on this woman, now that she hasn't got that skull-faced mage to shield her abuses.'

'I'm less concerned with his fate than I am about ours.' Kheda looked around at the throng of savages, now silent and motionless. 'Naldeth, do you want him dead, to show you're the wizard in charge here?'

As the young mage struggled for an answer, a scream back by the dead mage's hut made everyone jump. Kheda turned to see the second feather-crowned woman backing away from two men who were stealthily menacing her with spears.

'I won't have this,' Naldeth said wrathfully. A ring of crimson fire sprang up around the woman, protecting her from her attackers. One of them tried to stab at her through the brilliant flames. His spear flared and burned instantly to a charred stick that crumbled in his startled hands.

Kheda saw plenty of awe in the other savages' expressions and not a little fear. All the same, confusion was winning out on rather too many faces, and here and there the warlord saw unguarded annoyance. Kheda searched out the old woman and saw her narrow her eyes at him with impatience, before switching her exasperated gaze meaningfully to Naldeth.

He's not behaving as a newly triumphant wizard should. Because we don't know what a newly triumphant wizard should do. Regardless, that could put us all in danger.

'I won't kill her,' Naldeth insisted. 'I'm not her enemy.'

'You may not be her enemy,' Risala countered, 'but you're wagering all our lives on the hope she doesn't want to kill you to regain her status among her people.'

'Get rid of her, Naldeth,' Kheda said, calm and unhurried. 'However you want to do it, just get rid of her. She's trouble we don't need at present.'

Naldeth stared down at the ground for a moment. Looking up, he raised a hand and drew the circle of fire containing the feather-crowned woman towards him. She resisted until the unnatural red flames licked at her. At first the fire didn't seem to burn her and she stayed stubbornly still. Naldeth let a slow breath of exasperation hiss between his teeth and the flames burned gold for a moment. With a cry of pain, the woman yielded and the scarlet prison forced her across the encampment.

Some of the other savages jeered at her, nonetheless staying a discreet distance away. The feather-crowned woman walked as slowly as she could, face downcast yet looking this way and that. She stretched out a hand towards the flames, her fingers outspread. The fire flickered gold once again and she snatched back her hand with a frustrated cry. The mockery of the crowd grew louder as the bright red of elemental fire reasserted itself.

'What are you going to do?' Risala couldn't hide her growing unease.

'I'll get her out of this village,' Naldeth said grimly. 'Then she can take her chances.'

Kheda watched as the wizard steered his now apparently acquiescent captive towards the woven thorn barrier. 'You don't think she'll come back in the night to slit your throat?'

'Then at least I'll have some reason to fight her,' spat Naldeth, 'instead of murdering her in cold blood. Now open that sorry excuse for a gate!' he shouted, waving an authoritative hand at the bemused wild men. Three understood his meaning and immediately ran to do his bidding.

As her magical prison halted, the woman made another attempt to touch the scarlet flames. Naldeth narrowed his eyes and the fire surged higher and brighter. At the same time, the circle shrank and the woman cowered within its reduced confines. As soon as the busy savages had ripped an adequate gap in the thorny barrier, Naldeth set the fiery circle moving once more. Now the woman began struggling, shouting what could only be threats and forcing her hands against the flames, which burned white where she touched them.

'Just run, you stupid bitch, and good luck to you,' Naldeth muttered, frustrated, as he drove the circle of fire out onto the slope dotted with thistly plants and thorny spikes. He snapped his fingers and the fire extinguished itself.

'If she's stupid enough to try fighting you, at least make sure she dies a quick and painless death,' Velindre choked out with reluctance.

The woman stood, panting, blistered hands hanging by her sides. Sweat soaked her hide wrap, leaving it clinging to her body. The wax in her hair had melted and her feathers were all hanging askew. Trickles of red ochre ran down one side of her face and dripped on her bared shoulder. She stared back at Naldeth, utterly confused.

All around, wild warriors raised whoops and cheers that chilled Kheda's blood. Snatching up clubs and spears, they ran towards the gap in the thorny barrier. The boldest favoured Naldeth with enthusiastic, appreciative grins, the rest doing their best to at least bob a bow as they ran. The feather-crowned woman took to her heels, fleeing for her life.

'They're going to hunt her?' Appalled, Naldeth raised his hand.

'There's nothing you can do.' Kheda grabbed the wizard's wrist and forced his arm back down again. 'You wanted her gone. Let her take her chances.'

'Because that's her destiny?' spat Naldeth. 'You saw it in the stars?'

'Because there's nothing you can do to save her.' Kheda ruthlessly set aside his pity for the young wizard and the doomed wild woman alike. 'Not without putting the rest of us in danger.'

'She's heading for the hills.' Risala watched the woman skirting the thorny stockade.

'They'll catch her.' Velindre pointed to a group of wild men using their spears to rip a new hole in the barrier to take the most direct path after their fleeing quarry.

The feather-crowned woman was running as fast she could now, not looking back, heading for one of the this-tle-choked gullies cutting into the slope on the landward side of this stretch of higher ground. Kheda watched, a sick feeling gathering in his stomach.

Movement caught his eye. A deep shadow in another of the rock-strewn gullies shifted. Murky shapes melted, the lines of the random tumble of broken stone blurring and redrawing themselves into an ominously familiar shape. Darkness took on form and substance and the sun glittered on a deadly sheen of spines and scales. The earth dragon co-alesced out of gloom and dust into implacable black solidity.

The woman saw it and veered away, her terror-filled screams tearing the dry air. The wild men who'd been so keen to pursue her fell over each other in their haste to retreat, running headlong back to the spurious safety of the thorny palisade. Ignoring them, the dragon loped after the fleeing woman. It ran low to the ground like a lizard, feet set wide, with its broad, blunt head thrust forward and thick tail lashing behind.

She was running away down the long, shallow slope now, her arms flailing wildly as she tried to keep her balance. The dragon sprang forward with a flash of silver beneath its fold-ed wings. It didn't quite reach her, but as its forefeet landed the earth shivered like a living thing. An impossible ripple

405

reared up through the solid ground to fling the woman off her feet. The dragon took a quick step as she tried to get up and skewered her with a swift downward thrust of its metallic grey talons. Ducking its head, it bit, cutting short her scream of agony.

'Kheda, look.' Swallowing her revulsion, Risala pointed.

The woman's would-be hunters were tearing at their matted heads as they ran back, some even hacking at their mud-caked locks with stone knives pulled from their loincloths. They tossed unidentifiable lumps back over their shoulders as they fled.

'What are they doing?' As Kheda spoke he realised every man, woman and child still within the thorn barrier was drawing closer and closer to Naldeth.

Because the only thing that can protect you from a dragon is a wizard. So you indulge his whims and his brutality and his women's arrogance. Until someone strong enough to defeat him turns up out of the blue ocean.

The first of the men flung themselves through the gap in the spiny circle. Sweat was running down faces and bare chests, mingled here and there with blood. Hands and faces were bleeding freely where the razor-edged stone daggers had slipped.

'It's gems,' Velindre said suddenly. 'That's what they had hidden in their hair, stuck in all the mud and wax.'

Kheda saw she was right. Several of the erstwhile hunters still clutched rough stones that sparkled with the promise of an unpolished gem beneath the muck.

To throw to a dragon in hopes that the beast might just slow down to lick up a jewel and give them a chance of getting away. Which is pretty much what we did in Chazen, leaving caskets of jewels on the beaches to draw that fire dragon away from the inhabited islands.

'What do we do now?' Naldeth asked slowly.

The menacing black beast turned in a leisurely circle, deadly tail-spike dragging to carve a sweeping trough in the dust. Lifting its head, it looked towards the spread of flimsy huts within the pitiful thorny barricade. Eyes of burning amber unblinking, it advanced towards them. Every few paces it halted, sniffing in the dust before licking something up with its forked ebony tongue.

Accepting the savages' offerings. But I don't think that's going to persuade it to leave us alone.

'Can you call up another dragon to lure it away?' Risala didn't look at Velindre, all her attention fixed on the advancing dragon.

'I don't think this beast will fall for a trick like that,' the magewoman began.

'Then what are you going to do?' Kheda gripped his sword impotently. 'Naldeth?'

'I think—' The young wizard broke off with a choking sound.

The dragon stopped and reared back on its haunches, spreading its wings just a little. The smaller scales in the folds of its belly skin were the exact shade of the steel of Kheda's sword. It opened its mouth and growled low. Kheda didn't so much hear the sound as feel it vibrating through the ground beneath his feet, up through the leather soles of his sandals. It shook his bones, reverberating ominously inside the hollow drum of his chest. He rapidly felt light-headed and increasingly nauseous.

'Naldeth!' snapped Velindre. 'Fight it!'

With painful effort, Kheda forced his head around to look at the young mage.

Naldeth's soft brown eyes glittered like white crystal, all their colour drained away. His tanned skin shone with the implacable translucence of chalcedony, while his dirty white cotton clothes had taken on the rigidity of flow-stone. Only the metal of his false leg was moving.

The painstakingly fashioned steel flowed like quicksilver, rivets and folded seams melting away. The ungainly facsimile reshaped itself into a flawless limb, albeit one of living metal. The powerful muscles of a thigh formed above a sturdy knee where bone and tendons shone with amber magic beneath the silver flesh. Shin and calf emerged regular and straight and the liquid steel shaped itself around golden bones to make a strong high-arched foot, each separate toe tipped with a neatly trimmed nail that shone like quartz.

We're dead. We're all dead, except perhaps Naldeth, and he soon will be. Or he'll wish he was, if he suffers Dev's fate.

Kheda found he couldn't turn his head any more, not even to look back at the dragon. He could feel it approaching all the same, its every step sending tremors through the earth. Naldeth groaned like a man in torment and Kheda saw a faint red glint kindle in his crystalline eyes. Warmth wrapped itself around the warlord, not the sun's warmth but a harsh, punishing heat like the blast from an open furnace. Just when the heat was becoming too painful to bear, scorching his unprotected hands and face, Kheda found he could move again, albeit with every muscle screaming in protest.

How does that help me? Other than by letting me see my death coming?

He twisted his head to look for the dragon and saw it had halted on the far side of the thorny barrier. It crouched, cavernous mouth wide open, black tongue running around its grey metallic teeth. Golden fire burned in its amber eyes and the ebony ruff of spines around the back of its head bristled. Muscles rippled beneath its jet-black scales as it extended its steely talons, ripping gouges in the sandy ground. Dust rose from the holes the dragon's claws were making. Dust and then steam. The holes widened and belched hot metallic vapour. The dragon looked down and sniffed. It retreated a few paces, lowering its head to growl menacingly.

Kheda's head throbbed unbearably. The oppressive heat wrapped still tighter around him and every breath he took threatened to sear his lungs.

As the dragon's tongue flickered at the ground, sand and soil flowed into the gashes. Only as soon as one was filled, a new fissure opened up with a whiff of sulphur and a soft crack reverberating deep under the ground. The dragon growled more angrily and slapped at an importunate cleft with a murderous forefoot. The ground gaped to swallow its foreleg and the beast recoiled with a deafening roar. It would have taken a pace forward but a fissure split the earth just where its foot would have landed. Red fire from some unimaginable depth reflected off the polished black scales of the beast's chest. The dragon reared up to rattle its black and silver wings furiously.

The ground shook and the dry sandy soil fractured all around the beast. Thistly plants and spiny fingers toppled into crevices opening wider and wider. Unseen in the depths, the plants burst into flames, adding a homely note of wood ash to the rising smell of sulphur. The dragon retreated, head swinging from side to side, its ceaseless growl now ringing with wrath.

The crevices grew wider still and molten rock bubbled up to spill out over the barren ground. The trickles flowed faster down the slope, running together, merging into one swelling line of glutinous fire. The dragon walked slowly backwards, looking from one implacable stream to another. Each crawling line of burning red was curving slightly, not to follow the lie of the land but to take the most direct path to the black beast. It halted and crouched low, opening its mouth and growling so low that Kheda could barely hear it. The trickles of molten rock slowed and dulled and the murderous heat all around died away.

Intense cold replaced it as the air above them filled with twisting whiteness.

What are all these feathers?

As Kheda's bruised wits went begging for any explanation, the soft whiteness drifted down. It wasn't a cloud but something carried on the breeze. It wasn't feathers, nor, as he next guessed, ashes. As the flakes of this mysterious stuff landed on his skin, they instantly melted. He shivered violently, gooseflesh rising all over his body. Kheda found he could move freely now. The stuff was falling thicker now, blinding him. He wiped it away from his eyes, finding it turn to water at his touch. Where the stuff was falling into the crevices and onto the motionless trails of solidifying rock, it turned to steam.

Where's that accursed dragon?

The black shape was still visible among the storm of white and wreaths of vapour. It snapped at the swirling mystery, brutal head twisting this way and that. Abruptly it sprang into the air. The furious downdraught from its wings drove the whiteness into Kheda's face where it stung like wind-flung sand. The dragon roared, sending furious eddies spiralling through the clouds of steam. It soared away, its shadowy shape soon lost in the milkiness.

Kheda ached with cold, his teeth chattering. 'Risala?'

'I'm here.' As the wind died and the whiteness began falling precipitately to the ground, Kheda wrapped her in his arms. He could feel her shivering violently through her sodden, freezing clothes.

Velindre appeared as the blue sky cleared overhead. 'Where's Naldeth?'

'Over there.' Kheda couldn't resist a shudder as he looked over Risala's damp head.

The young mage was flesh and blood once again, his metal leg the same blacksmith's contrivance it had always been.

410

'Snow?' The wizard turned a ghastly gaze on Velindre. The tiny veins in both his eyes had ruptured, bleeding vivid red to utterly obliterate the whites.

'I didn't dare commit myself to anything more.' She shrugged. 'I just hoped any beast who'd spent its life hereabouts wouldn't have seen it.'

'Snow,' Kheda marvelled. 'I've read about it—'

'These people haven't.' Risala twisted in his embrace to watch the wild men and women staring astonished at the piles of white now melting rapidly as the fierce sun reasserted itself. Several matronly women ran to fetch hollow gourds as they realised this unknown stuff was turning to precious water that was just being wasted.

'How did the dragon take you unawares like that?' she snapped at Naldeth with sudden anger.

'What did it want?' Kheda asked in a more moderate tone. 'Before the snow came—'

'It's a stealthy beast, and I was concentrating on saving that woman—' The wizard stopped, closing his eyes momentarily to veil their bloodshot eeriness. 'It didn't want to kill me,' he continued painfully after a long moment. 'It wanted me to feed it. It would have been quite content to leave me here corralling these people and offering up whomever I chose when it felt hungry.' His face twisted with emotion. 'Now leave me alone. I want some peace and quiet.'

His voice rose perilously and he stumped away across the snow-covered ground. Stopping by the sodden corpse of the first feather-crowned woman, he made an angry gesture and scarlet flames leapt from the body. Flesh and bones were consumed with incredible swiftness, the snow all around shrinking away. The savages watched him disappear into the dead wizard's hut. Most were still looking stunned, fearful respect blended with awe in their faces.

'He's worked more magic today than he'd have done in a whole circle of the compass back in Hadrumal,' Velindre said slowly. 'He needs to rest, and to eat and drink, before he exhausts himself and collapses.'

Risala pulled herself free of Kheda's arms. 'I'll see if I can persuade him.' She went over to the communal hearth where various women were looking askance at the comprehensively quenched fire. Risala clapped her hands together and pointed authoritatively at the fat fleshy leaves. A woman immediately hooked a couple out of the wet ashes and offered them up. Nodding curt thanks, Risala went on her way.

Looking around, Kheda saw that nearly all the whiteness had vanished. He shivered. The sun was beating down as hot as ever before but some chill seemed to have got into the very marrow of his bones. He stripped off his sodden and clammy tunic. 'Are you recovered enough to drive off that black dragon if it comes back?'

'I very much doubt it,' Velindre said dryly. 'Still, let's have something to eat, before all the food goes.' The wild men and women were all delving in the wet ashes and salvaging whatever they could. The magewoman walked towards the dampened fire pit and an anxious girl hastily proffered a fat spiny leaf, wizened by the fire.

'Will it come back?' Kheda waved away an offer of inadequately cooked fowl flesh and took a stuffed spiny leaf instead.

'Eventually,' the magewoman said thoughtfully. 'We gave it plenty to think about. And it gave Naldeth plenty to think about.'

'What happened to him?' Kheda struggled with the memory of what he had seen.

'I don't know.' Velindre walked over to an empty space and sat cross-legged on the ground. 'He'll tell us when he's ready.' She drew her belt knife and slit open the spiny leaf.

'Oh.' Her prize proved to be filled with noisome coils of some worm or eel.

'You must have some idea.' Thanks to blind chance, the leaf Kheda opened contained fish, and he used his dagger to skewer a lump. It tasted sweeter than he had expected.

'You have to understand that a wizard must learn to live within the boundaries of his or her elemental affinity.' Velindre gingerly raised a twisted grey coil to her mouth, chewed and swallowed. 'Those wizards who cannot, who become totally enthralled with their element, lose all sense and caution as they go further and further, searching for the limits of their power.' She scowled. 'Only there aren't any limits. Those mages trying to find them either go utterly mad in the process and destroy themselves, or are destroyed by the Council and Archmages of Hadrumal.'

'What has this to do with dragons?' Kheda shook his head, confused.

'A dragon's power is utterly intoxicating.' Velindre closed her eyes, torn between longing and abhorrence. 'It offers a wizard the possibility of going beyond every constraint of elemental affinity that they have learned to live with, without penalty, without fear, to learn secrets undreamt of by countless generations of mages.'

'Do you think Naldeth can resist such temptation?' Kheda asked bluntly.

Velindre opened her eyes and scraped the rank contents from the inside of her leaf with her knife blade. 'Don't you think I could have found a competent mage with two flesh-and-blood feet to bring on this voyage?' She tasted the leaf pulp cautiously.

Kheda ate some more of his fish. 'What do you mean?'

'I've already told you. The puzzles of this place are not about magic, they're about power.' Velindre continued eating. 'Naldeth, of all the mages I know, understands only too well

413

what it's like to be utterly at the mercy of someone who is more than happy to abuse all the power within his reach.'

'You mean this pirate who cost him his leg?' Kheda prodded at the yellowish-grey pulp underneath his own fish.

'Exactly.' Velindre scraped down to the leathery outer skin of the leaf. 'He wouldn't take that dragon's power, not if the price was abusing these people for the beast's convenience. He didn't only lose his leg when those pirates captured him. He saw a wholly innocent friend clubbed to death.' Her gaze strayed towards the scorched black earth where no trace of the feather-crowned woman now remained.

'You thought other mages you might have brought on this voyage would have succumbed.' Kheda spoke his thoughts aloud without thinking. 'Dev would certainly have been looking for his own best advantage in such a situation.'

'Perhaps. Dev could be quite vile when the mood took him. Mages are just men and women like every Archipelagan or barbarian.' Velindre fixed him with a cold glare. 'Good-hearted or weak-willed and everything in between. Would every Aldabreshi you know behave with impeccable restraint and decorum if they were suddenly raised to a warlord's rank and privilege?'

'It's hardly the same.' Kheda wasn't about to be deterred from his questions. 'Do these wild mages command these dragons or do the dragons command the mages?'

'I don't think it's that simple,' Velindre said slowly. 'Or that complex, if you prefer. The dragons were drawn here by the confluences of elemental power. That's the key to this place, Kheda. Once the dragons arrived, they found easy prey in these people.' She gazed around at the savages in their crude garb with their mud-caked hair.

'Only with all the raw elemental power hereabouts, amplified through a dragon's aura, any mageborn among these savages would have found the magic to fight back out of sheer instinct. Using magic isn't the difficult part of being mageborn, it's controlling the magic before it kills you or you cause some catastrophe. That's why Hadrumal was founded, to save mageborn from themselves and from mobs who would stone them to death to be rid of them.'

She wiped her mouth with the back of her hand. 'But as we've seen, these dragons here don't necessarily want to fight each other to the death, despite what Azazir told me about the dragons of legend up in the mountains of the northern mainland. And however it happened, I think these dragons are content not to fight the mageborn either, as long as the mageborn don't stop them eating the lesser folk. Dragons aren't stupid, Kheda. Once one had learned how to live an easy life with easy prey, the rest would soon have copied it.'

'Like a jungle cat preying on villagers who can't run as far and as fast as deer,' the warlord said slowly. 'Where there's one man-eater, others will follow, not least because the mother will teach her kits the same tricks.'

Which is why a warlord will hunt down every spotted cat on an isle once one has turned man-eater. He'll skin the carcasses and nail the hides on the gates of his residence. Which is, as it happens, what we also customarily do with wizards.

Velindre was staring up into the cloudless sky, unblinking. 'That dragon I made from the air, the one that seized its chance for life by killing the sky dragon, it had no thought of preying on these people. All it wanted to do was fly after the most enticing coils of wind and weather. That sea dragon that we saw had no notion of coming ashore, not with plenty of fish in the sea for it to chase and eat. The dragons who prey on these people only do it because that's doubtless what they've learned from those who've gone before them. They're not responsible for the choices these wild mageborn have made, whether that be just saving themselves and their allies by offering up captives and slain enemies, or the evil of deliberately feeding anyone useless or burdensome to a dragon.' She forestalled any comment Kheda might have made. 'And that choice didn't arise from any inherent evil in the magic of this place either.'

'If mageborn have all this power, why do these people live like this?' Kheda glowered as he surveyed the dirty, inadequately clad savages. 'Even the poorest islanders in the most despoiled domains in the Archipelago live better.'

Velindre raised her brows at him. 'If you had Naldeth's abilities to shape the earth, just for a little while, could you make me a model of a Soluran keep and curtain wall?'

'I don't know what one of those might be.' As Kheda frowned, he realised he had fallen into her trap.

'Do you think these people know any better way to live? Magecraft is a tool.' Velindre waved her smeary blade to and fro at Kheda. 'Of itself, it's no more good or evil than this dagger, which can cut my food or cut your throat. What you do with magic depends on what you know and what you're taught.'

'Perhaps.' Kheda looked around the feeble excuse for a village. 'But as far as I can see, it's still these dragons and the rule of these wizards that keeps these people wretched.'

'If you can suggest any way to improve their lot, I'll be interested to hear it.' Velindre rose to her feet and went over to the cook pit again.

Kheda contemplated the spiny leaf in his hands and realised with some surprise that he had eaten nearly all the fish. He still had no appetite for the greyish-yellow pulp. Seeing a small child hovering hopefully, he smiled encouragingly and held out the soggy remnants to her.

The little girl approached, hesitantly at first, then snatched the fat, fleshy leaf from Kheda and immediately buried her face in it.

She eats like an animal. Is that because she is no more than an animal? These people don't farm any crops. They hunt, but matias

416

hunt together, to take on snakes too big for one to tackle alone. Loals use sticks or stones to smash stubborn nuts and they fight among themselves in bands led by the strongest. That doesn't make them men. But loals or matias couldn't have painted that cave.

The little girl looked up, ecstatic, her mouth and chin smeared with leaf pulp and fragments of fish. Too young to have her curly black hair caked with mud or wax to hold the rough gems that might buy her life from a dragon, she could have been an Aldabreshin child. The sweetness of her smile pierced Kheda as unbidden memories of his lost daughters assailed him.

Does this little one live like an animal because she knows no better? Could these people drag themselves out of filth and ignorance if their lives weren't brutalised by this accursed alliance between mageborn and dragons that makes them little more than geese penned for the slaughter?

Kheda watched Velindre standing by the fire pit and trying to convey her appreciation of the food to the women there with wordless gestures. The women were smiling tentatively. Kheda saw that the old woman whom they had first encountered was among them, looking more animated than he had yet seen her.

Emboldened, the old woman reached out to touch Velindre's golden hair. The magewoman stiffened for a moment, then bowed her head meekly. The other women laughed and several did the same. Velindre bore their curiosity with commendable patience. One of the other savage women rubbed the cotton of the magewoman's sleeve between finger and thumb, her expression marvelling.

Kheda got to his feet and walked past the fire pit and through the scatter of rough huts. He noted cautious eyes following him, and here and there he caught a thoughtful expression.

Ignorance is not the same as stupidity. I should remember that.

417

'Naldeth?' Kheda entered the dead mage's hut.

'Go away.' The young wizard's voice was muffled. He was lying on one of the heaps of grass and skins with his back to the door and the crude screens protecting him from breezes as well as the intrusive curiosity of the savages hovering outside the inadequate walls.

Not the dead mage's bed, nor yet the one where that murdered feathered girl offered herself to you as her old master's conqueror.

He glanced across the dim interior to see Risala sitting against one of the pillars supporting the roof. Her feet were drawn up and she was hugging her knees, her head resting on them and her face hidden by her arms. The food she had brought lay untouched on the ground beside her. Beyond her, Kheda saw a dull gleam in the shadows.

Why have you taken off your false leg?

It looked as if Naldeth had thrown the steel contrivance over there. One of the buckles had been almost wrenched off its strap.

'What exactly happened, with that black dragon?' Kheda asked quietly.

'It held me in thrall with its element so it could show me how to mend myself.' Naldeth's voice shook. 'They can do that, dragons, heal themselves. It could see how I was made and how I was injured and it knew how I could make myself whole again. You're a physician — you must know there are rare earths in our bones and blood, that we'll sicken for lack of them. That dragon would have taught me how to use my elemental power to draw what I needed to renew blood and bone and flesh and skin out of the earth around me.'

'What did it want in return?' Kheda already knew the answer.

'That I let it feed on whatever people I have no use for.' Naldeth's voice was thick with loathing.

'And you refused that trade,' Kheda said firmly. 'I can't think of one other man in a thousand who would have had the fortitude to do that. You fought free of whatever elemental thrall it wrapped you in. You have nothing to reproach yourself for.'

'I could only break free of its earth magic because it misread my affinity.' Naldeth refused to be comforted. 'And curse it, I want two whole legs again. It knew that. You've no idea—'

'Being cut off from my family in Daish has been like losing a part of me,' Kheda said without heat. 'Losing my children, born of my flesh. I live with it because I have to. You do the same. You could have curled up and died when you lost your leg. As you say, I'm a physician. I've seen men die not from wounds like that but from despair. You didn't succumb to either. You didn't capitulate to the dragon, despite temptation few could withstand.'

And I cannot allow you to give in to despair or self-pity just at the moment. You don't seem to realise it, but this fight has barely begun. If I cannot rekindle your spirit, we're all dead.

'I don't see much virtue in declining to become a murderer,' Naldeth groused, but the anger in his voice was blunted.

Kheda went to sit beside Risala, limbs leaden and fatigue tightening his neck. He rolled his head on his shoulders to ease his neck as best he could.

At least I'm not wearing armour.

Risala didn't move. Kheda put an arm around her rigid shoulders with some difficulty. Her tunic was cold and damp and unpleasant to embrace. She didn't yield to his attempt to draw her close. Surprised, he reached over to brush tousled hair from her forehead, trying to raise her face with a gentle hand. She refused to cooperate, shoulders hunching.

'I hate this,' she muttered with low vehemence. 'I hate this place and I hate these people and I hate being so scared and I hate seeing no end to this chaos.'

Kheda still did his best to hug her. 'We've survived death and magic before.'

'This is different.' Risala looked up, her eyes flinty and cold in the muted light. 'Before, we were among our own islands, with some hope of fleeing to our own people if worst came to worst. We were risking our lives to save our own people and, beyond them, the wider Archipelago. You were reading the signs in the skies and in the earthly compass that offered us some hope that we would see peace and safety again. All the omens reassured us we were doing the right thing, even if we were breaking every law and custom. What do we have to guide us now, if you've abandoned all trust in such lore? I thought if you got away from Chazen, from all the demands and debates and the burdens upon you, you'd see the compass clearly again, out on the ocean with nothing between you and the stars.'

She looked out of the bright rectangle that was the hut's entrance, her face smudged where tears had mingled with windblown dirt. 'We weren't even supposed to make landfall here, or to get involved with these people. These wizards were supposed to keep us safe and bring us home when we'd learned all we could to safeguard our own. What are we supposed to do now, Kheda? There's still a dragon and a wild mage between us and the *Zaise* and we've stirred up this place as thoroughly as if we'd stuck a stick in an anthill. How do we get out of here? How do we get back to the ship?'

Naldeth rolled over and sat up awkwardly. 'I know this isn't what we planned,' he began with some distress, 'but I'm sure we can leave soon enough. With the sky dragon gone and the skull-faced mage dead, I'm sure Velindre can work an effective translocation sooner or—'

'You don't think that black dragon will be back?' Risala looked angrily at the mage, flinging out a hand in the direction of the distant river. 'With his pet mage and as many spearmen as the tree dwellers can muster? Assuming it doesn't catch you off guard a second time, as soon as you're gone, these people will still be prey to the first wild wizard or hungry dragon that comes across them. Those who aren't killed outright will just be thrown into some foul stockade. You killed the mage who protected them, even if he was a monstrous man.'

She hunched her shoulders, hugging her knees again, refusing Kheda's embrace. 'Don't tell me you haven't realised all this, my lord of Chazen. And don't tell me you'll leave these people to death and torment, even if they are savages. I know you too well. What I don't know is how we're going to get out of this alive — and don't tell me you've any better idea, my lord, because you wouldn't accept an omen if it rose up in front of you. Not that that will stop you.' She pressed her mouth against her knees as if to stop herself saying anything more. Staring straight ahead, she refused to look at Kheda.

You're one of the most astute women I've ever known. It's only one of the reasons why I love you. And you're right. We're mired deeper in this with every step we take and I can't give you any answers, any more than I can give you any consolation read in the heavens or in omens.

Velindre appeared in the doorway. 'It's a good thing these people don't understand our tongue.'

'I want you to try scrying, to see exactly what lies between us and the *Zaise*,' Kheda ordered her without preamble. 'Which is almost certainly going to draw unwelcome attention, so you'll need to keep watch for that black dragon, Naldeth. Don't let anything else distract you.'

Velindre switched her gaze from the younger mage to the warlord. 'I'm not sure that's a good idea.'

'Then come up with a better one.' Abandoning his attempts to comfort Risala, Kheda got to his feet. He looked down at Naldeth, his expression implacable. 'We certainly won't get home to Hadrumal or Chazen if we're dead and in a dragon's belly, so you had better strap on that leg of yours and start thinking how best you two mages can defend us from the magical malice of beasts or wizards. I'll see if I can come up with some plan to get the better of their spears and slings. Between us, we must get back to the ship.'

'You honestly think we can?' Naldeth looked at him, half-sullen, half-hopeful.

'As long as we're not attacked in the meantime,' Risala said dourly. She glanced at the magewoman. 'Can you scry out for more immediate dangers yet?'

'I think so.' Velindre shrugged. 'But I'll need something to hold some water.'

'I'll get it.' Risala looked warily up at the sky as she went out of the doorway. She didn't have to go far before she reached a knot of women clutching straw-coloured gourds veined with brown. As she held out her hands, the sweetness of her beseeching smile pierced Kheda.

When will you smile at me like that again? How could I have been so blind to your distress at my rejection of both compasses and all omens?

The savage woman handed over her gourd, her scowl making it plain she begrudged it though she didn't dare refuse. Stony-faced once again, Risala brought it back to the mage woman.

Velindre took it with a sigh. 'Come on, Naldeth. How are we going to get past that black dragon without it noticing us? Unless you're going to change your mind and settle for a lifetime as the magical tyrant of this tribe.'

'I have no intention of staying here any longer than I have to.' Kheda managed a humourless smile. 'And as I see it, the only way we're going to get out of here is by cooperating and using all our skills. Let's get to it.'

Chapter 17

Are we any closer to getting out of here? Are we going to get back to the Zaise today? At least we were spared any more attacks yesterday. What good did that do us? How can we work together if we're barely even talking to each other?

Lying on his back as the morning light filtered through the doorway, Kheda looked up at the uncommunicative interior of the roof of the dead wizard's hut and sighed. In unspoken agreement the previous evening, they had dismantled the bed spaces of the dead mage and his women, dividing the hides and heaps of grass into four piles. Kheda had set himself between the open doorway and the four central pillars where the others were sleeping sheltered by panels of woven bark. Kheda had preferred to suffer the draughts, not wanting anything obstructing his view in case trouble came in the night. He rolled over as he heard footsteps outside the hut.

'It looks as if breakfast has arrived.' Risala sat upright as two small, naked children carefully set gourds down by the open doorway and took to their heels. It was apparent from her voice that she had already been wide awake as well.

Kheda retrieved the gourds and found them full of fluffy white pulp speckled with dark-green fragments. He scooped

424

up a cautious fingerful and held it on his tongue for a moment. It was surprisingly palatable, with an unexpected citrus flavour permeating the bland starchiness.

I don't suppose they'd be trying to poison us, not with Naldeth having proved himself so valuable a wizard.

He chewed and swallowed and bit down on something hard. Abrupt bitterness flooded his mouth. Grimacing, he used a grimy fingernail to dig fibres out from between two back teeth. 'Spit out the green bits,' he advised as he brought the gourds back into the hut, setting one down by the two wizards and offering the other to Risala.

Velindre was already reaching for the gourd full of water she had obtained the day before, her eyes distant. She said something to Naldeth in the Tormalin tongue, too fast and colloquial for Kheda to catch. She still looked drawn but the bruises of weariness beneath her eyes were less pronounced than they had been.

'So what are we doing today?' Naldeth tugged crossly at straps and buckles as he settled his stump in the leather cup of his metal leg. He looked up at Kheda with his grotesquely bloodshot eyes. 'Arguing round in circles until the sun sets again?'

'Velindre, I want you to keep scrying for any force of wild men coming over the river,' Kheda said. 'The tree-dwellers' wizard must know you've killed the skull-faced mage between the two of you. I'm sure he'll attack.'

'The only question is when,' Risala agreed as she took a handful of the fluffy pulp. 'Judging by what we saw in Chazen.'

'But the dragons—' Velindre broke off and Kheda narrowed his eyes with growing suspicion.

What about the dragons? What aren't you telling me?

'Velindre can do the scrying.' Naldeth struggled to rise. 'What can I do?'

Kheda offer him a hand. The wizard took it with a reluctant grimace and Kheda hauled him to his feet. 'Can you tell us where that black dragon might be?'

'Can you tell if it's hiding in the shadows anywhere close to spy on us again?' Risala shivered at the thought as she took a mouthful.

'Attune your affinity to earth and fire and do your best to sense any disruption,' Velindre interjected firmly.

'Naturally.' Naldeth tugged his grubby tunic straight. 'But I don't imagine I'll catch it out a second time with a simple trick like summoning up molten rock beneath it.'

Kheda glanced towards the magewoman. 'I take it that black dragon must know it was you who roused that snowstorm?'

She nodded. 'With air antithetical to earth, I as good as slapped the beast in the face.'

'Making it all the more hostile, no doubt.' Risala finished eating, then looked at her sticky hands with some exasperation. She rose and went out of the doorway without a backward glance.

Kheda looked after her.

What can I do to restore your peace of mind, my beloved? Nothing until I've solved the problems laid before me. That's what I've always done, whatever signs I may have thought were guiding me.

Kheda looked down and found he had little appetite for the remaining starchy pulp in the gourd. He forced himself to keep eating and nodded to Naldeth and Velindre. 'We can't afford to go hungry.'

'We can't afford to be caught unawares either.' Velindre plucked up gobbets of food with one hand as she sat cross-legged with the fat-bellied water gourd held between her legs and passed her other palm over the wide neck. Emerald radiance danced within, not quite strong enough to

426

escape. Frowning, Velindre peered into the gourd and faint green light played on her angular face.

Kheda realised a ragged circle of savages was watching them though the deceptive walls of the hut with mingled awe and apprehension. None was coming closer than a spear length. 'Do you suppose they know what she's doing?'

'I've no idea.' Naldeth was eating with little enthusiasm while watching the wild men and women with a curiosity to equal their own. 'We know so little about their wizardry, or what the non-mageborn here make of it.'

'There doesn't seem to be anyone between here and the river,' Velindre said slowly.

'What about the far bank?' Kheda moved closer to peer over the magewoman's shoulder. He struggled to make sense of the miniature vista shining in the mossy shadows within the gourd. Bright patches of brown and yellow and green shifted and blurred. 'Try to find those caves we told you about.'

'We don't know who those people might owe allegiance to.' The cleft between Velindre's golden eyebrows deepened as she concentrated.

'If the river's some kind of boundary, presumably they owe fealty to the tree-dwellers' wizard,' ventured Kheda.

'Kheda.' Risala appeared in the doorway, hastily shaking drops of water from her hands. 'There's something going on.'

He followed her outside to see a handful of men hurriedly tearing open a gap in the thorn barricades on the far side of the enclosure.

Naldeth joined them. 'It's not the dragon.' He sounded sure of that.

'They're getting ready to fight something.' Velindre came to the doorway still holding the gourd.

The men of the village were hurrying to gather their spears and clubs from their rickety huts as a group of new-comers waved their hands in animated conversation with those who had opened the woven thorns. The newcomers' voices were increasingly raised, and edged with urgency.

Kheda looked back into the scrying spell. The river valley reflected in the oscillating mossy water was empty. The water flowed sluggishly between the rich brown of the mudflats and nothing was stirring on the grassy plains, bird or lizard.

'Are they part of this village?' Risala didn't look reassured. 'Or from another? We've no idea who else might be living up here, have we?'

'Or how far word of our presence here has spread,' Kheda said thoughtfully.

Velindre looked up from her gourd. 'Do you suppose some other wizard we haven't encountered yet could have spies set among these people?'

'It's what we'd do,' Risala commented frankly.

Kheda noticed that a girl who had been standing near the arguing men was running over to the old woman whom they had first encountered. The girl began speaking rapidly, her hands lively. The old woman answered her, equally animated. Some of the men and women who had been hanging around the dead mage's hut began to drift towards this new commotion.

'I've found those caves.' Velindre focused all her attention on her gourd. 'There's nothing there.'

'Nothing?' Kheda frowned. 'No people? No fires?'

'No.' Velindre looked up. 'Nothing of what we saw when I scried there yesterday. The place looks deserted.'

'Wait.' Naldeth was looking down at the ground with growing alarm. 'There's something—'

'Something's wrong.' Risala walked forward to meet the old woman, who was making haste towards them, her wrinkled face creased still further with anxiety.

The old woman waved Risala away and hurried up to Kheda to tug at his elbow with her twig-like fingers.

How am I possibly supposed to understand you?

Detaching her hand, Kheda tried to look receptive. The old woman immediately seized his elbow again to urge him in the direction of the sizeable force now gathered by the gap in the thorn barricade. 'Velindre, are you sure there's nothing out there? Forget the caves. What's this side of the river?'

'Nothing that I can see.' Growing doubt tainted the mage-woman's words.

'You may not be seeing what there is to see.' Naldeth stooped awkwardly to spread his fingers on the sandy soil. 'I can feel something working with the water deep within the earth.'

'Is it the black dragon?' Kheda realised he had already taken ten or more steps at the old woman's insistence, Risala following a few reluctant paces behind.

'No,' Naldeth said confidently.

'I'll go and see if I can make any sense of this.' Seeing Kheda approaching, a few of the wild men dropped their crude weapons, holding out empty hands, their faces apprehensive. The old woman scolded them and pushed Kheda's hand towards the hilt of his sword.

Tension tightening his belly, he drew the blade, prompting a murmur of fearful wonder from the newly arrived wild men as they stared at the thin, bright steel. One of the men near the gap in the fence broke into voluble explanation. The other men of the village deferred to him, nodding their agreement. The newcomers' eyes grew wider still as they stared at Naldeth and at Velindre over by the dead mage's hut.

I have to learn how to tell these men apart.

Kheda studied the man who was doing the explaining. He was taller than most, his hair a solid mass of reddish mud. He carried a fire-hardened spear that reached to his shoulder and a worn leather sling tucked through his brief loincloth. His wiry arms and legs were sun-dried muscle and sinew while paler skin marred his flank, just above the hollow of his hip. Some time long since, some beast with vicious claws or teeth had bitten deep into his side. Age and experience shone in his dark-brown eyes, surrounded by the creases of a lifetime spent squinting in the bright sun.

A lifetime that you were lucky to see with that wound. How do I learn to understand what you want to tell me?

Kheda could see frustration to equal his own in the scarred spearman's face. The warlord gestured towards the gap in the thorn barrier with his sword and the wild men closest hurriedly retreated from the sunlit metal. Kheda kept his eyes fixed on the first spearman, raising his eyebrows in an exaggerated expression of enquiry.

The spearman licked his chapped lips and said something to his companions before nodding emphatically at Kheda. He moved towards the gap, jerking his head to indicate that Kheda should follow. The warlord complied, noting the newcomers and some of the men from the village following behind him.

The rest hurried away towards the huts, clapping their hands and summoning the women with urgent shouts. Kheda saw the old woman grab Risala, refusing to let go of her hand as she dragged her back towards the centre of the village. Brisk shouts brought more children than Kheda had expected running to the wide communal hearth. As the savages clustered together, they all looked anxiously at Naldeth and Velindre. The wizards didn't appear to notice. Velindre was still intent on her gourd. She had linked one hand with

Naldeth, who was kneeling awkwardly, the fingers of his other hand thrust deep into the hard earth.

There's trouble coming. Still, both wizards have proved themselves since we made the mistake of coming ashore here. Risala must be as safe with them as anywhere.

Kheda turned his back on the village and scanned the thistle-studded expanse beyond the thorny barrier. He could see no movement beyond the odd dusty stalk stirred by the breeze.

The scarred spearman loped ahead, ducking low and looking from side to side. Kheda followed and the rest of the men spread out around him. They reached the open plateau dotted with swollen barrel trees and the wild warriors split up to take advantage of the cover. Kheda looked to the scarred spearman for guidance. The wild man nodded and beckoned to him. Kheda joined him in pressing his back to the leathery bark and edging around the tree. The scarred spearman craned his neck to see what lay ahead and, catching Kheda by surprise, ran swiftly to the next tree. Kheda followed and saw that the other wild warriors were also advancing from tree to tree in groups of two and three, faces grim.

They reached the edge of the plateau where the rain-scored sandy ground fell away towards the grassy plain. The scarred spearman led Kheda to a vantage point off to one side. As they crouched behind another fat tree, he pointed, and the warlord saw movement down among the straw-coloured tussocks. Movement running contrary to the pleasant breeze bringing some relief from the heat. Concentrating, Kheda picked out smudges of dark skin and an incautious head breaking through the sea of fronds.

Four groups of attackers, possibly five, and spread out all along the plain. If we stay here, we'll be outflanked.

Kheda tapped the first spearman on the shoulder and pointed emphatically backwards towards the village. The wild man frowned and shook his head, reaching out to tap Kheda's sword hand with an encouraging grin.

You think a steel blade will make all the difference? There are plenty of dead in Chazen who could tell you otherwise. Though we did well enough against the invaders once they had no magic behind them.

Before Kheda could finish that thought, stifled commotion behind him demanded his attention. He whipped his head round to see Risala struggling in the hands of a burly savage who was doing his best to force her to the ground. Kheda retraced his steps as fast as he could, ducking low until he was sure he couldn't be seen from the plain.

By the time he reached her, Risala had freed herself from the wild man's grip and was standing at bay. Three savages ringed her, not daring to get within reach of her drawn dagger. The one who had seized her was sucking a shallow cut on his forearm. He looked at Kheda, openly apprehensive.

'There are savages out there.' Kheda pulled Risala into the shade of the nearest barrel tree. 'Velindre's scrying just isn't seeing them.'

I was right, and I didn't need any omen to tell me what to expect.

'That's what I came to tell you.' Still breathing hard from her exertions, Risala sheathed her dagger. 'That earth dragon is manipulating her spell against her — it's something to do with earth and water.' She dismissed the irrelevance with a shake of her head. 'And its pet wizard with the beaded cloak is working some kind of illusion, according to Naldeth. Only one of those bands of tree dwellers is real. The rest are just magical feints that you don't have to bother with, so Naldeth says anyway.'

'Which ones?' demanded Kheda. 'And how do I explain that to these men?'

'Velindre says she can hold the dragon's attention as long as it thinks she's being distracted,' Risala said resolutely. 'Naldeth says that will leave the wild mage working his magic without the beast's assistance, so Naldeth thinks he should be able to break the illusions and you can lead the spearmen against the real enemy.' She looked at Kheda with ill-concealed apprehension. 'You have to look for dust. That's what the wizard with the beaded cloak is using to make his illusions.'

'I should be able to do that.' Kheda felt strangely calm.

'Wooden spears and stone-studded clubs killed plenty of armoured men in Chazen.' Risala slid her arms around him, pressing her cheek against his shoulder. 'Promise me you'll be careful.'

'I promise, and I'll be the only one in the fight with steel weapons, won't I?' He brushed a kiss on her forehead and tasted the salt of the sweat slicking down wisps of her black hair. 'Now get back to the village and stay safe for my sake.'

She reached up a hand to draw his head down and pressed a fervent kiss on his lips. 'Be careful.' She didn't say anything more, simply turned away.

Apprehension fluttered in Kheda's belly as he watched her run back through the scrub, perilously exposed among the sparse thistly plants and upthrust spiny spikes. The wild men of the village crouching closest watched her go before turning their gaze on Kheda, some curious, some uneasy. The warlord nodded to them in turn, catching their eyes and trying to convey a confidence he didn't entirely feel before turning and darting swiftly from tree to tree to return to the scarred spearman's vantage point.

He crawled across the last gap on his belly. The enemy, be they real or illusions, were considerably closer now, far easier to pick out among the grasses. Kheda looked at the scarred spearman, who was intent on the slowly encroaching foes.

He didn't see any bloodlust in the savage's eyes, just a re-signed acceptance that this task must be done, coupled with grim resolve to defend his own.

Not so different from the men who laid down their lives to defend Chazen, even when they knew they were facing magic. Do you know what you're facing? Has this wizard across the river tested you with illusions before? How by all the stars and moons do I explain this to you?

Kheda looked back to see the enemy drawing closer still. He frowned as he saw a plume of dust flourish for a moment before dissolving in the breeze. Then he saw a second sandy smudge spiralling upwards to vanish, and a third. With sudden exultation, he realised there was only one column creeping low and stealthy through the grasses with no such betrayal trailing behind them. They weren't the closest, nor yet the ones looking to advance directly into the open ground dominated by the barrel trees. As far as he could tell, given the lie of the land, they were intent on slipping up the deep ravine choked with nut trees and thistly scrub that ran away inland on the far side of this higher ground.

So they can come up to attack our flank, or even bypass us altogether and strike at the village while all the spearmen are waiting here. That must be the real enemy. If Naldeth is right. Well, we'll just have to trust that he is, always assuming I can make myself understood.

Kheda shook the scarred spearman's shoulder. When the wild warrior looked at him, the warlord bent down and scored four marks in the dust roughly in keeping with the supposed enemy advancing down on the grasslands. The spearman nodded with cautious understanding. Kheda used his sandaled foot to obliterate three of the four marks, leaving just the one he hoped signified the real foe.

The spearman frowned at Kheda, baffled. Using the end of his spear, he redrew the three marks and pointed insistently out at the plain. Kheda shook his head emphatically, pointing at each of the false foes before he rubbed out the corresponding mark again. As the scarred spearman's frown grew more perplexed, Kheda swept his hand around to indicate all the spearmen from the village who were hiding behind the various fat trees. Drawing his hacking blade as well as his sword, he pointed first at the sole remaining mark on the ground with both murderous steel points and then over towards the scrub-choked ravine.

The spearman looked at Kheda, desperately wanting to understand — that much was plain in his eyes. Kheda gazed back at him, frustration burning in his throat. He set down his hacking blade and clapped a hand to his throat. Swiftly, he laid down his sword and unclasped Itrac's silver and turtleshell necklace. Redrawing the three marks that signified the false foes, he laid the necklace in the dust across them and then pointed back towards the village.

The scarred spearman nodded slowly, cautious understanding sparking in his intelligent eyes.

Kheda scooped up the necklace and a handful of dust, obliterating the marks as he did so. Opening his fingers, he let the dust blow away before closing his fist on the soiled necklace and stretching his arm out towards the unseen village again.

Do you understand? Do you see this as an adornment one of your mages might wear? Do you understand that those false enemies are the beaded wizard's work? Or that my wizards will defeat them for you? It comes to the same thing. Do you understand that the real enemy will be evading you by sneaking along that ravine?

The scarred spearman turned to gaze in that direction, new keenness brightening his eyes still further. He stooped to redraw the original marks showing all four putative foes and looked up at Kheda, unblinking. He tapped the side of one dark eye with a dusty forefinger and pointed at the first mark before pointing authoritatively at an individual spear-man lurking behind another tree. He did the same for the second and third, his expression now demanding Kheda's understanding. When it came to the fourth mark, he swept his hand around as if to gather up all the rest of the men and smacked his palm down hard to sweep the mark into oblivion.

You're trusting me this far. You'll leave men to keep watch on these three groups while the rest of us attack the force slipping up the ravine. That's good enough for me.

As Kheda nodded vigorously, the scarred spearman darted to the next tree and drew the men hiding behind it into a whispering huddle. Those three split up to run to different trees, beckoning and hissing to the wild warriors now alert on all sides. The scarred spearman hurried back to Kheda, new eagerness in his eyes.

The warlord turned to look at the fringe of the grassland at the base of the steep slope where dark figures were now obvious, squatting among the tussocks.

Too obvious, some of them. But I'd never have guessed they were a magical deceit if Naldeth hadn't sent word. Still, what wouldn't I trade for a decent bow and a quiver of broad-bladed arrows, so I could put a shaft into one of them, just to be sure?

He looked at the scarred spearman, who nodded back, his brown face implacable. At his sudden shout, the bulk of the spearmen from the village sprang out from behind the barrel trees and ran towards the ravine. Only a few remained behind the foremost trunks, clutching their spears as they looked down the slope of the plateau.

Kheda flinched as a shower of lethal-looking spears soared up from the enemies lurking in the bristling grasses. Before the shafts of fire-hardened wood had landed, several of the village's spearmen had stopped to hurl their own weapons down the slope in answer. Stones whizzed through

436

the air, apparently slung by the attackers below. Some fell short, others glanced off the swollen-bellied trees. More of the spearmen halted, stricken with doubt.

Can't you see their spears aren't landing anywhere close to us and that the stones from their slings aren't kicking up any dust?

Kheda shouted at the hesitating men with wordless anger, urging them on, his steel blades bright in his hands. Some yielded, turning to run for the ravine again. Too many scowled and skirted around him to reinforce the scattered men who had been left to watch the slope.

The scarred spearman shouted something, urgent and incomprehensible. Kheda gripped his sword and his hacking blade and they ran forward together. The first of the wild men whom the spearman had successfully co-opted had reached the brink of the ravine and were looking down with shouts of hate and menace. Kheda flinched as missiles soared up out of the thistly scrub. One of the village's spearmen, less wary than the rest, sank screaming to his knees clutching at a spear driven clean through his body just above the hip. A couple of others suffered wounds and bruises as sharp-edged rocks and smooth sling stones skittered and bounced across the hard earth. A wild warrior close by Kheda fell headlong, dead before he could make a sound as a slingshot buried itself in one of his eyes.

Kheda tried to look down into the ravine without exposing himself to danger. The twisted nut trees grew thickly there, protected from the winds and able to wind their roots down into a more constant water supply. It was difficult to make out the tree dwellers hiding beneath the fringes of pale-green leaves. Another shower of stones and sharpened sticks shot upwards, forcing Kheda and all the village spearmen to dodge backwards.

As they did so, a roar came from behind them, as if some mighty force was charging up the steep slope from the grasslands. The uncertain shouts from the spearmen left on guard rose to a panic that tore more spearmen away from the edge of the ravine. Kheda watched them go, exasperated. The scarred spearman shouted after them, to no avail.

Kheda looked back down into the ravine. He still couldn't make out where the tree dwellers were or what they were doing, but he could see enough dark curly heads to be sure there was a considerable force down there.

The warlord grabbed the scarred spearman's hand and wrapped his fingers around the hilt of the Aldabreshin hacking blade. Still gripping the man's hand, he used the broad blade to point down into the ravine, before jabbing an insistent forefinger into the spearman's chest and then down at the ground.

Do you understand me? You stay here and fight. I have to show the rest of your men that these attackers from the grassland are no more than illusion.

Kheda turned and ran for the slope at the edge of the plateau. To his intense relief, the scarred spearman didn't follow, shouting harsh rebuke instead at those others who took a pace after the warlord.

Over by the slope leading down to the grasslands, the village's spearmen were retreating from barrel tree to barrel tree, seeking shelter from a ceaseless hail of sticks and stones. Kheda forced himself not to hesitate, running onwards, flinching inwardly as the missiles continued to rain down.

It's an illusion. Just an illusion.

Just as he had convinced himself, a stone hit him hard on the shoulder, numbing his sword arm. In the same breath, a mob of tree dwellers, their faces twisted with hatred, appeared over the lip of the slope, brandishing their clubs and stone knives.

If they aren't an illusion, I'm a dead man.

438

An attacker ran towards Kheda, murderous club raised high. Kheda slashed at the man's midriff with his sword before driving upwards instinctively to parry the heavy club. The blade bit into neither flesh nor wood. As Kheda wondered how he had missed the savage, windblown dust blurred his vision. He blinked it away and saw the stone-studded club coming at his face. Kheda dodged to one side but the savage was still there in front of him.

Because it's an illusion.

Cursing himself for a fool, Kheda charged straight at the snarling wild man and found he passed straight through him. A second attacker appeared and Kheda ran full at him as well. A shiver of doubt shook the warlord at the very last moment but there was no way to stop. The attacker vanished, leaving a trace of fine dust sticking to the sweat on Kheda's face. There was no time for euphoria as the warlord realised he had gone too far down the perilously steep slope to stop safely. All he could do was carry on running until the dense tussocks of grass slowed him. Eventually he stopped, chest heaving, and turned to see what was happening behind him.

The last of the illusions dissolved into a cloud of pale dust as a spearman swept his weapon through it. A few of the village warriors were still on the lip of the plateau, looking down uncertainly. More had followed Kheda down the slope, some through choice, others with no more option than he had had. A couple were smeared with dust and blood where they had fallen but didn't seem to be slowed by their injuries. All regarded Kheda with respect tempered with awe. Looking around to get his bearings, he heard screams and shouts coming from the direction of the ravine.

'Let's see how those tree dwellers like being attacked from the flank,' he urged the spearmen. They looked back at him, uncomprehending. Kheda grinned and beckoned with his sword, moving towards the ravine. Grinning back ferociously as they realised his intent, the village spearmen made haste to follow.

Kheda hung back a little as he reached the mouth of the ravine. Walls of angled rocks loomed on either side, bristling with thorny plants clinging to the crevices. The nut trees grew thick and tangled in the uneven depths. He looked back and saw he had no need to caution the spearmen to move quietly. They were slipping through the scrub with practised stealth.

A lesson you learn on this hostile isle or die.

He did his best to match their deftness as they advanced deeper into the gully, drawing closer to the sounds of fighting. As they rounded a shoulder of red-veined stone, Kheda saw a double handful of the tree dwellers climbing up the rock face under cover of the slingshots and spear casts of the rest of their force.

A shaft of fire-hardened wood from somewhere behind whistled over Kheda's head, making him jump. The village spearman's aim was true and one of the climbers screamed as the point pierced his calf. As he reached instinctively down to the bloody wound, he lost his grip on the unforgiving rock. He fell backwards with a despairing shriek cut short as he landed with a sickening crunch somewhere unseen.

The other climbers froze on their perches, yelling back down to their allies. Attackers came running out of the thistly cover, their clubs studded with sharp shards of black stone and raised for the kill. The spearmen who'd followed Kheda ran forward as one man, shouting up to their allies on the brink of the ravine. Dark faces appeared up above and began hurling sticks and stones back down on the climbers. More lost their hold and fell to death or incapacitating injury.

Kheda raised his sword to parry a tree-dweller's club. This was no illusion. The sharp steel bit deep into the hard, dry wood and Kheda wrenched the weapon out of the savage's hand with an effort that tore deep into his shoulder muscles. The man ripped at Kheda with a stone knife clutched in his other hand. Kheda smashed downwards with the club and sword still locked in their deadly embrace. The impact as the man's forearm broke jarred the club free from the sword and Kheda turned the blade sideways instantly to rip the savage's belly open. The wild man screamed and doubled up, blood flowing down his thighs as he tried to close the gaping wound. Slate-blue loops of entrails bulged around his hands.

Kheda would have granted him a merciful beheading but another attacker threw himself forward, whirling his club two-handed and screaming incoherently. The warlord sidestepped and swept his sword round. He cut one of his opponent's hands clean through at the wrist and smashed the other to rags of flesh and white splinters. Blood sprayed from the savage's stump to stain the nut trees as he stumbled backwards, wailing.

Kheda wiped drops of red stickiness from his eyes and pursued the man. Another enemy interposed himself, jabbing with a spear. This one was alert enough to stay beyond reach of Kheda's deadly blade, darting forward to threaten him with the spear's blackened point before scurrying backwards. Kheda joined in the dance, blinking away blood. The savage matched his every move. Out of the corner of his eye, Kheda saw a second attacker slip sideways to come round behind him, club slowly lifting.

Kheda took a pace backwards, pulling his dagger from its sheath. Stepping forwards, he threw the knife full at the spearman's chest, startling him into an incautious leap backwards. Striking breastbone or a rib, the dagger had given the man little more than a flesh wound. The shock was enough, though, as he looked down to see what had happened.

Kheda dodged past the murderous point of the blood-stained spear just as the crushing club swept down behind him with a draught that raised the hairs on the back of his neck. Kheda cut the spearman's head half from his shoulders with a scything stroke of his sword, spinning around in the same movement to meet the man with the club. The savage recoiled, his second stroke faltering. Kheda rolled his hands to send the flat blade between the man's ribs and the savage staggered, bloody froth bubbling in his mouth.

Kheda ripped his sword backwards and the savage fell away dead. The one half-beheaded behind him was dead too. Kheda slipped as he wheeled around to see how the battle was going. There was so much blood that even this dry earth needed time to soak it up. A village spearman, one of many now climbing nimbly down the rocks to join in this battle, jumped the last stretch. He nodded grimly at Kheda as he scooped up the dead tree-dweller's club from the bloodied, muddied ground. A tree dweller ran towards them and then hesitated, fatally, unable to decide whether to attack Kheda or this new enemy. The village warrior's brutal club smashed into his head. The attacker fell without a sound, one whole side of his face grotesquely distorted.

Sword at the ready, Kheda took stock as best he could, ducking down briefly to recover his thrown dagger. The village spearmen's yells were turning from defiant to triumphant as they slaughtered the tree dwellers in the ravine, still more of their own climbing down the rock face to come to their aid.

How do I take control of this situation?

Village spearmen were emerging from the tangled nut trees, dragging dead and dying tree dwellers by their hands or feet. Where one moaned and struggled, a club put paid to his efforts and the warrior dragged him mercilessly onwards. A few of the attackers came walking out of the thickets, heads bowed between their upraised arms. The village warriors drove them on with vicious jabs from their spears, inflicting fresh wounds in their backs and legs.

As they passed by him on either side, Kheda realised the wild men of the village were taking all the dead and injured to the open space beyond the mouth of the ravine, their own included. Where the tree-dwellers' dead were simply dumped in a broken confusion of limbs and bodies, injured wild men from the village were carried carefully and laid gently down on the bare earth. Friends knelt to offer solace with a handclasp or a forehead pressed against the wounded man's, sweat and tears mingling.

Kheda watched as a kneeling spearman drew a knife of black stone from some fold in his loincloth and expertly slit the throat of the wounded man lying in his embrace. A broken shaft jutted from the man's belly, bright with life-blood and dark with ordure from his ripped bowels. Anguish twisted the spearman's face as he waited, unmoving, for his friend's blood to stop flowing down his chest and arm.

I feel your pain. I wish I could tell you you've done him the only service left to you. There would be nothing I could do for him even if I had every instrument and ointment known to Aldabreshin healers.

Kheda turned away to see that the prisoners were offered no such mercy. A spearman condemned one captive to an unnecessarily painful death with a cruel thrust deep into his belly. That prompted a murderous frenzy. Already noisy with flies, the air in the confines of the ravine grew rank with the stench of slaughter. All the bodies, friend or foe, were tossed onto the growing heap of carrion. A shadow crossed the sun and Kheda's blood ran cold. He looked up to see rusty-feathered birds with the keen eyes of predators circling overhead, barred tails fanning wide.

'Kheda!' Naldeth waved from the lip of the ravine, perilously exposed on an outthrust rock. 'What are they doing?'

'Are you sure they're all dead, the tree dwellers?' Kheda's voice cracked as he tried to shout back, his mouth as dry as the sandy ground.

Risala appeared beside the young mage and began climbing rapidly down the rock face.

'They're all gone,' Naldeth yelled. 'Dead or fled.'

All the same, Kheda searched the tangled nut trees for any sign of movement as Risala descended. She ran towards him, her complexion ashen with distress. 'You're hurt!'

Kheda looked down to see that his trousers were foul with blood. 'No, I'm not wounded.' His parched throat failed him.

'Here.' Risala thrust the brass water flask she had brought into his hands.

'What are they doing?' Velindre had joined Naldeth on the precipice.

Kheda let his head hang for a moment, then uncapped the flask and drank. The water was sweet and fresh and whatever enchantment had made it had conferred some lingering cool.

Time was when I would have died of thirst before drinking any water touched by magic.

'Kheda!' Naldeth shouted down at him again.

'Where's the dragon?' Kheda looked up, wiping his mouth with the back of his hand and instantly regretting it as he tasted some dead savage's blood.

Blue magelight swirled around both wizards before Naldeth could answer. Velindre walked composedly down from the heights on a stair of sapphire radiance, Naldeth following more slowly with an uneven gait. The village spearmen instantly threw themselves to the ground, hands outstretched and faces pressed into the dust.

'How can we tell them not to do that?' Naldeth looked exasperated.

'Where's the dragon?' Kheda repeated.

'It's gone to ground somewhere deep in the earth.' Velindre looked suspiciously down and around. 'It's a cursed clever beast. It was—'

Kheda waved her words away. 'Naldeth, if you want to let these people know you're not the kind of ruler they're used to, you had better do something about this.' He waved his bloody hand at the carnage. 'They're piling up the dead and killing off the wounded and if that black beast doesn't turn up, surely some other dragon will catch the scent of so much meat. Are either of you ready to cope with that?'

'This is vile.' Naldeth paled beneath his ruddy tan as he looked at the pile of corpses.

'Yes it is, but it's all these people know,' Kheda said mercilessly. 'What are you going to do about it?'

'Me?' Naldeth's mouth hung slack with dismay.

'Can't we just make a break for the *Zaise*?' Risala clung to Kheda's hand despite the blood clotted around his fingernails. 'If the dragon has gone and the tree dwellers are here, there won't be anything between us and the ship—'

Kheda saw the wizards exchange a swift guilty glance that told him they were thinking the same thing as him. 'Apart from the mage in the beaded cloak? And we can't leave these people like this. We started this, all of us, when we chose to come here—'

A squawk interrupted him as one of the rusty-coloured birds darted down to tear at a dead man's open wounds.

Another landed to peck at the unseeing eyes of the slain with its vicious hooked beak, cawing with pleasure.

'I can do something about that,' snarled Naldeth.

A searing wind sent the greedy birds tumbling through the air. They fled, screeching madly. Stray feathers floating after them were consumed in scarlet flashes. Then all of the dead bodies caught fire, each one burning with the fierce

445

crimson of magic, painfully bright. The village spearmen still lying prone on the ground hastily scrambled away from the scorching heat.

Naldeth clapped his hands, silencing the murmurs of consternation. All eyes turned to the young mage.

'What are you going to do now?' Velindre asked, curious.

'I haven't used earth in an illusion before.' Naldeth rubbed his hands together. 'But if that mage in the beaded cloak can, I'm sure I can do just as well if not better.'

Kheda saw the muscles tighten along Naldeth's jaw as the wizard gritted his teeth.

The mage spread his hands wide and drew a cloud of dust up from the scuffed and soiled ground. The village spearmen gasped as a figure formed in the empty air. It was the skull-masked mage, about as tall as a man's upheld forearm and complete in every detail, from his blue-feathered cloak to the hanks of hair hanging from the cord around his waist. Naldeth gave them a moment to recognise their erstwhile master before stepping forward to scatter the image with a violent blow, his face stern with anger. Stepping back, he smoothed the rage from his face as the dust formed itself into a miniature dragon. It wasn't the lithe sky dragon that the skull-faced mage had courted, nor yet the solid black earth dragon from across the river. A more sinuous creature, it was akin to the dragon Kheda had seen in the sea, albeit red-scaled rather than green.

The spearmen were kneeling in the dust now, all eyes fixed on the floating illusion. Still impassive, Naldeth wove another skein of dust into a pile of diminutive brown corpses. The dragon walked through the air with slow menace, sunlight glinting off its scarlet scales and golden claws.

Now scowling furiously, Naldeth stepped between the stalking dragon and the meat awaiting its pleasure. He smashed the little beast into sparkling shards with a clenched fist. As the glittering fragments dissolved into dust, the wizard sent illusory flames to wipe the image of the slain into oblivion, his face sorrowful.

'What exactly do you think you are telling them?' Kheda asked quietly.

'Hopefully that I'm no servant to any dragon.' Naldeth watched the dust blow away on the wind. 'That I won't see the dead dishonoured by filling some beast's belly.' He raised his hand and the flames of the woodless, scentless pyre sprang still higher, turning from wizardly scarlet to all-consuming white heat.

'I just hope that what he means is what they're understanding by all this,' Risala murmured as she and Kheda retreated. The wild men were getting slowly to their feet, talking quietly among themselves, eyeing all four of them with speculation and, here and there, suspicion.

'What are you doing?' Kheda saw Velindre holding her hands cupped before her, faint blue magelight wound between her fingers.

She didn't answer as Naldeth snapped his fingers and the incandescent white fire vanished. There was nothing left of the dead now but pale, gritty ash. Velindre spread her hands wide and released the magic she had been cherishing. It swept the feathery ashes up into a dancing spiral. Threaded with sapphire, the vortex rose high into the cloudless sky and dissolved into the radiant blue.

'So now they're utterly lost as well as dead.' Risala stared upwards, tears standing in her eyes.

'Perhaps not,' Velindre said quietly. 'Aldabreshi bury the humble dead to return their virtues to their domain but the bravest and best lie on the towers of silence so their merits may be spread wider.' She brushed lingering remnants of azure light from her hands. 'These ashes will be carried across this whole island.'

'My mother said the dead are burned so nothing is left to hold them here and stop them crossing to the Otherworld,' Naldeth said with a catch in his voice.

Risala favoured him with a quizzical glance. 'And you call us superstitious.'

'I wish I knew what these people thought about such things.' Kheda saw the wild men looking at each other with growing confusion and some unease. He took a deep breath. 'Let's get back to the village and discuss what we're going to do next. There's still a wizard and potentially a dragon between us and the *Zaise*.'

Just do the task that's laid before you and don't be distracted till it's done. That's what a warlord must always remember.

His uncompromising tone had silenced the other three and they followed him meekly back around to the open face of the bluff. With the spearmen trailing behind, they all struggled back up the steep slope in silence. No one spoke until the village came into sight. The open space within the thorny enclosure was wholly deserted.

'Where's everyone gone?' Naldeth wondered.

The spearmen started calling and whistling, clapping their hands. Slowly women and children began to emerge from thickets of spiny plants and thistles. Mothers had their babes strapped to their backs with lengths of stretched hide and all were carrying bundles. Even the youngest children clutched some burden.

'They were ready to run,' Kheda realised, 'in case we lost the fight.'

'Where were they going to go?' Risala wondered.

As the men spread out, arms wide to offer comforting embraces, the women did their best to smile through their lingering fears. Little children clung to their mothers' hands or hugged their fathers' legs. Kheda caught sight of the scarred spearman, the bloodied hacking blade still in his hand as he approached a woman, his expression sorrowful. She sank to her knees, pressing her hands to her face to stifle heart-rending sobs as she realised someone dear to her wasn't among the returning men. A young girl simply stood, her shocked face as immobile as carved wood. An infant wriggled in his mother's embrace as she tried to offer comfort to the bereaved girl. Other families clustered around a weeping mother and her bevy of distraught children.

These people are not animals to be prey for some beast. Or playthings to be tossed around by some wizard's whim. They could be so much more than savages.

'Is there anything we can do for them?' Risala's voice was tight with distress.

'Let's get out of this sun.' Kheda took her hand and began walking stiffly towards the skull-faced mage's hut.

'We won, didn't we?' Naldeth sounded less than convinced.

'We won that particular skirmish.' Kheda did his best but his words were still harsh and angry. 'That's all.'

They reached the dead mage's hut. The shade beneath the sturdy roof was welcome and the inadequate walls offered at least some diminution of the sounds of sorrow outside.

'So what do we do now?' Risala asked wearily.

'We think through exactly what we're doing here.' Kheda swatted at a couple of persistent flies that had pursued him into the gloom. 'We've barely taken time to draw breath since we set foot in this place.' He looked at Velindre. 'May I have some water for washing my hands?'

'Of course, my lord.' She mocked him with a low bow before picking up a gourd tucked in one of the bed spaces. She held a hand over its open neck and turquoise light dripped from her fingers. The sound of the drops hitting the empty bottom was loud in the silence.

449

'You were wondering why tyrants and brutes rule some domains within the Archipelago.' Kheda turned on Naldeth. 'It's because once you start a fight, it's nigh on impossible to stop it going further. We've started a war here today. I know we didn't mean to but we have. We've beaten back the tree dwellers but they'll attack again, doubtless with their mage in his beaded cloak coming looking to test himself against you.'

'Then we'll drive him off, or kill him if he won't take the hint,' Velindre said with distaste.

'We don't know anything about him,' protested Naldeth, sitting down awkwardly to massage his stump. 'We knew this skull wearer was evil, we saw him with that girl...' His words trailed off in confusion.

'We don't know anything about any of these people.' Kheda gestured towards the savages outside the hut. 'We don't know who deserves life or mercy, who's selfish or wicked. But I think we've all seen that they are more than mindless animals, more than savages. They're no different from Aldabreshi or barbarians in their suffering, and in their bravery.'

'Which is another reason why Aldabreshin warlords are always reluctant to wage war. Innocents always die, and every innocent life must be paid for.' Risala leaned against one of the pillars supporting the roof. 'The seeds of the future always lie buried in the past.'

'We didn't come here to fight in their battles.' Velindre handed Kheda the gourd, now full of water.

'No, we didn't.' Pouring a little water on his hands, he tried to rid himself of the dried blood. 'Which makes absolutely no difference to our current situation. We've started a war and we either have to abandon these people to certain death when that wizard and his dragon come to exact their revenge, or we have to work out how to drive this war to a rapid conclusion that leaves these people victorious, and safe as a consequence.' He looked at Naldeth again. 'Dev told me why you northerners think we're all savages in the Archipelago: because when we wage war, we do so relentlessly. But he came to understand that it saves more lives in the long run.'

Whereas, he told me, you northern barbarians have wars that have dragged on from generation to generation, wasting lives like waves of plague sweeping across your lands.

Velindre folded her arms and cocked her head to one side. 'So do you have a plan, my lord of Chazen?'

'These people live brutalised by magic.' Kheda bent to wash splashes of blood from his sandals. 'Their lot might improve if they looked to authority earned through wisdom and ability, rather than through whatever quirk of birth grants wizardry to otherwise undeserving individuals.' He looked at his soiled trousers and gave up on them without even trying.

'I find that an interesting perspective from a man born to his own position of absolute power,' Velindre said tersely.

'This isn't about me.' Kheda stood up straight and looked at her. 'It's about them, and this place, and how we get ourselves out of it. We didn't come to fight in their battles, you're right about that, and I still want to get home to Chazen.'

'How do you think we can do that?' interrupted Risala.

'We need to show these people that they can live without a wizard with his foot on their necks.' Kheda gazed out through the gaps between the stakes making up the wall of the hut. 'We need to convince them not to kill their enemies outright, but to offer them the choice of alliance instead of death.' He sighed. 'There will be those who will prefer to die, especially at first, but we can hope that the more intelligent ones will see the advantages to living free of magical tyranny.'

'Which all sounds very fine in theory.' Velindre couldn't curb her irritation. 'Just how do you propose to take magic out of the scales hereabouts?'

'By having you two kill as many mages as we come up against,' Kheda said with brutal frankness. 'And by having you two take no responsibility for these people beyond defending them by meeting wizardry with wizardry. Let them find leaders among themselves. And I can teach them things that will weight the balance heavily in their favour whenever it comes to a fight without magic.'

He paused for a moment. 'If we can make these people a power to be reckoned with, and the rest can see they can do it without magic, without the suffering that's the cost of having a wizard on your side, perhaps we won't need to fight too many battles. Perhaps other people here will want to share in a better life.'

'Perhaps,' scoffed Naldeth. He looked at Velindre. 'What about the dragons?'

'What about the dragons?' The magewoman looked at Kheda, her angular face severe. 'I won't kill them for you.'

'The first thing a warlord does if a jungle cat has turned man-eater is to make sure there are no men, women or children in the forest for it to catch. Every village locks its ducks and geese away and hogs and deer are driven out of the beast's territory.' He looked at Velindre. 'If you say these dragons are only here because they're used to easy meat, we deny it to them. We stop the slaughter of prisoners and wounded. You burn the dead to ashes every time.'

'It's not only the meat that keeps them here,' said Naldeth doubtfully. 'There's the confluence of elements.'

'You kept that black dragon distracted and out of the fight today.' Kheda looked from the young mage to Velindre. 'If you can keep that beast or any other from backing a wild wizard, I can give these people new tools to fight with, weapons that will give them a fair chance of killing an enemy mage without any magic of their own. Once that happens, everything changes.'

'You condemn them to death simply for being mage-born?' Naldeth protested. 'Besides, I thought you said only wizards kill wizards here. Isn't that the custom?'

'Then it's time to change the custom.' Kheda was un-moved. 'You were the ones decrying such magical tyranny. Don't you want to break this vile circle these people are trapped in?' he challenged Naldeth. 'Does it really favour these wizards and these dragons? Isn't their magic just as crude and makeshift as the wretched lives these lesser people lead? I thought you northern mages were all for advance-ment and learning.'

'It's a shame these people can't get the benefit of all the eloquence of an Aldabreshin warlord.' Velindre switched her gaze to Naldeth. 'We might be able to persuade these wild mages to surrender, short of killing them, if we stifle their magic. If we can drive the dragons away, there'll be no aura for them to draw on.'

'But how do we drive off dragons?' Naldeth shook his head. 'We should take this to Hadrumal and lay it before the Council. We've done all we can.'

'I still don't fancy my chances of working any spell over that distance,' Velindre told him with some chagrin. 'I'm definitely not about to try any translocation and I don't know what would happen if I tried a bespeaking. The fire dragon that attacked Chazen insinuated itself into my magic and looked right back through my spell at me when I was scrying for Dev once, before I ever came to the Archipelago. That black dragon could well do something similar.'

'Then what are we going to do?' Naldeth cried, exasperat-ed.

'We try using nexus magic to drive off the dragons,' Velin-dre said promptly.

Naldeth gaped at her. 'What?'

'You were working with Usara and Shiv, weren't you?' she demanded. 'I know they've been looking into blending sympathetic elements. You've a powerful fire affinity and working with Planir has honed your abilities with the earth. There are few wizards to equal me with the air, even if the Council decided Rafrid was a safer choice for Cloud Master.' She swallowed the bitterness tainting her words. 'And unwelcome as Azazir's attentions were, the mad old bastard taught me more about water magic than I ever expected to know.'

'Every scholar in Hadrumal would still say it takes four wizards to manipulate four elements.' Despite his reservations, Naldeth sounded tempted.

'Ordinarily, with the usual run of affinity and elemental power available.' Velindre nodded. 'But we will have the elemental congruencies here to draw on.'

'Nexus magic is best worked through a focus gem,' Naldeth said unguardedly.

'A ruby, perhaps?' Kheda asked bluntly.

Velindre surprised him with a sudden laugh. 'I imagined you'd go poking about in the holds.'

Kheda wasn't smiling. 'Are you sure you can do this? Overconfidence killed Dev just as surely as that fire dragon's egg.'

'We should be able to repel any dragon if we can draw the other elements into a nexus antithetical to its own affinity.' She sounded confident.

'Then we have to recover the *Zaise*,' Kheda said determinedly. 'And I can find good uses for the rest of that cargo. Our best chance of doing that is if we take the fight to the tree dwellers while they're still reeling from this defeat. Can you undertake to keep that dragon away, and curb their mage's power?'

Velindre nodded slowly, frowning. 'I'd like some time to think through a few ways of constraining that wizard's magic without killing him outright.'

'We should discuss this theory of nexus magic.' Naldeth didn't sound quite so sanguine as the magewoman.

'As long as we're not attacked, we can wait a day or so.' Kheda looked around. 'These people need time to recover a little.'

'What then?' Risala was gazing at Kheda, unblinking.

What are you expecting me to tell you? I'm sorry, my love, but I won't lie to you.

'Then we will have the *Zaise* and its cargo and we can decide how to make best use of both.' He swallowed unpalatable truths that he could not bring himself to voice just yet. 'Now, let's teach these people a few things that will give us the advantage in the fight.'

Chapter 18

The old woman was inexpressibly relieved when she final-ly saw dusk sweeping swiftly across the sky. After keeping the whole encampment busy all day, the strangers had finally gone back to the painted man's hut. The old woman accepted a piece of peeled vine from a shyly smiling child and spared the little girl a brief smile of her own. As the child scampered back to her mother, the old woman chewed on the sweetness coating the fibrous core, mindful of her sparse teeth. It soothed the qualms in her belly.

Was something wrong? The strangers had been harsh and curt as they spoke to each other ever since they had come back from defeating the men from across the river. Then the golden stranger and the red-faced one with the powers of painted ones had spent long periods just talking to each other, sitting in the hut, heads close together, murmur-ing like brooding birds. The tall stranger had been stirring all the men to action, making himself understood with wordless gestures and a frown that brooked no dissent. His woman had offered her helping hands to the women setting everything to rights again after their abortive flight to the uncertain safety of the thorn scrub.

People were still busy about their huts and enclosures. One or two smiled at her as they passed by. The old woman nodded obsequiously to acknowledge the mother of a healthy brood who'd earlier offered her shelter for the night. She knew why they were being so solicitous.

They wanted answers to their questions. How would they react when she finally had to admit that she had precious few answers? Would they still be as kind?

At least it still looked as if she didn't have to fear being tied up, to be kept barely alive with meagre scraps and water until some painted man demanded food for his beast. Everyone was still talking about the tale that the men had brought back from the battle. Neither the golden stranger nor the ruddy one had waited to woo a beast with the carrion. Instead they had shown the bodies of friend and foe alike the courtesy of fire. Of painted fire, at that.

She realised she had sucked the purple vine tasteless and her stomach growled with hunger. Welcome as it was, the sweetness hadn't filled her empty belly. She noted that the few men and women of her own age were sitting by the embers of the fire so they might warm their bones against the encroaching chill of the night. Perhaps they would be willing to share whatever softer food there might be, as long as she could conceal the full extent of her ignorance about the strangers.

As the old woman skirted the hearth, she watched some of the men of the village adroitly gutting and skinning a pair of the great grassland lizards with well-made blades of black stone. Emboldened by their victory over those who'd come from across the river, the hunters had ventured out to return with the scaly hissing creatures slain and slung on their spears. They were still boasting to each other of their prowess as they worked. Two men grasped the creature's clawed feet and lifted the naked carcass while another pulled the loosened hide down and slashed at the last webs of tissue along the lizard's backbone.

The village women were hacking the succulent meat from the first lizard. Dark lumps were already skewered on branches wedged with stones and propped with sticks to hold the meat safely above the flickering flames. Dripping juices spat in the embers while the hunters gnawed freshly flensed ribs and discussed whose valour had won the choicest pieces of the lizards' hides.

As she approached the elders, the old woman noted a young girl still with maiden hips kneeling where the hunters had carefully spilled the lizard's guts onto a length of blood-stained hide. The girl cut the convoluted bowel into slippery, pungent rings and dropped handfuls into a series of gourds. As she chopped up lungs and stomach, one of the hunters sat with a stone in his fist and obligingly smashed open the lizard's long bones so the maiden could scoop out the marrow and add it to the gourds. Topping each one up with water, she pushed them carefully into the embers around the edge of the fire, smiling at the grandmothers sitting a short distance away who querulously warned her not to let them burn instead of merely seething in the fire's heat.

The old woman sat slowly down, careful not to infringe on the elders' gathering. One old man and a couple of grandmothers, wizened as berries at the end of the dry season, eyed her keenly.

There were always more old women than old men. There were fewer ways a woman could die, as long as she survived childbirth. Men risked their lives every time they went out to hunt. Even a bite from a spotted scurrier cub could suppurate and kill the strongest spearman. So many men were lost in the painted men's battles. Women inevitably found themselves the playthings of the victors but they seldom died of it, even if they might wish it, at first. By the time the bruises and torn flesh had healed, most decided life was still better than walking out into the night to meet whatever death lurked in the darkness.

The old man and the grandmothers decided to notice the newly arrived old woman. The old man closest to her shuffled backwards and two women drew aside a little. Now she was more or less included in their erratic gathering. The old woman blinked away tears and nodded her gratitude.

As she sat quietly, she realised many of the elders were cherishing discreet excitement and not just because there was more than enough food for everyone to eat their fill tonight. The painted man who had worn the mountain-climber's skull was dead. These new painted strangers had shown no interest in offering up the dead of the battle to his blue beast. Indeed, the blue beast hadn't returned since it had flown away in pursuit of the white beast that none of them had seen before. Nor had the white beast come back. These painted strangers hadn't fed it with the dead of the battle against the men from across the river. What did all this mean?

Dark eyes shining bright in the firelight slid towards the old woman. She shook her head regretfully. She couldn't say where the white beast had come from, or where it had gone. She couldn't say, and she would keep her suspicions to herself.

The two wrinkled grandmothers who had made room for her, similar enough in features and mannerisms to be sisters, dismissed the question of the white beast with flapping hands. The blue beast was what they had feared and now it was gone. It hadn't even returned when the painted man's women were fighting with the red stranger.

Which was not to say it wasn't going to return. A wizened old man rubbed a swollen-knuckled hand thoughtfully over his ash-white hair. It could come back the very next morning. Or the black beast from across the river would be back.

They knew that black beast of old and it had only been the blue beast and the painted man that had protected them from it. He saw no reason to celebrate.

A grandsire further around the circle was more optimistic, though his mumbled words were difficult to understand. Perhaps these strangers were going to challenge the painted man who summoned the black beast next. At least two of these newcomers had the powers of painted ones. His son had been in the battle against those from across the river and he had seen fire and wind bend to fulfil the strangers' desires.

The white-haired old man wondered with some asperity just how these strangers could be doing such things without winning a beast's favour by feeding it carrion or captives. The mumbling man had no answer to that and stared into the hearth, sucking on his toothless gums.

Another old man with clouded eyes soon rallied. If they had no answers to their questions, they had the evidence of their own eyes. The red stranger with the mysterious leg had turned his face against the feathered women, there was no doubt about that. He had driven them out to take their chances against the clubs and spears of the village hunters. He had even driven off the black beast after it had appeared to claim the second woman for its own. He had used his powers to turn attackers to dust in the battle. He was plainly set on defending the village.

The white-haired old man wasn't convinced there was any such reason for optimism. How did they know the breaking and burning of the land and the strange white water that had fallen from the sky was the red stranger's doing? And he had taken the painted man's hut, even if he hadn't taken his women. Perhaps he had driven the woman out to be eaten by the beast, knowing it would be waiting for her. Perhaps that was the fate he had intended for the first one, and why he had been so furious when she had been slain. Perhaps

460

that was what these people did, in whatever strange land they came from. He turned to look at the old woman.

She considered her reply carefully before explaining how she had seen them floating along the coast on a strange raft. They had been coming along the sunrise coast and then turned the headland to continue along the sunset shore. Presumably they had dragged their raft ashore somewhere but she didn't know where that might be. She admitted she had simply seen them walking as she had been coming along the cliff tops herself and followed. The village elders gaped at her. Voluble, the sisters searched their joint memories for any tales of such things that might ever have been brought to the village. The white-haired old man hushed them, openly disbelieving. Piqued, the old woman told of the waterspout that had appeared out of an empty sky to draw away the water beast. That silenced him.

Then the old woman braced herself for someone asking just where she had come from, but no one did. The conversation faltered once again as all the elders wondered what to make of the mystery of the strangers' origins.

One of the sisters heaved a sigh and opined that there was nothing to be done but wait and see, so they might as well enjoy going to sleep on full bellies for a change. All eyes gazed greedily at the gourds now steaming copiously. The circle sat in silence for a while, the old woman wondering if she might expect an equal share.

The old man with the clouded eyes cleared his throat. What precisely was it that the tall stranger had sent the men and boys of the village to gather that afternoon? He explained that he had been occupied with other things. The old woman noted the other elders accepting this readily enough. Of course they would. No one would draw unwelcome attention to their own infirmities by mentioning another's failing sight or trembling hands. No one wanted the hunters or the matrons turning their thoughts to just what the elders offered the village in return for their usual meagre food.

The white-haired old man told him, his wrinkled face animated. First it had been sticks. Not firewood, he explained, but those rare tree limbs long and straight enough to be turned into spears. But he had stopped any of them sharpening the ends or hardening them in the hearth. The other old men looked at one another, shrugging bony shoulders in incomprehension.

That was not all, one of the sisters added unexpectedly. He had wanted grass. All the elders looked doubtfully at her. The tall stranger had wanted grass, she insisted, and not just for sleeping on. He had piled it inside the painted man's hut beside the sticks. Curious glances turned to the old woman once again. She had no choice but to admit her utter ignorance. Disappointment clouded various faces and she quailed inside.

The toothless old man sat up straight and pointed across the broad stone ring of the hearth as the tallest stranger came out of the painted man's hut, his woman at his side. The hunters of the village hastened to offer him both of the freshly killed lizard hides. The old men all agreed that was wise; any man carrying those knives like splinters of lightning should be placated even at such a cost.

The old woman watched the tall stranger lift up the first heavy lizard skin, turning it this way and that. He was frowning, but more in thought than in displeasure, unless she missed her guess. What was he going to do?

The tall stranger laid the skin carefully down and set the second next to it. He stood up, rubbing a hand across his beard. Snapping his fingers, he attracted the attention of one of the village's most revered hunters, who had been sitting close by the fire and waiting for first choice of the best of the meat, as was his right.

The old woman heard the white-haired old man whisper to his neighbour that the stranger had plainly recognised his son's merits. He had lent him one of his lightning knives during the battle with the men from across the river. The old woman thought privately that the white-haired man's son couldn't have been so clever in his youth, not if he'd so nearly fallen victim to whatever had dug its claws into his side.

The tall stranger was still deep in thought. Handing his two bright knives hidden in their wrappings to his woman, he untied the long strip of hide he wore doubled around his waist. The scarred hunter watched him closely. The stranger proffered the long strip of unknown hide and the hunter took it from him, bemused. Drawing his smallest blade, the stranger crouched and pretended to slice an equal length from the softer belly skin of the lizard hide. Standing up again, he pretended to pass the strip of lizard skin to the hunter, taking the unknown hide back in return. The hunter looked at him, baffled. Visibly trying to curb his exasperation, the stranger repeated his actions.

Several people around the hearth understood in the same moment and called out to the scarred hunter. The white-haired elder wondered aloud what the stranger could possibly want with strips of hide. The old woman saw younger women hurrying to bring old, worn hides from their huts. They weren't concerned with what he might want them for; they were just happy to exchange them for some claim on the highly prized lizard skin. The wrinkled sisters voiced their tart opinion that the tall stranger must be some kind of fool, to trade at such a disadvantage.

Was he a fool? The old woman wondered silently. She didn't think so. But he had had no idea how to find water roots and could have stood underneath the green-nut trees till he had starved before he had thought to eat them. She kept that recollection to herself.

463

The toothless old man was arguing with the wrinkled sisters. All of the village hunters had admired the tall stranger's bravery in the fight against the enemy from across the river. He had seen through their painted man's deceptions somehow, and led them on that courageous attack up the ravine. The other old men concurred. The tall stranger was definitely a man to have on your side in a fight, and not just because he carried those remarkable blades.

All conversation around the hearth circle died abruptly as the two pale strangers appeared, the ones with the painted men's powers. The golden-haired one exchanged a few words with the tall stranger before bending down to gather up an armful of the pieces of hide. As the tall man spoke briefly to the red stranger with the curious leg, the golden-haired one jerked her head back towards the painted man's hut and the two of them walked away. The tall stranger watched them go, exchanging a few words with his woman. She bent to help him sort through the remaining hides, her face drawn and tired.

The white-haired old man ventured his opinion that the tall stranger must also have the powers of a painted man, for the red stranger and the golden one both deferred to him. When did a painted man bow his head to anyone but a more powerful rival?

All eyes turned to the old woman again, so she told them she had seen no sign of the tall stranger using any painted man's powers. Yet, she freely admitted, he certainly seemed to be the leader of the four strangers.

The white-haired old man spoke over her, still insisting that the tall stranger must be a painted man. And his woman had such powers too, most likely. Apprehension deepened the creases in his aged face. Painted men only ever cooperated with each other. No wonder none of the strangers had shown any fear of the black beast. If they were going to attack the painted man across the river, perhaps it was so they

464

could feed him to the black beast, like the feathered woman, and win its favour that way.

Everyone fell silent. As the maiden returned and carried the gourds from the edge of the fire with hide-draped hands, no one spoke apart from offering the briefest thanks. She looked around the circle, concerned, but knew better than to ask. The wrinkled sisters and the white-haired old man let the old woman dip her hand into the gourd they were sharing between them. She fished out a hot slippery piece of intestine and ate it hungrily, waiting humbly to be offered the gourd again before taking another piece. Once all the offal was eaten, the white-haired old man seized the gourd and slurped at the ripe-smelling broth of the lizard's innards, stomach contents and bone marrow.

On the far side of the hearth, the scarred hunter was smiling ingratiatingly at the tall stranger, gesturing to the lizard meat cooking over the fire. The tall stranger took a whole branch heavy with meat away from the flames and drew his smallest lightning blade. The village women shared glances to reassure themselves there would still be plenty of meat for their children, even if the stranger was claiming such an unexpectedly large share.

The white-haired old man started saying something but then fell silent, his broth-stained mouth hanging open. The tall stranger wasn't keeping all the meat for himself. Instead he sliced it with his lightning knife and offered it all around, first to his woman and then to the other pale strangers who had now returned empty-handed from the painted man's hut. The white-haired man recovered himself sufficiently to argue this made his point for him. A painted man would only share his meat with others of his kind. Painted men would certainly only take orders to fetch and carry from another painted man.

Then the tall stranger took another lump of meat and cut a portion, which he offered to the scarred hunter on the point of his blade. The hunter squared his shoulders and took the meat with a shaking hand. As he stepped back to tear into it with his white teeth, the tall stranger offered a portion to the next hunter. The others promptly stepped forward. The circle of elders watched, mystified, as the tall stranger proceeded to cut up and apportion all the lizard meat. He continued until everyone had been fed. Even the smallest and weakest of the children got a share.

From the wonder on some of their little faces, the old woman guessed it was the first time they had tasted anything but offal. She almost wished she still had the teeth to manage meat like that. But at least she had a full belly. The second of the wrinkled sisters handed her the gourd and she drained the remaining pungent broth.

The scarred hunter walked around the hearth and sat down beside the white-haired old man. The old woman enviously noted the family resemblance that so safeguarded the old man. The hunter was watching the tall stranger, who was now sitting with his woman and the two pale strangers. The white-haired old man began telling his son her tale of seeing them on their strange raft on the sunrise coast.

The scarred hunter asked her bluntly what else she knew of these strangers. She repeated her tale of the waterspout that had lured away the water beast. The white-haired old man barely let her finish before insisting once again that all four strangers must be painted men, his voice rising.

The old woman looked down at the empty gourd. Well, if she was to die tonight, it would be with a full belly and warmth in her weary bones. So she told them about the painted cave. She slid over the dangerous truth that it was she who had led them to it, saying instead that they had seemingly stumbled upon it while she was merely following them. Though she admitted they had deliberately raised a path across the river for her. She assured the scarred hunter that the strangers had insisted she go inside the painted cave, mutely beseeching him not to kill her out of hand for profaning it.

He nodded reassurance. After all, who among them would dare refuse a painted man's order?

After that, it cost her nothing to admit she had been following the strangers out of fear of being captured and handed over to the local painted man, whoever he might be. Every wrinkled, toothless face showed that these elders understood such fears. What mystified them all was the old woman's insistence that the strangers had known nothing of such caves, that they had first marvelled at the paintings and then simply ignored them.

The hunter turned to his white-haired father and pointed out that none of the strangers were in fact painted in any way. For all their strange garb, none wore feathers or shells or bones or any of the signifiers anyone with the least pretensions to power adopted. The tall stranger's demeanour in the battle and now around the fire had convinced him that the man was a hunter among his own people, and one of great stature if he was accustomed to sharing meat so lavishly.

The white-haired old man shook his head, his face oddly troubled as he reminded them all that the tallest stranger wore something wrought of the same stuff as his knives and some kind of scale or shell around his neck. However strange their customs in whatever strange land they had come from, these were all still painted men as far as he could see. Only painted men could protect the unpainted from the beasts. He restated his conviction that it was simply the custom of these strangers only to feed their less powerful rivals to the beasts.

The scarred hunter had no answer to this. He stared into the fire, eloquent in his frustration at being unable to understand a word the tall stranger said.

The old man with the clouded eyes spoke up with a new concern. Surely they were all agreed that these strangers offered more protection for the village at less cost in lives and even in lizard meat than the painted man with the skull mask and his feather-crowned women. That could only be a good thing. But there were those among them who had not yet dared to claim paint or feathers as earnest of their abilities.

They would see the tall stranger's forbearance as weakness, and sooner or later would contemplate challenging the red stranger or the golden one. If these strangers were taken unawares by some attack, if their customs for such challenges were different, disaster might befall them and thus the rest of the village. None of those who wished them well would be able to warn them, not given that no one knew any common tongue with them.

The toothless man was similarly perturbed. Word of the death of the painted man who had worn the skull was soon going to spread among all the villages that he had ruled with the blue beast's connivance. Who knew how far beyond the river the news would reach? Sooner or later, some painted one who coveted this land and its people's blood and sweat would come to challenge the red stranger with the curious leg, or the golden-headed one. How could they stop such a thing happening, however much they might want to?

If any such challengers came, they would go to the painted cave first of all, the scarred spearman said slowly, whoever they were and wherever they came from. He fell silent and sat staring into the fire, unblinking even when a passing youth threw on a fresh bundle of twigs to strike bright sparks from the embers. Finally he got up and walked away without even a word to his father. The old woman watched him go to join a group of hunters sitting some distance from the strangers. After a short while, the men got up and one by one retreated into the darkness.

Chapter 19

Kheda realised he was awake, but this time it was nowhere near dawn. What had woken him? There was no sound to prompt instant alarm and he breathed a little easier.

He could hear the regular rhythm of Naldeth's exhausted sleep and the rasping that was usually a prelude to Velindre's penetrating snores. Then he heard movement: bare feet stealthy on the beaten earth. He opened his eyes and saw only blackness. Rolling onto his side, he raised himself up on one elbow. The darkness was barely relieved by the dying firelight slipping between the twisted sticks that made up the rudimentary walls of the dead mage's hut. A shadow slid across the bands of black and red, moving towards the doorway. It was Risala.

'What is it?' whispered Kheda. The bedding beneath him rustled as he made sure his sword and hacking blade lay ready to hand.

'I don't know,' Risala replied quietly.

Kheda rose and went to stand beside her. 'I thought they had all gone to sleep.'

I wouldn't have allowed myself to sleep otherwise.

'Not everyone.' Risala hugged herself against the chill of the night. The mage's hut was well beyond whatever warmth might still linger around the hearth's embers.

Kheda moved, partly to see more clearly, mostly to stand behind Risala and fold her in his arms. She leaned back against him. Kheda glanced upwards and noted the positions of the stars. 'It's not long till dawn.'

'Is there anything in the stars to help us?' Risala queried.

'Not that I can see.' Kheda looked out across the open ground.

We reached that outlying drowned island little more than a handful of days ago. The stars and heavenly jewels have barely moved. How could they possibly reflect this headlong run of startling events?

There was definitely movement out in the shadowy expanse. The savages' huts were blots of denser darkness in the night. The dim red glow lit on figures moving from one hut to another, crouching low. Stifled noises crept across the encampment. It was impossible to see what was going on, with the Lesser Moon still too new to make up for the loss of light now that the Greater Moon was definitely past full.

I don't need the Diamond riding with the Winged Snake in the arc of death to tell me I must find a way to evade these dragons or die. If the Spear in the arc of travel is telling me I came here to find a fight on my hands, that's hardly a surprise. I don't need the Amethyst to counsel calm and caution, nor the Opal in the same arc of the sky to promise that clear thinking will protect me and mine from the beasts.

All the same, a faint tremor stiffened his spine as stubborn recollection suggested more pertinent conjunctions in the heavenly compass.

The Ruby for friendship and talisman against fire rides with the Bowl that is symbol of sharing in the arc where we look for signs of wider brotherhood as well as with those born of our blood.

But I'd already concluded that these savages and we people of the Archipelago share a common humanity before I looked up at the sky just now. I don't need the Pearl as emblem of fertility combined with the stars of the Vizail Blossom in the arc of home and family to remind me of Itrac so far away.

Why should I cling to a fool's hope that the Pearl might truly be a talisman against dragons of air and water? It's talisman against sharks and I don't see any of those here.

The wizards stirred behind him and Velindre began snoring. Kheda tried to concentrate on the mysterious goings-on around the ramshackle huts. Unbidden thoughts persisted, disconcerting.

It was a shark that took Naldeth's leg. Time was when I would have spent long hours finding some significance in that. And wondering what new ideas the Topaz might validate as it rode in the arc of self and life with the Canthira Tree, whose seeds must suffer fire to sprout anew. No, this is just weariness distracting me.

Risala stood straighter, her body pressing back against his. 'Look, over there.'

Dark figures were dragging something from a hut. Hurrying, they headed for the thorny barrier. As two began ripping a hole in the spiny weave, the rest shouldered their limp, unresisting burden. It looked uncomfortably like a body, hard to say whether dead or unconscious.

'Stay here.' Kheda reluctantly let her out of his arms and quickly retrieved his scabbarded sword from beside his crude bed. As fast as he dared, he ran across the enclosure, trusting that it was as empty at night as it had been in the day. Nevertheless, by the time he had reached the void in the woven thorns, the dark shapes were through the barricade. Kheda drew his sword with a steely whisper. 'Who's there?'

Not that they'll understand, but their reactions might tell me something. Are they from this village or interlopers come to wreak havoc in the night?

He took a pace forward, his ready blade shining like blood in the fading light of the embers.

The group halted, indecisive, half-lost against the shadowy backdrop of the thickets of spiny fingers. A man stepped forward to stand tall in the fragile moonlight. Kheda recognised the scarred spearman. He walked towards Kheda, his expression sad yet implacably resolved. Moonlight silvered wetness on the wild man's arm and on his hand holding a knife of glossy black stone.

Who have they killed and why? Is this justice or revenge? How can I possibly tell? Can I trust this man who's proved himself in battle at my side? Do I have any other choice?

Kheda took a pace backwards and lowered his sword. The spearman nodded slowly and retreated into the darkness. Two other men crept forward, shooting nervous glances at Kheda as they dragged the spiky branches back together, securing the huts' defences. Kheda watched the dim figures disappear utterly into the impenetrable night, faint sounds of movement soon lost among the breeze-stirred rustles of thistly plants.

Where are they going? What are they doing? How could I hope to ask them?

Sliding his sword back into its scabbard, he walked slowly back to the dead mage's hut. As he passed the black entrances to the rickety huts, he caught the faint gleam of watchful eyes here and there. From one of the wretched dwellings he thought he heard stifled weeping.

Unfriendly silence fell over the enclosure like a pall. There were no sounds of night birds beyond the thorns, or any discreetly foraging animals. The air was cold and the ground beneath his bare feet damp with dew. The acrid taint of the embers in the hearth was overlaid with strange scents from unfamiliar plants. Something scuttling around the stones ringing the fire caught his eye. Long black beetles with twisted feelers scurried over and around the rank remnants of the lizard meat and the broken bones.

A faint breeze fingered his naked shoulders and Kheda felt dreadfully exposed standing all alone beneath the uncaring moons.

Do dragons come out at night?

Shivering, and not just from the pre-dawn chill, he broke into a half-run. Entering the dead mage's hut, he was breathing hard from more than exertion.

'What's going on?' Risala's urgent hands gripped his arms.

He slid his hands around her waist and drew her close. 'I don't know.' His soft words were muffled by her hair. 'It was men from the village, but I don't know what they were doing.'

Risala turned her face up to his. Kheda thought she was going say something, but she changed her mind and kissed him instead. He kissed her back and held her so close that he could feel her hip bones pressing into him. Her breath came faster, with a shudder of urgency as her kisses became more insistent, more demanding. He felt her fingertips digging into his shoulder blades.

Does this mean things are right between us? No, but this isn't a time for words. There are some things that need no words. We still have that understanding.

He matched her fierce kisses. There was a desperation in her passion and he recognised the same need in himself. Still embracing Risala and guiding her backwards, he walked step by slow step towards the rough heap of grass and skins where he had been sleeping. As the exhausted wizards slept on unseen in the darkness, he laid Risala gently down. He heard her wriggle free of her cotton trousers as he unknotted his own drawstring. Kneeling, he slid her tunic up over her stomach and her ribs, kissing her smooth, warm skin. He tarried over the yielding softness of her breasts as her breath came faster beneath his fingers and mouth and her hands

473

roamed around his head and shoulders. Neither of them let slip any sound.

Risala shifted beneath him and Kheda rose above her for a moment before claiming her lips with his own. Her hands slid up beneath his tunic and her fingers dug into the broad muscles of his back as she guided him to her. Holding tight, she drove him on with insistent hands, her back arching.

Kheda let go all the questions of these violent few days and the puzzles of this malevolent night. He abandoned himself to pure sensation, to the touch of skin on skin, the brush of lips on willing flesh. All his thoughts turned to riding the building swell of ecstasy sweeping them both along until he felt Risala break beneath him. As her body was rocked by waves of bliss transcending time or place, he let loose his own ardour and plunged on into the velvet darkness. Now it was Risala who matched her moves to his, willing him on. He threw himself into the endless instant where all consciousness was swept away.

Heart pounding, he came back to himself lying with Risala's arms cradling his head to her breasts. He could hear her heartbeat beneath her ribs, gradually slowing. Kissing her soft skin, he tasted salt and felt his sweat slowly mingle with hers. The cool of the night gradually asserted itself over the warmth between them but Kheda didn't want to leave her. Risala made no movement apart from gently stroking his hair.

Velindre exhaled noisily in her sleep and began snoring more loudly than ever. Beneath Kheda, Risala shook with suppressed giggles. He stifled her laughter and his own with a long fond kiss before withdrawing from her embrace. As he adjusted his clothing, Risala slipped back into her trousers. As they lay down together again, Kheda slipped one arm beneath her head and tucked the other around her waist, her thighs resting against his. After a soft kiss in the angle between her neck and shoulder, he gave himself up to the oblivion of dreamless sleep.

She had gone when he awoke. He blinked and realised the daylight outside was once more striping the gloomy interior of the hut. Even in the shade, the night's chill had long since been driven out by the harsh dry heat of this unfriendly land. Outside he could hear muted voices and a strange drumming sound.

Where's my body slave? I'll take a long bath with scented soap before I breakfast. Send word to the kitchens that I fancy honeyed saller bread stuffed with rustlenuts coated in tarit seed, and just a little fresh goat curd to cut the sweetness.

Kheda sat up on his crude bed, rubbing a hand over his hair and beard and feeling uncomfortably frowsty. His blood-stained trousers repelled him but he had nothing else to wear. Then he saw the lengths of wood that he had bidden the wild men gather the previous day, along with the heaps of grass and lengths of well-cured leather.

Do the task before you.

'You're awake.' Naldeth appeared in the doorway. The blood staining his eyes was beginning to discolour like bruises, but other than that he looked well rested.

'Let's get to work.' Kheda nodded at the grass and leather strips as he got to his feet and dressed.

'I'm intrigued,' the young mage said dryly. 'Just what is it you have in mind?'

'Where's Risala?' Kheda scanned the scatter of huts as he emerged, blinking, into the punishing sunlight. 'And Velindre?'

'Risala's making sure we all get a share of breakfast.' Naldeth pointed towards the hearth circle where the wild women were clustered.

Kheda saw they were raising sturdy sticks to pound down on something, making the muffled thumping sound he had noted. 'Where's Velindre?'

'Keeping watch for dragons,' Naldeth said succinctly. 'And as far as I can tell, the wild men have sent scouts to stand sentry by the river.'

'I take it she's recovered from yesterday.' Kheda saw the magewoman's golden hair, bright in the sunlight beyond the crude huts. She was standing still as a statue, her face turned to the sky, her eyes closed, her hands hanging loosely at her sides. 'She's not scrying?'

'We don't want to draw any dragon with magic, not just yet. We're not complete fools.' Naldeth's words were mild enough.

Kheda couldn't help gazing up at the cloudless blue. 'Can she alert us to any dragon approaching? Or just those of the sky?'

'She'll sense a dragon riding the air at the greatest distance and probably one manipulating water not far short of that.' Naldeth looked contemplatively at Velindre. 'But she'll know if the black dragon comes anywhere near.'

'Are you ready to tackle the creature and its mage, if we go across the river?' Kheda asked the youthful wizard.

Which is another task there's no benefit in delaying.

Naldeth squared his shoulders defiantly. 'Velindre and I have discussed how to stifle his magic rather than killing him outright.'

'As long as he's not killing our people, do as you see fit.' Kheda saw Risala emerge from the knot of women by the hearth. As they parted to let her pass, he saw they were pounding something in the hollow curve of an old tree trunk.

476

'What do you suppose is for breakfast today?' the mage wondered.

Risala was carrying crude bowls salvaged from old, cracked gourds. As she smiled at Kheda, reserve nevertheless shadowed her eyes.

So there's still distance between us, despite the closeness of last night. How can I put things right? I'm not going to lie to you and tell you the omens predict our safe return to Chazen, with our lives going back to the way they were.

He saw the bowls were full of the fluffy white pulp they had eaten before. 'Just what is this?'

Risala shrugged. 'They're beating it out of shoots that they cut from the bases of those spiny finger trees.'

Kheda wished for a spoon as he ate with his dirty fingers.

What wouldn't I give for that bath I was dreaming of? We had better find some way of washing before we all fall ill with some filth-borne disease.

'There are a lot more spearmen here this morning.' Risala looked discreetly around the enclosure. 'They've been coming in since first light, with their women and children.'

Kheda had already noted the increased numbers sitting around the ashy circle of the central hearth. 'It looks as if they intend to stay.' A group of men was breaking holes in the hard dry earth with the points of their wooden spears. Youths and young women stood ready with rough lattices of twisted tree branch and arms full of freshly cut fronds. 'Do you think we can persuade them to fight?'

'The more spears we have to call on, the better,' Naldeth said reluctantly. 'We have to get that ruby egg from the *Zaise.* Nexus magic is our only hope of driving away that black dragon.'

'Or any other beast that flies over and sees so much prey for the taking.' Risala looked up apprehensively.

477

Kheda felt the weight of the task before him descend on his shoulders. 'Then let's get these people ready to fight with some new tricks that will hopefully send more of the cave dwellers and tree dwellers running than will be willing to stand and fight.' He scraped up the last of the fluffy pulp and handed the rough bowl back to Risala.

'What tricks?' Naldeth followed the warlord back into the dead mage's hut.

'The cave dwellers aren't between us and the *Zaise*?' Risala protested.

'No,' Kheda agreed regretfully as he sorted through the most promising lengths of wood. 'But if they owe fealty to that mage over the river, they'll stab us in the back if we don't take them out of the balance. I told you, we've started a war here, whether these people realise that or not. The quickest way to end a war is to wage it without mercy.' He found a suitable length of worn leather and gathered up a handful of long, dry grasses.

'Which is what these people did in Chazen,' Naldeth said pointedly as they returned to the bright day outside. 'Are you sure you aren't taking revenge?'

'No.' Kheda sat down and drew his belt knife.

Risala sat a little distance away. 'No, you're not taking revenge, or no, you're not sure?'

'Weren't the people who came to Chazen just fleeing that drowned island?' Naldeth looked troubled.

'Perhaps, but they attacked first rather than trying to sue peaceably for sanctuary. And whoever they were, they were driven on by their wizards, who showed no one any mercy. This battle should free the cave dwellers from such tyranny.' Kheda began stripping the bark from the curved branch with deft knifestrokes. 'Risala, can you cut me some thong from those hide strips, please?'

'What are you making?' Naldeth watched him work, mystified.

'A bow.' Kheda worked his way around an irregularity in the wood.

Naldeth looked at him open-mouthed 'You can't be thinking you can teach these people archery in half a day?'

'They don't need to shoot the topknot off a palm pigeon.' Kheda looked down the length of the crude bow stave and resumed shaping it. 'A shower of arrows against people not expecting them doesn't need to be aimed. Now, can you summon water or do I need Velindre to do that?'

'I can summon water, but there's not much more I can do with that element,' Naldeth admitted. 'Not hereabouts anyway.'

Kheda looked up as the relentless pounding of the women's staves in the hollow tree slowed and faltered. Heads were turning all across the enclosure as the savages realised he was doing something. 'Can you find me a bone splinter that will make a decent needle? About as long as your smallest finger.'

'You'll be lucky to get a handful of shots out of that before it breaks,' Risala remarked as she tossed him a skein of thin leather strips.

'We don't have time to go hunting for decent wood or to craft proper bows.' Kheda used his dagger to scrape damp pith from the newly peeled wood and then carefully gouged deep notches in each end of the wood. 'We can hope that that mage in the beaded cloak is taking some time to try to fathom our presence here, but don't forget, he's hardly exerted himself as much as Velindre or Naldeth. We have to be ready for him and his followers to make another attack.'

Men were drifting towards them now, some with children hiding behind their legs while older boys came scampering ahead with lively curiosity. As Naldeth searched among the bones in the hearth, the women gathered round him, speculating audibly.

'Risala, do you think you could persuade these women to make us some strings?' Kheda cut a long strip, three fingers wide, from one of the hides offered the night before and used the tip of his dagger to pierce holes along both edges. 'And lend us a bowl, to soak the leather in?'

'I can try.' Risala teased some fibres from the discarded strips of bark. As she walked over to the village women, she began twisting them into two thin spirals. When she had a finger's length, she wound them together against themselves, so each one stopped the other from unravelling. The women clicked their tongues and smiled as they recognised what she was doing. As Risala touched the cords holding a gourd on one woman's shoulder, her expression beseeching, the women nodded readily.

'Well done,' Naldeth commented as she and he both returned together.

'It's hardly magecraft.' Risala was amused despite herself. She handed Kheda a shallow vessel roughly fashioned from a piece of hollowed log.

'Will this serve as a needle?' Naldeth diffidently proffered a sharp shard of bone unmistakably shaped and pierced by magic.

Did you learn how to do that from that black dragon's magic?

'I should think so. Can you fill this with water for me?' Kheda indicated the shallow trough.

As Naldeth nodded and steam gathered in the hollow of the wood to condense into shining droplets, the considerable crowd now gathered around them murmured, openly inquisitive. The wild men and women watched intently as Kheda laid the leather strip in the water to darken.

Patience. More haste makes for less speed.

As soon as he judged the leather was wet enough, he took it out and stretched it as best he could. Laying it down, he carefully arranged a dense layer of long, dry grass in the centre and put the bow stave precisely in the middle. Kneeling, he threaded a length of leather thong through the eye of the bone needle and bent over the bow stave to begin sewing the leather tightly around the wood and grass. 'It should dry fast enough in this heat,' he commented, 'so the leather will shrink still tighter.'

'It'll dry still faster and tighter if you let me do it with my magic,' Naldeth pointed out, somewhat exasperated.

'That's true enough.' Kheda looked up apologetically from his awkward task. 'Risala, do you think you can persuade these folk to find me some thin, straight sticks?'

'I can try.' She tossed him the coil of stout string that one of the women had just given her. She smiled briefly at Kheda and he felt memory of the night's passion twist deep in his stomach. He would have held her gaze longer but she turned away to her new task.

A few children followed at a respectful distance as Risala began searching the closest length of the thorn barrier for suitable twigs. The rest of the men and women continued to watch Kheda as he laboriously completed the finger-cramping task of sewing the leather tightly around the curved wood, compressing the grass inside. From time to time he tried to look around the enclosure but there were too many people moving about for him to get a clear sight of Velindre.

Kheda handed the stave in its case of damp leather to Naldeth. 'Very well then, Master Mage, dry that out for me.' He addressed himself to measuring a length of cord for a bowstring and tying tight loops in each end.

Naldeth took the bow stave, which immediately began steaming gently. Soon the darkness was fading fast from the leather. The savages murmured among themselves again and most took a pace or two back.

'Will these do?' Risala returned with a handful of long, whippy sticks.

Kheda nodded as he took the bow stave back from the young mage. 'Naldeth, help her, if you please. Strip off the bark and make me some arrows, about this long.' He indicated the standard shaft length reaching from his fingertips to his breastbone. 'Put a point on one end and a notch in the other.'

'I know I said I'm no hunter,' Naldeth complained mildly, 'but I have seen an arrow before.'

'How are you planning on fletching and barbing them?' Risala asked.

'Let's see what our new allies can offer us.' Kheda watched the wild spearmen edge closer to see more clearly as Naldeth took up one of the sticks. Some were intent on the dagger itself, others on the blade's action on the wood. As soon as the young mage set the first peeled wand down, one of the older hunters, bolder than the rest, immediately picked it up. He was short and stooped with some old, ill-healed injury twisting his back, his face wizened and his hair a thin grey fuzz on his fleshless skull. After studying it, he shrugged at his companions; their puzzlement was equally plain.

The whole circle of watchers took a pace backwards as Kheda stood up. He settled one loop of the string into the notch he had cut in one end of the improvised bow stave, tugging at it till the cord bit deep into the leather. Flipping the wood over, he braced the lower end against his foot and slowly leaned on the top, gradually bending it sufficiently to accept the second loop of the bowstring. His shoulder muscles protesting, he gently released the pressure until the string alone held the leather-encased wood in a new smooth curve.

So far, so good. It hasn't snapped at the first test. Risala can call that an omen if she wants to.

Kheda gave the string a tentative pull. The bow was stiff and the leather creaked but he couldn't feel any hint of the wood within cracking. 'Naldeth, some arrows please.'

The wizard complied. 'They're not very good, I'm afraid.'

'As long as they're good enough to show these people what we're doing.' Kheda moved to get a clear view across the upper end of the enclosure. There was plenty of space past the dead mage's hut where the skins of the lizards that had been slain the day before yesterday were drying stretched on stoutly lashed frameworks of wood. Drawing the crude bow in one fluid action, Kheda loosed the blunt, featherless shaft. It shot across the emptiness and vanished over one of the skins to be lost in the thorn barricade.

A murmur of surprise ran around the gathering. Before it ran its course, Kheda loosed a second rough shaft and this time he hit the lizard skin almost dead centre, the arrow bouncing off. Unmistakable interest lit the hunters' faces.

Naldeth rolled the next arrow between his fingers and the sappy point darkened and hardened. 'Why do you suppose none of them have ever contrived a bow?'

Kheda shot again and this time the arrow pierced the lizard hide to hang there quivering. 'I don't imagine their life offers much leisure for sitting and thinking.' He had to speak up to be heard over the hum of excitement all around.

Risala was still stripping bark from the thin sticks. 'And I don't see many elders around to turn their experiences into new ideas.'

'Do you imagine those wild mages let anyone showing more than usual intelligence live for long?' Kheda picked up another arrow. 'Tyrants like Ulla Safar soon cut down anyone with the wit to be a threat.'

'They certainly seem to like this idea—' Naldeth broke off as the stooping spearman who'd been the first to pick up a rough arrow tugged at his arm. 'What does he want?'

The wild man pointed over towards the ash-filled hearth and then tapped Naldeth's empty hand. He repeated the gesture a second time and then a third, looking a little frustrated at the mage's slowness.

'He wants you to light the fire.' Kheda's spirits rose.

If they can make themselves understood, surely so can we.

He shot again and missed the lizard skin, the arrow gouging a shallow groove in the dust. The crowd didn't care, their voices growing louder, edged with excitement. More savages came to see what was afoot.

'Be careful,' Risala said sharply as the mage held his hand up and a scarlet flame danced on his upturned palm. 'We don't want to draw any dragons.'

'A spark like this is lost in the confluence of elements around here, believe me.' Naldeth dropped the flame onto the ground and bent to pile the detritus from the bow-making on it. The red magelight shivered and turned to the comforting yellow of natural fire.

The stooped hunter glanced over his shoulder, wrinkled face expressive. Several of those behind him made encouraging sounds. The stooped hunter drew a deep breath and crouched down on his heels to hold the peeled stick out over the little fire. His hand was shaking so much that the wood wavered wildly in and out of the flickering flames. Grinning, Naldeth hunkered down and steadied the other end with his free hand. The hunter licked his lips nervously as he watched the wood intently. As the moisture that had lurked underneath the bark was drawn out of the wood, he snatched it back and deftly ran it through his leathery fingers. His hands steadier, he returned it to the flame. After a few such passes he was satisfied and, smiling shyly, he handed the arrow to Kheda.

'They know enough to understand that a straight shaft flies faster and truer.' Kheda rolled the blunt arrow between his fingers and looked down its length.

'It'll fly better still for some fletching—' Risala caught her breath on a recollection. 'And I know where to find some feathers.'

As she hurried into the dead mage's hut, Kheda loosed the newly straightened shaft at the lizard skin. It flew noticeably better than the first ones he had shot, striking the hard scales of the lizard's spine with a sharp snap. The stooped hunter shared a gleeful grin with his companions. Three of them set diligently to work straightening more sticks and two more sat to peel bark from the rest with their black-stone knives. One kept casting envious glances at Naldeth's dagger.

'Now we set these people making as many bows as they can before we find ourselves under attack.' Kheda watched Risala approaching with a twist of hide in one hand. 'What have you got there?'

'Feathers from those women.' She untwisted the soft leather to reveal a handful of vivid orange plumes.

A new sound ran through the crowd, this time of considerable disquiet.

'Is that wise?' Naldeth shared their unease. 'We've no real idea what the significance of such adornments might be, beyond marking out the mageborn. What will they make of us using such tokens like this?'

'I don't know.' Kheda set the bow down and took a feather from Risala. It had come from the wing of some as yet unseen, sizeable bird. 'But how else can we show them what we need?'

And we'll be showing them that such tokens have no meaning for us, no power in themselves, no more than the meaningless patterns we Aldabreshi men draw in the sky to comfort ourselves.

Using his dagger, he carefully stripped one side from the central quill and cut it into an arrow flight. He glanced at Risala. 'May I have some bark fibres, please.'

As she handed them to him, Kheda gave her the arrow shaft to hold. Lacking any kind of glue, he could only lick a finger and stick the strips of feather on with spittle. That was good enough to hold them as he began carefully tying the feather tightly to the wood, splitting the black-tipped orange barbs apart with the hair-thin binding. As he worked, an apprehensive murmur passed among the wild men and women. Here and there an emotional voice rose and was hastily hushed.

'What do you suppose they are saying?' Risala kept her face impassive.

'Does it matter?' Kheda tied off the bark fibres as solidly as he could and smoothed the fractured feather to a sleek smoothness once again. Looking down for the bow, he saw several of the older hunters were squatting beside it, stroking tentative fingers along the leather-bound wood and the taut string. Kheda grinned at them as he bent to retrieve the weapon.

'I could make some steel arrowheads if we can find something like ironstone.' Naldeth looked thoughtfully around.

'Which would use a lot more magic and might well catch a dragon's curiosity,' Risala said instantly.

Kheda carefully bent the bow, drawing the newly fletched arrow to his chin. 'Let's see what these people can come up with.' He let fly and the shaft soared over the lizard skin to clear the thorn barricade entirely and vanish into the distant thistly plants. The gathering hummed with excitement.

Perhaps they think there's magic in the feathers to make the arrow fly more true.

Kheda turned to the stooped hunter and offered him the bow. Everyone else immediately fell silent.

The stooped hunter licked his lips, blinking rapidly. His hands shook as he picked up a naked arrow. He mimicked Kheda's action in drawing the bow but lowered it awkwardly without loosing the unfletched shaft. Taking a deep breath he drew a second time and shot. The shaft flew across the enclosure to fall short of the lizard skin. The hunter looked at Kheda, plainly chagrined.

Kheda grinned back and nodded emphatic approval, pleased to see the man's face clearing. 'I think they've got the idea.'

Several of the other hunters shuffled closer, patently eager to try this new weapon themselves.

Naldeth looked at them with amusement. 'Where did you learn to make bows like that, Kheda?'

'My father taught me and my brothers,' the warlord said with a pang. 'He said we never knew when we might find ourselves without the trappings of privilege, so we needed to know how to keep ourselves alive with no more than a sharp knife and sharper wits.'

'A man of some forethought,' Naldeth said approvingly.

'Or one who foresaw you'd have need of such knowledge.' Risala challenged Kheda with a brief glance.

'Can you both help them make more bows, while I see if we can fashion any kind of arrowheads?' Kheda went back to the dead mage's hut. The wild men and women followed readily enough, though none would go inside. Kheda passed out handfuls of wood, leather and grass. Risala immediately had to stop the eager hunters layering them together without soaking the leather first. The women laughed as they sat in a

487

loose circle, twisting fresh lengths of cord from the grasses they had commandeered.

Finally convinced she had made her meaning clear, Risala sat back on her heels and glanced up at Kheda as she wiped sweat from her forehead. 'These people may lack knowledge but they don't lack wits or dexterity.'

'No,' Kheda agreed. 'Naldeth, can you make us some more of those bone needles without catching a dragon's attention, please?'

'Oh yes.' Naldeth hurried off towards the hearth with a few curious savages trailing after him.

Kheda turned to the stooped hunter and, drawing his own dagger from its sheath, he tapped it with one finger before tapping his own chest. Sheathing the steel, he tapped the hunter's bony breastbone and held out his empty hand expectantly.

Curiosity flickered across the man's brow as he delved in the folds of his ancient, stained loincloth to retrieve his crude knife of black stone. Seeing the fineness of the edge, Kheda couldn't resist trying it on the dark hairs dusting his forearm. The razor-sharp stone shaved his skin clean. He nodded his approval, then, raising his elbows and shrugging his shoulders, he mimicked trying to break the tip off the end. The hunter reached involuntarily for the knife before he realised Kheda wasn't actually damaging it. He frowned, trying to understand.

Kheda reached down and picked up a rough arrow shaft, holding the black-stone knife to it so that the tip jutted over the end of the wood. The hunter's face cleared and he nodded rapidly. Clapping his hands, he barked brisk instructions to someone at the back of the crowd.

'Let's hope they've got that idea.' Beyond the old men huddled round the stooped hunter, Kheda watched two men each carrying a bundle of spears rounding up a gaggle of lads. One waved an arrow shaft, self-evidently explaining what they would be seeking. With the hunters vigilant for any threat, they disappeared out beyond the thorn barrier. 'Now what I need is a good big gourd and a long forked stick.'

'What for?' Naldeth returned with a handful of long bone splinters pierced with smooth holes. Risala took them from him and set to work instructing the eager bow makers.

'Snakes.' Kheda frowned. 'How do you suppose we might identify the most venomous?'

'What do you want venomous snakes for?' Naldeth asked with misgiving.

'Are you any kind of shot with a bow?' Kheda watched the stooped hunter summon a few of his particular cronies and loftily allow them to try their hand with the first bow. One hit the lizard skin, to mingled envy and admiration.

'No,' said Naldeth tartly. 'I've generally found magic more effective.'

'Then it'll just be me and Risala with poisoned arrows.' Kheda challenged the distaste on the young mage's face. 'You don't think the cave dwellers and the tree dwellers will flee all the faster from the arrows if they see their strongest hunters dropping dead when they're hit?' He saw that the savages were readily understanding Risala as she showed them how to sew the damp leather tightly around the wooden staves. Eager hands reached for the bone needles. 'I don't want to kill any more of these people than we have to, Naldeth, and the best way to ensure that is to kill off anyone we can identify as a leader as early as we can. The sooner the battle ends, the fewer will die.'

The wizard sighed. 'I suppose I'm still not used to Aldabreshin ways of waging war.'

'I told you, we wage war hard because that's the way to keep wars short.' Kheda found the disdain in Naldeth's face was rousing his anger. 'Every warlord knows that the most effective defence is relentless aggression. That doesn't mean we relish it. And we find that knowing that no quarter will be given to them does tend to discourage hotheads from starting a fight in the first place.'

'These people don't know that,' Naldeth objected.

'Then they'll learn and I imagine they'll learn fast.' Now that he had allowed himself to vent his temper, Kheda found he was disinclined to stop. 'So I'll crush the heads of this land's venomous snakes to make poisons for my arrows, and if I had time and the right herbs, I'd bury the corpses in a jar to ferment with the venoms, to make a paste ten times more deadly than the snake's own bite.

'I'd show these people how to make scorpion pots to throw at their enemies, if they had clay, if I had the words to make them understand me and I knew which of this land's crawlers had the most lethal sting. When we retake the *Zaise*, you can have your ruby egg to work your magic and drive off the dragon while I'll take those barrels of naphtha and ground oil and that sulphur and resin and make sticky fire, just like we do in the Archipelago. That should show those tree dwellers across the river that these people are a force to be reckoned with, without a wizard to hide behind or a dragon to feed with their dead.'

'You think you have the right to show them such things?' Naldeth wasn't about to yield. 'All principles of warfare agreed in the north condemn sticky fire or any weapon like it as utterly immoral. Quite apart from anything else, such stuffs are hideously dangerous for friend and foe alike.'

'You expect me to believe that none of your barbarian war-captains has ever succumbed to temptation?' scoffed Kheda.

'There are cases recorded,' Naldeth admitted readily enough, 'mostly detailing how whoever was using the vile

490

stuff was attacked by every other local army, including those he thought were his allies.'

Risala looked up from helping with the bow-making to interrupt the mage. 'Velindre says that's less from fear of the sticky fire and more because the only safe way to use such stuff is to have a wizard on hand. And any barbarian war-captain suspected of drawing magic into a battle can expect to have his throat slit by his own men before his enemies can reach him to do it.'

'I'd be inclined to agree that's a wise precaution,' Kheda said dryly.

'No wizard with any conscience would ever use his magic in a war.' Naldeth flushed with growing anger. 'Yet you'll give these people sticky fire to use against their enemies. What else are you thinking of? Poisoned smokes? I've heard tell of Archipelagan battles where warlords have used those and killed off half their own men.'

'The fate of friend and foe alike would be considered an omen,' Risala said tightly. 'Token of the rightness of that warlord's course or proof that he was in grievous error.'

'Do these portents absolve you of every responsibility?' cried Naldeth.

'A warlord would only ever use poisoned smokes as a very last resort, and he'd study the winds and weather carefully beforehand.' Kheda realised the wild men and women had stopped working on the sticks and leather and cord and were watching this heated exchange with bemused incomprehension. He tried for a reassuring smile to encourage them back to their labours.

'Where will this stop?' Naldeth demanded passionately. 'Where will you stop, assuming we subdue the tree dwellers and those people in the caves?'

'You're finally starting to think this through.' Kheda congratulated the mage acerbically. 'There's every chance we'll have to take the fight to whatever wild men live beyond this valley, to their wizard, and to their dragon. I hope this nexus magic you and Velindre plan on working with that ruby is going to be all you claim.'

'We'll be using that to drive off dragons, not to kill people,' Naldeth said wrathfully.

'And I'll show these people how to make a better means to do the killing that must be done, so you can keep your hands and conscience clean—' Kheda broke off as he saw the scarred spearman approaching with a couple of the oldest wild men he'd yet seen. He smiled and nodded and beckoned the three of them to approach.

The old men muttered among themselves as they came closer and settled themselves stiffly on the ground. Unfolding the hides they were carrying, they revealed lumps of shiny black stone and a surprising array of pieces of bone and wood. The oldest man, with ash-white hair, began breaking delicate flakes off the ungainly stones with a bulbous knuckle of bone. His neighbour picked one up and, peering close, knocked infinitesimal slivers from it with another stone, his tongue caught between toothless gums as he concentrated. Faster than Kheda would have expected, he held up a leaf of stone, sharp edges finely translucent in the sunlight.

The warlord tested the edge with a cautious finger to find it was as sharp as any steel. 'That will make a fine arrowhead.' He smiled at the old men and hoped his tone conveyed his approval.

'And this looks like some kind of resin to stick them to the shafts.' Risala was peering into a gourd that the scarred spearman had pressed into her hands. She looked around with a half-smile. 'If we can only persuade the best men with a sling to bring down some birds, we'll have everything we need.'

Naldeth was still brooding darkly on Kheda's forceful words. 'Where does this stop? What happens once we've driven off whatever dragon lives beyond the tree dwellers and subdued those people and their mage?'

'Initially, we wait and see if driving them off sets them fighting whoever lies beyond their far borders.' Kheda pulled both his sword and his hacking blade from his double-looped sword belt and sat down not far from the old men diligently chipping at their lumps and flakes of stone. Unsheathing the wide hacking blade, he slipped a whetstone from a little pocket sewn into the scabbard and ran it firmly down the edge.

'You want this war to spread still further?' Naldeth wasn't giving up. 'I thought we were trying to improve the lot of these wretches.'

'In the longer term, I hope we shall.' Kheda concentrated on renewing the edge on the sturdy steel. 'In the short term, I'll settle for just not getting killed.'

Naldeth stared at the warlord. 'But where does this end?' he persisted.

Risala's gaze slid to Kheda, her expression unfathomable.

'Ultimately?' He concentrated on polishing out a shallow nick in the edge of the steel. 'I imagine we'll have peace when you've put all the dragons to flight and we've driven any remaining wizards off the edge of this island and any wild men who choose to stand against us rather than surrender are dead.'

Or when we have simply died through some mischance or fallen victim to a mage or a dragon's malice.

'You really mean that, don't you?' The young mage was incredulous.

Out of the corner of his eye, Kheda noticed the wild men and women growing increasingly restive, concerned at the wizard's agitation.

'You talk as if we have a choice. We don't.' He strove to sound unemotional. 'Either we take the battle to the tree dwellers and their wizard and his dragon or we wait for them to attack us. I prefer to fight on my own terms. I told you — this is a war now. Wars are very difficult to stop.' It was a challenge to hide both his sympathy for Naldeth's dismay and his irritation at the youth's naivety.

'This is why we bloodthirsty Aldabreshi so rarely start wars and in fact do all we can to avoid them, whatever your barbarian storytellers may say of us. Aldabreshin philosophers liken war to wildfire in a forest. Remember, we have no mages to curb such things.' He paused to lay down the hacking blade and drew his sword. 'It won't be safe to stop until we have imposed our new order on every last valley and cave redoubt. At least here we're dealing with just one island, even if it is larger than any in the Archipelago.' He swept the whetstone along the sword's curved edge. 'Though this whole debate will be irrelevant if you and Velindre can't keep the dragons from adding to the carnage. I suggest you concentrate on that particular task.'

Naldeth stared at him. 'How can you be so calm about this?'

Kheda shot him a stern look. 'It helps to remind myself that if battles are raging here, wild men and dragons can't be plundering the Archipelago.'

He glanced at Risala and saw that she at least understood that grim consolation.

'Is this all because you dislike magic so?' Naldeth demanded. 'Are you setting out on some quest to rid this place of wizardry, like the Archipelago?'

'Don't be a fool.' Risala's interruption was as unexpected as her scorn was withering. 'Weren't you the one decrying the perversion of magic governing the way these people live? Besides, we wouldn't even be here if you had left that skull-

494

faced mage well alone and we'd got back to the *Zaise* without being dragged into these people's travails. Just remember, Naldeth, you're the one who started this.'

The mage was as shocked as if she had physically struck him. He stared at her, his face colouring beneath his tan as if he had been slapped. Jaw clenched beneath his beard, he got to his feet with all the dignity he could muster, hampered as he was by his metal leg. Without a word, he turned his back and walked away towards Velindre. She was still standing looking up at the sky, apparently wholly oblivious to the activity on every side, and to the furious row that had been echoing across the enclosure.

Risala drew her own dagger, pulling a fine finger of whetstone from a slit in the sheath. 'How long do you suppose it will take to clear this whole island of wizards and dragons?'

'I have no idea,' Kheda admitted with a qualm of his own. 'But what other choice do we have?'

Risala didn't look up. 'We could take the *Zaise* and sail for home and leave these people to their fate.'

'And wait for some new plague of savages and dragons to appear on our western horizon?' Kheda sighed. 'Besides, I don't believe these people deserve this life, do you? I don't think they'd be so very different from us if they could be free from the thrall of magic and dragons. Do you?'

'No, I suppose not.' Risala began sharpening her own blade. 'But why must all this be our responsibility?'

Do you want me to lie to you? Do you want me to justify bringing you into such danger with some invented portent? Forgive me, my love, but I can't do that.

'Because we're here,' Kheda said simply. 'And even if Naldeth did start this particular crisis, we all chose to come on this voyage. We all bear a measure of responsibility.'

'And everything you've ever been taught as a warlord won't let you walk away from what you see as your duty.'

There was just a hint of despair in Risala's voice. 'Do you think we'll ever get home?'

'If we possibly can,' Kheda said resolutely.

They sat in silence amid the growing bustle until Kheda stood up and sheathed his newly sharpened blades. Leaving Risala still doggedly polishing her dagger, he went in search of a gourd and stick to catch snakes with.

Chapter 20

Is every snake on this accursed isle really poisonous? I can't see how I could have mistaken that old hunter's meaning. Pointing to a snake and then falling to the ground with your tongue lolling out is surely clear enough. Ideally I'd like the venom to fester for longer than half a day and a night but it's already past noon. Let's get this fight started on our own terms before we're attacked by the tree dwellers or their black dragon.

Kheda rubbed a curl of shaving from the gourd's woody surface and studied the image he had carved. A shadow fell across him and he looked up to see two inquisitive children watching him, one girl and one boy, naked but for strings of crude beads around their bellies. Another boy was looking with avid curiosity at the stack of white-fletched arrows laid beneath Kheda's leather-wrapped bow. Glutinous bloody paste marred the glistening points of deftly shaped black stone. Kheda studied the children as he sheathed his dagger.

You're probably about the same age as Efi and Vida, even if poor diet and a harsh life have left you both a head shorter. Are you as adept as they are at sneaking in where you're not expected and getting your hands on what's been forbidden to you?

Snapping his fingers to make sure he had the full attention of all three children, Kheda tapped a commanding finger on the carving he had just finished. A serpent wriggled across the curved belly of the gourd, crude mouth open to show larger-than-life fangs. Kheda pointed to the arrowheads, careful not to touch them, and grimaced with exaggerated fear. He fixed the children with a sternly questioning look and all three took a step backwards, tucking their hands behind their backs, eyes downcast. All the same, they exchanged an unreadable glance beneath their eyelashes.

'I think I had better make sure these are safely out of reach,' Kheda commented aloud. He tugged at the lizard-skin sleeve he had sewn to the pared-down neck of the gourd and carefully put the envenomed arrows into the crude quiver. As he tightened the grass cord threaded through the top of the uncured hide, he glanced up to check the position of the sun. Then he looked at the throng milling around the broad stone ring of the hearth. More wild men and women than ever were gathered around the scatter of rickety huts.

Where did they all come from? Can we possibly wage any kind of warfare with people we know so little about? Can I be sure they understand what I'm asking of them? Is Naldeth right? Is this madness? Is Risala right? Should we just fight our way through to the Zaise and leave this dreadful place behind us? Could I ever sleep easily in my bed if I did? And not just because my dreams would be full of dragons and savages' boats on the western horizon. How dare Naldeth think only northern barbarians have any kind of conscience?

Kheda realised the scarred spearman was looking keenly at him. Taking the warlord's nod of acknowledgement as some kind of invitation, the wild man hurried over, holding a gourd spattered with some pale substance. Kheda swallowed the sour apprehension that he recalled always preceded a battle.

I suppose I had better eat something. Strange, I can't decide if it's better or worse to be facing a fight with or without omens giving some prediction as to the outcome. Is it easier to be braver with even

498

false reassurance to cling to? What do these people have to stiffen their resolve beyond the brutal realities of their lives here?

The spearman dipped his hand into the gourd and rubbed it on his chest. He came to sit beside Kheda and set the gourd down between them, smearing more of the pallid stuff on his long legs. Kheda wiped a little from the rim and rubbed it between finger and thumb.

Pale yellow clay and grey ashes from the fire and some kind of grease.

The spearman nodded vigorously, continuing to coat himself with the ointment. It covered the darkness of his skin remarkably effectively. The savage reached for a strand of grass that had escaped the bow-making and laid it across his slickly shining thigh. Thanks to the streaky yellow clay, his skin was now virtually the same colour. Grinning, he took Kheda's hand and thrust his fingers into the gourd, plainly urging the warlord to anoint himself.

'They had the wits to devise ways to hide themselves down in the grasses long since, it would seem.' Risala arrived, holding her own bow and arrows. Hers were the only other white-fletched shafts and she too had painted the leather of her quiver with a charcoal-black snake's head, long fangs prominent. 'That might almost be an omen.'

'It should help us tell friend from foe so we don't make pincushions of the wrong people.' Kheda scooped up a glob of the stuff and smeared it along his forearm. The spearman smiled and rose to return to the hearth where the other warriors were gathered in urgent debate. A more sizeable force than Kheda could ever have expected had gathered. The women stood a little way off, children kept close, babies strapped to their backs and bundles of necessities close at hand.

'I've just about got the measure of that bow,' Kheda continued. 'If I'm not shooting at too great a distance. How about you?'

'I'm more likely to scare someone to death than hit them.' Risala set bow and quiver down and began spreading the concealing clay on her own arms.

'Are they ready to do this?' Kheda saw Velindre and Naldeth still deep in conversation beside the dead wild wizard's hut. 'They've been talking in that Tormalin tongue of theirs all morning. What is it they don't want me to understand?'

'Naldeth is still arguing that we don't have to attack the cave dwellers.' Risala's resigned tone nevertheless held some sympathy for the young mage. 'He says we have no quarrel with them. It's only the tree dwellers between us and the *Zaise*.'

'We cannot leave them free to attack us from behind,' Kheda said sternly.

'I know,' Risala responded with mild rebuke. 'And so does Velindre.'

'In any case, I don't think he'd manage to convince the men here to leave the cave dwellers alone.' Kheda managed a brief smile and nodded towards a circle of wild warriors on the far side of the fire circle. Already disguised with the pale grease, they were intent on the charcoal map he had drawn on the hard-baked earth.

'They certainly seemed to understand the plan quickly enough.' Risala sighed.

'If I took their meaning aright, they would expect the cave dwellers to cross the river and kill the women and children here while the warriors are away.' Kheda didn't hide his distaste.

'Do you think they'll be able to defend this place?' Risala looked across to the older men and half-grown boys gripping battered spears and those leather-cased bows that Kheda had rejected as too untrustworthy.

'If we do our job properly, they shouldn't have to. Besides, the women are ready to run and hide in the forest again.' Kheda rubbed the pale grease up under the sleeve of his tunic. 'I hope this stuff washes off.'

Risala surprised him with a faint grin. 'There's soap on the *Zaise*.'

'And clean clothes,' Kheda agreed fervently. He rose to his feet, holding out a hand to Risala. 'Be careful. I shall want you alive to wash my back for me.'

'You're the one who needs to be careful,' she said tartly as she took his hand and stood. 'I'll be back well beyond the wildest slingshot with our valiant wizards.'

Which must surely be the safest place for you, even if that black dragon shows itself.

'Try to make Naldeth think twice before he does anything too impulsive.' Kheda raised a hand to beckon to the mages. All the wild warriors watched alertly as the two fair-skinned wizards walked across the enclosure.

'Have you any notion where the black dragon might be?' Kheda asked them without preamble.

'No.' Naldeth was still looking mutinous, his bloodshot gaze more off-putting than ever.

'Let's hope it's gone looking for easier meat.' Kheda tried for a grin.

'I wouldn't count on it,' Velindre said darkly.

Kheda decided not to pursue that. 'If this all goes horribly wrong, do your best to get yourselves away through magic or whatever other means you can, all three of you. If we get separated, you can scry for me later as long as you're sure it's quite safe to use a spell. Otherwise, hide for a day or so in the cave with the *Zaise*, but only as long as it's safe to do so. That's where I'll make for, if I possibly can.' He looked at each of them. 'If I don't turn up, set sail for home.'

'If we can't devise any means to find you,' the mage-woman said mildly.

I suppose that's as close as I'll get to agreement. And I'll just have to trust you can keep your boy there in hand.

'Then let's be about it.' Settling his sword and hacking blade securely in his twin-looped belt, Kheda walked away.

The savage warriors instantly gathered around him, more than one glancing enviously at the warlord's weapons. Those who'd shown most aptitude over the day or so's practice with the crude bows held them proudly, quivers of new arrows slung over their shoulders. The rest held spears and clubs, each with at least two weapons, sometimes more, a bantering edge to their incomprehensible words. Some men twirled slings idly in experienced hands, bags of pebbles tied at their waists. All were deferring to the scarred spearman, both new-comers and those who'd originally dwelt in the village.

Where did you go, my scarred friend, while your fellow hunt-ers were making their bows and learning to shoot them? Were you recruiting all these others?

Kheda dismissed the irrelevance as they headed out of the enclosure. The warlord set as rapid a pace as he dared in the heat. The wild men matched him easily. As they passed through gaps in the spiny barrier, the older men left on guard called out encouragement before dragging the vicious thorns back together. The women waited in a silent group around the broad hearth, most faces impassive, a few betray-ing apprehension. An excited child earned an unduly sharp scolding from a tense grandmother. Once beyond the bar-ricade, the savages spread out to negotiate the thistly plants and the thickets of spiny fingers.

The mages followed a few paces behind Kheda, Risala at his side for the moment. He glanced at her as they reached

502

the open expanse dotted with the swollen barrel trees with their ridiculous crowns of inadequate branches. 'You don't have to come,' he said quietly.

'Who's going to keep those two barbarians honest if I don't?' She looked ahead, jaw resolutely set. 'Besides, I won't risk not knowing what's happened to you. It's not as if there are any omens as to the possible outcome.'

Kheda had found no answer to that by the time they reached the edge of the steep slope down to the river valley. He searched the gently waving fronds of sparse grass for any sign of movement. A dark shape appeared and his hand went to his quiver. The scarred spearman raised a hand and called out softly. An answer came from the indistinct figure and Kheda saw all the spearmen nod to each other, reassured. A handful of men emerged from the tall grass and beckoned the rest down the slope, their faces eager. As the main contingent joined them, the scouts reached for gourds of the pale-yellowish grease, smearing themselves as the whole force hurried on through the thick tussocks.

'If they were scouting, why didn't they colour themselves earlier?' wondered Risala.

'Perhaps doing so is some declaration of war,' Kheda suggested.

'Perhaps it's some kind of talisman.' Risala looked down at the clay cracking on the dry skin of her hands. 'Their wizards painted themselves after all.'

'And most of those who attacked Chazen.' Kheda shook his head. 'There's no point in guessing. We still know nothing of their customs.'

Crossing the grasslands, Kheda's view shrank to a few paces ahead and to either side. Looking back, he tried to determine if the wizards were still together. They were but he soon lost sight of them. Trying to keep track of the disparate groups of spearmen making their way through the grasses also proved impossible. The wild men were practised at moving with minimal sound or disturbance to the tall tussocks. Only the scarred spearman stayed close. He urged Kheda on with a jerk of his head, dark eyes as hard as the sharpened black stones that studded the club he carried.

Kheda tried to judge their speed to measure their progress across the plain. The thinning grasses as they arrived at the river bank still took him by surprise. He looked up and down the river to see Naldeth some distance upstream peering through the sparser concealment. The mage jumped down onto the muddy margin of the sluggish water and rapidly summoned up a walkway from the depths. The wild men pressed forward to run across this path and hide themselves once again in the grasses on the far northern side. Kheda scanned the sky apprehensively.

'They're splitting up,' Risala observed.

'It seems we did all understand the map I drew earlier.' Grim satisfaction took the edge off Kheda's trepidation.

The scarred spearman jumped down to the mud and Kheda followed, Risala close behind. The undercut edge of the far bank was already broken down by the hands and feet of the men gone before them. Kheda stood tall to try to make out the cave-dwellers' rocky outcrop. It was still hidden among the fringe of forest beyond the sere plain.

The scarred spearman clucked his tongue with irritation and forced the warlord down with an unforgiving hand. Risala was already crouching low. As the yellow grasses filled his vision, a rush of water made Kheda look round. With all the wild warriors safely across the river, Velindre was making her way along the silty path. Naldeth brought up the rear with the muddy waters swirling around his sandalled foot and his steel one as the river reclaimed its course to the sea.

Kheda took a moment to clasp Risala's hand. 'Stay with them now, please.'

As she slipped away backwards, the scarred spearman pushed Kheda on. Wild warriors on all sides were running faster now, sacrificing stealth for speed. A dun-coloured bird sprang up from the tussocks with a shrill cry of alarm and a rattle of wings. A horny-backed lizard dashed across Kheda's path, a thick mouthful of grass still clamped in its jaws.

Lizards that eat grass?

He had no time to ponder this puzzle as the scarred spearman drove him on with a shove in the small of his back. Kheda sweated uncomfortably beneath the greasy ointment disguising his face. His tunic clung to his back and a cloud of tiny black flies clustered around his head.

The scarred spearman drew level with the warlord, heedless of the insects crawling around his own eyes and nose. He was intent on the trackless grasses ahead. Kheda noted that the vicious grass blades were scraping at the grease coating his arms and legs but didn't appear to be drawing blood.

So it's protection in more ways than one.

Grateful nevertheless for his cotton tunic and trousers, Kheda pressed on, trying not to slow as the thick vegetation snagged his bow and quiver. Realising the ground was starting to slope gradually upwards, he risked standing a little straighter every few paces to search the rising forest ahead. Soon he could make out individual twisted nut trees and the pale-green sprawls of the fat spiny plants. The tussocks gradually thinned and disappeared, and they had reached the open space separating the grassland from the trees.

The wild men were running flat out, intent on their destination. Kheda spotted a contingent who had cut a diagonal path veering eastwards through the grasses to emerge some way ahead, deeper inland. The scarred spearman pushed past Kheda and the warlord followed, the breath pounding in his chest. As he ran, Kheda pressed one hand to the neck of his quiver, ready to pull out the first envenomed arrow.

The rocky outcrop reared up above the treetops. Mouth dry, Kheda scanned the hollows and shadows for any outline of the lurking dragon.

All you mages have to do is keep the beast off our backs. Then perhaps we can make this a rapid victory with the fewest possible deaths on either side.

Shouts broke out up ahead, startled and belligerent. Kheda heard the distinctive flick of bowstrings and the churr of inexpertly fletched arrows. Fearsome yells cut through the confusion as the fight spread among the trees. Slowing to a walk, Kheda carefully drew one poisoned arrow from his quiver. Wild men rushed past him, intent on joining the battle. Nocking his shaft, Kheda held the bow low, the lethal arrowhead angled away from himself. The scarred spearman looked back over his shoulder, grunting a clear question.

'Go on.' Kheda conveyed his meaning with a jerk of his head. The wild warrior didn't hesitate, hefting his spear up over one shoulder. The warlord took a moment to get his bearings and edged along the shallow slope. As the trees thinned, he saw the open space in front of the bottommost caves. The cave dwellers were mostly lurking in the shadows. A few were crouching behind the barricade of thorny branches they were used to defending from the predatory birds.

So much for drawing the enemy out into the open and scattering them with an arrow storm. Will Naldeth believe me when I tell him every Aldabreshin warlord knows that plans are generally the earliest casualties in any battle?

Arrows hissed through the air and clattered against the stone. Few found targets but the shock of such an unexpected attack clearly disconcerted the cave dwellers. Those in the shadows drew further back and those trapped behind the thorn barrier cowered lower. The village spearmen shouted and jeered triumphantly.

Those bows give our side confidence. That'll count for something. If I can pick off anyone who looks like a cave-dweller leader, that'll count for more.

Looking carefully, Kheda soon identified a man among those hiding behind the thorn barricade who was urging his companions back in the caves to action. The savage half-stood and shouted, waving his spear. Cave dwellers clutched spears and clubs and edged forward into the sunlight. Before Kheda could get a clear shot at the shouting man, the newly fledged archers waiting in the tree line loosed another flurry of reckless arrows.

The shouting man ducked hastily back down and the would-be relief force retreated back into the shadows. Taunts from the trees accompanied a second cascade of arrows, this time directed at the thorn barrier. The twisted branches brushed most of the missiles aside but some penetrated to provoke cries of pain. Angry yelling from the heights of the rocky outcrop drowned out a shouted exchange between those pinned behind the outer defences and whoever might be commanding the frustrated warriors in the caves.

Kheda watched intently, his poisoned arrow at the ready. Slingstones came raining down from the uppermost level of caves. The vicious hail tore at leaves and twigs, bouncing off branches and tree trunks. The defenders surged out of the lowest entrances, hurling spears at the attackers, who were now hastily retreating back among the trees.

Kheda saw that some of those fleeing for the safety of the caves were wounded, arms and legs pierced by the stone-tipped arrows. Few of the village archers were shooting with overmuch accuracy but with so many arrows in the air, some had inevitably struck unprotected flesh.

Two men dragged a third towards shelter who had a shaft wedged deep in his back. More arrows pursued them despite the best efforts of the slingshots in the heights. One man fell crazed with pain as he ripped an arrow from his thigh. He stared numbly as his life's blood gushed scarlet from the ragged wound and then collapsed to lie limp and still.

As a fresh shower of arrows clattered ineffectively against the rock face, Kheda let his white-fletched arrow fly. The apparent leader of the men behind the barricade had drifted too far from the safety of the thorns. The inadequacies of the makeshift bow meant that Kheda didn't strike the man in the chest as he had hoped. Instead, the stone head penetrated deep in his belly. The cave dweller looked down, face twisted with rage. Then the pain struck him and he gasped.

Kheda waited, his heart pounding. The cave dweller fell to his knees, hands hovering around the arrow. Men risked themselves to drag him back behind the thorn barricade. The cave dweller was past caring, his blank eyes staring up at the sky as his companions seized his nerveless hands, his slack legs sliding through the dust.

Village spearmen shouted exultantly from the edge of the trees, running forward, clubs raised in one hand as they flung their spears with the other. The cave dwellers defending the thorn barricade rose up to meet them, throwing their own shafts of fire-hardened wood. The slings in the uppermost caves sent down more lethal stones.

A flash of white feather told Kheda that Risala had seen some incautiously exposed foe and, sure enough, a moment later a corpse plummeted from the heights. He tried to find her along the margin of the forest. A haze of mage-light revealed her standing beside Naldeth and Velindre, the wizardry lurid in the shadows of the trees. A low growling made the air shudder. As one man, the village spearmen skidded to a halt and scrambled backwards for the illusory shelter of the trees.

The dragon.

Kheda felt a tremor in the ground beneath his feet. Mouth dry, he looked up as stones and dust began to fall from the top of the outcrop. He searched the broken edge for the dragon drawing itself out of the rocks. There was nothing there — or at least no sign of the black dragon's magic. The noise grew louder and men in the heights began to scream as the walls and floors of the caves broke apart beneath their feet. Men and women who had thought themselves safe in the lower levels began to cry out as the disintegration spread, sending cascades of shattered stone falling all around them.

The shards didn't drop to smash on the hard ground or break the limbs and skulls of the hapless defenders beneath. Kheda saw stones as big as his hand floating down like leaves slipping from trees in the dry season. Men and women from the heights were falling, but not to their deaths. Buoyed on clouds of dust with breezes snatching away their despairing cries, they tumbled slowly through the air, arms and legs flailing. They landed, some harder than others, within the thorny barricade where they cowered sobbing or simply lay frozen with fear.

Stones continued to rain down from the crumbling cliff. Piling in drifts like storm-driven leaves, they formed thick mounds blocking the mouths of the lowest caves. Panic-stricken shouts could be heard within, muffled as the walls grew higher.

Initially as startled as their foes, the village spearmen soon recovered themselves. Shouting exultantly, they emerged from the trees where they had so rapidly retreated, brandishing their weapons. Bolder than the rest, the scarred spearman hurled his spear at a cave dweller who had just staggered to his feet. A coil of wavering dust coalesced into a solid arm and plucked the weapon out of the air. Tightening around the wood, it snapped it into useless splinters. The sharp crack echoed back from the broken cliff face, the only sound in the stunned silence.

Naldeth and Velindre walked forward. Kheda returned the white-fletched arrow he was holding to his quiver and went to join them. No one else moved. Risala stayed standing prudently behind one of the thicker twisted nut trees. Slinging his bow over one shoulder, Kheda drew his sword and summoned up his most authoritative, intimidating scowl for the scarred spearman, who looked inclined to test the dusty magic with a second spear.

He looked from Naldeth to Velindre. 'What now?' Kheda asked caustically.

Amusement lifted one corner of the magewoman's mouth. 'What do you propose?'

The young mage's face hardened with defiance. 'We won't countenance a slaughter.'

'So I see.' Kheda glanced upwards. 'Can we expect a dragon to come and argue that point?'

'No,' Velindre assured him seriously. 'We wouldn't have risked this if there was the slightest hint of a beast anywhere close.'

'I suppose that's one way to knock the fight out of them.' Risala approached the three of them. Wild men and women watched her, the village spearmen and the stunned cave dwellers alike all waiting, wide-eyed. 'Some advance warning would have been welcome.'

'I felt there had been enough disagreement between us over these last few days,' Velindre said composedly.

Risala waved her words away. 'How are you planning to deal with the tree dwellers, so we can get to the *Zaise*?'

'How do you propose to avoid a massacre starting as soon as we leave here?' Kheda looked around to see the frustrated violence on the village warriors' faces. 'All these cave dwellers will most likely die now. Some might have escaped to hide in the forest in the confusion of the battle I was expecting to fight.'

'We must give these people a chance to surrender.' Jaw jutting obstinately, Naldeth waved a hand at the cowering cave dwellers. 'These spearmen will have to accept it, when they see that we do.'

'You'll risk their lives on that?' Kheda didn't hide his scepticism. 'When you've no way of explaining yourself?'

'Would you rather see their heads smashed in and be done with them?' retorted Naldeth.

Kheda did his best to curb his anger. 'This is warfare, Naldeth. It's ugly and cruel and relentless.'

'It doesn't have to be,' the wizard spat back.

'No, it doesn't, but it generally is in my experience,' snapped Kheda. 'And whatever we're going to do, we had best do it quickly. More on both sides will certainly die if that tree-dwellers' mage gets wind of our attack and whistles up his dragon while you're trying to find some compromise here to salve your conscience.'

'Kheda, some of these people have broken arms and legs and other wounds you could tend.' Risala spoke up before Naldeth could respond. 'If you want to convince everyone that you don't mean death for the cave dwellers, help them.'

'While we curb any of our allies who look inclined to dispute the point.' Velindre surveyed the village spearmen. Some were watching the cowering cave dwellers with unnerving intensity, weapons ready in their hands.

'What do you think will happen if you stop them when they've set their minds to killing these people?' Kheda didn't give either wizard a chance to respond. 'No question you could do it, but I very much doubt that any of these spearmen will follow you afterwards. Another lesson every warlord learns early is that a leader only commands as long as his men agree to obey. Do you want any spearmen backing you when we reach the tree-dwellers' valley? Or don't you think you need them?'

'Whether or not they come with us, I won't permit any more deaths than are absolutely unavoidable,' Naldeth said stubbornly.

Kheda saw the same obstinacy on both mages' faces.

How gratifying it must be to be master of powers that allow you the luxury of such magnanimity. Don't you understand that the rest of us never have such choices? But you're not going to give way on this and the longer I argue with you, the more time that gives some straggler to get word to that bead-cloaked wizard.

'I'll do what I can for the injured but only as long as our people are collecting spent arrows,' Kheda said brusquely. 'Then we move on the tree dwellers.'

Risala was looking at the cave mouths still blocked by the screes of broken stone. She rounded angrily on the youthful mage. 'How long are you going to leave those wretches walled up alive, Naldeth?'

Kheda saw the village spearmen gathering in knots beneath the trees, their low conversations indecisive, a slow stirring of irritation among some. 'Let your captives loose while I see if any of our allies are wounded. We won't win any friends by tending the enemy first.' He surveyed the wild warriors. To his surprise, while some had been painfully bruised by slingstones and hurled sticks, none had suffered any incapacitating injury.

I suppose that's something else we can thank Naldeth and Velindre for.

'Break down your walls, Naldeth, but don't give them room to come out more than one at a time.' Velindre smiled dangerously at the closest wild warriors. 'That should discourage anyone feeling overbold. If they don't attack, our allies should be less inclined to fight. I'll keep any hotheads in check.'

'I can bind broken bones.' Kheda bent to pick up a fallen arrow with brindled fletching and handed it to Risala. 'If I can find trees like those ones we saw back over the river, with the resinous bark.'

'That'll be better than nothing.' She waved the missile at the closest village spearman with a bow. The man came forward, his face uncertain. Risala thrust the arrow firmly into the quiver at his side and pointed to the ground. The would-be archer nodded obediently and began searching for more arrows.

'Get on with it, Naldeth.' Kheda drew his dagger and headed for the nearest tree. All around, the newly fledged bowmen joined in scavenging arrows to replenish their quivers. Spearmen went to recover their own thrown weapons, clubs at the ready. More than one sneered belligerently at the cringing cave dwellers, offering threatening gestures.

We have to get away from here before this whole enterprise dissolves into chaos.

Kheda kept half an eye on Risala as he stripped long lengths of bark from a dappled tree with his dagger, pleased to feel the stickiness of the sap. In between strokes, he tried to identify those cave dwellers who had obviously broken bones. Some were hugging the discomfort of cracked ribs and many bore cuts and bruises that could be hiding lesser fractures or more insidious injuries. Most sat apathetic, blank-eyed with shock.

Naldeth gestured towards the choked cave mouths and the rubble began trickling away. The warriors recovering their arrows and spears paused to watch the slithering stones apprehensively. The heads of imprisoned cave dwellers appeared as the barrier sank to waist height and then the steady flow of stones stopped.

'They can't come rushing out if they've got to negotiate that,' Naldeth said with satisfaction.

Risala straightened up, holding an arrow. 'They don't seem too keen to come out.'

The village spearmen began shouting, challenging, harsh and peremptory. The first of the cave dwellers climbed warily over the broken rock. The dust and sweat coating them made them much the same colour as their clay-smeared attackers. Their faces betrayed wretched fear, and seeing fallen friends or kinsmen, some began weeping. Injured defenders who'd been lying mute thus far couldn't help but succumb to their own misery and pain.

'Let's see if anyone can understand that we'd prefer to see mercy for the defeated.' Holding curling swathes of the sticky bark, Kheda headed for a youth sitting hunched over a forearm where both bones were plainly snapped. Kheda looked at Risala and grimaced. 'Of course, they may just think we're torturing him for our own amusement. I've no way of letting him know I mean no harm, nor anything to take the edge off his pain.'

The youth flinched and hunched down as Risala gripped his narrow shoulders tightly. 'Better this than leaving him in agony and with an arm that'll mend all crooked.'

Kheda took hold of the boy's upper arm, careful to support his wrist with his other hand. 'Naldeth, I need you too.'

'You want me to try mending those bones?' The wizard approached, looking unsure of himself. 'I didn't mind trying that dragon's magic to make those needles but I'm not at all sure about experimenting on a living person—'

'Just take the weight of his arm while I get the edges of the bones back in line,' said Kheda briefly.

The warlord set the broken limb with practised mercilessness. The boy's raw scream silenced every cave dweller's whimper as well as the belligerence of the village spearmen. Kheda concentrated on winding a length of the sappy bark around the break and up and down the fainting boy's forearm. He drew his dagger once again to slice a thin, fibrous length to serve as a tie and rubbed the back of his hand over

514

his own dry lips. 'Risala, can you tell Velindre he needs some water please?'

'They've worked that much out for themselves.' She pointed towards the cave-dweller women now emerging from the lowest caverns carrying dripping gourds filled from some underground cistern.

'Some for the rest of us wouldn't go amiss.' Naldeth had been absently winding a strip of bark around his hands. He looked down, surprised to find he had all but manacled himself as the resin rapidly dried.

'Pick five more wounded for me to help before we move on.' Kheda noted that the village spearmen had recovered all the weapons still worth having and no intact arrows remained on the ground.

The mage stared at him. 'Why do I have to choose?'

'Because you decided this fight would end this way.' Kheda stared at him, unblinking.

'Then start with her.' Naldeth pointed to a woman huddled beside a fallen boulder, one ankle grotesquely swollen. The youthful mage nodded more resolutely. 'We can come back here once we've recovered the *Zaise*. You can bring your physic chest.'

'And empty all my pots of salves before I'd treated half these abrasions, with no means of refilling them?' Kheda took no pleasure in rebuking the wizard. 'What do I do if you're injured? Or Risala? Or Velindre?' He knelt to probe the woman's ankle with careful fingers, trying to determine if any bones were broken.

Hearing a stir among the warriors in the shadows, he looked up to see Velindre hurrying towards them, visibly concerned. 'There's something—'

Kheda abandoned the woman's foot to stand up and search the trees. 'Is it the tree dwellers? The dragon?'

515

The village spearmen were spreading out, turning their backs on the cave dwellers as they raised their bows and clubs. A piercing cry rang through the forest and echoed back from the rock face. The cave dwellers murmured with new dismay.

'Those murderous birds have caught the scent of fresh blood.' Risala plucked a white-fletched arrow from her quiver.

Kheda saw the village spearmen disappearing into the trees. 'We have to go after them. If they get away from us, hunting or hunted, we'll never bring them back together to attack the tree-dwellers' valley.'

'I'm staying here,' Velindre said abruptly. 'There's something else in those woods. I wasn't talking about those birds. There's something wound around with elemental magic and quite close by. You don't want to leave that behind you any more than some enemy force.'

Risala looked around at the wretched cave dwellers. 'You can make sure none of these people come after us, out for revenge?'

Kheda looked at Naldeth and then at the magewoman. 'Is he up to defying that mage in the beaded cloak on his own?'

'What will you do when that dragon appears?' Risala demanded of the young wizard.

'Everything I did last time and more,' Naldeth snapped.

'You had better, or we're all dead.' Kheda nodded. 'Stay close to me.'

They hurried to catch up with the last of the village warriors slipping through the trees. Kheda searched for familiar faces. It was more difficult than ever to recognise individuals with the clay-tainted grease obscuring their features. As they left the clearing around the rocky outcrop behind, squawks erupted deeper in the forest. The killer birds' cries soon changed from aggression to panic and the village spearmen's shouts proclaimed successes.

'Do you suppose there are any tree dwellers hunting in these woods and hearing all this commotion?' Risala muttered savagely.

'Can their mages scry?' Kheda wondered.

'I've no idea.' Naldeth's metal foot stumbled on the uneven ground.

A spearman came hurrying towards them and Kheda recognised the stooped hunter by his twisted back. He grinned widely, waving a bloody blue wing. Kheda smiled back at the same time as pointing urgently in the direction of the tree-dwellers' valley with his sword. The spearman nodded with ready understanding and tossed the bird's wing at Naldeth before using his fingers and mouth somehow to send a piercing whistle through the forest. Similar signals answered him and Kheda's immediate fears receded as the fighting force re-formed. The savages were scooping up handfuls of leaf mould to smear on their arms and legs. Now their skins merged into the forest floor with its dappling of sun and shadow.

'What am I supposed to do with this?' Naldeth turned the bird's wing over, perplexed.

'I don't know.' Kheda ground dirt into his grubby tunic. His trousers couldn't be more soiled.

Risala was doing the same. 'Better not throw it away. We don't want to insult anyone.'

'I'm not about to stick the feathers in my hair.' Naldeth's attempt at a jest was half-hearted.

'Come on.' Kheda dismissed the irrelevance, turning all his attention to the trees ahead. He caught glimpses of heads, a back, an arm holding a spear aloft to better negotiate a patch of tortuous undergrowth. The village spearmen were moving faster through the dappled grey trees than they had raced over the grassy plains.

They don't need me to tell them we need every advantage of speed and surprise to stand a chance against the tree dwellers.

Kheda looked over his shoulder at Naldeth. 'As soon as you see their wizard, do whatever you can to stifle his magic or kill him outright.' He noticed that the wizard's face was a tense mask of determination and discomfort. 'Is your leg—'

Naldeth cut him off with a gesture. 'I'll manage.'

'I'll stay close to him.' Risala spared Kheda a brief smile before focusing intently on the forest ahead. She held her bow and quiver close to her body. 'I'll put a shaft into that wizard if I get the chance. The ones we fought with Dev were as vulnerable to an arrow in the belly as anyone else.'

'I remember.' Kheda didn't waste any more time on talk, pushing on over the undulating ground as fast as he felt Naldeth could manage.

Chapter 21

Naldeth's best speed was still barely sufficient to keep them from dropping behind the wild men. The village warriors were increasingly avid to join this new battle. Trying to find the sun whenever the meagre canopy of nut-tree branches grew thin over stretches of rocky earth, Kheda judged they were heading very nearly due west. He did his best to gauge their progress through the unfamiliar terrain but was still taken by surprise when the ground rose up and he saw the spearmen slipping over the crest of high ground that marked the eastern side of the tree-dwellers' dry valley. As they crouched to avoid being skylined, the tall trees with their dense, dark leaves barred their way down the slope, obscuring their view of the western bank.

Does this dry stream bed mark some boundary between the cave dwellers behind us and these people who owe fealty to the cloaked wizard and his black dragon?

Kheda looked northwards upstream and then down and saw the scarred spearman and the stooped hunter doing the same. Their eyes met and they nodded agreement. The warlord turned to Risala and Naldeth as the scarred spearman gave brisk orders to the village warriors.

'We'll make for that.' Kheda pointed upstream to a break in the tall buttressed trees. As they drew closer, he saw that some calamity had ripped through the forest, tossing the mighty trunks down the slope like twigs to leave a broad swathe of broken ground running down to the dry stream bed.

The village warriors gathered in the shade of the forest edging the destruction. On the western bank the tree-dwellers' broad fire pit smoked untended. The dry stream bed was entirely devoid of life. So was the sky. The scarred spearman slid beside Kheda and pointed to movement up among the platforms and shelters that clung to the trees on the far side of the stream and in the shadows around the thick boles.

'Where's their wizard?' Kheda asked Naldeth, not taking his eyes off the settlement. 'Where's that black beast of a dragon?'

'They got wind of our approach.' Risala shrugged that off. 'Do you think any of them will be circling around to attack us from behind?'

Kheda glanced over his shoulder to see the stooped hunter turning a reassuring number of spearmen and a few archers to look for just such a threat. Then he was startled by raucous shouts from their wild allies. A group of village spearmen advanced to stand at the top of the bare, broken slope, waving their spears and yelling defiance. The rest waited hidden, braced and ready. The scarred spearman grinned at Kheda.

Naldeth frowned. 'Those tree dwellers would be fools to launch any assault up this slope.'

'And our spearmen can't run into battle from here.' Risala was equally puzzled. 'They'll exhaust themselves crossing the stream bed before they get there.'

'I've no idea what they're thinking.' Kheda gave voice to his frustration. 'How am I supposed to be a warlord when I can't even talk to the men I'm sending into battle?'

'Don't worry.' The mage stared intently across the narrow valley. 'This is my battle.'

Risala carefully drew a white-fletched arrow from her quiver. 'Where is he?'

Fresh shouts from the village spearmen drowned out her words. Their tone turned from hostile to mocking. Some among the tree dwellers weren't proof against such taunting. A handful advanced from the darkness beneath the mighty trunks to wave their own spears and yell scathing retorts. This simply spurred the wild men on the ridge to new derision. A flash of colour startled Kheda, then another. The village wild men were hurling the wings they had hacked from the murderous birds down the slope, to lie dulled with dust on the dry stream bed's margin.

'What does that signify?' Risala was mystified.

Kheda slowly shook his head. 'They don't like it. Look.'

More tree dwellers advanced into the open, adding their angry shouts to the commotion echoing back and forth across the dry valley. Those village warriors armed with bows launched a storm of salvaged arrows into the sky. Tree dwellers looked up vacantly, wondering what the hissing rain might be.

'So they did understand me,' Kheda said with bitter relief.

Most of the tree dwellers had the wit to scurry backwards for the shelter of the trees. Those too slow fell screaming with wounds to arms and legs. A few thrashed in agony in the sandy stream bed as shafts driven deep into their bodies or faces were the death of them. The village spearmen roared, exultant, and the newly fledged archers launched a second flight of arrows. This time a cloud of dust sprang up from the dry stream bed to stop the missiles, weighing them down with dirt that matted their tousled fletching.

'Where is he?' Naldeth scoured the far bank for the wizard in the beaded cloak.

'Is the dragon anywhere close?' Risala was searching the rocks and shadows.

Kheda took an envenomed arrow and carefully nocked it on his bowstring.

'Leave their wizard to me.' Naldeth's bloodshot eyes were calm as he gazed over the valley.

'They are coming out to fight.' Risala readied her own bow as the clouds of sand in the stream bed subsided to show the tree dwellers rapidly advancing, shaking their spears and shouting with new boldness. The wild bowmen launched another cascade of arrows, thinner this time. Too many had already emptied their quivers. A curtain of dust swirled up just ahead of the advancing tree dwellers and the arrows slid down it, their threat blunted. By contrast, the tree-dwellers' slingstones shot straight and true through the haze and struck several village spearmen, prompting cries of pain.

'Naldeth?' Unable to see who had been wounded, Kheda tried in vain to pick out any obvious leader among the advancing enemy. 'The wizard?'

'I can't see him.' Risala was equally frustrated.

Naldeth stood motionless, rapt in remote contemplation.

Kheda staggered as the ground shook beneath his feet. The village spearmen's shouts turned to dismay as the hard-packed ridge crumbled beneath their feet. Torrents of flowing earth knocked men off their feet. As the soil turned to insubstantial sand around their roots, several of the lofty green trees fell too. They crashed downwards, ripping branches from their neighbours and crushing everything where they landed. The swathe of disintegration widened, splitting up the village spearmen. Some were forced down the face of the slope, others scrambling backwards away over the crest. Triumph edged the tree-dwellers' belligerence. Their leading spearmen broke into a run, now more than half-way across the stream bed.

Incongruous among the consternation spreading through the village spearmen, Naldeth chuckled. A glow of ochre light spread through broken ground and the powdery soil turned solid once again. The magic raced away down the slope and spread across the valley. The tree dwellers retreated apprehensively and Kheda saw they were right to be concerned. The sand of the dry stream bed swirled around them like water, ripples spreading. Soon they were sinking up to their knees. Ripples grew into steeper peaks, breaking with a spume of dust and surging mercilessly over the tree dwellers like a stormy sea.

As one man flailed frantically, he splashed the man next to him with great gouts of dirt that filled his eyes and mouth. Choking, the unfortunate clawed at his face, losing his own struggle to stay afloat. As he sank, he clutched at the nearest man, only to drag him down too. Both vanished beneath the flowing soil. Some had the presence of mind not to struggle, trying to float on the shallow waves of fluid earth, the boldest even using their spears as makeshift paddles.

'There he is.' The young wizard wasn't looking at the tree dwellers drowning in the sand. All his attention was focused on a solitary figure emerging from the shadows on the far bank.

The tree-dwellers' mage gestured wildly, his beaded cloak flapping. For an instant, there was silence in the valley. Then the surviving tree dwellers fought their way free of the clinging sand and ran back towards their wizard, pursued by the jeers of the village spearmen.

'Let's see what you make of this,' Naldeth murmured.

A surge of white water thick with broken timber and other detritus crashed down the valley. The flood drove ragged boulders to carve new channels, unearthing the bodies of tree dwellers overwhelmed by Naldeth's first spell. Those still alive and too slow to reach the far bank were unable to resist the torrent sweeping them away downstream towards the wide river bisecting the grassy plain.

The wild wizard strode forward, making throwing motions with his hands. Fissures gaped and gulped down the flood. Stream-tossed rocks ripped themselves from the mud to hurl themselves at Naldeth, shattering into a shower of lethal fragments as they came close. The young mage raised a hand to draw an arc of amber radiance over his head that spread in a flash to cover all the exposed spearmen. The rain of broken stones came thicker and faster, only to bounce off the magelight and rebound from tree to tree with dangerous speed.

'Kheda!' Risala pointed and the warlord saw that the tree-dwellers' warriors had regrouped and were making their way back across the muddy stream bed while the village spearmen could only cower beneath Naldeth's magic.

Kheda looked up at the amber shield. 'Can I fire through this?' he shouted urgently.

Naldeth didn't answer. Abruptly the hail of stones ceased. In the next breath, Naldeth's shield blinked away. Village spearmen raced down the slope to join battle with the foremost tree dwellers. With the enemy coated with mud and sand, it was impossible to tell friend from foe.

'I daren't fire anywhere close to that melee with this bow,' Risala spat with frustration.

As he looked in vain for the tree-dwellers' wizard, movement out on the stream bed caught Kheda's eye. He gaped and swallowed hard. 'Shoot that!'

'But he's already dead.' Risala stared in horrified disbelief.

The broken corpse of a tree dweller had staggered to its feet. The man's face was crushed to an anonymous ruin and the lower half of one arm had been torn away. As Kheda watched, the bones brightened with amber magic and lengthened into lethal spikes. The bones of the corpse's other hand burst through his dark fingers, curling into murderous claws. A second body lurched upright. Magelight shimmered around his head and his skull reshaped itself into a deadly maw somewhere between a terrible bird's beak and a lizard's crushing bite.

Risala's bowstring thrummed beside Kheda. He fired too. The white-fletched arrows both bit deep. Neither walking corpse flinched, or veered from their determined path towards the combat now spreading across the stream bed. Magelight flickered around more bodies, forging still more vile creations. All the village spearmen were charging down the slope now, shouting reassurance to their fellows and menace to their enemies.

'Wait!' Kheda shouted fruitlessly.

Only the scarred spearman halted, looking back.

Kheda ripped the hacking blade from his double-looped sword belt and tossed it down the slope. The spearman grinned and scrambled back up to get it before racing down into the fight with a blood-curdling yell.

'Kheda—' Risala choked with horror.

The first dead tree dweller had come up behind a village spearman who was intent on dodging a foe's crushing club. The corpse drove its bone claws deep into the village man's back, ripping out bloody handfuls of flesh. The man fell, writhing and screaming, as the monstrous corpse stepped over him to attack the next spearman. The village warrior drove his long spike of fire-hardened wood clean through the misshapen thing. It simply kept walking, the spear sliding through its body as it reached out gory talons to rip away the man's face.

'Naldeth!' Kheda found the breath frozen in his throat as the village spearman who had just died reared back up onto his feet. Dark ochre light racked the dead man, wrenching him this way and that. White bone shot out through his chest and back as his ribs thrust outwards, covering him in deadly spines. The corpse reached for a man who had just been fighting at his side and crushed him in a lacerating embrace.

'All right, Kheda, there are some evils that must be stopped.' All the young wizard's attention was concentrated on his outstretched hand. His unsheathed dagger stood upright, balanced on its pommel, slowly spinning. The steel blade burned with a searing gold that rivalled the sun.

'What are you going to do with that?' With the vivid outline of the dagger still scarring his vision, Kheda saw the tree-dwellers' wizard standing on the far bank. He blinked and knuckled his eyes.

No, my eyes aren't playing tricks on me.

One of the great trees on the far side of the dry valley was tilting drunkenly. It began to topple slowly over, silently, with no sound of snapping roots or breaking branches to betray it. The wild wizard was oblivious, all his attention consumed by the burning metal still balanced on Naldeth's palm. The ensorcelled blade was spinning so fast it was a blur.

Kheda saw with relief that the degraded corpses the wild wizard had driven into battle had fallen back down, quite dead — for the moment, at least. He braced himself as the ground throbbed beneath his feet. Risala dropped to one knee, still looking for some target for her ready arrow. The throbbing became a low pulsing noise and grew louder, rapidly building to a physical torment. Kheda found himself fighting violent nausea and a swelling, inexorable dread.

Tears of pure terror streamed down Risala's face, her hands trembling so much she couldn't have hit any target even if her numbed fingers had managed to loose her arrow.

The whole fight down on the stream bed had broken into confusion. The village spearmen were fleeing, scrambling over the fallen trees or cowering, hands covering their ears, clubs and spears abandoned. The archers had thrown away their bows. The tree dwellers were faring no better. Several of the wild men had collapsed, vomiting. Others were curled like animals on the ground, hiding their heads in their arms, knees drawn up, heedless of any enemy. The pulsing noise went on, unrelenting.

'Naldeth—' Kheda choked on bile flooding his mouth as the tormenting sound rose to a new pitch. He threw away his makeshift bow and wrapped his arms around Risala, as if his own body might protect her from whatever catastrophic magic was about to engulf them.

The noise stopped. In the silence, the giant tree behind the wild wizard finally collapsed. It fell toward the stream, swift and true. The upper stretch of its trunk struck the wild wizard unerringly on the top of his head and the branches threw a swishing pall over his bloody remains.

Naldeth said something heartfelt and incomprehensible in his native Tormalin and threw away his dagger. He wrung his hands, wincing.

Kheda saw the deep scar burned into the young wizard's flesh. 'What did you do?'

'I tricked him.' His clothes rank with sweat and his blood-shot gaze ghastly, Naldeth nevertheless grinned like a boy caught in mischief. 'These wizards draw all the elemental power that they can find into themselves and then just throw it out in whatever way seems best. So I drew as much earth magic as I could reach into that dagger. There's no subtlety to their battles, so all he could imagine me doing was somehow turning that weapon and the power within it back against him. So he put all his efforts into trying to steal back the magic.'

Kheda glanced at the dagger and saw that the steel of the blade was blackened and distorted while the sandy soil around it had fused into a dirty-brown glass lump. 'So he didn't notice a tree about to fall on his head.'

'Unfortunately for him.' Naldeth sniffed with a disdain reminiscent of Velindre.

'You managed another victory without a slaughter of innocent women and children.' Risala was still standing within the circle of Kheda's arms.

'That's something, isn't it?' Naldeth smiled crookedly.

'Let's hope Velindre's managed to keep the cave dwellers alive.' Kheda looked around to see how their allies were faring. Most were scrambling to their feet, ashen beneath their coating of dirt and grease, grabbing spears more to lean on them for support than with any intent of fighting. Across the valley, the tree-dwellers' women and children were climbing slowly down from their platforms and shelters, wailing and throwing themselves to the ground in abject surrender.

Risala looked up and down the dry stream bed now so drastically reshaped by flood and magic. 'Where was his dragon when he needed it?'

'I don't know.' Naldeth shivered involuntarily. 'I couldn't have pulled off that trick if it had been anywhere close.'

'Would you know if it was attacking Velindre?' Kheda looked at the forest back beyond the crest of the valley's eastern edge.

'Oh yes,' Naldeth assured him.

'Has it truly just given up and gone away?' Disbelieving, Risala was still looking around.

'There must be other places on this island with easier pickings.' All the same, Kheda wasn't convinced.

'Perhaps.' From his tone, neither was Naldeth. 'But dragons aren't known for backing away from a fight.'

'So if it returns to finish this fight, you and Velindre will need that ruby egg.' Kheda looked out across the valley beyond the tree-dwellers' settlement.

'Then let's make for the *Zaise*.' Risala pulled free of his embrace.

'How do we do that without taking this army with us?' Naldeth wondered.

'Let's just go.' Kheda searched for the scarred spearman among the village warriors and beckoned him forward. The warrior stepped up readily, dirty face alert. He clutched Kheda's hacking blade, the broad steel clotted with blood. Kheda encompassed the whole force with a sweeping gesture and then cut down with one hand to divide them. He found the stooped hunter in one half and pointed over to the abject tree dwellers. Holding the man's gaze, he pointed to the bloody hacking blade and shook his head slowly, his expression forbidding. The stooped hunter nodded slowly, some unidentifiable emotion clouding his brown eyes. Hoping he had made himself clear, Kheda turned his attention to the scarred spearman standing with the remaining warriors and made as if to push them all away, back towards the caves and Velindre. The scarred spearman nodded readily and called out to other hunters. The wild men began moving away, purposefully, some with a definite spring in their step.

'I think they appreciate a victory where they're not leaving half their friends dead behind them,' Risala observed.

Kheda looked at Naldeth. 'Are you fit to fight any more today, if we do run into that dragon?'

'If it's that or be blasted into dust.' The young mage rubbed at his beard, bruises of tiredness under his discoloured eyes looking as if the bloodstains were spreading. 'But I'd rather not, if we can possibly avoid it. And the sooner we recover that ruby the better.'

'Come on, then.' Kheda turned to tackle the treacherous slope down to the stream bed.

Naldeth let slip an incomprehensible Tormalin oath.

Turning, Kheda expected to see the young mage struggling with his false leg on the broken ground. Instead he saw a fiery ring of elemental magic shimmering on Naldeth's steel thigh.

A bespeaking. Kheda recalled Dev's name for the spell.

'What's happened?' Velindre's voice echoed through the magic of fire and steel, harsh and tinny.

'We've killed their wizard and sent the tree dwellers running in all directions.' Naldeth sounded more resigned than proud. 'We're on our way to recover the *Zaise*.'

'Some of our spearmen are taking charge of the tree dwellers but the rest should be making their way back to you.' Kheda wasn't sure if the magewoman could hear him.

'Get back here with the ship as fast as you can.'

Even allowing for the distortion of the spell, Kheda could hear strain in Velindre's clipped words. 'Has something happened?'

Naldeth peered into the scarlet circle, frowning with growing concern. 'What's the matter?'

'Just get back here. We need the *Zaise*—' This time there was no mistaking the catch of a sob in Velindre's voice.

'Is it the dragon?' Naldeth clenched impotent fists.

'No.' Velindre rallied. 'There's no dragon or any wild mage here and I can hold off anything short of that till you get back.' A treacherous quaver shook her voice and the spell blinked into nothingness.

'Give me an arrow, a feather, something to burn.' Naldeth held out a hand to Kheda 'I'll bespeak her and—'

'There's something wrong.' Risala looked uncertainly at Kheda.

'Yes.' He waved away Naldeth's hand. 'But whatever it is, it's not so wrong that Velindre couldn't use her magic to speak to us, and she didn't ask us to come straight back to her.' Kheda began walking cautiously down the slope. 'And she's right. We need the *Zaise*. We can probably get back to her as quickly with the ship as we could by walking.'

'Naldeth,' Risala said abruptly, 'what gemstone would an earth dragon seek above all others for its egg?'

'Amber,' the wizard replied readily. 'Not rubies.'

'I think we'd know if the black dragon had found the *Zaise*.' Kheda drew his sword as they advanced across the mud. The stooped hunter and his contingent of spearmen were just reaching the tree-dwellers' settlement. A few looked curiously at the mage and the two Aldabreshi but none made any move to follow them.

'We can be grateful for the awe that wizards inspire around here,' Naldeth said sardonically.

'They all appreciate that you're well able to take care of yourself.' Kheda was relieved to find that he could see clearly through the tall forest on the far side of the stream bed for a reassuring distance.

The spiny underbrush thinned out as they left the bank behind and the sturdier, more densely leaved trees soon gave way to the twisted nut trees with their scanty foliage. Kheda kept his sword drawn all the same, Risala tense with vigilance at his side. The dappled, spindly trees grew sparser still and Kheda saw grey rock and parched brown earth ahead ending abruptly in the knife-like cliff. He searched the ragged edge outlined against the western sky for any possible hint of a lurking dragon.

'Do you remember exactly where that cave is?' He tossed the question back over his shoulder.

'Yes.' Naldeth was toiling up the slope with scant breath to spare.

'Which way do we go from here?' Gripping the hilt of his sword, Kheda walked warily out into the open. The sun beat down with unrelenting fury and the sea breeze offered no more than an illusion of coolness. A moment after it brushed Kheda's forehead, he realised it was as hot as a furnace breath. The headache that had been stubbornly lingering since the assault of the cloaked wizard's magic assailed him with new force.

'There.' Naldeth pointed unerringly to a rocky protrusion.

They made haste towards it, fresh sweat beading every brow.

A thought chilled Kheda despite the punishing heat. 'Naldeth, can you get the *Zaise* out of that cave on your own? If Velindre was using magic on the waters to keep it there—'

'It's easier to unpick an antipathetic element than it is to work with it,' the young mage said curtly. 'I see you're learning something about magic,' he added with the faintest of smiles.

They reached the bluff and gathered in what little shade it offered There was no lessening of the heat.

'I haven't the energy or the inclination to be subtle about this.' Naldeth's chest heaved as he laid both hands on the rock and pressed his face up against the stone. The rock cracked with a violence that shook the barren cliff top. Ochre light shimmered around Naldeth's fingers and the solid rock turned to glittering sand that flowed down to heap up around the wizard's feet. A shift in the wind blew a pale plume out over the cliff edge. Naldeth spread his hands and the void in the rock widened, ruddy-golden magic still pouring from his hands.

'There you are.' He coughed, brushing dust from his filthy tunic. Wincing, he blew on the raw score burned deep into his palm.

'I've salves for that on the ship.' Kheda saw that a narrow passage had been driven through the rock to join the irregular stairway Naldeth had made for them when they'd landed.

It feels as if that was half a lifetime ago.

'Let's get the *Zaise* and see what's upsetting Velindre.' Naldeth went ahead of them into the darkness, a dutiful breeze clearing away the dust for him.

'Let's hope nothing's gone seriously awry.' Kheda held out a hand to Risala. She took it and they followed the young wizard.

'Watch your step.' Naldeth's voice echoed eerily up from the depths of the cave. 'I've marked your path.' Amber footprints glowed on the rock, casting just enough light to show them where to tread.

'So I see.' Kheda moved slowly, waiting for his eyes to grow more accustomed to the gloom. The cool of the cave was welcome after the heat outside, though it did little to relieve his headache and the aftertaste of bile still burned his throat.

I've herbs in my physic chest to brew a cure for that too. We are returning to some sort of normality.

He saw a lantern casting a pool of light onto the *Zaise*'s deck. Naldeth was taking the lid off the water cask lashed to the rear mast. The wizard dipped a cupful and the distant splash of the falling drops echoed softly before the sound of his thirsty drinking drowned it out.

Kheda concentrated on walking safely down the dark stair. Behind them, the gloom deepened as the footsteps Naldeth had left glowing on the rock snuffed out one by one. Looking back, Kheda saw the narrow entrance like a white blade cutting through the darkness.

'Watch where you're walking,' Risala chided him. 'You've no cure for a broken neck in your physic chest.'

Kheda turned obediently to catch up with the fading footsteps. He finally reached the lowest ledge and jumped down onto the deck of the ship with Risala, still holding her hand. The thud of their landing reverberated in the confines of the cave. The deck felt stiff and dead beneath his feet, none of the movement of a living ship stirring.

Naldeth handed them both cups of water. 'I'll unpick the anchoring spell as soon as we get the ruby up on deck.'

Risala drained her cup. 'Are you sure it won't draw the black dragon to us?'

'Why do you need it on deck?' Kheda drank deep, relishing the cool water cutting through the sour dryness closing his throat!

'After opening up this cave, I can't work any more magic without it,' Naldeth retorted. 'You've no idea how exhausting magecraft can be.'

'We do.' Risala lifted the lantern from its hook on the mast.

Kheda saw that Naldeth's face was more drawn than ever. 'We saw what wizardry cost Dev.'

Naldeth said nothing, disappearing into the dark stern cabin. Kheda followed, with Risala's lantern throwing soft light and harsh shadows to either side. As they dropped down into the rearmost hold, Kheda tasted a breath of home in the still air. There were the herbs Beyau favoured for keeping the Chazen household's clothing chests free of weevils and an unexpected sweet scent of preserved velvet berries.

He looked into the blackness where his physic chest lay. 'Let me get you something for that burn on your hand.'

'Later. We have to get back to Velindre.' Naldeth was opening the door into the middle hold. The penetrating mineral smell of ground oil and sulphur overwhelmed all the other scents.

Kheda suddenly imagined the whole boat catching fire in the blackness of the cavern. 'Stay here with that lantern.' As Risala waited, he went after the young mage.

He found Naldeth waiting in the fore hold. The wizard was leaning on a rough-hewn wooden chest, all his weight resting on his hands, his head hanging.

Kheda looked at the sacking lump behind the chest that was the unnatural ruby. 'Is it still dead?'

'As dead as Dev,' Naldeth said bleakly.

What do we do if Naldeth collapses on us? I can't see the two of us getting the Zaise *out of this cave without magical aid.*

'Are you all right?' As Kheda asked the question, he was struck by its pointlessness.

The mage heaved a sigh that shook him from his tousled head to his steel toes and dirty sandal and forced himself upright. 'I'll feel better when we can get this gemstone further away from the water and closer to the rocks. Then I can draw on the sympathy between elemental fire and the earth.'

'If you say so.' Kheda tried to pull the rope-bound bundle out from its hiding place. It was heavier than he had expected and solidly wedged. He heaved and it came free with a jerk. Hefting it in his arms, Kheda returned to the welcome glow of Risala's lantern in the rearmost hold.

She eyed the awkward bundle with misgiving. 'Let me go up first, and you can pass it up to me.'

'It's heavier than you think,' Kheda warned her.

She climbed up and crouched to reach down through the trap door. Hauling himself one-handed half-way up the ladder wasn't easy, nor was swinging the sacking bundle up so that Risala could grab the binding ropes. Kheda gave it a shove to help Risala drag the weight over the edge of the trap and climbed up after it. Naldeth pressed close behind him on the ladder. Kheda saw an unwelcome eagerness on the mage's tired face as he reached for the ropes to help the warlord carry the burden while Risala led the way out onto the deck with her lantern.

'Let the air touch it.' Naldeth reached for his dagger only to find an empty scabbard.

'Here.' Reluctantly, Kheda handed over his own belt knife.

Thumping the dust-caked knee joint of his metal leg to make it bend, Naldeth knelt and slashed at the hemp bindings. The sacking fell away to reveal the crazed glassy surface of the ruby egg. Licking his cracked lips, the wizard rubbed his hands over the dulled jewel, heedless of his burned palm.

Kheda caught his breath as an infinitesimal scarlet spark stirred in the heart of the gem.

The lantern light flickered as Risala trembled. 'Are we sure this won't bring a dragon down on us?'

'There are dragons here whatever we might do.' The wizard leaned forward, sliding his hands down the curved sides of the egg as if he were caressing a naked woman. 'If I'm going to hold them off, I'll need this.' The glow strengthened. Naldeth sank down and laid his face on the egg's upper surface. He closed his bloodshot eyes as the ruby light cast strange shadows, disfiguring his amiable features.

Kheda's throat closed as his memory irresistibly recalled the horrific fire that had consumed Dev. The scarlet flames had burned the flesh from his face, making a death mask of his skull and boiling his eyes in their sockets, all while the wizard had still been drawing breath. And Dev had relished the embrace of the devouring fires, lost in the ecstasy that was his communion with the element even as it was stealing his life away.

But then the fire in the egg was alive, with a pulse like the beat of a heart. That spark of life would have become a new dragon. This new flame is steady. It doesn't even flicker like a normal fire.

Kheda tried to hold on to that frail reassurance as the crimson glow strengthened.

The deck lurched suddenly and he staggered sideways. Risala's lantern went swinging to throw crazy shadows in all directions. Water slapped against the rocks in the cave and Kheda realised he could hear the sound of surf breaking against the rocks outside for the first time.

Naldeth knelt upright and grinned, quite his old self. 'That's Velindre's spell over the sea broken. Give me a hand up.'

Kheda helped the mage to his feet. 'Can you get us out of here?'

'Not as smoothly as she would have done,' Naldeth said wryly, 'but this ship is solidly built.'

'What do we do with that?' Risala looked mistrustfully at the ruby egg, though the scarlet glow within it had faded to little more than a pinprick of light.

'Put it in the stern cabin.' Naldeth headed for the stair to the steering oars platform with a new spring in his step. 'That'll be close enough for me to use it for elemental focus.'

Kheda bent to take a handful of the sacking that the ruby egg was nested in.

Risala stooped on the other side to do the same. 'It would be easier to toss it in the water if it draws a dragon to us if it's on deck,' she muttered.

'I don't know if that would save us,' Kheda replied as they dragged the uncanny egg through the doorway into the stern cabin and wedged it as best they could between bundles of bedding.

'What do we do now?' Risala asked in the shadows. 'Are we staying to see how far and how fast the bloodshed we've started today spreads through these wretched people? We can't just blame Naldeth now. There's blood on all our hands.'

'I know,' Kheda acknowledged frankly, 'but at least fewer died than might have. We can thank their magic for that. As for what happens next—' He shook his head. 'First, we had better find out what's distressing Velindre. Then we can make plans—'

He held Risala tight as the *Zaise* lurched. The ship's wooden sides scraped along the rocky ledge as Naldeth's magic forced the vessel out of the narrow anchorage.

'Plans to go home?' Risala looked up at him, her face tense.

He looked down at her. 'How can we leave these people now we've started this? If they go into battle without a wizard, if there's a wizard or a dragon set against them, they'll just be slaughtered.'

'How can you be any kind of warlord here when you can barely make yourself understood and you don't understand a word of their language?' she protested. 'What about Chazen?'

'What's best for Chazen, as far as I can see at the moment, is having turmoil spread in this land to keep men and dragons alike occupied here.' He gazed at her helplessly. 'I wish we hadn't got ourselves into this, but we did and I can't see a way out of it, not yet.'

Risala pulled herself free of his embrace, her expression lost in the gloom. 'Naldeth will need our help rigging the sails.'

Back out on deck, eerie magelight glowed purple around the masts and side rails as Naldeth's wizardry dragged the *Zaise* towards the cave entrance. As the daylight strengthened, the colours of the ship emerged from shades of black and grey. The magelight lightened to lavender and then to a clear blue as the ship slid out onto the open ocean. Surf seethed around the hull as Naldeth wove skeins of wizardry around stern and prow to force the vessel around. Seabirds wheeled overhead, their shrill cries rising above the sound of the waves.

Risala heaved a sigh and looked at her soiled garments. 'At least we can celebrate our victory with some clean clothes.'

Kheda couldn't recall ever hearing anyone sound less joyful. He followed her into the stern cabin and pulled up the trap door once again as she delved into a bundle of creased cotton. 'I'll tend to that burn of Naldeth's.'

After the awkwardness of fetching up the dead dragon's egg, carrying his physic chest up the ladder was comparatively simple. As he climbed back up, the coffer under one arm, he averted his eyes from the ruby. He could not ignore it, though. Scarlet brilliance was seeping through the lattice of cracks on its surface to throw a web of mage-light around the wooden walls. Risala followed him back out on deck, her arms full of clothes, kicking the stern cabin door shut to slam behind her.

Up on the stern platform, Naldeth was smiling broadly, eyes distant as he wove blue magic with an amethyst hint around the *Zaise*. The ship cut a straight path through the submissive seas, scorning the waves that would have pushed her towards the merciless rocks.

'You don't need the sails?' Kheda knelt to set his physic chest down and snapped open the latches.

'Not now.' Naldeth chuckled, his weariness seemingly quite forgotten.

'That egg was the death of Dev.' Kheda searched for the particular pot of leatherspear salve that he wanted.

'I know,' the mage acknowledged, somewhat sobered, 'but you don't know how good I feel now, Kheda. It's not just being able to focus my fire affinity through the gemstone.

Velindre was right — I've been using more magic in these past few days than I've done all year. The more I exercise my affinity, the stronger my magic becomes.' He smiled wryly. 'Now I understand just why our esteemed Archmage spends so much of his time finding unimpeachable reasons for all wizards, himself included, to use the bare minimum of magic required.'

'Power is always a temptation, whatever its nature, as I believe you've reminded me before.' Kheda stood up with a scrap of cotton and a stoppered vial of feathereye tincture. 'Let me see your hand.'

Naldeth flinched as the warlord cleansed the burn. 'I had my hands read by a soothsayer when I was sailing the Archipelago with Velindre.' He looked down at the shiny red score obliterating the creases of his palm.

'Did he foresee any of this?' Risala wondered, looking up from the deck, a clean tunic in one hand.

Naldeth shrugged. 'He did say my life would be taking an unexpected course.'

'Show me a seer that doesn't.' Kheda restoppered the vial of astringent lotion. 'All they have is vagueness to swap for their meat and drink on the trading beaches.'

'How can you say that?' Risala was more puzzled than angry. 'How can you say the beliefs of generations and countless domains mean nothing, just because you have lost your faith in them? Don't you think we might not have got so mired in this mess if you had been reading the right omens?'

'I did meet one soothsayer who had some very interesting predictions.' Naldeth was ready to explain.

Kheda found himself disinclined to listen. 'This is hardly the time or the place to debate such things.' He dressed Naldeth's burn with the leatherspear salve and a light bandage of fine gauze.

'No—' Then Naldeth stammered and blushed, retreating back to the tiller.

Kheda realised Risala was stripping naked down on the deck. She slung a bucket into the sea and washed herself briskly. He slid down the ladder-like stair and returned his physic chest to the stern cabin. Wordlessly, Risala offered him the bucket and he washed in turn, gasping at the bracing chill of the water on his warm body. Still not speaking, she tossed him clean clothes, redolent of different herbs used to ward staleness from stored cottons in some other reach of the Archipelago.

It would be so easy to tell Naldeth simply to turn this ship's prow to the south, to round that cape and sail away east, leaving this strange and dangerous land. Velindre could find us with her magic, couldn't she? But when we return to the Archipelago, will I arrive to find I've lost Risala?

Kheda fetched scouring paste, rag and oil and cleaned his sword and his dagger, polishing them till they shone. Risala brought dried meat and fruit from some store, taking a share to Naldeth, still without a word. They ate, all remaining silent, watching the broken cliffs subside and the broad mouth of the river open up before them. The *Zaise* bucked as Naldeth's magic drove the ship through the turbulent water where the river's muddy flow forced itself out into the surging sea. The wide mudflats stretched away on either side.

'Watch the skies.' Kheda searched the sandbanks with their tangled tussocks of grasses.

Risala shaded her eyes with her hand. 'There's nothing to see, not even birds.'

Kheda noted the same lack of life across the fertile mudbanks. There were no birds, no sign of any animals. He called up to Naldeth. 'Has all the wizardry used in this valley today frightened everything away? How far does magic's influence reach? Does it taint the water, or the air?'

'Look over there.' Risala pointed at a pillar of smoke that was rising from the far edge of the grasslands on the northern bank, just a little eastwards of their own position.

'It's an ordinary fire,' Naldeth called, unperturbed.

Kheda tried to judge the intervening distance. 'And nowhere near the cave dwellers.'

'Isn't it near where we left Velindre?' Risala stood beside him, tense.

'She could let us know if she were in trouble, couldn't she?' Kheda tried to swallow his own apprehension as he realised Risala was right. 'Come on, we'll see more from the stern.'

They climbed up the ladder to join Naldeth.

'Isn't that the tree-dwellers' valley?' Risala turned to point to a shallow notch in the undulating land where it ran away towards the broken shore.

'I think so.' Still looking inland, Kheda saw that the fire was rather more than half-way between the caves and the tree-dwellers' settlement.

That's the direction we fled in the night, when we met that old woman and she showed us shelter.

'Naldeth, if Velindre were in trouble, could she use this magic of yours to find the *Zaise*? Or would the spell just carry her to the cave where we left it?'

'I don't think anyone's ever tried translocating to a boat while it's under sail.' This new idea evidently intrigued Naldeth. 'What—'

A gang of wild spearmen appeared on the north bank. Shouting and waving their spears, they beckoned to the *Zaise* and Kheda recognised several faces, even through their covering of grease and filth.

'I take it those are our friends?' Naldeth wrapped a skein of blue light around his burned hand and hauled the prow around towards the north shore regardless.

'They don't look too happy to see us,' Risala said slowly.

'No,' Kheda agreed, 'but they don't look as if they're about to attack us either.'

'They look more apprehensive than anything.' Naldeth's newfound high spirits faltered for the first time. 'Velindre would have found a way to warn us, if there was danger.'

'There's definitely some kind of trouble.' Kheda studied the faces of the men waiting on the bank.

A good number of the men offered a studied blankness just short of defiance. Others were more openly nervous, their eyes flickering from Kheda to Naldeth. A few gazes slid to Risala with a hint of guilty appeal.

'Velindre had better not be hurt.' Naldeth's tone hardened.

Chapter 22

The *Zaise* juddered as the keel sliced into the river bed. A ramp of mud reared up to bridge the gap between the ship's rail and the bank.

Kheda saw some of the spearmen on the bank react with violent surprise while the rest merely took a step back, more concerned with beckoning the three mariners ashore. 'Some of these warriors must be cave or tree dwellers. They haven't seen Naldeth's bridging trick.'

'Then Velindre has found some way to convince them to cooperate rather than fight.' Nonetheless, Risala looked uncertain.

'We can ask her once we find her.' Growing concern was rapidly quelling Naldeth's good humour. He swung himself over the rail and hurried to the bank.

Kheda noted which spearmen looked agog at the wizard's metal leg. He gestured to Risala to go on ahead, keeping one hand on his sword hilt as he brought up the rear.

The spearmen had trampled a broad path down to the river. They retraced their steps along it, noisily beating the stubborn tussocks with their spears and stamping down already crushed blades of the razor-sharp grass.

Kheda looked around in hopes of finding the scarred spearman or the stooped hunter. Neither wild man was anywhere to be seen. He recognised some faces, and registered all too clearly the beseeching glances that slid his way.

Whatever this trouble is, they're hoping I'll take their side.

Kheda hurried after Risala, who was walking as fast as she could to keep up with Naldeth. The joints and rivets of the wizard's metal leg glowed with scarlet fire. As the grasses thinned, they reached a line of straggling nut trees cut off from the main sprawl of the forest by a stony slope. Wild men were busy dragging fallen wood to add to a long fire that was the source of the smoke they had seen.

Just as Kheda realised this was familiar ground approached from an unfamiliar direction, Risala pointed to a shallow cluster of rocks. 'That's the cave we hid in, the one with the paintings.'

'There's Velindre.' Naldeth nodded at the magewoman, profoundly relieved. 'She's not hurt.'

Velindre was sitting on the bare earth hugging her knees some distance below the entrance to the cave. He recognised the scarred spearman standing some distance away, ringed by a band of warriors whom he identified as having come from the village across the river.

'What do you suppose they've done?' Risala wondered.

Kheda saw the wild men who'd met them at the river spread out to join the warriors on the far side of the cave or those gathering firewood, demonstrably disassociating themselves from the scarred spearman and his band. The shunned men hadn't a spear or a club between them. He caught an ominous breath of sickly putrefaction.

'Velindre!' Naldeth called out as the magewoman got slowly to her feet. 'Are you all right?'

'Yes,' she answered wearily, 'but there's something you have to see.' Her face was tearstained, her eyes red-rimmed.

'You remember I said there was something strange in these woods, something elemental gone all awry?'

The scent of decay grew stronger and Kheda's stomach roiled. 'What is it?'

'You can see all you need to from here.' Velindre approached the cave's entrance with visible reluctance.

Naldeth pushed past her. 'There's magical—' He recoiled, retching.

Kheda looked into the cave to see a tangle of bloodied corpses. The only movement was the crawling of black flies. Dark clots of insects shifted like shadows across the bodies. More clung to the cave's walls where gouts of blood utterly obscured the delicate paintings. It was difficult to estimate the numbers of dead, but it was all too easy to see the slender legs of women among the confusion of limbs. Children's hands stuck out from the crush as if they were scrabbling at the cave walls.

Risala gasped with horror, pressing her hands to her face.

'This is what they were doing in the night.' Kheda didn't even realise he was speaking aloud.

'You knew about this?' Furious, Velindre berated the warlord. 'You did nothing?'

'I knew something was happening.' Kheda glared accusingly at the scarred spearman and the other weaponless warriors. 'I didn't know what—' His rage strangled any further words.

Tears stood in Risala's eyes. 'Why were these people killed?'

'Because they were mageborn.' Naldeth spat vomit into the dust. 'Every last one of them.'

'You wanted these people to free themselves from magical tyranny.' Kheda regretted the words as soon as he spoke. He made no move to defend himself as Naldeth's fist smashed

546

into his cheek. He staggered backwards, struggling not to fall over. The mage came after him, ready to hit him again.

'I didn't know what they were doing!' Kheda shouted. 'How could I? I couldn't ask any of them!' He waved a hand at the scarred spearman and his band. 'Don't you think I would have stopped them if I'd known?'

'You Archipelagans think all wizards are better off dead,' snarled Naldeth. He turned on the motionless warriors, brandishing a handful of scarlet fire. The pyre roared with shocking intensity.

'I know better than that now.' Kheda took a step forward to place himself between the irate wizard and the wild warriors. 'And you know better than this.'

'But why did they do this?' Risala gazed into the charnel cave, a tear trickling down her face.

'They did it to please us.' Velindre's voice was thick with loathing. 'You should have seen their smiles when I came here. I think Kheda's right — they're looking to rid themselves of all their wizards. And all because we killed their mages and drove the dragons away instead of pandering to the beasts and using their power to assert our own domination over these wretches.'

'You think that's what we should have done?' Aghast, Naldeth let his hand fall and the scarlet fire flickered out, the flames of the pyre dying back.

'No.' Velindre turned her back on the stinking cavern, scrubbing fresh tears from her eyes. 'I don't know what else we could have done. But we don't know what we've started here, and we sure as curses don't know how to stop it. We can't even talk to these people!'

'At least we have shown them that not all wizards are necessarily tyrants.' Kheda tried to keep the despair he felt out of his voice.

'What good will that do? Who have we shown this marvellous revelation? A couple of hundred of however many thousands live on this accursed rock?' Velindre retorted with angry dejection. 'And they think the best way to please us is to slaughter these innocents. What good are we doing here? I should have listened to you, Naldeth. We should go back to Hadrumal and lay this all before the Council.'

'If we leave, all this will have been for nothing,' Kheda objected. 'All these people will be crushed under the heel of the first wild wizard to learn there's land and dragon fodder here for the taking.'

'Who made you their warlord?' Velindre snapped.

'You were the one lecturing me about responsibility,' countered Kheda.

He fell silent as a spearman he recognised from the village slowly approached. He was holding the hacking blade that Kheda had given the scarred spearman. He offered it to Kheda. As the warlord took the weapon, still bemused, the scarred spearman took a few paces away from his companions. He dropped to his knees and raised his chin, leaning back to offer his naked throat to Kheda. A nerve twitched in his cheek as he screwed his eyes tight shut in anticipation of the killing blow.

'I can't do this,' Kheda said helplessly. 'I can't condemn a man when I don't know what he's done.'

'You know what he's done.' But Velindre wasn't condemning the man either. 'He just didn't think it was a crime until he saw my reaction.'

Kheda swallowed. 'They can be the ones to drag out the bodies and give them to the fire—'

'Be quiet.' Naldeth's soft words nevertheless commanded everyone's attention.

'Where is it?' Risala's voice was harsh with dread.

Behind the scatter of rocks where the cave entrance lay, the forest sloped upwards. Grouped in sparse clusters, the nut trees cast meagre shadows on the dry earth. Kheda saw a golden glint in a patch of darkness blink out and reappear. Now that he saw it was an eye, he could see the rest of the earth dragon's head. The random shadows beneath the trees ran together or melted away as the ground shifted and blurred. The beast appeared fully, crouched between two thickets, its belly pressed to the dusty soil. It moved one forefoot, extending steely claws to crush a sapling with purposeful menace.

'I can't drive it away without the ruby closer to hand,' Naldeth said evenly.

'Where is it?' Unblinking, Velindre was watching the dragon.

'On the *Zaise*.' Out of the corner of his eye, Kheda could see the wild men frozen with fear.

'We'll never get to the ship before the beast attacks,' Risala whispered.

'That depends on what it's here for.' Kheda swallowed sour revulsion. 'Do you suppose it's come to eat those dead in the cave?'

'No.' Naldeth's voice echoed as if he were hidden deep in a cavern. 'It's come for me.'

Kheda forced his eyes away from the dragon to look at the wizard. Naldeth's leg was melting again, the liquid metal rippling. The mage staggered and the stony soil around him glowed with ochre magic. The limb re-formed, misshapen and discoloured.

'It knows I killed that wild wizard in the beaded cloak. It didn't come to help him because it wanted to see what I would do to him.' The magelight still suffused the patch of ground where Naldeth stood. 'And I didn't yield to it before, so that makes me a rival. It's come to kill me.'

'It's come to kill us both,' Velindre said thoughtfully. 'I really don't think it liked my snowstorm.'

Kheda saw the magewoman was standing precariously astride a cleft that had opened noiselessly between her feet.

The gap opened wider. A few moments more and she would lose her balance. Suddenly clenching her fists on her breastbone, Velindre drew up slatey-blue magelight from the depths to crisscross the void. She sprang backwards, traversing an impossible distance, further than a wild man could launch a spear. Landing painfully on her rump, she stretched both hands out before her to ward off the black dragon's magic. The rift in the ground snaked towards her, fast as a whip. Sapphire fire burned around her fingers as she shuffled backwards, shooting through the air to strengthen the magelight webbed across the cleft. The thrusting point of the rift slowed and stopped just short of her scrambling feet.

'Is there anything we can do?' Kheda gripped sword hilt and hacking blade.

The dragon fixed him with its burning amber gaze and opened its black maw to hiss at him. Its black tongue tasted the air before licking around its shiny metallic teeth. Kheda's sword and the hacking blade melted like wax, the steel dripping to the ground in useless gobbets.

The wild men broke and ran, village spearmen and cave dwellers alike, whimpers of terror escaping them as they fled in all directions. The scarred spearman and his band made a dash into the nut trees, skidding and slipping on the dusty slope.

A low detonation sent shivers through the woods. The dry air was rent in the next heartbeat by agonised screams. Kheda felt a furnace breath on the back of his neck. The menace of the earth dragon notwithstanding, he turned to look. The fire lit to burn the dead had run in all directions and the grassy plain was ablaze. The wild warriors who had fled that way were not merely caught in the conflagration. The burning tussocks were coiling around their arms and legs, pinioning them with crimson fire. Kheda choked as the sickly scent of roasting flesh joined the vile smell of smouldering hair and leather to overwhelm the innocent odour of burning grass.

A second dragon came stalking through the inferno. Its head was broad and blunt, armoured with dull maroon scales, ruby eyes lit with pinpoints of white-hot flame, red tongue flickering over teeth as long as swords and shining like polished copper. It stooped to snatch a burning corpse from the blazing ground and reared up, its forefeet lifting from the ground. The paler golden scales of its throat and chest bulged as it devoured the blackened carcass in a few swift bites. As the dragon dropped back to stand on all four feet, the ground trembled. The beast roared, showing dark rags of flesh clinging to its burnished teeth. Smoke and flames behind it swept to and fro as it lashed its spiked tail.

We're dead. We're all dead. That's bigger than the red dragon that came to plague Chazen and that beast was as long as a trireme. That black dragon knew enough to go and look for an ally, when it realised it had two wizards to fight. What was it Naldeth said? Fire and earth are sympathetic? And what a prize that ruby egg will make for this new beast.

White light closed in all around him and sucked the air from his lungs. Swept off his feet, Kheda was chilled to the marrow of his bones. He opened his mouth and his teeth ached with the cold. His lips and tongue were numbed and useless before he could attempt to speak. Then the white fire vanished and he fell hard onto the deck of the *Zaise*. He barely felt the impact on his frozen hands and knees.

'Risala?' he grated.

'Here,' she gasped.

Kheda sat back on his heels, rubbing frantically at his eyes. He found frost crystals riming his brows. Risala's dark hair was misted with icy vapour as she lay sprawled on the planks.

'The egg?' Velindre's frozen tunic crackled as she whirled around.

'In the stern cabin.' Naldeth was already tugging at the door. The warped joints in his metal leg split, the brittle steel fracturing. He cursed and clutched at his thigh. Ruddy magic flowed from his fingers, mending the metal with ugly bulbous seams.

'You two watch for the dragons.' Kheda ran, Risala close behind him. Throwing open the door, they seized the sacking and dragged the ruby out onto the deck. Sunlight sparkled in the cracks patterning the dulled surface.

The fire dragon came gliding across the burning grassland on massive wings, maroon bones dark against the red-gold membranes. It had barely taken flight, simply springing into the air to cross the scorched expanse. It roared, first with rage and then with challenge as it landed, throwing up a cloud of ash and cinders. The embers brightened with new fire and spun upwards. As the dragon swept its head around, the incandescent storm shot through the air towards the *Zaise*.

Naldeth threw up a commanding hand and the fiery cloud stopped dead. Velindre added sapphire skeins of magelight winding all around it. Her magic flared white before turning scarlet and evaporating into nothing. The crimson dragon roared with triumph. The burning hail edged over the river between the *Zaise* and the bank. The water all around the ship steamed and fled, leaving moist brown mud that instantly parched to cracked earth.

'I can't hold it much longer,' Naldeth warned, uncannily calm.

'Let's see if this works.' The magewoman narrowed her eyes and azure magelight dripped from her hands to flow across the ship's deck and drip through the scuppers.

With a bubbling rush, the muddy waters returned from upstream and down. Meeting in a surge of dirty foam, the river leapt up to slap at the burning cloud. The fire glowed with jade light and exploded. Blazing embers flew in all directions to hiss and die in the river or clatter dull and devoid of magic against the *Zaise*'s deck and sides.

Kheda dodged the searing fragments as the crimson dragon spread its awesome wings and sprang. A wall of emerald magelight shot upwards from the river to surround the boat, reaching as high as the top of the masts. The dragon bellowed and soared more steeply upwards, clawed feet abruptly drawn tight to its underside where before it had been reaching out with its lethal talons. The ridged spike that tipped its broad tail brushed against the curtain of green wizardry. The dragon roared with pain and anger as it rolled backwards through the air, a dark stain marring its tail.

Kheda felt the planking rise and fall beneath his feet as the whole river shivered. A bulge of water swept down from upstream and his heart missed a beat. 'Naldeth!'

'Wait.' The wizard was standing over the ruby egg, bent with both hands pressed to its sides. Scarlet fire suffused it. The sacking and ropes were crumbling to ash and a scorch mark was spreading across the deck. Naldeth gazed into the gemstone, utterly absorbed in the spark building at its heart.

Are we going to lose him the same way we lost Dev? Where do I hide now? Where do any of us run to? We should never have come here. We should never have stayed.

'Naldeth, look in the water!' Kheda yelled desperately.

The black dragon's head broached the silty surface. Muddy ooze outlined the scales of its back as the rest of the beast emerged. It crouched in the middle of the river chan-

553

nel, the opaque water lapping around its belly, hiding its legs and feet. It thrashed its long tail and dark magic boiled up from the depths, threading steely radiance through the water. Tendrils reached for the *Zaise*, knotting and swelling, brightening to a putrid grey-green. The first touched the hull and the planking cracked. The dragon hissed with malicious satisfaction.

Velindre grabbed the ship's rail with both hands. The curtain of emerald magic slid down through the air to soak into the wood, making the ship shine as brightly as new leaves. The river gurgled protestingly. The *Zaise* lurched and tilted.

'Are we sinking?' demanded Kheda.

'Not if I can help it,' Velindre grunted through gritted teeth.

The red dragon landed back on the bank with a resounding thud. It roared with fiery rage and flames sprang up from the dead ashes all along the grasslands. Like a shower of spears, flames appeared in the air, flung straight at the *Zaise*'s masts. Ropes flared into lines of scarlet fire. The spars smouldered and molten pitch dripped onto the decking. The fire dragon took a pace forwards, the undercut edge of the bank crumbling beneath its weight. It stretched out its massive head and breathed a snapping coil of fire towards the ship.

'Oh no you don't.' Naldeth's head jerked up from his rapt contemplation of the ruby egg. Unseen wind tousled his brown hair before sweeping across the river to blow the red dragon's fire back into its face. The creature recoiled, spitting furiously. Naldeth raised a hand and a golden haze floated up from his fingers towards the *Zaise*'s masts where scarlet flames crackled gleefully as they gnawed on blackened wood. The foggy yellow magelight glowed and smothered the dragon's fires.

'Kheda! Remember the cargo!' Risala had found a bucket somewhere and hurried to toss it over the rail.

Kheda saw that the sailcloth covers held down by the battens nailed over the deck hatches were burning.

Before he could move, Risala screamed and tried to let go of her rope. It struck back like a snake, tying itself around her wrists and wrenching her forward.

Kheda ran to her, drawing his dagger to cut the rope. The blade struck the cable with a dull thud and the steel dented. Catching Risala around the waist, he braced his feet against the side of the ship and hacked at the rope. Every stroke notched the edge of his knife but the transmuted hemp began splintering. Risala's face twisted with pain, her hands bloodless, the vicious binding biting deep into her forearms. Just when Kheda thought the ruined dagger was going to break clean in two, the rope snapped and they both fell backwards. The bucket plummeted downwards to strike the water with an odd clunk instead of a splash.

'Are you all right?' Kheda cut the snare from Risala's wrists, thankfully now no more than braided hemp once again.

She nodded, muddy-faced and biting her lip against the pain. 'Kheda, the fire!'

All the young wizard's attention was on the ship's masts where the charred spars now writhed like living things. Swinging this way and that, they were fighting to escape the stifling haze so that the greedy flames could blossom anew. Ominous splintering sounds filled the air above Kheda's head.

'Naldeth!' he shouted urgently.

Naldeth glanced down for a moment and the ruby egg at his feet glowed brilliantly. A billow of golden vapour rolled along the deck. The flames burning insidious holes in the canvas-covered deck hatches died as the magic swept over them, but they sprang to life once again as soon as it had passed. Naldeth spat some unintelligible Tormalin oath and the cloud of magelight bounced back from the upswept timbers of the blunt prow to snuff the fires a second time. This time they stayed dead.

'Velindre, we need water.' Kheda moved to look down over the ship's side.

There was no water to be seen. The bucket Risala had cast overboard lay on top of a thick layer of dead fish. A gasping eel writhed among their pale bellies. A tide of oily blackness oozed over the stricken creatures, like nothing Kheda had ever seen before. Wisps of grey followed the darkness, gathering into a dense layer of vapour. As Kheda watched, the bucket grew indistinct and vanished. He looked upstream to see the black dragon crouching in the midst of this unnatural mire, mouth agape. Amber eyes glowing, it breathed out dense clouds of the heavy mist that rolled across the glistening mud. The greyness was gathering around the *Zaise*. As it grew thicker, it began mounting higher up the sides of the ship. The green magelight that Velindre was still forcing into the timbers flickered and dulled.

She gasped with pain. 'Naldeth, we're going to tire before they do!'

The fire dragon angrily pacing up and down the river bank interrupted her with an ear-splitting roar. The black dragon in the water answered with a bellow that made the air throb.

'If we could just wound one, we might drive the other off—' Naldeth stooped awkwardly to press one hand onto the ruby egg. It was now entirely filled with scarlet magelight. He flicked his other hand towards the red dragon and fire sprang up around its forefeet. The beast growled and stamped on the crimson flames, ripping up clods of earth with its coppery claws.

'How do we do wound either of them without the other one killing us outright?' Velindre yelled hoarsely.

'We can give that red one something else to fight.' Naldeth stood upright and a distant stand of trees burst into flames.

Roaring, the crimson dragon whirled around, its trailing tail throwing up a cloud of ash. Barely a heartbeat later, it spun back towards the river, breathing a fresh curl of fire straight at Naldeth.

Green wizardry sprang up from the ship's rail to deflect it. 'It knows that was you.' For the first time, despair dulled Velindre's defiance.

Kheda saw a grey finger slide over the side of the ship. He looked down over the rail where the green magelight had dimmed almost to nothing and saw that the rising tide of vapour was level with the deck. The black dragon was an ominous shadow edging slowly closer.

'Can you do anything with the cargo?' he shouted desperately. 'Can you use that to set one of the beasts alight?'

'Let's try.' Velindre might have said more but the ship rocked violently. She spun around to draw a spear of lightning down from the sky to shatter the glaucous tendril snaking across the deck. 'Get the hatches open, Kheda. Naldeth, if I can keep that beast busy, you—'

'I know,' the mage yelled.

The battens and canvas holding down the hatches were already more than half-burned through. Kheda tore at them, heedless of fire or splinters. Risala helped as best she could with one hand, the other pressed tight beneath her breasts, weeping with silent anguish.

That cursed rope broke her wrist.

Kheda had barely cleared one hatch when a barrel shot upwards through the broken laths. Velindre swept one hand through the air and the barrel rode a swirl of sapphire light towards the crimson dragon. Naldeth threw an arrow of scarlet fire after it and the barrel exploded into a ball of flame right in the creature's face. It recoiled, roaring furiously. Kheda scrambled away from the gaping hole in the deck as more barrels and casks forced their way up. He grabbed Risala and sought what little shelter the foremast offered.

Velindre whirled a sling of sapphire light around to fling a barrel upstream. The black dragon reared up on its hind legs and swiped at it with steely claws. The wood splintered and dark sticky oil splashed a rainbow sheen over the creature's forelegs and chest. Naldeth threw another dart of fire and the oil ignited. The dragon hissed malevolently, breathing dark smoke that instantly quenched the flames. The crimson dragon's roar took on a note of triumph, unbothered by the flames dancing along its own spine and flanks.

'Naldeth?' Velindre's blue magic drove a flurry of caskets and chests up from the *Zaise*'s hold. Pale dust hovered in the air together with an eye-watering smell of naphtha.

'Do it.' The youthful wizard was looking at the black dragon, his hands outstretched as if to ward off the tide of grey vapour it was now breathing out, the miasma building faster than before.

Velindre sent a cask flying at the maroon dragon so hard and so fast that it shattered on the beast's massive flank. Sticky pine resin oozed down its hind quarter. The creature had barely turned its head when a cask of white powder and one of brilliant yellow broke across its spine. The dragon tasted the air with its tongue and growled. As it glowered at the *Zaise*, a second barrel ripped itself apart above its tail, showering the creature with liquid. The first drops had barely landed when the sticky mess coating the dragon ignited.

Bellowing with fury, the beast turned away to scour this importunate blaze from its scales with its own white-hot fiery breath. Velindre sent more barrels and chests to smash on the ground around its feet, each one adding fuel to the infernal alchemy. She drew winds threaded with blue magelight from all directions to fan the flames still higher.

Kheda could feel the heat where he stood on the deck. The wood was steaming.

Naldeth was standing stock still, all his attention focused on the black dragon. It crouched low in the lifeless mire it had made of the river, breathing out billows of the grey mist that rapidly threatened the *Zaise*'s rails. The mage knelt and laid gentle hands palm down on the massive ruby. A golden haze began gathering around the gem once again and flowed across the deck to slip through the scuppers as Velindre's magic had done earlier. The radiance spread over the ominous grey vapour, moving faster than the dead greyness, questing, challenging. Where the dragon's breath left coils slow to subside, the golden magic insinuated itself into the voids. The greyness roiled around the brightness, agitated. The brilliance forced fingers into the dullness, tearing off rags of grey that floated up to vanish in the empty air.

Naldeth slid his hands together atop the ruby egg. The shimmering gold forced the deadly grey vapour inexorably back towards the black dragon. It growled and crouched low, breathing a paler whiteness that dissolved the grey. The white mist evaporated almost instantly, revealing the glutinous mess of sludge and dead fish. The dragon sank lower and inky darkness flowed into the mud all around it. Its outline became indistinct.

'Oh no you don't,' Naldeth breathed.

Kheda heard a cavernous echo in the mage's voice again and tore his gaze away from the dragon. Naldeth's skin was shining, not with sweat but with a crystalline lustre. The metal of his leg was moulding itself into the contours of living flesh once again. The warlord looked past the mage to Velindre. She was still tangling the fire dragon in snares of air to keep the flames surging ever higher around it. Kheda realised he could see the timbers of the *Zaise* through her. Flesh, bone and clothing fading, the magewoman was becoming translucent. She didn't seem to notice. Insane serenity shone in her eyes and she laughed as if she didn't have a care in the world.

'Stay here.' Kheda hugged Risala hard and left her clinging to the foremast, forcing himself across the deck towards Velindre. He dared not look back to Risala lest his courage fail him, but he had to spare a glance for Naldeth and the black dragon lurking in the river. The amber magelight had set the noxious ooze boiling around the beast. Naldeth was now bathed in a ruby glow coming from the great gem. The dragon reared up out of the searing mud, its every scale as hard and sharp-edged as if it had been carved out of jet.

'Velindre.' Kheda reached out towards the mage-woman's arm. Close to, she looked as insubstantial as fog. A shock of lightning sprang from her to numb his whole hand. 'Velindre!' he yelled frantically.

'What?' She half-turned, still keeping her gaze fixed on the crimson dragon raging in the blaze ashore. Her eyes were no longer the soft hazel that had looked so striking against her blonde hair. They were blue like Risala's, but wholly blue, without white or iris. A pinpoint of lightning fire lit the deep sapphire.

Like dragon's eyes. Like Dev's eyes, just before his magic was the death of him.

Kheda tried to reach her again and once more stinging lightning sparked between them. 'This will kill you!' he bellowed.

Velindre didn't seem to hear him. She turned back to beatific contemplation of the lattice of sapphire light she was weaving through the flames mocking the crimson dragon.

Wringing his seared and throbbing hands, Kheda stumbled towards Naldeth. The red glow from the gem bathed him with heat. He reached recklessly for the mage regardless. Naldeth's shoulder was as cold as marble and as unyielding as any statue.

'What is it?' Naldeth looked briefly at Kheda. His gaze was all ruddy brown but at least that was just the blood still staining the whites of his eyes. Before Kheda could answer, the wizard gasped and his head snapped round towards the black dragon.

The golden magelight was fading from the clinging morass of boiling mud. The black dragon was extricating itself from friable rock that splintered and cracked all around it. With a triumphant growl, it pulled its hind legs and tail free, leaving dark holes. Hissing venomously, it took a menacing step across the solid surface.

Naldeth narrowed his eyes and the rock began to glow red while the fire within the great ruby burned with a new intensity. The dragon took another pace and its dull grey claws sank into newly molten lava viscous beneath its feet. Pulling its forefoot free, the creature roared, its steely talons glowing white hot at their tips. The dragon coughed pale mist at its claws and the whiteness dulled.

Kheda reached out again and tried to shake the mage's arm. 'You can't win this!' he cried.

'I know,' Naldeth said desperately. 'What do we do?'

'Nexus magic.' Velindre's words were a whisper of winter wind. 'To poison the well.'

She was barely more than an eerie white shadow outlined with sapphire magelight. Kheda took a step backwards as the magewoman sank to her knees beside the glowing ruby. She laid her pale hands on it and the fiery light dimmed abruptly.

Naldeth gasped and stumbled sideways. Kheda caught him; the wizard's flesh was warm and his clothes soft cotton.

Naldeth shook him off. 'You don't want to be caught up in this.' His voice sounded as if it was coming from some great distance.

561

Kheda backed away towards Risala as fast as he dared, trying to keep both of the dragons in view and still watch what the two wizards were doing.

They knelt on either side of the ruby egg, their hands resting upon it. The fire at its heart was now wholly quenched. The crimson dragon on the river bank screeched triumphantly as it wrested command of the fires from the dissipating sapphire magic. The black dragon replied with a snarl of elation and the river's waters returned to drown the slough of lava in a cloud of reeking steam.

The *Zaise* rocked violently. Kheda stumbled backwards to wrap one arm around the foremast and the other around Risala. Naldeth and Velindre took no notice. All their attention was focused on the great ruby. New lights kindled deep inside it, scarlet and blue, gold and green, rising and falling and rising once more to glow ever stronger.

The fire dragon roared and sprang into the air, the downdraught of its wings buffeting Kheda and Risala mercilessly. It flew inland, straight as an arrow, and Kheda saw that the distant mountain tops were belching white smoke high into the air.

The ship rocked again. This time the entire river was shaken by a shudder deep beneath its bed. Birds rose shrieking from the distant forests as tremor after tremor racked the plain. The banks on either side collapsed, sending great lumps of earth splashing into the water. A gaping crack opened in the barren slope leading up to the plateau. The most violent tremor so far nearly broke Kheda's grip on the mast and he saw a broad swathe of the grassland drop bodily down, leaving a scar of raw earth as tall as a man.

The black dragon took to the air, clumsy and reluctant. It flew over the *Zaise*, barely clearing the tops of the masts. It growled relentless hatred at the two wizards still kneeling motionless on the scorched planks, though there was a new note in the creature's snarls.

Fear.

Kheda wrapped his arms around Risala and around the foremast as the waters convulsed beneath the ship. The river surged for the sea, sweeping the *Zaise* along. As they swept past the riverbanks at dizzying speed, Kheda saw that the plumes of white from the mountains far inland were darkening to mottled grey. Clouds were spreading in all directions over the island, as fast as the terrifying rush of the water beneath them. The *Zaise* reached the maze of channels and mud banks that made up the mouth of the river and grounded with a bone-shaking thud. They were stranded between sandflats stripped glistening and naked as the river disappeared. The ocean itself was fleeing the shore as the cliffs were forced upwards higher and higher, ragged cracks splitting the rocks with penetrating shocks. The clouds rising from the mountains far inland were now black and riven with brilliant white lightning.

More snow?

The sunlight dimmed as white flakes drifted down to the deck. Kheda tasted sulphur that had nothing to do with the *Zaise*'s lost cargo and realised this was a fall of ashes from a burning fire mountain. Ash fell thicker and faster and drifted around their feet, stirred by a hot breeze. Stones began falling, as riddled with holes as a sea sponge. Cinders dropped from the grey clouds, glowing red. Kheda saw one strike Velindre's shoulder.

She didn't even flinch as the ember burned a dark score in her tunic.

The noise far inland sounded like the worst thunders of every rainy season that Kheda had ever known all recalled together. The lightning that ripped through the massive black clouds grew ever more violent. Close at hand, silent spheres of phosphorescence blinked around the *Zaise*'s mast-heads before vanishing as suddenly as they had appeared.

The ship twisted this way and that as the sands and silts of the river mouth convulsed. Kheda looked up to see that the sky was black as ink, as if night had driven out the day. The air was stifling, poisonous. His chest burned with it. Red light rippled along the sooty pall of the clouds.

On the deck between the two wizards, answering scarlet fire blazed in the gem. The rumbling in the far distance rose to a deafening pitch as the shoreline's paroxysms lifted the *Zaise* upwards. The ship shivered from stem to stern, assailed by brutal pulses of air. Spars split and crashed to the deck while such ropes as remained were ripped from the masts.

Far inland, one of the mountains threw up a flaming column of white-hot rock to rip into the swollen black belly of the cloud. A second eruption followed, and a third. The clouds blazed.

The ruby egg exploded in a coruscating flash. Kheda screwed his shut, blinded with tears. He didn't dare let go of the mast to try clearing his vision. Blinking and gasping for breath, he tried desperately to see what had befallen the wizards.

Velindre lay sprawled in the thick layer of ash coating the deck, her legs twisted awkwardly beneath her. She was bleeding from countless gashes, lacerated by razor-sharp shards of the shattered gem. Her eyes were open, staring unmoving.

Naldeth was slumped on his side, his head hidden in his outstretched arms. His hands had taken the brunt of the explosion, the bones of broken fingers white in the uncanny half-light. Blood glistened where his torn tunic revealed his pale flank.

'Are they dead?' Risala cried.

'I don't know.' Kheda didn't think he could prise his own hands from the mast and he certainly wasn't going to risk losing Risala as she clung to him with her one sound hand knotted in the cloth of his tunic.

He watched gold and scarlet torrents pouring from ragged craters in the distant mountains. The forests were burning, flames spreading even faster than the molten rock. The ash was still falling. Now, wholly unexpectedly, rain began falling with it. Soon the deck was coated with a thick layer of gritty mud. Kheda shifted his feet and found that the stuff was hardening with horrifying speed.

'If they're not already dead, Velindre and Naldeth will suffocate under this.' He had to shout to make himself heard, even with Risala inside the circle of his arms.

'Will we be any safer in the stern cabin?' she screamed back.

Kheda's throat ached with the effort of replying. 'There's nowhere else to go.'

Summoning up all his courage, he wrenched his fingers apart and let go of the mast, immediately clamping one hand around Risala's sound wrist. Slipping and stumbling, sick with terror, he forced his way across the deck. Risala struggled along with him. As he bent to grab the front of Velindre's mud-caked tunic, Risala twisted her one good hand free of his grip and reached down for Naldeth's outstretched arm. Somehow between them, they dragged the comatose wizards into the stern cabin.

Leaning against the cabin door to force it shut, they clung together. As the storm of fire and air and the earth's convulsions assailed the ship, they were shaken from side to side, buffeted by bundles of clothing and bedding tossed all around them. Hard-edged objects anonymous in the darkness struck more painful blows. Rocks or other things entirely thumped against the deck and sides of the ship, making the whole hull resound like a drum. The noise was deafening, the fear incapacitating. The ground shook and shook again, unceasing.

It was some moments after the tremors stopped before Kheda actually realised that the *Zaise* had come to rest. The planks sloped beneath him at an ominous angle and the loose items that had been thrown around the cabin slid down to the floor. He found he was shaking from head to toe, aching with bruises, the pain of his wrenched shoulders indescribable. All was silent.

'Kheda?' Risala's whisper was shockingly loud in the darkness.

'Here.' He held her tight.

'Where are we?' A spasm of coughing racked her.

Kheda's own throat was burning in the acrid air. Finally convincing himself that any sensation of movement was no more than an echo in his shocked mind, he forced the stern cabin's door open. He had to push hard against the setting slurry of ash-laden rain still clogging the deck.

The *Zaise* was wedged between two sandbanks, the channels all around choked with ash and debris. There was no sign whatsoever of the muddy river's flow.

Kheda looked over his shoulder at Risala. 'Are they still alive?'

'I think so,' she said shakily. She was kneeling between the two wizards, bent with her ear over Velindre's mouth and her fingers pressed to the pulse in Naldeth's neck.

'We won't get out of here without them.' Kheda surveyed the flood plain as best he could in the dim light. While the air was hot and foul and the grasslands were ablaze, there was no immediate sign of a torrent of molten rock pouring down the valley to consume them. There was no sign of any other living creature.

Risala sat back on her heels. 'Then all we can do is wait.'

Kheda leaned his forehead against the frame of the door. 'Will you ever forgive me for agreeing to come here?'

'I hardly think you're responsible for this catastrophe.' Risala looked at the comatose mages with fearful awe. 'Do you think they will wake up?'

'I have no idea,' Kheda said helplessly.

Chapter 23

The old woman sat in the shade of the swollen-bellied tree on the edge of the plateau and looked down the steep slope towards the river. Only now there was a steadily swelling flood spreading over the burned plain. She looked out towards the sunset shore where the land had raised itself up in broken sharp-edged ridges that now blocked the river's meandering path to the boundless water.

But the waters still flowed from the hills inland, and with nowhere to go, the flood was now reaching the nut-tree thickets in the ravine. The trees were dying anyway, smothered by the black mud that had rained down. The open expanse where the swollen-bellied trees stood was strewn with the oddly light stones that had fallen from the sky. Down below, the valley was rank with a smell of decay that grew stronger day by day. The air hummed with the drone of the clouds of biting insects that were hatching in the stilled waters.

She sat still and quiet, the breath catching in her aching chest. Sharp-tailed red flyers wheeled through the clouds of insects, gorging themselves. Down on the flood's margin, she could see brown and pink waders probing the turgid waters with their long beaks. Closer to hand, she saw a striped

568

lizard nosing among the sodden remnants of the grasses. It had found some carrion, its tail lashing enthusiastically as it gorged.

Had it found one of the men still missing from the village? So many had gone with the strangers on the day the world had changed so utterly. If they hadn't returned by now, surely they must be given up as lost? The old woman looked up at the sky. Where were the beasts? The men who had made their way back to the village had spoken of a fearsome creature of red and flame joining forces with the black beast from across the river. Yet a day for every wrinkled finger on one of her hands had passed now and there had been no sign of any great beast, of any hue, not even one flying overhead.

She sat in the shade and wondered if they would return in days to come. Would it be safe to stay up here on the high ground? It had been terrifying in the village, in the deafening darkness with the stifling air swirling thick with ash. Great chasms had opened up in the earth. Two of the swollen-bellied trees at the very edge of the high ground had fallen all askew. Yet one was putting out bright new leaves on its twisted, stubby branches, vivid green against the dark bark. A yellow bird with bright-blue wingtips trilled as it perched in the tree's tilted crown.

The old woman got stiffly to her feet. Even amid all this calamity, she felt content. The villagers had accepted her as one of their own. Every man or woman was valued now, even those weakened by age and infirmity. And she had more status than the men and women from the devastated settlements across the river.

She was still a little surprised that village spearmen who had gone with the strangers had straggled back with captives, muddy and bruised and as shocked as everyone else. The spearmen were adamant that the painted man who had lived over the river had been utterly defeated by the strangers before the cataclysm struck. Certainly none of those men or women denied this, properly humble as they begged for their lives. Besides, the caves that had sheltered them had shattered and the life-giving springs in their depths had dried up overnight. The dry valley had become a lethal confusion of pits and fissures.

The old woman was relieved that none of the villagers on this side of the valley had raised more than a token objection to the newcomers joining them. And happier still that no one was interested in humiliating the defeated men with meaningless tasks or degrading their women. There was nothing to be gained by it now that there was no painted man anywhere in the whole valley. The painted cave across the river was lost beneath broken rocks, according to the hunters who had been the first to venture across the spreading waters. Did that mean painted men could no longer step out of the pictures on the walls to reach them all? The old woman certainly hoped so.

There was no one left in the whole river valley who might aspire to the status of a painted man either. She hadn't realised that the scarred hunter had led his men to cull all those suspected of such powers before the ground had broken. Had they truly been afraid one of them might challenge the strangers and bring their astounding powers down to devastate the village?

She rose stiffly to her feet. Everyone was expected to bring food to the hearth, however slowly in the case of the elders. At least she had an easier task than most. She took a moment to count the swollen-bellied trees as the village woman had shown her and walked towards one of the oldest. This one had grown hollow over the years, hiding a dark void within while the leathery walls still bore a twisted green tangle. She had to duck to get through the split in the trunk, with a twist that set her back aching.

Her eyes stung with unexpected tears as a different pain assailed her. She had given birth in the safe embrace of a

570

mighty tree, just like the village women. She had come back when the eyes of the sky were closed to bury the tie that had bound the child into her belly. Did any of her children still live? How far had this catastrophe reached? Certainly the most distant mountains still burned and smoked. Had the green forest where she had lived for so long been burned to ashes?

She screwed her eyes shut and refused to give way to weeping. Her daughters, wherever they might be, were grown and might have had some chance to save themselves. There were enough women grieving for their little children lost in the confusion of the calamitous night. Every day some woman broke down, inconsolable when the man who had begotten babies on her wasn't among the latest group to make their way back, battered and dazed.

And there were still children to be fed, so they might grow to be hunters and mothers in times to come. The old woman opened her eyes. She could just make out bulbous shapes hanging in the folds of the tree's interior. She tugged at one but it refused to come loose. A crawler ran down her arm and she recoiled, shaking it away. It took a few moments for her heart to stop pounding.

But it had not bitten her, she realised, so she would not die today. Taking a deep breath, even though her chest still ached from the after-effects of that choking night, she reached up and pulled on one of the dark bulges as hard as she could. The vine snapped and she clutched the precious lump to her bony breast. As she wormed her way out of the hollow tree, the bright sunlight outside prompted fresh tears.

She looked at her prize. The lizard's stomach had wizened to a hard casing, the sinew tying it tight darkened by the smoke that had first dried it. She examined it carefully for any sign that some curious creature or insect had eaten its way through to the pounded meat and fat and herbs within. No, it looked as secure as the day that the village woman had hidden it, against those hungry seasons when such caches might be all that would save the children she had borne there.

The women of the village had all agreed that food hoarded for an uncertain future was best eaten now. They had need of it, and besides, who knew what might lie ahead? The old woman gazed inland to the distant peaks still belching pale smoke into the soiled skies. Was it her imagination, her old bones and meagre flesh failing and her eyes clouded by age? Or were the days truly darker and cooler since the mountains had caught fire?

A shout startled her so badly that she nearly dropped her precious burden. She crouched, ready to duck back inside the tree, for all the protection that might afford her. Two figures came closer, close enough for her to recognise them and feel her racing heart slow for a second time.

It was the white-haired old man from the village. He waved a sturdy stick in greeting. One of the aged sisters was with him, carefully carrying a gourd full of fat white grubs. She congratulated the aged sister and secretly hoped the village woman who had taken her in would share instead some of the wind-dried meat cut from a lizard that one of the hunters had found crushed beneath a fallen tree. And she had heard one of them say the great lizards were returning to the flooded plain, to lurk among the decaying grasses. The hunters had agreed that the waters were too deep and too perilous to wade in now. They were talking of going inland to try to find trees large enough to make boats.

The white-haired old man was shrill with irritation as he was explaining how he had very nearly stunned an immature stalking bird that the two of them had startled from its hiding place. The old woman commiserated with him as they walked back to the village together. The aged sister was less sympathetic. She was more concerned that one such marauder might mean that more and bigger birds had found a way across the flooded valley. How long would it be before some child was taken by their cruel beaks?

The white-haired old man dismissed such fears. Let the biggest, most ferocious birds come, he scoffed. The village's hunters would slay them with the new weapons the tall stranger had shown them and everyone would go to bed with a belly full of sweet meat.

The aged sister would not be reassured. How far were the floods going to reach now that the river's path to the sea was blocked by the upthrust broken land? And the hunters who had ventured towards the sunset, to what had been the edge of the cliffs, had found the ground impassable with no water visible beyond. The sands and rocks lay bereft. They would go hungry, she predicted sourly, in the driest season. The fish from the great water and the shells from the rocks had often been all that they had had to eat.

The white-haired old man shook his head resolutely. If the waters towards the sunset were gone, they must turn their attentions inland. There were still birds and lizards to eat.

The aged sister wasn't listening, continuing her querulous complaints. Where, she wanted to know, were those strangers who had shown the village hunters how to make those curious weapons that flung sharpened and feathered sticks so hard and so far? They had not returned, had they? Who was going to protect their village now? Strangers they might have been, but the red man and the golden woman had undeniably had the powers of the painted men, even if they used them in such a puzzling fashion.

The old woman shrugged as both elders looked questioningly at her. She had no idea where the strangers were and that saddened her. They had shared the spoils of the hunt instead of fastening on the villagers like leeches, as any other painted man would have done. She struggled not to feel despondent as the three of them trudged on through the clotted ash, past thistly plants defaced by dirty smears and scored with deep burns from the rain of searing embers. The wind had had less chance to scour away the thick carpet of fallen stones here and they crunched through drifts of clinker.

The aged sister had a point. Who was going to defy any painted man if one did arrive somehow to claim the village for his own? She tried not to think of her likely fate if a beast and a painted man appeared together. She and all the elders would be sacrificed to satisfy the beast's hungers. That would please the painted man, and a contented painted man could summon clean water out of the dry earth and kill birds or lizards and roast them over fire that needed no fuel.

The upthrust fingers of the spiny thickets were burdened with dried black mud like the nut thickets. A group of children were trying to salvage something from a sprawl of fleshy-leaved plants choked with ash. The hunter with the stooped back was keeping watch. He carried a spear as well as one of the new curved weapons the tallest stranger had made. He grinned at the elders and held up a feathered stick that had skewered a dappled scratching fowl.

The old man congratulated him and tarried to tell of his own near-capture of a much greater prize. The aged sister and the old woman walked on to the village. Most of the able-bodied men were still busy repairing the thorny barrier that had been ripped asunder by the violent winds on the night of the catastrophe. Arms and legs bloodied from countless scratches, they paused to let the old women pick their way through the gap they were mending.

They paused to look past the broad fire pit to the charred ruin of the great hut that had belonged to the dead painted man with the skull mask. Falling cinders had set fire to the thickly grassed roof that these villagers had built him with so much time and effort. The hut had blazed with a ferocity to rival one of the distant peaks. The lesser huts had suffered as well. Several had collapsed under the weight of the rain of mud. Others had gaping holes in their roofs where falling rocks had crashed through to terrify those within. But they could be rebuilt, and new huts built beside them.

Then the old woman realised there were newcomers gathered around the central hearth. She squinted as she drew nearer and felt a tightness in her chest as if the ash-laden winds had returned. The leader of the newcomers was a man wearing strings of coiled seashells, white and gold. He waved a demanding hand at the racks of meat set to dry in the sun. One of his followers seized a gourd of water from a young girl and drank greedily, one hand fending off his two companions who would plainly have snatched it if they could.

The village women and the spearmen who had returned over the past few days didn't look impressed. The tallest, the scarred warrior who was the white-haired elder's son, stepped forward. Fearful yet desperate to hear what was being said, the old woman edged closer, clutching the stuffed lizard stomach so tight that her swollen knuckles ached.

The scarred hunter was denying the newcomers any share in the salvaged meat, or in the roots that the children had gathered from the torn earth, or even in the boring beetle grubs that were feasting on the fallen trees. If they were hungry, he told them bluntly, they could forage for themselves.

The man wearing the strings of shells scowled and promised that the scarred hunter would regret such arrogance. Who was there to defy him here? He wanted to know. He turned to the women standing silently around the ring of blackened stones. Didn't they want his protection for their children?

The old woman wondered if she was the only one who saw the tremor in the man's hand. One of the elders, the man with the clouded eyes, spat into the dust with deliberate contempt. Who did these newcomers think they were, to demand food from the village's hearth without offering anything in return? Peering up at the sky, he allowed that he might not have seen a beast flying overhead given the webs blurring his sight, but he had heard their wings often enough in his long life. Why had these people come here? What could have driven them out of their home if they had a painted man to call on?

Several of the newcomers spoke up. Their village had been beyond that ridge of high ground. They pointed, their hands shaking. The stream in their valley had run backwards when the land towards the sunset had reared upwards and the day had turned to night. It had disappeared utterly into the sands and dig as they might, they had not been able to find any water.

Why were they trying to take food and water from the mouths of this village's children, the scarred hunter challenged, when they had a painted man to satisfy their hunger and thirst?

The youth who had snatched the gourd of water lowered it, drops glistening on his chin, and stared at the man wearing strings of shells. Evidently that question hadn't occurred to him. But the old woman noticed several of those who stayed silent looking at the man with growing disillusion, their eyes dark with sorrow and loss.

The man with the shells raised a threatening hand towards the scarred hunter. The newcomers looked eager, even those who hadn't spoken. The old woman bit her lip and felt the tears that came so easily since the cataclysm prick her eyes. The scarred hunter was the best spearman in the village and the strongest willed. Without him to defend them, for the sake of his white-haired father, surely all the elders were doomed.

The man wearing the shells screwed up his eyes and turned his face to the sky. His upthrust hand began to tremble and soon his whole body was shaking. Nothing happened. No murderous shards of ice stabbed the spearman. No painted fire split his scarred skin anew or melted his flesh and burned his bones to ash. He didn't collapse, frothing at the mouth as he drowned where he stood, or clawing at his throat as the very breath of life was denied him. Instead, taking everyone by surprise, he sprang forward and struck the newcomer a brutal blow with his clenched fist.

The newcomer fell sideways, knocked clean off his feet. He didn't try to get up, just cowered in the black dirt, weeping now, utterly desolate. When the scarred hunter took a pace towards him, he scrambled away on hands and knees, wailing like a child. His followers recoiled, some blank-faced with this new shock. Other faces were more resigned, showing that a fear they had dared not voice had now been realised. A few turned around and began trudging back the way they had come.

The scarred hunter didn't let the supposed painted man escape. In a few strides, he caught him and ripped the strings of shells from his neck. The pale shells scattered across the dark mud. One of the newcomers stamped on one, crushing it with vehement fury. A village spearman stepped up to offer the scarred hunter his club. The scarred hunter raised it above his head and the powerless newcomer curled up in futile protest. The stone-studded club crashed down, not to dash out the powerless man's brains but to thud into the earth beside his ear.

The scarred hunter said something the old woman didn't catch as he handed the club back to the spearman, his face twisted with strange regret. He turned to the rest of the newcomers, spurning the powerless man grizzling at his feet with a vicious kick. Raising his voice, he told them firmly that if they wished to stay, they could. If they did their best for the village, then naturally they could share in whatever food or water they brought to the hearth. There was a catch in his voice as he acknowledged that this village had recently lost more people than it could easily spare in the fires that had swept through the grassy plain.

Though no one living here had any interest in being subject to anyone who might claim to be a painted man, he said firmly. The village men and women voiced their agreement. Several of the newcomers looked anxiously at the sky as if they expected a beast to appear to avenge their leader's humiliation. None appeared. The scarred hunter looked as if he might have said more but shut his mouth resolutely instead.

One of the newcomers ducked his head submissively as he assured the scarred spearman that he would work hard for his food and water, and fight for this village besides, if he were to be trusted with a spear. The newcomer gazed down at the powerless man still huddled on the ground, his head hidden in his arms. Their painted man hadn't been able to slow the burning rock that had spilled from a fissure and consumed their village. Whatever he had done for them in the past, he had been helpless against this new calamity.

They had been walking for days, one of the women said angrily, and whenever they had asked him to use his powers to find them water or bring them food he had refused, saying they hadn't yet reached a place that pleased him. The powerless man whimpered.

The scarred spearman shrugged and said that if the newcomers wished to eat now, they should start working. The broad-hipped mother who had taken the old woman in stepped up beside him. Indicating salvaged gourds by the hearth, she suggested the newcomers begin by fetching water. Though it wasn't an easy walk inland, she warned, to find the point where the river still flowed rather than stood still and spoiled. All the other springs had dried up here as well.

One of the newly arrived women clutching a limp and dull-eyed baby to her breast fell to her knees, sobbing with gratitude. The old woman joined the rest of the village mothers as they welcomed the newcomers with assurances that the worst of their trials were over. The hunters paired off with the newly arrived men, some heading off to help rebuild the defences, others explaining how the lie of the land had been so dramatically changed. No one spared a second glance for the wretched man still lying in the dirt and keening softly, clutching one of his golden shells in his filthy hand.

What did it mean, the old woman wondered, if the painted men and women had truly lost their powers? And had the beasts gone for ever?

Chapter 24

Kheda drew his hand back slowly, his eye fixed on the plump bird insouciantly probing the sandbank with its fine spike of a beak. He threw the stone hard and true and the bird fell in a flurry of feathers.

'Well done.' Risala gave a soundless clap from the slanted deck of the *Zaise*, careful of her splinted and bandaged wrist.

Kheda grinned up at her. 'You wouldn't care to go and get it, would you?'

She smiled down with a shake of her head. 'You shot it, you fetch it. I've done enough today carrying water.'

Kheda looked inland to the pit he had dug in the deepest channel that was still nonetheless as dry as a bone. At least there was water far beneath in the sand. And ironically, more water than they wanted was edging up the slope that the upheaval had made of the river mouth. The floods filling the grassy plain were slowly reclaiming the channels. His pleasure in securing fresh meat abated somewhat.

We're not drinking that water, stagnant and tainted with whatever's rotting beneath it. And it's bringing far too many insects to bite us and that could lay us low with whatever foul fevers this land might harbour.

He tried for a reassuring smile as he turned back to Risala. 'Did you see anyone?'

'No one.' Risala sighed. 'Nothing alive bar a few new birds, those little striped lizards and far too many flies.'

'Those people who stayed back on the higher ground must have been safe,' Kheda said stubbornly. 'We saw smoke from a fire, didn't we?'

'Who's to say who or what lit it?' Risala glanced involuntarily over her shoulder. 'If you want to find that village again, you'll have to go and look for yourself.'

'I think we can wait until someone finds us, if someone risks those floodwaters. I can't see any easy path for us inland, not if we have those two to help along.'

It's no bad thing that the twists of this channel hide us from view from inland. I don't suppose those wild men and women would be too impressed if they came to us looking for help and found our vaunted mages wholly incapable. And I don't think any of us want to get entangled in their affairs again.

Kheda followed Risala's gaze towards the stern cabin. 'Is she trying to scry again?' he asked quietly.

'For the third time today.' Risala nodded, half-concerned, half-exasperated. 'I told her she should wait till tomorrow, or at least until after noon.'

'You don't imagine she'll listen, do you?' Kheda shook his head, resigned. 'How's Naldeth?'

Risala answered with a shrug. 'Still just sitting and staring at his hands.'

Kheda shook his head, frustrated. 'I wish he'd let me see what's happening under those bandages. Or take some poppy syrup. He must be suffering agonies.'

'You don't think he's afraid of how much it might hurt if you need to re-splint his fingers?' Risala suggested with a shudder.

Kheda gave another sigh. 'I'd better go and find that bird before green ants eat it.' He trudged over the desiccated sand and picked up the dead bird. Digging a shallow pit with the square end of the single hacking blade they still had between them, he gutted it carefully with Risala's dagger and buried the entrails. Pausing to wipe the sweat from his forehead before it drew too many flies, he looked back at the *Zaise*, wedged in a curved hollow, masts broken, her deck a hollow ruin. Then he looked back out to the west. The ship rested high and dry an astounding distance from the sea.

What are we going to do if both wizards' powers continue to fail them? Risala and me are hardly going to carry the Zaise over those exposed reefs and out to the sea between us. Though the ship's not going to be seaworthy, even if we could.

Retracing his steps, he threw the bird up to thud onto the deck and pulled himself up the dangling rope ladder. Sitting on the rail, he began plucking the bird, letting the feathers drift idly away to be lost on the steady breeze coming in from the distant ocean.

Risala studied him. 'What are you thinking about?'

Kheda continued stripping away feathers. 'Arrogance,' he said after a long moment. 'I keep wondering how I could have been so arrogant as to think I could just change what didn't suit me about this place, because I was a warlord and that's what I wanted.'

'It wasn't just you,' Risala protested quietly. 'They were at least as determined to work their will here.'

'And we all just dragged you along with us.' Kheda tried to rid himself of down sticking to the blood on his fingers.

'I had a choice,' Risala reminded him. 'I came because I wanted to, because I believe in you, because I believed we had to find out just what might threaten Chazen.'

Kheda glanced at her. 'At least they had their magic to encourage them to think they might actually be able to do something about any dangers lurking here.'

'You don't think their magic just made them more arrogant?' countered Risala. 'Do you honestly think they intended to raise up the coastline like this? I don't think they had any idea what would happen when they let their magic loose like that.'

'Well, we're all more humble now.' Kheda tore viciously at a particularly stubborn quill. 'And at least they saved us all from those dragons.'

'Do you think you might have been a little arrogant in setting your face against omens and portents?' Risala fiddled with the bandage around her broken wrist.

Kheda didn't answer, simply ripping more feathers from the partially denuded bird.

'When we get back to the Archipelago,' Risala persisted, 'will you at least look again at all the records, all the philosophers' writings, and listen to the epic poets who discuss their misgivings? You're hardly the first one to have doubts. Just to see if there's a chance you might be mistaken, before you throw all that away?'

Kheda cleared his throat. 'All right. I can do that much for you.'

When we get back to the Archipelago? If we ever get back to the Archipelago. That's an easy promise to make, because I don't see how we're ever going to get home.

'Kheda! Risala!'

The shout from the stern cabin made them both jump.

Risala looked at Kheda. 'Naldeth wants us.'

'Let's see why.' He swung his legs inboard. Traversing the slanted deck was a question of half-crawling, half-walking. The door to the stern cabin was hinged on the uphill side and awkward to manage. Splinters from the shattered ruby egg were driven deep into the wood.

Kheda forced a cheerful tone as he looked inside the cabin and flourished the dead bird. 'Fresh meat tonight, and I'll see if—'

He swallowed the rest of his words as he saw that the cabin wasn't just lit by the harsh sunlight filtering through the holes in the broken planking. A green glow rose from the dented silver bowl that Velindre cradled, illuminating her face.

The magewoman sat cross-legged on the haphazard collection of clothing and bedding that they had piled in the angle of the sloping deck and the tilted wooden wall to make a vaguely level surface for sleeping. Looking up, she smiled at Kheda. Where her face had been thin before, the mage-woman was now positively gaunt and the green light made the bruises all down one cheek look black against her pallor.

'How far can you scry?' Kheda tossed the dead bird back out onto the deck and stepped into the cabin. Risala followed him, her face alive with curiosity.

'So far I've seen that our friends in the village over on that higher ground escaped the worst of it.' Velindre sounded weary yet exultant.

'Some of their warriors have even made their way home.' There was no mistaking Naldeth's guilty relief. He still looked as exhausted as Velindre. His tan had faded to an unhealthy sallow and deep lines were now fixed between his brows and either side of his mouth. The blood staining his eyes had decayed to ghastly yellow and purple.

Kheda sneaked a discreet look at the young wizard's stump. The convulsions that had racked Naldeth during the mountains' eruptions had left his metal leg a misshapen ruin. As the mage had lain unconscious, Kheda had forced himself to see what had happened to his bleeding thigh. Relieved to find metal and flesh separate once more, he had forced the contrivance off the blistered stump and thrown it into a corner. Naldeth hadn't spoken of it since recovering his senses. Nor had he allowed Kheda to re-dress his broken scars.

At least there's no sign of suppuration, and if the flesh was rotting, we'd all smell it in here.

Then he realised that the young mage's hands were clasping his remaining knee. He had discarded all the splints and bandages Kheda had used to painstakingly reconstruct his broken bones.

'Naldeth, your hands,' the warlord said, astounded.

The young mage looked down and flexed his fingers, wincing. The torn flesh was still thickly scabbed and odd lumps bulged beneath the skin. 'I thought I had better make use of that black dragon's bone magic,' he said, swallowing hard. 'If my hands don't mend sufficiently to be useful, I really will be a cripple for the rest of my life.'

So such knowledge has its uses, however vile the uses that cloaked wizard might have put it to.

'Indeed.' Kheda kept his voice neutral.

'What have you seen?' Risala peered into the ensorcelled bowl.

'Rather more pertinent is what we haven't seen,' Velindre said slowly. 'We've seen no wild wizards working any magic to help the people or to help themselves. Some villages have gathered up their dead, but there's no sign that any dragon has been tempted to dine.'

'Neither of us have had any sense of a dragon within miles of here.' Naldeth gazed inland as if he could see through the splintered planks. 'And there's a warlord's ransom in rubies studding the deck. That would surely have drawn any beast attuned to fire.'

'I think we did it.' Velindre broke into a coughing fit that left her wheezing painfully.

The confusion plaguing Kheda resolved itself into one simple question. 'What exactly did you do?'

'We poisoned the well.' Velindre's smile was as cheerful as a death's-head rictus. 'That's another respected tactic in Aldabreshin warfare, according to what I heard as I sailed the Archipelago, one of the best ways to end a fight quickly.'

'We realised we couldn't beat the dragons.' Naldeth shuddered. 'We must have been mad to think we ever stood a chance. We couldn't match them without destroying ourselves.'

'They were drawing on the elemental confluences that underpin this place.' Velindre gazed around as if she too could see through the broken hull of the *Zaise*. 'Or used to underpin it, I should say.'

'But what did you do?' Risala asked again.

'There was a degree of instability already inherent in the elements,' Naldeth said briskly. 'Water was seeping into the fissures in the sea bed, reaching all the way to the point where the fire came up out of the earth into the mountains. The pressures would have built up to an eruption long since if the dragons and the wild mages hadn't been drawing the elemental potential away with their wizardry, crude as it was. We simply accelerated events.'

Kheda wasn't wholly sure what the wizard was talking about but he knew self-justification when he heard it.

'Perhaps,' Velindre said dryly. 'The crucial thing was that we could use that ruby to work nexus magic. Between us we could draw all four elements together. Only there was no point in trying to use that quintessence against the dragons.'

'So we turned it against the instabilities in the elemental confluences and tipped the whole balance.' Naldeth rubbed a hand over his unkempt beard. 'I have to say, I wasn't expecting quite such dramatic results,' he added, contrite.

As Risala tucked herself under his arm, Kheda groped for understanding. 'How did this poison the elements?'

'They're all running into each other at the moment.' As Velindre looked up, the emerald light in the water dulled. 'Like dyestuffs bleeding into each other in cheap cloth. Any dragon with any sense will have gone in search of a purer, stronger elemental focus. All this confusion will repel them.'

'None of these wild wizards will have a chance of working their magic' Satisfaction warred with apprehension in Naldeth's words. 'It's proved nigh on impossible for us these past few days and we're used to working complex wizardry. These wild mages only know how to draw on a single element and their spells are little more than pure instinct.'

'I think we've both learned that all the strictures and warnings about working nexus magic are more than valid, certainly without a full quartet of mages.' Velindre looked down at the silver bowl, frowned, and the radiance rallied.

'I thought I had burned out my own affinity,' Naldeth said, voice hollow.

Velindre shivered with sympathy. 'This was ten times worse than that potion you fed me and Dev, Kheda.' She closed her eyes, bloodless lips pressed tight together.

'But as you can see, it was just a matter of time.' Naldeth rubbed at the crease between his brows with the ball of his thumb 'We still have our affinities.'

'What do you think you can do?' Kheda asked carefully. 'Without exhausting yourselves. You mustn't risk overtaxing yourselves.'

'Dev told us how dangerous that could be,' Risala agreed anxiously.

'Don't you want to know if we can get us all home?' Naldeth's smile was unnerving in the eerie light.

'That's not my only concern,' Kheda said frankly, 'but yes, since you mention it.'

'Haven't we done all we came here to do,' Risala demanded, 'and more?'

'Rather more than we intended,' commented Velindre sardonically. 'I don't know if I can work a translocation over such a distance,' she went on, abruptly serious. 'Not until I have some better understanding of the elemental changes we've wrought around here.'

'We can give you all the time you need. The *Zaise* isn't going anywhere and we've seen no sign of savages making their way in this direction.' Kheda returned Risala's supportive hug that inevitably found some of his bruised ribs. 'I'd be grateful, though, when you think you're strong enough, if you could try to see what's happening in Chazen.'

If I'm stuck here, at least show me that no disasters have struck there because I abandoned my responsibilities to Itrac and my new children.

'I can try now.' Velindre looked into her glowing bowl, the tip of her tongue toying with a split in her chapped lower lip. 'If you'll let me raid your physic chest.'

'Of course.' Kheda crawled over the unkempt layer of quilts and blankets to retrieve the ebony coffer.

Naldeth shifted so that Risala could sit beside him. Kheda carefully negotiated the yielding surface to sit opposite the two mages. Velindre set the silver bowl carefully down between the four of them.

Kheda opened the physic chest. 'What do you want?'

'Whatever it is that you've been using to ease my chest pains.' Velindre held out her hand.

Kheda gave her the crystal vial of pungent silver-leaf oil.

Velindre managed a thin smile. 'It's close enough to the aids we offer inadequate apprentices, and this is no time for me to be too proud to accept a little assistance.'

She let a few drops fall onto the water and the emerald radiance glowed through the slowly dissipating circles. As the oil spread into a fine film, the green light dimmed and a new brightness grew in the depths of the water.

Kheda saw the garden in the centre of Itrac's pavilion.

The logen vine was in full bloom and silken basket flowers clustered thick. The white-sand paths were neatly raked and in the central bower, Itrac and the baby girls were taking their ease on a green carpet patterned with fire-creeper and striol flowers. Chazen's lady wore a simple tunic and trousers of white silk, her bare feet kicking idly as she lay on her front, propped up on her elbows. The baby girls were lying on their backs on either side of their mother, each little face flushed with laughter. Itrac was using the end of her long plait to tickle first Olkai and then Sekni. The babies kicked lustily, trying to grab the teasing thing.

Assuming we ever get home, how will I ever explain any of this to you? Now I have still more secrets to come between us. We're further apart than ever.

'I wouldn't mind being there,' Naldeth said softly.

'Nor me.' Kheda ran a hand through his unkempt hair. 'Can you show me whether all is well around the lagoon?'

'I'll try,' Velindre said cautiously.

The spell flickered so violently that Kheda thought her magic had failed her. Then the emerald light returned and a new image floated on the surface. The lagoon around the Chazen dry-season residence was thick with ships — merchant galleys from all the neighbouring domains and a profusion of the dispatch boats and triangular-sailed traders that plied the sea lanes within the domain. Heavy triremes were manning the key stations that governed entry and departure from the heart of the domain. In the open seas beyond, fast triremes carved deceptively lazy circles in the blue waters, ready to pursue any importunate vessel.

Risala gazed down at this picture of abundant trade with longing. 'Do you suppose the pearl harvest is as rich as last year's?'

'I haven't given that a moment's thought.' Kheda shook his head in wonder.

Risala hugged him. 'There'll be time enough to find out when we get home.'

'I'm sorry.' Velindre shook her head as the emerald light faded and died with ominous finality.

'Do you think you could scry as far as Hadrumal? When you're fully rested, of course.' Naldeth ran a thoughtful finger around the rim of the bowl. 'Do you think we should try bespeaking the Archmage?'

'Are you that eager to have the Council asking endless awkward questions?' Velindre looked askance at him. 'Don't you think that can wait until we get back there?'

'We are going to have an unholy amount of explaining to do, aren't we?' Naldeth managed a crooked smile.

Kheda saw a faint green radiance rekindled in the bottom of the scrying bowl and frowned. 'Velindre, he's right — you should rest before you try that.'

'What?' She looked at him puzzled.

Naldeth looked down at the bowl. 'That's not your spell and it's certainly not mine.'

'Do you think the Archmage is looking for us?' Velindre looked like an unwed girl who'd been caught in some mischief.

'Is he?' Kheda forced himself to look into the bowl.

'No,' said Velindre softly. 'Oh dear.'

Words failed Kheda as he saw a pale-green dragon with turquoise spines crouching on a beach of yellow sand. The dragon's head whipped around and looked straight at them through the magic. It bared jade teeth in a soundless snarl, its aquamarine tongue tasting the air.

'That's the dragon we saw off the southernmost headland.' Velindre was astonished, 'The one I sent chasing the water spout.'

'Then it got the taste of your magic from that,' Naldeth said.

'That's a trading beach in the Archipelago.' Risala jabbed a finger at the wreckage of boats large and small drifting in the lapping surf. Cloth was tangled around one of the beast's forefeet and it was tentatively crushing metal wares and pottery under its talons. There was no sign of any people, dead or alive.

'Where exactly?' demanded Kheda.

'I've no idea,' Velindre said slowly.

The dragon continued to look straight at them, its head growing larger and larger as it filled their vision. The creature was stalking towards them.

'No!' Naldeth plunged his hand into the scrying bowl, sending the water slopping to soak the coverlets and wet everyone's knees. The emerald light flashed a sickly yellow and died.

'I think we had better bespeak Planir.' Velindre was trembling. 'Just as soon as we can.'

'What are we going to do after that?' Risala demanded.

'We rid Chazen of one dragon.' The magewoman sighed heavily. 'We know how to drive that one off. Without killing it,' she added determinedly.

'You can't think of attempting anything like that until all your bruises have healed and you've both recovered your full

591

strength,' Kheda said angrily. 'How many people will it kill in the meantime?'

'Hopefully none,' Velindre said thoughtfully. 'That dragon had no interest in eating carrion, if you recall. It should find plenty of fish in Aldabreshin waters. Perhaps I can lure it away with a sea serpent as bait,' she said hopefully.

'Perhaps,' Kheda echoed with distinctly less optimism.

Risala was still wide-eyed. 'How many others have flown for the Archipelago? Can you tell what happened to the white one you made, that ate the blue sky dragon's heart?'

'I thought they'd go into the northern wilds to find un-contaminated focuses of elemental power...' Words failed Velindre.

Kheda closed his eyes and took a long, slow breath. 'Can you find out, without risking yourself?'

'As long as I'm ready to shatter the spell if it's subsumed into a dragon's magic again.' Naldeth stared into the empty bowl. 'We had better discuss all the possible tactics we might use against dragons of every colour,' the younger wizard said suddenly. 'And bespeak Planir and every other wizard we trust in Hadrumal, be they friend or rival, and seek their advice. The Council must insist that everyone share any relevant learning they can dig out of the libraries.'

'The time for keeping this all as our little secret has obviously passed.' Velindre was plainly not sorry about that.

'I share some measure of responsibility for all this.' Kheda took Risala's hand and held it tight. 'I had better come with you, when you find out where that beach is.'

'You'll come and help me fight a dragon again?' Velindre tried to sound incredulous. 'Even when it's not in Chazen, or anywhere close by the looks of things?'

'You'll need someone to help you convince the lord and people of whatever domain that might be that you're able to help them.' Kheda glanced at Risala, wordlessly beseeching.

She nodded resolutely, not even seeing his appeal as she looked at Velindre. 'If anyone suspects you're a mage, you'll just see your own hide flayed from your back and nailed to a gate in hopes that will be enough to deter the beast.'

Velindre closed her eyes as a tear glistened behind her lashes. 'I can scry for dragons with an air or a water affinity. Naldeth, if I work the scrying with you, can you look for those tied to fire and earth?'

'I'll help you scry for them but I don't think I'm going back with you to fight them.' His words stunned them all to silence. 'Someone has to stay here and I don't see that I have any choice.' Naldeth's voice strengthened, determined. 'I started all this. I have to see it through.'

'See what through?' Velindre shifted to look severely at him.

Naldeth met her gaze without flinching. 'The mageborn here will be incapable of working magic for a good long while, but sooner or later the echoes of these eruptions will finally die away. Instinctive magic will spark fires when someone's angry or freeze the water in the cup they're holding, just like some apprentice back on the mainland who's over-ready to be sent to Hadrumal. Once that happens, they'll soon stumble into some more powerful spellcraft. You know that.'

'What happens then?' Velindre asked brusquely. 'What will you do?'

'Won't that depend on the people here?' Kheda said tentatively.

'What do you suppose they will do?' Naldeth challenged him. 'Will they have become sufficiently used to living without magical tyranny that they'll refuse to bow their heads to

someone crowning himself with feathers or cloaking himself
in some lizard's hide because he's discovered some inborn
prowess? What if the dragons come back when the elemental
confusion subsides? Will the whole sorry system that kept
these people in their ignorance and filth simply be resur-
rected? A generation or more will have to die before all those
customs are forgotten.'

Distress flickered across his face. 'Or do you suppose the
people will be so determined not to be enslaved again that
they will kill all the mageborn — those they know were guilty
of abusing them in the past and any others, however young
or innocent, that they fear might grow to be tyrants? They
have some way of telling the mageborn from the mundane,
we know that much. Do you suppose there are enough of
those painted caves to hold all the bodies?'

'I don't know.' The bitter memory of the slaughter the
scarred spearman had ordered soured Kheda's stomach. 'But
how will you help them, when you don't speak their language
or understand their lives?'

'I'll find ways around that.' Naldeth looked at Velindre.
'There will be innocent mageborn here and we're always told
that all wizards have a responsibility for all others.'

She looked troubled. 'That's usually in the context of one
mage making sure another doesn't misuse his magic to the
detriment of all wizardry.'

'Who else is going to teach innocent mageborn here not
to follow in the corrupt practices of their forebears?' Naldeth's resolve was unshakeable. 'I'll have an advantage over
them long enough to be sure of that.'

'Do you think the Archmage will approve?' Velindre plainly had her doubts.

'Do you want to try explaining to him that we've left
mageborn here to either be slaughtered or sucked into a life
dependent on abusing their affinity?' Naldeth took a moment

to consider his next words carefully. 'Don't you think he will have concerns, when some of the wizards currently on the Council learn of this island and the elements that underpin it? When they learn there have been dragons here, with all the potential power that implies? I'm sure you'll find plenty willing to join you in establishing whether or not more dragons have flown to the Archipelago but there'll be some who'd rather make their way here, if they think there'll be no one to see what they do.'

'I can think of at least two,' Velindre said reluctantly, 'who I really don't trust.'

'If I'm here, there can't be any clandestine visits.' Naldeth gestured vaguely towards the wreckage of his metal leg. 'Not when I can bespeak Planir at a moment's notice with steel and magefire.'

'That might well be advisable,' Velindre agreed slowly.

'What if the dragons come back?' Kheda said sharply. 'They'll see you as a rival, won't they?'

'Then I'll have no qualms about calling for the Archmage's help, and that of any other wizard I can bespeak.' Naldeth smiled humourlessly. 'That will be no time for pride.'

'I see you're quite set on this.' Kheda held out his hand to the young mage. 'Then I won't argue with you. But you should be proud of yourself. This is a courageous choice.'

Naldeth clasped the warlord's hand. 'I don't imagine pursuing dragons through the Archipelago will be any task for a coward.'

'With any luck, there'll only be the one,' the mage-woman ventured. 'I'm sure the others will have flown north to find the purer elements.'

'I've given up trusting to luck.' Kheda looked at Velindre. 'Have you any idea at all how long it will be before you've recovered your magic sufficiently to get us home? You mustn't risk it until you're quite certain,' he added hastily.

'I won't,' she promised fervently. 'But no, I don't know how soon that will be. I'm sorry.'

'What can't be cured must be endured,' Risala said quietly. 'That's what the healers say.'

'And as Naldeth pointed out, we can make our plans while we wait,' Kheda said resolutely.

Risala looked at him. 'Will you look for omens in the heavenly compass tonight, please, just for me? You don't know what you might see.'

Kheda nodded slowly.

If it can't help, it can't hurt. That's something else that healers say, when they have precious little idea what they're actually doing.

And the compass will turn full circle as we go back to the Archipelago. Where will that leave me, always assuming I don't finally end up in a dragon's belly?

It will leave me doing the task that's before me, as always. But what will I do once that task's done? Perhaps it's time to look beyond it. My life has certainly swung far out of the paths I always assumed I would follow.

About the Author

Juliet E McKenna is a British fantasy author living in the Cotswolds, UK. Loving history, myth and other worlds since she first learned to read, she has written fifteen epic fantasy novels so far. Her debut, *The Thief's Gamble*, began The Tales of Einarinn in 1999, followed by The Aldabreshin Compass sequence, The Chronicles of the Lescari Revolution, and The Hadrumal Crisis trilogy. *The Green Man's Heir* was her first modern fantasy inspired by British folklore, followed by *The Green Man's Foe* and *The Green Man's Silence*. She also writes diverse shorter stories that include forays into dark fantasy, steampunk and science fiction. She promotes SF&Fantasy by reviewing, by blogging on book trade issues, attending conventions and teaching creative writing. She has also written historical murder mysteries set in ancient Greece as J M Alvey.

www.julietemckenna.com

@JulietEMcKenna

The Tales of Einarinn

1. The Thief's Gamble (1999)
2. The Swordsman's Oath (1999)
3. The Gambler's Fortune (2000)
4. The Warrior's Bond (2001)
5. The Assassin's Edge (2002)

The Aldabreshin Compass

1. The Southern Fire (2003)
2. Northern Storm (2004)

3. Western Shore (2005)

4. Eastern Tide (2006)

Turns & Chances (2004)

The Chronicles of the Lescari Revolution

1. Irons in the Fire (2009)

2. Blood in the Water (2010)

3. Banners in The Wind (2010)

The Wizard's Coming (2011)

The Hadrumal Crisis

1. Dangerous Waters (2011)

2. Darkening Skies (2012)

3. Defiant Peaks (2012)

A Few Further Tales of Einarinn (2012) (ebook from Wizards Tower Press)

Challoner, Murray & Balfour: Monster Hunters at Law (2014) (ebook from Wizards Tower Press)

Shadow Histories of the River Kingdom (2016) (Wizards Tower Press)

The Green Man (Wizards Tower Press)

1. The Green Mans Heir (2018)

2. The Green Man's Foe (2019)

3. The Green Man's Silence (2020)

4. The Green Man's Challenge (2021)

The Philocles series (as J M Alvey)
   1. Shadows of Athens (2019)
   2. Scorpions in Corinth (2019)
   3. Justice for Athena (2020)

WESTERN SHORE

Printed in November 2021
by Rotomail Italia S.p.A., Vignate (MI) - Italy